The Critics Hail Ma̲̅ ̲̅ ̲̅ ̲̅
Darkov̲̅ ̲̅ ̲̅ ̲̅

"A rich and highly co̲̅ ̲̅ ̲̅ ̲̅ ̲̅ ̲̅ ̲̅ ̲̅ ̲̅ ̲̅ ̲̅ and
magic, courage and pressure . . . Topflight
adventure in every way!"
—Lester Del Rey in *Analog*
(for *THE HERITAGE OF HASTUR*)

"May well be [Bradley's] masterpiece."
—*New York Newsday*
(for *THE HERITAGE OF HASTUR*)

"Literate and exciting."
—*New York Times Book Review*
(for *CITY OF SORCERY*)

"Suspenseful, powerfully written, and deeply
moving."
—*Library Journal* (for *STORMQUEEN!*)

"A warm, shrewd portrait of women from
different backgrounds working together under
adverse conditions."
—*Publishers Weekly* (for *CITY OF SORCERY*)

"I don't think any series novels have succeeded
for me the way Marion Zimmer Bradley's
Darkover novels did."
—*Locus* (general)

"Delightful . . . a fascinating world and a great
read."
—*Locus* (for *EXILE'S SONG*)

**"Darkover is the essence, the quintessence, my
most personal and best-loved work."**
—Marion Zimmer Bradley

A Reader's Guide to the Novels of Darkover

THE FOUNDING

A "lost ship" of Terran origin, in the pre-empire colonizing days, lands on a planet with a dim red star, later to be called Darkover.
  DARKOVER LANDFALL

THE AGES OF CHAOS

A thousand years after the original landfall settlement, society has returned to the feudal level. The Darkovans, their Terran technology renounced or forgotten, have turned instead to freewheeling, out-of-control matrix technology, psi powers and terrible psi weapons. The populace lives under the domination of the Towers and a tyrannical breeding program to staff the Towers with unnaturally powerful, inbred gifts of *laran*.
  STORMQUEEN!
  HAWKMISTRESS!

THE HUNDRED KINGDOMS

An age of war and strife retaining many of the decimating and disastrous effects of the Ages of Chaos. The lands which are later to become the Seven Domains are divided by continuous border conflicts into a multitude of small, belligerent kingdoms, named for convenience "The Hundred Kingdoms." The close of this era is heralded by the adoption of the Compact, instituted by Varzil the Good. A landmark and turning point in the history of Darkover, the Compact bans all distance weapons, making it a matter of honor that one who seeks to kill must himself face equal risk of death.
  TWO TO CONQUER
  THE HEIRS OF HAMMERFELL
  THE FALL OF NESKAYA

THE RENUNCIATES

During the Ages of Chaos and the time of the Hundred Kingdoms, there were two orders of women who set themselves apart from the patriarchal nature of Darkovan feudal society: the priestesses of Avarra, and the warriors of the Sisterhood of the Sword. Eventually these two independent groups merged to form the powerful and legally chartered Order of Renunciates or Free Amazons, a guild of women bound only by oath as a sisterhood of mutual responsibility. Their primary allegiance is to each other rather than to family, clan, caste or any man save a temporary employer. Alone among Darkovan women, they are exempt from the usual legal restrictions and protections. Their reason for existence is to provide the women of Darkover an alternative to their socially restricted lives.

THE SHATTERED CHAIN
THENDARA HOUSE
CITY OF SORCERY

AGAINST THE TERRANS

—THE FIRST AGE (Recontact)

After the Hastur Wars, the Hundred Kingdoms are consolidated into the Seven Domains, and ruled by a hereditary aristocracy of seven families, called the Comyn, allegedly descended from the legendary Hastur, Lord of Light. It is during this era that the Terran Empire, really a form of confederacy, rediscovers Darkover, which they know as the fourth planet of the Cottman star system. The fact that Darkover is a lost colony of the Empire is not easily or readily acknowledged by Darkovans and their Comyn overlords.

REDISCOVERY (*with Mercedes Lackey*)
THE SPELL SWORD
THE FORBIDDEN TOWER
STAR OF DANGER
THE WINDS OF DARKOVER

AGAINST THE TERRANS
—THE SECOND AGE (After the Comyn)

With the initial shock of recontact beginning to wear off, and the Terran spaceport a permanent establishment on the outskirts of the city of Thendara, the younger and less traditional elements of Darkovan society begin the first real exchange of knowledge with the Terrans—learning Terran science and technology and teaching Darkovan matrix technology in turn. Eventually Regis Hastur, the young Comyn lord most active in these exchanges, becomes Regent in a provisional government allied to the Terrans. Darkover is once again reunited with its founding Empire.

THE BLOODY SUN
HERITAGE OF HASTUR
THE PLANET SAVERS
SHARRA'S EXILE
WORLD WRECKERS
EXILE'S SONG
THE SHADOW MATRIX
TRAITOR'S SUN

THE DARKOVER ANTHOLOGIES

These volumes of stories edited by Marion Zimmer Bradley strive to "fill in the blanks" of Darkovan history, and elaborate on the eras, tales and characters which have captured readers' imaginations.

THE KEEPER'S PRICE
SWORD OF CHAOS
FREE AMAZONS OF DARKOVER
THE OTHER SIDE OF THE MIRROR
RED SUN OF DARKOVER
FOUR MOONS OF DARKOVER
DOMAINS OF DARKOVER
RENUNCIATES OF DARKOVER
LERONI OF DARKOVER
TOWERS OF DARKOVER
MARION ZIMMER BRADLEY'S DARKOVER
SNOWS OF DARKOVER

THE FORBIDDEN CIRCLE

THE SPELL SWORD

THE FORBIDDEN TOWER

Marion Zimmer Bradley

DAW BOOKS, INC.
DONALD A. WOLLHEIM, FOUNDER
375 Hudson Street, New York, NY 10014

ELIZABETH R. WOLLHEIM
SHEILA E. GILBERT
PUBLISHERS
http://www.dawbooks.com

First Printing, November 2002
1 2 3 4 5 6 7 8 9

DAW TRADEMARK REGISTERED
U.S. PAT. OFF. AND FOREIGN COUNTRIES
—MARCA REGISTRADA
HECHO EN U.S.A.

PRINTED IN THE U.S.A.

The Spell Sword

This one is for Caradoc.

The Forbidden Tower

For Diana L. Paxson who asked the question which
directly touched off this book;

And for Theodore Sturgeon, who first explored the
questions which, directly or indirectly, underlie
almost everything I have written.

Author's Note On Chronology

I am always being asked by those who have read anywhere from three to nine of the Darkover books to tell them exactly when and where any given book fits, chronologically, into the series. While I am always grateful for the interest of my readers, usually the only answer I can give is a shrug. I have always tried to make each of the Darkover books so complete that each one can be read by itself, even if the reader has never seen any of the other books before.

I do not really think of them as a "series" but rather of Darkover as a familiar world about which I like writing novels, and to which the readers seem to like returning. Where absolute consistency might damage the self-sufficiency of any given book, I have quite frankly sacrificed consistency. I make no apologies for this.

Nothing is more frustrating to me than to read the second, or fourth, or sixth book of a series, and to have the author blandly assume that I have read all his other books and know the whole background. When readers start nitpicking, demanding to know (for instance) why two locations are a day's journey apart in one book, and three days' ride in another, I begin to understand why Conan Doyle attempted to throw Sherlock Holmes over the Reichenbach falls, and why Sax Rohmer repeatedly tried to burn, drown, or dismember Fu Manchu so thoroughly that even the publishers could not resurrect him for another book.

But for those who have followed, or tried to follow, the chronology of the Terrans on Darkover, I think of this book as coming perhaps thirty years before STAR OF DANGER while Lorill Hastur still ruled Comyn Council and while Valdir Alton, a younger brother of Ellemir and Callista, was away at Council. Readers of the earlier books will remember that Valdir's adolescent son, Kennard, played an important part in STAR OF DANGER; that Valdir and his Terran foster-son Larry Montray reappeared in WINDS OF DARKOVER, about four years after the previous book. Kennard, grown to manhood, was an important character in THE BLOODY SUN.

Lerrys Ridenow—a grandson, perhaps, of the *Damon* in this book—appeared, with Regis Hastur, in THE PLANET SAVERS. Regis Hastur appeared again, with Lew Alton, son of Kennard, in THE SWORD OF AL-DONES; and yet again, as a major character, in WORLD WRECKERS which was, so far, the last in chronology of the novels. Some general sense of the elapsed time may be gained by the knowledge that Desideria, who appears in WINDS OF DARKOVER as a girl of sixteen, appears (as a minor character) in WORLD WRECKERS as a woman of great age, possibly over a hundred years old.

The books were not written in chronological order. SWORD OF ALDONES, late in the series, was actually written first. DARKOVER LANDFALL, which dealt with how the planet was colonized, long before the coming of the Terran Empire, was actually written *after* WORLD WRECKERS, which otherwise was the last in the series. I prefer to think of it as a loosely interrelated group of novels with a common background—the Terran Empire against the world and culture of Darkover—and a common theme: the clash of two warring cultures, apparently irreconcilable and in spite of all, closely akin. If the books have any message at all, which I personally doubt, it is simply that for a man nothing of mankind is alien.

                                        Marion Zimmer Bradley

THE SPELL SWORD

CHAPTER ONE

He had followed a dream, and it had brought him here to die.

Half conscious, he lay on the rocks and thin moss of the mountain crevasse, and in his dazed state it seemed to him that the girl he had seen in that earlier dream stood before him. *You ought to be laughing*, Andrew Carr said to her imagined face. *If it weren't for you I'd be halfway across the galaxy by now.*

Not lying here half dead on a frozen lump of dust at the edge of nowhere.

But she was not laughing. It seemed that she was standing at the very edge of the lip of rock, the bitter mountain wind blowing her thin blue draperies about her slender body, her hair bright red and gleaming, long about her delicate features. Just as he had seen her before, in the dream, but she was not laughing. Her delicate face looked pale and stern.

And it seemed that she spoke, although the dying man knew—*knew*—that her voice could not be anything but the echo of the wind in his fevered brain.

"Stranger, stranger, I did not mean you harm; it was none of my calling or my doing that brought you to this pass! True, I called you—or rather I called to anyone who could hear me, and it was you. But those above us both know that I meant you no ill! The winds, the storms, these are not under my command. I will do what I may to save you, but I have no power in these mountains."

It seemed to Andrew Carr that he flung angry words back at her. *I'm mad*, he thought, *or maybe already dead, lying here exchanging insults with a ghost-girl.*

"You say you called me? But what of the others in my ship? You called them too, perhaps? And brought them here to die in the crosswinds of the Hellers? Does death by wholesale give you any pleasure, you ghoul-girl?"

"That isn't fair!" Her imagined words were like a cry of anguish and her ghost-face on the wind twisted as if she were about to weep. "I did not call them; they came in the path where their work and their destiny led. Only you had the choice to come, or not to come, because of my call; you chose to come, and to share whatever fate their destiny held for them. I will save you if I can; for them, their time is ended and their destiny was never at my disposal. You I can save, if you will hear me, but you must rouse yourself. Rouse yourself!" It was like a wild cry of despair. "You will die if you lie here longer! Rouse yourself and take shelter, for the winds and the storms are not mine to command. . . ."

Andrew Carr opened his eyes and blinked. As he had known all along, he was alone, lying battered on the mountain ledges in the wreckage of the mapping plane. The girl—if she had ever been there at all—was gone.

Rouse yourself and take shelter, for the winds and the storms are not mine to command. That was, of course, a damn good idea, if he could manage it. Shelter. Where he lay, under a fragment of the smashed cabin of the mapping plane, was no place to meet the bitter night of this strange planet. He'd been warned about the weather here when he first came to Cottman IV—only a lunatic would stay out in the nights during the storm season.

He fought again, with a last desperate effort, to free the ankle which was caught, like the leg of a trapped animal, in twisted metal. This time he felt the metal crumple and give a little, and, although the ripping pain grew greater, tearing skin and flesh, he wrenched grimly at the caught foot in the darkness. Now he could move enough to bend over and move the leg with his hands. Torn clothing and torn flesh were slippery with blood which was already beginning to stiffen in the icy cold. When he touched the jagged metal his bare hands burned like fire, but now he could guide the wounded leg upward, avoiding the worst jagged edges of metal. Now, with a gasp of mingled agony and relief, his foot was free; blood-covered, boot and clothing torn, cut to the bone, but free; he was trapped no longer. He struggled to his feet, to be beaten again to his knees by a gust of the icy, sleet-laden wind that whipped around a corner of the rock-ledge.

Crawling, to present less body surface to the wind, he crept inside the cabin of the mapping plane. It was swaying dangerously in the battering wind, and he immediately abandoned any thought of taking shelter in here. If the wind got any worse, the whole damn thing would catapult down at least a thousand feet into the invisible valley below. Part of it, he thought, had already gone with the first crash. But finding himself still alive, beyond all expectations, he had to be sure there was no other survivor.

Stanforth was dead, of course. He must have been killed in the very first shock; nothing could survive with that gaping hole in its forehead. Andrew shut his eyes against the ghastly sight of the man's brains frozen and spilled all over his face. The two mappers—one was called Mattingly; he had never known the other's name—were twisted limp on the floor, and when he cautiously crawled across the jiggling balance of the cabin to find if any spark of life remained in either, it was only to feel the bodies already cold and stiffened in rigor. There was no sign of the pilot. He must have gone down with the nose of the plane, into that awful chasm below them.

So he was alone. Cautiously, Andrew backed out of the cabin; then, steeling himself, reentered it again. There was food in the plane—not much, a day's rations, lunches, Mattingly's hoard of sweets and candies, which he had so generously passed around and which they had all laughingly refused; emergency supplies in a marked panel behind the door. He dragged them all out, and, shaking with terror, set himself to wrench Mattingly's huge topcoat off the stiffening corpse. It made his stomach turn—*robbing the dead!*—but Mattingly's topcoat, a great expensive fur thing, was of no use to its owner and it might mean the difference between life and death in the terrible oncoming night.

When he edged out of the hideously shaking cabin for the last time, he was trembling and sick, and his torn, cut leg, no longer mercifully numb, was beginning to tear at him with claws of pain. He carefully backed away against the inner edge of the cliff, piling his hard-won provisions close to the rock-face.

It occurred to him that he should make one final essay inside the plane. Stanforth, Mattingly, and the nameless other man had carried identification, their disks from the Terran Empire Service. If he lived, if he came again to the Port, this would serve as proof of their death and mean something to their kinfolk. Wearily, he dragged himself forward.

And she was there again, the girl, the ghost, the ghoul who had brought him here, white with terror, standing directly in his way. Her mouth seemed drawn with screaming.

"No! No!"

Involuntarily he stepped back. He knew she was not there, he knew she was only air, but he stepped back and his lamed foot crumpled under him; he fell against the rock-cliff as a gust of wind struck it, howling like a damned thing. The girl was gone, was nowhere, but before he could drag himself to his feet again, there was a great howling blast of wind and icy sleet, a sound like a thunderclap. With a final rattling, rocking clash the cabin of the wrecked plane slid free from its resting place and overbalanced, tipped, slid down the rocks, and crashed into the chasm below. There was a great roar like an avalanche, like the end of the world. Andrew clung, gasping, to the face of the cliff, his fingers trying to freeze to the rocks.

Then it quieted and there was only the soft roaring of the storm and the snow spray, and Andrew huddled in Mattingly's fur topcoat, waiting for his heart to quiet to normal.

The girl had saved him again. She had kept him from going into the cabin, that last time.

Nonsense, he thought. *Unconsciously I must have known it was ready to go.*

He shelved the thought for later pondering. Just now he had escaped, by the second in a series of miracles, but he was still very far from safe.

If that wind could blow a plane right off a cliff, it could blow him, too, he reasoned. He had to find some safer place to rest, shelter.

Cautiously, clinging to the inner part of the ledge, he crept along the wall. Ten feet beyond where he lay, in one direction, it narrowed to nothing and ended in a dark rock-fall, slippery with the falling sleet. Painfully, his foot clawing anguish, he retraced his steps. The darkness seemed to be thickening and the sleet turning to white, soft thick snow. Aching and tired, Andrew wished he could lie down, wrap himself in the fur coat, and sleep there. But to sleep was death, his bones knew it, and he resisted the temptation, dragging himself along the cliff-ledge in the opposite direction. He had to avoid the fragments of torn metal which had held him trapped. Once he gave his good leg a painful shin-blow on a concealed rock which bent him over, moaning in pain.

But at last he had traversed the full length of the ledge, and at the far end, he found that it widened, sloping gently upward to a flat space on which thick underbrush clung, root-fast to the mountainside. Looking up in the thickening darkness, Andrew nodded. The clustered, thick foliage would resist the wind—it had evidently been rooted there for years. Anything which could grow here would have to be able to hang on hard against wind and storm, tempest and blizzard. Now, if his lamed foot would let him haul himself up there . . .

It wasn't easy, burdened with coat and food supplies, his foot torn and bleeding, but before the darkness closed in entirely, he had dragged himself and his small stock of provision—crawling, at last, on both hands and one knee—up beneath the trees, and collapsed in their shelter. At least here the maddening wind blew a little less violently, its strength broken by the boughs. In the emergency supplies there was a small battery-operated light, and by its pale glimmer he found concentrated food, a thin blanket of the "space" kind, which would insulate his body heat inside its shelter, and tablets of fuel.

He rigged the blanket and his own coat into a rough lean-to, using the thickest crossed branches to support them, so that he lay in a tiny dugout scooped beneath the tree-roots and boughs, where only occasional snow-spray reached him. Now he wanted nothing more than to collapse and lie motionless, but before his last strength left him, he grimly cut away the frozen trouser-leg and the remnants of his boot from his damaged leg. It hurt more than he had ever dreamed anything could hurt, to smear it with the antiseptic in the emergency kit and bandage it tightly up again, but somehow he managed it, although he heard himself moaning like a wild animal. He dropped at last, exhausted beyond weariness, in his burrow, reaching out finally for one of Mattingly's candies. He forced himself to chew it, knowing that the sugar would warm his shivering body, but in the very act of swallowing, he fell into an exhausted, deathlike sleep.

For a long time, his sleep was like that of the dead, dark and without dreams, a total blotting-out of mind and will. And then for a long time he was dimly aware of fever and pain, of the raging of the storm outside. After it diminished, still in the darkening fever-drowse, he woke raging with thirst, and crawled outside, breaking icicles from the edge of his shelter to suck them, staggering away from the shelter to answer the needs of his body. Then he dropped exhausted inside his hollowed-out shelter to swallow a little food and fell again into deep pain-racked sleep.

When he woke again it was morning, and he was clearheaded, seeing clear light and hearing only a faint murmur of wind on the heights. The storm was over; his foot and leg still pained him, but endurably. When he sat up to change the bandages, he saw the wound was clean and unfestered. Above him the great blood-red sun of Cottman IV lay low in the sky, slowly climbing the heights. He crept to the edge and looked down into the valley, which lay wrapped in mist below. It was wild, lonesome country and seemed untouched by any human hands.

Yet this was an inhabited world, a world peopled by humans who were, as far as he knew, indistinguishable from Earthmen. He had somehow survived the crash which had wrecked the Mapping and Exploring plane; it should not be wholly impossible, somehow, to make his way back to the spaceport again. Perhaps the natives would be friendly and help him, although he had to admit it didn't seem too likely.

Still, while there was life there was hope . . . and he

still had his life. Men had been lost, before this, in the wild and unexplored areas of strange worlds, and had come out of it alive, living to tell about it at Empire Central back on Earth. So that his first task was to get his leg back in walking shape, and his second, to get out of these mountains. *Hellers*. Good name for them. They were hellish all right. Crosswinds, updrafts, downdrafts, storms blowing up out of nowhere—the plane wasn't made that could fly through them unscathed in bad weather. He wondered how the natives got across them. Pack mules or some local equivalent, he thought. Anyway, there would be passes, roads, trails.

As the sun rose higher, the mists cleared and he could look down into the valleys below. Most of the slopes were tree-clad, but far below in the valley a river ran, and across it there was some darkening which could only be a bridge. So he wasn't in entirely uninhabited country, after all. There were blotches which might well be plowed lands, squared fields, gardens, a pleasant and peaceful countryside, with smoke rising from chimneys and houses—but very far away; and between the cultivated lands and the cliffside where Andrew clung were seemingly endless leagues of chasms and foothills and crags.

Somehow, though, he'd get down there, and then back to the spaceport. And then, damn it, off this ghastly inhospitable planet where he never should have come in the first place, and having come, should have left again within forty-eight hours. Well, he'd go now.

And what about the girl?

Damn the girl. She never existed. She was a fever-dream, a ghost, a symbol of his own loneliness. . . .

Lonely. I've always been alone, on a dozen worlds.

Probably every lonely man dreams that someday he will arrive at a world where someone is waiting, someone who will stretch out a hand to him, and speak to something inside, saying "I am here. We are together. . . ."

There had been women, of course. Women in every port—what was the old saying, starting with sailors and transferred to spacemen, always a new one in every port? And there were men who thought that state of affairs was enviable, he knew.

But none of them had been the right woman, and at heart he knew all the things the Psych Division had told him. They ought to know. You look for perfection in a woman to protect yourself against a real relationship. You take refuge in fantasies to avoid looking at the hard realities of life. And so forth and so on. Some of them even told him that he was unconsciously homosexual and found ordinary sexual affairs unsatisfactory because it wasn't really women he wanted at all, he just couldn't admit it to himself. He'd heard it all, a hundred times, yet the dream remained.

Not just a woman for his bed, but one for his heart and his heart-hungry loneliness. . . .

Maybe that was what the old fortune-teller in the Old Town had been playing on. Maybe so many men shared that romantic dream that she handed it out to every-body, as psi-quacks back on Earth told romantic teen-age girls about a tall dark stranger they would surely meet someday.

No. It was a real girl. I saw her and she—she called me.

All right. Think about it now. Get it all straight. . . .

He had come to Cottman IV en route to a new assign-ment, and it was simply a port of call, one of a series of crossroads worlds where routings were changed in the great network of the Terran Empire. The spaceport was large, as was the Trade City around it, to cater to the spaceport personnel, but it was not an Empire world with established trade, travel, tours. It was, he knew, an inhabited world, but most of it was off limits to Earthmen. He didn't even know what the natives called it. The name on the Empire maps was enough for him, Cottman IV. He hadn't intended to stay there more than forty-eight hours, only long enough to arrange transit to his final destination.

And then, with three others from the Space Service, he had gone into the Old Town. Ship fare got tiresome; it always tasted of machines, with a strong acrid taste of spices to cover the pervasive tang of recycled water and hydrocarbons. The food in the Old Town was at least natural, good grilled meat such as he had not had since his last planetside billeting, and fresh fragrant fruits, and he had enjoyed it more than any meal he had tasted in months, with the sweet clear gold-colored wine. And then, out of curiosity, he and his companions had strolled through the marketplace, buying souvenirs, fingering strange rough-textured fabrics and soft furs, and then he had come to the booth of the fortune-teller, and out of amused curiosity he had paused at her words.

"Someone is waiting for you. I can show you the face of your destiny, stranger. Would you see the face of the one who waits for you?"

He had never dreamed that it was more than a standard pitch for a few coins; amused, laughing, he had given the wrinkled old woman the coins she asked for, and followed her inside her small awning-covered canvas booth. Inside she had looked into her crystal—strange how on every world he had ever known the crystal ball was the chosen instrument of pretended far-seeing—and then, without a word, shoved the ball toward him. Still half in laughter, half in disgust, ready to walk away, Andrew had bent to see the pretty face, the shining red hair. *A pitch for a high-class call-girl,* he thought cynically, and was prepared to ask what the old madam was charging for the girl that day, and if she made a special price for Earthmen. Then the girl in the crystal raised her eyes and met Andrew's, and . . .

And it happened. There were no words for it. He stood there, half-crouched and unmoving over the crystal, so long that his neck, unheeded, was stabbed with cramp in the muscles.

She was very young, and she seemed to be both frightened and in pain. It seemed that she cried out to him for help that only he could give, and that she touched, deliberately, some secret thing known only to both of them. But he could not, later, understand what it had been, only that she called to him, that she needed him desperately. . . .

And then her face was gone and his head was aching. He gripped at the edge of the table, shaking, desperate to call her back. "Where is she? Who is she?" he demanded, and the old woman turned up a blank, frowning face. "No, now, how do I know what you saw, off-worlder? I saw nothing and no one, and others are waiting. You must go now."

He had stumbled out, blank with despair.

She called to me. She needs me. She is here. . . .

And I am leaving in six hours.

It hadn't been exactly easy to break his contract and stay, but it hadn't been all that hard either. Places on the world to which he was going were in high demand, and there wouldn't be more than three days' delay in filling his position. He'd have to accept two downgrades in seniority, but he didn't care. On the other hand, as Personnel told him, volunteers for Cottman IV weren't easy to find. The climate was bad, there was almost no trade, and although the pay was good, no career man really wanted to exile himself way out here on the fringes of the Empire on a planet which stubbornly refused to have any dealings with them except for leasing the spaceport itself. They offered him a choice of work in the computer center, or in Mapping and Exploring, which was high-risk, high-pay work. For some reason, the natives of this world had never mapped it, and the Terran Empire felt that presenting them with finished maps which their native technology could not, or would not, encompass might be a very good thing for public relations between Cottman IV and the Empire.

He chose Mapping and Exploring. He already knew—in the first week he had seen every girl and woman in the spaceport—that she was none of the workers in Medic or Personnel or Dispatch. Mapping and Exploring enjoyed certain concessions which allowed them to go outside the severely limited preserve of the Empire. *Somewhere, somehow, she was out there waiting. . . .*

It was an obsession and he knew it, but somehow he could not break the spell, and didn't want to.

And then, the third time he'd gone out with the mapping plane, the crash . . . and here he was, no closer than ever to his dream girl if she had ever existed, which he doubted.

Exhausted by the long effect of memory, he crawled back into his shelter to rest. Time enough tomorrow to work out a plan for getting down off the ledge. He ate emergency rations, sucked ice, fell into an uneasy sleep. . . .

She was there again, standing before him, both in and

not quite in the little dark shelter, a ghost, a dream, a dark flower, a flame in his heart. . . .

I do not know why it is you I have touched, stranger. I sought for my kinfolk, those who love me and could help me. . . .

Damsel in distress, Andrew thought, *I just bet. What do you want with me?*

Only a look of pain, and a sorrowful twisting of the face.

Who are you? I can't keep calling you ghost-girl.

Callista.

Now I know I'm freaked out, Andrew said to himself. *That's an Earth name.*

I am no Earth sorceress, my powers are of air and fire. . . .

That made no sense. *What do you want with me?*

Just now, only to save the life I unwittingly endangered. And I say to you: avoid the darkened land.

She faded abruptly from sight and hearing, and he was alone, blinking.

"Callista" means simply "beautiful," as I remember, he thought. *Maybe she is simply a symbol of beauty in my mind. But what is the darkened land? And how can she help to save me? Oh, rubbish, I'm treating her as if she were real again.*

Face it. There's no such woman, and if you're going to get out of here, you'll have to go it alone.

And yet, as he lay back to rest and make plans, he found himself trying, again, to call up her face before his eyes. . . .

CHAPTER TWO

The storm still raged on the heights, but here in the valley daylight shone through, and lowering sunlight; only the thick anvil-shaped clouds to the west showed where the peaks of the mountains were wrapped in storm.

Damon Ridenow rode with head down, braced against the wind that ripped his riding-cloak, and it felt like flight. As if he fled before a gathering storm. He tried to tell himself, *The weather's getting into my bones, maybe I'm just not as young as I was*, but he knew it was more than that. It was an unease, something stirring, nagging at his mind, something wrong. Something rotten.

He realized that he had been keeping his eyes turned from the low tree-clad hills which lay to the east, and deliberately, trying to break the strange unease, made himself twist in his saddle and look up and down the slopes.

The darkened lands.

Rubbish, he said to himself angrily. There was war there, last year, with the cat-people. Some of his folk were killed and others were driven away, forced to resettle in the Alton country, around the lakes. The cat-people were fierce and cruel, yes, they slaughtered and burned and tormented and left for dead what they could not kill outright. Maybe what he felt was simply the memory of all the suffering there during the war. *My mind is open to the minds of those who suffered. . . .*

No, it was worse than that. The things he'd heard about what the cat-people did.

He glanced behind him. His escort—four swordsmen of the Guard—were beginning to draw together and murmur, and he knew he should call a halt to breathe the horses. One of them spurred and came to his side, and he reined his mount in to look at the man.

"Lord Damon," the Guardsman said, with proper deference—but he looked angry. "Why do we ride as if foemen rode hard at our heels? I have heard no word of war or ambush."

Damon Ridenow forced his pace to slacken slightly, but it was an effort. He wanted to spur his mount hard, to race away for the safety of Armida beyond them. . . .

He said somberly, "I think we *are* pursued, Reidel."

The Guardsman warily swept his eyes from horizon to horizon—it was his trained duty to be wary—but with open skepticism. "Which bush, think you, hides ambush, Lord Damon?"

"That you know no more than I," said Damon, sighing.

The man looked stubborn. He said, "Well, you are a Comyn Lord, and it is your business, and mine to carry out your orders. But there is a limit to what man and horseflesh can do, Lord, and if we are attacked with wearied horses and saddle sores, we will fight the less."

"I suppose you're right," Damon said, sighing. "Call halt if you will, then. Here at least there is little danger of attack in open country."

He was cramped and weary, and glad to dismount, even though the nightmare urgency still beat at him. When the Guard Reidel brought him food, he took it without smiling, and his thanks were absentminded. The Guardsman lingered with the privilege of an old acquaintance.

"Do you still smell danger behind every tree, Lord Damon?"

"Yes, but I can't say why," Damon said, sighing. Afoot he was little more than medium height, a thin pale man with the fire-red hair of a Comyn Lord of the Seven Domains; like most of his kindred he went unarmed except for a dagger, and under his riding-cloak he wore the light tunic of an indoor man, a scholar. The Guardsman was looking at him solicitously.

"You are unused to so much riding, Lord, and in such haste. Was there so much need for it, so swiftly?"

"I do not know," the Comyn Lord said quietly. "But my kinswoman at Armida sent me a message—a guarded one—begging me to come to her with all speed, and she is not of that fearful kind who start at shadows

and lie awake nights fearing bandits in the courtyard
when her menfolk are away. An urgent summons from
the Lady Ellemir is nothing to treat lightly, so I came at
once, as I must. It may well be some family trouble,
some sickness in her household; but whatever it is, the
matter is grave or she could deal with it on her own."

The Guardsman nodded slowly. "I have heard the
lady is brave and resourceful," he said, "I have a brother
who is a part of her household staff. May I tell my fellows this much, Lord? They may grumble less, if they
know it is grave trouble and no whim of your own."

"Tell them and welcome, it is no secret," Damon said,
"I would have done so myself, if I had thought to do so."

Reidel grinned. "I know you are no man-driver," he
said, "but none of us had heard rumors, and this is not
a country any man cares to ride in without need." He
was turning away, but Damon kept him, a hand on his
sleeve.

"Not a country to ride in without need—what do you
mean, Reidel?"

Now that he was asked a direct question, the man
fidgeted.

"Unchancy," he said at last, "and bad luck. It lies
under a shadow. They call it, now, the darkening lands,
and no man will ride there or travel there unless he
must, and not even then unless he carries mighty
protections."

"Nonsense."

"You may laugh, Lord, you Comyn are protected by
the Great Gods."

Damon sighed. "I had not thought to find you so superstitious, Reidel. You have been a Guardsman for a
score of years, you were paxman to my father. Do you
still think we Comyn are otherwise than other men?"

"You are luckier," Reidel said, his teeth clenched,
"but now, when men ride into the darkening lands, they
return no more, or return with their wits astray. No,
Lord, do not laugh at me, it befell my mother's brother
two moons ago. He rode into the darkened lands to visit
a maid he would make his second wife, having paid
bride-price when she was but nine. He came not when
he was expected, and when they told me he had gone

forever into the shadow, I too laughed and said he had, no doubt, delayed to bed the girl and get her with child. Then one night, Lord, after overstaying his leave a full ten days, he rode into the Guardroom at Serré late one night. I am not a fanciful man, Lord, but his face—his face—" He gave up struggling for words, and said, "He looked as if he'd been looking straight down into Zandru's seventh hell. And he said nothing that made sense, Lord. He raved of great fires, and of death in the winds, and withered gardens, and witch-food that took a man's wits, and of girls who clawed at his soul like cat-hags; and though they sent for the sorceress, before she could come to heal his mind, he sank, and died raving."

"Some sickness in the mountains and foothills," Damon said, but Reidel shook his head.

"As you reminded me, Lord, I have been Guardsman in these hills a score of years, and my uncle twoscore. I know the sicknesses that strike men, and this was none of them. Nor do I know any sickness which strikes a man only in one direction. I myself rode a little way into the darkened lands, Lord, and I saw for myself the withered gardens and untended orchards, and the folk who live there now. It is true they live on witch-food, Lord."

Damon interrupted again. "Witch food? There are no such things as witches, Reidel."

"Call it what you will, but this is no food from grain, root, berry, or wholesome tree, Lord, nor flesh of any living thing. I would not touch a grain of it, and I think this is why I escaped unscathed. I saw it come from the air."

Damon said, "Those who know their business can prepare food from things which look inedible, Reidel, and it is wholesome. A matrix technician—how can I explain this? He breaks down the chemical matter which cannot be eaten with safety, and changes its structure so that it can be digested and will nourish. It is not sufficient to sustain life for many months, but it will keep life for a little while in urgency. This I can do myself, and there is no witchery to it."

Reidel frowned. "Sorcery of your starstone—"

"Sorcery be damned," Damon said testily. "A skill."

"Then why can no one do it but you Comyn?"

He sighed. "I cannot play upon the lute; my ears and fingers have neither the inborn talent nor the training. But you, Reidel, were born with the ear, and the fingers were trained in childhood, and so you make music as you wish. So it is with this. The Comyn are born with talent, as it might be a talent for music, and in childhood we are trained to change the structure of matter with the help of these matrix stones. I can do only a few small things; those well-trained can do much. Perhaps someone has been experimenting with such imitation food in those lands, and not knowing his skill full well, has wrought poison instead, a poison which sets men's wits running wild. But this is a matter for one of the Keepers. Why has no one brought this to them for their mending, Reidel?"

"Say what you like," the Guardsman said, and his clenched and stubborn face said volumes. "The darkened lands lie under some evil, and men of goodwill should avoid them. And now, if it pleases you, Lord, we should be a-horse again if we would reach Armida before nightfall. For even if we stay clear of the darkening lands, this is no road to ride by night."

"You are right," said Damon, and mounted, waiting while his escort gathered again. He had plenty to think about. He had, indeed, heard rumors about the lands at the fringes of the cat-country, but nothing, as yet, like this. Was it all superstition, rumor based on the gossip of the ignorant? No; Reidel was no fanciful man, nor was his uncle, a hard-bitten soldier for twenty years, any man to fall prey to vague shadows. Something very tangible had killed him; and he'd have bet the old fellow would have taken a lot of killing.

They had topped the summit of the hill, and Damon looked down into the valley, alert for any sign of ambush; for his sense of being watched, pursued, had grown to an obsession by now. This would be a good place for an ambush, as they came up over the hill.

But the road and the valley lay bare before them in the cloudy sunlight, and Damon frowned, trying to loosen his tense muscles by an act of will.

You're getting to where you jump at shadows. Much

*good you'll be to Ellemir, unless you can get your nerves
in order.*

His gloved hand went to the chain about his neck;
there, wrapped in silk inside a small pouch of leather,
he could feel the hard shape, the curious warmth of the
matrix he carried. Given to him when he had mastered
its use, the "starstone" Reidel had spoken about, it was
keyed to his mind in a way no one but a Darkovan—
and Comyn-telepath could ever understand. Long training had taught him to amplify the magnetic forces of his
brain with the curious crystalline structure of the stone;
and now the very touch of it quieted his mind to calm;
the long discipline of the highly trained telepath.

Reason, he told himself, *all things in order*. As the
disquiet lessened, he felt the quiet pulse and slow euphoria which meant his brain had begun to function at what
the Comyn called basic, or "resting," rhythm. From this
moment of calm, above himself, he looked at his fears
and Reidel's. Something here to be examined, yes; but
not to be chewed over restlessly from confused tales as
he rode. Rather, something to be set aside, thought
about, then systematically investigated, with facts rather
than fears, happenings rather than gossip.

A wild shout ripped into his mind, crashing his artifi-
cial calm like a stone flung through a glass window. It
was a painful, shattering shock, and he cried aloud with
the impact of fear and agony on his mind, half a moment
before he heard a hoarse male scream—a fearful scream,
a scream which comes only from dying lips. His horse
plunged and reared upward beneath him; his hand still
clutching the crystal at his throat, he hauled desperately
at the reins, trying to get control of his pitching mount.
The animal stopped short under him, standing stiff-
legged and trembling, as Damon stared in amazement,
watching Reidel slide slowly to the ground, limp and
unmistakably dead, his throat a single long gash, from
which blood still spouted in a crimson fountain.

And no one was near him! A sword from nowhere, an
invisible claw of steel to rip out the throat of a living,
breathing man.

"Aldones! Lord of Light deliver us!" Damon whispered to himself, clutching the hilt of his knife, struggling

for self-control. The other Guardsmen were fighting, their swords sweeping in great gleaming arcs against them.

Damon clutched the crystal in his fingers, fighting a silent battle for mastery of this illusion—*for illusion it must be!* Slowly, as through a thick veil in his mind, he saw shadowy forms, strange and hardly human. The light seemed to shine *through* them, and his eyes went in and out of focus, trying hard to keep them before him.

And he was unarmed! No swordsman at best—

He gripped the reins of his horse, struggling against the impulse to rush in against the invisible opponents. Red fury pulsed in his blood, but an icy wave of reason told him, coldly, that he was unarmed, that he could only plunge in and die with his men, and that his duty to his kinswoman now came first. Was her house besieged by some such invisible terrors? Were they, perchance, lying in wait to keep any of her kinfolk from coming to her aid?

His men were fighting wildly against the invisible assailants; Damon, clutching the matrix, wheeled his mount and swerved, dashing away from the attackers at a hard gallop, and down the path. His throat seemed to crawl. For all he knew some invisible blade might sweep out of empty air and strike his head from his shoulders. Behind him the hoarse cries of his men were like a knife in his heart, clutching at him, clawing at his conscience. He rode, head down, cloak clutched about him, as if indeed demons pursued him; and he did not slacken pace until he came to a halt, his horse trembling and streaming sweat, his own breath coming in great ragged heaving gasps, on the next hill rise, two or three miles below the ambush, and above him the high gates of Armida.

Dismounting, he drew the crystal from its protective leather pouch and unwrapped the silk within. *Naked, this could have saved us all*, he thought, looking down despairingly at the blue stone with the strange, curling gleams of fire within; his trained telepathic power, enormously amplified by the resonating magnetic fields of the matrix, could have mastered the illusion; his men might have had to fight, but they would have fought free of illusions, against foes they could see, who could match them fairly. He bowed his head. A matrix was never carried bare; its resonating vibrations had to be insulated from what was around it. And by the time he could have freed it from its insulation, his men would have been dead, anyway, and him with them.

Sighing, and thrusting the crystal back into the silk, he patted his exhausted horse on the flank, and, not mounting to spare the gasping, trembling beast any further exertion, he led him slowly up the rise toward the gates. Armida was not besieged, it seemed. The courtyard lay quiet and bare in the dying sunlight, and the nightly fog was beginning to roll in from the surrounding hills; serving men came to take his horse and cried out in alarm at the state of it.

"Were you pursued? Lord Damon, where is your escort?"

He shook his head slowly, not trying to answer. "Later, later. Tend my horse, and let him not drink until he is cooled; he has ridden too far at a gallop. Send for the Lady Ellemir to tell her I have come."

If this mission is not of grave importance, he said to himself grimly, *we shall quarrel. Four of my faithful men dead, and horribly. Yet she is under no siege or trouble.*

Then he became aware of the grim quiet that lay over the courtyard. Surely there were splotches of blood on the stones. A strange disquiet, a sickening unease— which he knew was in his mind, sensed from something not on this mundane level at all—crept slowly over him.

He raised his eyes to see Ellemir Lanart standing before him.

"Kinsman," she said half audibly. "I heard something— not enough to be sure. I thought it was you, too—" Her voice failed, and she threw herself into his arms.

"Damon! Damon! I thought you were dead, too!"

Damon Ridenow held the girl gently, stroking the shaking shoulders. Her bright head dropped heavily for a moment against him, and she sighed then, fighting for control, raised her head. She was very tall and slender, her fire-red hair proclaiming her a member of Damon's own telepath caste; her features were delicate, her eyes brilliant blue.

"Ellemir, what has happened here?" he asked, his apprehension growing. "Are you under attack? Has there been a raid?"

She lowered her head. "I do not know," she said "All I know is that Callista is gone."

"Gone? In God's name what do you mean? Carried off by bandits? Run away? Eloped?" Even as he spoke he knew that was madness; Ellemir's twin sister Callista was a Keeper, one of those women trained to handle all the power of a circle of skilled telepaths; they were vowed to virginity, and surrounded with a circle of awe which meant no sane man on Darkover would raise his eyes to one. "Ellemir, tell me! I thought her safe in the Tower at Arilinn. Where? How?"

Ellemir was fighting for self-control. "We cannot talk here on the doorstep," she said, withdrawing from him and regaining her self-possession. Damon felt a moment of regret—her head against his shoulder had seemed to belong there somehow. He told himself incredulously that this was neither the time nor the place for such thoughts, and resisted the impulse to touch her hand lightly again, following her at a sedate pace into the great hall. But she was barely inside before she turned to him.

"She was here for a visit," Ellemir said in a shaking voice. "The Lady Leonie has sought to lay down her Keeper's place and return to her home at Valeron, and Callista was to take her place in the Tower; but she came for a visit to me first, and she wished to persuade me to come to Arilinn and stay there with her, that she might not be so terribly alone. In any case, to see me for a little before she must be isolated for the making of the Tower Circle. All went well, although she seemed uneasy. I am no trained telepath, Damon, but Callista and I were twin-born and our minds can touch, a little, whether we will it or not. So I sensed her unease, but she said only that she had evil dreams of cat-hags and withering gardens and dying flowers. And then one day—" Ellemir's face paled and, hardly knowing what she did, she reached her hand to Damon's, gripping desperately as if to lean her weight upon him.

"I woke, hearing her scream; but no one else had

heard any sound, even a whisper. Four of our people lay dead in the court, and among them—among them was our old foster mother Bethiah. She had nursed Callista at her breasts as a babe and she slept always on a cot at her feet, and she lay there with her eyes—her eyes clawed out of their sockets, still just alive." Ellemir was sobbing aloud now. "And Callista was gone! Gone, and I could not reach her—I could not reach her even with my mind! My twin, and she was gone, as if Avarra had snatched her alive into some otherworld."

Damon's voice was hard; he kept it that way with a fierce effort. "Do you think she is dead, Ellemir?"

Ellemir met his eyes with a level blue gaze.

"I do not. I did not feel her die; and my twin could not die without my sharing her death. When our brother Coryn died in a fall from the aerie, taking hawks, both Callista and I felt him pass from life into death; and Callista is *my twin*. She lives." Then Ellemir's voice broke and she wept wildly.

"But where? Where? She is gone, gone, gone as if she had never lived! And only shadows moving since then— only shadows. Damon, Damon, what shall I do, what shall I do?"

CHAPTER THREE

He would never have thought that going downhill could be so difficult.

All day Andrew Carr had climbed, scrambled, and slid around on the sharp rocks of the slope. He had looked down into an incredibly deep ravine where the remnants of the mapping plane lay smashed, and written off any lingering hope of salvaging food, protective clothing, or the identity disks of his companions. Now, as darkness fell and a light fall of snow began to drift across the slopes, he huddled inside the thick fur coat and sucked the last few of the sweets he had with him. He scanned the horizon below him for lights or any other signs of life. There must be some. This was a thickly inhabited planet. But out in the mountains here, it might be miles or even hundreds of miles between settled areas. He did see pale gleams against the horizon, one clustered group of lights which might even have been a town or village. So his only problem was to get down to it. But that might take some doing. He knew nothing—less than nothing, really—of woodcraft or survival skills. Finally, remembering something he had read, he half buried himself in a heap of dead leaves and pulled the flap of the fur coat over his head. He wasn't warm, and he found his thoughts dwelling lovingly on food, great steaming platefuls of it, but finally he did sleep; after a fashion, waking almost hourly to shiver and pull himself more deeply into his heap of leaves, but he did sleep. Nor did he see, anywhere in his confused dreams, the face of the ghostly girl he identified with his vision.

All the next day, and the day after, he struggled his way through, and down, a long slope covered with dense thorny underbrush, twice lost his way in the thickly wooded valley at the bottom, and finally toiled his way up the far side of the slope. From the bottom of the valley he had no way to ascertain which way he should be going, and from there, he saw no sign of human or other habitation. Once he came across remnants, in extreme disrepair, of a split-rail fence, and wasted a couple of hours walking its length—the existence of a fence usually postulated something to be fenced in, or kept out. But it lead him only into thick, tangled dry vines and he decided that whatever strange kind of livestock had been fenced in at one time, both the stock and their keeper had been long, long gone. Near the spot where he had first found the fence was a dry creek bed, and he surmised that he could probably follow it down out of the mountains. Civilizations, especially farmlands, had always built their settlements along watercourses, and he believed that this planet would hardly be an exception. If he followed the stream down along its natural course, it would certainly lead him out of the hills and probably to the abodes of whatever people had built the fence and herded the stock. But after a few miles the course of the dry stream bed was obscured by a rock slide, and try as he might, he could not find it on the other side. Maybe that was why the fence-builders had moved their livestock.

Toward the end of the second day he found a few withered fruits clinging to a gnarled tree. They looked and tasted like apples, dry and hard but edible; he ate most of them and gathered the last few to be eaten later. He felt miserably frustrated. Probably there were other edibles all around him, everything from the bark of certain trees to the mushrooms or fungi he found growing on fallen wood. The trouble was that he couldn't tell the wholesome food plants from the deadly poisonous ones, and therefore he was only tantalizing himself by thinking about it.

Late that night, as he was searching for a windbreak in which to sleep, snow began to fall again, with a strange and persistent steadiness that made him uneasy. He had heard about the blizzards of the hills, and the thought of being caught out in one, without food or protective clothing or shelter, scared him out of his wits. Before long the snow became so heavy that he could hardly see his hand before his face, and his shoes were wet through and caked with the cold and gluey mass.

I'm finished, he thought grimly. *I was finished when the plane crashed, only I didn't have the sense to know it.*

The only chance I had—the only chance I ever had—was good weather, and now that's broken.

The only thing that made sense now was to pick out a comfortable place, preferably out of the damned wind that howled like a lost thing around the rocky crags above him, lie down, make himself comfortable, and fall asleep in the snow. That would be the end of it all. Considering how deserted this part of the world looked, it was likely to be so many years before anyone stumbled over his body, that no one would be able to tell whether he was a Terran or a native of this planet.

Damn that wind! It howled like a dozen wind machines, like a chorus of lost souls out of Dante's *Inferno*. There was a curious illusion in the wind. It sounded as if, very far away, someone was calling his name.

Andrew Carr! Andrew Carr!

It was an illusion, of course. No one within three hundred miles of this place even knew he was here, except maybe the ghostly girl he had seen when the plane crashed. If she *was* actually within three hundred miles of this place. And of course he had no idea if she actually knew his name, or not. Damn the girl, anyway, if she even existed. Which he doubted.

Carr stumbled and fell full length into the deepening snow. He started to rise, then thought, *Oh, hell, what's the use*, and let himself fall forward again.

Someone *was* calling his name.

Andrew Carr! Come this way, quickly! I can show you the way to shelter, but more I cannot do. You must take your own way there.

He heard himself say fretfully, against the dim voice that was like an echo inside his mind, "No. I'm too tired. I can't go any farther."

"Carr! Raise your eyes and look at me!"

Resentfully, shielding his eyes against the howling wind and the sharp needles of the snow, Andrew Carr braced himself with his palms and looked up. He already knew what he would see.

It was the girl, of course.

She wasn't really there. How could she be there, wearing a thin blue gown that looked like a torn nightdress, barefoot, her hair not even blowing in the bitter snow-laden wind?

He heard himself say aloud—and heard the words ripped by the wind from his mouth and carried away, so that the girl could not possibly have heard them from ten feet away, "What are you doing now? Are you really here? Where are you?"

She said precisely, in that low-pitched voice which seemed always to carry just to his ear and not an inch farther, "I do not know where I am, or I would not be there, since it is nowhere I wish to be. The important thing is that I know where you are, and where the only place of safety is for you. Follow me, quickly! Get up, you fool, get up!"

Carr stumbled to his feet, clutching his coat about him. She stood, it seemed, about eight feet ahead of him in the storm. She was still clad in the flimsy and torn night-dress, but although her bare feet and shoulders gleamed palely through the rents in the garment, she did not seem to be shivering at all.

She beckoned—now that she knew she had his attention, it seemed, she would not waste any more effort trying to make herself heard—and began to walk lightly across the snow. Her feet, he noticed with a weird sense of unreality, were not quite touching the ground. *Yeah, that figures, if she's a ghost.*

Head down, he stumbled after the retreating figure of the girl. The wind tore at his coat, sent it flapping out wildly behind him. His shoes were thick, half-frozen lumps of wet snow, and his hair and the stubble of beard were icy streaks of roughness against his face. Now that the snow had obscured the ground to even whiteness, covering the lumps and shadows, two or three times he tripped over some hidden root or unseen chuckhole, and measured his length on the ground; but each time he struggled up and followed the shadow ahead of him. She had saved his life once before. *She must know what she's doing.*

It seemed a very long time that he floundered and stumbled in the snow, although he thought afterward that it was probably not more than three-quarters of an hour, before he blundered full into what felt like a brick wall. He put out his hand, incredulous.

It *was* a brick wall. Or, anyway, it felt like one. It felt like the side of a building, and feeling about a little, he found a door which was made of placed wood, worn smooth, and fastened with stiff leather straps, hauled through a rough-cut wooden latch, and knotted. It took him some time to tease the wet leather knot apart, and he finally had to take off his gloves and fumble with stiff bare fingers which were blue and bleeding by the time the knot finally yielded. The door creaked open and Carr cautiously stepped inside. For all he knew he might have found light, fire, and people sitting around a supper table; but the place was dark and cold and deserted. But not half as cold as the outdoors, and at least it was dry. There was something like straw on the floor, and the dim light of reflected snow from outside showed him vague shapes that might have been cattle stanchions, or furniture. He had no way of making a light, but it was so quiet that he knew neither the animals which had once been stabled here, nor their keepers, still inhabited the place.

Once again the girl had led him to safety. He sank down on the mercifully dry floor, scooped a comfortable place in the straw, took off his sopping wet shoes, dried his chilled and numb feet on the straw, and lay down to sleep. He looked around for the ghostly form of the girl who had guided him here, but as he had expected, she was gone.

He woke, hours later, out of the deep sleep of exhaustion, to a raging snow-whitened world, a howling inferno of blowing sleet and ice battering against the building where he lay. But enough light filtered through the heavily fastened wooden shutters so that he could see the inside of the building where he lay: empty except for the thick straw and the uprights of stanchions. It smelled, very faintly, of long-dried animal dung, a sharp but not unpleasant pungency.

In the far corner was a dark mass of something, which he curiously explored. He found a few rags of strangely fashioned clothing. One, a warm, blanketlike cloak of ragged and faded tartan cloth, he took to wrap himself in. Under the heaped clothing—which was ragged but, because of the dryness of the building, untouched by mold or mildew—he found a heavy chest fastened shut with a hasp, but not locked. Opening it, he discovered food; forgotten, or most likely left over for another herding season by the keepers of whatever strange beasts had once been kept here. There was a form of dried bread—actually more like hardtack or crackers—wrapped in oiled paper. There was some leathery unrecognizable stuff which he finally decided must be dried meat; but neither his teeth nor his palate could cope with it. Some pasty, fragrant stuff reminded him of peanut butter, and it went well on the hardtack, made of crushed seeds or nuts with dried fruit mashed up in it. There was some kind of dried fruit, but it, too, was so hard that, although it smelled good, he decided it would need a good long soak in water, preferably hot water, before approaching anything like edibility.

He satisfied his hunger with the hardtack and the nut-and-fruit-butter paste, and after hunting around, discovered a crude water tap that ran into a basin, apparently for watering the beasts. He drank, and splashed a little cold water on his face. It was far too cold for any more meticulous washing, but he felt better even for that much. Then, wrapped in the tartan blanket, he explored the place end to end. He was much relieved, when he found the final convenience, a crude earth-closet latrine roughly enclosed at the far end. He had not relished the thought of either venturing out into the storm, even for a moment, or of defiling the place against the possible future return of its owners. It crossed his mind that the conveniences, and the stored provisions, must have been provided against just such blizzards as this, when neither man nor beast could live without some shelter.

So this world was not only inhabited, it was civilized, at least after a fashion. *All the comforts of home*, he thought, returning to his bed of piled straw. Now all he had to do was to wait out the blizzard.

He was so weary, after days of climbing and walking, and so warm in the thick blanket, that he had no trouble at all in falling asleep again. When he woke again, the light was declining, and the noise of the storm was lessening a little. He guessed, by the gathering darkness, that he had slept most of the day away.

And it's early fall. What must it be like here in the winter? This planet might make a great winter-sports resort, but it's not fit for anything else. I pity the people who live here!

He made another meager meal of hard crackers and fruit-and-nut paste (good enough, but boring for a regular diet), and because it was too cold and dark to do anything else, he wrapped himself up again, and stretched out in the straw.

He had slept his fill, and he was no longer cold, nor very hungry. It was too dark to see much, but there was not a great deal to see in any case. He thought randomly, *Too bad I'm not a trained xenologist. No Terran has ever been let loose on this world before.* He knew there were skilled sociologists and anthropologists who, with the artifacts he had seen (and eaten), could skillfully analyze the exact level of this planet's culture, or at least of those people who lived in this area. The sturdy brick or stone walls, squarely mortared together, the cattle stanchions constructed of wood and nailed together with wooden pegs, the water tap of hardwood which ran into a stone basin, the unglazed windows covered only with tight wooden shutters, said one thing about the culture: it went with the fence rails and the rude earth-closet latrine, a low-level agricultural society. Yet he wasn't sure. This was, after all, a herdsman's shelter, a bad-weather retreat for emergencies, and no civilization wasted much technical accomplishment on them. There was also the kind of sophisticated foresight which built such things at all, and stocked them with imperishable food, against need, even guarding against the need to go out momentarily for calls of nature. The blanket was beautifully woven, with a craftsmanship rare in these days of synthetics and disposable fabrics. And so he realized that the people of this planet might be far more civilized than he thought.

He shifted his weight on the crackling straw, and blinked, for the girl was there again in the darkness. She was still wearing the torn, thin blue dress that gleamed with a pale, icelike glitter in the dimness of the dark barn. For a moment, even though he still half believed that she was a hallucination, he could not help saying aloud, "Aren't you cold?"

It is not cold where I am.

This, Carr told himself, was absolutely freaky. He said slowly, "Then you're not here?"

How could I be where you are? If you think I am there—no, here—try to touch me.

Hesitantly, Carr stretched out his hand. It seemed that he must touch her bare round arm, but there was nothing palpable to the touch. He said doggedly, "I don't understand any of this. You're here, and you're not here. I can see you, and you're a ghost. You say your name is Callista, but that's a name from my own world. I still think I'm crazy, and I'm talking to myself, but I'd love to know how you can explain any of this."

The ghost-girl made a sound that was like soft childlike laughter. "I do not understand it either," she said quietly. "As I tried to tell you before, it was not you I attempted to reach but my kinswoman and my friends. But wherever I search, they are not there. It is as if their minds had been wiped off this world. For a long time I wandered around in dark places, until I found myself looking into your eyes. It seemed that I knew you, even though my eyes had never looked on you before. And then, something in you kept drawing me back. Somewhere, not in this world at all, we have touched one another. I am nothing to you, but I had brought you into danger, so I sought to save you. And I come back because"—for a moment it seemed that she was about to weep—"I am very much alone, and even a stranger is better than no companion. Do you want me to go away again?"

"No," Carr said quickly, "stay with me, Callista. But I don't understand this at all."

She was silent for a minute, as if considering. *God*, Carr thought, *how real she seems*. He could see her breathing, the faint rise and fall of her chest beneath the thin, torn dress. One of her feet was smudged: no, bruised and reddened and bloodstained. Carr said, "Are you hurt?"

"Not really. You asked me how I could be there with you. I suppose you know that we live in more than one way, and that the world you are in now is the solid world, the world of *things*, the world of hard bodies and physical creations. But in the world where I am, we leave our bodies behind like outgrown clothing or cast snake-skins, and what we call *place* has no real being. I am used to that world, I have been trained to walk in it, but somehow I am being kept in a part of it where no other of my people's minds may touch. As I wandered in that gray and featureless plain, your thoughts touched mine and I felt you clearly, like hand clasping hand in the darkness."

"Are you in darkness?"

"Where my body is being kept, I am in darkness, yes. But in the gray world, I can see you, even as you can see me. That is how I saw your flying machine crash and knew it would fall into the ravine. And I saw you lost in the snowstorm and I knew you were near to this herdsman's hut. I came here now to show you where food was kept if you had not found it."

"I found it," Carr said. "I don't know what to say. I thought you were a dream and you're acting as if you were real."

It sounded again like soft laughter. "Oh, I assure you, I am just as real and solid as you are yourself. And I would give a great deal to be with you in that cold, dark herdsman's hut, since it is only a few miles from my home, and as soon as the storm subsides I could be free and by my own fireside. But I—"

In the middle of a word, she was abruptly gone, winked out like a breath. For some strange reason this did more to convince Carr of her reality than anything she had said. If he'd been imagining her, if his subconscious mind had hallucinated her, as men cold and alone and in danger *did* hallucinate strangers from their deepest wishes, he'd have kept her there; he'd at least have let her finish what she was saying. The fact that she'd vanished in the middle of a phrase tended to indicate not only that she had really been there, in some intangible sense, but that some unknown third party had a superior power over her comings and goings.

She was frightened, and she was sad. *I am very much alone, and even a stranger is better than no companion.*

Cold and alone on a strange and unfamiliar world, Andrew Carr could understand that very well. It was just about the way he felt himself.

Not that she'd be all that bad as a companion, if she were really here. . . .

Not a great deal of satisfaction out of a companion you can't touch. And yet . . . even though he couldn't lay a hand on her, there was something surprisingly compelling about the girl.

He'd known lots of women, at least in the Biblical sense. Known their bodies and a little about their personalities, and what they wanted out of life. But he'd never got close enough to any one of them that he felt bad when the time came for them to go off in opposite directions.

Let's face it. From the minute I saw this girl in the crystal, she's been so real to me that I was willing to turn my whole life around, just on the off chance that she was something more than a dream. And now I know she's real. She's saved my life once: no, twice. I wouldn't have lasted long out in that blizzard. And she's in trouble. They're keeping her in the dark, she says, and she doesn't even know for sure where she is.

If I come out of this alive, I'm going to find her, if it takes me the rest of my life. Lying wrapped in his fur coat and blanket, in a musty heap of straw, alone on a strange world, Carr suddenly realized that the change in his life, the change that had begun when he saw the girl in the crystal and had thrown over his job and his life to stay on her world, was complete. He had found his new direction, and it led toward the girl. *His* girl. His woman, now and for the rest of his life. Callista.

He was cynic enough to jeer a little at himself. Yeah. He didn't know where she was, who she was, or what she was; she might be married with six children (well, hardly, at her age); she might be a ghastly bitch—who knew what women were like on this world? All he knew about her was . . .

All he knew about her was that in some way she'd touched him, come closer to him than anyone had ever come before. He knew that she was lonely and miserable and frightened, that she couldn't get in touch with her own people, that for some reason she needed him. All he knew about her was all he needed to know about her: she needed him. For some reason he was all she had to cling to, and if she wanted his life she could have it. He'd hunt her up somehow, get her away from whoever was keeping her in the dark, hurting her, and frightening her. He'd get her free. (*Yeah*, sneered his cynical other self, *quite the hero, slaying dragons for your fair lady*, but he turned the jeer off harshly.) And after that, when she was free and happy—

After that, well, we'll cross that bridge when we come to it, he said firmly, and curled down to sleep again.

The storm lasted, as nearly as he could tell (his chronometer had evidently been damaged in the crash and never ran again), for five days. On the third or fourth of those days he woke in dim light to see the girl's shadowy form, stilled, sleeping, close beside him; still disoriented, rousing to sharp, intense physical awareness of her—round, lovely, clad only in the flimsy, torn thin garment which seemed to be all she was wearing—he reached out to draw her close into his arms; then, with the sharp shock of disappointment, he realized there was nothing to touch. As if the very intensity of his thoughts had reached her, awareness flashed over her sleeping face and the large gray eyes opened; she looked at him in surprise and faint dismay.

"I am sorry," she murmured. "You—startled me."

Carr shook his head, trying to orient himself. "I'm the one to be sorry," he said. "I guess I must have thought I was dreaming and it didn't matter. I didn't mean to offend you."

"I'm not offended," she said simply, looking straight into his eyes. "If I were here beside you like this, you would have every right to expect— I only meant, I am sorry to have unwittingly aroused a desire I cannot satisfy. I did not do it willingly. I must have been thinking of you in my sleep, stranger. I cannot go on simply thinking of you as *stranger*," Callista said, a flicker of faint amusement passing over her face.

"My name's Andrew Carr," he said, and felt her soft repetition of the name.

"Andrew. I am sorry, Andrew. I must have been thinking of you in my sleep and so drawn to you without waking." With no further sign of haste or fluster, she drew her clothes more carefully around her bare breasts and smoothed the diaphanous folds of her skirt down around her round thighs. She smiled and now there was a glimmer almost of mischief in her sad face. "Ah, this is sad! The first time, the very first, that I lie down with any man, and I am not able to enjoy it! But it's naughty of me to tease you. Please don't think I am so badly brought up as all that."

Deeply touched, as much by her brave attempt to make a joke as anything else, Andrew said gently, "I couldn't think anything of you that wasn't good, Callista. I only wish"—and to his own surprise he felt his voice breaking—"I wish there was some real comfort I could give you."

She reached out her hand—almost as if, Andrew thought in surprise, she too had forgotten for a moment that he was not physically present to her—and laid it over his wrist. He could see his own wrist through the delicate appearance of her fingers, but the illusion was somehow very comforting, anyhow. She said, "I suppose it is something, that you can give companionship and"— her voice wavered; she was crying—"and the sense of a human presence to someone who is alone in the dark."

He watched her weep, torn apart by the sight of her tears. When she had collected herself a little, he asked, "Where are you? Can I help you somehow?"

She shook her head. "As I told you. They have kept me in the dark, since if I knew exactly where I was, I could be elsewhere. Since I do not know precisely, I can leave this place only in my spirit; my body must perforce stay where they have confined it, and they must know that. *Curse them!*"

"Who are *they*, Callista?"

"I don't know that, exactly, either," she said, "but I suspect they are not men, since they have offered me no physical harm except blows and kicks. It is the only thing for which a woman of the Domains may be grateful when she is in the hands of the other folk—at least with them she need not fear ravishment. For the first several days in their hands, I spent night and day in hourly terror of rape; when it did not come, I knew I was not in human hands. Any man in these mountains would know how to make me powerless to fight them . . . whereas the other folk have no recourse except to take away my jewels, lest one of them should be a starstone, and to keep me in darkness so I can do them no harm with the light of sun or stars."

Andrew didn't understand any of that. Not in human hands? Then who were her captors? He asked another question.

"If you are in the dark, how can you see me?"

"I see you in the overlight," she said quietly, telling him nothing at all. "As you see me. Not the light of this world—look. You know, I suppose, that the things we call solid are only appearances, tiny particles of energy strung together and whirling wildly around, with much more of empty space than of solidness."

"Yes, I know that." It was an odd way to explain molecular and atomic energy, but it got her meaning across.

"Well, then. Strung to your solid body by these energy webs there are other bodies, and if you are taught, you can use them in the world of that level. How can I say this? Of the level of solidness where you are. Your solid body walks on this world, this solid planet under your solid feet, and you need the solid light of our sun. It is powered by your mind, which moves your solid brain, and the solid brain sends messages that move your arms and legs and so forth. Your mind also powers your lighter bodies, each one with its own electric nerve-net of energy. In the world of the overlight, where we are now, there is no such thing as darkness, because the light does not come from a solid sun. It comes from the energy-net body of the sun, which can shine—how can I say this?—right through the energy-net body of the planet. The solid body of the planet can shut out the light of the solid sun, but not the energy-net light. Is that clear?"

"I suppose so," he said slowly, trying to cope with it.

It sounded like the old story of astral duplicates of the body and astral planes, in her own language, which he supposed was reaching his mind directly from hers. "The important thing is that you can come here. There have been times when I've wanted to step out and leave my body behind."

"Oh, you do," she said literally. "Everyone does in sleep, when the energy-nets fall apart. But you have not been trained to do it at will. Someday, perhaps, I can teach you how it is done." She laughed a little ruefully. "If we both live, that is. If we both live."

CHAPTER FOUR

Outside the thick walls of the great house at Armida, the white blizzard raged, howling and whining around the heights as if animated by a personal fury against the stone walls which kept it at bay. Even inside, in the great hall, the windows were grayed with its blur and the wind reached them as a dulled roar. Restless and distraught, Ellemir paced the length of the hall. With a nervous glance at the raging storm outside, she said, "We cannot even search for her in this weather! And with every hour that passes, it may be that she is farther and farther away." She turned on Damon like a fury, and demanded, "How can you sit there so calmly, toasting your toes, when Callista is somewhere in this storm?"

Damon raised his head and said quietly, "Come and sit down, Ellemir. We may be reasonably sure that wherever Callista may be, she is not out in the snowstorm. Whoever went to so much trouble to steal her from here did not do it to let her die of exposure in the hills. As for searching for her, were the weather never so good, we could not go out and quarter the Kilghard Hills on horseback, shouting her name in the forests." He had spoken with wry humor, but Ellemir whirled on him angrily.

"Are you saying we can do nothing, that we are helpless, that we must abandon her to whatever fate has seized her?"

"I am saying nothing of the sort," Damon told her. "You heard what I said. We could not search for her at random in these hills, even if the weather would allow it. If she were in any ordinary hiding place, you could touch her mind. Let us use these days of the storm to begin the search in some reasonable way, and the best way to do that is to sit down, and think about it. Do come and sit down, Ellemir," he pleaded. "Pacing the floor, and tearing your nerves to shreds, will not help

Callista. It will only make you less fit to help her when the time comes. You have not eaten; you look as if you have not slept. Come, kinswoman. Sit here by the fire. Let me give you some wine." He rose and led the girl to a seat. She looked up with her lips trembling and said, "Don't be kind to me, Damon, or I'll break down and melt."

"It might do you good if you could," he said, pouring her a glass of wine. She sipped it slowly, and he stood by the fireplace, looking down at her. He said, "I have been thinking. You told me Callista complained of evil dreams—withering gardens, cat-hags?"

"That is so."

Damon nodded. He said, "I rode from Serrais with a party of Guards, and Reidel—a Guardsman of my company—spoke of misfortune that had fallen on his kinsman. He was said to have raved—listen to this—of the darkening lands, and of great fires and winds that brought death, and girls who clawed at his soul like cathags. From many men, I would have dismissed this as mere babble, imagination. But I have known Reidel all my life. He does not babble, and as far as I have ever been able to determine, he has no more imagination than one of his own saddle bags. *Had*, I should say; the poor fellow is dead. But he was speaking of what he had seen and heard, and I think it more than coincidence. And I told you of the ambush, when we were struck by invisible attackers with invisible swords and weapons. This alone would tell me that something very strange is going on in the heights they have begun to call the darkening lands. Since it is rather less than unlikely that there would be two complete sets of bizarre happenings in one part of the country, it makes sense to begin with the assumption that what happened to my Guardsmen is somehow associated with what happened to Callista."

"That seems likely," she said. "This tells me something else. It was no human being who tore out old Bethiah's eyes as she fought to save her fosterling." She shuddered, wrapping her arms around her shoulders as if she were icy cold. "Damon! It is possible, can it be, that Callista is in the hands of the cat-people?"

"It seems not impossible," Damon said.

"But what could they want with her? What will they do with her? What—what—"

"How should I know, Ellemir? I could only guess. I know so little of those folk, even though I fought them. I have never seen one of them, except lying as a corpse on a battlefield. There are those who believe that they are as intelligent as mankind, and there are those who believe they are little more than the brutes. I do not think that anyone since the days of Varzil the Good really knows anything about them for certain."

"No, there is one thing we know for certain," Ellemir said grimly, "that they fight like men, and sometimes even more fiercely."

"That, yes," said Damon, and was silent, thinking of his Guard, ambushed and lying dead on the hillsides below Armida. They had died so that he could sit here by the fireside with Ellemir. He knew he could have done nothing to save them, and sharing their death would have done no good to anyone, but all the same guilt, tore at him and would not be eased. "When the storm subsides I must make shift somehow to go back and bury them," he said, adding after a moment, "If there is enough left of them to bury."

Ellemir said, quoting a well-known mountain proverb, "The dead in heaven is too happy to grieve for indignities to his corpse; the dead in hell has too much else to grieve for."

"Still," said Damon stubbornly, "for the sake of their kinfolk, I would do what I can."

"It is Callista's fate that troubles me now," Ellemir said. "Damon! Can you possibly be serious? Can you really believe that Callista is in the hands of nonhumans? Beyond all other considerations, what could they possibly *want* with her?"

"As for that, child, I know no more than you do," said Damon. "It is just possible—and we must accept the possibility—that they stole her for some unexplainable reason, comprehensible only to nonhumans, which we, being human, can never know or comprehend."

"That is no help at all!" Ellemir said angrily. "It sounds like the horror tales I heard in the nursery! So-and-so was stolen by monsters, and when I asked why the monsters stole her, Nurse told me that it was because they were monsters, and monsters were evil—" She broke off and her voice caught again. "This is *real*, Damon! She's my *sister!* Don't tell me fairy stories!"

Damon looked at her levelly. "Nothing was further from my mind. I told you before; no one *really* knows anything about the cat-folk."

"Except that they are evil!"

"What is evil?" Damon asked wearily. "Say they do evil to our own people, and I will agree heartily with you. But if you say that they are evil in themselves, for no reason and just for the pleasure of doing evil, then you are making them into those fairy-story monsters you're talking about. I only said that since we are human and they are cat-people, we may have to accept that we may not be able to understand, now or ever, what their reasons for taking her may have been. But that is simply something to keep in mind—that any reasons we might guess for her kidnapping may simply be human approximations of *their* reasons, and not the whole truth. Apart from that, though, why do any folk steal women, and why Callista in particular? Or, for that matter, any beasts steal? I have never heard that they were cannibal flesh-eaters, and in any case the forests are filled with game at this season, so we may assume it was not that."

"Are you trying to give me the horrors?" Ellemir still sounded angry.

"Not a bit of it. I'm trying to do *away* with the horrors," Damon said. "If there was any vague thought in your mind that she might have been killed and eaten, I think you can dismiss it. Since they killed her guards, and disabled her foster mother, it was not just *any* human being they wanted, or even any woman. So they took her, not because she was human, not just because she was female, but because she was one specific female human: because she was Callista."

Ellemir said, low, "Bandits and trail-raiders steal young women, at times, for slaves, or concubines, or to sell in the Dry Towns—"

"I think we can forget that too," said Damon firmly. "They left all your serving-girls; in any case, what would cat-men want with a human female? There are stories of crossbreeds between man and *chieri*, back in the ancient times, but even those are mostly legends and no man living can say whether or not they have any foundation in fact. As for the other folk, our women are no more to them than theirs to us. Of course, it is possible that they have some human captive who wanted a wife, but even if they were so altruistic and kind as to be willing to provide him with one, which I admit I find hard to believe, there were a dozen serving girls in the outbuildings, as young as Callista, just as beautiful, and infinitely easier to come at. If they simply wanted human women, as hostages, or to sell somewhere as slaves, they would have taken them as well. Or taken them, and left Callista."

"Or me. Why take Callista from her bed and leave me sleeping untouched in mine?"

"That, too. You and Callista are twins. *I* can tell you one from the other, but I have known you since your hair was too short to braid. A casual stranger could never have known you apart, and might easily have taken Callista for you. Now it's barely possible that they were simply wanting a hostage, or someone to hold to ransom, and snatched the one who came first to hand."

"No," Ellemir said, "my bed is nearest the door, and they walked very quietly and carefully around me to come at her."

"Then it comes to the one difference between you," Damon told her. "Callista is a telepath and a Keeper. You are not. We can only assume that in some way they knew which of you was the telepath, and that for some reason they wanted specifically to take the one woman here who fitted that description. Why? I know no more than you do, but I am sure that was their reason."

"And all this still leaves us no nearer to a solution," Ellemir said, and she sounded frantic. "The facts are that she is gone, and we don't know where she is! So all your talk is no good at all!"

"No? Think a little," said Damon. "We know she has probably not been killed, except by accident; if they went to such great pains to take her, they will probably treat her with great care, feed her well, keep her warm, cherish her as a prize. She may be frightened and lonely, but she is probably neither cold, hungry, nor in pain, and it is very unlikely that she has suffered physical abuse or molestation. Also, it is quite probable that she has not been raped. That, at least, should ease your mind."

Ellemir raised the forgotten wine glass and sipped at it. She said, "But it doesn't help us get her back, or even know where to look." Just the same, she sounded calmer, and Damon was glad.

He said, "One thing at a time, girl. Perhaps, after the storm—"

"After the storm, whatever tracks or traces they might have left would be blotted out," Ellemir said.

"From all I hear, the cat-folk leave no tracks a man could read; hardly traces for another cat. In any case, I'm no tracker," Damon said. "If I can help you at all; that won't be the way."

Her eyes widened and suddenly she clutched at his arm.

"Damon! You're a telepath too, you've had some training—can you find Callista that way?"

She looked so excited, so happy and alive at the prospect, that it crushed Damon to have to smash that hope, but he knew he must. He said, "It isn't that easy, Ellemir. If you, her twin, can't reach her mind, there must be some reason."

"But I've had no training, I know so little," Ellemir said hopefully, "and you were Tower-trained—"

The man sighed. "That's true. And I'll try," he said. "I always meant to try. But don't hope for too much, *breda*."

"Will you try *now?*" she pleaded.

"I'll do what I can. First, bring me something of Callista's—jewelry she wears a good deal, a garment she has often worn, something of that sort."

While Ellemir went to fetch it, Damon drew his starstone from the protective silk wrappings about it, and gazed at it, broodingly. Telepath, yes, and Tower-trained in the old telepath sciences of Darkover—for a little while. And the hereditary Gift, the *laran* or telepathic power of the Ridenow family, was the psychic sensing of extrahuman forces, bred into the genetic material of the Ridenow Domain for just such work as this, centuries ago. But in these latter days, the old Darkovan noncausal sciences had fallen into disuse; because of intermarriage, inbreeding, the ancient *laran* Gifts rarely bred true. Damon had inherited his own family Gift in full measure, but all his life he had found it a curse, not a blessing, and he shied away from using it now.

As he had shied away from using it—he faced the fact squarely now, and his own guilt—to save his men. He had sensed danger. The trip which should have been peaceful, routine, a family mission, had turned into a nightmare, reeking with the feel of danger. Yet he had not had the courage to use his starstone, the matrix stone given him during his Tower training, and too intimately keyed to the telepath patterns of his mind to be used or even touched by anyone else.

Because he feared it . . . he had always feared it.

Time reeled, slid momentarily away, annihilating fifteen years that lay between, and a younger Damon stood, with bowed head, before the Keeper Leonie, that same Leonie now aging, whose place Callista was to have taken. Not a young woman even then, Leonie, and far from beautiful, her flame-colored hair already fading, her body flat and spare, but her gray eyes gentle and compassionate.

"No, Damon. It is not that you have failed, or displeased me. And all of us—I myself—love you, and value you. But you are too sensitive, you cannot barricade yourself. Had you been born a woman, in a woman's body," she added, laying a light hand on his shoulder, "you would have been a Keeper, perhaps one of the greatest. But as a man"—faintly, she shrugged—"you would destroy yourself, tear yourself apart. Perhaps, free of the Tower, you may be able to surround yourself with other things, grow less sensitive, less"—she hesitated, groping for the exact word—"less vulnerable. It is for your own good that I send you away, Damon; for your health, for your happiness, perhaps for your very sanity." Lightly, almost a breath, her lips brushed his forehead. "You know I love you; for that reason I do not want to destroy you. Go, Damon."

From that there was no appeal, and Damon had gone, cursing the vulnerability, the Gift he carried like a curse.

He had made a new career for himself in Comyn Council, and although he was no soldier and no swordsman, had taken his turn at commanding the Guardsmen: driven, constantly needing to prove himself. He never admitted even to himself how deeply that hour with Leonie had torn at his manhood. From any work with the starstone (although he carried it still, since it had been made a part of him), he had shied away in horror and panic.

And now he must, though his mind, his nerves, all his senses, were screaming revolt. . . .

He jolted back to present time as Ellemir said tentatively, "Damon, are you asleep?"

He shook his head to clear it of the phantoms of past failure and fear. "No, no. Preparing myself. What have you for me of Callista's?"

She opened her hand; a silver filigree butterfly lay within, daintily starred with multicolored gemstones. "Callista always wore this in her hair," Ellemir said, and indeed a strand or two of long, silken hair was still entangled in the clasp.

"You are sure it is hers? I suppose like all sisters you share your ornaments—my own sisters used to complain of that."

Ellemir turned to show him the butterfly-shaped clasp at the nape of her own neck. She said, "Father always had her ornaments fashioned in silver and mine in gilt, so that we could tell them apart. He had these made for us in Carthon years ago, and she has worn it in her hair every day since then. She does not care much for jewelry, so she gave me the bracelet to match it, but the clasp she always wears."

That sounded circumstantial and convincing. Damon took the silver clasp between his fingers, closing his eyes, tentatively trying to sense what he could from it. "Yes, this is Callista's," he said after a moment, and she said, "Can you really tell?"

Damon shrugged. "Give me yours for a moment," he said, and Ellemir turned and drew the matching clasp from her own hair, turning modestly aside so that he caught only the faintest glimpse of her bare neck. He was so sensitized to her at that moment that even that momentary and fleeting glimpse jerked a string of sensual awareness and response deep in his body; firmly he put it away on a deeper level of consciousness. No time for that now. Ellemir laid the gilded ornament in his hand. It tingled with the feel of her very self. Damon drew a deep breath and forced the awareness below conscious level again. He said, "Close your eyes."

Childishly, she screwed them up tight.

"Hold out your hands. . . ." Damon laid one of the ornaments in each small pink palm. "Now, if you cannot tell me which is your own, you are no child of the Alton Domain. . . ."

"I was tested for *laran* as a child," Ellemir protested, "and told I had none, compared with Callista—"

"Never compare yourself with anyone," Damon said, with a sudden rough thrust of anger. "Concentrate, Ellemir."

She said, with a queer strange note of surprise in her voice, "This is mine—I am sure."

"Look and see."

She opened her blue eyes, and gazed in astonishment at the gilt butterfly clasp in her hand. "Why, it is! The other one felt strange, this one— How did I do that?"

Damon shrugged. "This one—yours—has the impress of your personality, your vibrations, on it," he said. "It would have been simpler still if you and Callista were not twins, for twins share much in vibration. That was why I wanted to be quite, quite sure you had never worn hers, since it is difficult enough to tell twin from twin by their telepathic imprint alone. Of course, since Callista is a Keeper, her imprint is more definite." He broke off, feeling a sudden surge of anger. Ellemir had always lived in her twin's shadow. And she was too good, too gentle and good, to resent it. Why should she be so humble?

Forcibly, he calmed the irrational surge of rage. He said quietly, "I think you have more *laran* than you realize, although it is true that, in twins, one seems always to get more than her fair share of the Gift, and the other rather less. This is why the best Keepers are often one of a twin-pair, since she has her own and a part of her sister's share of the psi potentials."

He cupped the starstone between his hands; it winked

back at him, blue and enigmatic, little ribbons of fire crawling in its depth. *Fires to burn his soul to ashes.* . . . Damon clamped his teeth against the cold nausea of his dread. "You'll have to help," he said roughly.

"But how? I know nothing of this."

"Haven't you ever kept watch for Callista when she went *out?*"

Ellemir shook her head. "She never said anything to me of her training or her work. She said it was difficult and she would rather forget it when she was here."

"A pity," Damon said. He settled himself comfortably in his chair. He said, "Very well, I'll have to teach you now. It would be easier if you were experienced in this, but you have enough to do what you must. It is simple. Here. Lay your hands against my wrists, so that I can still see the starstone, but—yes, there, at the pulse spots. Now—" He reached out, tentatively, trying to make a light telepathic contact. She flinched physically, and he smiled. "Yes, that's right, you can perceive the contact. Now all you must do is to keep watch over my body while I am out of it hunting for Callista. When I first go *out*, I will feel cold to your touch, and my heart and pulse will slow slightly. That is normal; don't be afraid. But if we are interrupted, don't let anyone touch me; Above all, don't let anyone move me. If my pulse begins to quicken and race, or if the veins at my temples swell, or my body begins to grow either deathly cold or very waxen, then you must wake me."

"How do I do that?"

"Call my name, and put your whole force behind it," Damon said. "You don't have to speak aloud, just project your thoughts at me, calling my name. If you cannot wake me, and it gets worse—for instance, if I show any difficulty in breathing—wake me *at once*; don't delay any further. At the last, but only if you cannot wake me any other way, touch the stone." He winced as he said it. "Only as a last desperate expedient, though; it is painful and might throw me into shock." He felt her hands tremble as they gripped his wrists, and felt her fear and hesitation like a faint fog obscuring the clarity of his own thought.

Poor child. I shouldn't have to do this to her. Damn

the luck. If Callista had to get herself into trouble—He forced himself to be fair, and tried to still his pounding heart. This wasn't Callista's fault either. He should save his curses for her kidnappers.

Ellemir said timidly, "Don't be angry, Damon," and he thought, *It's a good sign she can feel that I'm angry.* He said aloud, "I'm not angry at you, *breda.*" He used the intimate word which could mean simply *kinswoman* or, more closely, *darling.* He settled himself as comfortably as he could, sensitizing himself to the feel of Callista's hair-clasp between his hands, the starstone above it, pulsing gently in unconscious rhythm with his own nerve currents. He tried to blur everything else, every other sensation, the feel of Ellemir's cold hands on his wrists and her warm breath against his throat, the faint woman-scent of her closeness; he blotted these out, blotted out the flicker of fire and candle beyond them, dimmed the shadows of the room, let vision sink into the blue pulsing of the starstone. He sensed, rather than physically felt, the relaxing of his muscles as his body went insensible. For an instant nothing existed except the vast blue of the starstone, pulsing with the beating of his heart, then his heart stopped, or at least he was no longer conscious of anything except the expanding blueness: a glare, a blue flame, a sea rushing in to drown him. . . .

With a brief, tingling shock, he was out of his body and standing over it, looking down from above, with a certain ironic detachment, on the thin, slumped body in the chair, the frail, frightened-looking girl kneeling and grasping its wrists. He was not really seeing, but perceiving in some strange, dark way through closed eyelids.

In the overlight forming around him he cast a swift downward look. The body in the chair had been wearing a shabby jerkin and leather riding breeches, but as always when he stepped *out* he felt taller, stronger, more muscular, moving with effortless ease as the walls of the great hall thinned and moved away. And this body, if it could be called a body, was wearing a glimmering tunic of gold and green that flickered with a faint firelight glow. Leonie had told him once, "this is how your mind sees itself." He was bare-armed and barefoot, and he felt an incongruous flicker of amusement. *To go out in the blizzard like this?* But of course the blizzard was not *here*, not at all, although if he listened, he could hear the faint howl of the wind, and he knew the violence of the storm must be intense indeed if even its echo could penetrate into the overworld. As he formulated that thought he felt himself begin to shiver and quickly dismissed the thought and memory of the blizzard; his consciousness of it could solidify it on this plane and bring it here.

He moved, gliding, not conscious of separate steps. He was conscious of Callista's jeweled butterfly still between his hands, fluttering like a live thing, beating with the impress of her mental "voice." Or rather, since the jewel itself was in the hands of his body, "down there," the mental counterpart of the ornament, which he bore "here." He tried to sensitize himself to the special reverberations of that "voice," adding to it his call, a shout that felt to him like a commanding bellow.

"Callista!"

There was no answer. He had not really expected an answer; if it had been that simple, Ellemir would have already made contact with her twin. Around him the overworld was as still as death, and he looked around, all the time aware that the world, and himself, were only comfortable visualizations, for some intangible level of reality. . . . That he saw it as a "world" because it was more convenient to see and feel it that way than as an intangible mental realm; that he visualized himself as a body, striding across a great barren empty plain, because it was easier and less disconcerting than visualizing himself as a bodiless point of thought adrift in other thoughts. At the moment it looked to him like an enormous flat horizon, stretching away dim and bare and silent into endless spaces and skies. In the far distance shadows drifted, and as his curiosity was roused about them, he moved rapidly, without the need to take steps, in their direction.

As he came nearer, they became clearer, human forms which looked oddly gray and unfocused. He knew that if he spoke to them, they would immediately vanish—if they had nothing to do with him or his quest—or immediately come into sharp focus. The overworld was never empty: there were always minds out on the astral for one reason or another, even if they were only sleepers out of their bodies, their minds crossing his in the formless realm of thought. He saw a few faces, dimly, like reflections in water, of people he vaguely recognized. He knew that these were kinsmen and acquaintances of his who were sleeping or deep in meditation, and that he had somehow come into their thoughts; that some of them would wake with a memory of having seen him in a dream. He passed them without any attempt to speak. None of them could have any bearing on his search.

Far in the distance he saw a great shining structure which he recognized from previous visits to this world, and knew it was the Tower where he had been trained, years before. Usually he bypassed it, in such journeys, without passing near; now he felt himself drifting nearer and nearer to it. As he came closer it took on form and solidity. Generations of telepaths had been trained here, exploring the overworld from this base and background. No wonder the Tower stood firm as a landmark in the overworld. Surely Callista would have come here, if she was out on the planes and was free, he thought.

Now he stood on the plain, just below the looming structure of the Tower. Grass, trees, and flowers had begun to formulate around him, his own memory and the joint visualizations of everyone who came into the overworld from the Tower keeping them relatively solid here. He walked amid the familiar trees and scented flowers now with an aching sense of loss, of nostalgia, almost of homesickness. He passed through the dimly shining gateway, and stood briefly on the remembered stones. Suddenly, before him, stood a veiled woman, but even through her veils he knew her: Leonie, the sorceress-Keeper of the Tower during his years there. Her face was a little blurred: half, he knew, the face he remembered; half, the face she wore now.

"Leonie," he said, and the dim figure solidified, took on more definite and clear form, even to the twin copper bracelets, formed like serpents, which she always wore. "Damon," she said, with gentle reproach, "what are you doing out here on this plane tonight?"

He held out the silver butterfly clasp, and felt it cold

and solid between his fingers. He said, and heard his own voice strangely thinned, "I am looking for Callista. She is gone, and her twin cannot find her anywhere. Have you seen her here?"

Leonie looked troubled. She said, "No, my dear. We, too, have searched, and she is nowhere on any plane we can reach. From time to time I can feel her somewhere, her living presence, but no matter where I look I cannot come to her."

Damon felt deeply disquieted. Leonie was a powerful, trained telepath, and all the accessible levels of the overworld were known to her. She walked in that world as readily as in the solid world of the body. The fact that Callista's distress was known to her, and that she herself could not locate her pupil and friend, was ominous. Where, in any world, was Callista hiding?

"Perhaps you can find her where I cannot," said Leonie gently. "Blood kin is a deep tie, and may link kindred when friendship or affinity fails. Somehow I think she is there." Leonie raised a shadowy arm and pointed. Damon turned in the direction indicated, and saw only a thick, foggy darkness.

"The darkness is new on this plane," Leonie said, "and none of us can breach it, at least not yet. When we move in that direction we are flung back, as if by force. I do not know what new minds move on this level, but they have not come here by our leave."

"And you think Callista may have strayed into that level and be held there, unable to penetrate that shadow with her mind?"

"I fear so," Leonie said. "If she were kept drugged, or entranced; or if her starstone had been taken from her, or she had been so ill-treated that her mind had been darkened by madness; then it might appear to us, on this level, as if she were imprisoned in a great and impenetrable darkness."

Quickly, with the swiftness of thought, Damon told Leonie what he knew of the abduction of Callista, from her very bed at Armida.

"I do not like it," Leonie said. "What you tell me frightens me. I have heard that there are strange men from another world at Thendara, and that they have come there by permission of the Hasturs. Now and again one of them strays in a dream on to the overworld, but their forms and their minds are strange and mostly they vanish if one speaks to them. They are only shadows here, but they seem harmless enough, men like any others, without much skill at moving in the realms of the mind. I find it hard to believe that these Terrans—that is what they call themselves—can have had any part in what has happened to Callista. What reason could they have had? And since they are on our world by sufferance, why would they antagonize us by such conduct? No; there seems more purpose to it than that."

Damon became conscious that he was cold again, and shivering. The plain seemed to tremble under his feet. He knew that if he wished to remain in the overworld, he must move on. Speaking to Leonie had been a comfort, but he must not linger here if he hoped to carry on his search for Callista. Leonie seemed to follow his resolution, and said, "Search, then. Take my blessing." even as she raised her hand in the ritual gesture, her form faded and Damon discovered that he had receded a great distance and was no longer standing on the familiar courtyard stones of the Tower, but had come a long way over the gray plain toward the darkness.

The cold grew and he shuddered with the recurrent blasts, like icy winds, that beat out from that dark place. The darkening lands, he thought grimly, and against the cold he quickly visualized himself dressed in a thick gold and green cloak. The cold lessened, but only slightly, and his motion toward the darkness grew ever slower, as if some pressure from that darkness were flowing out, pushing him backward, backward. He struggled against it, calling out Callista's name again. *If she's anywhere out on the planes, she'll hear that*, he thought. But if Leonie had sought in vain, how could *he* hope to succeed?

The darkness flowed, like thick boiling cloud, and seemed suddenly peopled with dark twisted shapes, menacing half-seen faces, threatening gestures made by bodiless limbs that were seen for a moment in the darkness and vanished again. Damon felt a spasm of fear, an almost anguished longing for the solid world and his solid body and the fireplace at Armida. . . . The world seemed full of half-heard threats and cries. *Go back! Go back or you will die!*

He slogged painfully onward, forcing his way hard against the pressure. Callista's butterfly clasp, between his hands, seemed to shine, and flutter, and vibrate, and he knew that he was coming nearer to her, nearer. . . .

"Callista! Callista!"

For an instant the thick dark cloud thinned, and almost, for a moment, he saw her, a shadow, a wisp, in a thin, torn nightdress, her hair loose and tangled, her face dark and bruised with pain or tears. She stretched out her hands to him, in appeal, and her mouth moved, but he could not hear. Then the darkness boiled up again, and for a moment he saw flashing sword-blades, curiously shaped, slashing.

Quickly, Damon shifted ground again, and with a swift thought, transformed the thick warm cloak into a gleaming coat of armor. None too soon. He heard the half-visible sword-blades clash against it and a nightmarish stab of pain came and went, momentarily, near his heart.

The swords retreated into the darkness, and again he tried to press forward. Then the darkness began to boil up again, like the whirling of a tornado, and out of the thick bubbling whorl of the maelstrom of cloud came a thin, malevolent voice.

"Go back. You cannot come here."

Damon stood his ground, working hard to make the feel of the surface beneath his boots solid, to formulate familiar paving stone so that he and his invisible antagonist stood on ground of his choosing. But beneath him the surface rippled and flowed like water until he felt dizzy, and again the invisible voice spoke, in tones of command.

"Go, I tell you. Go while you still can."

"By what right do you tell me to go?"

The indifferent voice said thinly, "I know nothing of right. I have the power to make you go, and I shall do so. Why provoke such a struggle without need?"

Damon stood his ground, although it seemed as if he were swaying in a sickening up-and-down rhythm, his head pounding with pain. He said, "I will go if my kinswoman comes with me."

"You will go, at once, and that is all I intend to say," the voice said, and Damon felt an enormous thrust of power, a great blow that sent his head reeling. He struggled inside the boiling darkness, and cried out, "Show yourself! Who are you? By what right do you come here?" The starstone—or its mental counterpart—was still between his fingers; he swung it over his head, like a lantern, and the darkness was illuminated by a dazzling blue glare. By that light he beheld a tall, strangely robed figure, with a savage cat's head, and great claws. . . .

And at that moment there was another of those savage blows. The darkness receded, into a great howling, screaming wind, and Damon found himself alone on what felt like a slippery hillside. Around him was the buffeting wind, the razor-needles of sleet driving into his face . . . the thick driving snow, the storm. . . .

He struggled to regain his footing, knowing that out here he had met something he had never before encountered on this plane. His flesh seemed to crawl, and he tensed himself, knowing that now he must fight for his sanity, his very life. . . .

The telepaths of Darkover were trained to work with the starstones, which had the power, assisted by the human mind, of transforming energies directly from one form to another. In the realms where their minds traveled to encompass this work, there were strange things, intelligences which were not human, or material, but came from other realms of existence. Most of them had nothing to do with humankind at all. Others were prone, when touched by human minds come seeking in the realms to which they, the alien intelligences belonged, to meddle with those human minds. A few of them, reached by human minds trained to reach their levels, remained in contact with the human levels, and were visualized as demons, or even as gods. The Ridenow Gift, Damon's Gift, had been deliberately bred into the minds of his family, to allow them to scent and make contact with these alien presences.

But he'd never seen one who took that form . . . *the great cat.* . . . It was deliberately malevolent, not just indifferent. It had thrust him here, into the level of the blizzard. . . .

He forced himself to search for rationality. The blizzard was not real. It was a thought blizzard, solidified here by thought, and he could take refuge in other realms where it did not blow. He visualized warm sunshine, a sunlit mountainside . . . for a moment the snow-needles thinned, then began to rage with renewed force. Someone was projecting it at him . . . someone or *something*. The catmen? Was Callista in their power, then?

The gusts of wind strengthened, forcing his weakening body to its knees. He struggled, slipped, and fell on rugged ice, which cut him. He felt himself bleeding, freezing, weakening. . . .

Dying. . . .

He thought, with icy rationality, *I've got to get off this level, I've got to get back to my body.* If he was trapped here, out of his body, his body would live a while, spoon-fed and helpless, slowly withering, and finally die.

Ellemir, Ellemir, he sent out the call that sounded like a scream. *Wake me, bring me back, get me out of here!* Again and again he shouted, feeling the howling of the winds carry his cry away into the snow-cut needled darkness. His face was cut, his hands bleeding as he struggled again and again to get to his feet in the snow, to raise himself to his knees, to crawl even. . . .

His struggles grew fainter and fainter, and a sense of total hopelessness, almost of resignation, came over him. *I should never have trusted to Ellemir. She isn't strong enough. I'll never get out.* It seemed he had been sliding, slipping, floundering in the nightmare blizzard for hours, days. . . .

Agony lanced through him, and an icy pain squeezed his head. A glare of blue fire sprang up wildly around him, there was a shock like a thunderclap, and Damon, weak and gasping and exhausted, was lying in the armchair in the great hall at Armida. The fire had long burned down, and the room was icy cold. Ellemir, pale and terrified, her lips blue and chattering, looked down at him. "Damon, oh, Damon! Oh, wake up, wake up!"

He gasped, painfully. He said, "I'm here, I'm back." Somehow, she had reached into the nightmare of the overworld and brought him back. His head and heart were pounding; and his teeth chattering. He looked around. Daylight was beginning to steal through the long windows; outside, the courtyard lay quiet and peaceful in the daybreak; the storm was over, inside and out. He blinked and shook his head. "The blizzard," he said, dimly.

"Did you find Callista?"

He shook his head. "No, but I found whatever has her, and it nearly took me too."

"I couldn't wake you—and you were blue and gasping, and moaning so. Finally I grabbed the starstone," Ellemir confessed. "When I did, I thought you were having a convulsion. I thought I'd killed you—"

She nearly had, Damon thought. But better that than leaving him to die in the raging blizzard of the overworld. She had been crying. "Poor girl, I must have frightened you out of your wits," he said tenderly, and drew her down to him. She lay across his knees, still trembling; he became aware that she was nearly as cold as he was. He caught up a fur lap-robe that lay across the back of the settle, and wrapped it around them both. Soon he would mend the fire; just now it was enough to huddle within its comforting warmth, to feel the girl's icy stiffness begin to lessen a little and her shivering quiet. "My poor little love, I frightened you, and you're half dead with cold and fright," he murmured, holding her tight against him. He kissed her cold, tear-wet cheeks and became aware that he had been wanting to do that for a long, long time; he let his kisses move slowly from her wet face to her cold lips, trying to warm them with his own. "Don't cry, darling. Don't cry."

She stirred a little against him, not in protest but in returning awareness, and said, almost sleepily, "The servants are still abed. We should make up the fire, call them—"

"Damn the servants." He didn't want anyone interrupting this new awareness, this new and beautiful closeness. "I don't want to let you go, Ellemir."

She lifted her lips and kissed him on the mouth. "You don't have to," she said softly, and they lay quietly, close together in the great fur robe, barely touching, but warmed by the contact. Damon was conscious of deathly weariness and of hunger, the terrible depletion of nervous force which was the inevitable penalty of telepathic work. Rationally he knew he should get up, mend the fire, have some food brought, or he might pay in hours or days of lassitude and illness. But he could not bring himself to move, was deeply reluctant to let Ellemir out of his arms. For a moment, letting the exhaustion have its way, he lapsed into brief sleep or unconsciousness.

Ellemir was shaking him, and in the bright hall there was a pounding, a sound, a strange shouting. "Someone is at the door," Ellemir said dazedly. "At this hour? And the servants . . . ? What—"

Damon untangled himself from the robe and stood up, going through the hall to the inner court and through that to the great bolted outer doors. Stiffly, with unpracticed fingers, he struggled with the bolt and drew it back.

On the doorstep stood a man, wrapped in a great fur coat of an unfamiliar pattern, clad in ragged and strange clothing. He said, and his accent was strange and alien, "I am a stranger and lost. I am with the mapping expedition from the Trade City. Can you give me shelter, and send a message to my people?"

Damon looked at him confusedly for a moment. He said at last, slowly, "Yes, come in, come in, stranger; be welcome." He turned to Ellemir and said, "It is only one of the Terrans from Thendara. I have heard of them, they are harmless. It is the wish of Hastur that we show them hospitality when needful, though this one is far astray indeed. Call the housefolk, *breda*; he is probably in need of food and fire."

Ellemir collected herself and said, "Come in; be welcome to Armida and the hospitality of the Alton Domain, stranger. We will help you as we may—" She broke off, for the stranger was staring at her with wide, frightened eyes. He said shakily, "Callista! Callista! You are real!"

She stared at him, as confused as he. She stammered, "No. No, I am not Callista, I am Ellemir. But what can you—what can *you* possibly know of Callista?"

CHAPTER FIVE

"I may as well tell you at once that I don't believe a word of it," the girl who called herself Ellemir said.

It's still hard to accept that she isn't Callista. They are so damned *alike!*, thought Andrew Carr. He sat back on the heavy wooden bench before the fire, drinking in the growing warmth. It was good to be inside a real house again, even though the storm was over. He could smell food cooking somewhere, and that was wonderful too. It could have been entirely wonderful, except for the girl, who looked so much like Callista and so strangely wasn't; she was standing in front of him, looking down with bleak hostility and repeating, "I don't believe it."

The slender red-haired man, kneeling on the hearth to feed the gnawing fire (he looked tired, too, and cold, and Carr wondered if he were ill), said without raising his head, "That is unfair, Ellemir. You know what I am. I can tell when I am being lied to, and he's not lying. He *recognized* you. Therefore he must have seen either you, or Callista. And where would one of the *Terranan* have seen Callista? Unless, as he says, his story is true."

Ellemir's face was stubborn. She said, "How do we know that it is not *his* people who have imprisoned Callista? He comes to us with a wild story that Callista has somehow reached him, guided him when he was lost in the mountains, and saved him from the storm. Are you trying to make me believe that Callista could reach this outworlder, this stranger, when you could not find her in the overworld, and when she could not come through to me, her twin sister? I'm sorry, Damon, I simply cannot believe it."

Carr looked straight at the girl. He said, "If you're going to call me a liar, do it *to* me, not over my head. This story of mine, as you call it, is no pleasure to be telling. Do you think I like to sound like a madman? At first I thought the girl was a ghost, as I told you; or that

I was dead already and seeing whatever it is that comes
after. But when she saved me from falling with the
plane, and then when she guided me to a safe place to
wait out the storm, I believed that she was real. I *had*
to believe it. I don't blame you for doubting me. I
doubted myself, long enough. But it's true. And I suppose you are Callista's kinsfolk; heaven knows you look
enough like her for a twin."

Too bad, he found himself thinking, *that this one
hasn't a little of Callista's sweet disposition*. Well, at least
the man seemed to believe his story.

Damon stood up, leaving the fire to fend for itself now
that it was burning well, and turned to Carr. He said, "I
apologize for my cousin's lack of courtesy, stranger. She
has endured some difficult days since her sister was
taken away, in the night and unseen. It is not easy for
her to accept what you say, that Callista could reach
your mind when she could not reach her own twin; the
bond of the twin-born is believed to be the strongest
bond known. I cannot explain it either, but I am old
enough to know that there are too many things in this
life for any man, or any woman either, to understand
them all. Perhaps you can tell us more."

"I don't know what I can tell you," Carr said. "I don't
understand it either."

"Perhaps you know something you don't realize you
know," Damon said. "But for now, stop badgering him,
Ellemir. Whoever and whatever he is, or whatever the
many truths of all this may be, he is a guest, and weary
and cold, and until he has had his fill of warmth and
food, and sleep if he needs it, it is a failure in hospitality
to question him. You do the Alton Domain no honor,
kinswoman."

Carr followed all this sketchily; there were words that
he only partially understood, though in Thendara he had
been taught to speak the *lingua franca* of the Trade City,
and he could make himself understood well enough.
Nevertheless, he realized that Damon was upbraiding
the girl who looked like Callista; and she flushed to the
roots of her coppery hair. She said (speaking slowly, so
that he would be sure to understand), "Stranger, I meant
no offense. I am sure that any misunderstandings will

become clear in time. For now, accept the hospitality of our house and Domain. Here is fire; food will be brought to you as soon as it is cooked. Have you any other need I have neglected to supply?"

"I'd like to get out of this wet coat," Carr said. It was beginning to steam and drip in the growing warmth of the fire. Damon came to help him unwrap it, and laid it aside. He said, "None of your clothing is fit for the storms of our mountains, and those shoes, now, are fit only for the trashpile. They were never built for travel-ing in the mountains."

Carr said, with a wry grimace, "I wasn't exactly plan-ning on this trip. As for this coat, it belongs to a dead man, but I was damned glad to have it."

Damon said, "I was not intending to insult your man-ner of dress, stranger. The fact remains that you are unsuitably clothed, even indoors, and dangerously ill-clad for any return journey. My own clothes would hardly fit you"—Damon looked up with a laugh at the tall Earthman, a head taller than he was and probably half again his weight and girth—"but if you have no objection to wearing the clothes of a servant or one of the stewards, I think I can find something which will keep you warm."

"That's very kind of you," Andrew Carr said. "I've been wearing these since the crash, and a change wouldn't feel bad at all. I could use a wash, too."

"I don't doubt it. Very few, even of those who live in the mountains, survive being caught out in our mountain storms," Damon said.

"I wouldn't have lived through it, if it hadn't been for Callista," he answered.

Damon nodded. "I believe it. The very fact that you, a stranger to our world, survived one of our storms, says much for the truth of what you have told us. Come with me, and I'll find you fresh clothes and a bath."

Andrew followed Damon through the broad corridors and spacious rooms and up a long flight of shallow stairs. He conducted him at last into a suite of rooms with wide windows, covered with heavy woven draperies against the cold. Opening from one of the rooms was a large bathroom with a huge stone tub, sunk deep in the floor.

Steam was rising from a fountain in the middle of the room.

"Have a hot bath, and wrap up in a blanket or something," Damon said. "I'll go wake up a few more of the servants, and find some clothes to fit you. Shall I send someone to help you bathe, or can you manage by yourself? Ellemir keeps few servants, but I am sure I can find someone to wait on you."

Andrew assured Damon that he was accustomed to bathing himself without assistance, and the young man withdrew. Andrew took a long, luxurious bath, soaking to the neck in the scalding hot water *(And I thought this place was primitive, good God!)*, meanwhile wondering a little about the heating system. The ancient Romans and Cretans on Earth managed to have the most elaborate baths in history, so why shouldn't these people? Downstairs they'd been lighting wood fires, but why not? Fireplaces were considered the height of luxury even in some societies that didn't need them. Maybe they used natural hot springs. Anyhow, the hot water felt good, and he lingered, soaking out the stiffness of days spent sleeping on stone floors, clambering around in the mountains. Finally, feeling incredibly refreshed, he climbed out of the deep tub, dried himself, and wrapped himself in a blanket.

Soon afterward Damon returned. He looked as if he, too, had taken advantage of the time to bathe and put on fresh clothes; he looked younger and less exhausted and spent. He brought an armful of clothing, saying almost in apology, "These are poor enough garments to offer a guest; it is the hall-steward's holiday suit."

"At least they're dry and clean," Andrew said, "so thank him for me, whoever he is."

"Come down to the hall when you're ready," Damon said. "There will be food cooked by then."

Left alone, Andrew got himself into the "hall-steward's holiday suit." It consisted of a shirt and knee-length underdrawers of coarse linen; over which went suedelike breeches, flared somewhat from knee to ankle; a long-sleeved finely embroidered shirt with wide sleeves gathered in at the wrist; and a leather jerkin. There were knitted stockings that tied at the knee, and over them low felt boots lined with fur. In this outfit, which was more comfortable than he had thought when he looked at it, he felt warm for the first time in days. He was hungry, too, and when he opened his door to go downstairs, it was only necessary to follow the good smell of food that was rising. He did wonder, a little tardily, if this would take him, not to the hall, but to the kitchens; but the stairway ended in a corridor from which he could see the door to the Great Hall, where he had been welcomed.

Damon and Ellemir were seated at a small table, and a third chair, empty, was drawn up before it. Damon raised his head in welcome and said, "Forgive us for not waiting for you. But I was awake all night, and very hungry. Come and join us."

Andrew took the third chair. Ellemir looked him over with mild surprise as he sat down, and said, "In those clothes you look quite like one of us. Damon has been telling me a little about your people from Terra. But I had thought that men from another world would be very different from us, more like the nonhumans in the mountains. Are you human in every way?"

Andrew laughed "Well, I seem human enough to myself," he said. "It would seem more rational for me to ask, are *you* people human too? Most of the worlds of the Empire are inhabited by people who seem to be more or less human, at least as far as the casual observer can tell. Most people believe that all the planets were colonized by a common human stock, a few million years ago. There's been plenty of adaptation to environment, but on planets like Terra, the human organism seems to stay fairly stable. I'm not a biologist, so I can't answer for things like chromosomes and such, but I was told before I came here that the dominant race on Cottman Four was basically human, though there were a couple of sapient peoples that weren't." With a shock, he remembered what Callista had said: that she was in the hands of nonhumans. Surely she would want her kinsfolk to know. But should he spoil their breakfast? Time enough to tell them later.

Damon held a dish toward him, and he served himself with what looked—and later, tasted—like an omelet. It had herbs and unfamiliar vegetables in it, but it was good. There were fruits—the nearest analogy to what he was accustomed to were apples and plums—and a drink he had tasted in the Trade City, with the taste of bitter chocolate.

He noticed, while he ate, that Ellemir was watching him surreptitiously. He wondered if by their standards his table manners were atrociously bad, or whether it was more complicated than that.

Ellemir was still unsettling to him. She was so very like Callista, and yet in some subtle way so unlike. He could look at every feature of her face, and not see a hair's difference from Callista: the broad high forehead, with the hair growing in small delicate tendrils at the hairline, too short to be tucked into the neat braids at the back; the high cheekbones and small straight nose with a dusting of amber freckles; the short upper lip and small determined mouth; and the small, round dimpled chin. Callista had been the first woman he had seen on this planet who had not been abundantly and warmly clad, except for the women working in the central heated spaceport offices, and those were women of the Empire.

Yes, that was the subtle difference. Callista, every time he had seen her, had been in definite undress, in her flimsy blue nightgown. He had seen almost all of her that there was to see. If any other woman had shown herself to him in that kind of attire—well, all his life Carr had been the kind of man who took his fun where he found it, without getting particularly involved. And yet when he woke and found Callista apparently sleeping at his side, and still half-sleeping had reached for her, he had been distressed and had shared her own embarrassment. Quite simply, he didn't really want her on those terms at all. No, that wasn't quite right. Of course he wanted her. It seemed the most natural thing that he should want her, and she had accepted it that way. But what he wanted was something more. He wanted to know her, to understand her. He wanted her to know and understand him, and care about him. At the very thought that she might have reason to fear some crude or thoughtless approach from him, Andrew had gone hot and cold all over, as if by his own clumsy reactions he might have spoiled something very sweet and precious, very perfect. Even now, when he remembered the brave little joke she had made ("Ah, this is sad! The very first time, the very first, that I lie down with any man, and I am not able to enjoy it!"), he felt a lump in his throat, an immense and completely unfamiliar tenderness.

For this girl, this Ellemir, he felt nothing of that sort at all. If he had waked up and found her asleep in his bed, he would have treated her like any other pretty girl he found there, unless she had some strenuous objection—in which case she probably wouldn't have been there at all. But it would have meant no more than that to him, and when it was over, she would have meant no more to him than any of the various other women he had known and enjoyed for a little while. How could twins have such a subtle difference? Was it simply that intangible known as *personality?* But he hardly knew anything at all of Ellemir's.

So how could Callista rouse in him that enormous and unqualified *yes*, that absolute self-surrender, and Ellemir simply a shrug?

Ellemir put down her spoon. She said uneasily, "Why are you *staring* at me, stranger?"

Andrew dropped his eyes. "Didn't realize I was."

She flushed to the roots of her hair. "Oh, don't apologize. I was staring too. I suppose, when first I heard of men who had come here from other planets, I halfway expected them to be strange, weird, like the strange creatures of horror stories, things with horns and tails. And here you are, quite like any man from the next valley. But I am only a country girl, and not as accustomed to new things as people who live in the cities. So I am staring like any peasant who never sees anything but his own cows and sheep."

For the first time Andrew sensed a faint, a very faint likeness to Callista: the gentle directness, the straightforward honesty, without coquetry or wariness. It warmed him to her, somehow, for all the hostility she had shown before.

Damon leaned forward, laying his hand over Ellemir's, and said, "Child, he does not know our customs. He meant no offense. . . . Stranger, among our people it is offensive to stare at young girls. If you were one of us, I would be in honor bound to call challenge on you. Ignorance can be forgiven in a child or a stranger, but I can tell you are not a man who would deliberately offend women; so I instruct you without offense." He smiled, as if anxious to reassure Carr that he really meant none.

Uneasily, Carr looked away from Ellemir. That was a hell of a custom; it would take some getting used to.

"I hope it's polite to ask questions," Andrew said. "I could use some answers. You people live here—"

"It is Ellemir's home," Damon said. "Her father and brothers are at Comyn Council at this season."

"You are her brother? Her husband?"

Damon shook his head. "A kinsman; when Callista was taken, she sent for me. And we, too, would like to ask some questions. You are a Terran from the Trade City; what were you doing in our mountains?"

Andrew told them a little about the Mapping and Exploring expedition. "My name's Andrew Carr."

"Ann'dra," Ellemir repeated slowly, with a light inflection. "Why, that is not so outlandish; there are Anndras and MacAnndras back in the Kilghard Hills, MacAnndras and MacArans—"

And that was another thing, Andrew thought, *the names on this planet. They were a lot like Terran names.* Yet, as far as he had ever heard, this wasn't one of the colonies settled by Terran Empire ships and societies. Well, that wasn't important now.

"Have you had quite enough to eat?" Damon asked. "You are sure? The cold here can deplete your reserves very fast; you must eat well to recuperate."

Ellemir, nibbling at a plate of dried fruit resembling raisins, said, "Damon, you eat as if you had been out in the blizzard for days."

"Believe me, it felt that way," Damon said wryly, and shivered. "I did not tell you everything, because he came and we were distracted, but I was thrust into a place where the storm had gone on, and if you had not brought me back—" He stared at something invisible to Carr or the young woman. "Why don't we move to the fire, and be comfortable," he said, "and then we can talk. Now that you are warm and, I hope, comfortable—" He paused.

Andrew, guessing some formal remark was expected, said, "Very. Thank you."

"Now it is time to go over your story again, from the beginning, and in detail." They moved to the fireside, Andrew on one of the high-backed benches, Ellemir in a low chair. Damon dropped to the rug at her feet, and said, "Now begin, and tell us everything. Especially I want to hear every word you exchanged with Callista; even if you did not understand it, there may be some clue in it which would mean something to us. You said that you saw her first after your plane crashed—?"

"No, that was not the first time," Andrew said, and told them about the fortune-teller in the Trade City, and the crystal, and how he had seen Callista's face. He hesitated at the thought of trying to tell them exactly how deep that random contact had gone, and finally left it without comment.

Ellemir asked, "And did you accept her as real, then?"

"No," Andrew said. "I thought it was a game—the fortune-telling. Maybe even that the old dame was a procuress, showing me women for the usual reasons. Fortune-telling is usually a swindle."

"How can that be?" Ellemir said. "Anyone who pretended to psi powers which she did not in fact possess would be treated as a criminal! That is a very serious offense!"

Andrew said dryly, "My people don't believe there are any psi powers which are *not* pretended. At that time I thought that the girl was a dream. A wish-fulfillment, if you like."

"Yet she was real enough for you to change your plans and decide to stay here on Darkover," Damon said shrewdly.

Andrew felt uncomfortable under his knowing gaze, and said, "I had nowhere special to go. I'm—what's the old saying? 'I'm the cat who walked by himself and all places are alike to me.' So this place was as good as any other and better than most." (As he said it, he remembered Damon saying, "I know when I'm being lied to," but he couldn't explain it and felt foolish trying.)

"Anyhow, I stayed. Say it seemed like a good idea at the time. Call it a whim."

To Carr's relief, Damon left it at that. He said, "In any case, and for whatever reasons, you stayed. Exactly when was this?" Andrew figured out the time, and Ellemir shook her head in puzzlement.

"At that time, Callista was safe in the Tower. She would hardly have sent any psi message for help and comfort, certainly not to a stranger!"

Carr said stubbornly, "I don't ask you to believe it. I'm trying to tell you just exactly what happened, the way I felt it. *You're* supposed to be the ones who understand psychic things like this." Again, their eyes met in that queer hostility.

Damon said, "In the overworld, time is often out of focus. There may have been some element of precognition, for both of you."

Ellemir flared, "You're acting as if you believe his story, Damon."

"I'm giving him the benefit of the doubt, and I suggest you do likewise. I remind you, Ellemir: neither you nor I can reach Callista. If this man has done so, he may very well be our only link with her. It would be best not to anger him."

She dropped her eyes and said curtly, "Go on. I won't interrupt again."

"So. Andrew, your next contact with Callista was when the plane crashed—?"

"After the plane crashed. I was lying half conscious on the ledge, and she called to me, and told me to take shelter." Slowly, trying to recall word by word what Callista had said to him, he told of how she had saved him from trying to reenter the plane a moment before it crashed down into the bottom of the ravine.

"Do you suppose you could find the place again?" Ellemir asked.

"I don't know. The mountains are bewildering, when you're not used to them. I suppose I could try, though the trip was bad enough one way."

"I see no reason why it's necessary," Damon said. "Go on. When did she next appear to you?"

"After the snow began. In fact, just about the time it was working up to blizzard proportions, and I was ready to give up and decide it was all completely hopeless, and the best thing to do was to pick out a comfortable spot to lie down and die."

Damon thought that over a moment. He said, "Then the link between you is two-way. Possibly *her* need established a link with you, the first time. But *your* need and danger brought her to you that time, at least."

"But if Callista is free in the overworld," Ellemir cried out, "why could she not come to you there, Damon? Why could Leonie not reach her? It makes no sense!"

She looked so distressed, so frantic, that Carr could not endure it. It was too much like Callista's weeping. "She told me she did not know where she was—that she was being kept in darkness. If it is any comfort to you, Ellemir, she came to me only because she had tried, and failed, to reach you." He tried to reconstruct her exact words. It wasn't easy, and he was beginning to suspect that Callista had reached his mind directly without too much need for words. "She said something like—I think—it was as if the minds of her kinsfolk and friends had all been erased from the surfaces of this world, and that she had wandered around a long time in the dark looking for you, until she had found herself in communication with me. And then she said that she kept coming back to me because she was frightened and alone"—he heard his own voice thicken and catch—"and because a stranger was better than no one at all. She said she thought she was being kept in a part of that level—overworld you call it?—where her people's minds could not reach."

"But how? Why?" Ellemir demanded.

"I'm sorry," Carr said humbly. "I don't know a thing about it. Your sister had a dreadful time trying to explain even that much to me, and I'm still not sure I've got it straight. If what I say isn't accurate, it's not because I'm lying, it's because I just don't have the language to put it in. I seemed to understand it when Callista was telling me about it, but it's something else to try to tell it in your language."

Ellemir's face softened a little. "I don't think you're lying, Ann'dra," she said, again mispronouncing his name in that strange soft way. "If you'd come here with some evil purpose, I'm sure you could tell much better lies than those. But anything you can tell us about Callista, please try to say it somehow. Has she been hurt, did she seem to be in pain, had she been ill-treated? Did you actually see her, and how did she look? Oh, yes, you must have seen her if you recognized me."

Andrew said, "She did not seem to be injured, although there was a bruise on her cheek. She was wearing a thin blue dress, it looked like a nightgown; no one in her right senses would have worn it out-of-doors. It had—" He closed his eyes, the better to visualize her. "It had some kind of embroidery around the hem, in green and gold, but it was torn and I could not see the design."

Ellemir shivered faintly. "I know the gown. I have one like it. Callista wore it to bed the night we were—raided. Tell me more, quickly!"

"Proof of the truth of his tale," Damon said. "I saw her, only for an instant, in the overworld. She still wore that nightdress. Which tells me two things. He has in fact seen Callista. And—a little more ominous—she cannot, for some reason, although she walks in the overworld as if it were her own courtyard, clothe herself in anything more suitable, even in thought. When I have seen her before this in the overworld, she was clothed as befits a *leronis*—a sorceress," he added to Andrew, in explanation, "in her crimson robes, and veiled as a Keeper should be." He repeated, unwillingly, what Leonie had said: "If she were drugged, or entranced, or her starstone taken from her, or if she had been so ill-treated that her mind had darkened into madness—"

"I can't believe that," Andrew said. "Everything she did was too—too sensible, too *purposeful*, if you will. She guided me to one specific place, in the blizzard; and she came back again, so she could show me where to find food that had been stored there for emergencies. I asked her if she was cold, and she told me it was not cold where she was. Also—when I saw the bruise on her face—I asked, and she told me she had not been hurt or really ill-treated."

Damon said, "Try to remember everything she said to you."

"She told me that the herdsman's hut where I sheltered from the storm was not more than a few miles from here. What she said was, she wished she were there with me in body, so that when the storm was over, in a little while she could be—" he frowned, again trying to remember a communication which now seemed to be more in thoughts than words—"warm and safe and at home."

"I know the place," Damon said. "Coryn and I slept there, when we were boys, on hunting trips. It is something, that Callista could come there in thought." He frowned, trying to add it all up. "What else did Callista say to you?"

It was after that, that I woke and found her sleeping almost in my arms, Andrew thought, *but I'm damned if I'm going to tell you about that. That's strictly between me and Callista.* And yet, if some random thing she had said to him might give Damon a clue to her actual whereabouts— He paused, irresolute.

Damon could clearly see the conflict in his face, and followed it more accurately than Andrew would have believed. He said kindly, trying to spare him, "I can well believe that alone in the dark, and both of you in strange and hostile places, you may well have exchanged—" He paused, and Andrew, sensitized to his mood, knew that Damon was searching for a word which would not trespass too strongly on his emotions. "Exchanged—confidences. You don't have to tell us about that."

Funny, how these people can get so close to you, know almost what you're thinking. Andrew was aware of Damon's attempt not to trespass on his privacy, or on the more intimate things he had shared with Callista. *Intimate . . . funny word when I've never set eyes on her. To have come so close, so close to a woman I've never seen.* He was also aware of Ellemir's sullen face and knew that she, too, sensed something of how close he had come to her twin; and that she did not approve.

Damon, too, sensed Ellemir's resentment. "Child, you should be grateful that anyone, anyone at all, could reach Callista. Just because you could not come to her and comfort her, are you going to resent the fact that a stranger could? Would you rather that she should be all alone in her prison?" He turned back to Andrew and said, as if apologizing for Ellemir, "She is very young, and they are twins. But for your kindness to my kinswoman, I am ready to be your friend. Now, if you can tell me anything she said, about her captors—"

"She said she was in the dark," Andrew said, "and that she did not know precisely where she was, that if she knew precisely, she could have left the place somehow. I didn't quite understand that. She said that since she did not know exactly, her body—that's how she seemed to differentiate it—had to stay where they had confined it. And she cursed them."

"Did she say who they were?" Damon asked.

"What she said made no sense to me," Andrew answered. "She said that they were not men."

"Did she tell you how she knew that? Did she say that she had seen them?" Damon asked eagerly.

"No," Andrew answered. "She said that she had *not* seen them, that she suspected they had kept her in darkness so that she should *not* see them. But she suspected they were not men because—" Again he hesitated a little, trying to find a way to phrase it, and then thought, *Oh hell, if Callista didn't mind talking about it to a stranger it can't be anything to be so embarrassed about.* "She said she knew they were not men because none of them had attempted to rape her. She took it for granted that any man would have done just that, which says something funny about the men of your planet!"

Damon said, "We knew already that whoever would stoop to kidnapping a *leronis*, a Keeper, would be no friend to the people of the Domains. I had surmised that she was stolen, not as any woman might be kidnapped, for revenge, or slavery, but quite specifically because she was a trained telepath. They could not have hoped that she could be forced to use her Keeper's powers against her own people. But if she was kept a prisoner, and her starstone taken from her, she could not be used against them, either. And kidnappers, if they were men, would know that a Keeper is always a virgin; that there was a simpler, less dangerous way to make a Keeper powerless to use her skills against them. A Keeper in the hands of her people's enemies would not long remain a virgin."

Carr shuddered in revulsion. *What a hell of a world, where this kind of war against women is taken for granted!*

Once again Damon followed his thoughts and said, with a little wry twist of his mouth, "Oh, it's neither that easy nor that one-sided, Andrew. The man who tries to ravish a *leronis* has no easy or innocent victim, but takes his very life, not to mention his sanity, in his hands. Callista is an Alton, and if she strikes with her full Gift, she can paralyze, if not kill. It *can* be done, it *has* been done, but it's a more equal battle than you would imagine. No sane man lays hands on a Comyn sorceress except at her own desire. But to anyone who has good reason to fear that a Keeper's powers will be used against him, it may seem worth the danger."

"But," Ellemir said, "she has not been touched, you say."

"She said not."

"Then," Damon said, "I think my first surmise is true. Callista is in the hands of the cat-men, and now we know why. I guessed earlier, when I spoke to Reidel, that somewhere in the darkening lands, someone or something is experimenting with unlicensed and forbidden matrix stones, trying to work with telepath powers; to harness these forces outside the wardenship of the Comyn and the Seven Domains. Men have done this before. But as far as I know, this is the first time any nonhuman race has tried to do so."

Suddenly Damon shuddered, as if with cold or fear. He reached blindly for Ellemir's hand, as if to reassure himself of something solid and warm.

As if, thought Andrew, *he were in darkness and fear like Callista's.*

"And they have done it! They have made the darkening lands uninhabitable to mankind! They can come on us with invisible weapons, and even Leonie could not find Callista when they had hidden her under their darkness! And they are strong, Zandru seize them with scorpions! They are strong. I am Tower-trained, but they flung me out of their level, into a storm I could not overcome. They mastered me as if I were a child! Gods! Gods! Are we helpless against them, then? Is it hopeless?"

He buried his face in his hands, shuddering. Andrew looked at him in surprise and consternation. Then, slowly, he spoke, reaching out to lay his hand on Damon's shoulder.

"Don't do that," he said. "That doesn't help anybody. Look, you just pointed out that Callista still has her powers, whatever they are. And she can reach *me*. Maybe, just maybe— I don't know anything about this kind of thing, or whatever wars and feuds you have in your world, but I do know about Callista, and I—I care a lot about her. Maybe there's some way I can find out where she is—help get her back for you."

Damon raised his face, white and drawn, and looked at the Earthman in wild surmise. "You know," he said to Andrew, "you're right. I hadn't thought of that. *You* can still reach Callista. I don't know why, or how, it happened; or even what we can do with it, but it's the one hope we have. *You can reach Callista.* And she can come to you, when another Keeper can't reach her, when her own twin is barred away from her. It may not be completely hopeless after all."

He reached out and gripped Andrew's hands, and somehow the Terran sensed that for him this was a very unusual thing, that touch, among telepaths, was reserved for close intimacy. It put him almost unendurably in touch with Damon for an instant—Damon's exhaustion and fear, his desperate worry about his young cousins, his own deeper doubts and terrors about his own inability to meet this challenge, his horror of the overworld, his deep and desperate doubts of his very manhood. . . . For a moment Andrew wanted to withdraw, to reject this undesired intimacy which Damon, at the end of his endurance, had thrust on him; then he met Ellemir's eyes, and they were so much like Callista's now, pleading, no longer scornful, so full of fear for Damon (*Why, she loves him*, Andrew thought in a flash; *he doesn't seem much of a man to me either, but she loves him, even if she doesn't know it*) that he could not refuse their plea. They were Callista's people, and he loved Callista, and for better or worse he was entangled in their affairs. *I'd better get used to it now*, he thought, and in a clumsy surge of something almost like affection, he put his arm around Damon's shoulders and hugged the other man roughly. "Don't you worry so much," he said. "I'll do what I can. Sit down, now, before you collapse. What in the hell have you been doing to yourself, anyway?"

He shoved Damon down on the bench before the fire. The unendurable contact lessened, dropped away. Andrew felt confused and a little dismayed at the intensity of the emotion that had surged up. It was like having a kid brother, he thought, cloudily. *He's not strong enough for this kind of thing.* It struck him that Damon was older than he was and far more experienced in these curious contacts, but he still felt older, protective.

Damon said, "I'm sorry. I was out all night in the overworld, searching for Callista. I—I failed."

He sighed, with a sense of utter relief. He said, "But now we know where she is, or at least how to get into contact with her. With your help—"

Andrew warned, "I know nothing about these things."

"Oh, that." Damon shrugged it aside. He looked completely exhausted. He said, "I should have more sense; I'm not used to the overworld anymore. I'll have to rest and try again. Just now, I haven't any more strength. But when I can try again"—he straightened his back—"the damned cat-men had better look to themselves! I know, now, I think, what we can do."

And that, Andrew thought, *is one hell of a lot more than I know. But I guess Damon knows what he's doing, and that's enough for me, for now.*

CHAPTER SIX

Damon Ridenow woke and lay for a moment staring at the ceiling. Day was waning; after the strenuous all-night search within the overworld, and the confrontation with Andrew Carr, he had slept most of the day. His weariness was gone, but apprehension was still there, deep within. The Earthman was their one link with Callista, and this seemed so unlikely, so bizarre, that one of these men from another world should be able to make this subtle telepathic contact with one of their own, Terrans, with Comyn *laran* powers! Impossible! No, not impossible: it had *happened*.

He felt no revulsion for Andrew personally, only for the idea that the man was an alien, an off-worlder. As for the man himself, he was inclined rather to like him. He knew that was, at least in part, a consequence of the mental rapport they had, for an instant, shared. In the telepath caste, it was often the accident of possessing *laran*, the specific telepath Gift, which determined how close a relationship would come. Caste, family, social position, all these became irrelevant compared to that one compelling fact; one had, or one did not, that inborn power, and in consequence one was stranger or kinsfolk. By that criterion alone, the most important one on Darkover, Andrew Carr was one of them, and the fact that he was an Earthman was a small random fact without any real importance.

Ellemir, too, had suddenly taken on a new importance in his life.

Being what he was, born telepath and Tower-trained telepath, the touching of minds created closeness, above and beyond anything else. He had felt this for Leonie—twenty years his senior, pledged by law to remain virgin, never beautiful. During his time in the Tower, and for long after, he had loved her deeply, hopelessly, with a passion that had spoiled him for other women. If Leonie had known this—and she could hardly have helped knowing, being what *she* was—it had never made any difference to her. Keepers were trained, by methods incomprehensible to normal men or women, to be unaware of sexuality.

Thinking of that brought him around to thinking again of Callista—and of Ellemir. He had known her most of her life. But he was almost twenty years older than she was. His parents had many times urged him to marry, but the devotion of his first youth had gone up in the white heat of smokeless flame for the unattainable Leonie. Later he had never thought of himself as having much to offer any woman. The intimacy he had known with the others, men and women, in the Tower Circle, minds and hearts open to one another—seven of them come together in a closeness where nothing, however small, could be hidden—and nothing refused or rejected, had spoiled him for any contact lesser than this. Cast out of the Tower, he had known such a desolate loneliness that nothing could dispel it.

Lonely, lonely, all my life alone. And I never dreamed . . . Ellemir, my kinswoman, but a child, only a little girl. . . .

Rising swiftly from his bed, he strode to the window and looked down into the courtyard. *So* young Ellemir was not. She was old enough to care for this vast Domain when her kinsmen were away at Comyn Council. She must be nearly twenty years old. Old enough to have a lover; old enough, if she chose, to marry. She was *Comynara* in her own right, and her own mistress.

But young enough to deserve someone better than I; torn by fear and incompetence. . . .

He wondered if she had ever thought of him as a lover, if perhaps she had known other lovers. He hoped so. If Ellemir cared for him, he hoped it was built on awareness, experience, knowledge of men: not the infatuation of an unawakened girl, which might well dissipate when she knew other men. He wondered. Twin sister to a Keeper, she might somehow have picked up some of Callista's conditioned unawareness of men.

In any case, it was now a full-blown thing between them which had to be faced. The sensitivity, the almost-sexual awareness between them, was something they could no longer ignore, and there was not, of course, any reason to ignore it. It would also heighten their ability to work together in whatever lay ahead; they were committed to find Callista, and the rapport between them would only heighten their contact and strength. Afterward—well, they might never be able to get free of one another. Smiling gently, Damon faced the knowledge that they would probably have to marry; they might never be able to remain apart after this. Well, that would not displease him too much either, unless Ellemir was for some reason unhappy about it.

The awareness of this was still on the surface of his mind when he went downstairs, but the moment he saw Ellemir in the Great Hall it was no longer an apprehension. Even before she raised her serious eyes to his, he knew that all this was something she too had come to realize and accept. She dropped the needlework in her hands and came up to him, snuggling in his arms without a word. He drew a deep breath of absolute relief. After a long time, during which neither of them spoke aloud, standing with linked fingers before the fire, he said, "You don't mind, *breda*—that I'm nearly old enough to be your father?"

"You? Oh, no, no—only if you had been too old to father children, like poor Liriel when they married her off to old Dom Cyril Ardais; *that* would trouble me a little. But you, no, I've never stopped to think whether you were old or young," she said, very simply. "I do not think I would want a lover who could not give me children. That would be too sad."

Damon felt an incongruous ripple of inner laughter. That he had never thought about; trust a woman to think of the important things. It was not an unpleasant thought, and it would please his family. He said, "I think we need not worry about that, *preciosa*, when the proper time comes."

"Father will be displeased," Ellemir said slowly, "with Callista in the Tower. I think he had hoped I would stay here and keep his house while he lived. But I have completed my nineteenth year, and by Comyn law I am free to do as I will."

Damon shrugged, thinking of the formidable old man who was the father of the twins. "I have never heard that Dom Esteban disliked me," he said, "and if he cannot bear to lose you, it matters little where we choose to live. Love . . ." He broke off, then with swift apprehension, "Why are you crying?"

She curled closer into his arms. "I had always thought," she said bleakly, "that when I chose, Callista would be the first I would tell."

"You are very close to Callista, beloved?"

"Not as close as some twins," Ellemir said, "since when she went to the Tower, and was pledged, I knew we could never, as so many sisters do, share a lover, or a husband. Yet it seems so sad that this thing that means so much to me, she will not know."

He tightened his clasp on her.

"She shall know," he said. "Be sure of this: she will know. Remember, now we know she is alive, and there is one who can reach her."

"Do you really think this Earthman, this Ann'dra, can help us to find her?"

"I hope so. It won't be easy, but then we never thought it would be easy," he said. "Now, at least, we know it's possible."

"How can it be? He's not one of us. Even if he has some powers or gifts like our *laran*, he doesn't know how to use any of it."

"We'll have to teach him," Damon said. That wouldn't be easy either, he thought. He closed his hand over the starstone on its cord around his neck. It must be done if they were to have the faintest hope of reaching Callista; and he, Damon, would have to be the one to do it. But he dreaded it, Zandru's hells, *how* he dreaded it. But he said calmly, trying to give Ellemir confidence, "Until last night, you yourself never thought you could use *laran*; yet you used it, you saved my life with it."

Her smile wavered, but at least she was smiling again. He said, "So for now let us take what we can have of happiness, and not spoil it with worry, Ellemir. As for the law and the formalities, I expect Dom Esteban will return sometime soon." As he spoke the cold awareness rushed over him again, so that he caught his breath for a moment. *Sooner than I think, and it will not be well for any of us*, he thought but he closed his mind to it, hoping Ellemir had not picked up the thought. He continued: "When your father comes, we can tell him our plans. Meanwhile, we will have to teach Andrew what we can. Where is he?"

"Asleep, I suppose. He, too, was very weary. Shall I send to him?"

"I suppose you must. We have little time to lose," Damon said, "although now we have found each other, I would rather be alone with you a while." But he smiled as he said it. They already shared more than he had ever known with any other woman, and for the rest, there was no urgency. He was no raw youth clutching his girl in haste, and they could wait for the rest. Briefly he picked up a shy thought from Ellemir, *But not too long*, and it warmed him; but he let her go, and said, "There is time enough. Send a steward to bid him come down to us, if he is rested enough. And now, I must think." He moved away from Ellemir and stood looking into the blue-green flames that shot up from the piled resin-treated fuel in the fireplace.

Carr was a telepath, and a potentially powerful one. He had found and held rapport with a stranger, not even blood-kin. A part of the overworld barred even to the Tower-trained might be accessible to him. Yet he was wholly untrained, wholly untaught, and not even inclined to believe very much of these strange powers. With all his heart Damon wished someone else were here to teach this man. The awakening of latent psi powers was not an easy task even for those trained to it, and for an off-worlder, with an unthinkably strange background, without even belief and confidence to help him, it was likely to be a difficult and painful business. Damon had shied away from such contacts ever since he had been dismissed from the Tower Circle. It wouldn't be easy to take them up again, to drop his barriers for this stranger. Yet there was no one else.

He looked around the room, searching. He said, "Have you *kirian* here?" *Kirian*, a powerful drug compounded of the pollen of a rare plant from the mountains, had a tendency, in carefully regulated dosage, to lower the barriers against telepathic rapport. He was not sure whether he meant to give it to Andrew Carr or take it himself, but one way or the other it might make it easier to get through to a stranger. Most deliberate telepathic training was done by the Keepers themselves, but *kirian* could heighten the psi powers, temporarily, enough to make contact possible even with non telepaths.

Ellemir said doubtfully, "I don't *think* so. Not, at least, since Domenic outgrew the threshold sickness. Callista never needed it, nor I. I will look and see, but I fear not."

Damon felt the cold shudder of fear, gnawing deep in his belly. Blurred a little by the drug, he might have been able to endure the difficult business of directing and disciplining the arousal of *laran* in a stranger. The thought of going through it without some help was almost unendurable. Yet, if it was Callista's only chance—

"You have a starstone," Ellemir said. "You used it to show me what little I could do—"

"Child, you are my blood-kin and we are close enough emotionally—even so, when you gripped the stone, it was agony, more than I can tell you," Damon said gravely. "Tell me. Has Callista any other of the matrix jewels, unused?" If he could get for Carr a blank, unkeyed jewel, perhaps he could work more easily with him.

"I am not sure," Ellemir said. "She has many things I have never seen, nor asked about, because they have to do with her work as Keeper. I wondered why she had brought them here rather than leaving them in the Tower."

"Perhaps because—" Damon hesitated. It was hard to speak of his own days in the Tower Circle; his mind kept shying and skittering away like a frightened horse. Yet somehow he must overcome this fear. "Perhaps because a *leronis*, or even a matrix technician, prefers to keep his, or her, working gear close at hand. I don't quite know how to explain it, but it feels better, somehow, to have it within reach. I do not use my own starstone twice in a year," he added, "yet I keep it here, around my

neck, simply because it has been made into a—a part of
me. It is uncomfortable, even physically painful, to have
it too far from me."

Ellemir whispered, verifying swiftly his guess about
her own fast-developing sensitivity: "Oh, poor Callista!
And she told Andrew that they had taken her starstone
from her—"

Grimly, the man nodded. "So even if she has not been
ravished or ill-treated, she is suffering now," he said.
*Why should I shrink from a little pain or trouble, to spare
her worse?* he thought. "Take me to her room; let me
look through her things."

Ellemir obeyed, without question, but when they
stood in the center of the room the twin sisters shared,
with the two narrow beds at opposite ends of the room,
she said in a frightened whisper, "What you said—won't
it hurt Callista for you to touch her—the things she uses
as a Keeper?"

"It's a possibility," said Damon, "but no worse than she
has been hurt already, and it may be our only chance."

*My men died because I was too cowardly to accept the
thing that I was: a Tower-trained telepath. If I let Callista
suffer because I fear to use my skills . . . then am I
worthless to Ellemir, then am I a lesser thing than any
off-worlder . . . but, God, I am afraid, afraid. . . . Blessed
Cassilda, mother of the Seven Domains, be with me
now. . . .*

His even, neutral voice betrayed nothing. "Where
does Callista keep her belongings? I can tell yours from
hers by their feel, but I would rather not waste time or
strength on that."

"The dressing table there, with the silver brushes, is
hers. Mine is the other, with the embroidered scarves
and the ivory-backed brushes and combs." He could feel
the tension and fear in Ellemir's voice, but she was trying to match his cool, dispassionate manner. Damon
looked on the dressing table, and rummaged briefly in
the drawers. "Nothing here but rubbish," he said. "One
or two small matrix jewels, first-level or less, good for
fastening buttons, no more. You're sure you never saw
where she keeps anything of the kind?" But even before
he saw her shake her head, he knew the answer.

"Never. I tried not to—to intrude on that part of her life."

"What a pity I'm not the Terran," Damon said sourly. "I could ask her directly." He clasped his hand, reluctantly, over the starstone which hung on its cord, slowly drew it from the leather pouch, closing his eyes, trying to sense something. As always when he touched the cold, smooth jewel he felt the strange sting of fear. After a moment, hesitantly, he moved toward Callista's bed. It lay still tangled and the bedclothing crumpled, as if no one, servant or mistress, had had the heart to disturb the last imprint of her body there. Damon wet his lips with his tongue, bent and reached under the pillow, then drew back, lifting the pillow gingerly. Beneath it, against the fine linen sheet, lay a small silk envelope, almost— but not quite—flat. He could see the shape of the jewel through the silk.

"Callista's starstone," he said slowly. "So her captors did not take it from her."

Ellemir was trying to remember Andrew's exact words. "He said—Callista did not say her starstone had been taken from her," she repeated slowly. "She said, '*They* could only take my jewels from me lest one of them should be my starstone.' Something like that. So it has been here all along."

"If I had had it, maybe I could have seen her in the overworld," Damon mused aloud, then shook his head. No one but Callista could use her stone. Yet it explained one thing. Without her starstone, she could be concealed in the darkness. If she had been touching it, he could probably have located her; he could have focused his own stone on it. . . . No good thinking about that now. He stretched out his hand to take it, then drew back.

"You take it," he directed, and as she hesitated, "You are her blood-kin, her twin; your vibrations are closer to hers. You can handle it with less pain to her than anyone living. Even through the silk insulation there is some danger, but less from you than anyone else."

Gingerly, Ellemir picked up the silk envelope and slipped it into the bosom of her dress. *For all the good that would do*, Damon thought. Callista, with her starstone, might have been better able to resist her captors. Or maybe not. He was beginning to surmise that it could be she was held prisoner by someone using one of these matrix jewels, someone stronger than herself, who wished mostly to hold her powerless; someone who knew that, free and armed, she would be a danger.

The cat-men. The cat-men, Zandru help them all! But how, and where, did the cat-men get together enough skill and power even to experiment with the matrix jewels? *The truth is*, he thought, *none of us knows a damn thing about the cat-men, but we've made the bad mistake of underestimating them. A fatal mistake? Who knows?*

Well, at least the starstone was not in nonhuman hands.

They were halfway down the stairs when they heard the commotion in the courtyard, the sounds of riders, the great bell in the court. Ellemir gasped and her hand flew to her heart. Damon felt for an instant that prickle of tense fear; then he relaxed.

"It cannot be another attack," he said. "I think it is friends or kinsfolk, or an alarm would have been rung." *Besides*, he thought grimly, *I felt no warning!*

"I think it is Lord Alton come home," he said, and Ellemir looked startled.

"I sent a message to Father when I sent to you," she said, "but I did not believe he would come during Comyn Council, whatever the need." She ran down the stairs, picking up her gray skirt about her knees; Damon followed more slowly through the great doors into the bricked-in courtyard.

It was a scene of chaos. Armed men, covered in blood, swaying in their saddles. *Too few men*, Damon thought swiftly, *for Dom Esteban's bodyguard, any time*. Between two horses, a litter rudely woven of evergreen boughs had been slung, and on the litter lay the motionless body of a man.

Ellemir had stopped short on the courtyard steps, and as Damon came up, the pallor of her face struck him like a blow. Her hands were clenched into fists at her sides, nails driven into the palms. Damon took her gently by the arm, but she seemed not to know he was there, frozen into herself with shock and horror. Damon went down the steps, looking quickly around the pale, strained faces of the wounded men. *Eduin . . . Conan . . . Caradoc . . . where is Dom Esteban? Only over their dead bodies . . .* Then he caught a glimpse of the swarthy aquiline profile and iron-gray hair of the man in the litter, and it was like a blow to the solar plexus, so painful that he physically swayed with the shock of it. *Dom Esteban! By all the hells—what a time to lose the best swordsman and commander in all the Domains!*

Servants were running about in what looked like confusion; two of the blood-soaked men had slid from their horses, and were cautiously unstrapping the litter. The horses carrying it shied away—*The smell of blood, they never get used to it!*—and there was a sharp cry; the man in the litter began to curse, fluently, in four languages.

Not dead, then, but very much alive. But how badly hurt? Damon thought.

"Father!" Ellemir cried out, and began to run toward the litter. Damon caught and held her before she banged into it. The cursing stopped, like a faucet turned off.

"Callista, child—" The voice was harsh with pain.

"Ellemir, Father—" she murmured. They had managed to get the litter down to the ground now, and Damon saw the healer-woman pushing her way through the crowding servants. She said, in her crisp voice, "Move back, this is my business. Domna"—to Ellemir—"this is no place for you, either." Ellemir disregarded the woman, kneeling beside the wounded man. His lips drew back harshly in a grimace meant for a smile.

"Well, *chiya*, I'm here." The bushy eyebrows writhed. "I should have brought more men, though." Damon, looking down over Ellemir's bent back, could see on his face the marks of a long struggle with pain, and something worse. Something like fear. Although, since no one living had ever seen fear on the face of Esteban-Gabriel-Rafael Lanart, Lord Alton, no one knew how fear would have looked on that grim and controlled face. . . .

"Away with you now, child. Battle scenes and blood—no place for a little maiden. Damon, is it you? Kinsman, take the child away from here."

And, besides, you can't curse until she's gone, Damon thought wryly, seeing the old man's teeth worrying his lip and knowing Dom Esteban's iron prejudices. He laid his hand on Ellemir's shoulder as the healer-woman knelt down beside Lord Alton, and after a moment she permitted him to draw her away.

Damon looked swiftly around the courtyard. Dom Esteban was not the only wounded, he saw; not even the most gravely wounded. One of the men was helped down from his horse and supported, half carried, by two men, toward the stone seat at the center, where they laid him out full length. His leg was wrapped with a crude bandage, blood soaking through; Damon's stomach turned at the thought of what must lie beneath.

Ellemir, pale but controlled now, was quickly giving orders for hot water, bandage linen, cushions. "The Guardroom is too cold," she said to Dom Cyril, the grizzled old *coridom*, or chief steward. "Carry them into the Great Hall; have beds moved in there from the Guardroom. They can be tended there more easily."

"A good thought, *vai dumnu*," said the old man, and hobbled toward the leader of the Guard—now that Esteban was out of it—the *seconde*, or chief officer of the Armida Guardsmen; Eduin the man's name was. He was small and gnarled in stature, broad-shouldered and hawk faced, a long bloody gash now lending a fierce, wild look to his features. There were rips and slashes in the sleeve of his tunic.

"—invisible!" Damon heard him saying. "Yes, yes, I *know* it's not possible, but I swear, you couldn't see them until they were killed, and then they just—they—well, they fell out of the air. Sir, I swear it's true. You could hear them moving, you could see the marks they left in the snow, you could see them *bleeding*—but they weren't *there!*" The man was shaking all over with reaction, and under the smeared blood his face was dead white. "If it hadn't been for the *vai dom*—" He spoke Dom Esteban's name in his own far-mountain dialect, calling him *Istvan*. "Except for the Lord Istvan, we'd all have been killed."

"No one doubts you," said Damon, stepping forward to grasp the man by the arms; he seemed about to fall. "I met them myself, crossing the darkening lands. How did you escape?" *Not as I did, running away and leaving my men to die.* Suddenly his disgust with himself and his own cowardice rose up and sickened him. He felt for a moment as if he would choke. Before Eduin's words he forced himself to be calm and listen.

"I'm not sure. We were walking our horses, and all at once they all shied, started to bolt. While I was trying to get mine under control, there was this—this *howl*, and Dom Istvan had his sword out and there was blood on it. And this cat-man just—just *materialized* out of the air and fell dead. Then I saw Marcos fall with his throat cut, and heard Dom Istvan yell, *'use your ears,'* and Caradoc and I got back-to-back and started swiping at the air with our swords. There was a sort of a hiss, and I thrust at it, and I felt the blade go in, and there was this cat-thing, dying in the snow, and I— Somehow I got the blade free, and kept cutting at everything I could hear. It was like night fighting—" His eyes fell shut as if for a moment he fell asleep where he stood. "Can I have a drink, Lord Damon?"

Damon broke the eerie paralysis that held him. Servants were running into the court with pails of hot water, blankets, bandages, steaming jugs. He beckoned quickly to one of them, wondering who had had sense enough to order a hot brew of *firi* at this hour. He poured a cupful and thrust it at Eduin. The man swilled down the hot raw spirit as if it were watered wine at a banquet, and stood shuddering. Damon said, "Go into the Hall, man; your wounds can be tended better there." But Eduin shook his head. "Nothing much wrong with me, but Caradoc—" He gestured toward the heavyset brown-bearded man who lay, fists clenched, on the stone bench. "He took a wound in the leg." He strode toward his friend and bent over him.

"The Lord Alton—" Caradoc muttered between clenched teeth. "Is he still alive? I heard him cry out when they picked him up."

"He is alive," Damon said, and Eduin held a cup of the strong liquor to Caradoc's lips. The man gulped at it greedily, and Eduin said, low-voiced, "He'll need it when we move him. Give me a hand, *vai dom*. I'm still strong enough to help carry him, and I'd rather help him myself than leave him to the servants; he took the stroke that was meant for me."

Moving as carefully as he could, Damon helped Eduin support Caradoc's great weight up the stairs and into the Great Hall. Caradoc moaned and muttered, half coherently, as if the raw spirit had loosened his control over himself. Damon heard him mumbling, "Dom Esteban was fighting with his eyes closed . . . killed near a dozen of them . . . a lot of us were dead, and more of them . . . heard them running away, can't blame them, felt like running myself, but one of them got him, he crashed into the snow . . . we were sure he was dead until he started swearing at us. . . ." Caradoc's head fell forward on his chest and he slumped, unconscious, between the two who were carrying him.

With Damon's help, Eduin arranged his comrade carefully on one of the camp-beds which had been hastily set up in the hall, and covered him tenderly with warm blankets. He refused help for himself when Dom Cyril offered bandages and ointments, saying that he was almost unhurt. "—But Caradoc will bleed to death unless someone gets to him at once! Help *him!* I did what I could, but it wasn't much in the cold."

"I'll do what I can," Damon said, gritting his teeth. He felt sick, but like all Comyn Guardsmen commanding even small detachments, he had had sound training in field-hospital techniques; he had, perhaps, had more than most because his deficiencies in swordplay had made him feel he should have a special skill to counterweight his shortcomings. He saw, out of the corner of his eye, that Andrew Carr had come down into the Great Hall and was staring at the scene of carnage with wonder and horror. He caught a glimmer of thought, *Swords and knives, what sort of a place have I landed in*; then he forgot him completely again. "The healer is with Dom Esteban, but this can't wait. Dom Cyril, give me a hand with these bandages."

For the next hour he had not a breath to spare in thinking of Andrew Carr or even of Callista. Caradoc had a wound in the calf of the leg and another in the upper thigh, from which, despite the rough tourniquet Eduin had tied on, blood still oozed slowly. It was a struggle to stanch the bleeding, and an awkward spot for a pressure bandage: one of the great blood vessels in the groin had been nicked. At last he thought it would hold, and he turned to sewing up the flesh wound in the calf— a messy business and one that always made him feel sick; but by the time he had finished that, blood was oozing again from the wound in the groin. He looked down at the man, bitterly, thinking. *One more for the damned cat-things*, but under Eduin's pleading glance he shook his head.

"No more I can do, *com'ii*. It's a bad place."

"Lord Damon, you're Tower-trained. I have seen the *leronis* stop worse wounds than this with her jewel-stone. Can't you do anything?" Eduin pleaded. He had withstood all attempts to get him to rest, or eat, or leave his friend for a moment.

"Oh, God," Damon muttered. "I haven't the skill or the strength—it's delicate work. I could just as easily stop his heart, kill him—"

"Try, anyway," begged Eduin. "He'll die, anyhow, in a few minutes if you can't stop the bleeding."

No, damn it, Damon wanted to lash out. *Let me be, I've done as much as I can. . . .*

Caradoc didn't run from the cat-men. He probably saved Esteban's life. Thanks to him Ellemir is not this moment fatherless. Is he still alive? I have had not even an instant to go and see! Reluctantly, he said, "I'll try. But don't hope for too much. It's just a bare chance."

He fumbled with tense fingers for the jewel around his neck, drew it out. *Now I must do the work of a sorceress*, he thought bitterly. *Leonie said it, as a woman I would have made a Keeper. . . .*

He stared into the blue stone, concentrating savagely on controlling the magnetic fields. Slowly, slowly, he focused his heightened psi awareness, carefully down and down, to the molecular level and beyond, feeling the pulsing blood cells, the fumbling heart . . . *careful, careful. . . .* For an instant his mind merged with the unconscious man's, a dim swirl of fear and agony, a growing weakness as the precious life's blood oozed away . . . down and down, into the cells, the molecules . . . the blood vessel severed, broken, the gush, the pressure. . . .

Pressure, now, directly against the severed vessel . . .

telekinetic psi force, to hold together, together . . . cells knitting; careful, don't stop the heart; ease up just there . . . . He knew he had not moved a muscle, but it felt as if his hands were *inside* the man's body, gripping tight on the severed vessel. He knew he was holding pure energy against the flowing blood. . . .

With a long sigh, he withdrew. Eduin whispered, "I think the bleeding's stopped."

Damon nodded, exhausted. He said hoarsely, "Don't move him for an hour or so, until the clot's strong enough to hold by itself. Put sandbags around him to keep him from moving accidentally." Once the bleeding was stopped, the wound was no great matter. "Bad place, but it could be worse. Half an inch to one side and he'd have been castrated. Keep him from moving, now, and he'll be all right. In hell's name, man, get up. What are you about—"

Eduin had dropped to his knees. He murmured the ritual formula, "There is a life between us, *vai dom.*"

Damon said sharply, "There may be times coming when we're going to need brave men like the pair of you. Save your life for that! Now, damn it, if you don't go and get yourself some food and rest, I'll knock you down and sit on you. Go on, *teniente*—that's an order!"

Eduin muttered groggily, "Dom Istvan—"

"I'll see what's with him. Go and have your own wound seen to," Damon ordered, and looked around, coming up to sharp focus again. Ellemir, white-faced, was still supervising the placing of beds and coverings for the wounded men, and the bringing of food to the less severely wounded. The healer-woman still sat beside Dom Esteban. Damon went slowly toward her, and noticed, as if his body belonged to someone else, that he swayed as he walked. *I'm not used to this anymore, damn it.*

The healer-woman raised her head at Damon's question. "He's sleeping; he won't answer any questions this day. The wound missed his kidneys, by just a fraction; but I think something's hurt in the nerves of the spine. He can't move his legs at all, not even wriggle a toe. It *could* be shock, but I fear it's something worse. When he wakes—well, either he'll be perfectly all right, or else he'll spend the rest of his life dead from the waist down. Wounds in the spine don't heal."

Damon walked away from the healer-woman in a daze, slowly shaking his head. Not dead, no. But if, indeed, he was paralyzed from the waist, he might as well be, would probably rather be. He didn't envy whoever it was that would have the task of telling the formidable old man that his daughter's rescue must be left in other hands.

Whose hands? Mine? Damon realized, with shock, that ever since he had realized that Esteban lived, he had hoped that his older kinsman who, after all, was Callista's father, her nearest kinsman, and thus in honor bound to avenge any hurt or dishonor to her—would be able to take over this frightful task. But it hadn't happened like that.

It was still up to him—and to the Earthman, Andrew Carr.

He turned resolutely and left the Great Hall to go in search of Andrew Carr.

CHAPTER SEVEN

What kind of a world is this, anyway? Swords and knives—bandits, battles, kidnappings. Carr had seen the wounded men, but had quickly discovered that he was only in the way, that his hosts had no time or thought for him now, and had retreated upstairs to the room where they had taken him. He had felt strange about not offering to help, but the place was crawling with people and they all knew more about what to do than he did. He decided the best thing he could do was to keep out of the way.

What was going to happen now? He had gathered, from what little he could understand of the servants' talk—mostly in a dialect he could barely follow—that this was the Lord of this estate: Ellemir's father. With the owner returned, would Damon still be in charge of whatever arrangements could be made for Callista's rescue? It was Callista he was thinking about, almost to the exclusion of everything else. Then, almost as if his thoughts had drawn her to him (maybe they had, she seemed to think there was some such bond between them), he saw her standing before his bed.

"So you are safe, safe and well now, Andrew. Have my kinsfolk been hospitable to you?"

"They couldn't have been kinder," Andrew said. "But if you can come into their house, why can't *they* see you?"

"I wish I knew. I cannot see them, I cannot feel their thoughts; it is as if the house were empty, without even a ghost to haunt it! Or as if I were the ghost haunting it—my own house!" Her face crumpled with sobbing. "Somehow, someone has been able to barricade me from everyone, everyone I know. I wander in the overworld and I see only strange, drifting faces, never even a glance from any familiar face. I wonder if I have gone mad . . . ?"

Andrew said slowly, trying to explain the things Damon had told him, "Damon believes you are in the hands of the cat-men; it seems that they have attacked others, and that they keep you prisoner so that you cannot use your starstone against them."

Callista said slowly, "Before I left the Tower, Leonie said something of this. She said that something was amiss is the darkening lands and she suspected that some unmonitored stones were being used—or misused—there. You are a Terran—do you know what I mean by the stones?"

"Not a word of it," Andrew confessed.

"It is the ancient knowledge—science, you would say—of this world. The matrix stones, starstones we call them among ourselves, can be attuned to the human mind, and amplify what you call psi powers. They can be used to change the form of energy. All matter, all energy and force, is nothing but vibration, and if you change the rate at which it vibrates, then it takes another form."

Andrew nodded. He could follow that. It sounded as if she were trying, without the scientific training of the Terran Empire, to explain the atomic field theory of matter and energy; and doing it better than he could do it with the scientific training he had had. "And you can use these stones?"

"Yes. I am a Keeper, and Tower-trained; the leader of a circle of trained telepaths who use these stones for the transmutation of energy. And all the stones we use, keyed to our own individual brains, are monitored from one or another of the Towers; no one is allowed to use them unless he has been personally trained by an older Keeper or technician, and we are sure he will damage nothing. The stones are very, very powerful, Andrew. The higher-level ones, the larger ones, could shatter this planet like a roasting bird bursting in the oven. This is why we were frightened when we discovered that someone, or some*thing*, in the darkening lands was probably using a very powerful stone, or stones, unmonitored and without training."

Andrew was trying to recall Damon's words. "He said men have done this before, but nonhumans never."

"Damon has forgotten his history," Callista said. "It is well-known that our ancient forebears first received the Stones from the *chieri* folk, who knew how to use them when we were savages, and have gone so far beyond them that they no longer need them. But the *chieri* have little to do with mankind these days, and few men living have so much as seen one. I wish I might say the same of the cat-things, curse them!" She drew a long, exhausted breath. "Oh, I am weary, weary, Andrew. Would to Evanda I might *touch* you. I think I shall go mad, alone in the darkness. No, I have not been ill-treated, but I am so tired, so tired of the cold stone, and the dripping water, and my eyes ache with the darkness, and I cannot eat the food or drink the water they give me, it is foul with their stink—"

It drove Andrew half mad to hear her sobbing, and to be unable to reach her, touch her, comfort her somehow. He wanted to take her in his arms, hold her close, quiet her crying. And she stood there before him, looking so real, so solid, he could see her breathing and the tears that kept rolling down her face, and yet he could not so much as touch her fingertips. He said helplessly, "Don't cry, Callista. Somehow Damon and I will find you, and if he won't, I'll damn well try it myself!"

Raising his eyes suddenly, he saw Damon standing in the doorway. Damon's eyes were wide. He said, on an in-drawn breath of amazement, "Is Callista *here?*"

"I can't believe you can't see her," Andrew said, and felt again that strange, tentative outreach of contact, like a touch directly on his mind—he didn't resent it. At least Damon could know that he was telling the truth.

"I never really doubted you," Damon said, and his eyes were wide with wonder and dismay.

"Damon is here? Damon!" Callista said, and her lips trembled "You say he is here and I cannot see him. Like a ghost, a ghost in my own house and my brother's room—" She made a desperate attempt to control her weeping. Andrew felt the desperation of her struggle to stay calm. "Tell Damon he must find my starstone. *They* did not find it; I was not wearing it. Tell him I do not wear it around my neck as he does his own."

Andrew repeated this aloud to Damon. He felt uncomfortably like a trance medium supposedly relaying messages from a disembodied spirit. The thought made him shudder; they were usually dead.

Damon touched the thong around his neck and said, "I had forgotten she knew that. Tell her Ellemir has it, she found it beneath her pillow, and ask—"

Andrew repeated his words, and Callista interrupted him. "That explains why—I knew *someone* had touched it, but if it was Ellemir—" Her shadowy form wavered and flickered, as if the effort to stay present with them had taxed her beyond endurance. To Andrew's quick cry of concern she whispered, "I am very weak—I feel as if I were dying—or perhaps . . . Watch the stone," and she was gone. Andrew stood looking, in terror, at the place where she had disappeared. When he repeated her words Damon ran down the corridor, shouting for Ellemir.

"Where were you?" he demanded irascibly, when finally she appeared.

She looked at him in astonishment and annoyance. "What is the matter with you? My clothes were soaked in blood; I have been tending wounded men. Have I no right to a bath and clean garments? I sent the very servants for so much!"

How like and how unlike Callista, Andrew thought, and felt a completely irrational resentment, that this one was walking around free, enjoying a bath and fresh clothes and Callista was alone and crying in the dark somewhere.

"The starstone, quickly," Damon demanded. "We can see in it if Callista is alive and well." He explained to Andrew, quickly, that when a trained matrix worker died, his starstone "died" too, losing color and brilliance. Ellemir drew it out, handling it gingerly through the insulating silk, but it pulsed as brightly as ever.

Damon said, "She is exhausted and frightened, it may be, but she is physically very strong, or the stone could not shine so brightly. Andrew! When she comes to you again, tell her that she must somehow force herself to eat and drink, to be strong, to keep her strength up until we can somehow come to her! I wonder why she was so insistent that we must find her starstone?"

Andrew stretched out his hand to it, and said, "May I—?"

"It is hardly safe," Damon said hesitantly. "No one can use a stone keyed to another." Then he remembered. Callista was a Keeper, and they were so highly trained that, sometimes, they could key themselves in to someone else's stone. Leonie had held his in her hands many times, and while Ellemir's lightest touch on it, even though it had saved his life, had been agony, Leonie's had hurt him no more than the touch of Leonie's hand on his cheek. During his training, before they taught him how to key his own starstone to the rhythm of his own brain and energies, he had been trained with his Keeper's stone; and for that time he had been so in touch with Leonie that they were wide open to one another. *Even now a thought will bring her to me,* he thought.

Andrew knew what Damon was thinking. *It's as if he were broadcasting his thoughts to me. I wonder if he knows it?* He said quietly, "If Callista and I weren't awfully close in touch somehow, I don't think she'd keep coming back to me." He hesitated a moment, reluctant to reveal more, then realized that for Callista's sake, for all their sakes, it was unfair to keep back even what should have been private and highly personal. He said, trying to keep his voice even, "I—I love her, you know. I'll do whatever you think is best for her, no matter what it takes. You know more about this kind of thing than I do. I'm completely in your hands."

For an instant Damon felt a sting of revulsion (*This alien, this stranger, even his thoughts defile a Keeper*), then he made himself be fair. Andrew was not a stranger. However it had happened, however it came about, this alien, this Earthman, had *laran*. As for loving a Keeper, he himself had loved Leonie all his life, and she had never been angry about it or felt it an intrusion, even though she had never responded even a breath to his desire; his love she had accepted, although in an entirely sexless way. Callista was probably equally capable of defending herself, if she wished, against this stranger's emotions.

Andrew was getting very tired of seeing everything

that happened through Damon's eyes. "One thing I
don't understand," he said. "Why must a Keeper neces-
sarily be a virgin? Is it a law? Something religious?"

"It has always been so," said Ellemir, "from the most
remote past."

That, of course, Andrew thought, wasn't a reason.

Damon sensed his dissatisfaction and said, "I don't
know if I can explain it properly—it's a matter of nerve
energies. People have only so much. You learn to protect your energy currents, how to use them most effec-
tively, how to relax, to safeguard your strength. Well,
what uses most human energy? Sex, of course. You can
use it, sometimes, to channel energy, but there are limits
to that sort of thing. And when you're keyed into the
matrix jewels—well, the energy *they* will carry is lim-
itless, but human flesh and blood and brainwaves can
stand only so much. For a man it's fairly simple. You
can't overload with sex because if you're too heavily
overloaded, you simply can't function sexually at all. Matrix telepaths find that out fairly early in the game. You
have to go on short rations of sex if you want to keep
enough energy to do your work. For a woman, though,
it's easy to—well, to overload. So most of the women
have to make up their minds to stay chaste, or else be
very, very careful not to key into the more complex matrix patterns. Because it can kill them, very quickly, and
it's not a nice death."

He remembered a story Leonie had told him, early in
the training. "I told you, once, that it wasn't easy to
ravish a Keeper, unwilling—but that it could be done, it
had been done. There was a Keeper once—she was a
princess of the House of Hastur—and it was during one
of the wars, when such women could be used as pawns.
So the Lady Mirella Hastur was kidnapped, and they
flung her out at the city gates, believing she was now
useless to work against them. But the other Keeper in
the Tower had been killed outright, and there was no
one to act against the invaders who were storming Arilinn. So the Lady Mirella concealed what had been done
to her, and went into the screens, and fought for hours
against the forces mustered against them. But when the
battle was over and the invaders lay, all of them, dying

or dead at the city gates, she came down from the screens, and fell dead at their feet, burned out like a spent torch. Leonie's grandmother was a *rikhi*, and Under-Keeper, at that time, and she saw the Lady Mirella die, and she said that not only was her starstone blasted and blackened, but that the Lady's hands were burned as with fire and her body scorched by the energies she could no longer control. There is a monument to her in Arilinn," he concluded. "We pay our respects to her memory each year at Festival Night, but I still believe it is there as a warning to any Keeper who trifles with her powers—or her chastity."

Andrew shuddered, thinking, *Maybe it's just as well I couldn't touch Callista even for a moment. I wonder, though, if Damon told this story to keep me from getting ideas later on!*

Damon gestured to Ellemir and said, "Give him the stone, child. Touch it lightly at first, Andrew. Very lightly. Your first lesson," he added wryly. "Never grasp a starstone hard in your hands. Handle it, always, as if it were a living thing." *Must I, too, work as a Keeper? To train him, as Leonie trained me?*

Andrew took the stone from Ellemir's outstretched fingers. He had caught Damon's resentful thought and wondered what the slender Comyn Lord was angry about. Were all the telepaths women here, so Damon felt that being one made him less of a man? No, it couldn't be that, or he wouldn't have one of the stones himself, but Andrew felt there was *something*. The starstone felt faintly warm, even through the silk. He had somehow expected it to feel like any other jewel, cold and hard. Instead it had the warmth of a live thing in his palm.

Damon said, in a low voice, "Now take off the silk. Very gently and slowly. Don't look at the stone right away."

He unwrapped the insulating silk, and saw Ellemir flinch. She said in a low voice, "I felt that."

Damon said swiftly, "Cover it again, Andrew." He obeyed, and Damon asked, "Did it hurt when he touched it?"

Can we use Ellemir as a barometer to Callista's reactions? Andrew thought.

"It didn't exactly *hurt*," Ellemir said, her brow knitted, evidently trying to be very exact about her reactions. "Only—I *felt* it. Like a hand touching me. I'm not sure where. It wasn't even really unpleasant. Just—somehow, intimate."

Damon frowned slightly. "You're developing *laran*," he said. "That's evident. That may be helpful."

She looked frightened and said, "Damon! Is it—dangerous for me? I am no virgin."

Twin to a Keeper and so ignorant? Damon thought in exasperation, then saw that she was really afraid. He said quickly, "No, no, *breda*. Only for those women who work at the highest levels in the screens or with the most powerful stones. You might, if you overworked—and you were exhausted with lovemaking, or pregnant—get a bad headache or a fainting fit. Nothing worse. There are women, Tower-trained, working among us there, who need not live by a Keeper's laws."

She looked relieved and faintly embarrassed. It was evidently not, Andrew thought, the kind of thing girls here usually blurted out in front of strangers. Although sexual taboos here seemed to be different than they were among Terrans, they seemed to have plenty of them.

Damon said, "Ellemir, touch my stone a moment. Lightly—careful," he said, gritting his teeth as he unwrapped the stone.

Andrew, watching, thought he was braced as if for a low blow. Ellemir laid her fingertip lightly on the stone, and Damon only sighed a little.

So Ellemir and I are keyed together somehow, he thought. *It's understandable. It always happens in sympathy like this. If we came closer still, if I took her to my bed, perhaps she could even learn to use it. Well, if I needed a good reason . . .* He laughed a little, harshly, aware that once again he was broadcasting his thoughts both to the woman who was their subject and to the man who was still, by ordinary standards, a stranger. Well, they'd all better get used to it. It would be worse before it was better.

"For what it's worth," he said aloud, and Andrew heard the tension and fear in his voice, "it seems Ellemir can handle my stone without hurting me. Which helps. As for you, Andrew, I *think* I can key you into Callista's stone without danger to her. It's a risk we'll have to take. You're our one link with her. For what we're going to have to do—"

Andrew looked quizzically at the older man and asked, "Precisely what *are* we going to do?"

"I'm not sure yet. I can't make definite plans until Dom Esteban wakes. Her father has a right to share in any plans we make." *Besides*, Damon thought grimly, *by then we'll know whether or not he can take any part in the rescue*. "But whatever we do, Callista will have to know about it. And, anyway"—he saw Ellemir flinch as he said it—"even if Callista should be hurt, or killed, we would still have to go out against whomever is doing this in the darkening lands."

Andrew thought, *I'm only in this for Callista's sake; I want no other part of it*. But before Damon's haggard face he could not bring himself to say so. He was still holding the wrapped stone.

Damon sighed deeply and said, "Unwrap it again. Touch it—lightly. Ellemir?" He glanced at the woman, and she nodded.

"Yes. I feel it when he touches it, still."

Andrew gingerly held the stone between his palms. He was seated on a low chair near the window, Damon standing before him. Damon said grimly, "I'd better guard against what happened last time." He dropped cross-legged on the thick carpet, drawing Ellemir down beside him.

Andrew, watching Damon's face, thought, *He's afraid. Is it that dangerous?*

Damon's gray eyes met the Earthman's, as he said, "Don't deceive yourself; yes, it is. People who use these skills without adequate training can do immense harm. I ought to tell you there's some risk to you, too. Usually the business of keying anyone into a matrix is handled by a Keeper. I'm not." *Leonie said, if I had been born a woman, I'd have made a Keeper*. For the first time this thought did not bring Damon the usual ration of self-contempt, doubt of his own manhood. Instead, he felt faintly grateful. It could save all their lives.

Andrew leaned over him, Callista's stone still cradled in his hands, and said, "Damon. You know what you're doing, don't you? If I didn't trust you, I'd never have let you start this. Let's take the risk for granted and go on from there."

Damon sighed and said, "I guess that's the only thing we can do. I wish—" but he did not finish the sentence.

I wish there was time to send for Leonie, bring her here. But would she approve of what I am doing—keying in a stranger, a Terran, into a Keeper? Even to save Callista's life? Callista knew what risks a Keeper must take, before ever she pledged to the Tower. Leonie does not know this Earthman as I do, as Callista does.

I have never done anything against Leonie's will, in all my life. Yet she set me free to use my own judgment, and that is exactly what I must do now.

Andrew said, in a low voice, "Exactly what do I have to do? Don't forget I don't know a damned thing about these psychic things." His fingers moved unsteadily on the starstone; remembering Damon's caution, he carefully relaxed his fingers. He thought, *It's as if—I must be as cautious as if it were Callista's own life I were holding between my hands.* The thought filled him with an inexpressible tenderness, and Ellemir raised her head and her gray eyes met his in a brief moment of sympathy. *She is more like Callista than I thought.*

Damon said, "I'm going to go into your mind—make my brain waves, the electrical force-field of my brain, resonate in the same wavelength as yours, if it's easier to understand it that way—and then try to adjust the field of *your* brain to that of Callista's stone, so that you'll be able to function on that exact frequency. This will put you in closer contact with her, so that, perhaps, you can lead us to her."

"You don't know where she is?"

"I know only in a general way," Damon said. "You told me she spoke of dripping water and darkness. That sounds to me like the caves of Corresanti; they are the only caves within a day's ride, and they would not dare to keep her aboveground and in the light of the sun. And the village of Corresanti is within the borders of the darkening land. But if you are keyed into her starstone, you will be able to use it as a beacon, and find out *exactly* where they have hidden her. And then you can tell us."

Andrew followed all this with some difficulty. He said, "You are evidently an expert with these stones. Why can't you find her with it?"

"Two reasons," Damon said. "Whoever's holding her prisoner is not only holding her body prisoner, and in darkness, but they've managed to barrier her mind on a level of the overworld none of us can reach. Don't ask me how they did it. Whoever's doing this is evidently using a very powerful matrix himself." *The Great Cat I saw*, he thought. *Well, maybe we'll singe his whiskers for him.*

"Second reason. She's evidently in very close touch with you, emotionally. So that half our work is done already. If we had a blank stone for you, I could simply key *your* frequencies into it, and you could lead us to Callista because you are already in touch with her. But since we must use Callista's own stone, which is keyed into *her*, body and brain, we must take into account that only someone in deep sympathy with her can use it without danger. Without you, I might have tried it with her twin. But the fact that Callista can come directly to you means you are the logical one." Abruptly Damon said, "I'm putting it off again. Look into the stone."

Andrew lowered his eyes to the flashing luminescence of blue. Deep inside the stone small ribbons and worms of color moved, slowly, like a beating heart. Callista's heart.

"Ellemir. You'll have to monitor us both." Damon longed, with an almost physical longing, for the trained women from the Tower Circles, who knew this work and could keep in touch, almost automatically, with up to seven or eight telepaths working in the Circle at once. Ellemir was new to laran, just awakened, and untrained. "If either of us forgets to breathe, if we seem to be in any deep physical distress, you'll simply have to bring us out of it."

She looked scared, too. "I'll—try."

"You'd better do more than try. You have the talent. *Use* it, Ellemir, as you value your sister's life. Or mine.

If you had training, you could step in and regulate our breathing and our heartbeats if they began to go astray; but I'll manage if you can just bring us up to surface if that happens."

"Don't scare her," Andrew said gently. "I know she'll do the best she can."

Damon drew a deep breath, focused deeply on the stone. Fear surged up like a struck flame on flint, and he felt his heartbeat catch, then he forced it back. *I can do this. I used to. Leonie said I could.* He felt his breathing quiet as he relaxed, felt his heartbeats quiet into the slow pulsing rhythm of the stone. He began to try to formulate his instructions to Andrew. *Watch the lights in the stone. Try to quiet your mind, to feel your whole body pulsing in that rhythm.*

Andrew felt the thought—*pick up the beat*—and wondered exactly how it was done. Could you change your own heartbeat that way? Well, in the Medic and Psych Center he'd been taught on a biofeedback machine to initiate alpha rhythms for sleep or deep relaxation. This wasn't all that different. He watched, trying to relax, as he tried to feel and sense the exact rhythmic pulse of the stone. *It's like feeling Callista's heartbeat.* He became conscious of his own heartbeat, of the rhythm of the blood in his temples, of all the small interior noises and feelings and rhythms. The pulse of the starstone between his palms quickened and brightened, quickened and brightened, and he was conscious of his own internal rhythms in a definite, out-of-phase counterpoint. *I guess what I have to do is match those rhythms.* He began breathing deep and slow, trying to match his breathing, at least, to the rhythm of the starstone. *Callista's rhythm? Don't think. Concentrate.* He managed to match his breathing to the exact rhythm of the stone. For an instant it faltered, went ragged, and he felt the spurt of adrenalin through him—*Callista?*—and realized that Ellemir had drawn a deep breath, audible, almost a gasp. He steeled himself to quiet again, tried to pick up the ragged rhythm, slowly returned it to normal. To his own detached wonder, he saw that as his breathing quieted the pulse in the starstone quieted, too.

Now breathing and the pulse of the stone were one

rhythm, but his heartbeat was a strong counter-rhythm against the matched beat of stone and breath. *Concentrate. Pick up the beat.* His eyes were aching, and a wave of nausea rippled through him. The stone was spinning—he squeezed his eyes shut, fighting the surging sickness, but the light and the crawling colors persisted through his closed eyelids.

He moaned aloud, and the sound broke the growing beat to fragments. Damon quickly raised his head, and Ellemir looked up in apprehension.

"What's wrong?" Damon asked softly, and Andrew muttered with difficulty, "Seasick." The room seemed to be swinging in slow circles around him and he held out one hand to brace himself. Ellemir looked pale, too.

Damon wet his lips and said, "That happens. Damn. You're too new to this. I wish—Aldones! I wish we had some *kirian*. Failing that—Ellemir, are you sure there is none here?"

"I honestly don't think so."

Damon thought, *I'm not feeling so good myself. It's not going to be easy.*

Andrew asked him, "Why should it have that effect?" Then he felt Damon's surge of impatience: *Is this the time for asking foolish questions?* His anger, Andrew thought in slow incredulity, looked like a pale red glow around him. "The room's—ragged," he said, and leaned back, closing his eyes.

Damon forced himself to be calm. This was not going to be easy even if they were all in total harmony. If they started arguing, it wasn't even going to be *possible*. And he couldn't expect Andrew, doing a difficult and unexpected thing with total strangers, and struggling against the sickness and pain of having the unused psi centers of his brain forced open, to stay in control. The job of staying in control was strictly up to him. That was a Keeper's job, holding everyone in rapport. *A woman's job. Well, man or woman, right now it's my job.*

He forced himself to relax, deliberately quieted his breathing. He said, "I'm sorry, Andrew. Everybody goes through it sometime or other. I'm sorry it's so rough on you; I wish I could help. You're feeling sick because, first, you're using part of your brain that you usually *don't* use. And, second, because your eyes, and your balance centers, and all the rest of it, are reacting to your effort to bring some—well, some automatic functions under deliberate, voluntary control. I don't mean to be irritable. There's a certain degree of physical irritability I can't quite control either. Try not to focus your eyes on anything, if you can help it, and lie back against the cushions. The sickness will probably go away in a few minutes. Do the best you can."

Andrew stayed still, eyes closed, until the swaying sickness receded a little. *He's trying to help.* The physical sensations were like bad side effects of some drug, a nausea that wasn't even definite enough to be relieved by vomiting, a strange sensation of crawling in his very bowels, strange flashes of light against the inside of his eyes. Well, it wouldn't kill him; he'd had bad hangovers that were worse. "I'm all right," he said, and caught Damon's surprised, grateful glance.

"Actually it's a good sign you should be sick at this stage," he said. "It means something's actually *happening.* Ready to try again?"

Andrew nodded and, without instructions this time, tried to focus on the beat and rhythm within the matrix stone. It was easier now. He realized he did not have to look into the stone; he could sense the pulsation through the tips of his fingers. No, the sensation was not exactly physical; he tried to identify exactly where it came from and lost it again. Did it *matter* where it came from? The important thing was to stay open to it. He picked it up again (*A part of my brain I've never used before?*) and felt how quickly the breathing went into synchronization with the invisible pulsation. After a short, slow time, during which he felt as if he were groping in the dark for an elusive rhythm, the heartbeat followed.

He fought in the dark for what seemed a long time against the elusive cross-rhythms which seemed now to be inside him, now outside. No sooner would he tame one rhythm of the multiplex percussion orchestra and subdue it into the pervasive harmony, than another would escape him and start up a rebellious tickety-tock pattern against it; then he had to listen and analyze them and, somehow, delicately, try to fasten on where in his body the alien rhythm was beating, and try to tune it, beat by rebellious beat, into the proper harmony. After a long, long time he was conscious of beating all in one pulsation, other rhythms quieted, swaying up and down as if cradled inside the vast ticking heart, swaying in a ceaseless, tideless sea, his body and brain, his flowing pulsing blood, the incessant motion of the cells inside his muscles, the slow gentle pulse inside his sexual organs, all pulsing in rhythm. . . . *As if I were inside the jewel, flowing with all the little lights. . . .*

Andrew—the most delicate of whispers, part of the great rhythm.

Callista? Not a question. No answer needed. *As if we lay cradled together in a vast swaying darkness. Yes, that will come too. Cradled like twins in one womb.* He had no conscious thoughts at that moment, lying deep below the level of thought where there was only a sort of unfocused *awareness*. With a small detached level of fragmentary thought, he wondered if this was what was meant by being attuned to someone else's mind. Not conscious of the answer as a separateness, he knew, yes, he was close in contact with Callista's mind. For an instant he sensed Ellemir, too, and without really willing it, a thought tangled through his mind, a flash of faintly disturbing intimacy, as if in this pulsating darkness he lay naked, stripped as he had never been, entangled in intimacy that was like a pounding rhythm of sex. He was aware of both women, and it seemed completely natural, a part of reality without surprise or embarrassment. Then he slipped one notch farther up into awareness and knew his body was there again, cold and soaked in sweat. At that moment he was aware of Damon close by, a disturbing intimacy, not wholly welcome because it thrust between his intense emotional closeness to Callista. He didn't want to be that close to Damon: it wasn't the same, his texture was different somehow, disturbing. For an instant he struggled and felt himself gasp, almost retching, and it was as if the heart between his hands struggled and beat hard for an instant, and then, abruptly, there was a short bright flare of light and a fusion. (For an instant he saw Damon's face and it felt terrifyingly like looking into a mirror, a swift touch and grip and flare.) Then, abruptly and without transition, he was fully conscious of his body again and Callista was disappearing.

Andrew lay back in his chair, aware that he still felt sick. But the acute sickness was gone. Damon was kneeling upright beside him, looking down into his eyes with anxious concern.

"Andrew, are you all right?"

"I'm—fine," he managed to say, feeling a tardy embarrassment. "What the hell—"

Ellemir—he realized suddenly that her hand lay in his, and the other hand in Damon's—gave his fingers a soft little squeeze. She said, "I couldn't see Callista. But she was *there* for a moment. Andrew, forgive me for doubting you."

Andrew felt strangely embarrassed. He knew perfectly well that he had not moved from the chair, that he had not touched anything except Ellemir's fingertips, that Damon had not touched him at all, but he had the definite feeling that something profound and almost sexual had happened among all of them, including Callista, who was not there at all. "How much of what I felt was real?" he demanded.

Damon shrugged. "Define your terms. What's *real*? Everything and nothing. Oh, the images," he said, apparently picking up the texture of Andrew's embarrassment. "That. Let me put it this way. When the brain—or the mind—has an experience like nothing *else* it's ever experienced, it visualizes it in terms of familiar things. I lost contact for a few seconds—but I imagine you felt strong emotion."

"Yes," Andrew said, almost inaudibly.

"It was an unusual emotion, so your mind instantly associated it with a familiar but equally strong one, which just happened to be sexual. My own image is like walking a tightrope without falling off, and then finding something to hang on to, and brace myself with. But"—he grinned suddenly—"an awful lot of people think in sexual images, so don't worry about it. I'm used to it and so is anyone who's ever had to find their way around in direct *rapport*. Everybody has his own individual set of images; you'll soon recognize them like individual voices."

Ellemir said, almost in a murmur, "I kept hearing voices in different pitches, that suddenly slid in to close harmony and started singing together like an enormous choir."

Damon leaned over and touched her cheek lightly with his lips. "So that was the music I heard?" he murmured.

Andrew realized that somewhere in the back of his mind he too had heard something like far-off voices blending. Musical images, he thought a little wryly, were safer and less revealing than sexual ones. He looked tentatively at Ellemir, sounding out his own feelings, and found he was thinking on two levels at once. On one level he felt an intimacy with Ellemir, as if he had been her lover for a long time, a comprehensive goodwill, a feeling of sympathy and protectiveness. On another level, even clearer, he was perfectly aware that this was a girl unfamiliar to him, that he had never touched more than her fingertips, and had no intention of ever doing any more than that and it confused him.

How can I feel this almost sexual acceptance *of her, and at the same time have no sexual interest in her at all, as a person? Maybe Damon's right and I'm just visualizing unfamiliar feelings in familiar terms. Because I have that same sort of profound intimacy and acceptance toward* Damon*, and that's* really *confusing and disturbing.* It gave him a headache.

Damon said, "I didn't see Callista either, and I wasn't really in touch with her, but I could feel that Carr was." He sighed, with the weariness of physical fatigue, but his face was peaceful.

But the peaceful interlude was short-lived. Damon knew that, so far, Callista was well and safe. If anyone harmed her now, Andrew would know. But how long would she remain safe? If her captors had any idea that Callista had reached anyone outside, anyone who could lead rescuers to her—well, there was one obvious way to prevent that. Andrew couldn't reach her if she was dead. And that was so simple, and so obvious, that Damon's throat squeezed tight in panic. If they caught any hint of what he was trying to do, if they had the faintest

notion that rescue was on the way, Callista might not
live long enough to be rescued.

Why had they kept her alive this long? Again Damon
reminded himself not to judge the cat-men by human
standards. *We really know nothing of why they do
anything.*

He rose, and swayed where he stood, knowing that
after taxing, demanding telepathic work he needed food,
sleep, and quiet. The night was far gone. The hideous
need for haste beat at him. He braced himself to keep
from falling and looked down at Ellemir and Andrew.
*Now that things have begun moving again, we must be
ready to move with them,* he thought. *If I'm going to act
as Keeper, this is my responsibility—to keep them from
panicking. I'm in charge, and I've got to look after them.*

"We all need food," he said, "and sleep. And we can't
do a thing until we know how badly Dom Esteban is
hurt. Everything, now, depends on that."

CHAPTER EIGHT

When Damon came down into the Great Hall the next morning, he found Eduin prowling around in front of the doors, his face pale and drawn. To Damon's question he nodded briefly. "Caradoc's doing well enough, Lord Damon. But the Lord Istvan—"

That told Damon all he needed to know. Esteban Lanart had awakened—and was still unable to move. So that was *that*. Damon felt a sickening sensation as if he stood on quicksand. What now? *What now?*

Then it was up to him. He realized, hardening his jaw, that he had really known this all along. From the moment of premonition (*You will see him sooner than you think and it will not be well for any of you*) he had known that in the end it would be his task. He was still not sure how, but at least he knew he could not let the burden slide onto the stronger shoulders of his kinsman.

"Does he know, Eduin?"

Eduin's hawklike face twisted in a grimace of compassion, and he said briefly, "Do you think anyone'd need to tell him? Aye. He knows."

And if he didn't, he'd know the minute he saw me. Damon began to push aside the doors to enter, but Eduin gripped his arm.

"Can't you do for his wound what you did for Caradoc's, Lord Damon?"

Pityingly, Damon shook his head. "I'm no miracle worker. To stop the flow of blood is nothing. That done, Caradoc would heal. I healed nothing; I did only what Caradoc's wound would have done of itself if anyone could have reached it. But if the spinal nerve is severed—no power on this world could repair it."

Eduin's eyes closed briefly. "That I feared," he said. "Lord Damon! Is there news of the Lady Callista?"

"We know she is safe and well, at this moment,"

Damon said, "but there is need for haste. So I must see Dom Esteban at once, and make plans."

He pushed the door open. Ellemir was kneeling by her father's bedside; the other wounded men had evidently been moved out to the Guardroom, except for Caradoc, who lay under blankets far at the back of the Hall, and seemed fast asleep. Esteban Lanart lay flat, his heavy body immobilized in sandbags so that he could not turn from side to side. Ellemir was feeding him, not very expertly, with a child's spoon. He was a tall, heavy, red-faced man, with the strongly aquiline features of all his clan, his long sideburns and bushy eyebrows graying but his beard still brilliantly red. He looked angry and incongruous with drops of gruel in his beard; his fierce eyes moved to Damon.

"Good morning, kinsman," Damon said.

Dom Esteban retorted, "Good, you say! When I lie here like a tree struck by lightning and my daughter— my daughter—" He raised a clenched fist in rage, struck the spoon, upset more of the gruel, and snarled, "Take that filthy stuff away! It's not my belly that's paralyzed, girl!" He saw her stricken face and moved his hand clumsily to pat her arm. "Sorry, *chiya*. I've cause enough for anger. But get me something decent to eat, not that baby-food!"

Ellemir raised helpless eyes to the healer-woman who stood by; she shrugged, and Damon said, "Give him anything he wants, Ellemir, unless he's feverish."

The girl rose and went out, and Damon came to the bedside. It seemed inconceivable that Dom Esteban would never again rise from that bed. That harsh face should not lie on a pillow, that powerful body should be up and moving about in its usual brisk military way.

"I won't ask you how you feel, kinsman," Damon said. "But are you in much pain now?"

"Almost none, strange as it seems," said the wounded man. "Such a little, little wound to lay me low! Hardly more than a scratch. And yet—" His teeth clenched in his lip. "I've been told I'll never walk again." His gray eyes sought out Damon's, in an agony of pleading so great that the younger man was embarrassed. "Is it true? Or is the woman as much a fool as she seems?"

Damon bent his head and did not answer. After a moment the older man moved his head in weary resignation. "Tragedy stalks our family. Coryn dead before his fifteenth year, and Callista, Callista—so I must seek help, humbly, as befits a cripple, from strangers. I have no one of my own blood to help me."

Damon knelt on one knee beside the old man. He said deliberately, "The gods forbid you should seek among strangers. I claim that right—father-in-law."

The bushy eyebrows went up, almost into the hairline. At last Dom Esteban said, "So the wind blows from that quarter? I had other plans for Ellemir, but—" A brief pause, then, "Nothing goes, I believe, as we plan it, in this imperfect world. Be it so, then. But the road will be no easy one, even if you can find Callista. Ellemir has told me something—a confused tale of Callista and a stranger, a Terran, who has somehow gained *rapport* with her and has offered his sword, or his services, or some such thing. He must talk of it with you, whoever he is, although it seems strange that one of the Terranan should show proper reverence for a Keeper." He scowled fiercely. "Curse those beasts! Damon, what has been happening in these hills? Until a few seasons ago the cat-men were timid folk who lived in the hills, and no one thought them wiser than the little people of the trees! Then, as if some evil god had come among them, they attack us like fiends, they stir up the Dry Towns against us—and lands where our people have lived for generations lie under some darkness as if bewitched. I'm a practical man, Damon, and I don't believe in bewitchments! And now they come invisible out of the air, like wizards from some old fairy tale."

"All too real, I fear," Damon said, and knew his face was grim. "I met them, crossing the darkening lands, and only too late did I realize that I could have made them visible with my starstone." His hand sought the leather pouch about his throat. "They slaughtered my men. Eduin said you saved them, that almost alone you cut your way out of the ambush. How—?" Damon felt suddenly awkward.

Dom Esteban lifted the long, squarish swordsman's hand from the bed and looked at it, as if puzzled. "I hardly know," he said slowly, looking at his hand and moving the fingers back and forth, turning it to look at the palm, and then back again. "I must have heard the other sword in the air—" He hesitated and an odd note of wonder crept into his voice as he spoke again. "But I didn't. Not till I had my sword out and up to guard." He blinked, puzzled. "It's like that sometimes. It's happened before. You suddenly turn, and block, and there's an attack coming that you'd never have seen unless you'd found yourself guarding it." He laughed again, raucously. "Merciful Avarra! Listen to the old man bragging." Suddenly the fingers knotted into fists. His arm trembled with anger. "Boast? Why not? What else can a cripple do?"

From the greatest swordsman in the Domains to a helpless invalid—horrible! And yet, Damon thought reluctantly, there was an element of justice in it. Dom Esteban had never been tolerant of the slightest physical weakness in anyone else. It had been in proving his courage to his father, climbing the heights he feared, that Coryn had fallen to his death. . . .

"Zandru's hells," the old man said after a moment. "The way my joints have stiffened, these last three winters, the bone-aches would have done it in another year or so, anyway. Better to have one last terrific fight."

"It won't be forgotten in a hurry," Damon said, and turned quickly away so the old man would not see the pity in his eyes. "Zandru's hells, how we could use your sword now against the accursed cat-men!"

The old man laughed mirthlessly. "My sword? That's easy—take it and welcome," he said with a bitter grimace meant to be a grin. "Afraid you'll have to use it yourself, though. I can't go along and help."

Damon caught the unspoken contempt—*There's no sword ever forged could make a swordsman of you*—but at the moment he felt no anger. Dom Esteban's only remaining weapon was his tongue. Anyway, Damon had never prided himself on his skill at arms.

Ellemir was returning with a tray of solid food for her father; she set it down beside the bed and began cutting up the meat. Dom Esteban said, "Just what are your plans, Damon? *You're* not planning to go up against the cat-men?"

He said quietly, "I see no alternative, Father-in-law."

"It will take an army to wipe them out, Damon."

"Time enough for that next year," Damon said. "Just now our first problem is to get Callista out of their hands, and for that we have no time to raise an army. What's more, if we came up against them with an army, their first move would be to kill her. Time presses. Now that we know where she is—"

Dom Esteban stared, forgetting to chew a mouthful of meat and gravy. He swallowed, choked a little, gestured to Ellemir for a drink, and said, "You know. Just how did you manage that?"

"The Terranan," said Damon quietly. "No, I don't know how it happened either. I never knew any of the strangers had anything like our *laran*. But he has it, and he is in contact with Callista."

"I don't doubt it," Esteban said. "I met some of them in Thendara when they negotiated to build the Trade City. They are more like us. I heard a story that Terra and Darkover are of common stock, far back in history. They rarely leave their city, though. How did this one come here?"

"I will send for him and you can hear it from his own lips," said Ellemir. She beckoned a servant and gave the message, and after a little while Andrew Carr came into the Great Hall. Damon, watching the Earthman bowing to Dom Esteban, thought that at least these people were no savages.

Prompted by Damon, Carr gave a brief account of how he had come into contact with Callista. Esteban looked grave and thoughtful.

"I cannot say that I approve of this," he said, "For a Keeper to make such close contact with a stranger from outside her own caste is unheard-of, and scandalous. In the old days of the Domains, wars were fought on Darkover for less than this. But times change, whether we like the changes or not, and perhaps as things stand now it is more important to save her from the cat-men than from the disgrace of such a *rapport*."

"Disgrace?" Andrew Carr said, flushing deeply. "I mean her no harm or dishonor, sir. I wish her nothing but the best, and I have offered to risk my life to set her free."

"Why?" Esteban asked curtly. "She can be nothing to you, man; a Keeper is pledged a virgin."

Damon hoped Carr would have sense enough not to say anything about his own emotional attachment to Callista; but not trusting Andrew to hold his tongue, he said, "Dom Esteban, he has already risked his life to make contact with her; for a man of his age, untrained, to work through a starstone is no light matter." He scowled at Andrew, trying to convey "Shut up, let well enough alone."

In any case, Dom Esteban, whether from pain or worry, did not pursue the topic, but turned to Damon. "You know, then, where Callista is?"

"We have reason to believe she is in the caves of Corresanti," Damon said, "and Andrew can lead us to her."

Dom Esteban snorted. "There's a lot of countryside between here and Corresanti, and all of it chock full of cat-men, and blasted villages," he said. "It lies half a day's ride into the darkening lands."

"That can't be helped," Damon said. "You managed to get through them, which proves it can be done. At least they cannot come on us veiled by invisibility, while I have my starstone."

Esteban thought about that; nodded slowly. "I had forgotten you were Tower-trained," he said. "What about the Earthman? Will he come with you?"

Andrew said, "I'm going. I seem to be the only link to Callista. Besides, I swore to her that I would rescue her."

Damon shook his head. "No, Andrew. No, my friend. Just *because* you are the only link with Callista, we dare not risk you. If you were killed, even accidentally, we might never make our way to her, or recover only her dead body, too late. You stay at Armida, and maintain contact with me, through the starstone."

Stubbornly, Carr shook his head. "Look, I'm *going*," he said. "I'm a lot bigger and tougher than you think. I've knocked around on half a dozen worlds. I can take care of myself, Damon. Hell, man, I'd make two of *you!*"

Damon sighed, and thought, *Maybe he can; he got here*

through the blizzard. I couldn't have done that well if I were lost on a strange world. "Possibly you're right," he said. "How good are you with a sword?"

Damon saw the faint surprise and hesitation in the Earthman's face. "I don't know. My people don't use them except for sport. I could learn, though. I learn fast."

Damon raised his eyebrows. "It's not that easy," he said. *His people use swords only for sport? How do they defend themselves, then? Knives, like the Dry-Towners, or fists? If so, they may be stronger than we are. Or have the Terrans gone beyond the Compact, and banned all weapons that can kill at all?*

He said, "Eduin," and the big Guardsman, lounging near the door, sprang to attention. *"Vai dom?"*

"Step over to the armory, and get a couple of practice swords."

After a moment Eduin returned, bearing two of the wood-and-leather weapons used for training in swordsmanship. Damon took one in his hand, extended the other to Carr. The Earthman looked curiously at the long blunt stick of springy wood, with braided leather covering the edge and tip, then experimentally gripped it in his palm. Damon, frowning at the unpracticed grip, asked bluntly, "Have you ever touched a sword before in your life?"

"A little fencing for sport. I'm no champion."

I can well believe that, Damon thought, slipping on the leather headpiece. He looked at Carr over his right shoulder through the grillwork that protected his face: the practice swords bent easily enough that there was not much danger of damaging a bone or an internal organ, but eyes and teeth were more vulnerable. Carr faced him straight on. *Chest exposed,* Damon thought, *and he handles the thing as if he were poking the fire.*

Andrew stepped forward; Damon lifted his sword only slightly, brushing the weapon aside. As the big man went off balance, the leather tip caught Carr in the chest. Then Damon relaxed, lowering the tip to the floor. He slowly shook his head. He said, "You see, my friend? And I'm no swordsman. I wouldn't last half a dozen strokes against anyone even halfway competent; Dom

Esteban, or Eduin here, would have had the sword out of my hand before I got it up."

"I'm sure I could learn," Carr protested stubbornly.

"Not in time," Damon said. "Believe me. Andrew, I began to train with these swords before I was eight years old. Most lads begin at least a year before that. You're strong—I can see that. You're even fairly fast on your feet. But we couldn't even teach you enough, in a week, to keep you from getting killed. And we haven't got a week. We haven't even got a day. Forget it, Andrew. You've got something more important to do than carrying a sword."

"And do you think *you're* going to lead a party of swordsmen against the cat-people?" Dom Esteban asked sardonically. "Eduin here could do to you what you did to the Earthman, in seconds."

Damon looked around at the man lying motionless. Esteban had motioned the tray of food away, and was watching them fixedly, his eyes bright with something like anger. He said, "Show some sense, Damon. I kept you in the Guards because the men like you and you're a good organizer and administrator. But this is a job for a master swordsman. Are you so blind to facts that you think you could go up against swordsmen who could cut down the whole castle Guard here at Armida and steal Callista right out of her bed? Am I marrying my daughter to a fool?"

Ellemir said in a rage, "Father, how dare you! You cannot talk like that to Damon!"

Damon motioned to her to be quiet. He faced the older man straightforwardly, and said, "I know that, kinsman. I probably know more about my own deficiencies than you do. Just the same, no man can do more than his best, and this is my right. I am now Callista's closest kinsman, except for Domenic, and he is not yet seventeen."

Esteban smiled grimly. He said, "Well, my son, I admire your spirit; I wish you had the skill to go with it." He raised his fists and beat them against the pillow, in a fit of fury. "Zandru's hells! Here I lie, broken-down and useless as Durraman's donkey, and all my skill and all my knowledge—" The fit subsided at last and he said, his voice weaker than before, "If I had time to teach you, you're not so hopeless—but there's no time, no time. You say with your starstone you can throw off their accursed illusion of invisibility?"

Damon nodded. Eduin came forward to the bedside and knelt there. He said, "Lord Istvan. I owe the Lord Damon a life. Let me go with them to Corresanti."

Damon said, deeply moved, "You're wounded, man. And you've been through one battle."

"All the same," Eduin protested, "you have said my skill with a sword is greater than your own. Let me go to guard you, Lord Damon; your task is to bear the starstone."

"Merciful Avarra," Dom Esteban said almost under his breath, "*that* is the answer!"

"I will gladly have your company and your sword, if you are able," Damon said, laying his hand on Eduin's shoulder. In his sensitized state he was overwhelmingly aware of the man's outpouring of loyalty and gratitude, and he felt almost abashed by it. "But you owe your service to the Lord Esteban; it is for him to give you leave to go with me."

Both men turned to Esteban, who lay motionless; his eyes were closed and his brow knitted as if deep in thought. For a moment Damon wondered if they had exhausted the wounded man too much, but he could feel that beneath the closed eyes there was some very active thinking going on. Esteban's eyes suddenly flew open.

"Just how good are you with that starstone, Damon?" he asked. "I know you have *laran*, you spent years in the Tower, but didn't Leonie kick you out again? If it was for incompetence, this won't work, but—"

"It wasn't for incompetence," Damon said quietly. "Leonie did not complain of my skill, only that I was too sensitive, and my health, she felt, would suffer."

"Look me in the eye. Is that truth or vanity, Damon?"

There were times, Damon thought, when he positively detested the brutal old man. He met Esteban's eyes without flinching and said, "As I remember, *you* have enough *laran* to find out for yourself."

Esteban's lips flicked in that mirthless grin again. He said, "From somewhere, you've gotten courage enough to stand up to me, kinsman, and that's a good sign. As a lad you were afraid of me. Is it only because I'll never move out of this bed again that you've got courage to confront me now?" He returned Damon's gaze for an instant—a harsh touch like a firm grip—and then said tersely, "My apology for doubting you, kinsman, but this is too important to spare anyone's feelings, even my own. Do you think I like confronting the fact that someone else will rescue my favorite daughter? Just the same. You are skilled with a starstone. Have you ever heard the story of Regis the Fifth? The Hasturs were kings in those days; it was before the crown passed into the Elhalyn line."

Damon frowned, searching in memory of old legends. "He lost a leg in the battle of Dammerung Pass—?"

"No," said Dom Esteban, "he lost a leg by treachery, when he was set on in his bed by assassins; so that he could not fight in a duel and would forfeit a good half of the Hastur lands. Yet he sent his brother Rafael to the battle, and Rafael, who was a monkish man with little knowledge of swordplay, nevertheless fought in single combat with seven men and killed them all. To this day Castle Hastur stands in Hastur hands at the edge of the mountains. And this he could do because, as Regis lay in his bed not yet able to rise and hobble about on crutches, he made contact through his brother's starstone with his sword, and the monkish Rafael bore the sword of Regis into the fight, wielding it with all of Regis' skill."

"A fairy tale," said Damon, but he felt a strange prickle go up and down his spine.

Dom Esteban moved his head as much as he could for the sandbags and said vehemently, "By the honor of the Alton Domain, Damon, it is no fairy tale. The skill was known in the old times, but in these days few of the Comyn have the strength or the wish to dare so much. In these days the starstones are left mostly to women. Yet, if I thought you had the skills of our fathers with such a stone—"

With a slow prickle of wonder, Damon realized what Dom Esteban was suggesting. He said, "But—"

"Are you afraid? Do you think you could stand the

touch of the Alton Gift?" Dom Esteban demanded. "If it enabled you to fight your way through the cat-men with my own skill?"

Damon shut his eyes. He said honestly, "I'd have to think about it. It wouldn't be easy."

Yet—might it be Callista's one chance?

Dom Esteban was the only living man to cut his way out of a cat-man ambush. He himself had run like a rabbit from them, leaving his men to die. He had to be sure about this. He knew it was the kind of decision no one else could make for him. For a moment no one else in the room existed but Esteban and himself.

He stepped close to the bed and looked down at the prostrate man. "If I refuse, kinsman, it is not because I am afraid, but because I doubt your power to do this, sick and wounded as you are. I knew not that you had the Alton Gift, bred true."

"Oh, yes, I have it," said Esteban, staring up with a fearful intensity, "but in such days as I am living in, I always believed, I needed no gift other than my own strength and skill with weapons. Where do you suppose Callista got it in such measure that she was chosen from all the girls of the Domains to be Keeper? The Alton Gift is the ability to force rapport, and I had some training in my own youth. Try me, if you will."

Ellemir came and slid her hand into Damon's. She said, "Father, you can't do this dreadful thing."

"Dreadful? Why, my girl?"

"It's against the strongest law of the Comyn: that no man may dominate another's mind and soul."

"Who said anything about his mind and soul?" asked the old man, his gray bushy eyebrows crawling up like giant caterpillars to his hairline. "It's his sword-arm and reflexes I'm interested in dominating, and I *can* do it. And I'll do it by his free will and consent, or not at all." He began to reach out, winced, and lay still between the sandbags. "It's your choice, Damon."

Andrew looked pale and worried; Damon himself felt much the same way, and Ellemir's hand, tucked in his, was trembling. He said slowly, "If it's Callista's best chance, I'd agree to more than that. If you are strong enough, Lord Esteban."

"If my damned useless legs would only move, I've *fought* with worse wounds than this," Dom Esteban said. "Take the practice sword. Eduin, you take the other."

Damon slipped on the basketwork headpiece, turned his right side to Eduin. The Guardsman saluted, standing very casually, legs apart, sword-tip resting on the ground. Damon felt a sharp spasm of fear.

Not that Eduin could hurt me much with these wooden swords, not that I care so much for a few bumps and bruises. But all my life that damnable old man has been baiting me about my lack of skill. To make a fool of myself before Ellemir . . . to let him humiliate me once again. . . .

Esteban said in a strange, faraway voice, "Your starstone is insulated, Damon. Uncover it."

Damon fumbled with the leather pouch, drew it off, letting the warm heaviness of the matrix jewel rest against the base of his throat. He gave the pouch to Ellemir to hold, and the quick brush of her warm fingers against his was a reassurance.

Esteban said, "Stand back, Ellemir. And you too, Terranan. By the door, and see that no servants come in here. They can't do much harm with the practice foils, but even so—"

They withdrew slowly, and the two men faced one another, the heavy wooden swords in hand, circling slowly. Damon was faintly conscious of the harsh grip-touch that was Dom Esteban's *(What did I tell Andrew, you get to recognize people by their images as well as by their voices?)* and felt a strange droning in his ears, a sense of harsh pressure. He saw Eduin's sword come up, and before he knew what he was doing, he felt the flexing of his own knees, his arm moving without his knowledge in a quick whirling stroke. He heard the rapid-fire *whack! whack! whack!* of wood-and-leather clashing, then saw an incongruous whirl of images: Eduin's astonished face, with its seamed raw wound; Andrew's flare of amazement; his own arm coming up and a rapid backward step and feint; Eduin's sword flying out of his hand and across the room, landing almost at Andrew Carr's feet. The Earthman bent and picked it up as the droning suddenly receded from Damon's head.

Esteban said quietly, "Now do you believe me, kinsman? Have you ever been able to touch Eduin before, let alone disarm him?"

Damon realized that he was breathing fast and his heart beating like a smith's hammer at the forge. He thought, *I never moved that fast in my life*, and felt a mingled fear and resentment. *Someone else's hand, someone else's mind . . . in control . . . control of my very body.*

And yet— To get back at the damned cat-things who killed his Guardsmen, Dom Esteban would have been the logical choice to lead swordsmen against them. And he would if he could.

Damon had never especially wanted to be a swordsman. It wasn't his game. Just the same, he owed the cat-men something. His men were relying on him, and he'd left them to die. And Reidel had been his friend. If with Dom Esteban's help he could do it, did he have the right to refuse?

Esteban was lying quite still, passive between his sandbags, just flexing and unflexing his fingers thoughtfully. He did not speak, only met Damon's eyes with a look of triumph.

Damon thought, *Damn the man, he's enjoying this. But after all, why shouldn't he? He's proved to himself that he's not completely useless, after all.*

He put down the practice sword. From the naked jewel against his throat he was picking up flashing impressions, wonder and terror from Eduin, a sort of bemusement from Andrew, dismay from Ellemir. He tried to shut them all out, and went toward the bed again.

He said slowly, steadily—but he had to force the words out—"I agree, then, kinsman. When can we start?"

CHAPTER NINE

They started later that day, near to high noon, and Andrew, watching them ride away from the roof of Armida, thought they were a small party to go up against an army of nonhumans. He said so to Ellemir, who stood beside him wrapped to the earlobes in a heavy plaid shawl of green and blue. She shook her head, saying in an odd faraway voice, "Force alone wouldn't get them through. Damon has the only weapon that matters— the starstone."

"It looks to me like he'll be doing some fairly tough fighting—or your father will," Andrew said.

Ellemir answered, "Not really. That will just—if he's lucky—keep him from getting killed. But swordsmen have failed, before this, to get into the darkening lands. The cat-men know it, too. I am sure they took Callista in the hope of capturing her starstone as well. The cat people who are using a matrix unlawfully must have discovered that she was here—in a general way one matrix-user can spy out another—and hoped to gain her stone. Perhaps they even hoped they could force her to use it against us. Men would have known better—they would have known that any Keeper would die first. But the cat-people are apparently just beginning to learn about these things—which is why there is still some hope."

Andrew was thinking, grimly, that was lucky; if they had known more about Keepers, the cat-people would not have kidnapped Callista, but simply left her lying with her throat cut, in her bed. He saw from Ellemir's grimace of horror that she had followed his thoughts.

The woman said in a low voice, "Damon blames himself for running away and leaving his men to be slaughtered. But it was the right thing to do. If they had captured him, *and his starstone*—alive—"

"I thought no one could use another's stone except under very special circumstances."

"Not without hurting its owner terribly. But do you think the cat-men would have hesitated to do that?" she asked, almost with contempt, and was silent.

The riders had virtually disappeared now, only three small dots on the horizon: Damon and two swordsmen of the guard.

Andrew thought bitterly, *I should have been with them. Rescuing Callista is my job; instead I sit here at Armida, no more use than Dom Esteban. Less. He's fighting along with them.*

He had wanted to go. He had thought until the last that he would ride with them, that he would be needed to guide them to Callista, at least when they got inside the caves. After all, he was the only one who could reach her. Damon, even with his starstone, couldn't. But Damon had absolutely refused.

"Andrew, no, it's impossible. The best bodyguard in the world wouldn't be able to ensure you against getting killed accidentally. You are absolutely helpless to defend yourself, let alone help anyone else. It's not your fault, my friend, but all our energies have to go to getting inside the caves and getting Callista out. The spare minute we might take to defend you might make the difference between getting out alive—or not. And—let me remind you—if we get killed," he said, his lips tightening, "someone else can try. If *you* get killed, Callista will die inside the caves, from starvation, or ill-treatment, or with a knife in her throat when they discover she's no good to them." Damon had laid his hand on Andrew's shoulder, regretfully. "Believe me, I know how you feel. But this is the only way."

"And how will you find her without me there? You can't, even with your starstone; you just said so!"

"With Callista's starstone," Damon said. "*You* have access to the overworld. And you can reach me, too. Once I am inside the caves, you can lead us to her through the starstone."

Andrew still wasn't sure how that would be done. He had, in spite of yesterday's demonstration, only the foggiest notion of *how* it worked. He had *seen* it work, he had *felt* it work, but twenty-eight years of not believing in such things weren't wiped away in twenty-eight hours.

At his side, on the parapet, Ellemir shivered and said, "They're gone. There's no sense standing out here in the cold." She turned and went in through the doorway that led into the upper corridor of Armida, and slowly, Carr followed.

He knew Damon was right—or more accurately, he had faith that Damon knew what he was doing—but it was still galling. For days now, ever since he had realized that if he lived through the storm, somehow he would find Callista and rescue her, he had sustained himself with a mental picture of Callista, alone in the darkness of her prison, of himself coming to her side and sweeping her up in his arms, and carrying her away. . . . *Some damn romantic dream,* he thought sourly. *Where's the white horse to carry her away?*

He had never envisioned a world where men took swords seriously. For him a sword was either something to look at on the wall of a museum, or something to play with for exercise. He had wished for a gun or a blaster—*that* would make short work of a cat-man, he'd bet—but when he had said so, Damon had looked at him with as much horror as if he'd suggested gang-rape, cannibalism, and genocide, and mentioned something called the Compact. Before signing his contract with the Empire on Cottman IV, Andrew *had* fuzzily noted that they did have something there called the Compact, which as near as he could understand—he hadn't paid much attention to it, you never paid much attention to technicalities of native culture—forbade any lethal weapons which didn't bring the user within an equal risk of being killed in return. Damon had spoken of it, saying it had been universally accepted on Darkover, which seemed to be his name for the planet, for either a few hundred years or a few thousand. Andrew wasn't sure which; his command of the language was improving, but still wasn't perfect. So guns were definitely out, although swordplay had become a fine art.

No wonder they start training their kids in fighting before they're out of short pants. He wondered, in view of the ghastly cold weather on this planet, if children ever wore short pants at all, and cut off the thought with impatience. He went into the guest-room they had assigned him earlier and walked to the window, drawing aside the curtain to see if he could still catch a glimpse of Damon's party disappearing. But evidently they had ridden away past the crest of the hill.

Andrew lay down on the bed, hands tucked behind his neck. He supposed sooner or later he should go down and say a few polite words to his host. He didn't much like Dom Esteban; the man had tried hard to humiliate Damon, but the man was an invalid, and his host. Also, he felt some sense of obligation toward Ellemir. He didn't know what he could say to her, torn as she was between fear for Callista, fear for Damon, and anxiety about her father. But if he could do anything, or say anything, to let her know he shared her anxiety, he ought to do it.

Callista, Callista, he thought, *it's some world you brought me into.* Nevertheless, he felt a curious acceptance of what he would find here.

Callista's starstone around his neck felt reassuringly warm, like a live thing. *It's like touching Callista herself,* he thought, *the nearest to touching her that I've ever come.* Even through the silk insulation, there was an intimacy in the touch against his throat. He wondered where she was, if it was well with her, if she was crying alone in the darkness?

Damon seemed to think I could reach her through the stone, Andrew thought, and he drew it from his shirt front. The grayish silk envelope in which it was wrapped protected it from a careless touch. Carefully, mindful of Damon's warning, he unwrapped it with infinite caution, and a curious sense of hesitation. *It's almost as if I were undressing Callista,* he thought with a tender embarrassment, and at the same time he was ready to explode with hysterical laughter at the incongruity of the idea.

As he cradled the stone in his palm, he suddenly saw her close beside him. She was lying on her side, her lovely hair tangled—he could see her in a strange bluish light quite unlike the dim red sunlight in the room—and her face blotched and swollen as if she had been crying again. Quite without surprise, she opened her eyes and looked at him.

"Andrew, is it you? I had wondered why you had not came to me before," she said softly, and smiled.

"Damon is on his way to you," Andrew said, and the urge of resentment that he was not with them, that *he* would not be the one to find her, boiled over. He tried to conceal it from her and realized too late that he could not, that in this kind of close touching of minds no thought could be concealed.

She said very tenderly, "You must not be jealous of Damon; he has been as a brother to me since we were children."

Andrew felt ashamed of his own jealousy. *It's no good to pretend not to be jealous, I'll just have to get beyond thoughts like that.* He tried to remember how much he had liked Damon, how close he had felt to him for a little while, that in the deepest way of all he was grateful to Damon for doing what he himself couldn't, and he saw Callista smiling gently at him. He sensed somehow that he had overcome one of the first major barriers to acceptance on their own terms as one of themselves in a telepath culture, that because of this he was somehow less of an alien to Callista than he had been before.

She said, "You can come to me in the overworld now."

He looked at her helplessly. "I don't know how."

"Take the stone and look into it," she said. "I can see it, you know. I can see it like a light in the darkness. But you must not come to me *here*, where my body is. If my captors should see you, they might kill me to keep me from being rescued. I will come to you." Abruptly, without transition, the girl lying wearily on her side in the dark cave was standing before him at the foot of the bed. "Now," she said. "Simply leave your solid body behind; step out of it."

Andrew focused on the stone, fighting back the faint, crawling inner nausea, the perceptible surge of terror. Callista held out her hand to him, and suddenly, with a strange, tingling sensation, he was standing upright (he had not moved at all, he thought), and below him he could see his body, clad in the heavy unfamiliar garments Damon had given him, lying motionless on the bed, the stone between his hands.

He reached out his hand on the overworld level, and for the first time touched Callista's. It felt faint, and ethereal, hardly a physical touch at all, but it *was* a touch, he could *feel* it, and he saw from Callista's face that she felt it, too.

She whispered, "Yes, you are real, you are here. Oh, Andrew, Andrew—" For an instant she let herself fall against him. It was like embracing a shadow, but still, for an instant, he felt her light weight against him, felt the warmth and fragrance of her body in his arms, the wispy feel of her hair. He wanted to crush her in his arms and cover her with kisses, but something in her— a faint sense of hesitation, a drawing away—kept him from acting on his impulse.

I'm not even supposed to think about a Keeper. They're sacrosanct. Untouchable.

She raised her shadowy fingers to lay them gently against his cheek. She said very gently, "There will be time enough to think about all that later, when I am with you—really with you, really close to you."

"Callista. You know I love you," he said hesitantly, and her mouth trembled.

"I know, and it is strange to me, and I suppose under any other conditions it would be frightening to me. But you have come to me when I was so terribly alone, and fearing death, or torment, or ravishment. Men have desired me before," she said very simply, "and of course I have been taught, in ways I couldn't even begin to explain to you, not to respond to them in any way, even in fancy. With some men, it has made me feel—feel sick, as if insects were crawling on my body. But there have been a few that I have almost wished—wished, as I wish now with you—that I knew how to respond to their desire; even, perhaps, that I knew how to desire them in return. Can you understand this at all?"

"Not really," Andrew said slowly, "but I'll try to understand what you're feeling. I can't help how I feel, Callista, but I'll try not to feel anything you don't want me to." To a telepath girl, he was thinking, a lustful thought must have some of the quality of a rape. Was that why it was rude to look at a young woman here? To protect them against one's thoughts?

"But I want you to," Callista said shyly. "I'm not sure what it would feel like to—to love anyone. But I want you to go on thinking about me. It makes me feel less lonely somehow. Alone in the dark, I feel as if I am not real, even to myself."

Andrew felt an infinite tenderness. Poor child; brain-washed and conditioned against any emotion, what had they made of her? If only he could do something, anything to comfort her. . . . He felt so damned helpless, miles and miles away from her, and Callista alone in the dark and frightened. He whispered to her, "Keep up your courage, my darling. We'll have you out of there soon," and as the words escaped him he found himself back in his body, lying on the bed, feeling sick and faint and somehow drained. But at least he knew Callista was alive, and well—as well as she could possibly be, he amended—until Damon got her out of there.

He lay quiet for a moment, resting. Evidently tele-pathic work was a lot more strenuous than physical ac-tivity; he felt about like he had when he'd been fighting his way through the blizzard.

Fighting. But Damon was doing the real fighting. Somewhere out there, Damon had the really serious task, fighting his way through the cat-men—and from what he'd seen downstairs, when Dom Esteban's party had dragged themselves home, wounded and broken, the cat-men were damned formidable antagonists.

Damon had told him that it was for him to lead them to Callista, once Damon was inside the caves. He sup-posed he could do that, now that he knew how to step outside his body—what Callista had first called his "solid" body—and into the overworld. Then a frighten-ing thought struck him.

Callista was in some level of the overworld where she could not reach, or even see, Damon, or Ellemir, or any of her friends. He, Carr, could reach her, somehow; but did that mean that he was on *her* part of the overworld, the only one the cat-men had left open to Callista? If that was true, then *he* couldn't reach Damon either! And how in *hell*—in that case—could he lead Damon anywhere?

Once the thought had come into his mind it would

not be dispelled. *Could* he reach Damon? Even through the starstone? Or would he find himself, like Callista, wandering like a ghost in the overworld, unable to reach any familiar human face?

Nonsense. Damon knew what he was doing. They had been in contact, last night, through the stones. (Again the memory of that curiously intimate moment of fusion warmed and disturbed him.)

Just the same . . . the doubt lingered, would not be chased away. Finally he realized there was only one way to be sure, and once again he drew forth the starstone from its silk envelope. This time, he did not attempt to physically move out of his body into the overworld, but concentrated, with all his strength, on Damon, repeating his name.

The stone clouded. Again the curious creeping sickness (Would he ever get past that stage? Would he ever be free of it?) surged up and he struggled for control, trying to focus his thoughts on Damon. Deep in the depths of the blue stone—as he had seen Callista's face, so long ago now in the Trade City—he saw tiny figures, like riders, and he knew that he saw Damon's party, the swirling cloak of green-gold, which Damon had told him were the colors of the Ridenow family, the two tall riders on either side. Over them, like a menace, hovered a dark cloud, a dimness, and a voice, not his own, whispered in Andrew's thoughts: *The edge of the darkening lands.* Then there was a curious flare and touch, and Andrew felt himself merging with another mind—he *was* Damon. . . .

Damon's body sat his horse with careless, automatic skill; no one who did not know him well would have realized that his body was empty of consciousness, that Damon himself rode somewhere *above*, his mind sweeping over the land before him, seeking, seeking.

The shadow rose before him, a thick darkness to his mind as it had been to his eyes, and again he felt the memory of fear, the apprehension which he had felt on leading his men into ambush, unawares. . . . *Is this fear for now, or a memory of that fear?* Briefly, dropping back into his body, he felt Dom Esteban's sword, which lay loosely held in his right hand, twitch slightly, and knew he must control himself and react only to real dangers. It was Dom Esteban's sword, rather than Damon's own, because, as Dom Esteban put it, "I have carried it in a hundred battles. No other sword would come so ready to my hand. It knows my ways and my will." Damon had carried out the old man's wishes, remembering how the silver butterfly Callista wore in her hair carried the mental imprint of *her* personality. How much more, then, a sword on which Dom Esteban had depended for his very life, for over fifty years spent in battles, feuds, raiding parties?

In the hilt of the sword, Damon had set one of the small, unkeyed first-level matrixes which he had dismissed, at first, as being only fit to fasten buttons; small as it was, it would resonate in harmony with his own starstone and allow Dom Esteban to maintain contact not only with the energy-nets of his muscles and nerve centers, but with the hilt of his sword.

Spell sword, he thought, half derisively. But the history of Darkover was full of such weapons. There was the legendary Sword of Aldones in the chapel at Hali, a weapon so ancient and so fearful—that no one alive knew how to wield it. There was the Sword of Hastur, in Castle Hastur, of which it was said that if any man drew it save in defense of the honor of the Hasturs it would blast his hand as if with fire. And that in turn reminded him of the Lady Mirella, whose body and hands had been burned and blackened as if with fire. . . .

His hand trembled faintly on the hilt of Dom Esteban's sword. Well, he was as well prepared for such a battle as any living man could be; Tower-trained, strong enough that Leonie had said that as a woman he would have been a Keeper. And as for the rest—well, he was riding in defense of his own kinswoman, taking up a duty for his father-in-law-to-be, and thus safeguarding the honor of his future wife's family.

And as for being a virgin, Damon thought wryly, *I'm not, but I'm as nearly chaste as any adult male my age could be. I didn't even bed Ellemir, although Evanda the Fair knows that I would have liked to.* To himself he recited the Creed of Chastity taught him at Nevarsin

Monastery, where he had been schooled, like many sons of the Seven Domains, in childhood. The creed was adhered to by men working in the Tower Circles: never to lay hands on any unwilling woman, to look never with lewd thoughts on child or pledged virgin, to spend oneself never on such women as are common to all.

Well, I learned it so thoroughly in the Tower that I never unlearned it, and if it makes it safer for me on what is, basically, work for a Keeper—well, so much the better for me and so much the worse for the cat-men, Zandru seize them for his coldest hell!

He dropped back into his body, opened his eyes, and watched the land ahead of him. Then, carefully and slowly, he raised his consciousness again, leaving his body to react with long habit to the motion of the horse. He used the link of those open, staring eyes to send himself out over the physical landscape ahead, still brooding beneath that dark mist.

It was as darker clots of blackness just at the edge of that shadow that he saw them first; then the fine web of force that bound them to some other power, hidden in a depth of shadow that neither his eyes nor the power of the starstone could yet pierce.

Then he could see the furred bodies that those forces hid, crouched silent and motionless among little shrubs which could hardly have hidden them, visible.

Cats. Stalking mice. And we're the mice. He could see his own little group of men, moving steadily toward that ambush. He began to lower himself toward his body again. *Change their route. Avoid that ambush.*

But no. He blinked, staring between his horse's ears, realizing that the prowling cat-men would, doubtless, follow after them; and if another ambush lay ahead, they would be trapped between the two parties. He contented himself with turning his head to Eduin and warning, tersely, "Cat-men ahead. Better be ready."

Then he willed out of his body once more, focused deep on the starstone, and was again floating above the cat-men, studying the tenuous nets of force that hid their bodies from his physical eyes, noting the way those strands fanned out from the shadow. Just where and when could those webs be broken?

He saw it, reflected in the tension of the cat bodies which he could see clearly in the overworld, when he and his men came into view. He saw them drawing short, curved swords—like claws. And still he waited, till the crouching cat-men came up to their feet and began to run quietly and swiftly over the snow, noiseless on their soft pads. Then he drew deep into the starstone and hurled a sudden blast of energy like a lightning bolt, focused on the carefully spun net of energies, ripping it apart.

Then he was back in his body as the cat-men, not yet realizing that their magical invisibility was gone, came running toward them over the snow. But before he regained full control of his body, his horse reared and screamed in terror, and Damon, reacting a split second too late to the horse's movement, slid off into the snow. He saw one of the cat-men bounding toward him, and felt a tightening surge of something—not quite fear—as he fumbled his hand into the basket hilt of Dom Esteban's sword .

. . . Miles away, in the Great Hall at Armida, Dom Esteban Lanart stirred in his sleep. His shoulders twitched, and his thin lips curled back in a smile—or a snarl—that had been seen on countless battlefields. . . .

Damon found himself rolling to his feet, his hand whipping the sword from its sheath in a long slash. His point ripped through the white-furred belly and there was blood on the blade outstretched beyond, the blade that was already pointed at a second cat-man.

As that one slashed at his middle, he saw and felt his wrist turn slightly to move his point down, into the path of the cut; as steel rang, he felt his leg jerk in a little kick step, and suddenly his point was buried in the furred throat.

He caught a brief glimpse of Eduin and Rannan, superb horsemen like all the men of the Alton Domain, whirling their frightened horses, slashing down at the gray furred bodies surrounding them. One went down under a kick from Rannan's horse, but he had no more time to spare for them; wide green eyes glared at him, and a mouth of needlelike fangs opened in a menacing hiss. Tufts of black fur twitched atop the wide ears as the creature whipped its blade around to knock his point aside, and spun on, the scythe-blade flashing toward his eyes. Damon felt a spasm of terror, but his own blade had already whirled at the head; the two swords clashed and he saw a spark leap in the cold. The snarling cat face lurched forward at him, and for a second he was fighting empty air.

It flickered in and out of visibility; whatever power lurked behind the dark edge of shadow was trying to hide its minions again. Stark terror and despair clawed at him for a moment, so painfully that he half wondered if he had been wounded. Then, with a deep breath, he realized what he had to do, and focused on the starstone. As he abandoned his body wholly to Esteban's skill, he prayed momentarily that the link would hold. Then he forgot his body (either it was safe with Esteban or it wasn't, either way he couldn't help much) and hurled himself upward into the overworld.

The shadow lay blank and terrible before him, and from it questing tendrils were weaving, seeking to cloak the angry red shadows of the cat things that fought there.

He reached blindly into the energy-nets and found that without conscious thought he had brought a blade of pure force into his hand. He brought it down on the fine shadow-stuff and the half-woven net of darkness shriveled and burned away. Severed tendrils, quivering, recoiled into the shadow, and their ends faded and vanished. The shadow swirled and eddied, drew back, and out of the midst of the darkness a great cat-face glared at him.

He raised his glowing blade and stood fronting that great menace. Somewhere near his feet he was dimly aware of tiny forms fighting below him, four cats tinier than kittens, three little men, and one of those men . . . surely it was Dom Esteban, surely that was his sidestep, his twirling disengage . . . ?

The dark mist swirled again, veiling the great cat, and now only the glowing eyes and the fierce evil grin stared at him, and somewhere in the back of his mind, a lunatic whisper in Damon's voice muttered half aloud, "I've often seen a cat without a grin, but a grin without a cat . . . ?" and Damon for a split second wondered if he were going mad.

Only two of the little solid cat-things were still on their feet and fighting below him. Unconcerned, he saw one of them go down, spitted on the sword of the man who fought afoot. One of the horsemen struck down the second. The swirling shadow covered the great glaring eyes, their green glow changing, behind the gray wall of mist, to a red glow, like distant, burning coals; then the gray wall blotted them out. A black arrow of force hurled at him and he caught it on his flaming blade. He waited, but the grayness remained, unrippled, even the last glimpse of the glowing cat-eyes gone, and finally he permitted himself to sink earthward, into his body. . . .

There was blood on his sword, and blood on the pale grayish fur of the twisted dead things in the snow. He rested the point of his sword on the ground, and suddenly became aware that he was shaking all over.

Eduin wheeled his horse and rode toward him. He had broken open his face-wound and, from the blue unguent smeared over it to keep out the cold, drops of blood were trickling; otherwise he seemed unhurt. "They're gone," he said, and his voice sounded oddly faraway and weary. "I got the last of them. Will I catch your horse, Lord Damon?"

The sound of his name recalled Damon from a blind, baseless anger, directed at Eduin, an anger he could not understand. Shaking, he realized he had been about to curse the man, to scream at him with rage for riding down *his* prey, an anger so great that he was shaking from head to foot, with a strange half-memory of charging the last of the cat-men, and the other had thundered past him and stolen the last of the quarry from him.

"Lord Damon!" Eduin's voice was stronger now, and alive with concern. "Are you wounded? What ails you, *vai dom*?"

Damon passed his sweating palm over his forehead. He realized for the first time that there was a scratch, hardly more than a razor-cut, on the back of his left hand. He said, "I've cut myself worse at shaving," and in that instant . . .

           *   *   *

. . . In that instant Andrew Carr sat up, shaking his head, sweating and trembling with the memory of what he—*he?*—had done and seen. He had lived through the entire battle in Damon's mind and body.

Damon was safe. And Andrew could keep contact with him—*and* with Callista.

CHAPTER TEN

The afternoon clouds were gathering when Damon and his party rode down a narrow and grass-grown roadway toward a little cluster of cottages lying in a valley at the foot of a cliffside.

"Is this the village of Corresanti?" Eduin asked. "I am not overfamiliar with this countryside. And besides"—he scowled—"everything looks strange in this damnable mist. Is it really there—the shadow and darkness—or have they done something to our minds to make us *think* it's darker?"

"I think it's really there," Damon said slowly. "Cats are not sunlight animals but nocturnal ones. It may be that whoever is doing this to these lands feels discomforted by the light of the sun, and has spread a mist over it, to ease the eyes of his people. It's not a complicated piece of work with a starstone, but of course none of our people would want to do it: we have little enough sunlight even in summer.

Not a complicated bit of work. But it takes power. Whoever their cat-adept may be, he has power, and it is growing rapidly. If we cannot disarm him swiftly, he may become too powerful for anyone to do so. Our task is to rescue Callista. But if we rescue her and leave these lands lying beneath the shadow, others will suffer. Yet we cannot move against him until Callista is free, or his first act will be to kill her.

He had been half prepared for what he was to see by the memory of Reidel's words—"withered gardens"— but not for any such scene of blight and disaster as met his eyes as he rode past the little houses and farms. The fields lay shadowed beneath the dimmed sun, straggling plants withering in the ground, the drainage ditches fouled and filled with rotting fungus, the great sails of the windmills broken and torn, gaping useless. Here and there, from one of the barns, came the doleful sound of untended and starving beasts. In the middle of the road, almost beneath Eduin's hooves, a ragged child sat listlessly gnawing on a filthy root. As the horsemen passed, he raised his eyes, and Damon thought he had never seen such terror and hopelessness in any face that could vaguely be called human. But the child did not cry. Either he was long past tears or, as Damon suspected, he was simply too weak. The houses seemed deserted, except for blank, listless faces now and again at a window, turned incuriously to the sound of their hooves.

Eduin raised his hands to his face, whispering, "Blessed Cassilda, guard us! I have seen nothing like this since last the trailmen's fever raged in the lowlands! What has come to them?"

"Hunger and terror," Damon said briefly. "Terror so great that even hunger cannot drive them into the darkened fields." He felt a fury and rage which threatened to spill out into furious cursing, but he clutched at his starstone and deliberately stilled his breathing. Another score against the Great Cat and his minions, the cat-folk he had let loose to amuse themselves in this innocent village.

The other Guardsman, Rannan, had no such aid to calm. He said, and his face looked green with sickness, "Lord Damon, can't we do something for these people—anything?"

Damon said, torn with pity, "Whatever we could do would be a small bandage on a deathwound, Rannan, and we could help them but little before whatever had overcome them turned its strength on us and we joined them, creeping into a doorway to lie down and die in despair. We can only strike at the heart of the cancer, perhaps; and we dare not do that until my kinswoman is safe."

"How do we know she is not dead already, Lord?"

"I will know through the stone," Damon said. It was easier than explaining that Andrew would somehow manage to communicate it. "And I swear to you, if once we hear she is dead, we will turn all our forces to attack and exterminate this whole nest of evil—to the last claw and whisker!" Resolutely he turned his eyes away from the horror of blight and ruin. "Come. First we must reach the caves."

And once there, he thought grimly, *we're likely to have our troubles getting inside, or finding out where belowground they keep Callista hidden.*

He focused his mind on the stone, looking across at the base of the hillside where, he remembered from a boyhood excursion years ago, a great doorway led into the caves of Corresanti. Years ago they had been used for shelter against the severest winters, when snow lay so deep on the Kilghard Hills that neither man nor animal could survive; now they were used for storage of food, for cultivation of edible mushrooms, for the aging of wines and cheeses, and similar uses. Or they had been used for these things until the cat-people came into this part of the world. There should be food stored there, Damon thought, to tide these starving folk over until their next harvest. Unless the cat-folk had destroyed their hoards of food out of sheer wantonness. They could bring the villagers through. Assuming, that was, that they came through themselves.

It seemed to him now that a great and palpable darkness beat outward from the dark edge of the cliff, some miles from them, where the doorway of the caves of Corresanti was hidden. He had been right in his conjecture, then. The caves of Corresanti were the very heart of the shadow, the focus at the heart of the darkening lands. Somewhere in there some monstrous intelligence, not human, experimented blindly with monstrous, unknown power. Damon was a Ridenow, and the Ridenows had been bred to scent and deal with alien intelligences, and that ancient Gift in his very blood and cells tingled with awareness and terror. But he mastered it, and rode steadily on through the deserted streets of the village.

He looked around, searching for any human face, any sign of life. Was everyone here terrified into insensibility? His eyes fell on a house he knew; he had stayed here one summer, as a boy, so long, so very long ago. He pulled up his horse, a sudden ache clutching his heart.

I haven't seen any of them for years. My foster mother married one of the MacArans, a paxman to Dom Es-

teban, and I used to come here in the summer. Her sons were my first playmates. Suddenly Damon could stand it no longer. He had to know what fared in that house!

He pulled the horse to a stop and dismounted, tying the horse to the post. Eduin and Rannan called questioningly, but he did not answer; slowly, they dismounted, but did not follow him toward the steps of the cottage. He knocked; only silence followed the knocking, and he pulled the door open. After a moment a man slouched toward the door, his eyes vacant; he cringed away as if by habit. Damon thought, confused, *This is surely one of Alanna's sons. I played with him as a boy, but how changed!* He fumbled for the name. Hjalmar? Estill?

"Cormac," he said at last, and the blank eyes looked up at him, an idiotic smile touching the features briefly.

"Serva, dom," he muttered.

"What has come to you? What—what do they want of you, what is happening here?" Words came tumbling out by themselves. "Do you see the cat-men often? What do they—"

"Cat-men?" the man mumbled, a hint of question in his dull voice. "Not men—women! Cat-hags . . . they come in the night and tear your soul to ribbons. . . ."

Damon shut his eyes, sickened. Blank-faced, Cormac turned back into the house; the visitors had ceased, for him, to exist. Damon stumbled back into the street, cursing.

The sound of hooves caught his ears; turning, he glimpsed the riders, coming swiftly in single file down a road that ran from a hill above the village. Here in the ruined village they had seen no horses, or cattle, nor any domestic beasts of any kind.

They were near enough now to be clearly seen; they wore shirt-cloaks and breeches of a strange cut, and they were all tall, thin men, with thick, rough pale hair, but they were men. Human men, not cat-folk, unless this was another of the illusions cast. . . .

Damon focused through his starstone, through the dimming haze which still seemed to obscure, like murky water, everything that was not close to him. But these were real men, on real horses. No horse ever foaled would stand quiet for a cat-man to mount. Nor were these the mindless faces of the villagers, terrorized into immobility and apathy.

"Dry-Towners," muttered Eduin. "Lord of Light be with us!"

Now Damon knew where he had seen tall, pale, rangy men like that before. The desert folk rarely penetrated to this part of the world, but now and again he had seen a solitary caravan of them, traveling silent and swift toward their own part of the world.

And our horses are already wearied; if the Dry-Town men are hostile . . . ?

He hesitated. Rannan leaned across to grasp his arm. "What are we waiting for? Let's get out of here!"

"They may not be enemies," Damon began. Surely humans would not join the cat-folk in this plunder and terror?

Eduin's mouth was a grim, set line. "There were small bands of them fighting among the cat-folk last year, and I've heard there were cat-men helping the Dry-Towners in that trouble down Carthon way. They trade with the cat-men, I've heard. Zandru knows *what* they trade, or what they get in return, but the trading's a fact."

Damon's heart sank. They should have fled at once. Too late now, so he made the best of it. "These may be traders," he said, "and have nothing to do with us." In any case they were so close now that the leading Dry-Towner was reining in his mount. "We'll just have to bluff it through; stay ready, but don't draw swords unless I give you the signal, or unless they attack us."

The leader of the Dry-Towners looked down at them, lounging in his saddle, the faint trace of a sneer on his face—or was that just the normal cast of his features? "*Hali-imyn*, by Nebran! Who would have thought it?" His gaze swept over the empty streets. "What are you folk still doing here?"

"Corresanti has been a village of the Alton Domain for more years than Shainsa has stood on the plains," said Damon; he was trying to count the horsemen reined in behind the leader. Six, eight—too many! "I might as well ask you if you are astray from your normal trading paths, and demand you show safe-conduct from the Lord Alton."

"The days of safe-conducts are over in the Kilghard Hills," the leader said. "Before long it will be you folk who learn you must ask leave to ride here." His teeth bared in a lazy grin. He slid from his horse, the men behind him following suit. Damon's hand slid into the basket-hilt of his sword, and the small matrix there felt smooth and hot in his palm. . . .

. . . Dom Esteban laid down the meat-roll he had been eating, and leaned back against his pillow, his eyes wide, staring. The servant who had brought him the food spoke to him, but he did not reply. . . .

"It will be long before I ask leave to ride in my kinsmen's lands," Damon said. "But what are *you* doing here?" His voice sounded oddly shrill and weak in his own ears.

"We?" said the Dry-Towner. "Why, we're peaceful traders, aren't we, comrades?" There was a chorus of assent from the men behind him. They did not look particularly peaceful (*Of course*, Damon thought in a split second, *Dry-Towners never did*), their swords jutting from their hips at an aggressive angle ready to draw, swaggering like tavern brawlers. The horses behind them began to paw the ground nervously, and frightened snorts filled the air.

"Peaceful traders," insisted the leader, fumbling with the clasp of his shirt-cloak, "trading here by permission of the Lord of these lands, who has given us a few small commissions." The hand whipped out of his shirt-cloak, holding a long ugly knife, and then he jerked his long, straight sword free of its sheath. "Throw down your weapons," he grated, "and if you're fool enough to think you can resist, look behind you!"

Eduin's hand caught Damon's arm in an agonizing grip. Out of the corner of his eye, a quick backward-flipped glance over the shoulder, Damon saw why. Out of the thick forest at the edge of the road, spreading out behind the three Guardsmen to cut them off, cat-men were padding quietly on large, soft paws. Too many cat-men. Damon couldn't begin to count them and didn't try. He found that Dom Esteban's sword was in his hand, but despair took him. Even Dom Esteban could never fight his way out of such an ambush!

The Dry-Towners were closing in slowly, knife and sword in each hand. Damon had forgotten the dagger hanging at his own belt; he was startled as his left hand plucked it out and extended it toward the enemy. He found himself in a stance almost the direct opposite of the one he had been trained to, looking over his left shoulder at his foe past the point of the extended dagger, his sword-hilt cold against his right cheek. *Of course. Esteban had traveled beyond the Dry-Towns, knew how the desert people fought. . . .*

He thought, coldly, that there must have been an ambush back there. If they had mounted and fled, as the Dry-Towners must have expected, they would have ridden straight into the cat-men.

"Take them!" the Dry-Town leader snarled.

There was no escape; the alternatives were death or surrender. Damon's mind hung undecided, not knowing what to do, but his body knew. As the two blades of the Dry-Towner came at him Damon saw the tip of his own sword dip suddenly, sweeping sharply across the sword and dagger, driving them aside; felt his feet shift and his body dip.

So Dom Esteban thinks we can cut down ten men and get away, he thought, ironic and detached, watching somehow without involvement as his sword and dagger drove both points at the same time into the Dry-Town leader's side. He heard the clatter of steel on both sides of him, and saw another one circling toward his back.

His head turned and as his sword jerked free a simple motion of his forearm brought it around. The other man, running, had let his guard slip. Damon felt his own weight shift suddenly, and then his sword went between the man's ribs. He caught a glimpse of Eduin, his sword red in the last glare of sunlight, running to meet another man who was falling back, fear on his face . . . and then he was spinning away, dagger lifting to fend off a thrust that had been coming straight at his throat. His sword flashed at an elbow and the Dry-Towner was screaming at his feet and Damon's stomach turned at the sight of the raw horror where the man's arm had been torn half through. . . .

"They're demons," one of the Dry-Towners shouted. "They're not men at all. . . ." Damon saw that the Dry-Towners still alive were falling back, jostling up against the restive horses which made a wall behind them. They had never seen five men die that fast before. . . .

Demons . . . the Dry-Towners were known to be a superstitious lot. . . .

One of the remaining Dry-Towners shouted something in his own language, trying to rally his remaining comrades, and ran toward Eduin. Damon ignored him, diving deep into the focus of the starstone, even noticing the man's hand was too high. . . . Damon's body whirled and stepped, and his sword went between the man's elbows, slicing so expertly that it touched no bone, and the man fell. Damon himself did not notice. He reached deep into his subconscious, into the dark closet where he had locked away the nightmares of his childhood, and brought forth a demon. It was gray and scaly, horned and taloned, smoke and flame gushing from its nostrils; he hurled the picture into the lens of the starstone, focusing it between him and the Dry-Towners. . . .

The Dry-Towners screamed and ran, trying to catch their wildly plunging horses, which were now running wild, maddened by the smell of blood and the musk of cat. Wild screeching rose from the cat men behind them. Damon pictured—knowing they all saw—the demon turning, charging down the village street toward the cat-people, roaring, fire shooting from its mouth and nostrils. Some of the cat-men broke and ran. Others, perhaps sensing it was not quite what it seemed, tried to dodge around it.

Damon reached blindly for the bridle of his horse; the rearing, fear-maddened beast kicked and plunged, but Damon, his mind still on the demon he had set off ravening among the cat-men (it was stalking them now, reaching out right and left with a great stench of burning cat-fur), found himself tearing the reins loose and vaulting to the saddle with a command of horsemanship as much beyond his own as—*as Dom Esteban's, of course.*

One of the cat-men was too close, and he had to guard

against a slash from the deadly claw-curved sword. He lopped at it; saw sword and paw fall together, twitching convulsively, and lie still. He never saw what happened to the cat-man's body; he was already pulling his horse around.

Something like a lightning bolt struck the gray scaled monster Damon had created, and it flared up in a column of gray dust and smoke and vanished. Damon's mind reeled with horrid shock.

It was Esteban who guided the terrified horse, who cut down the few cat men who ran at the beast's heels and tried to hamstring him, who guided the horse along the road upward to the caves. Dimly, distantly, Damon knew what Esteban was doing with his body and his horse, but he himself was flying above the overworld, borne swiftly and unwillingly through ever-thickening, boiling mist toward the black heart of the shadow, from which glared, unveiled, and blazing out like the fires at the heart of a volcano, the terrible eyes of the Great Cat.

With the eyes, blazing and scorching, were claws, claws that reached, snatched at Damon where he wheeled and turned, dodging, evading them. Damon knew that if even the tip of one of those deadly claws touched him, raked into his heart, he would be forced back into his body and the Great Cat could do with that as he would, blast him lifeless with a single scorching breath.

Damon thought, *What are cats afraid of?* His body, in the overworld, shot up; he dropped on all fours, and knew that where he had flown and dodged from the claws of the cat, now a great, wavering dark wolf-shape grew and solidified before the cat. He plunged at the cat, hearing the terrifying werewolf-howl reverberating through the overworld, a paralyzing cry before which the cat thing dimmed and wavered for a moment. A scorching breath seared the wolf's eyes, and he howled with rage as Damon felt himself tremble with the blood lust. He flung himself at the throat of the cat-thing, great dripping jaws closing, the teeth of the werewolf-thing fastening over the cat's throat, the stink of cat-musk—

The great furred threat thinned and vanished from between the teeth; Damon heard himself howl again and tried to spring at the darkness, maddened with the insane hunger to tear, to bite, to feel the blood burst out under his fangs. . . .

But the cat was gone, melted away, and Damon, shaking and drained, sick to his very toenails, and retching with the taste of blood in his throat, sat swaying in his saddle. The cat-adept had been forced off the astral plane by Damon's werewolf-form. For the first time, it looked as if the Great Cat might not be invulnerable, after all. For the road lay bare ahead to the caves, with nothing before them except bodies of the dead.

CHAPTER ELEVEN

A brief sharp shock, like the shock of falling, brought Andrew Carr awake. The brief winter day was waning, the room was dim, and by the fading light of the window he saw Callista at the foot of his bed. He saw for a moment, with relief, that she was dressed in a skirt and loose tunic, and her hair braided. No, it was Ellemir, and she had a tray of food in her hands. She said, "Andrew, you must eat something."

"I'm not hungry," Andrew muttered, still disoriented with sleep and confused dreams—giant cats? Werewolves? How did it fare with Damon? Was Callista still safe? How could he have slept? How could Ellemir speak of food at a time like this?

"No, you must," Ellemir said, accurately following his thoughts. That would take some getting used to. Well, he'd better get used to it, he told himself.

She sat down on the edge of the bed and said, "Matrix work is terribly draining; you must keep up your strength or you'll overload. I knew you wouldn't feel like it, so I brought you some soup, and things like that which are easy to swallow. I know how you feel, but *try*, Andrew." She said, shrewdly, the one thing which would have persuaded him.

"Damon cannot reach Callista. Once inside the caves of Corresanti, he may not be able to find her in the darkness; it's a dreadful labyrinth of dark passages. I was there once, and I heard of a man who wandered there until he came out months later, blinded and with his hair turned white with fear. So you must be ready when he needs you, to guide him toward Callista. And for that you must be strong."

Reluctantly, but convinced by her argument, Andrew picked up the spoon. It was a meat soup with long noodles in it, very strong and good. With it was a nut bread and sharp jelly. Once he tasted it, he realized that he was half starved and he ate up everything on the tray.

"How is your father?" he asked for courtesy's sake.

She giggled faintly. "You should have seen the meal *he* put away an hour or so ago, telling me between bites how many cat-men he had killed—"

Andrew said soberly, "I saw it. I was *there*. They are terrible!" He shuddered, knowing that part of what he thought a dream had been his mind wandering among the villages blighted by the shadow of the Great Cat. He put down the last bread crust. Briefly, turning his mind inward to the starstone and the contact with Damon, he saw them . . . nearing the caves, the slope clear before them. . . .

This time it was easier to step into the overworld, and because the dim light of the winter day was fading, he discovered that he could see better in the dim blue glimmer of what Callista had called the "overlight." Blue? he thought. Was that because the stones were blue and somehow cast the light through his mind? He looked down at himself and saw his body slumped back on the bed, and Ellemir, setting the tray on the floor, knelt beside him and laid her hand on his body's pulse as she had done with Damon.

He realized briefly that in the overworld he had left behind the heavy fur-and-leather garments he had borrowed from Ellemir's servant, and was wearing the thin gray nylon tunic and trousers he wore around the office at Terran HQ, with the narrow band of jewels on his collar, eight of them, one for each planet where he had seen service.

Damn cold for this planet. Oh, hell, this is the overworld. If Callista can go around in her torn nightie without freezing to death, what difference does it make? He realized that he had moved an immense distance from Ellemir and he was outside Armida, on a gray and featureless plain with distant, shimmery, miragelike hills in the distance. *Now, which way to the caves of Corresanti?* he asked himself, trying to orient himself in the gray distances, and as if by the wings of thought he found himself borne swiftly over the spaces between.

He found that between his fingers he still held the

starstone, or rather whatever referent to it existed in
the overworld, and that here it gleamed like a firework,
sending off brilliant sparkles of fire. He wondered if it
would take him directly toward Callista. Yes, he was
moving, and now he could see the hills clearly, a great
darkness seeming to emanate from their very center.
Was it behind that darkness that Damon had seen the
Great Cat? Was it he who held Callista captive beneath
the great illegal matrix jewel?

Andrew shuddered, trying not to think of the Great
Cat. Or rather, to transform him, in his thoughts, to the
Cheshire cat of Terran children's tales, the great harmless cat which grinned enormously and made amusing
conversation. Or Puss-in-Boots. *He's just a character out
of a fairy tale*, Andrew told himself, *and I'm damned if
I'll let him get on my nerves.* Instinctively he knew that
was the safest way to protect himself from the power of
the Great Cat. *Puss in Boots*, he reminded himself. *I
hope Damon doesn't meet him again.* . . .

As if the thought of Damon had given him a definite
direction, he discovered that he was standing (though his
feet were not quite touching the ground) on a slope just
outside a great dark cave-mouth, and a little below him,
Damon and his two men, swords drawn and ready, were
slowly working their way toward the cave-mouth. He
tried to wave to him, to make Damon see him, and then
that curious *merging* happened again; and again he was
seeing out from behind Damon's eyes. . . .

. . . Scarcely breathing, placing his feet as silently as
possible. *As we had to do, scouting, in the campaigns
last year.* . . .

He could see the great indolent cats sprawled before
the entrance of the cave, drowsing at their post; secure
in their faith that the Power they served would guard
them in return.

But they were still cats, and their great tufted ears
lifted suddenly at the soft brushing of boots through
grass, and instantly they were on their feet, the claw-
swords ready. Damon found himself leaping forward,
sword already alive in his hand, driving toward the nearest in a long lunge. The cat's curved blade whipped

down in that curious, circling guard they used, blurring
to a half-moon before its body, driving his point down
and away, and Damon saw bright steel flash toward his
side.

Then he was looking at the back of his wrist as his
arm jerked up, and felt the blade trembling in his hand
as the other struck its earth-aimed point; he heard its
edge hissing past his ear as it whirled around his body,
slashing at the furred shoulder. The cat-man's sword
lifted to meet it; he leaped back, and saw the blurred
point of the scythe-sword slice the air an inch in front
of his eyes. The great circling blows of the curved blade
looked clumsy, and yet it seemed to take all Esteban's
skill to find a weakness in that whirling defense. Eduin
and Rannan were engaged nearby—he heard their
swords clashing and battering behind him. He felt his
arm snap forward in a feint—he knew it was a feint
because his feet did not move. The curved claw-sword
whistled down; Dom Esteban's sword dropped out of its
path, whirling back and up, and came down between the
tufted ears.

He jerked his sword from the bloody skull with an
expert tug and ran to where Rannan, his shirt ripped
and wet with blood, was falling back before one of the
whirling blades. His own blade whirled and danced, raining cut after cut at the creature's head. He jumped back
from a great whistling stroke that could have sliced him
in half at the waist, felt the blade coming around in an
enormous circling cut that he thought was another head
cut, until he felt his wrist drop and the long, thin blade
sliced through the cat-creature's knee. His arm jerked
again and as the squalling creature fell forward the point
jabbed into its throat. Eduin and Rannan were standing
over the lifeless body of the last of the guards and again,
for an instant, Damon felt that same strange baseless
surge of Dom Esteban's anger. . . .

Damon shook his head. He felt oddly dizzy, as if he
were drunk. What was he doing? He opened his eyes
and sheathed his sword, aware as he did so of aching
muscles at the base of his thumb and in his wrist: muscles he'd never known he had. Swaying a little, he turned
his back on the grisly heaps of bloody fur lying on the

ground, and tottered toward the cave-mouth, motioning to Eduin and Rannan to follow. As he ran, he saw a strange man's form before him, clad in thin, gray unfamiliar clothing. It was a moment before he recognized Andrew Carr . . . and as the realization of who it was came into Damon's mind, Andrew was back in his own mind again, standing a few feet away from Damon and motioning him forward.

It seemed a little strange to Andrew to be able to see Damon when Damon was not in the overworld, but after all, he, "down there," had seen Callista. He stepped ahead of him into the entrance of the cave. It was a great dark chamber, and for a moment, even in the overlight, it was hard to see. Damon was through the doorway now and was motioning, impatiently, for his swordsmen to follow; they seemed to be pressing against some barrier invisible to Andrew—and evidently invisible to Damon, too.

For a moment the Darkovan looked puzzled, then—and neither then nor later did Andrew know whether Damon spoke aloud or whether he heard him *thinking*—Damon said, "Oh, of course. There's a first-level barrier across the entrance, which means no one can get in and out unless either he's carrying a matrix, or the operator *lets* him in or out." Of course. It was just what the Great Cat would do. But it might mean an extra vulnerability. He couldn't be everywhere at once, even with a matrix. But if they were lucky, he might not know that yet.

Slowly, Damon moved through the huge vaulted chamber which was the entrance to the caves. Somewhere at the back he heard water dripping, and his eyes saw only the little bit of daylight admitted from the cavemouth, which faded as he went farther. The cold terror of the dark was on him, and he hesitated, remembering, *When I came here as a boy, there were torches, there were lights mounted by which we could see the walls and the pathways.* Then he saw, seemingly emerging from the very wall itself, the spectral figure of Andrew. The Earthman's figure seemed to glow with faint blue light, and between his hands he bore what looked like a great sparkling blue torch. *The matrix, of course. Will it alert*

*that cat-thing? If I must go into the overworld, to find
my way, will he see my starstone?*

Now he seemed to hear a droning, humming sound,
like some gigantic hive of bees. Out of the dim chambers
of memory, he recognized it now: a powerful, unshielded
matrix. A cold spasm of fear squeezed his heart in an
iron band that was almost physical pain. *That cat-thing
must be mad! Mad or more powerful than any man or
any Keeper! It would take a Circle of at least four minds
to handle a matrix-screen that size!*

They never came that way in nature. They had made
them artificially, in the heyday of starstone technology.
Had he found this one, a freak, or could he have *made*
it? *How in Zandru's nine hells does he handle the thing?
I wouldn't touch it for my life!* Damon thought.

Again he saw Andrew's figure, beckoning dimly in the
bluish glow. By the light of his starstone, he saw massive
crystalline pillars, great stony spikes that jutted from floor
to ceiling or down from ceiling to floor. Everywhere was
the dark dampness and the sound of failing water, and
the terrifying drone of the matrix. Damon thought he
could find his way down to it by sound alone. But that
would come later. Right now he had to find Callista and
get her out of here before the cat-thing knew he was here
and sent one of his henchmen to cut her throat.

At the back of the chamber two passages ran back
into darkness and dim far-off glimmers. He paused a
moment, irresolute, before seeing, far down the left hand
passage, the form of Andrew Carr. He followed the dim
spectral figure, and after stumbling twice on the rocky
floor—of course, Andrew in the overworld couldn't stub
his toes—he focused on his own starstone, warm and
heavy and naked against his throat, to focus a ball of
witchlight in front of him. It was hard and sluggish and
Damon suspected that its power was being damped by
proximity to the enormous one nearby, but he did manage to focus enough power to make a little light. *Damn
good thing too. How could I fight my way through, in
case I have to, and hold a torch in my other hand?*

Andrew's figure had vanished again, going far ahead.
*Yes, that was right. He should find Callista. Tell her help's
on the way*, Damon reasoned.

In the shadow beyond the faint witchlight something moved, and a voice spoke in the mewing speech of the cat-men. The voice changed to a sudden snarl. Damon saw one of the curved blades flash outside the circle of light. The droning in his head was maddening, painful. He drew out his sword, raised it, but it seemed a dead, awkward weight in his hand. *Dom Esteban* . . . he reached frantically for that contact, but there was nothing, only that droning, blurring sound, that *pain*.

The curved blade came whistling down. Somehow he got the inert metal thing in his hand aloft, into the path of the cut, a barrier of steel. Fear choked him as he forced his weary body into stance, parrying automatically, not daring to expose himself to attack. He was alone, fighting with only his own meager skill!

The barrier at the cave-mouth! Dom Esteban couldn't reach him through it! And he thought, *I'm dead!*

In a split second he remembered years of tedious lessons—always the worst swordsman in his age-group, the clumsy boy, the one never meant for the arts of war. The coward. Feeling sluggish with terror, feeling as if his sword dragged through thick syrup, he parried the skilled, circling strokes. He was doomed. He could not defend himself adequately against men fighting in the style to which he was trained. How then could he stand against these masters of a wholly alien technique? He backed away frantically, seeing out of the corner of his eye that a second guard was running to join the first, and in a moment he would face two of them—if he lived that long. He saw the terrible scythe-blade spinning in a blow he could never have caught, even though he knew how Esteban would have blocked it.

The blade came up in the deft block he had pictured, and, with a wild thrill of relief he saw the weakness in the cat-man's position, and at the same instant drove his sword into it. The second guard ran up just as Damon, gasping, pulled his sword free. He turned to face it, knowing perfectly well how Esteban would attack this one, and as the thought formed in his mind his arm jabbed out, back; the claw-sword whirred down in that circling guard they all seemed to use; Damon launched himself in a long lunge, piercing the furred throat even as the sickle-sword reversed, striking his blade weakly in a feeble attempt to guard.

He whipped the sword free, and the third cat-guard stopped crouching warily, and began to back away across the cave floor, its down-curved blade poised beside its head, ready to sweep down in that strange, spinning defense. Damon stepped toward it, warily, and waited. . . .

Seconds crawled by, and his body did nothing he didn't tell it to. He focused on the link . . . nothing. Only the pulsing, throbbing overload from the giant matrix, somewhere down deep in the cave, out of sight, almost out of knowledge, but there, present, dreadful. Dom Esteban could not reach him here. *Had not* reached him here. Damon nearly dropped his sword as realization shocked him. He had not been in touch with Esteban at all, yet he had killed two of the cat-men.

And he would kill a third. Now.

Why not? He had always understood all the tricks, he had been taught by master swordsmen, even though the practice eluded him . . . perhaps that was the problem. He had thought about life more than he had lived it, always his body and his mind had been separated; perhaps the contact with Esteban had taught his nerves and muscles directly how to react. . . .

The cat-man snarled and launched itself at him, and he hurled himself down, sword extended before him, catching himself with his other hand on the floor. The claw-sword hissed above his head, a clean miss, and something wet and sticky gushed over his arm. He pulled his own sword free with a sharp tug and raised himself. Now which way to Callista? Quickly, before the Great Cat finds . . .

He looked around for Andrew, and saw him, a split second flash at the far end of the passage, and then Andrew was gone. . . .

Andrew, wrapped up, sharing the battle with Damon, suddenly heard something like a cry, and in a flash he saw Callista. It seemed that she was lying on the floor at his feet and he realized abruptly that he had moved far down, into a deeper level of the caves, where the walls glowed faintly with pale greenish phosphorescence. Callista was lying in the darkness, but as she opened terrified eyes, Andrew saw, sneaking toward her and only a dim shadowy form in the darkness, the form of one of the cat-creatures. Callista scrambled to her feet and backed away, helplessly defending herself with her outthrust arms. The cat-thing had a curved dagger in its paws, and Andrew ran toward it helplessly, struggling.

I need my body, I cannot defend her from the overworld. . . . For an instant he wavered between the cave where Callista blindly fled from the cat man's knife, between the upper room at Armida where his body lay guarded by Ellemir, back and forth, struggling, torn. *I cannot go back, I must stay with Callista.* . . . Then there was a blue flash and a painful, dazzling electrical shock, and Andrew felt himself drop hard on his feet in the cave, in pitch-dark except for the glow of fungus, his ankle twisting as he came down.

He yelled a warning, ran blindly toward the cat-thing. *(How did I get here? How? Am I really here at all?)* He stumbled, his toes agonizingly banged on loose rock. He scooped up the rock; the cat-man whirled, snarling, but Andrew raised the rock and brought it down hard against the thing's temple. It fell heavily, with an ear-splitting yowl, twitched feebly, and lay still. The force of the blow had spilled its brains all over the floor; Andrew found himself slipping in them and almost falling.

He said, idiotically, "I guess that settles that, I really *am* here." Then he ran toward Callista, who was crouched against the wall, staring up at him in wonder and terror.

"Darling," he cried out. "Callista—darling—are you all right? Have they hurt you?" He caught her in his arms, and she fell heavily against him. She was solid and real and warm in his arms, and he held her hard, feeling her whole body shake with deep, terrifying sobs.

"Andrew—Andrew—it's really you," she repeated.

He pressed his mouth to her wet cheek and repeated again, "It's me, and you're safe now, beloved. We'll have you out of here in a few minutes—can you walk?"

"I can walk," she said, recovering a little of her composure. "I don't know my way out, but I have heard there are ropes along the walls; we can feel our way along and come at last to the entrance. If you will give me the starstone, I can make a light," she said, remembering it at last, and Andrew gently took it out and handed it to her. She cupped it almost tenderly between her palms. In the pale blue light of the stone, paler than the overworld light but still enough to show him quite clearly in its radiance, her lovely delicate features were contorted with fear.

"Damon," she whispered. "Oh, no—Andrew! Andrew, help me—" and in a single moment her fingers reached out for his hand and her thoughts were linked with his as they had been before.

Then, with another of those harsh, painful electric shocks, he was standing on the door of a great, partially lighted cave chamber, at the far end of which glowed, with a painful radiance, a jewel like the starstone—but a huge one, glowing and sparkling like an arclight, hurting his eyes. Damon, looking very small, was striding toward it, and then Andrew's mind flowed into Damon's again, and he saw, through Damon's eyes, the crouching figure kneeling behind the great stone. Its paws were blackened, and its whiskers scorched away, and huge patches of fur had been singed from its hide. Damon raised his blade—

And found himself in the overworld, while before him, towering in majesty and menace, the Great Cat, taller than a tree, glared down at him, with great red eyes like giant coals, and snarled, a great space-filling roar. It raised one paw and Damon flinched, feeling how the stroke of that paw would fling him aside like a feeble mouse. . . .

At that moment Callista cried out, and two giant dogs—one huge and bull-throated, the other slender and whippet-quick—with great gleaming fangs, leaped at the cat-thing's throat and began worrying it, snarling. *Andrew and Callista!* Without stopping to think, Damon dropped back into his body and ran forward, whipping up his sword. He lunged down on the prone, crouching cat-creature, feeling the droning rise to a scream, to wild snarling howls, to confused yelps and spitting hisses that filled all space. The sword wobbled as Damon, holding it steady with all his might, his hands scorching and seared, ran Dom Esteban's sword through the body of the cat-thing.

It screeched and writhed, screaming, on the sword. The great matrix flared and spat sparks and great sheets of flame. Then abruptly the lights died and the cavern was dull and silent, except for the pale glimmer of Callista's starstone. The three of them were standing close together on the stone floor, Callista sobbing shakily and clinging to them. On the floor at their feet a burned and blackened thing lay, scorched and stinking of burning fur, which bore only the faintest resemblance to a catman, or to anything else which had ever been alive.

The great matrix stood before them in its frame, with a burned, dead, glassy glimmer. It rolled free, fell with a tinkle to the floor of the cave, and shattered into nothingness.

CHAPTER TWELVE

"So what will happen to the darkening lands now?" Andrew asked, as they rode slowly back through the dusk toward Armida.

"I'm not sure," Damon said slowly. He was very weary, and drooped in his saddle, but he felt at peace.

They had found food and wine in the caves—evidently the cat-men had not bothered to explore the lower levels—and had eaten and drunk well. There had been clothing there, too, of a sort, including great fur blankets, but Callista had shuddered away from the touch, saying that nothing would induce her to wear fur again as long as she lived. In the end Damon had given the fur cloak to Eduin and wrapped Callista in the swordsman's heavy wool cape.

She rode now on the front of Andrew's saddle, clinging to him, her head against his shoulder, and he rode with his head lowered so that his cheek lay against her hair. The sight made Damon lonely for Ellemir, but that could wait. He wasn't sure Andrew even heard the answer to his question, but he answered, anyway.

"Now that the matrix is destroyed, the cat-men have no abnormal weapons of fear or darkness. We can send out soldiers against them and cut them down. The villagers, most of them, will recover when the darkness is gone and there is no more fear."

Below them, in the valley, Damon could see the lights of Armida. He wondered if Ellemir knew he was returning, with Callista safe, and the darkening lands cleansed. Damon smiled faintly. The old man must be fretting himself sick with impatience to know what had happened since he lost contact with Damon at the barrier. Dom Esteban probably believed—he had been contemptuous of Damon for so long as a weakling—that he, Damon, had been cut down seconds after. Well, it would be a pleasant surprise for the old man, and Dom Esteban would need a few pleasant surprises to make up for the inevitable shock he'd get when he found out about Callista and Andrew. That wasn't going to be pleasant, but the old man owed them something, and Damon was going to twist his arm until he gave in. He realized, with a deep and profound pleasure, that he was looking forward to it, that he wasn't afraid of Dom Esteban anymore. He wasn't afraid of *anything* anymore. He smiled, and dropped back to ride by Eduin and Rannan who shared a horse's broad back, having given up a mount to Andrew and Callista.

Andrew Carr did not even notice Damon go. Callista was warm in his arms, and his heart was so full that he could hardly think clearly. He whispered, "Are you cold, beloved?"

She nestled closely against him. "A little," she said softly. "It's all right."

"It won't be long, and we'll have you where it's warm, and Ellemir will look after you."

"I'd rather be cold in the clean air, than be warm in those foul, stinking caves! Oh, the stars!" she said almost ecstatically.

He tightened his arm around her, aware that she was so weary that she might fall. He could see the lights of Armida, warm and beckoning, below.

She murmured, "It won't be easy. My father will be angry. He thinks of me as a Keeper, not a woman. And he would be angry if I chose to lay down my post and marry anyone, anyone at all, and it will be that much harder, since you are a Terran." But she smiled and curled closer to him. "Well, he'll just have to get used to the idea. Leonie will be on our side."

They were taking it all for granted, Andrew thought. Somehow, he would have to send a message to the Trade City that he was alive—that would be easy enough—and a message that he wouldn't be coming back. That wouldn't be so easy. With this new ability he had discovered—well, somehow or other he'd have to learn how to use it. After that—well, who could tell? There must be something he could do, to hasten the day when Terrans and Darkovans no longer looked on each other as alien species.

They *couldn't* be so alien. The names alone must tell

him that. Callista. Damon. Edwin. Caradoc. Esteban. He could buy a lot of coincidence, but that he couldn't believe in. He wasn't a linguist, but he simply refused to accept that these people could independently have evolved names so identical with Terran names. Even *Ellemir* was not outlandish; the first time he heard it, he'd thought it was *Eleanor*. Not only Terran names, but Western European ones, from the days when those distinctions applied on Terra.

Yet this planet had been discovered by the Terran Empire less than a hundred years ago, and the Trade City built less than fifty years ago. The little he knew about this planet showed him that its history was longer than that of the Empire.

So what was the answer? There were stories of "Lost Ships," taking off from Terra itself in the days before the Empire, thousands of years ago, disappearing without trace. Most of them had been believed destroyed— the ships of those days had been ridiculous contraptions, running on primitive atomic or matter-antimatter drives. But one of them *might* somehow have survived. He faced the fact that he'd probably never know, but he had the rest of his life to find out. Anyway, did it matter? He knew all he needed to know.

He clasped Callista closer in his arms; she made a small involuntary movement of protest, then smiled and deliberately moved against him. He thought, *I really know nothing about her*. Then, remembering that incredible four-way moment of fusion and total acceptance, he realized that he knew all he needed to know about her, too. Already he had noticed that she no longer shrank from a casual touch. He thought, with great tenderness, that if she had been conditioned against desire or sensual response, at least the conditioning was not irrevocable, and they had time enough to wait. Already, he suspected, it had been breached by days of terror alone in the darkness, and by her hunger for any other human presence. But they already belonged to one another in the way that mattered most. The rest would come in time. He was sure of that, and he found himself wondering, whimsically, if precognition was among the new psi talents he'd be exploring.

As they rode through the great looming gates of Armida, a light snow had begun to fall; and Andrew remembered that less than a week ago he had been lying on a ledge in a howling storm, waiting to die.

Callista shivered—did she remember it too?—and he bent down and murmured tenderly, "We're almost home, my beloved." And already it did not seem strange to think of it as home.

He had followed a dream, and it had brought him here.

THE FORBIDDEN TOWER

CHAPTER ONE

Damon Ridenow rode through a land cleansed.

For most of the year, the great plateau of the Kilghard Hills had lain under the evil influence of the catmen. Crops withered in the fields, under the unnatural darkness which blotted out the light of the sun; the poor folk of the district huddled in their homes, afraid to venture into the blasted countryside.

But now men worked again in the light of the great red sun of Darkover, garnering their harvests against the coming snows. It was early autumn, and the harvests were mostly in.

The Great Cat had been slain in the caves of Corresanti and the giant illegal matrix which he had found and put to such frightful use had been destroyed with his death. Such catmen as still lived had fled into the far rain forests beyond the mountains, or fallen to the swords of the Guardsmen that Damon had led against them.

The land was clean again and free of terror, and Damon, most of his army dismissed to their homes, rode homeward. Not to his ancestral estates of Serrais; Damon was an unregarded younger son and had never felt Serrais his home. He rode now to Armida, to his wedding.

He sat his horse now at the side of the road, watching the last few men separate themselves according to their way. There were uniformed Guardsmen bound for Thendara, in their green and black uniforms; there were a few men bound northward to the Hellers, from the Domains of Ardais and Hastur; and a few riding south to the plains of Valeron.

"You should speak to the men, Lord Damon," said a short, gnarled-looking man at Damon's side.

"I'm not very good at making speeches." Damon was a slight, slender man with a scholar's face. Until this campaign he had never thought himself a soldier and was still surprised at himself, that he had led these men successfully against the remnants of the catmen.

"They expect it, lord," Eduin urged, and Damon sighed, knowing what the other man said was true. Damon was Comyn of the Domains; not Lord of a Domain, or even a Comyn heir, but still Comyn, of the old telepathic, psi-gifted caste which had ruled the Seven Domains from time unknown. The days were gone when Comyn were treated as living gods, but there was still the respect, near to awe. And Damon had been trained to the responsibilities of a Comyn son. Sighing, he urged his horse to a spot where the waiting men could see him.

"Our work is done. Thanks to you men who have answered my call, there is peace in the Kilghard Hills and in our homes. It only remains for me to give you my thanks and farewell."

The young officer who had brought the Guardsmen from Thendara rode toward Damon, as the other men rode away. "Will Lord Alton ride to Thendara with us? Shall we await him?"

"You would have long to wait," Damon said. "He was wounded in the first battle with the catmen, a small wound, but the spine was injured past healing. He is paralyzed from the waist down. I think he will never ride anywhere again."

The young officer looked troubled. "Who will now command the Guardsmen, Lord Damon?"

It was a reasonable question. For generations the command of the Guardsmen had lain in the hands of the Alton Domain; Esteban Lanart of Armida, Lord Alton, had commanded for many years. But *Dom* Esteban's oldest surviving son, Lord Domenic, was a youth of seventeen. Though a man by the laws of the Domains, he had neither the age nor the authority for command. The other remaining Alton son, young Valdir, was a boy of eleven, a novice at Nevarsin Monastery, being schooled by the brothers of St.-Valentine of-the-Snows.

Who would command the Guards, then? It was a very reasonable question, thought Damon, but he did not know the answer. He said so, adding, "It will be for Comyn Council to decide next summer, when Council meets in Thendara." There had never been war in winter on Darkover; there never would be. In winter there was a fiercer enemy, the cruel cold, the blizzards which swept down across the Domains from the Hellers. No army could move against the Domains in winter. Even bandits were kept close to their own homes. They could wait for the next Council season to name a new commander. Damon changed the subject.

"Will you reach Thendara by nightfall?"

"Unless something should delay us by the way."

"Then don't let me delay you further," Damon said, and bowed. "The command of these men is yours, kinsman."

The young officer could not conceal a smile. He was very young, and this was his first command, brief and temporary as it was. Damon watched with a thoughtful smile as the boy mustered his men and rode away. The boy was a born officer, and with *Dom* Esteban disabled, competent officers could expect promotions.

Damon himself, though in command of this mission, had never thought of himself as a soldier. Like all Comyn sons he had served in the cadet corps, and had taken his turn as an officer, but his talents and ambitions had been far otherwise. At seventeen he had been admitted to the Arilinn Tower as a telepath, to be trained in the old matrix sciences of Darkover. For many, many years he had worked there, growing in strength and skill, reaching the rank of psi technician.

Then he had been sent from the Tower. No fault of his own, his Keeper had assured him, only that he was too sensitive, that his health, even his sanity might be destroyed under the tremendous stresses of matrix work.

Rebellious but obedient, Damon had gone. The word of a Keeper was law, never to be questioned or resisted. His life smashed, his ambitions in ruins, he had tried to build himself a new life in the Guardsmen, though he was no soldier, and knew it. He had been cadet master for a time, then hospital officer, supply officer. And on this last campaign against the catmen he had learned to bear himself with confidence. But he had no desire to command, was glad to relinquish it now.

He watched the men ride away until their forms were lost in the dust of the roadway. Now for Armida and home. . . .

"Lord Damon," Eduin said at his side, "there are riders on the road."

"Travelers? At this season?" It seemed impossible. The winter snows had not yet begun, but any day the first of the winter storms would sweep down from the Hellers, blocking the roads for days at a time. There was an old saying, Only the mad or the desperate travel in winter. Damon strained his eyes to make out the distant riders, but he had been somewhat shortsighted since childhood, and could make out only a blur.

"Your eyes are better than mine. Are they armed men, do you think, Eduin?"

"I do not think so, Lord Damon; there is a lady riding with them."

"At this season? That seems unlikely," Damon said. What could bring a woman out into the uncertain traveling of the approaching winter?

"It is a Hastur banner, Lord Damon. Yet Lord Hastur and his lady would not leave Thendara at this season. If for some reason they rode to Castle Hastur, they would not be on this road. I cannot understand it."

Yet even before he finished, Damon knew the identity of the woman who rode with the little party of Guardsmen and escorts toward him. Only one woman on Darkover would ride alone beneath a Hastur banner, and only one Hastur would have reason to ride this way.

"It is the Lady of Arilinn," he said at last, reluctantly, and saw Eduin's face light up with wonder and awe.

Leonie Hastur. Leonie of Arilinn, Keeper of the Arilinn Tower. Damon knew that in courtesy he should ride to meet his kinswoman, to welcome her, yet he sat his horse as if frozen, fighting for self-mastery. Time seemed annihilated. In a frozen, timeless, echoing chamber of his mind, a younger Damon stood trembling before the Keeper of Arilinn, head bowed to hear the words which shattered his life:

"It is not that you have failed us or displeased me. But you are all too sensitive for this work, too vulnerable. Had you been born a woman, you would have been a Keeper. But as things stand now . . . I have watched you for years. This work will destroy your health, destroy your reason. You must leave us, Damon, for your own sake."

Damon had gone without protest, for there was guilt in him. He had loved Leonie, loved her with all the despairing passion of a lonely man, but loved her chastely, without a word or a touch. For Leonie, like all Keepers, was a pledged virgin, never to be looked upon with a sensual thought, never to be touched by any man. Had Leonie somehow known this, feared that some day he would lose his control, approach her—even if only in thought—in a way no Keeper might be approached?

Shattered, Damon had fled. It seemed now, years later, that a lifetime stretched between the young Damon, thrust into an unfriendly world to build himself a new life, and the Damon of today, in command of himself, veteran of this successful campaign. The memory was still alive in him—it would be raw till his death—but Damon armed himself, as Leonie drew near, with the memory of Ellemir Lanart, who awaited him now, at Armida.

I should have wedded her before ever I came on this campaign. He had wanted to, but *Dom* Esteban had felt that a marriage in such haste was unseemly for gentlefolk. He would not have his daughter hurried to her marriage bed like a pregnant serving wench! Damon had agreed to the delay. The reality of Ellemir, his promised bride, should now banish even the most painful of memories. Summoning the control of a lifetime, Damon finally rode forward, Eduin at his side.

"You lend us grace, kinswoman," he said gravely, bowing from the saddle. "It is late in the year for journeying in the hills. Where do you ride at this season?"

Leonie returned the bow, with the excessive formality of a Comyn lady before outsiders.

"Greetings, Damon. I ride to Armida, and so, among other things, I ride to your wedding."

"I am honored." The journey from Arilinn was long, and not lightly undertaken at any season. "But surely it is not only for my wedding, Leonie?"

"Not only for that. Although it is true that I wish you all happiness, cousin."

For the first time, momentarily, their eyes met, but Damon looked away. Leonie Hastur, Lady of Arilinn, was a tall woman, spare-bodied, with the flame-red hair of the Comyn, now graying beneath the hood of her riding cloak. She had, perhaps, been very beautiful once; Damon would never be able to judge.

"Callista sent me word that she wishes to lay down her oath to the Tower and marry." Leonie sighed. "I am no longer young; I wished to give back my place as Keeper, when Callista was a little older and could be Keeper."

Damon bowed in silence. This had been ordained since Callista had come, a girl of thirteen, to the Arilinn Tower. Damon had been a psi technician Callista's first year there, and had been consulted about the decision to train her as a Keeper.

"But now she wishes to leave us to marry. She has told me that her lover"—Leonie used the polite inflection which made the word mean "promised husband" — "is an off-worlder, one of the Terrans who have built their spaceport at Thendara. What do you know of this, Damon? It seems to me fanciful, fantastic, like an old ballad. How came she to know this Terran? She told me his name, but I have forgotten. . . ."

"Andrew Carr," Damon said as they turned their horses toward Armida, riding side by side. Their escorts and Leonie's lady-companion followed at a respectful distance. The great red sun hung low in the sky, casting lurid light across the peaks of the Kilghard Hills behind them. Clouds had begun to gather to the north, and there was a chill wind blowing from the distant, invisible peaks of the Hellers.

"I am not certain, even now, how it all began," Damon said at last. "I only know that when Callista was kidnapped by the catmen, and she lay alone, in darkness and fear, imprisoned in the caves of Corresanti, none of her kinsmen could reach her mind."

Leonie shuddered, pulling her hood closer about her face. "That was a dreadful time," she said.

"True. And somehow it happened that this Terran, Andrew Carr, linked with her in mind and thought. To this day I do not know all of the details, but somehow he came to bear her company in her lonely prison; he alone could reach her mind. And so they grew close together in heart and mind, although they had never seen one another in the flesh."

Leonie sighed and said, "Yes, such bonds can be stronger than bonds of the flesh. And so they came to love one another, and when she was rescued, they met—"

"It was Andrew who aided most in her rescue," Damon said, "and now they have pledged one another. Believe me, Leonie, it is no idle fancy, born of a lonely girl's fear, or a solitary man's desire. Callista told me, before I went on this campaign, that if she could not win her father's consent and yours, she would leave Armida, and Darkover, and go with Andrew to his world."

Leonie shook her head sorrowfully. "I have seen the Terran ships lying in the port at Thendara," she said. "And my brother Lorill, who is on the Council and has dealings with them, says that they seem in every way men like to ourselves. But marriage, Damon? A girl of this planet, a man of some other? Even if Callista were not Keeper, pledged virgin, such a marriage would be strange, hazardous for both."

"I think they know that, Leonie. Yet they are determined."

"I have always felt very strongly," Leonie said, in a strange faraway voice, "that no Keeper should marry. I have felt so all my life, and so lived. Had it been otherwise . . ." She looked up briefly at Damon, and the pain in her voice struck at him. He tried to barricade himself against it. *Ellemir*, he thought, like a charm to guard himself, but Leonie went on, sighing. "Even so, if Callista had fallen so deeply in love with a man of her own clan and caste, I would not impose my belief on her; I would have released her willingly. No—" Leonie stopped herself. "No, not willingly, knowing what troubles lie ahead for any woman trained and conditioned as Keeper for a matrix circle, not willingly. But I would, at the last, have released her, and given her in marriage with such good grace as I must. But how can I give her to an alien, a man from another world, not even born of our soil and sun? The thought makes me cold with horror, Damon! It makes my skin crawl!"

Damon said slowly, "I, too, felt so at first. Yet Andrew is no alien. My mind knows that he was born on another world, circling the sun of another sky, a distant star, not even a point of light in our sky from here. Yet he is not inhuman, a monster masquerading as a man, but truly one of our own, a man like myself. He is foreign, perhaps, not alien. I tell you, I know this, Leonie. His mind has been linked to mine." Without being aware of the gesture, Damon placed his hand on the matrix crystal, the psi-responsive jewel he wore around his neck in its insulated bag, then added, "He has *laran*."

Leonie looked at him in shock, disbelief. *Laran* was the psi power which set the Comyn of the Domains apart from the common people, the hereditary gift bred into the Comyn blood! *"Laran!"* she said, almost in anger. "I cannot believe that!"

"Belief or disbelief do not alter a simple fact, Leonie," Damon said. "I have had *laran* since I was a boy, I am Tower-trained, and I say to you, this Terran has *laran*, I have linked with his mind and I can tell you he is no way different from a man of our own world. There is no reason to feel horror or revulsion at Callista's choice. He is only a man like ourselves."

Leonie said, "And he is your friend."

Damon nodded, saying, "My friend. And for Callista's rescue we linked together—through the matrix." There was no need to say more. It was the strongest bond known, stronger than blood-kin, stronger than the tie of lovers. It had brought Damon and Ellemir together, as it had brought Andrew and Callista.

Leonie sighed. "Is it so? Then I suppose I must accept it, whatever his birth or caste. Since he has *laran*, he is a suitable husband, if any man living can truly be a suitable husband for a woman Keeper-trained!"

"There are times when I forget he is not one of us,"

Damon said. "Then there are other times when he seems strange, almost alien, but the difference is one only of custom and culture."

"Even that can make a great difference," Leonie said. "I remember when Melora Aillard was stolen away by Jalak of Shainsa, and what she endured there. No marriage even between Domains and Dry Towns has ever endured without tragedy. And a man from another world and sun must be even more alien than this."

"I am not so sure of that," Damon said. "In any case Andrew is my friend and I will support him in his suit."

Leonie slumped in her saddle. "You would not give your friendship, nor link through a matrix, with one unworthy," she said. "But even if all you say is true, how can such a marriage be anything but disaster? Even if he were one of our own, fully understanding the grip of the Tower on a Keeper's body and mind, it would be near to impossible. Would *you* have dared so much?"

Damon flinched away from the question. She could not have meant it, not as he thought she meant it.

They were not living in the days before the Ages of Chaos, when the Keepers were mutilated, even neutered, made less than women. Oh, yes, the Keepers were still trained, Damon knew, with a terrible discipline, to live apart from men, reflexes deeply built into body and brain. But no longer changed. And surely Leonie could not have known . . . or, Damon thought, he was the one man she would never have asked that question. Surely it was innocent, surely she never knew. He steeled himself against Leonie's innocence, forced himself to look at her, to say in a low voice, "Willingly, Leonie, if I loved as Andrew loved."

As hard as he fought to keep his voice steady and impassive, something of his inward struggle communicated itself to Leonie. She looked up, quickly and for a bare moment, a second or less. Their eyes met, but Leonie quickly looked away.

Ellemir, Damon reminded himself desperately. *Ellemir, my beloved, my promised wife.* But his voice was calm. "Try to meet Andrew without prejudice, Leonie, and I think you will see that he is such a man as you would willingly have given Callista in marriage."

Leonie had mastered herself again. "All the more for your urging, Damon. But even if all you say is true, I am still reluctant."

"I know," Damon said, looking down the road. They were now within sight of the great front gates of Armida, the hereditary estate of the Domain of Alton. Home, he thought, and Ellemir waiting for him. "But even if all *you* say is true, Leonie, I do not know what we can do to stop Callista. She is no silly young girl in the grip of infatuation; she is a woman grown, Tower-trained, skilled, accustomed to having her own way, and I think she will do her will, regardless of us all."

Leonie sighed. She said, "I would not force her back unwilling; the burden of a Keeper is too heavy to be borne unconsenting. I have borne it a lifetime, and I know." She seemed weary, weighed down by it. "Yet Keepers are not easy to come by. If I can save her for Arilinn, Damon, you know I must."

Damon knew. The old psi gifts of the Seven Domains, bred into the genes of the Comyn families hundreds or thousands of years ago, were thinned now, dying out. Telepaths were rarer than ever before. It could no longer be taken for granted that even the sons and daughters of the direct line of each Domain would have the gift, the inherited psi power of his House. And now, not many cared. Damon's elder brother, heir to the Ridenow family of Serrais, had no *laran*. Damon, himself, was the only one of his brothers to possess *laran* in full measure, and he had been in no way specially honored for it. On the contrary, his work in the Tower had made his brothers scorn him as something less than a man. It was hard to find telepaths strong enough for Tower work. Some of the ancient Towers had been closed and stood dark, no longer teaching, training, working with the ancient psi sciences of Darkover. Outsiders, those with only minimal Comyn blood, had been admitted to the lesser Towers, though Arilinn kept to the old ways and allowed only those closely related by blood to the Domains to come there. And few women could be found with the strength, the psi skill, the stamina—and the courage and willingness to sacrifice almost everything which made life dear to a woman of the Domains—to endure the terrible discipline of the Keepers. Whom would they find to take Callista's place?

Either way, then, was tragedy. Arilinn must lose a Keeper—or Andrew a wife, Callista a husband. Damon sighed deeply and said, "I know, Leonie," and they rode in silence toward the great gates of Armida.

CHAPTER TWO

From the outer courtyard of Armida, Andrew Carr saw
the approaching riders. He summoned grooms and atten-
dants for their horses, then went into the main hall to
announce their coming.

"That will be Damon coming back," Ellemir said in
excitement and ran out into the courtyard. Andrew followed more slowly, Callista close at his side.

"It is not only Damon," she said, and Andrew knew,
without asking, that she had used her psi awareness to
guess at the identity of the riders. He was used to this
now, and it no longer seemed uncanny or frightening.

She smiled up at him, and once again Andrew was
struck by her beauty. He tended to forget it when he
was not looking at her. Before he ever set eyes on her,
he had come to know her mind and heart, her gentleness, her courage, her quick understanding. He had
come to know, and value, her gaiety and wit, even when
she was alone, terrified, imprisoned in the darkness of
Corresanti.

But she was beautiful too, very beautiful, a slender,
long-limbed young woman, with coppery hair loosely
braided down her back, and gray eyes beneath level
brows. She said as she walked at his side, "It is Leonie,
the *leronis* of Arilinn. She has come, as I asked."

He took her hand lightly in his own, though this
was always a risk. He knew she had been trained and
disciplined, by methods he could never guess, to avoid
the slightest touch. But this time, although her fingers
quivered, she let them lie lightly in his, and it seemed
that the faint trembling in them was a storm which
shook her, inwardly, through her schooled calm. He
could just see, faintly, on the slender hands and wrists,
a number of tiny scars, like healed cuts or burns. Once
he had asked her about them. She had shrugged them
away, saying only, "They are old, long healed. They

were . . . aids to memory." She had not been willing
to say more, but he could guess what she meant, and
horror shook him again. Could he ever truly know
this woman?

"I thought *you* were Keeper of Arilinn, Callista," he
asked now.

"Leonie has been Keeper since before I was born. I
was taught by Leonie to take her place one day. I had
already begun to work as Keeper. It is for her to release
me, if she will." Again there was the faint shivering, the
quickly withdrawn glance. What hold did that terrible
old woman have over Callista?

Andrew watched Ellemir running toward the gate.
How like she was to Callista—the same tall slenderness,
the same coppery-golden hair, the same gray eyes, dark-
lashed, level-browed—but so different, Ellemir, from her
twin! With a sadness so deep he did not know it was
envy, Andrew watched Ellemir run to Damon, saw him
slide from his saddle and catch her up for a hug and a
long kiss. Would Callista ever be free enough to run to
him that way?

Callista led him toward Leonie, who had been carefully assisted from her saddle by one of her escorts. Callista's slim fingers were still resting in his, a gesture of
defiance, a deliberate breaking of taboo. He knew she
wanted Leonie to see. Damon was presenting Ellemir to
the Keeper.

"You lend us grace, my lady. Welcome to Armida."

Andrew watched intently as Leonie put back her
hood. Braced for some hideous domineering crone, he
was shocked to see that she was only a frail, thin, aging
woman, with eyes still dark-lashed and lovely, and the
remnants of what must have been remarkable beauty.
She did not look stern or formidable, but smiled at Ellemir kindly.

"You are very like Callista, child. Your sister has
taught me to love you; I am glad to know you at last."
Her voice was light and clear, very soft. Then she turned
to Callista, holding out her hands in a gesture of
greeting.

"Are you well again, *chiya*?" It was enough of a surprise that anyone could call the poised Callista "little

girl." Callista let go of Andrew's hand; her fingertips just brushed Leonie's.

"Oh, yes, quite well," she said, laughing, "but I still sleep like a nursery-child, with a light in my room, so I will not wake to darkness and think myself again in the accursed caverns of the catmen. Are you ashamed of me, kinswoman?"

Andrew bowed formally. He knew enough of Darkovan manners now not to look at the *leronis* directly, but he felt Leonie's gray eyes resting on him. Callista said, with a little thrill of defiance in her voice, "This is Andrew, my promised husband!"

"Hush, *chiya*, you have no right to say so yet," Leonie rebuked. "We will speak of this later; for now I must greet my host."

Recalled to her duty as hostess, Ellemir dropped Damon's hand and conducted Leonie up the steps. Andrew and Callista followed, but when he reached for Callista's hand she drew it away, not deliberately but with the absent habit of years. He felt she did not even know he was there.

The Great Hall of Armida was an enormous stone-floored room, furnished in the old manner, with benches built in along the wall, and ancient banners and weapons hung above the great stone fireplace. At one end of the hall was a fixed table. Near this, *Dom* Esteban Lanart, Lord Alton, was lying on a wheeled bed, flattened against pillows. He was a huge, heavy man, broad-shouldered, with thick, curly red hair liberally salted with gray. As the guests came in he said testily, "Dezi, lad, put me up for my guests," and a young man seated on one of the benches sprang up, skillfully piled pillows behind his back and lifted the old man to a sitting position. Damon had thought at first that the boy was one of Esteban's body-servants, then he noticed the strong family resemblance between the old Comyn lord and the youngster who was lifting him.

He was only a boy, whiplash thin, with curly red hair and eyes more blue than gray, but the features were almost those of Ellemir.

He looks like Coryn, Damon thought. Coryn had been *Dom* Esteban's first son, by a long-dead first wife. Older

than Ellemir and Callista by many years, he had been
Damon's sworn friend when they were both in their
teens. But Coryn had been dead and buried for many
years. And he had not been old enough to leave a son
this age—not quite. *The boy is an Alton, though*, Damon
thought. *But who is he? I've never seen him before!*

Leonie, however, seemed to recognize him at once.
"So, Dezi, you have found a place for yourself?"

The boy said with an ingratiating grin, "Lord Alton
sent for me, to come and make myself useful here, my
lady."

Esteban Lanart said, "Greetings, kinswoman, forgive
me that I cannot rise to welcome you to my hall. You
lend me grace, *Domna*." He caught the direction of Damon's gaze and said offhandedly, "I'd forgotten you
don't know our Dezi. His name is Desiderio Leynier.
He's supposed to be a *nedestro* son to one of my cousins,
though poor Gwynn died before he could get around to
having him legitimated. We had him tested for *laran*—he
was at Arilinn for a season or two—but when I needed
someone around me all the time, Ellemir remembered
he was home again, and so I sent for him. He's a good
lad."

Damon felt shocked. How casually, even brutally,
Dom Esteban had spoken, in Dezi's very presence, of
the boy's bastardy and his poor-relation status! Dezi's
mouth had tightened but he kept his composure, and
Damon warmed to him. So young Dezi also knew what
it was to find the warmth and closeness of a Tower circle, and then be shut out from it again!

"Damn it, Dezi, that's enough pillows, stop fussing,"
Esteban commanded. "Well, Leonie, this is no way to
welcome you under my roof after so many years, but
you must take the will for the deed and consider yourself
bowed to, formally welcomed, and all courtesies duly
done, as I should indeed do if I could rise from this
accursed bed!"

"I need no courtesies, cousin," Leonie said, coming
closer. "I only regret to find you like this. I had heard
you were wounded, but did not know how serious it
was."

"I didn't know either. It was a small wound—I've had

deeper and more painful ones from a fishhook—but small or large, the spine was damaged, and they say I will never walk again."

Leonie said, "It is often so with spinal injuries; you are fortunate to have the use of your hands."

"Oh, yes, I suppose so. I can sit in a chair, and Damon devised a brace for my back so that I can sit without drooping like a baby too small for his high chair. And Andrew is helping to supervise the estate and the livestock, while Dezi is here to run errands for me. I can still run things from my chair, so I suppose I am fortunate, as you say. But I was a soldier, and now . . ." He broke off, shrugging. "Damon, my lad, how went your campaign?"

"There is little to tell, Father-in-law," Damon said. "Such catmen as are not dead have fled to their forests. A few made a last stand, but they died. Beyond that, nothing."

Esteban chucked wryly. "It is easy to see you are no soldier, Damon! Even though I have reason to know you can fight when you must! Some day, Leonie, it will be told everywhere, how Damon bore my sword into Corresanti against the catmen, linked in mind through the matrix—but another time for that! For now, I suppose if I want details of the campaign and the battles, I will have to ask Eduin; he knows what I want to hear! As for you, Leonie, have you come to bring my foolish girl back to her senses, and take her back to Arilinn where she belongs?"

"Father!" Callista protested. Leonie smiled faintly.

"It is not as easy as that, cousin, and I am sure you know it."

"Forgive me, kinswoman." Esteban looked abashed. "I am remiss in hospitality. Ellemir will show you to your rooms—damn the girl, where has she gone to now?" He raised his voice in a shout. "Ellemir!"

Ellemir came hastily through the door at the back, wiping flour stained hands on a long apron. "The maids called me to help with the pastries, Father—they are young and unskilled. Forgive me, kinswoman." She dropped her eyes, hiding her floury hands. Leonie said kindly, "Don't apologize for being a conscientious housekeeper, my girl."

Ellemir struggled for composure. She said, "I have had a room made ready for you, my lady, and another for your companion. Dezi will see to the housing of your escort, won't you, cousin?" Damon noted that Ellemir spoke to Dezi in the familiar mode, that of family intimacy; he had also noticed that Callista did not. Damon said, "We'll see to it, Ellemir," and went with Dezi to make the arrangements.

Ellemir led Leonie and her lady-companion (without whom it would have been scandalous for a woman of Comyn blood to travel so far) up the stairs and through the wide halls of the ancient house. Leonie asked, "Do you manage this great estate all alone, child?"

"Only in Council season, when I am alone here," Ellemir said, "and our *coridom* is old and well experienced."

"But you have no responsible woman, no kinswoman nor companion? You are too young to bear such a weight alone, Ellemir!"

"My father has not complained," Ellemir said. "I have kept house for him since my older sister was married; I was fifteen then." She spoke with pride, and Leonie smiled.

"I was not accusing you of any lack of competence, little cousin. I meant only that you must be very lonely. If Callista does not stay with you, I think you must have some kinswoman or friend come and live here for a time. You are overburdened already, now that your father needs so much care, and how would you manage if Damon made you pregnant at once?"

Ellemir colored faintly and said, "I had not thought of that. . . ."

"Well, a bride must think of that, soon or late," Leonie said. "Perhaps one of Damon's sisters could come to bear you company—Child, is *this* my room? I am not used to such luxury!"

"It was my mother's suite," Ellemir said. "There is another room there where your companion can sleep, but I hope you brought your own maidservant, for Callista and I have none to send you. Old Bethiah, who was our nurse when we were little, was killed in the raid when Callista was kidnapped, and we have been too heartsore to put anyone else in her place as yet. There are only kitchen-women and the like on the estate now."

"I keep no maidservant," Leonie said. "In the Tower, the last thing we wish for is the presence of outsiders near to us, as I am sure Damon must have told you."

"No, he never speaks of his time in the Tower," Ellemir answered, and Leonie said, "Well, it is true, we keep no human servants, even if the price is having to look after ourselves. So I will manage very well, child." She touched the girl's cheek lightly, a feather-touch in dismissal, and Ellemir went down the stairs, thinking, in surprise, *She's kind; I like her!* But many things Leonie had said troubled her. She was beginning to be aware that there were things about Damon she did not know. She had taken it for granted that Callista did not want servants about, and humored her twin sister, but now she realized that Damon's years in the Tower, those years of which he never spoke—and she had learned that it made him unhappy if she asked about them—would always lie like a barricade between her and Damon.

And Leonie had said, "If Callista does not stay with you." Was there a question? Could Callista actually be sent back to Arilinn, persuaded against her will that her duty lay there? Or—Ellemir shivered—was it possible that Leonie would refuse to release Callista from the Tower, that Callista would be forced to carry through her threat, desert Armida and even Darkover, and run away with Andrew to the worlds of the Terrans?

Ellemir wished she had even a flash of the occasional precognition which turned up, now and again, in those of Alton blood, but the future was blank and closed to her. Try as she would to throw her mind forward, she could see nothing but a disquieting picture of Andrew, his face covered with his hands, bent, weeping, his whole body shaken with unendurable grief. Slowly, worried now, she turned toward the kitchen, seeking forgetfulness among her neglected pastries.

A few minutes later, the lady-companion—a dim and colorless woman named Lauria—came to say, deferentially, that the Lady of Arilinn wished to speak alone with *Donna* Callista. Reluctantly Callista rose, stretching her fingertips to Andrew. Her eyes were frightened, and he said in a grim undertone, "You don't have to face her alone if you don't want to. I won't have that old woman frightening you! Shall I come and speak my mind to her?"

Callista moved toward the staircase. Outside the room, in the hall, she turned back to him and said, "No, Andrew, I must face this alone. You cannot help me now." Andrew wished he could take her in his arms and comfort her. She seemed so small, so fragile, so lost and frightened. But Andrew had learned, painfully and with frustration, that Callista was not to be comforted like that, that he could not even touch her without arousing a whole complex of reactions he did not yet understand, but which seemed to terrify Callista. So he said gently, "Have it your way, love. But don't let her scare you. Remember, I love you. And if they won't let us marry here, there's a whole big world outside Armida. And a hell of a lot of other worlds in the galaxy beside this one, in case you've forgotten that."

She looked up at him and smiled. Sometimes she thought that if she had first seen him in the ordinary way, rather than as she had come to know him, through his mind-link with hers in the matrix, he would never have seemed handsome to her. She might even have thought him ill-favored. He was a big, broad man, fair-haired as a Dry-Towner, tall, untidy, awkward, and yet, beyond this, how dear he had become to her, how safe she felt in his presence. She wished, with a literal ache, that she could throw herself into his arms, hold herself to him as Ellemir did so freely with Damon, but the old fear held her motionless. But she laid her fingertips, a rare gesture, lightly across his lips. He kissed them and she smiled. She said softly, "And I love you, Andrew. In case you've forgotten *that*," and went away up the stairs to where Leonie was waiting for her.

CHAPTER THREE

The two Keepers of Arilinn, the young and the old, faced one another. Callista stood considering Leonie's appearance: never beautiful, perhaps, except for the lovely eyes, but with serene, regular features; her body flat and spare, sexless as any *emmasca*; the face pale and impassive as if carved in marble. Callista felt a faint shiver of horror as she knew that the habit of years, the discipline which had gone bone-deep, was smoothing away her own expression, turning her cold, remote, as withdrawn as Leonie. It seemed that the face of the old Keeper was a mirror of her own across the many dead years which lay ahead. *In half a century I will look exactly like her. . . . But no! No! I will not, I will not!*

Like all Keepers, she had learned to barricade her own thoughts. She knew, with an odd clairvoyance, that Leonie was expecting her to break down and weep, to beg and plead like an hysterical girl, but it was Leonie herself who had armored her, years ago, with this icy calm, this absolute control. She was Keeper, Arilinn-trained; she would not show herself unfit. She laid her hands calmly in her lap and waited, and finally it was Leonie who had to speak first.

"There was a day," she said, "when a man who sought to seduce a Keeper would have been torn on hooks, Callista."

"That day is centuries past," Callista replied in a voice as passionless as Leonie's own, "nor did Andrew seek to seduce me; he has offered honorable marriage."

Leonie gave a slight shrug. "It is all one," she said. She was silent for a long time, the silence stretching into minutes, and again Callista felt that Leonie was willing her to lose control, to plead with her. But Callista waited, motionless, and it was again Leonie who had to break the silence.

"Is this, then, how you keep your oath, Callista of Arilinn?"

For a moment Callista felt pain clutch at her throat. The title was used only for a Keeper, the title she had won at such terrible cost! And Leonie looked so old, so sad, so weary!

Leonie is old, she told herself. *She wishes to lay aside her burden, give it into my hands. I was traind so carefully, since I was a child. Leonie has worked and waited so patiently for the day I could step into the place she prepared for me. What will she do now?*

Then, instead of pain, anger came, anger at Leonie, for playing so on her emotions. Her voice was calm.

"For nine years, Leonie, I have borne the weight of the Keeper's oath. I am not the first to ask leave to lay it down, nor will I be the last to do so."

"When I was made Keeper, Callista, it was taken for granted that it was a lifetime decision. I have borne my oath lifelong. I had hoped you would be willing to do no less."

Callista wanted to weep, to cry out *I cannot,* to plead with Leonie. She thought, with a forlorn detachment, that it would be better if she could. Leonie would be readier to believe her unfit, to free her. But she had been taught pride, had fought for it and armored herself with it, and she could not now surrender it.

"I was never told, Leonie, that I must give my oath lifelong. It was you who told me that it is too heavy a burden to be borne unconsenting."

With stony patience, Leonie said, "That is true. Yet I had believed you stronger. Well, then, tell me about it. Have you lain with your lover?" The word was scornful; it was the same she had used before, meaning "promised husband," but this time Leonie used the derogatory inflection which gave it, instead, the implication of "paramour," and Callista had to stop and steady her voice before she could summon up calm enough to speak quietly.

"No. I have not yet been given back my oath, and he is too honorable to seek it. I asked leave to marry, not absolution for betrayal, Leonie."

"Truly?" Leonie said, disbelief in the word, and her cold face scornful. "Having resolved to break your oath, I wonder you waited for my word!"

It took all of Callista's self-control, this time, to keep from bursting into angry defense of herself, of Andrew— then she realized that Leonie was baiting her, testing to see if she had indeed lost control of her carefully disciplined emotions. This game she knew from her earliest days at Arilinn, and relief at the memory made her want to laugh. Laughter would have been as unthinkable as tears in this solemn confrontation, but there was merriment in her voice, and she knew Leonie was aware of it, as she said with calm amusement, "We keep a midwife at Armida, Leonie; send for her, if you wish, and let her certify me virgin."

It was Leonie who lowered her eyes, saying at last, "That will not be necessary, child. But I came here prepared to face, if need be, the knowledge that you had been raped."

"In the hands of nonhumans? No, I suffered fear, cold, imprisonment, hunger, abuse, but rape I was spared."

"It would not really have mattered, you know," Leonie said, and her voice was very gentle. "Of course, a Keeper need not, in general, have to fear rape very much. You know as well as I that any man who lays hands on a Keeper trained as you have been trained takes his life in his hands. Yet rape is possible. Some women have been overpowered by sheer might, and some fear at the last moment to invoke that strength to protect themselves. So it was this, among other things, I came to tell you: even if you had truly been raped, you still had a choice, my child. It is not the physical act which makes the difference, you know." Callista had *not* known, and was vaguely surprised.

Leonie went on, dispassionately: "If you had been taken unwillingly, wholly without consent, it would make no difference that could not be quickly overcome by a little time in seclusion, for the healing of your fears and hurts. But even if it was not a question of rape, if you had lain with your rescuer afterward, in gratitude or kindness, without any genuine involvement—as you might well have done—even that need not be irrevocable. A time of seclusion, of retraining, and you could be as before, unchanged, unharmed, still free to be Keeper.

This is not widely known; we keep it secret, for obvious reasons. But you still have a choice, child. I do not want you to think that you are cast out from the Tower for all time because of something which happened without your will."

Leonie still spoke quietly, almost impassively, but Callista knew she was pleading. Callista said, wrung with pity and pain, "No, it is not like that, Leonie. What has happened between us . . . It is quite different. I came to know him, and love him, before I ever saw his face in this world. But he is too honorable to ask that I break an oath given, without leave."

Leonie raised her eyes, and the steel-blue gaze was suddenly like a glare of lightning.

"Is it that he is too honorable," she said harshly, "or is it that you are afraid?"

Callista felt a stab of inward pain, but she kept her voice steady. "I am not afraid."

"Not for yourself perhaps—I acknowledge it! But for him, Callista? You can still return to Arilinn, without penalty, without harm. But if you do not return—do you want your lover's blood on your head? You would not be the first Keeper to bring a man to death!"

Callista raised her head, opened her lips to protest, but Leonie gestured her to silence and went on mercilessly, "Have you been able even to touch his hand, even so much as that?"

Callista felt relief wash through her, a relief so great that it was like physical pain, draining her of strength. With a telepath's whole total recall, the image in her memory returned, annihilating everything else that lay between. . . .

Andrew had carried her from the cave where the Great Cat lay dead, a blackened corpse beside the shattered matrix he had profaned. Andrew had wrapped her in his cloak and set her before him on his horse. She felt it again, in complete recall, how she had rested against him, her head on his breast, folded close into the curve of his arms, his heart beating beneath her cheek. Safe, warm, happy, wholly at peace. For the first time since she had been made Keeper, she felt free, touching and being touched, lying in his arms, content to be there.

And all during that long ride to Armida she had lain there, folded inside his cloak, happy with such a happiness as she had never guessed.

As the image in her mind communicated itself to Leonie, the older woman's face changed. At last she said, in a gentler voice than Callista had ever heard, "Is it so, *chiya?* Why, then, if Avarra is merciful to you, it may be as you desire. I had not believed it possible."

And Callista felt a strange disquiet. She had not, after all, been wholly truthful with Leonie. Yes, for that little while she had been all afire with love, warm, unafraid, content—but then the old nervous constraint had come back little by little, until now she found it difficult even to touch his fingertips. But surely that was only habit, the habit of years, she told herself. It would certainly be all right. . . .

Leonie said gently, "Then, child, would it indeed make you so unhappy, to part from your lover?"

Callista found that her calm had deserted her. She said, and knew that her voice was breaking and that tears were flooding her eyes, "I would not want to live, Leonie."

"So . . ." Leonie looked at her for a long moment, with a dreadful, remote sadness. "Does he understand how hard it will be, child?"

"I think—I am sure I can make him understand," Callista said, hesitating. "He promised to wait as long as we must."

Leonie sighed. After a moment she said, "Why, then, child . . . child, I do not want you to be unhappy. Even as I said, a Keeper's oath is too heavy to be borne unconsenting." Deliberately, a curiously formal gesture, she reached out her hands, palm up, to Callista; the younger woman laid her hands against the older woman's, palm against palm. Leonie drew a deep breath and said, "Be free of your oath, Callista Lanart. Before the Gods and before all men I declare you guiltless and unloosed from the bond, and I will so maintain."

Their hands slowly fell apart. Callista was shaking in every limb. Leonie took her kerchief and dried Callista's eyes. She said, "I pray you are both strong enough, then." She seemed about to say something more, but stopped herself. "Well, I suppose your father will have a good deal to say about this, my darling, so let us go and listen to him say it." She smiled and added, "And then, when he has said it all, we will tell him what is to be, whether he likes it or not. Don't be afraid, my child; I am not afraid of Esteban Lanart, and you must not be either."

Andrew waited in the greenhouse which stretched behind the main building at Armida. Alone, he looked through the thick and wavy glass toward the outline of the faraway hills. It was hot here, with a thick scent of leaves and soil and plants. The light from the solar collectors made him narrow his eyes till he got used to it. He walked through the rows of plants, damp from watering, feeling isolated and unfathomably alone.

It struck him like this, now and again. Most of the time he had come to feel at home here, more at home than he had ever felt anywhere else in the Empire; more at home than he had felt since, at eighteen, the Arizona horse ranch where he had spent his childhood had been sold for debts, and he had gone into space as an Empire civil servant, moving from planet to planet at the will of the administrators and computers. And they had welcomed him here, after the first few days of strangeness. When they heard that he knew something of horse-breaking and horse-training, a rare and highly paid field of expertise on Darkover, they had treated him with respect, as a highly trained and skilled professional. The horses from Armida were said to be the finest in the Domains, but they usually brought their trainers up from Dalereuth, far to the South.

And so, in general, he had been happy here, in the weeks since he had come, as Callista's pledged husband. His Terran birth was known only to Damon and *Dom* Esteban, to Callista and Ellemir; the others simply thought him a stranger from the lowlands beyond Thendara. Beyond belief, he had found here a second home. The sun was huge and blood-tinged, the four moons that swung at night in the curiously violet sky were strangely colored and bore names he did not yet know, but beyond all this, it had become his home. . . .

Home. And yet there were moments like this, moments when he felt his own cruel isolation, knew it was only Callista's presence that made it home to him. Under the noonday glare of the greenhouse, he had one of those moments. Lonely for what? There was nothing in the world he had been taught to call his own, the dry and barren world of the Terran HQ, nothing he wanted. But would there be a life for him here after all, or would Leonie snatch Callista back to the alien world of the Towers?

After a long time, he realized that Damon was standing behind him, not touching him—Andrew was used to that now, among telepaths—but close enough that he could sense the older man as a comforting presence.

"Don't worry this way, Andrew. Leonie's not an ogre. She loves Callista. The bonds of a Tower circle are the closest bonds we know. She'll know what Callista really wants."

"That's what I'm afraid of," Andrew said through a dry throat. "Maybe Callista doesn't know what she wants. Maybe she turned to me only because she was alone and afraid. I'm afraid of that old woman's hold on her. The grip of the Tower—I'm afraid it's too strong."

Damon sighed. "Yet it can be broken. I broke it. It was hard—I can't begin to tell you how hard—yet I have built another life at last. And if you should lose Callista that way, better now than when it's too late to return."

"It's already too late for me," Andrew said, and Damon nodded, with a troubled smile.

"I don't want to lose you either, my friend," Damon said, but to himself he thought: *You are part of this new life I have built with so much pain. You, and Ellemir, and Callista. I cannot endure another amputation.* But Damon did not speak the words; he only sighed, standing beside Andrew. The silence in the greenhouse stretched so long that the red sun, angling from the zenith, lost strength in the greenhouse and Damon, sighing, went to adjust the solar collectors. Andrew flung at him, "How can you wait so calmly? What is that old woman *saying* to her?"

Yet Andrew had already learned that telepathic eavesdropping was considered one of the most shameful crimes possible in a caste of telepaths. He dared not even try to reach Callista that way. All his frustrations went into pacing the greenhouse floor.

"Easy, easy," Damon remonstrated. "Callista loves you. She won't let Leonie persuade her out of that."

"I'm not even sure of that anymore," Andrew said in desperation. "She won't let me touch her, kiss her—"

Damon said gently, "I thought I had explained that to you; she *cannot*. These are . . . reflexes. They go deeper than you could imagine. The habit of years cannot be undone in a few days, yet I can tell that she is trying hard to overcome this . . . this deep conditioning. You know, do you not, that in a Tower, it would be unthinkable for her to take your hand, as I saw her do, to let you kiss even her fingertips. Have you any idea what a struggle that must have been, against years of training, of conditioning?"

Against his will Damon was remembering a time in his life he had taught himself, painfully, *not* to remember: a lonely struggle, all the worse because it was not physical at all, to quench his own awareness of Leonie, to control even his thoughts, so that she should never guess what he was concealing. He would never have dared to imagine a fingertip-touch such as Callista bestowed on Andrew in the hall, just before she went up to Leonie.

With relief, he saw that Ellemir had come into the greenhouse. She walked between the rows of green plants, knelt before a heavily laden vine. She rose with satisfaction, saying, "If there is sunlight for another day, these will be ripened for the wedding." Then her smile slid off as she saw Damon's strained face, Andrew's desperate quiet. She came and stood on tiptoe, putting her arms around Damon, sensing he needed the comfort of her presence, her touch. She wished she could comfort Andrew too, as he said in distress, "Even if Leonie gives her consent, what of her father? Will *he* consent? I do not think he likes me much. . . ."

"He likes you well," Ellemir said, "but you must understand that he is a proud man. He thought me too good for Damon, but I am old enough to do my own will. If he had offered me to Aran Elhalyn, who warms the throne at Thendara, Father would still have thought him not good enough. For Callista, no man ever born of woman would be good enough, not if he was rich as the Lord of Carthon, and born bastard to a god! And of course, even in these days, it is a great thing to have a child at Arilinn. Callista was to be Keeper at Arilinn, and it will go hard with him, to renounce that." Andrew felt his heart sink. She said, "Don't worry! I think it will be all right. Look, there is Callista now."

The door at the top of the steps opened, and Callista came down into the greenhouse. She held out her hands toward them, blindly.

"I am not to return to Arilinn," she said, "and Father has given his consent to our marriage—"

She broke down then, sobbing. Andrew held out his arms, but she turned away from him and leaned against the heavy glass wall, hiding her face, her slender shoulders heaving with the violence of her weeping.

Forgetting everything except her misery, Andrew reached for her; Damon touched him on the arm, shook his head firmly. Distressed, Andrew stood looking at the sobbing woman, unable to tolerate her misery, unable to do anything about it, in helpless despair.

Ellemir went to her and turned her gently around. "Don't lean on that old wall, love, when there are three of us here with shoulders to cry on." She dried her sister's tears with her long apron. "Tell us all about it. Was Leonie very horrible to you?"

Callista shook her head, blinking her reddened eyes hard. "Oh, no, she couldn't have been kinder. . . ."

Ellemir said, with a skeptical headshake, "Then why are you howling like a banshee? Here we wait, in agony lest we be told you'll be whisked away from us and back to the Tower, and then when you come to us, saying all is well, and we are ready to rejoice with you, you start blubbering like a pregnant serving wench!"

"Don't—" Callista cried. "Leonie . . . Leonie was kind, I truly think she understood. But Father—"

"Poor Callie," said Damon gently. "I have felt the rough side of his tongue often enough!"

Andrew heard the pet name with surprise and a sudden, sharp jealousy. It had never occurred to him, and the pretty abbreviation which Damon used so naturally seemed an intimacy which simply pointed up his isolation. He reminded himself that Damon, after all, had been an intimate of the household since Callista was a small child.

Callista raised her eyes and said quietly, "Leonie freed me from my oath, Damon, and without question." Damon sensed the anguished struggle behind her controlled calm, and thought, *If Andrew makes her unhappy, I think I will kill him.* Aloud he only said, "And your father, of course, was another story. Was he very terrible, then?"

For the first time, Callista smiled. "Very terrible, yes, but Leonie is even more stubborn. She said that you cannot bind a cloud in fetters. And Father turned on me. Oh, Andrew, he said dreadful things, that you had abused hospitality, that you had seduced me—"

"Damned old tyrant!" Damon said angrily. Andrew set his mouth in quiet wrath. "If he believes that—"

"He does not, now," Callista said, and her eyes held a hint of their old gaiety. "She reminded him that I was not now thirteen years old; that when the doors of Arilinn first closed behind me, he had surrendered forever all right to give or refuse me in marriage; that even if Leonie had found me unfit and sent me from the Tower before I was of legal age and declared a woman, it would have been *her* right, and not his, to find me a husband. And many other home truths which he did not find pleasant hearing."

"Evanda be praised that you are laughing again, darling," Ellemir said, "but how did Father take these unkind truths?"

"Well, he did not like it, as you can imagine," Callista said, "but in the end there was nothing he could do but accept it. I think he was even glad to have Leonie to quarrel with; we have all humored him too much since he was wounded! He began to act like himself, and maybe he began to feel a little more like himself too. Then when he had grumbled himself into accepting it, Leonie set herself to charm him—told him how lucky he was to have two full-grown sons-in-law to manage the estate for him so that Domenic could take his place in Council, and two daughters to live here and bear him

company. At last he said Leonie had made it clear that
I needed no blessing to marry, but he bade you come
to take his blessing."

Andrew was still angry. "If the old tyrant thinks I give
a damn for his blessing, or his curse either—" he began,
but Damon laid a hand on his wrist, interrupting him.

"Andrew, this means he will accept you as a son in his
house, and for Callista's sake I think you should accept it
with such grace as you can. Callie has already lost one
family when she chose, for your sake, not to return to
Arilinn. Unless you hate him so much you cannot dwell
in peace under his roof . . ."

"I don't hate him at all," Andrew said, "but I can
care for my wife in my own world. I do not want to
come to him penniless, accepting his charity."

Damon said quietly, "The charity, Andrew, is on your
side, and mine. He may live many years, but he will
never again set foot to the ground. Domenic must take
his place in Council. His younger son is a child of eleven.
If you take Callista from him, you leave him at the
mercy of such strangers as he can hire for a price, or
distant kinsmen who will come through greed to see
what bones they can pick. If you remain here and help
him manage this estate, and give him the companionship
of his daughter, you bestow far more than you accept."

Thinking it over, Andrew realized that Damon was
right. "Still, if Leonie wrung consent from him
unwillingly . . ."

"No, or he would never have offered his blessing,"
Damon said. "I have known him all my life. If he still
grudged you consent, he would have said something like
take her and be damned to both of you. Would he
not, Callista?"

"Damon is right: he is terrible in anger, but no man
to hold a grudge."

"Less than I," Damon said. "With Esteban, it is
one flare of anger, then all's well, and he will take you
to his heart as readily as he kicked you a moment ago.
You may quarrel again—you probably will—he is harsh-
tempered and irritable. But he will not serve you up old
grudges like stale porridge!"

When Damon and Ellemir had gone Andrew looked

at Callista and said, "Is this truly what you want, my
love? I don't dislike your father. I was only angry because he had bullied you and made you cry. If you want
to stay here . . ."

She looked up at him, and the closeness came over
them again, the old touch that had drawn them together
before they met, the touch so much more real to him
than the hesitant and frightened physical touch which
was all she could ever permit. "If you and Father could
not have agreed, I would have followed you anywhere
on Darkover, or anywhere among your Empire of the
stars. But only with such grief as I could never measure.
This is my home, Andrew. The dearest wish of my heart
is that I should never leave here again."

He raised her fingertips gently to his lips. He said
softly, "Then it shall be my home too, beloved.
Forever."

By the time Andrew and Callista followed the other
couple into the main house they found Damon and Ellemir seated side by side on a bench beside *Dom* Esteban. As they came in Damon rose and knelt before
the old man. He said something Andrew could not hear,
and the Alton lord said, smiling, "You have proved
yourself a son to me many times, Damon, I need no
more. Take my blessing." He laid his hand for a moment
on Damon's head. Rising, the younger man bent and
kissed his cheek.

Dom Esteban looked over Damon's head with a grim
smile. "Are you too proud to kneel for my blessing,
Ann'dra?"

"Not too proud, sir. If I offend against custom, in this
or anything else, Lord Alton, I ask that you take it as
ignorance of what is considered proper, and not as will-
ful offense."

Dom Esteban gestured them to a seat beside Damon
and Ellemir. "Ann'dra," he said, still giving the name
the Darkhovan inflection, "I know nothing really bad of
your people, but I know little of them that is good. I
suppose they are like most people, some good and some
bad, and most of them neither one nor the other. If you
were a bad man, I do not think my daughter would be

so ready to marry you, against all custom and common sense. But you cannot blame me if I am not quite happy about giving my best-loved child to an out-worlder, even one who has shown himself honorable and brave."

Andrew, next to Ellemir on the bench, felt her hands clench tight as he spoke of Callista as his best-loved child. That was cruel, he thought, in her very presence. It had been Ellemir after all who had stayed at home, a dutiful and biddable daughter, all these years. Indignation at the old man's tactlessness made his voice cool.

"I can only say, sir, that I love Callista and I will try to make her happy."

"I do not think she will be happy among your people. Do you intend to take her away?"

"If you had not consented to our marriage, sir, I would have had no choice." But could he really have taken this sensitive girl, reared among telepaths, to the Terran Zone, to imprison her among tall buildings and machines, to expose her to people who would regard her as an exotic freak? Her very *laran* would have been regarded as madness or charlatanry. "As matters stand, sir, I will remain here gladly. Perhaps I can prove to you that Terrans are not as alien as you think."

"I know that already. Do you think me ungrateful? I know perfectly well that if it had not been for you, Callista would have died in the caverns, and the lands would still lie under their accursed darkness!"

"I think that was more Damon's doing than mine, sir," Andrew said firmly. The old man laughed a short, wry laugh.

"And so it is like the fairy-tale, fitting that you two should be rewarded with the hands of my daughters, and half my kingdom. Well, I have no kingdom to give, Ann'dra, but you have a son's place here while you live, and if you wish, your children after you."

Callista's eyes were brimming. She slipped off the bench and knelt beside her father. She whispered, "Thank you," and his hand rested, for a moment, on her fine, copper-shining braids. Over her bent head he said, "Well, come, Ann'dra, kneel for my blessing." The harsh voice was kind.

With a sense of confusion, half embarrassment, half

ineradicable strangeness, Andrew knelt beside Callista.
On the surface of his mind were random thoughts, such
as how damn silly this would seem at Headquarters, and
when in Rome . . . but on a deeper level, something in
him warmed to the gesture. He felt the old man's square,
calloused hand on his head, and with the still-strange,
newly opened telepathic awareness with which he had
not yet wholly made his peace, picked up a strange me-
lange of emotions: misgivings, blended with a tentative,
spontaneous liking. He was sure that what he sensed was
what the old man felt about him; and to his own surprise,
it was not too unlike what he himself felt for the
Comyn lord.

He said, trying to keep his voice neutral, though he
was perfectly sure the old man could read his thoughts
in turn, "I am grateful, sir. I will try to be a good son
to you."

Dom Esteban said gruffly, "Well, as you can see, I'm
going to need a couple of good ones. Look here, are
you going to keep calling me *sir* for the rest of our
lives, son?"

"Of course not, kinsman." He used the intimate form
of the word now, as Damon did. It could mean "uncle,"
or any close relative of a father's generation. He rose,
and as he moved away he encountered the curious stare
of the boy Dezi, silent behind Esteban, filled with an
angry intensity—yes, and what Andrew could feel as resentment, envy.

Poor kid, he thought. *I come here a stranger, and they
treat me like family. He's family—and the old man treats
him like a servant, or a dog! No wonder the kid's jealous!*

CHAPTER FOUR

It had been decided that the marriage would take place four days hence, a quiet one, with only Leonie for honored guest, and a few neighbors who lived on nearby estates to celebrate with them. The brief interval allowed just time for word to be sent to *Dom* Esteban's heir, Domenic, at Thendara, and for one or more of Damon's brothers to come from Serrais if they wished.

On the night before the wedding, the twin sisters lay awake late, in the room they had shared as children, before Callista went to the Arilinn Tower. Ellemir said at last, a little sadly, "I had always believed that on my marriage day there would be much feasting, and fine gowns, and all our kinfolk to celebrate with us, not a hasty marriage with a few countryfolk! Well, with Damon for husband I can manage without the rest, but still . . ."

"I am sorry too, Elli, I know it is my fault," Callista said. "You are marrying a Comyn lord of the Ridenow Domain, so there is no reason you should not be married by the *catenas*, with all the festivity and merrymaking you might wish. Andrew and I have spoiled this for you." A Comyn daughter could not marry *di catenas*, with the old ceremony, without permission of Comyn Council, and Callista knew there was no chance whatever that Council would give her to a stranger, a nobody—a Terran! So they had chosen the simpler form known as freemate marriage, which could be solemnized by a simple declaration before witnesses.

Ellemir heard the sadness in her sister's voice and said, "Well, as Father is so fond of saying, the world will go as it will, and not as you or I would have it. In the next Council season, Damon has promised, we shall journey to Thendara and there will be enough merrymaking for everyone."

"And by that time," Callista added, "my marriage to

Andrew will be so long established that nothing can alter it."

Ellemir laughed. "It would be just my ill fortune to be heavy with child then, and unable to enjoy it! Not that I would think it ill fortune, to have Damon's child at once."

Callista was silent, thinking of the years in the Tower, where she had put aside, unregretted because unknown, all the things a young girl dreams of. Hearing these things in Ellemir's voice now she asked, hesitating, "Do you want a child at once?"

Ellemir laughed. "Oh, yes! Don't you?"

"I had not thought about it," Callista said slowly. "There were so many years when I never thought of marriage, or love, or children. . . . I suppose Andrew will want children, soon or late, but it seems to me that a child should be wanted for herself, not only because it is my duty to our clan. I have lived so many years in the Tower, thinking only of duty toward others, that I think I must first have a little time to think only of myself. And of . . . of Andrew."

This was puzzling to Ellemir. How could anyone think of her husband without thinking first of her desire to give him a child? But she sensed that it was otherwise with Callista. In any case, she thought with unconscious snobbery, Andrew was not Comyn; it did not matter so much that Callista should give him an heir at once.

"Remember, Elli, I spent so many years thinking I was not to marry at all. . . ."

Her voice was so sad and strange that Ellemir could not bear it. She said, "You love Andrew, and your choice was freely made," but there was a hint of question too. Had Callista chosen to marry her rescuer only because it seemed the simplest thing?

Callista followed that thought, and said, "No, I love him, more than I can tell you. Yet there is another old saying, I never knew till now how true: no choice goes wholly unregretted, either way will bring more, both of joy and sorrow, than we can foresee. My life had seemed unchanging to me, already settled, so simple: I would take Leonie's place in Arilinn and serve there until death or age freed me from the burden. And that too

seemed a good life to me. Love, marriage, children—
these things were not even daydreams to me!"

Her voice was trembling. Ellemir got out of bed and
went to sit on the edge of her sister's, taking her hand in
the darkness. Callista moved, an unconscious, automatic
gesture, to draw it away, then said ruefully, more to
herself than Ellemir, "I suppose I must learn not to do
that."

Ellemir said gently, "I do not think Andrew will ap-
preciate it."

She felt Callista flinch from the words. "It is a . . .
reflex. I find it as hard to break as it was hard to learn."

Ellemir said impulsively, "You must have been very
lonely, Callista!"

Callista's words seemed to come up from some barricaded depth. "Lonely? Not always. In the Tower we are
closer than you can imagine. So much a part of one
another. Even so, as Keeper I was always apart from
them, separated by a . . . a barrier no one could ever
cross. It would have been easier, I think, to be truly
alone." Ellemir felt that her sister was not speaking to
her at all, but to remote and unsharable memories, trying to put words to something she had never been willing
to speak about.

"The others in the Tower could . . . could give some
expression to that closeness. Could touch. Could love.
A Keeper learns a double separateness. To be close,
closer than any other, to each mind within the matrix
circle, and yet never . . . never quite real to them. Never
a woman, never even a living, breathing human being.
Only . . . only part of the screens and relays." She
paused, her mind lost in that strange, barricaded, lonely
life which had been hers for so many years.

"So many women try it, and fail. They become involved, somehow, with the human side of the other
men and women there. In my first year at Arilinn, I
saw six young girls come there, to be trained as
Keeper, and fail. And I was proud because I could
endure the training. It is . . . not easy," she said, knowing the words ridiculously inadequate. They gave no
hint of the months of rigid physical and mental discipline, until her mind was trained to unbelievable

power, until her body could endure the inhuman flows and stresses. She said at last, softly and bitterly, "Now I wish I had failed too!" and stopped, hearing her own words and horrified by them.

Ellemir said softly, "I wish we hadn't grown so far apart, *breda*." Almost for the first time, she spoke the word for sister in the intimate mode; it could also mean darling. Callista responded to the tone, rather than the word.

"It was never that I didn't . . . didn't love you, or remember you, Ellemir. But I was taught—oh, you can't imagine how!—to hold myself apart from every human contact. And you were my twin sister—I had been closest to you. For my first year, I cried myself to sleep at night because I was so lonely for you. But later . . . later you came to seem like all the rest of my life before Arilinn, like someone I had known only in a dream. And so, later, when I was allowed to see you now and again, to visit you, I tried to keep you distant, part of the dream, so that I would not be torn apart with every new separation. Our lives lay apart and I knew it must be so."

Her voice was sadder than tears. Impulsively, eager to comfort, Ellemir lay down beside her sister and took her in her arms. Callista went rigid against the touch, then, sighing, lay still; but Ellemir sensed the effort her sister was making not to pull away from her. She thought, with a violent surge of anger, *How could they do this to her? It's deforming, as if they'd made her a cripple or a hunchback!*

She hugged her and said, "I hope we can find our way back to each other!"

Callista tolerated the gesture, though she did not return it. "So do I, Ellemir."

"It seems dreadful, to think you have never been in love."

Her sister said lightly, "Oh, it is not as bad as that. We were so close in the Towers that I suppose, in one way or another, we were always in love." It was too dark to see Callista's face, but Ellemir sensed the smile as she added, "What if I should tell you that when I first came to Arilinn, Damon was still there, and for a little

I fancied myself in love with him? Are you very jealous, Ellemir?"

Ellemir laughed. "No, not very."

"He was a senior technician, he taught me monitoring. Of course, I was not a woman to him, just one of the little girls in training. Of course for him there was no woman alive, save for Leonie—" She stopped herself and said quickly, "That is long over, of course."

Ellemir laughed aloud. "I know Damon's heart is all mine. How could I be jealous of such love as a man can give a Keeper, a pledged virgin?" Ellemir heard her own words and broke off in consternation. "Oh, Callista, I did not mean—"

"I think you did," Callista said gently, "but love is love, even without any hint of the physical. If I had not known that before, I would have learned it in the caves of Corresanti, when I came to love Andrew. It is love, and it was real, and if I were you I would not smile at it, nor scorn Damon's love for Leonie, as if it were a boy's green fancy." She thought, but did not say, that it had been real enough to disturb Leonie's peace, even if no one but Callista herself had ever guessed it.

She did right to send Damon away. . . .

"It seems strange to me to love without desire," Ellemir said, "and not quite real, whatever you say."

"Men have desired me," Callista said quietly, "in spite of the taboo. It happens. Most of the time it aroused nothing in me, it only made me feel as if . . . as if dirty insects were crawling on my body. But there were other times when I almost wished I knew how to desire them in return."

Suddenly her voice broke. Ellemir heard a wild note in it, very like terror. "Oh, Ellemir, Elli, if I shrink even from your touch—if I shrink from the touch of my twin-born sister—what will I do to Andrew? Oh, merciful Avarra, how much will I have to hurt him?"

"*Breda*, Andrew loves you, surely he will understand—"

"But it may not be enough to understand! Oh, Elli, even if it were someone like Damon, who knows the ways of the Towers, knows what a Keeper is, I would be afraid! And Andrew does not know, or understand,

and there are no words to tell him! And he too has abandoned the only world he has ever known, and what can I give him in return?"

Ellemir said gently, "But you have been freed from a Keeper's oath." The habit of many years, she knew, could not be broken in a day, but once Callista freed herself from her fears, surely all would be well! She held Callista close, saying with quiet tenderness, "Love is nothing to fear, *breda*, even if it seems strange to you, or frightful."

"I knew you did not understand," Callista said, sighing. "There were other women in the Towers, women who did not live by a Keeper's laws, who were free to share the closeness we all shared. There was so much . . . so much love among us, and I knew how happy it made them, to love, or even to satisfy desire, when there was not love but only . . . need, and kindness." She sighed again. "I am not ignorant, Ellemir," she said with a curious, forlorn dignity, "inexperienced, yes, because of what I am, but not ignorant. I have learned ways to . . . not to be much aware of it. It was easier that way, but I knew, oh, yes, I knew. Just as I knew, for instance, that you had lovers before Damon."

Ellemir laughed. "I never made any secret of it. If I did not speak of it to you, it was because I knew the laws under which you lived—or knew as much as any outsider can know—and that seemed a barrier between us."

"But you must surely have known that I envied you that," Callista said, and Ellemir sat up in bed, looking at her twin in surprise and shock. They could see one another only dimly; a small green moon, the dimmest of crescents, hung outside their window. At last Ellemir said, hesitating, "Envy . . . me? I had thought . . . thought surely . . . that a Keeper, pledged so, would surely despise me, or think it shameful, that I—that a *comynara* should be no different than a peasant woman, or some female animal in heat."

"Despise you? Never," Callista said. "If we do not talk much about it, it is for fear we would not be able to endure our differences. Even the other women in the Towers, who do not share our isolation, look on us as alien, almost inhuman. . . . . Separateness, pride, become our only defense, pride, as if to conceal a wound, conceal our own . . . our own incompletion.''

Her voice sounded shaken, but Ellemir thought that her sister's face, in the dim moonlight, was inhumanly impassive, like something carved in stone. It seemed that Callista was almost heartbreakingly distant, that they were trying to talk across a great and aching chasm which lay between them.

All her life Ellemir had been taught to think of a Keeper as something remote, far above her, to be revered, almost worshiped. Even her own sister, her twin, was like a goddess, far out of reach. Now for a moment she had an almost dizzying sense of reversal, shaking her certainties; now it was Callista who looked up to her, envied her, Callista who was somehow younger than herself and far more vulnerable, not clothed in the remote majesty of Arilinn, but a woman like herself, frail, unsure. . . . She said in a whisper, "I wish I had known this about you before, Callie.''

"I wish I had known it about myself," Callista said with a sad smile. "We are not encouraged to think much about such things, or about much of anything but our work. I am only beginning to discover myself as a woman, and I . . . do not quite know how to begin.'' It seemed to Ellemir an incredibly sad confession. After a moment Callista said softly in the darkness, "Ellemir, I have told you what I can of my life. Tell me something of yours. I don't want to pry, but you have had lovers. Tell me about that.''

Ellemir hesitated, but sensed that there was more behind the question than simple sexual curiosity. There was that too, and considering the way in which Callista had been forced to stifle this kind of awareness during her years as Keeper, it was a healthy sign and augured well for the coming marriage. But there was more too, a desire to share something of Ellemir's life during the years of their separation. Responding impulsively to that need, she said, "It was the year Dorian was married. Did you meet Mikhail at all?''

"I saw him at the wedding." Their older sister Dorian had married a *nedestro* cousin of Lord Ardais'. "He seemed a kind, well-spoken young man, but I exchanged no more than, a few dozen words with him. I had seen Dorian so seldom since childhood."

"It was that winter," said Ellemir. "Dorian begged me to come and spend the winter with her; she was lonely, and already pregnant, and had made few friends of the mountain women. Father gave me leave to go. And later in the spring, when Dorian grew heavy, so it was no pleasure to her to share his bed, Mikhail and I had grown to be such friends that I took her place there." She giggled a little, reminiscently.

Callista said, startled, "You were no more than fifteen!"

Ellemir answered, laughing, "That is old enough to marry; Dorian had been no more. I would have been married, had Father not wanted me to stay home and keep his house!"

Again Callista felt the cruel envy, the sense of desperate alienation. How simple it had been for Ellemir, and how right! And how different for her! "Were there others?"

Ellemir smiled in the darkness. "Not many. I learned there that I liked lying with men, but I did not want to be gossiped about as they whisper scandal about Sybil-Mhari—you have heard that she takes lovers from Guardsmen or even grooms—and I did not want to bear a child I would not be allowed to rear, though Dorian pledged that if I gave Mikhail a child she would foster it. And I did not want to be married off in a hurry to someone I did not like, which I knew Father would do if there was scandal. So there are not more than two or three men who could say, if they would, that they have had more of me than my fingers to kiss at Midsummer night. Even Damon. He has waited patiently—"

She gave an odd, excited little laugh. Callista stroked her twin's soft hair.

"Well, now the waiting is nearly over, love."

Ellemir cuddled close to her sister. She could sense Callista's fears, her ambivalence, but she still misunderstood its nature.

She has been pledged virgin, Ellemir thought, *she has lived her life apart from men, so it is not surprising that*

*she should be afraid. But once she has come to under-
stand that she is free, Andrew will be kind to her, and
patient, and she will come at last to happiness . . . happiness like mine . . . and Damon's.*

They were lightly in rapport, and Callista followed Ellemir's thoughts, but she would not trouble her sister by
telling her that it was not nearly as simple as that.

"We should sleep, *breda*, tomorrow is our wedding
day, and tomorrow night," she added mischievously,
"Damon may not let you sleep very much."

Laughing, Ellemir closed her eyes. Callista lay silent,
her twin's head resting on her shoulder, staring into the
darkness. After a long time she sensed, as the thread of
rapport between them thinned and Ellemir moved into
dreams, that her sister slept. Quietly she slid from the
bed and went to the window, looking out over the moon-
flooded landscape. She stood there till she was cramped
and cold, until the moons set and a thin fine rain began
to blur the windowpane. With the hard discipline of
years, she did not weep.

*I can accept this and endure it, as I have endured so
much. But what of Andrew? Can I endure what it will
do to him, what it may do to his love?* She stood motionless, hour after hour, cramped, cold, but no longer
aware of it, her mind retreating to one of the realms
beyond thought which she had been taught to enter for
refuge against tormenting ideas, leaving behind the
cramped, icy body she had been taught to despise.

Rain had given way to thin sleet in the dawn hours,
rattling the pane. Ellemir stirred, felt about in the bed
for her sister, then sat up in consternation, seeing Callista
motionless at the window. She got up and went to her,
calling her name, but Callista neither heard nor stirred.

Alarmed, Ellemir cried out. Callista, hearing the voice
less than the fear in Ellemir's mind, came slowly back
to the room. "It's all right, Elli," she said gently, looking
at the frightened face turned up to hers.

"You're so cold, love, so stiff and cold. Come back to
bed, let me warm you," Ellemir urged, and Callista let
her sister lead her back to bed, cover her warmly, hold
her close. After a long time she said, almost in a whisper,
"I was wrong, Elli."

"Wrong? How, *breda*?"

"I should have gone to Andrew's bed when first he brought me from the caves. After so much time alone in the dark, so much fear, my defenses were down." With an aching regret she remembered how he had carried her from Corresanti, how she had rested, warm and unafraid, in his arms. How, for a little while, it had seemed possible to her. "But there was so much confusion here, Father newly crippled, the house filled with wounded men. Still, it would have been easier then."

Ellemir followed her reasoning, and was inclined to agree. Yet Callista was not the kind of woman who could have done such a thing in the face of her father's displeasure, against her Keeper's oath. And Lord Alton would have known it, as surely as if Callista had shouted it aloud from the rooftop.

"You were ill yourself, love. Andrew surely understood."

But Callista wondered: had the long illness which came upon her after her rescue been somehow a reaction to this failure? Perhaps, she thought, they had lost an opportunity which might never come again, to come together when they were both afire with passion and had no room for doubts and fears. Even Leonie thought it likely that she had done so.

Why did I not? And now, now it is too late. . . .

Ellemir yawned, with a smile of pure delight.

"It is our wedding day, Callista!"

Callista closed her eyes. *My wedding day. And I cannot share her gladness. I love as she loves, yet I am not glad. . . .* She felt a wild impulse to tear at herself with her nails, to beat herself with her fists, to turn on and punish the beauty which was so empty a promise, the body which looked so much like a lovely and desirable woman's body—a shell, an empty shell. But Ellemir was looking at her in troubled question, so she made herself smile gaily.

"Our wedding day," she said, and kissed her twin. "Are you happy, darling?"

And for a little while, in Ellemir's joy, she managed to forget her own fears.

CHAPTER FIVE

That morning Damon came to assist *Dom* Esteban into the rolling chair that had been made for him. "So you can be present at the wedding sitting upright, not lying flat on a wheel-bed like an invalid!"

"It feels strange to be vertical again," said the old man, steadying himself with both hands. "I feel as dizzy as if I were already drunk."

"You've been lying flat too long," Damon said matter-of-factly. "You'll soon get used to it."

"Well, better to sit up than go propped on pillows like a woman in childbed! And at least my legs are still there, even if I can't feel them!"

"They are still there," Damon assured him, "and with someone to push your chair, you can get around well enough on the ground floor."

"That will be a relief," Esteban said. "I am weary of looking at this ceiling! When spring comes, I will have workmen come here, and let them do over some rooms on the ground floor for me. You two," he added, gesturing Andrew to join them, "can have any of the large suites upstairs, for yourselves and your wives."

"That is generous, Father-in-law," Damon said, but the old man shook his head.

"Not at all. No room above ground level will ever be of the slightest use to me again. I suggest you go and choose rooms for yourselves now; leave my old rooms for Domenic when he takes a wife, but any others are for your own choice. If you do it now, the women can move into their own homes as soon as they are married." He added, laughing, "And while you do that, I shall have Dezi wheel me about down here and get used to the sight of my house again. Did I thank you, Damon, for this?"

On the upper floor, Damon and Andrew sought out Leonie. Damon said, "I wanted to ask you, out of earshot. I understand enough to know *Dom* Esteban will never walk again. But otherwise how is he, Leonie?"

"Out of earshot?" The Keeper laughed faintly. "He has *laran*, Damon; he knows all, though perhaps he has wisely refused to understand what it will mean to him. The flesh wound has long healed, of course, and the kidneys are not damaged, but the brain no longer communicates with legs and feet. He retains some small control over body functions, but doubtless as time passes and the lower part of his body wastes away, that will go too. His greatest danger is pressure sores. You must be sure his body-servants turn him every few hours, because, since there is no feeling, there will be no pain either, and he will not know if a fold in his clothing, or something of that sort, puts pressure on his body. Most of those who are paralyzed die when such sores become infected. This process can be delayed, with great care, if his limbs are kept supple with massage, but sooner or later the muscles will wither and die."

Damon shook his head in dismay. "He knows all this?"

"He knows. But his will to live is strong, and while that remains, you can keep his life good. For a while. Years, perhaps. Afterward . . ." A small, resigned shrug. "Perhaps he will find some new will to live if he has grandchildren about him. But he has always been an active man, and a proud one. He will not take kindly to inactivity or helplessness."

Andrew said, "I'm going to need a hell of a lot of his help and advice running this place. I've been trying to get along without bothering him—"

"By your leave, that is mistaken," said Leonie gently. "He should know that his knowledge is still needed, if not his hands and his skill. Ask him for advice as much as you can, Andrew."

It was the first time she had addressed him directly, and the Terran glanced at the woman in surprise. He had enough rudimentary telepathy to know that Leonie was uncomfortable with him, and was troubled to feel there was something more now in her regard. When she had gone away he said to Damon, "She doesn't like me, does she?"

"I don't think it is that," Damon said. "She would feel uneasy with any man to whom she must give Callista in marriage, I think."

"Well, I can't blame her for thinking I'm not good enough for Callista; I don't think there's any man who is. But as long as Callista doesn't think so . . ."

Damon laughed. "I suppose no man on his wedding day feels worthy of his bride. I must keep reminding myself that Ellemir has agreed to this marriage! Come along, we must find rooms for our wives!"

"Shouldn't it be up to them to choose?"

Damon recalled that Andrew was a stranger to their customs. "No, it is custom for the husband to provide a home for his wife. In courtesy *Dom* Esteban is giving us a way to find such a place and ready it before the wedding."

"But they know the house—"

Damon replied, "So do I. I spent much of my boyhood here. *Dom* Esteban's oldest son and I were *bredin*, sworn friends. But you, have you no kinsmen in the Terran Zone, no servants sworn to you and awaiting your return?"

"None. Servants are a memory out of our past; no man should serve another."

"Still, we'll have to assign you a few. If you're going to be managing the estate for our kinsman"—Damon used the word usually translated as "uncle"—"you won't have leisure to handle the details of ordinary life, and we can't expect the women to do their own cleaning and mending. And we don't have machines as you do in the Terran Zone."

"Why not?"

"We're not rich in metals. Anyhow, why should we make people's lives useless because they cannot earn their porridge and meat at honest work? Or do you truly think we would all be happier building machines and selling them to one another as you do?" Damon opened a door off the hallway. "These rooms have not been used since Ellemir's mother died and Dorian was married. They seem in good repair."

Andrew followed him into the spacious central living room of the suite, his mind still on Damon's question.

"I've been taught it is degrading for one man to serve another, degrading for the servant—and for the master."

"I'd find it more degrading to spend my life as servant to some kind of machine. And if you own a machine, you are in turn owned by it and spend your time serving it." He thought of his own relationship to the matrix, and every psi technician's on Darkover, to say nothing of the Keepers'.

Instead, he opened doors all around the suite. "Look, on either side of this central living room is a complete suite: each with bedroom, sitting room and bath, and small rooms behind for the women's maids when they choose them, dressing rooms and so forth. The women will want to be close together, and yet there's privacy too, for when we want it, and other small rooms nearby if we need them someday for our children. Does this suit you?"

It was far more space than any young couple would have been assigned in Married Personnel HQ. Andrew agreed, and Damon asked, "Will you have the left-hand or right-hand suite?"

"Makes no difference to me. Want to flip a coin?"

Damon laughed heartily. "You have that custom too? But if it makes no difference to you, let us have the left-hand suite. Ellemir, I have noticed, is always awake and about with the dawn, and Callista likes to sleep late when she can. Perhaps it would be better not to have the morning sun in your bedroom window."

Andrew blushed with pleasant embarrassment. He had noticed this, but had not carried it far enough in his mind to think ahead to the mornings when he would be waking in the same room as Callista. Damon grinned companionably.

"The wedding's only hours away, you know. And we'll be brothers, you and I—that's a good thought too. It seems sad, though, that you should not have a single kinsman or friend at your wedding."

"I've no friends on this planet anyway. And no living relatives anywhere."

Damon blinked in dismay. "You came here without family, without friends?"

Andrew shrugged. "I grew up on Terra—a horse

ranch in a place called Arizona. When I was eighteen or so, my father died, and the ranch was sold for his debts. My mother didn't live long after that, and I went into space as a civil servant, and a civil servant goes where he's sent, more or less. I wound up here, and you know the rest."

"I thought you had no servants among you," Damon said, and Andrew got into a tangle of words trying to explain to the other man the difference which made a civil servant other than a servant. Damon listened skeptically and finally said, "A servant, then, to computers and paperwork! I think I had rather be an honest groom or cook!"

"Aren't there cruel masters who exploit their servants?"

Damon shrugged. "No doubt, just as some men ill-treat their saddle horses and whip them to death. But a reasoning man may some day learn the error of his ways, and at the worst, others may restrain him. But there is no way to teach a machine wisdom after folly."

Andrew grinned. "You know, you're right. We have a saying, you can't fight the computer, it's right even when it's wrong."

"Ask *Dom* Esteban's hall-steward, or the estate mid-wife Ferrika, if they feel ill-used or exploited," Damon said. "You're telepath enough to know if they're telling the truth. And then, perhaps, you'll decide you can honorably let some man earn his wages as your body-servant and your groom."

Andrew shrugged. "No doubt I will. We have a saying, When in Rome, do as the Romans do. Rome, I think, was a city on Terra; it was destroyed in a war or an earthquake, centuries ago, only the proverb remains. . . ."

Damon said, "We have a similar saying; it runs, Don't try to buy fish in the Dry Towns." He walked around the room he had chosen for his bedroom and Ellemir's. "These draperies have not been aired since the days of Regis the Fourth! I'll get the stewards to change them." He pulled a bell-rope, and when the steward appeared, gave orders.

"We'll have it done by tonight, my lord, so you and your ladies can move in when you like. And, Lord

Damon, I was asked to let you know that your brother, Lord Serrais, has come to witness your wedding."

"Very good, thank you. If you can find Lady Ellemir, ask her to come and approve what arrangements we have made," Damon said. When the servant went away, he grimaced.

"My brother Lorenz! Such good will as he has for my wedding, I suspect, could be dropped into my eyes without pain! I had hoped for my brother Kieran, at least, or my sister Marisela, but I suppose I should be honored, and go to say a word of thanks to Lorenz."

"Have you many brothers?"

"Five," Damon said, "and three sisters. I was the youngest son, and my father and mother had already too many children when I was born. Lorenz—" He shrugged. "I suppose he is relieved that I have taken a bride of family so good that he need not haggle about patrimony and a younger son's portion. I am not wealthy, but I have never wished for much wealth, and Ellemir and I will have enough for our needs. My brother Lorenz and I have never been overly friendly. Kieran—he is only three years older than I—Kieran and I are *bredin*; Marisela and I are only a year apart in age, and we had the same foster-mother. As for my other brothers and sisters, we are civil enough when we meet in Council season, but I suspect none of us would grieve over much if we never met again. My home has always been here. My mother was an Alton, and I was fostered near here, and *Dom* Esteban's oldest son went with me into the Cadets. We swore the oath of *bredin*." It was the second time he had used this word, which was the intimate or family form of brother. Damon sighed, looking into space for a moment.

"You were a cadet?"

"A very poor one," Damon said, "but no Comyn son can escape it if he has two sound legs and his eyesight. Coryn was like all Altons, a born soldier, a born officer. I was something else." He laughed. "There's a joke in the cadet corps about the cadet with two right feet and ten thumbs. That was me."

"Awkward squad all the way, huh?"

Damon nodded, savoring the phrase. "Punishment detail eleven times in a tenday. I'm right-handed, you see. My foster-mother—she was midwife to my mother—used to say I was born upside-down and ass-backward, and I've been doing everything that way ever since."

Andrew, who had been born left-handed into a right-handed society and only on Darkover had found things arranged in a way that made sense to him, everything from silverware to garden tools, said, "I can certainly understand that."

"I'm a bit short-sighted, too, which didn't help, though it was a help in learning to read. None of my brothers have any clerical skills, and they can't do much more than spell out a placard or scrawl their names to a deed. But I took to it like a rabbithorn to the snow, so when I finished in the cadets I went to Nevarsin, and spent a year or two learning to read and write and do some map-making and the like. That was when Lorenz decided I'd never make a man. When they accepted me at Arilinn, it only confirmed him in his decision: half monk, half eunuch, he used to say." Damon was silent, his face set in lines of distaste. Finally he said, "But for all that he was no better pleased when they sent me from the Tower, a few years ago. For Coryn's sake—Coryn was dead then, poor lad, killed in a fall from the cliffs—but for his sake, *Dom* Esteban took me into the Guards. I was never much of a soldier, though, hospital officer, cadet-master for a year or two." He shrugged. "And that's my life, and enough of that. Listen, the women are coming, we can show our wives around before I have to go down and try to be polite to Lorenz!"

Andrew saw, with relief, that the lonely, introspective sadness slid off his face as Ellemir and Callista came in.

"Come, Ellemir, see the rooms I have chosen for us."

He took her through a door at the far end, and Andrew sensed, rather than heard, that he was kissing her. Callista followed them with her eyes and smiled. "I am glad to see them so happy."

"Are you happy too, my love?"

She said, "I love you, Andrew. I do not find it so easy to rejoice. Perhaps I am naturally a little less light of heart. Come, show me the rooms we are to have."

She approved of nearly everything, though she pointed

out half a dozen pieces of furniture which, she said, were so old they were not safe to sit on, and called a steward, directing that they be taken away. She called the maids and gave directions about what things were to be brought from the household storerooms for bedroom and bath linens, and sent another to have her clothing brought and stored in the enormous clothes-press in her dressing room. Andrew listened in silence, finally saying, "You are quite a homemaker, Callista!"

Her laugh was delightful. "It is all pretense. I have been listening to Ellemir, that is all, because I do not want to sound ignorant in front of her servants. I know very little about such things. I have been taught to sew, because I was never allowed to let my hands sit idle, but when I watch Ellemir about the kitchens, I realize that I know less of housekeeping than any girl of ten."

"I feel the same way," Andrew confessed. "Everything I learned in the Terran Zone is useless to me now."

"But you know something of horse-breaking—"

Andrew laughed. "Yes, and in the Terran Zone that was considered an anachronism, a useless skill. I used to take Dad's saddle horses and break them, but I thought when I left Arizona that I'd never ride again."

"Does everyone on Terra walk, then?"

He shook his head. "Motor transit. Slidewalks. Horses were an exotic luxury for rich eccentrics." He went to the window and looked out on the sunlit landscape. "Strange, that of all the known worlds of the Terran Empire, I should have come *here*." A faint shudder went through him at the thought of how narrowly he could have missed what now seemed his fate, his life, the true purpose for which he had been born. He wanted desperately to reach out and draw Callista into his arms, but as if his thought had somehow reached her, she went tense and white. He sighed and stepped a pace away from her.

She said, as if completing a thought that no longer interested her much, "Our horse-handler is already an old man, and without Father at hand, it may be up to you to teach the younger ones." Then she stopped and looked up at him, twisting the end of one long braid.

"I want to talk to you," she said abruptly.

He had never decided whether her eyes were blue or gray; they seemed to vary with the light, and in this light they were almost colorless. "Andrew, will this be too hard on you? To share a room when we cannot—as yet—share a bed?"

He had been warned of this when they first discussed marriage, that she had been conditioned so deeply that it might be a long time before they could consummate their marriage. He had promised her then, unasked, that he would never hurry her or try to put any pressure on her, that he would wait as long as necessary. He said now, touching her fingertips lightly, "Don't worry about it, Callista. I promised you that already."

Faint color crept slowly across her pale cheeks. She said, "I have been taught that it is . . . shameful to arouse a desire I will not satisfy. Yet if I stay apart from you, and do *not* rouse it, so that in turn your thoughts may act on me, then things may never be different at all. If we are together, then, slowly perhaps, things may be different. But it will be so hard on you, Andrew." Her face twisted. She said, "I don't want you to be unhappy."

Once, once only, and with great constraint, and briefly, he had spoken of this with Leonie. Now, as he stood looking down at Callista, that brief meeting, difficult on both sides, came back to his mind as if again he stood before the Comyn *leronis*. She had come to him in the courtyard, saying quietly, "Look at me, Terran." He had raised his eyes, unable to resist. Leonie was so tall that their eyes were on a level. She had said, in a low voice, "I want to see to what manner of man I am giving the child I love." Their eyes had met, and for a long moment Andrew Carr felt as if every thought of his entire life had been turned over and rummaged through by the woman, as if in that one glance, and not a long one, she had drawn the very inmost part from him and left it to dangle there, cold and withering. Finally—it had not been more than a second or two, but it had seemed an age—Leonie had sighed and said, "So be it. You are honest and kind and you mean well, but have you the faintest idea of what a Keeper's training means, or how hard it will be for Callista to lay it down?"

He had wanted to protest, but instead he had only shaken his head and said humbly, "How can I know? But I will try to make it easy for her."

Leonie's sigh had seemed ripped up from the very depths of her being. She had said, "Nothing you could do, in this world or the next, could make it easy for her. If you are patient and careful—and lucky—you may make it *possible*. I do not want Callista to suffer. And yet in the choice she has made, there will be much suffering. She is young, but not so young that she can put aside her training without pain. The training that makes a Keeper is long; it cannot be undone in a little while."

Andrew had protested. "I know—" and Leonie had sighed again. "Do you? I wonder. It is not only a matter of delaying the consummation of your marriage for days, or perhaps for seasons; that will be only the beginning. She loves you, and is eager for your love—"

"I can be patient until she is ready," Andrew had sworn, but Leonie had said, shaking her head, "Patience may not be enough. What Callista has learned cannot be unlearned. You do not want to know about that. Perhaps it is better for you not to know too much."

He had said again, protesting, "I'll try to make it easy for her," and again Leonie had shaken her head and sighed, repeating, "Nothing you could do could make it easy. Chickens cannot go back into eggs. Callista will suffer, and I fear you will suffer with her, but if you are—if you *both* are lucky, you may make it possible for her to retrace her steps. Not easy. But possible."

Indignation had burst out of him then. "How can you people do this to young girls? How can you destroy their lives this way?" But Leonie had not answered, lowering her head and moving noiselessly away from him. When he blinked she was gone, as swiftly as if she had been a shadow, so that he began to doubt his sanity, began to wonder if she had ever been there at all, or if his own doubts and fears had constructed an hallucination.

Callista, standing before him in the room that—tomorrow—would be theirs to share, raised her eyes again, slowly, to his. She said in a whisper, "I did not know Leonie had come to you that way," and he saw her hands clench tightly, so tightly that the small knuckles were white as bone. Then she said, looking away from him, "Andrew, promise me something."

"Anything, my love."

"Promise me. If you ever . . . desire some woman, promise me you will take her and not suffer needlessly. . . ."

He exploded. "What kind of man do you think I am? I love you! Why would I want anyone else?"

"I cannot expect—It is not right or natural. . . ."

"Look here, Callista," and his voice was gentle, "I've lived a long time without women. I never found it did me all that much harm. A few, here and there, while I was knocking around the Empire on my own. Nothing serious."

She looked down at the tips of her small dyed-leather sandals. "That's different, men alone, living away from women. But here, living with me, sleeping in the same room, being near me all the time and knowing . . ." She ran out of words. He wanted to take her into his arms and kiss her till she lost that rigid, lost look. He actually laid his hands on her shoulders, felt her tense under the touch, and let his hands drop to his sides. Damn anyone who could build pathological reflexes into a young girl this way! But even without the touch, he felt the grief in her, grief and guilt. She said softly, "You have no bargain in a wife, Andrew."

He replied gently, "I have the wife I want."

Damon and Ellemir came into the room. Ellemir's hair was tousled, her eyes shining; she had that glassy-eyed look which he associated with women aroused, excited. For the first time since he had seen the twins, he saw Ellemir as a woman, not merely as Callista's sister, and found her sensually attractive to him. Or was it that for a moment he saw in her the way Callista might, one day, look at him? He felt a flicker of guilt. She was his promised wife's sister, in a few hours she would be his best friend's wife, and of all women, she was the one at whom he should not look with desire. He looked away as she collected herself, slowly coming back to ordinary awareness.

She said, "Callie, we must have new curtains brought in; these have not been aired or washed, since—since"—

she groped for analogy—"since the days of Regis the Fourth." Andrew knew that she had been in close contact with Damon, and smiled to himself.

Just before high noon a clatter of hooves sounded in the courtyard, a commotion like a small hurricane, riders, sounds, cries, noises. Callista laughed. "It is Domenic; no one else ever arrives with such a fury!" She drew Andrew down to the courtyard. Domenic Lanart, heir to the Domain of Alton, was a slight, red-haired boy, tall and freckled, astride an enormous gray stallion. He flung the reins to a groom, jumped down, grabbed Ellemir and hugged her exuberantly, then threw his arms around Damon.

"Two weddings for one!" he exclaimed, drawing them up the steps at his side. "You've been long enough about your wooing, Damon. I knew last year that you wanted her; why did it take a war to bring you to the point of asking her hand? Elli, will you have a husband so reluctant?" He turned his head from side to side, kissing both of them, then broke away and turned to Callista.

"And for you a lover insistent enough to win you from the Tower! I am eager to meet this marvel, *breda*." But his voice was suddenly gentle, and when Callista presented him to Andrew, he bowed. For all the exuberant noise and boyish laughter, he had the manners of a prince. His hands were small and square, calloused like a swordsman's.

"So you are to marry Callista? I suppose that crowd of old ladies and graywigs in the Council won't like it, but it's time we had some new blood in the family." He stood on tiptoe—Callista was a tall woman, and for all his lanky height, Domenic was not, Andrew thought, quite full-grown yet—and brushed her cheek lightly with his lips. "Be happy, sister. Avarra's mercy! You deserve it, if you can dare to marry like this, without Council permission or the *catenas*."

"*Catenas*," she said scornfully. "I had as soon marry a Dry-Towner and go in chains!"

"Good for you, sister." He turned to Andrew as they went into the hall. "Father said in his message that you were a Terran. I have talked with some of your people in Thendara. They seem good enough folk, but lazy.

Good Gods, they have machines for everything, to walk
on, to lift them up a flight of stairs, to bring them food
at table. Tell me, Andrew, do they have machines to
wipe themselves with?" He shouted boisterous boyish
laughter, while the girls giggled.

He turned to Damon. "So you're not coming back to
the Guards, cousin? You're the only decent cadet-master
we've had in ages. Young Danvan Hastur's trying his
hand at it now, but it's not working. The lads are all too
much in awe of him, and anyway, he's too young. It
needs a man of more years. Any suggestions?"

"Try my brother Kieran," Damon suggested, smiling.
"He likes soldiering more than I ever did."

"You were a damn good cadet-master, though," Domenic said. "I'd like you back, though I suppose it's no
job for a man, being a sort of he-governess to a pack of
half-grown boys."

Damon shrugged. "I was glad enough to have their
liking, but I am no soldier, and a cadet-master should
be one who can inspire his cadets with a love of a soldier's trade."

"Not too much love of it, though," said *Dom* Esteban,
who had listened with interest as they approached, "or
he'll harden them and make them brutes, not men. So
you have come at last, Domenic, my lad?"

The boy laughed. "Why, no, Father, I am still carous-
ing in a Thendara tavern. What you see here is my
ghost." Then the merriment slid off his face as he saw
his father, thin, graying, his useless legs covered with
a wolfskin robe. He dropped to his knees beside the
wheelchair. He said brokenly, "Father, oh, Father, I
would have come at any moment, if you had sent for
me, truly—"

The Alton lord laid his hands on Domenic's shoulders.
"I know that, dear lad, but your place was in Thendara,
since I could not be there. Yet the sight of you makes
my heart more glad than I can say."

"I too," said Domenic, scrambling up and looking
down at his father. "I am relieved to see you so well
and hearty; reports in Thendara had you at the point of
death, or even dead and buried!"

"It is not as bad as that," *Dom* Esteban said, laughing.

"Come sit here beside me, tell me all that goes on in Guard-hall and Council." It was easy to see, Andrew thought, that this merry boy was the very light of his father's eyes.

"I will, and gladly, Father, but this is a wedding day and we are here for merrymaking, and there is little mirth to that tale! Prince Aran Elhalyn thinks I am all too young to have command of the Guards, even while you lie here sick at Armida, and he whispers that tale night and day into the ears of Hastur. And Lorenz of Serrais—forgive me for speaking ill of your brother, Damon—"

Damon shook his head. "My brother and I are not on the best of terms, Domenic, so say what you will."

"Lorenz, then, damn him for a warped scheming fox, and old Gabriel of Ardais, who wants the post for that bullying wretch of a son of his, are quick to sing the same chorus, that I am all too young to command the Guards. They are about Aran night and day with flattery and gifts that stop just that one step short of being bribes, to persuade him to name one of them Commander while you are here in Armida! Will you be back before Midsummer festival, Father?"

A shadow passed over the crippled man's face. "That must be as the Gods will have it, my son. Would the Guards be commanded, think you, by a man chairbound, with legs of no more use than fish-flippers?"

"Better a lame commander than a commander who is no Alton," Domenic said with fierce pride. "I could command in your name, and do all for you, if you were only *there*, to command as the Altons have done so many generations!"

His father gripped his hands, hard. "We shall see, my son. We shall see what comes." But even that thought, Damon could see, had fired the Alton lord with a sudden hope and purpose. Would he, indeed, be able to command the Guards again from his chair, with Domenic at his side?

"Alas that we have now no Lady Bruna in our family," Domenic said gaily. "Say, Callista, will you take up the sword as Lady Bruna did, and command the Guardsmen?"

She laughed, shaking her head. Damon said, "I do not know that tale," and Domenic repeated it, smiling. "It was generations ago—how many I do not know—but her name is written in the rolls of Commanders, how Lady Bruna Leynier, when her brother, who was Lord Alton then, was slain, leaving a son but nine years old, took the lad's mother in freemate marriage to protect her, as women may do, and ruled the Guards till he came of age to command. In the annals of the Guards, it says she was a notable commander too. Would you not have that fame, Callista? No? Ellemir?" He shook his head with mock sadness as they declined. "Alas, what has come to the women of our clan? They are not what they were in those days!"

Standing around *Dom* Esteban's chair, the family resemblance was overwhelming. Domenic looked like Callista and Ellemir, though his hair was redder, his curls more riotous, his freckles a thick golden splotch instead of a faint gilt sprinkle. And Dezi, quiet and unregarded behind the wheeled chair, was like a paler reflection of Domenic. Domenic looked up and saw him there, giving him a friendly thump on the shoulder.

"So you are here, cousin? I heard you had left the Tower. I don't blame you. I spent forty days there a few years ago, being tested for *laran*, and I couldn't get away fast enough! Did you get sick of it too, or did they chuck you out?"

Dezi hesitated and looked away, and Callista interposed. "You learned nothing there of our courtesies, Domenic. That is a question which must never be asked. It is between a telepath and his own Keeper, and if Dezi chooses not to tell, it is inexcusably rude to ask."

"Oh, sorry," said Domenic good-naturedly, and only Damon noticed the relief in Dezi's face. "It's just that I couldn't get out of the place fast enough, and wondered if you felt the same way. Some people like it. Look at Callista, she had nearly ten years of it, and others—well, it wasn't for me."

Damon, watching the two lads, thought with pain of Coryn, so like Domenic at this age! He seemed to taste again the half-forgotten days of his own boyhood, when he, the clumsiest of the cadets, had been accepted as one of them because of his sworn friendship with Coryn, who, like Domenic, had been the best liked, the most energetic and outrageous of them all.

That had been in the days before failure, and hopeless love, and humiliation had burned so deep . . . but, he thought, it was also before he knew Ellemir. He sighed and clasped her hand in his. Domenic, feeling Damon's eyes on him, looked up and smiled, and Damon felt the weight of loneliness slip away. He had Ellemir, and he had Andrew and Domenic for brothers. The isolation and loneliness were gone forever.

Domenic took Dezi's arm in a companionable way. "Look here, cousin, if you get tired of hanging around here at my father's footstool, come to Thendara. I'll get you a commission in the cadet corps—I can do that, can't I, Father?" he asked. At *Dom* Esteban's indulgent nod, he added, "They always need lads of good family, and anyone can see to look at you that you've got Alton blood, haven't you?"

Dezi said quietly, "I have always been told so. Without it I could never have passed through the Veil at Arilinn."

"Well, it doesn't matter a damn in the cadets. Half of us are some nobleman's bastard"—he laughed again uproariously—"and the rest of us poor devils are some nobleman's legitimate son suffering and sweating to prove ourselves worthy of our parents! But I lived through three years of it, and you will too, so come to Thendara and I'll find you something. Bare is back that has no brother, they say, and since Valdir's with the monks at Nevarsin, I'll be glad to have you with me, kinsman."

Dezi's face flushed a little. He said in a low voice, "Thank you, cousin. I will stay here while your father has need of me. After that, it will be my pleasure." He turned quickly, attentively to *Dom* Esteban. "Uncle, what ails you?" For the old man had gone white and slumped against the back of his chair.

"Nothing," *Dom* Esteban said, recovering himself. "A moment of faintness. Perhaps, as they say in the hills, some wild thing pissed on the ground for my grave. Or perhaps it is only that this is my first day upright after lying flat for so long."

"Let me help you back to bed, then, Uncle, to rest until the wedding," Dezi said. Domenic said, "I'll come help," and as they fussed around him, Damon noticed that Ellemir was watching them with a strange look of dismay.

"What is it, *preciosa*?"

"Nothing, a premonition, I don't know," said Ellemir, shaking, "but as he spoke I saw him lying like death here at this table—"

Damon recalled that now and again in the Altons, a flash of precognition accompanied the gift of *Laran*. He had always suspected that Ellemir had more of the gift than she had ever been allowed to believe. But he stilled his unease and said lovingly, "Well, he is not a young man, my darling, and we are to make our home here. It stands within reason that we would some day see him laid to rest. Don't let it trouble you, my beloved. And now, I suppose, I must go and pay my respects to my brother Lorenz, since he has chosen to honor my wedding with his presence. Do you suppose we can keep him and Domenic from coming to blows?"

And as Ellemir became enmeshed again in thoughts of guests and the celebration to come, her pallor lessened. But Damon wished he had shared her prevision. What had Ellemir seen?

Andrew watched, with a sense of unreality, as the wedding drew near. Freemate marriage was a simple declaration before witnesses, and it was to be made at the end of the dinner for the guests and neighbors from adjoining estates who had been invited to take part in the celebration. Andrew had no kinsmen or friends here, and although he had dismissed the lack easily enough, as the moment approached, he found he even envied Damon the presence of the dour-looking Lorenz, standing at his side for the solemn declaration which would make Ellemir, by law and custom, his wife. What was the proverb Damon had quoted? "Bare is back that has no brother." Well, his was bare indeed.

Around the long table of the Great Hall of Armida, laid with the finest cloths and decked out with holiday ware, all the farmers, small-holders and noblemen within

the day's ride were gathered. Damon looked pale and
tense, handsomer than usual in a suit of soft leather,
dyed and richly embroidered, made in what Andrew had
heard were the colors of his Domain. The orange and
green looked gaudy to Andrew. Damon reached his
hand to Ellemir, who came around the table to join him.
She looked pale and serious, in a green gown, her hair
coiled into a silver net. Behind her two young girls—she
had told Andrew they had been her playmates when she
and Callista were children, one a noblewoman from a
nearby holding, one a village girl from their own estates—came to stand behind her.

Damon said steadily, "My friends, nobles and gentlefolk,
we have called you together to witness our pledging. Be
you all witness that I, Damon Ridenow of Serrais, being
freeborn and pledged to no woman, take as freemate this
woman, Ellemir Lanart-Alton, with the consent of her kin.
And I proclaim that her children shall be declared the
legitimate heirs of my body, and shall share in my heritage
and estate, be it large or small."

Ellemir took his hand. Her voice sounded like a
child's in the huge room. "Be witness all of you that I,
Ellemir Lanart, take Damon Ridenow as freemate, with
consent of our kin."

There was an outcry of applause and laughter, congratulations, hugs and kisses for both bride and groom.
Andrew clasped Damon's hands in his own, but Damon
put his arms around Andrew for the embrace that was
customary here, between kinsmen, his cheek briefly
touching his friend's. Then Ellemir pressed herself
lightly against him, standing on tiptoe, her lips for a moment on his. For a moment, dizzied, it was as if he had
received the kiss Callista had never yet given him, and
his mind blurred. For a moment he was not sure which
of them had actually kissed him. Then Ellemir was
laughing up at him, saying softly, "It is too early for you
to be drunk, Andrew!"

The newly married couple moved on, accepting other
kisses, embraces, good wishes. Andrew knew that in a
moment it would be his turn to make the declaration,
but he must stand alone.

Domenic leaned close to him and whispered, "If you

wish, I will stand as your kinsman, Andrew. It is only anticipating the fact by a few moments."

Andrew was touched by the gesture, but hesitated to accept. "You know nothing of me, Domenic . . ."

"Oh, you are Callista's choice, and that is quite enough testimony to your character," Domenic said lightly. "I know my sister, after all." He rose with him, seeming to accept it as settled. "Did you see the sour face on *Dom* Lorenz? It's hard to imagine he's Damon's brother, isn't it? I don't suppose you've seen the woman *he* married! I think he envies Damon my pretty sister!" As they moved around the table, he murmured, "You can use the words Damon used, or any others which happen to occur to you—there is no set formula. But leave it to Callista to declare your children legitimate. Without offense, that is for the parent of higher rank to do or leave undone."

Andrew whispered his thanks for the advice. Now he was standing at the head of the long table, facing the guests, dimly aware of Domenic behind him, of Dezi facing him across the long table, of Callista's eyes steadily before him. He swallowed, hearing his own voice roughened and hoarse.

"I, Ann'dra"—a double name in Darkovan denoted at least minor nobility; Andrew had no lineage any of them would have recognized—"declare that in your presence, as witnesses, I take Callista Lanart-Alton as freemate, with consent of her kin. . . ." It seemed to him that there should be something more than this. He remembered a sect on Terra which had performed their own marriages this way, before witnesses, and out of vague memory he paraphrased, translating the words from an echo in his mind:

"I take her to love and to cherish, in good times and bad, in poverty and wealth, in health and in sickness, while life shall last, and thus I pledge before you all."

Slowly she came around the table to join him. She was wearing flimsy draperies of crimson embroidered with gold. The color quenched her pale hair, made her look paler still. He had heard that this was the color and the dress reserved for a Keeper. Leonie, behind her, was similarly garbed, solemn and unsmiling.

Callista's quiet voice was, nevertheless, the voice of a trained singer. Soft as it was, it could be heard throughout the room. "I, Callista of Arilinn," and her fingers tightened on his almost convulsively as she spoke the ritual title aloud for the last time, "having laid down my holy office forever with the consent of my Keeper, take this man, Ann'dra, as freemate. I further declare"—her voice trembled—"that should I bear him children they shall be held legitimate before clan and council, caste and heritage." She added, and it struck Andrew that there was defiance in the words, "The Gods witness it, and the holy things at Hali."

At that moment he saw Leonie's eyes fixed on him. They seemed to hold a fathomless sadness, but he had no time to wonder why. He bent his head, taking Callista's hands in his own, touching his lips lightly to hers. She did not shrink from the touch, but he knew that she was barricaded against it, that it did not truly reach her, that somehow she had managed to endure this ritual kiss here before witnesses, only because she knew it would have been scandalous if she did not. The desolation in her eyes was agony to him, but she smiled and murmured, "Your words were lovely, Andrew. Are they Terran?"

He nodded, but had no time to explain further, for they were swept into a round of hugs and congratulations like that which had encompassed Damon and Ellemir. Then they were all kneeling for *Dom* Esteban's blessing, and for Leonie's.

It was quickly apparent, as the festivities began, that the real purpose of this celebration was for the nearby neighbors to meet and judge *Dom* Esteban's sons-in-law. Damon, of course, was known by name and reputation to all of them: a Ridenow of Serrais, an officer in the Guards. Andrew, however, was pleasantly surprised at how he was welcomed and accepted, how little attention he attracted. He suspected—and later knew he was right—that in general whatever a Comyn lord did was assumed to be beyond question.

There was a lot of drinking, and he was quickly drawn into the dancing. Everyone joined in this, even the staid Leonie taking the arm of Lord Serrais for a measure.

There were some boisterous games. Andrew was dragged into one which involved a lot of kissing, under confusing rules. In a quiet moment on the edge of the game, he voiced some of his confusion to Ellemir. Her face was flushed; he suspected that she had been drinking quite a lot of the sweet, heavy wine. She giggled. "Oh, it's a compliment to Callista, that these girls should show that they find her husband desirable. And besides, they see no one from Midwinter to Midsummer but their own brothers and kinsmen; you're a new face and exciting to them."

That seemed reasonable enough, but still, when it came to playing kissing games with drunken girl children, many of whom were hardly into their teens, he suspected he was simply too old for this kind of party. He had never cared much for drinking anyhow, even among his own compatriots where he knew all the jokes. He looked longingly at Callista, but one of the unwritten rules seemed to be that a husband was not to dance with his own wife. Every time he came near her, others rushed between them and kept them apart.

It finally grew so obvious that he hunted up Damon to ask about it. Damon chuckled and said, "I had forgotten that you are a stranger to the Kilghard Hills, brother. You don't want to cheat them of their fun, do you? It's a game at weddings, to keep husband and wife apart so they cannot slip away and consummate their marriage in private, before being put to bed together. Then everybody can have the fun of making the kind of jokes that are traditional here at weddings." He chuckled, and Andrew wondered suddenly what he was in for!

Damon followed his thoughts accurately and said, "If the marriages had been held in Thendara—they are more sophisticated there, and more civilized. But here they keep country customs and I'm afraid they're very near to nature. I don't mind all that much, myself, but then, I was fostered here. At my age I'll take a little extra teasing—most men marry when they're about Domenic's age. And Ellemir was brought up in the hill-country, too, and she's teased the bride at so many weddings, I suppose she'll enjoy the fun as much as any of them. But I wish I could spare Callista this. She's been . . . sheltered. And a Keeper giving up her place is fair game for dirty jokes; I'm afraid they'll think up something really tough for her."

Andrew looked at Ellemir, laughing and blushing in a crowd of girls. Callista was similarly surrounded, but she looked withdrawn and miserable. Andrew noticed, however, with relief that while many of the women were giggling, blushing, and shrieking with laughter, a substantial number of them—mostly the youngest ones—were like Callista, red-faced and shy.

"Drink up!" Domenic thrust a glass into Andrew's hands. "You can't be sober at a wedding, it's disrespectful. Anyhow, if you didn't get drunk, you might be too eager and mishandle your bride, eh, Damon?" He added some kind of joke about moonlight which Andrew failed to understand, but it made Damon snort with shamed laughter.

"I see you are consulting Andrew for advice about later tonight. Tell me, Andrew, do your people have a machine for that too? No?" He pantomimed exaggerated relief. "That's something! I was afraid we'd have to arrange a special demonstration."

Dezi was staring at Damon with concentrated attention. Was the youngster drunk already? Dezi said, "I am glad you declared your intention of legitimating your sons, or are you? At your age, do you mean to tell me you have no sons, Damon?"

Damon said with a good-natured smile, a wedding being no time to take offense at intrusive questions, "I am neither monk nor *ombredin*, Dezi, so I suppose it is not impossible, but if I have, their mothers have neglected to inform me of their existence. But I would have welcomed a son, bastard or no." Abruptly his mind touched Dezi's; drunkenly, the boy had failed to barricade himself, and in the flood of bitterness Damon understood the one relevant thing, realizing for the first time what lay at the core of Dezi's bitterness.

The boy believed himself to be *Dom* Esteban's son, and never acknowledged. But would Esteban have done that to any son of his, however begotten? Damon wondered. He recalled that Dezi had *laran*.

Later, when he mentioned this to Domenic the other

said, "I don't believe it. My father is a just man. He acknowledged his *nedestro* sons by Larissa d'Asturien, and has settled property on them. He has been as kind to Dezi as to any kinsman, but if Dezi had been his son, he would surely have said so."

"He sent him to Arilinn," Damon argued, "and you know that no one except those of the pure Comyn blood may come there. It is not so at the other Towers, but Arilinn—"

Domenic hesitated. "I will not discuss my father's doings behind his back," he said at last, firmly. "Come and ask him."

"Is this the time for such a question?"

"A wedding is the time for settling questions of legitimacy," Domenic said firmly, and Damon followed him, thinking that this was very like Domenic, to have such a question settled as soon as it was raised.

Dom Esteban was sitting on the sidelines, talking to a painfully polite young couple who slipped away to dance as his son approached. Domenic asked it bluntly:

"Father, is Dezi our brother or not?"

Esteban Lanart looked down at the wolfskin covering his knees. He said, "It might well be so, my boy."

Domenic demanded fiercely, "Why, then, is he not acknowledged?"

"Domenic, you don't understand these things, lad. His mother—"

"A common whore?" Domenic demanded in dismay and disgust.

"What do you take me for? No, of course not. She was one of my kinswomen. But she . . ." Oddly, the rough old man colored in embarrassment. He said at last, "Well, the poor lass is dead now and cannot be shamed further. It was Midwinter festival, and we were all drunk, and she lay that night with me—and not with me alone, but with four or five of my cousins. So when she proved to be with child, none of us was willing to acknowledge the boy. I've done what I could for him, and it's obvious to look at him that he has Comyn blood, but he could have been mine, or Gabriel's, or Gwynn's—"

Domenic's face was red, but he persisted. "Still, a Comyn son should have been acknowledged."

Esteban looked uncomfortable. "Gwynn always said he meant to, but he died before he got around to it. I have hesitated to tell Dezi that story, because I think it would hurt his pride worse than simple bastardy. I do not think he has been ill-used," he said, defending himself. "I have had him here to live, I sent him to Arilinn. He has had everything of a *nedestro* heir save formal acknowledgment."

Damon thought that over as he went back to the dancing. No wonder Dezi was touchy, troubled; he obviously sensed some disgrace which bastardy alone would not have given. It was disgraceful for a girl of good family to be promiscuous that way. He knew Ellemir had had lovers, but she had chosen them discreetly and one, at least, had been her sister's husband, which was long-established custom. There had been no scandal. Nor had she risked bearing a child no man would acknowledge.

When Damon and Domenic had left him, Andrew went moodily to get another drink. He thought, with a certain grimness, that considering what lay ahead of him this night, he might do well to get himself as drunk as possible. Between the country customs Damon thought so much of a joke, and the knowledge that he and Callista could not consummate their marriage yet, it was going to be one hell of a wedding night.

On second thought he would have to walk a narrow line, drunk enough to blur his awareness of embarrassment, but sober enough to keep in mind his pledge to Callista, never to put the slightest pressure on her, or try to hurry her. He wanted her—he had never wanted any woman in his life as much as he wanted her—but he wanted her willingly, sharing his own desire. He knew perfectly well that he wouldn't get the slightest pleasure out of anything remotely approaching rape; and in her present state, it couldn't be anything but.

"If you do not get drunk, you might be overeager and mishandle your bride." Damn Domenic and his jokes! Fortunately none of them except Damon, who understood the problem, knew what he was going through.

If they did know, they'd probably think it was funny! Andrew considered. Just one more dirty joke for a wedding!

Abruptly he felt distress, dismay . . . Callista! Callista in trouble somewhere! He hurried in her direction, letting his own telepathic sensitivity guide him.

He found her at one end of the hall, pinned against the wall by Dezi, who had one arm at either side of her so she could not dodge away and escape. He was leaning forward as if to kiss her. She twisted to one side and then the other, trying to avoid his lips, imploring him. "Don't, Dezi, I do not want to defend myself against a kinsman—"

"We are not now in the Tower, *domna*. Come now, one real kiss. . . ."

Andrew grabbed the boy by one shoulder and plucked him away, lifting him clear of the floor.

"Damn it, leave her alone!"

Dezi looked sullen. "It was but a jest between kinfolk."

"A jest Callista seemed not to share," Andrew said. "Get lost! Or I'll—"

"You'll *what*?" Dezi sneered. "Challenge me to a duel?"

Andrew looked down at the slight youngster, flushed, angry, obviously drunk. Abruptly his anger melted away. There was something to be said, he thought, for the Terran custom of a legal age for drinking. "Challenge, hell," he said laughing, looking down at the angry boy. "I'll put you over my knee and spank you for the nasty little boy you are. Now go away and sober up and stop bothering the grown-ups!"

Dezi gave Andrew a look like murder, but he went, and Andrew realized that for the first time since the declaration he was alone with Callista.

"What the hell was that all about?"

She was as crimson as her light draperies, but she tried to make a joke of it. "Oh, he said that now I was Keeper no more, I was free at last to give way to the irresistible passion he is sure he must arouse in any female breast."

"I should have mopped up the floor with him," Andrew said.

She shook her head. "Oh, no, I think he's simply drunk a bit more than he can carry. And he is a kinsman, after all. It's not unlikely he's my father's son."

Andrew had, after all, half guessed this when he saw Domenic and Dezi side by side. "But would he so misuse a girl he believes to be his sister?"

"Half-sister," Callista answered, "and in the hills, half-brothers and half-sisters can lie together if they will, or even marry, though it is considered luckier for them to bear no children so close akin. And horseplay and dirty jokes are expected at a wedding, so what he did was only rude, not shocking. I am too sensitive, and after all he is very young."

She still looked shaken and distressed, and Andrew still thought he should have wiped the floor up with the boy; then, tardily, he wondered if he had been too hard on Dezi. Dezi wasn't the first kid or the last to drink more than he could handle and make himself obnoxious.

He said gently, looking at her tired, strained face, "This will be over soon, love."

"I know." She hesitated. "You do know . . . the custom . . . ?"

"Damon told me," he said wryly. "I gather they put us to bed together, with plenty of rough jokes."

She nodded, coloring. "It is supposed to encourage the begetting of children, and in this part of the world that is very important to a young family, as you can imagine. So we must simply . . . make the best of it." She glanced at him, crimson, and said, "I am sorry. I know this will make it worse—"

He shook his head. "Actually, I don't think so," he said, smiling. "If anything, that kind of thing would tend to put me off anyhow." He saw the flicker of guilt again in her face, and ached to comfort and reassure her.

"Look," he said gently, "think of it this way: let them have their fun, but we can do as we please, and that will be our secret, as it should be. In our own time. So we can sit back and ignore their nonsense."

She sighed and smiled at him. She said softly, "If you really think of it that way . . ."

"I do, love."

"I'm so glad," she said in a whisper. "Look, Ellemir is being pulled away by all the girls." She added quickly, at his look of dismay, "No, they're not hurting her, it's only the custom that a bride should struggle and fight a little. It comes from the days when girls were married off without consent, but it's only a joke now. See, Father's body-servants have taken my father away, and Leonie will withdraw too, so the young folk can make all the noise they like."

But Leonie was not withdrawing; she came and stood beside them, still and somber in her crimson draperies.

"Callista, child, do you want me to stay? Perhaps in my presence the jokes will be a little more restrained and seemly."

Andrew could sense how much Callista longed for this, but she smiled and touched Leonie's hand, the feather-touch customary among telepaths. "I thank you, kinswoman. But I . . . I must not start by cheating everyone of their fun. No bride ever died of embarrassment, and I am sure I shall not be the first." And Andrew, looking at her, bravely steeled to endure without complaint whatever obscene horseplay they had created for a Keeper who gave up her ritual virginity, remembered the gallant girl who had made brave little jokes, even when she was a prisoner, alone and terrified in the caves of Corresanti.

It is for this that I love her so, he told himself.

Leonie said, very gently, "As you will, then, darling. Take my blessing." She bowed gravely to them both and went away.

As if her withdrawal had loosed the floodgates, a tide of young men and girls came surging up to them in full flood.

"Callista, Ann'dra, you waste time here, the night is wearing away. Have you nothing better to do this night than talk?"

He saw Damon being pulled along by Dezi; Domenic grasped his own hand and he was drawn away from Callista, saw the flood of young girls surge up around her and conceal her from him. Someone shouted out, "We'll make sure she's ready for you, Ann'dra, so you needn't defile these holy robes of hers!"

"Come along, both of you," Domenic cried, in high good spirits. "These fellows would rather stay here drinking all night, I am sure, but now they must do their duty, a bride must not be kept waiting."

He and Damon were hauled up the stairs, shoved into the living room of the suite they had prepared this morning. "Don't get them mixed up now," the Guardsman Caradoc called out drunkenly. "When the brides are twins, how is a mere husband, and drunk at that, to know if he lies in the arms of the right woman?"

"What difference does it make?" asked a strange young man. "That is for them to settle among themselves, is it not? And when the lamp is out, one woman is like another. If they are confused between left hand and right, what difference does it make?"

"We must start with Damon. He has lost so much time that he must make haste to do his duty to his clan," Domenic said gaily. Damon was quickly stripped of his clothing and wrapped in a long robe. The bedroom door was opened with ceremony and Andrew could see Ellemir, thinly gowned in spider-silk, her copper hair unbound and streaming over her breasts. She was red-faced, giggling uncontrollably, but Andrew sensed that it was on the ragged edge of hysterical sobbing. It was enough, he thought. It was too much. Everyone should get out and leave them alone.

"Damon," Domenic said solemnly, "I have made you a gift."

Andrew saw with relief that Damon was just drunk enough to be good-natured. "That is kind of you, brother-in-law. What is your gift?"

"I have made you a calendar, marked with the days and the moons. If you do your duty this night, see, I have marked in crimson the date when your first son will be born!"

Damon was red with stifled laughter. Andrew could see that he would rather have thrown it at Domenic's head, but he accepted it, let them ceremoniously help him into bed at Ellemir's side. Domenic said something to Ellemir which made her duck down and smother her face in the sheets, then conducted the watchers to the door, with mock solemnity.

"And now, so that we may pass our night in peaceful drinking, undisturbed by whatever goes on beyond these doors, I have another gift for the happy couple. I shall set up a telepathic damper just inside your doors—"

Damon sat up in bed and flung a pillow at them, finally losing patience. "Enough is enough," he shouted. "Get the hell out of here and leave us in peace!"

As if that had been what they were waiting for—perhaps it was—the whole crowd of men and women began to withdraw quickly toward the doors. "Really," Domenic rebuked, drawing his face into reproving lines, "can you not contain your impatience a little longer, Damon? My poor little sister, at the mercy of such unseemly haste!" But he closed the door, and behind him Andrew heard Damon come to the door and bolt it. At least there was a limit to the jokes considered proper, and Damon and Ellemir were alone.

But now it was his turn. There was, he thought grimly, only one good thing about all this. By the time the drunken men were finished with their horseplay, he was going to be too tired—and too damn mad—for anything except sleep.

They thrust him into the room where Callista waited, surrounded by the young girls, friends of Ellemir, their own servants, young noblewomen from the surrounding countryside. They had taken away her somber crimson draperies, put her into a thin gown like Ellemir's, her hair unbraided, streaming over her bare shoulders. She looked quickly up at him, and somehow it seemed to Andrew for a moment that she looked much younger than Ellemir: young, lost, and vulnerable.

He sensed that she was fighting to keep back tears. Shyness and reluctance were part of the game, but if she really broke down and cried, he knew, they would be ashamed and resentful of her for spoiling their fun. They would despise her for her inability to join in the game.

Children could be cruel, he told himself, and so many of these girls were only children. Young as she looked, Callista was a woman. She was, perhaps, never a child; she had her childhood stolen by the Tower. . . . He steeled himself against whatever was coming, knowing that however rough it was for him, it was worse for Callista.

How soon can I get them out of here, he wondered,

before she breaks down and cries, and hates herself for it? Why should she have to endure this nonsense?

Domenic took him firmly by the shoulders and turned him around, facing away from Callista.

"Pay attention," he admonished. "We have not finished with you yet, and the women have not yet made Callista ready for you. Can you not wait a few minutes?" And Andrew let Domenic do as he would, preparing to give courteous attention to the jokes he did not understand. But he thought longingly of the time when he and Callista would be alone.

Or would that be worse? Well, whether or not there was this to get through, somehow, first. He let Domenic and the men lead him into the adjoining room.

CHAPTER SIX

There were times when it seemed to Andrew that Damon's contentment was a visible thing, something which could be seen and measured. At such times, as the days lengthened and winter came on in the Kilghard Hills, Andrew could not help feeling a bitter envy. Not that he grudged Damon a moment of his happiness; it was only that he longed to share it.

Ellemir too looked radiant. It made him cringe, sometimes, to think that the servants at Armida, strangers, *Dom* Esteban himself, noticed this difference and blamed him, that forty days after their marriage Ellemir looked so joyous, while day by day Callista seemed to grow more pale and grave, more constrained and sorrowful.

It was not that Andrew was unhappy. Frustrated, yes, for it was sometimes nerve-racking to be so close to Callista—to endure the good-natured jokes and raillery which were the lot, he supposed, of every newly married man in the galaxy—and to be separated from her by an invisible line he could not cross.

And yet, if they had come to know one another by any ordinary route, there would have been a long time of waiting. He reminded himself that they had married when he had known her less than forty days. And this way he could be with her a great deal, coming to know the outward girl, Callista, as well as he had come to know her inwardly, in mind and spirit, when she had been in the hands of the catmen, imprisoned in darkness within the caves of Corresanti. Then, when for some strange reason she could reach no other mind on Darkover save Andrew Carr's, their minds had touched, so deeply that years of living together could have created no closer bond. Before he had ever laid eyes on her in the flesh he had loved her, loved her for her courage in the face of terror, for what they had endured together.

Now he came to love her for outward things as well: for her grace, her sweet voice, her airy charm and quick wit. She could make jokes even about their present frustrating separation, which was more than Andrew could do! He loved too the gentleness with which she treated everyone, from her father, who was crippled and often peevish, to the youngest and clumsiest of the household servants.

One thing for which he had not been prepared was her inarticulateness. For all her quick wit and easy repartee, she found it difficult to speak of things which were important to her. He had hoped they could talk freely together about the difficulties which faced them, about the nature of her training in the Tower, the way in which she had been taught never to respond with the slightest sexual awareness. But on this subject she was silent, and on the few occasions Andrew tried to get her to speak of it she would turn her face away, stammer and grow silent, her eyes filling with tears.

He wondered if the memory was so painful, and would be filled again with indignation at the barbarous way in which a young woman's life had been deformed. He hoped, eventually, she would feel free enough to talk about it; he could not think of anything else that might help free her from the constraint. But for the present, unwilling to force her into anything, even to speaking against her will, he waited.

As she had foreseen, it was not easy to be so close to her, and yet distant. Sleeping in the same room, though they did not share a bed, seeing her sleepy and flushed and beautiful in the morning, in her bed, seeing her half-dressed, her hair about her shoulders—and yet not daring more than the most casual touch. His frustration took strange forms. Once, when she was in her bath, feeling foolish but unable to resist, he had picked up her nightgown and pressed it passionately to his lips, breathing in the fragrance of her body and the delicate scent she used. He felt dizzy and ashamed, as if he had committed some unspeakable perversion. When she returned, he could not face her, knowing that they were open to one another and that she knew what he had done. He had avoided her eyes and gone quickly away, unwilling to face the imagined contempt—or pity—in her face.

He wondered if she would have preferred him to sleep elsewhere, but when he asked her, she said shyly, "No, I like to have you near me." It occurred to him that perhaps this intimacy, sexless as it was, was a necessary first step in her reawakening.

Forty days after the marriage the high winds and snow flurries gave way to heavy snows, and Andrew's time was taken up, day after day, in arranging for the wintering of the horses and other livestock, storing accessible fodder in sheltered areas, inspecting and stocking the herdmen's shelters in the upland valleys. For days at a time he would be out, spending days in the saddle and nights in outdoor shelters or in the far-flung farmsteads which were part of the great estate.

During this time he realized how wise *Dom* Esteban had been to insist on the wedding feast. At the time, knowing the wedding would have been legal with one or two witnesses, he had been angry with his father-in-law for not letting it take place in privacy. But that night of horseplay and rough jokes had made him one of the countryfolk, not a stranger from nowhere, but *Dom* Esteban's son-in-law, a man whom they had seen married. It had saved him years of trying to make a place for himself among them.

He woke one morning to hear the hard rattle of snow against the window, and knew the first storm of the oncoming winter had set in. There would be no riding out today. He lay listening to the wind moaning around the heights of the old house, mentally reviewing the disposition of the stock under his care. Those brood mares in the pasture under the twin peaks—there was fodder enough stored in windbreak shelters, and one stream, the old horse-master had told him, which never completely froze over—they would do well enough. He should have separated out the young stallions from the herd—there might be fighting—but it was too late now.

There was gray light outside the window, through a white blur of snow. There would be no sunrise today. Callista lay quiet in her narrow bed across the room, her back to him so that he could see only the braids on her pillow. She and Ellemir were so different, Ellemir always awake and astir at dawn, Callista never waking until the sun was high. He should soon be hearing Ellemir moving in the other half of the suite, but it was early even for that.

Callista cried out in her sleep, a cry of terror and dread, again some evil nightmare of the time when she had lain prisoner of the catmen? With a single stride Andrew was beside her, but she sat up, abruptly wide awake, staring past him, her face blank with dismay.

"Ellemir!" she cried, catching her breath. "I must go to her!" And without a word or a look at Andrew she slid from her bed, catching up a chamber robe, and ran out into the center part of the suite.

Andrew watched, dismayed, thinking of the bond of twins. He had been vaguely aware of the telepathic link between Ellemir and her sister, yet even twins respected one another's privacy. If Ellemir's distress signal had reached Callista's mind it must have been powerful indeed. Troubled, he began to dress. He was lacing his second boot when he heard Damon in the sitting room of their suite. He went out to him, and Damon's smiling face dispelled his fears.

"You must have worried, when Callista ran out of here so quickly, I think Ellemir was frightened too, for a moment, more surprised than anything else. Many women escape this altogether, and Ellemir is so healthy, but I suppose no man can tell much about such things."

"Then she's not seriously ill?"

"If she is, it will cure itself in time," Damon said, laughing, then sobered quickly. "Of course, just now she's miserable, poor girl, but Ferrika says this stage will pass in a tenday or two, so I left her to Ferrika's ministrations and Callista's comforting. There's little any man can do for her now."

Andrew, knowing that Ferrika was the estate midwife, knew at once what Ellemir's indisposition must be. "Is it customary and proper to offer congratulations?"

"Perfectly proper." Damon's smile was luminous. "But somewhat more customary to offer them to Ellemir. Shall we go down and tell *Dom* Esteban he's to expect a grandchild some time after Midsummer?"

Esteban Lanart was delighted at the news. Dezi commented, with a malicious grin, "I see you are all too anxious to produce your first son on schedule. Did you really feel so much obliged by the calendar Domenic made for you, kinsman?"

For a moment Andrew thought Damon would hurl his cup at Dezi, but he controlled himself. "No, I had rather hoped Ellemir could have a year or two free of such cares. It is not as if I were heir to a Domain and had urgent need of a son. But she wanted a child at once, and it was hers to choose."

"That is like Elli, indeed," Dezi said, dropping the malice and smiling. "Every baby born on this estate, she has it in her arms before it is a tenday old. I'll go and congratulate her when she is feeling better."

Dom Esteban asked, as Callista came into the room, "How is she, then, Callista?"

"She is sleeping," Callista said. "Ferrika advised her to lie abed as long as she could in the mornings, while she still feels ill, but she will be down after midday."

She slipped into her seat beside Andrew, but she avoided his eyes, and he wondered if this had saddened her, to see Ellemir already pregnant? For the first time it occurred to him that perhaps Callista wanted a child; he supposed some women did, though he himself had never thought very much about it.

For more than a tenday the storm raged, snow falling heavily, then giving way to clear skies and raging winds that whipped the snow into deep, impenetrable drifts, then changing to snowfall again. The work of the estate came to a dead halt. Using undergrown tunnels, a few of the indoor servants cared for the saddle horses and dairy animals, but there was little else that could be done.

Armida seemed quiet without Ellemir bustling about early in the mornings. Damon, idled by the storm, spent much of his time at her side. It troubled Damon to see the ebullient Ellemir lying pale and strengthless, far into the mornings, unwilling to touch food. He was worried about her, but Ferrika laughed at his dismay, saying that every young husband felt like this when his wife was first pregnant. Ferrika was the estate midwife at Armida, responsible for every child born in the surrounding villages. It was a tremendous responsibility indeed, and one for which she was quite young; she had only succeeded her mother in this office in the last year. She was a calm, firm, round-bodied woman, small and fair-haired, and because she knew she was young for this post, she wore her hair severely concealed in a cap and dressed in plain sober clothing, trying to look older than she was.

The household stumbled without Ellemir's efficient hands at the helm, though Callista did her best. *Dom* Esteban complained that, though they had a dozen kitchen-women, the bread was never fit to eat. Damon suspected that he simply missed Ellemir's cheerful company. He was sullen and peevish, and made Dezi's life a burden. Callista devoted herself to her father, bringing her harp and singing him ballads and songs, playing cards and games with him, sitting for hours beside him, her needlework in her lap, listening patiently to his endless long tales of past campaigns and battles from the years when he had commanded the Guardsmen.

One morning Damon came downstairs late to find the hall filled with men, mostly those who worked, in better weather, in the outlying fields and pastures. *Dom* Esteban in his chair was at the center of the men, talking to three who were still snow-covered, wearing bulky outdoor clothing. Their boots had been cut off, and Ferrika was kneeling before them, examining their feet and hands. Her round, pleasant young face looked deeply troubled; there was relief in her voice as she looked up to see Damon approaching.

"Lord Damon, you were hospital officer in the Guards at Thendara, come and look at this!"

Troubled by her tone, Damon bent to look at the man whose feet she held, then exclaimed in consternation, "Man, what happened to you?"

The man before him, tall, unkempt, with long wiry hair in still-frozen elf-locks around his reddened, torn cheeks, said in the thick mountain dialect, "We were weathered in nine days, *Dom*, in the snow-shelter under the north ridge. But the wind tore down one wall and we couldna' dry our clothes and boots. Starving we were

with food for no more than three days, so when the
weather first broke we thought best to try and win
through here, or to the villages. But there was a snow-
slide along the hill under the peak, and we spent three
nights out on the ledges. Old Reino died o' the cold and
we had to bury him in the snow, against thaw, with
n'more than a cairn o' stones. Darrill had to carry me
here—" He gestured stoically at the white, frozen feet
in Ferrika's hands. "I can't walk, but I'm not so bad off
as Raimon or Piedro here."

Damon shook his head in dismay. "I'll do what I can
for you, lad, but I can't promise anything. Are they all
as bad as this, Ferrika?"

The woman shook her head. "Some are hardly hurt
at all. And some, as you can see, are worse." She gestured at one man whose cut-off boots revealed black,
pulpy shreds of flesh hanging down.

There were fourteen men in all. Quickly, one after
another, Damon examined the hurt men, hurriedly sorting out the least injured, those who showed only minor
frostbite in toes, fingers, cheeks. Andrew was helping the
stewards bring them hot drinks and hot soup. Damon
ordered, "Don't give them any wine or strong liquor
until I know for certain what shape they are in." Separating the less hurt men, he said to old Rhodri, the hall-
steward, "Take these men to the lower hall, and get
some of the women to help you. Wash their feet well
with plenty of hot water and soap, and"—he turned to
Ferrika—"you have extract of white thornleaf?"

"There is some in the still-room, Lord Damon; I will
ask Lady Callista."

"Soak their feet with poultices of that, then bandage
them and put plenty of salve on them. Keep them warm,
and give them as much hot soup and tea as they want,
but no strong drink of any kind."

Andrew interrupted. "And as soon as any of our people can get through, we must send word to their women
that they are safe."

Damon nodded, realizing that this was the first thing
he should have remembered. "See to it, will you,
brother? I must care for the hurt men." As Rhodri and
the other servants helped the less injured men to the

lower hall, he turned back to the remaining men, those
with seriously frozen feet and hands.

"What have you done for these, Ferrika?"

"Nothing yet, Lord Damon; I waited for your advice.
I have seen nothing like this for years."

Damon nodded, his face set. A hard freeze such as
this, when he was a child near Corresanti, had left half
the men in the town with missing fingers and toes,
dropped off after severe freezing. Others had died of
the raging infections or gangrene which followed. "What
would you choose to do?"

Ferrika said hesitantly, "It is not the usual treatment
here, but I would soak their feet in water just a little
warmer than blood-heat but not hot. I have already forbidden the men to rub their feet, for fear of rubbing off
the skin. The frost is deep in the flesh. They will be
fortunate if they lose no more than skin." A little encouraged that Damon did not protest, she added, "I
would put hot packs about their bodies to encourage
circulation."

Damon nodded. "Where did you learn this, Ferrika?
I feared I would have to forbid you to use old folk remedies which do more harm than good. This is the treatment used at Nevarsin, and I had to struggle to have it
used in Thendara, for the Guards."

She said, "I was trained in the Amazon Guild-house
in Arilinn, Lord Damon; they train midwives there for
all the Domains, and they know a good deal about healing and caring for wounds."

Dom Esteban frowned. He said, "Women's rubbish!
When I was a lad, we were told never to bring heat near
a frozen limb, but to rub it with snow."

"Aye," broke in the man whose feet were pulpy and
swollen, "I had Narron rub *my* feet wi' snow. When
my grandsire froze his feet in the reign of old Marius
Hastur—"

"I know your grandfather," Damon interrupted. "He
walked with two canes till the end of his life, and it
looks to me as if your friend tried to make sure you had
the same good fortune, lad. Trust me, and I will do better for you than that." He turned to Ferrika and said,
"Try poultices, not hot water alone, but black thornleaf,

very strong; it will draw the blood to the limbs and back to the heart. And give them some of it in tea too, to stimulate the circulation." He turned back to the injured man, saying encouragingly, "This treatment is used in Nevarsin, where the weather is worse than here, and the monks claim they have saved men who would otherwise have been lamed for life."

"Can't *you* help, Lord Damon?" begged the man Raimon, and Damon, looking at the grayish-blue feet, shook his head. "I don't know, truly, lad. I will do as much as I can, but this is the worst I have seen. It's regrettable, but—"

"Regrettable!" The man's eyes blazed with pain and fury. "Is that all you can say about it, *vai dom*? Is that all it means to you? Do you know what it means to us, especially this year? There's not a house in Adereis or Corresanti but lost a man or maybe two or three to the accursed catfolk, and last year's harvest withered ungathered in the fields, so already there is hunger in these hills! And now more than a dozen ablebodied men to be laid up, certainly for months, maybe never to walk again, and you can't say more than 'It is regrettable.'" His thick dialect angrily mimicked Damon's careful speech.

"It's all very well for the likes of you, *vai dom*, you willna' go hungry, what may happen or no! But what of my wife, and my little children? What of my brother's wife and *her* babes, that I took in when my brother ran mad and slew himself in the Darkening-lands, and the cat-hags made play wi' his soul? What of my old mother, and her brother who lost an eye and a leg on the field of Corresanti? All too few ablebodied men in the villages, so that even the little maids and the old wives work in the fields, all too few to handle crops and beasts or even to glean the nut-trees before the snow buries our food, and now a good half of the ablebodied men of two villages lying here with frozen feet and hands, maybe lame for life—regrettable!"

His voice struggled with his rage and pain, and Damon closed his eyes in dismay. It was all too easy to forget. Did war not end, then, when there was peace in the land? He could kill ordinary foes, or lead armed men against them, but against the greater foes—hunger, disease, bad weather, loss of ablebodied men—he was powerless.

"The weather is not mine to command, my friend. What would you have me do?"

"There was a time—so my grandsire told me—when the folk of the Comyn, the Tower-folk, sorceresses and warlocks, could use their starstones to heal wounds. Eduin"—he gestured to the Guardsman at *Dom* Esteban's side—"saw you heal Caradoc so he didna' bleed to death when his leg was cut to the bone by a catman sword. Can't you do something for us too, *vai dom*?"

Without conscious thought, Damon's fingers closed over the small leather bag strung round his neck which held the matrix crystal he had been given at Arilinn, as a novice psi technician. Yes, he could do some of those things. But since he had been sent from the Tower—he felt his throat close in fear and revulsion. It was hard, dangerous, frightening, even to think of doing these things outside of the Tower, unprotected by the electromagnetic Veil which protected the matrix technicians from intruding thoughts and dangers. . . .

Yet the alternative was death or crippling for these men, indescribable suffering, at the very least, hunger and famine in the villages.

He said, and knew his voice was trembling, "It has been so long, I do not know if I can still do anything. Uncle . . . ?"

Dom Esteban shook his head. "Such skills I never had, Damon. My little time there was spent working relays and communications. I had thought most of those healing skills were lost in the Ages of Chaos."

Damon shook his head. "No, some of them were taught at Arilinn even when I was there. But I can do nothing much alone."

Raimon said, 'The *domna* Callista, she was a *leronis*. . . ."

That was true too. He said, trying to control his voice, "I will see what we can do. For now, the important thing is to see how much of the circulation can be restored naturally. Ferrika," he said to the young woman who had come back, carrying vials and flasks of herb salves and extracts, "I will leave you to care for these men, for now. Is Lady Callista still upstairs with my wife?"

"She is in the still-room, *vai dom*, she helped me to find these things."

It was in a small back passage near the kitchens, a narrow, stone-floored room, lined with shelves. Callista, a faded blue cloth tied over her hair, was sorting bunches of dried herbs. Others hung from the rafters or were stuffed into bottles and jars. Damon wrinkled his nose at the pungent herb-smell of the place, as Callista turned to him.

"Ferrika tells me you have some bad cases of frostbite and freezing. Shall I come help put hot-packs about them?"

"You can do better than that," Damon said, and laid his hand, with that involuntary gesture, over his insulated matrix. "I am going to have to do some cell-regeneration with the worst ones, or Ferrika and I will end by having to cut off a dozen fingers and toes, or worse. But I can't do it alone; you must monitor for me."

"To be sure," she said quickly, and her hands went automatically to the matrix at her throat. She was already replacing the jars on the shelf. Then she turned— and stopped, her eyes wide with panic.

"Damon, I cannot!" She stood in the doorway, tense, a part of her already poised for action, a part stricken, drooping, remembering the real situation.

"I have given back my oath! I am forbidden!"

He looked at her in blank dismay. He could have understood it if Ellemir, who had never lived in a Tower and knew little more than a commoner, had spoken this old superstition. But Callista, who had been a Keeper?

"Breda," he said gently, with the feather-light touch on her sleeve that the Arilinn people used among themselves, "it is not a Keeper's work I ask of you. I know you can never again enter the great relays and energon rings—that is for those who live apart, guarding their powers in seclusion. I ask only simple monitoring, such work as any woman might do who does not live by the laws of a Keeper. I would ask it of Ellemir, but she is pregnant and it would not be wise.

Surely you know you have not lost that skill; you will never lose it."

She shook her head stubbornly. "I cannot, Damon. You know that everything of this sort which I do will reinforce old habits, old . . . old patterns which I must break." She stood unmoving, beautitful, proud, angry, and Damon inwardly cursed the superstitious taboos she had been taught. How could she believe this nonsense? He said angrily, "Do you realize what is at stake here, Callista? Do you realize the kind of suffering to which you condemn these men?"

"I am not the only telepath at Armida!" she flung at him. "I have given years of my life to this, now it is enough! I thought you, of all men living, would understand that!"

"Understand!" Damon felt rage and frustration surge up inside him. "I understand that you are being selfish! Are you going to spend the rest of your life counting holes in linen towels and making spices for herb-breads? You, who were Callista of Arilinn?"

"Don't!" She flinched as if he had struck her. Her face was drawn with pain. "What are you trying to do to me, Damon? My choice has been made, and there is no way to go back, even if I would! For better or worse, I have made my choice! Do you think—" Her voice broke, and she turned away so that he would not see her weeping. "Do you think I have not asked myself—asked myself again and again—what it is that I have done?" She dropped her face into her hands with a despairing moan. She couldn't speak, she couldn't even raise her head, her whole body convulsing with the terrible grief he could feel, tearing her apart. Damon felt it, the agony which was threatening to overwhelm her, which she kept at bay only with desperate effort.

You and Ellemir have your happiness, already she is bearing your child. And Andrew and I, Andrew and I . . . I have never been able even to kiss him, never lain in his arms, never known his love. . . .

Damon turned, blindly, and went out of the still-room, hearing the sobs break out behind him. Distance made no difference; her grief was *there*, with him, *inside* him. He was wrung and wrenched by it, fighting to get his barriers together, to cut off that desperate awareness of her anguish. Damon was a Ridenow, an empath, and Callista's emotions struck so deep that for a time, blinded by her pain, he stumbled along the hall, not knowing where he was or where he was going.

Blessed Cassilda, he thought, *I knew Callista was unhappy, but I had no idea it was like this . . . The taboos surrounding a Keeper are so strong, and she has been reared on tales of the penalties for a Keeper who breaks her vow. . . . I cannot, I cannot ask anything of her which would prolong her suffering by a single day. . . .*

After a time he managed to cut off the contact, to withdraw into himself a little—or had Callista managed to rebuild her taut control?—and to hope against hope that her anguish had not reached Ellemir. Then he began to think what alternatives he had. Andrew? The Terran was untrained, but he was a powerful telepath. And Dezi—even if he had been sent from Arilinn after only a season or so, he would know the basic techniques.

Ellemir had come downstairs and was helping Dezi with the work of washing and bandaging the feet of the less seriously hurt men in the lower hall. The men were groaning and crying out in pain as the circulation was restored in their frostbitten limbs as but, although their sufferings were dreadful, Damon knew they were far less seriously injured than the other men.

One of the men looked up at him, his face contorted with pain, and begged, "Can't we even have a drink, Lord Damon? It might not help the feet any, but it sure would dull the pain!"

"I'm sorry," Damon said regretfully. "You can have all the soup or hot food you want, but no wine or strong drink; it plays hell with the circulation. In a little while, Ferrika will bring you something to ease the pain and help you sleep." But it would take more than this to help the other men, the ones whose feet were seriously frozen.

He said, "I must go back and see to your comrades, the ones who are worst hurt. Dezi—"

The red-haired boy looked up, and Damon said, "When these men are taken care of, come and talk to me, will you?"

Dezi nodded, and bent over the man whose feet he was smearing with strong-smelling salve and bandaging. Damon noticed that his hands were deft and that he worked quickly and with skill. Damon stopped beside Ellemir, who was winding a length of bandage around frozen fingers, and said, "Be careful not to work too hard, my darling."

Her smile was quick and cheery. "Oh, it is only early in the morning that I am ill. Later in the day, like this, I have never felt better! Damon, can you do anything for those poor fellows in there? Darrill and Piedro and Raimon played with Callista and me when we were little girls, and Raimon is Domenic's foster-brother."

"I did not know that," Damon said, shaken. "I will do all I can for them, love."

He came back to where Ferrika was working with the worst of the hurt men, and joined her in the preliminary bandaging and soaking, giving them strong drugs to ease or blunt the worst of the pain. But this, he knew, was only a beginning. Without more help than Ferrika and her herb-medicines could give, they would die or be crippled for life. At the very best they would lose toes, fingers, lie helpless and lamed for months.

Callista had recovered her cool self-possession now, and was working with Ferrika, helping to put hot-packs about the injured men. Restoring the circulation was the only way to save any of their feet, and if feeling could be restored in any part of their limbs, it was a victory. Damon watched her with a remote sadness, not really blaming her. He found it hard to overcome his own disquiet at the need for returning to matrix work.

Leonie had told him that be was too sensitive, too vulnerable, that if he went on, it would destroy him.

She also said that if he had been a woman, he would have made a good Keeper.

He told himself firmly that he hadn't believed it then and that he refused to believe it now. Any good matrix mechanic could handle a Keeper's work, he reminded himself. He felt a chill of dread at doing this work outside the safe confines of a Tower.

But here was where it was needed, and here was where it must be done. Perhaps there was more need

for matrix mechanics outside a Tower than within. . . .
Damon realized where his random thoughts were taking him, and shuddered at the blasphemy. The
Towers—Arilinn, Hali, Neskaya, Dalereuth, the others
scattered about the Domains—were the way in which
the ancient matrix sciences of Darkover had been
made safe after the terrible abuses of the Ages of
Chaos. Under the safe supervision of the Keepers—
oath-bound, secluded, virgin, passionless, excluded
from the political and personal stresses of the Comyn—
every matrix worker was trained carefully and tested
for trustworthiness, every matrix monitored and
guarded against misuse.

And when a matrix was used illegally, outside a Tower
and without their leave, then such things happened as
when the Great Cat cast darkness through the Kilghard
Hills, madness, destruction, death. . . .

He let his fingers stray to his own matrix. He had used
it, outside a Tower, to destroy the Great Cat and cleanse
the Hills of their terror. *That* had not been misuse. And
this healing he was about to do, *this* was not misuse; it
was legitimate, sanctioned. He was a trained matrix
worker, yet he felt queasy and ill at ease.

At last all the men, slightly or seriously hurt, had been
salved, bandaged, fed, and put to bed in the back halls.
The worst ones had been dosed with Ferrika's pain-
killing potions, and Ferrika, with some of her women,
stayed to watch over them. But Damon knew that while
many of the men would recover, with no more treatment
than good nursing and healing oils, there were a few
who would not.

A noonday hush had settled over Armida. Ferrika
watched over the hurt men; Ellemir came to play cards
with her father, and at *Dom* Esteban's request, Callista
brought her harp, laid it across her lap and began tuning
the strings. Damon, watching her closely, saw that while
she seemed calm, her eyes were still red, and her fingers
less steady than usual as she struck the first few chords.

What sound was that upon the moor?
    Hear, O hear!
What sound was that in the darkness here?

It was the wind that rattled the door,
    Child, do not fear.

Was that the noise of a horseman's hoof,
    Hear, O hear!
Was it the sound of a rider near?
It was but branches, astrike on the roof,
    Child, do not fear!

Was that a face at the window there?
    Hear, O hear!
A strange dark face . . .

Damon rose silently, beckoned to Dezi to follow him. As they withdrew into the corridor, he said, "Dezi, I know perfectly well that one never asks why someone left a Tower, but would you care to tell me, in complete confidence, why you left Arilinn?"

Dezi's face was sullen. "No, I wouldn't. Why should I?"

"Because I need your help. You saw the state those men were in, you know that with nothing more than hot water and herb-salves, there are at least four of them who will never walk again, and Raimon, at least, will die. So you know what I am going to have to do."

Dezi nodded, and Damon went on: "You know I will need someone to monitor for me. And if you were dismissed for imcompetence, you know I could not dare use you."

There was a long silence. Dezi stared at the slate-colored slabs of the floor, and inside the Great Hall they heard the sound of the harp, and Callista singing:

Why lies my father upon the ground?
    Hear, O hear!
Stricken to death with a foeman's spear . . .

"It was not incompetence," Dezi said at last. "I am not sure why they decided I must go." He sounded sincere, and Damon, enough of a telepath to know when he was being lied to, decided he probably was sincere. "I can only think that they didn't like me. Or perhaps"—he raised his eyes, with an angry steel glint in them—"they knew I was not even an acknowledged *nedestro*, not good enough for their precious Arilinn, where blood and lineage are everything."

Damon thought that no, the Towers didn't work that way. But he was not so sure. Arilinn was not the oldest of the Towers, but it was the proudest, claiming more than nine hundred generations of pure Comyn blood, claiming too that the first Keeper had been a daughter of Hastur's self. Damon didn't believe it, for there was too little history which had survived the Ages of Chaos.

"Oh, come, Dezi, if you could pass the Veil they would know you were Comyn, or of Comyn blood, and I don't think they would care that much." But he knew nothing he said could get past the boy's wounded vanity. And vanity was a dangerous flaw for a matrix mechanic.

The Tower circles depended so much on the character of the Keeper. Leonie was a proud woman. She was when Damon knew her, with all the arrogance of a Hastur, and she had grown no less so in the years between. Perhaps she was personally intolerant of Dezi's lack of proper pedigree. Or perhaps he was right, and they simply didn't like him. . . . In any case, it made no difference here. Damon had no choice. Andrew was a powerful telepath, but essentially untrained. Dezi, if he had lasted even half a year in a Tower, would have had meticulous training in the elemental mechanics of the art.

"Can you monitor?"

Dezi said, "Try me."

Damon shrugged. "Try, then."

In the hall, Callista's voice rose mournfully:

> What was that cry that rent the air?
>   Hear, O hear!
> What dreadful shriek of dark despair,
> A widow's curse and an orphan's prayer . . .

"Zandru's hells," *Dom* Esteban exploded, at the top of his voice, "why such a doleful song, Callista? Weeping and mourning, death and despair. We are not at a funeral! Sing something more cheerful, girl!"

There was a brief harsh sound, as if Callista's hands had struck a dissonance on the harp. She said, and her voice faltered, "I fear I am not much in the mood for singing, Father. I beg you to excuse me."

Damon felt the touch on his mind, swift and expert, so perfectly shielded that if Damon had not been watching Dezi, he would not have known by whom he had been touched. He felt the faint, deep probing, then Dezi said, "You have a crooked back tooth. Does it bother you?"

"Not since I was a boy," Damon said. "Deeper?"

Dezi's face went blank, with a glassy stare. After a moment he said, "Your ankle—the left ankle—was broken in two places when you were quite young. It must have taken a long time to heal; there are scars where bone fragments must have worked out for some time afterward. There is a fine crack in your third—no, the fourth—rib from the breastbone. You thought it was only a bruise and did not tell Ferrika when you returned from the wars with the catmen last season, but you were right, it was broken. There is a small scar—vertical, about four inches long—along your calf. It was made by a sharp instrument, but I do not know whether knife or sword. Last night you dreamed—"

Damon nodded, laughing. "Enough," he said, "you can monitor." How in the name of Aldones had they been willing to let Dezi go? This was a telepath of surpassing skill. With three years of Arilinn training, he would have matched the best in the Domains! Dezi picked up the thought and smiled, and again Damon had the moment of disquiet. Not lack of competence, or lack of confidence. Was it his vanity, then?

Or had it been only some personality clash, someone there who felt unable or unwilling to work with the youngster? The Tower circles were so intimate, a closer bond than lovers or kinfolk, that the slightest emotional dissonance could be exaggerated into torture. Damon knew that Dezi's personality could be abrasive—he was young, touchy, easily offended—so perhaps he had simply come at the wrong time, into a group already so intimate that they could not adapt to any outsider, and not enough in need of another worker that they would work hard enough at the necessary personal adjustments.

It might not have been Dezi's fault at all, Damon considered. Perhaps, if he did well at this, another Tower would take him. There was a crying need for strong natural telepaths, and Dezi was gifted, too gifted to waste. He saw the smile of pleasure, and knew Dezi had picked up the thought, but it didn't matter. A moment's reproving thought, that vanity was a dangerous flaw for a matrix technician, knowing that Dezi picked that up too, seemed enough.

"All right," he said, "we'll try. There's no time to lose. Do you think you can work with me and Andrew?"

Dezi said sulkily, "Andrew doesn't like me."

"You're too ready to think people don't like you," Damon reproved gently, thinking that it was bad enough for Dezi to know he chose him because Callista refused. But he could not betray Callista's grief. And Ellemir should not try to do this work, so early in pregnancy. Pregnancy was about the only thing which could seriously interrupt a matrix worker's capability, with its danger to the unborn child. And in the last day or two, linked with Ellemir, he had begun to pick up the first, faintest emanations of the developing brain, still formless, but *there*, real, enough to make their child a distinct separate presence to him.

He thought that there ought to be a way to compensate for this too, to protect a developing child. But he didn't know of any, and he wasn't going to experiment with his own! So it was himself, Andrew, and Dezi.

Andrew, a little while later, when Damon broached the subject, frowned and said, "I can't say I'm crazy about the idea of working with Dezi." But, at Damon's remonstrance, admitted it was hardly worthy of an adult, to hold a grudge against a boy in his teens, a youngster who had, admittedly, been drunk at the time of the offense.

"And Dezi's young for his age," Damon told Andrew. "If he'd been acknowledged *nedestro*, he would have been given responsibilities to equal his privileges, all along. A year or two in the cadets would have made all the difference, or a year of good, hard, monkish discipline at Nevarsin. It's our fault, not Dezi's, that he's turned out the way he has."

Andrew did not protest further, but he still felt disquiet. No matter whose fault it was, if Dezi had flaws of character, Andrew did not feel right about working with him.

But Damon must know what he was doing. Andrew watched Damon making his preparations, remembering when he had first been taught to use a matrix. Callista had been part of the linkage of minds then, though she was still prisoner in the caves, and he had never seen her with his physical eyes. And now she was Keeper no more, and his wife. . . .

Damon held his own matrix cradled between his hands, finally saying aloud, with an ironic smile, "I am always afraid to do this outside a Tower. I never lose the fear that it is not safe. An absurd fear, perhaps, but a real one."

Dezi said gently, "I am glad you are afraid too, Damon. I am glad to know it is not only me."

Damon said, in a shaking voice, "I think anyone who is not afraid to use this kind of force probably should not be trusted with it at all. The forces were so misused in the Ages of Chaos that Regis Hastur the Fourth decreed that from his day, no matrix circle should presume to use the great screens and relays outside the established Towers. That law was not made for such work as this, but there is still the sense of . . . of violating a taboo." He turned to Andrew and said, "How would they treat frostbite in *your* world?"

Andrew answered thoughtfully, "The best treatment is arterial injection of neural stimulators: acetylcholine or something similar. Possibly transfusion, but medicine isn't really my field."

Damon sighed and said, "I seem to have been thrust into such work more often than I intended. Well, let us get on with it." He let his mind sink deep into the matrix, reaching out for contact with Andrew. They had been linked before, and the old rapport quickly reestablished itself. For a moment there was a shadow-touch from Ellemir, only a hint, like the faint memory of a kiss, then she dropped gently out of the rapport at Damon's admonition: she must guard herself and their child. For an instant Callista too lingered, a fragmentary touch, in the old closeness, and Andrew clung to the contact. For so long she had not touched even his hand, and now they were linked together, close again—then, with a poignant sharpness, she broke the link, dropping away. Andrew felt empty and cold without the touch of her mind, and he sensed the wrenching aftertaste of grief. He was glad, for a moment, that Dezi was not yet in the rapport. Then Damon reached out and Andrew felt Dezi in the linkage, was momentarily aware of him, barriered, yet very much *there*, a cool firm strength, like a handclasp.

The threefold link persisted for a moment, Damon getting the feel of the two men with whom he must work so closely linked. With his eyes closed as always in a circle, he saw behind them the blue crystalline structure of the matrix gems which held them linked together, amplifying and sending out the individual, definite, electronic resonances of their brains, and beyond that, the purely subjective feel of them. Andrew was rocklike and strong, protective, so that Damon felt with a sigh of relief that his own lack of strength did not matter, Andrew had plenty for both of them. Dezi was a quick, darting precision, an awareness flicking here and there like reflections of light playing from a prism. Damon opened his eyes and saw them both; it was difficult to reconcile the actual physical presence with the mental *feel* within the matrix.

Dezi was so much—physically—the image of Coryn, his long-dead friend, his sworn brother. For the first time Damon let himself wonder how much of his love for Ellemir arose from that memory, the brother-friend he had loved so deeply when they were children, whose death had left him alone. Ellemir was like Coryn, and yet unlike, uniquely herself—He cut off the thought. He must not think of Ellemir in this strong link or he would be picking her up telepathically, and this strong rapport, this flow of energons, could overpower and deform their child's developing brain. Quickly, picking up the contact with Dezi and Andrew, he began to visualize—to create on the thought-level where they would work—a strong and impregnable wall around them, so that no other person within Armida could be affected by their thoughts.

When we work with the men, healing them, we will bring them one by one behind this wall, so that nothing will overflow to damage Ellemir or the child, or trouble Callista's peace, or disturb the sleep of Dom *Esteban.*

It was only a psychological device, he knew, nothing like the strong electrical-mental net around Arilinn, strong as the wall of the Tower itself, to keep out intruders in body or mind. But it had its own reality on the level where they would be working: it would protect them from outside interference, shielding those in Armida who might pick up their thoughts, and dilute or distort them. It would also focus the healing on the ones who needed it.

"Before we start, let's have it clear what we're going to do," he said. Ferrika had some rather well drawn anatomical charts. She had been giving classes in basic hygiene to the women in the villages, an innovation of which Damon completely approved, and he had borrowed the charts she used, discarding the ones she used to teach pregnant women, but keeping the one which diagramed the circulation. "Look here, we have to restore circulation and healthy blood flow into the legs and feet, liquefy the frozen lymph and sluggish blood, and try to repair the nerve fibers damaged by freezing."

Andrew, listening to the matter-of-fact way in which Damon spoke, in much the same way as a Terran medic would have described an intravenous injection, looked uneasily at the matrix between his hands. He did not doubt that Damon could do everything he said he could, and he was perfectly willing to help. But he thought they were a most unlikely hospital team.

The men were lying in the room where they had been taken. Most of them were still in their drugged sleep, but Raimon was awake, his eyes bright with fever, flushed and pain-racked.

Damon said gently, "We have come to do what we can for you, my friend."

He bared the matrix in his hands; the man flinched.

"Sorcery," he muttered, "such things are for the Hali'imyn. . . ."

Damon shook his head. "A skill which anyone with the inborn talent can use. Andrew here is no Comyn-born, nor of the race of Cassilda, yet he is skilled in this work, and has come to help."

Raimon's feverish eyes fixed on the matrix. Damon saw the twisting sickness pass over his face, and even through his own growing euphoric rapport with the jewel, he somehow found enough separateness and detachment to say gently, "Do not look directly into the matrix, friend, for you are not trained to the sight, and it will trouble your eyes and brain."

The man averted his eyes, making a superstitious gesture, and Damon felt annoyed again, but he controlled it. He said, "Lie down, try to sleep, Raimon," and then, firmly, "Dezi, give them another dose of Ferrika's sleeping medicine. If they can sleep while we work, they will not interfere with the healing." And if they slept, they would feel no fear, and thoughts of fear could interfere with the careful, delicate work they would be doing.

It was a pity Ferrika could not be taught this work, Damon thought. He wondered if she had even minimal *laran*. With her knowledge of healing, and the ability to use matrix skills, she would indeed be valuable to all the people on the estate.

That was what Callista ought to be doing, he decided, not work any stupid housewife could do!

As Raimon swallowed the sleeping medicine and sank back drowsily against his pillows, Damon gently reached out with his mind and picked up the threads of contact. Andrew, watching the lights in his matrix brightening and dimming in pulse with his breathing, felt Damon reach out, center his consciousness between himself and Dezi. To Andrew, subjectively, though Damon did not move or touch any of them, it was as if he leaned on them both, carefully supported, and then lowered his awareness into the wounded man's body. Andrew could sense, could feel, the tension in the damaged flesh, the broken blood vessels, the blood which lay thick and sluggish in the bruised and torn tissues, distended or flaccid, pulpy, like meat frozen and then thawed. He felt Damon's awareness of this, felt him search out, with something like the fingers of his mind, the damaged nerve sheathing in the bundles of fibers in ankle, toes, arches, tendons. . . . *Not much to be done there.* As if they were against his own fingertips, Andrew could feel the tight tendons, feel the way in which Damon's pressure relaxed them, feel impulses streaming again through the fibers, brokenly, damaged. The surface of the fibers would never wholly heal, but once again the impulses were moving, feeling had been restored. Damon flinched at the awareness of pain in the restored nerve fibers. *It is a good thing I had them give Raimon sleeping medicine; he could never have endured the pain if he were awake.* Then, with delicate, rhythmic pulsations, he began to stimulate the pulse of blood, the flow through arteries and veins nearly choked by the thick blood. Andrew felt Damon, intent on the delicate work deep in the layers of cells, falter and hesitate, his breathing ragged. He felt Dezi reach out and steady Damon's heartbeat. Andrew felt himself reach out—the image in his mind was of a rock, strong behind Damon where the other man could lean his weight against him—and was conscious of something around them. Walls? Thick walls, enclosing them? Did it matter? He concentrated on lending strength to Damon, seeing, with his eyes shut, the blackened feet slowly changing color, reddening, paling. Finally Damon sighed, opened his eyes. Letting the rapport drop, except for a slender thread of contact, he bent over Raimon, who lay somnolent, touching the feet carefully with his fingers. The blackened skin was sloughing off in patches; below it lay reddened flesh, whealed and bruised-looking, but, Andrew knew, free of gangrenous taint or poison.

"He'll have a hell of a lot of pain," Damon said, bending to touch one of the smaller toes, where the nails had sloughed away with the broken and blackened skin, "and he might still lose a toe or two; the nerves were dead there, and I couldn't do much. But he'll recover, and he'll have the use of his feet and hands. And he was the worst." He tightened his mouth, sobered by the responsibility, and knew, ashamed of himself, that he had almost, somewhere inside himself, hoped for failure. It was too much, he thought, this kind of responsibility. But he could do it, and there were other men in the same danger. And now that he knew he *could* save them . . . He made his voice deliberately harsh as he turned to Dezi and Andrew.

"Well, what are we waiting for? We'd better get on to the others."

Again, the picked-up threads of rapport. Andrew had the knack of it now, knew just how and when to flood Damon with his own strength when the other man faltered. They were working as a team, as Damon sank his consciousness into the second man's feet and legs, and Andrew, some small part of him still apart from this, felt the walls enclosing them so that no random thought from outside intruded. He felt with Damon the descent, cell by slow cell, through the layers of flesh and skin and nerves and bone, gently stimulating, sloughing aside, reawakening. It was more effective than a surgeon's knife, Andrew thought, but what a cost! Twice more the descent into raw, blackened frozen flesh before Damon finally let the last rapport go, separating them, and Andrew felt as if they had slipped outside an enclosed space, a surrounding wall. But four men lay sleeping, their legs and feet raw, sore, damaged, but healing. Definitely healing, without danger of blood poisoning or infection, clean and healthy wounds that would mend as quickly as possible.

They left the men sleeping, warning Ferrika to stay near them, and went back to the lower hall. Damon staggered, and Andrew reached out and supported him physically, feeling that he was repeating, in the physical world, what he had done so often in thought during the long rapport. Not for the first time, he had the feeling that Damon, so much older, was somehow the younger, to be protected.

Damon sat on the bench, exhaustedly leaning back against Andrew, the dead weariness and draining of matrix work settling down over him. He picked up some bread and fruit which had been left on the table after the evening meal, and chewed at it with ravenous hunger, feeling his depleted body demanding a renewal of energy. Dezi too had begun to eat hungrily.

Damon said, "You should eat something too, Andrew; matrix work depletes your energies so much, you'll collapse." He had almost forgotten that terrible drained feeling, as if his very life had gone out of him. At Arilinn he had been given technical explanations about the energy currents in the body, the channels of energy which carried physical as well as psychic strength. But he was too weary to remember them long.

Andrew said, "I'm not hungry," and Damon replied with the ghost of a smile, "Yes you are. You just don't know it yet." He put out his hand to stop Dezi as the boy poured a cup of wine. "No, that's dangerous. Drink water, or fetch some milk or soup from the kitchens, but no drink after something like this. Half a glass will make you drunk as a monk at Midwinter feast!"

Dezi shrugged and went off to the kitchen, returning with a jug of milk which he poured all around. Damon said, "Dezi, you were at Arilinn, so you don't need explanations, but Andrew should know: you should eat about twice as much as usual, for a day or so, and if you have any dizziness, nausea, anything like that, come and tell me. Dezi, do they keep *kirian* here?"

Dezi said, "Ferrika does not make it, and with Domenic and myself both past threshold sickness, and Valdir in Nevarsin, I do not think anyone here has had need of it."

Andrew asked, "What's *kirian*?"

"A psychoactive drug which is used in the Towers, or among telepathic families. It lowers the resistance to telepathic contact, but it can also be helpful in cases of overwork or telepathic stresses. And some developing telepaths have a lot of sickness at adolescence, physical and psychic, when all the development is taking place at once. I suppose you're too old for threshold sickness, Dezi?"

"I should think so," the boy said scornfully. "I had outgrown it before I was fourteen."

"Still, being away from matrix work since you left Arilinn, you might have a touch of it when you try to go back to it," Damon warned. "And we still don't know how Andrew will react." He would ask Callista to try to make *kirian*. There should be some kept in every household of telepaths, against emergencies.

He put aside his cup of milk, half finished. He was

deathly weary. "Go and rest, Dezi lad . . . you are worthy of Arilinn training, believe me." He gave the boy a brief embrace and watched him go off toward his room near *Dom* Esteban's, hoping the old man would sleep through the night so the boy could rest undisturbed.

Whatever Dezi's faults, Damon considered, at least he had nursed the old man as filially as an acknowledged son would have. Was it affection, he wondered, or self-interest?

He let himself lean on Andrew as they climbed the stairs, making a rueful apology, but Andrew brushed it aside. "Forget it. You think I don't know you pulled the whole weight of that?" So Damon let Andrew help him up the stairs, thinking, *I lean on you now as I did in the matrix.* . . .

In the outer room of their suite he hesitated a moment. "You aren't Tower-trained, so you should be warned of this, too: matrix work . . . you'll be impotent for a day or two. Don't worry about it, it's temporary."

Andrew shrugged, with a twist of wry amusement, and Damon, remembering abruptly the real state of affairs between Andrew and Callista, knew that a word of apology would only reemphasize the tactlessness of his words. He asked himself how in hell he could have been groggy enough to have forgotten that.

In their room, Ellemir lay half asleep on the bed, wrapped in a fleecy white shawl. She had taken down her braids and her hair was scattered like light on the pillow. As Damon looked down at his wife, she sat up, blinking sleepily, then, as Ellemir always did, moving from sleep to waking without transition, she held out her arms. "Oh, Damon, you look so weary, was it very terrible?"

He sank down beside her, resting his head against her breast. "No. Only I am no longer used to this work, and there is such a need for it, such a terrible need! Elli—" He sat bolt upright, looking down at her. "So many people here on Darkover are dying, when they should not die, suffering, being crippled, dying of minor injuries. It should not be so. We do not have the kind of medical services Andrew tells me that his Terrans have. But there are so many things that a man—or a woman—with a matrix can heal. And yet how are the injured to be taken to Arilinn or Neskaya or Dalereuth or Hali, to be treated in the Towers there? What do the matrix circles in the great Towers care for a poor workman's frost bite, or some poor hunter clawed by a hunting-beast or kicked in the head by an *oudrakhi*?"

"Well," said Ellemir, puzzled, but trying to follow his vehemence, "in the Towers they have other things to do. Important things. Communications. And . . . and mining, and all of those things. They would have no time to look after wounds."

"That's true. But listen, Elli, all over Darkover there are men like Dezi, or women like Callista, or like you. Women and men who cannot, do not *want* to spend their lives in a Tower, away from the ordinary lives of humankind. But they could do any of these things." He sank down on the bed beside Ellemir, realizing he was more fatigued than after any battle he had fought in the Guards. "One need not be Comyn, or have enormous skill, to do these things. Anyone with a little *laran* could be trained so, to help, to heal, and no one does!"

"But Damon," she said reasonably, "I have always heard—Callista has told me—it is dangerous to use these powers outside the Towers."

"Flummery!" Damon exclaimed. "Are you so superstitious, Elli? You yourself have been in contact with Callista. Did you find it so dangerous?"

"No," she said uneasily, "but during the Ages of Chaos, so many terrible things were done with the great matrix screens, such terrible weapons—fire-forms, and wind-creatures to tear down castles and whole walls, and creatures from other dimensions walking abroad in the land—that they decreed in those days that all matrix work should be done only in the Towers, and only under safeguards."

"But that time is past, Ellemir, and most of those enormous, illegal matrix weapons were destroyed during the Ages of Chaos, or in the days of Varzil the Good. Do you really think that because I healed four men's frozen feet and restored to them the ability to use their limbs, that I am likely to send a fire-form raging in the forest, or raise a cave-thing to blight the crops?"

"No, no, of course not." She sat up, holding out her arms to him. "Lie down, rest, my dearest, you are so weary."

He let her help him undress, and lay down at her side, but he went on, staring stubbornly into the darkness.

"Elli, there is something very wrong with the use we are making of telepaths here on Darkover. Either they must live guarded all their lives within the Towers, hardly human—you know that it nearly destroyed me when I was sent from Arilinn—or else they must give up everything they have learned. Like Callista—Evanda pity her," he added, a flicker of consciousness still in link with Andrew, looking down at the sleeping Callista, traces of tears still on her face. "She has had to give up everything she ever learned, everything she has ever done. She is afraid to do anything else. There ought to be a way, Elli, there ought to be a way!"

"Damon, Damon," she entreated, holding him close, "it has always been so. The Tower-trained are wiser than we are; they must know what they are about when they ordain it so!"

"I am not so sure."

"In any case, there is nothing we can do about it now, my dearest. You must rest now, and calm yourself, or you will disturb *her*," she said, taking Damon's hand in her own and laying it against her body. Damon, knowing he was being deliberately diverted, but willing to go along with it—after all, Ellemir was right—smiled, letting himself begin to pick up the formless, random emanations—not yet thoughts—of the unborn child. "*Her*, you said?"

Ellemir laughed softly in delight. "I am not sure how I know, but I am certain of it. A little Callista, perhaps?"

Damon thought, *I hope her life will be happier. I would not wish to see the hand of Arilinn laid on any daughter of mine. . . .* Then he suddenly shuddered, in a flick of precognition seeing a slender red-haired woman, in the crimson robes of a Keeper in Arilinn. . . . She tore them from neck to ankle, rending them, casting them aside. . . . He blinked. It was gone. Precognition? Or was it a dramatization, an hallucination, born of his own disquiet? Holding his wife and child in his arms, he tried to put it all aside for the time.

CHAPTER SEVEN

The frostbitten men were recovering, but with so many men disabled, an extra share of the actual physical work fell on Andrew, and even Damon took a hand now and then. The weather had moderated, but *Dom* Esteban told them this was only a break before the real winter storms would sweep down from the Hellers, layering the foothills deep in snow for months.

Damon had offered to ride to Serrais with Andrew, and bring back some surplus men from the estate there, to work for the estate through the winter, and help with the crops in the early spring. The journey would last more than a tenday. They were making plans in the Great Hall of Armida that morning. Ellemir's morning sickness had subsided, and, as usual, she was in the kitchens, supervising the women with their work. Callista was seated beside her father when suddenly she sat upright with a look of disquiet. She said, "Oh—Elli, Elli—oh, no—!" But even before she was on her feet Damon's chair crashed over backward and he ran toward the kitchens. At that moment there were cries of dismay from the other rooms.

Dom Esteban grumbled, "What's wrong with those women?" but no one was listening. Callista had run toward the kitchen door. After a moment Damon came hurrying back, beckoned to Andrew.

"Ellemir has fainted. I do not want any stranger touching her now. Can you carry her?"

Ellemir lay in a crumpled heap on the kitchen floor, surrounded by staring, crowding women. Damon motioned them away, and Andrew picked up Ellemir. Her pallor was frightening, but Andrew knew nothing about pregnant women, and fainting like this, he supposed, was not so alarming.

"Carry her to her room, Andrew. I will go and call Ferrika."

By the time Andrew laid Ellemir on her own bed Damon was there with the woman. His hands closed on Ellemir's as he slipped into rapport with her, searching for the faint, formless contact with the unborn. Even as he felt in his own body the painful spasms racking Ellemir's, he knew, in anguish, what was happening. He begged, "Can't you do anything?"

Ferrika said gently, "I will do all I can, Lord Damon," but over her bent head, Damon met Callista's eyes. They were full of tears. She said, "Ellemir is not in danger, Damon. But it's already too late for the baby."

Ellemir clutched at Damon's hands. "Don't leave me," she begged, and he murmured, "No, love. Never. I'll stay with you." This was custom; no telepath Comyn of the Domains left his wife alone while she bore their child, or shrank from sharing her ordeal. And now he must strengthen Ellemir for their loss, not for joy. Fighting back his own anguished grief, he knelt beside her, holding her in his arms, cradling her against him.

Andrew had gone downstairs again to *Dom* Esteban, with nothing to tell except that Damon was with her, and Callista, and they had sent for Ferrika. He felt the pall that lay over the estate, all that day. Even the maids clustered in frightened huddles. Andrew wanted to reach out for Damon, to try to strengthen him, reassure him, but what could he do or say? Once, looking up the stairs, he saw Dezi coming from the outer hall, and Dezi asked "How is Ellemir?" and Andrew's resentment against the youngster overflowed.

"Much *you* care!"

"I don't wish Elli any harm," Dezi said, queerly subdued. "She's the only one here who's ever been decent to me." He turned his back on Andrew and went away, and Andrew had the odd sense that Dezi, too, was near to tears.

Damon and Ellemir had been so happy about their baby, and now this! Andrew wondered wildly if his own ill luck had somehow proved contagious, if the trouble of his own marriage had somehow rubbed off on the other couple. Realizing that this was absolute insanity, he went down to the greenhouse and tried to lose himself in giving orders to the gardeners.

Hours later, Damon came out of the room where Ellemir lay, asleep now, pain and grief alike forgotten in one of Ferrika's sleeping draughts. The midwife, pausing for a moment beside him, said gently, "Lord Damon, better now than for the poor little thing to live to birth and be born deformed. The mercy of Avarra takes strange forms."

"I know you did what you could, Ferrika." But Damon turned away, unstrung, not wanting the woman to see him weeping. She understood, and went quietly down the stairs, and Damon went blindly along the hall, shrinking from the need to tell *Dom* Esteban. By instinct he headed toward the greenhouse, finding Andrew there. Andrew came toward him, asking gently, "How is Ellemir? Is she out of danger?"

"Should I be here if she were not?" Damon asked, then, remembering, dropped down on a crate, covered his face with his hands, and gave way to his grief. Andrew stood beside him, his hand on his friend's shoulder, trying without words to give Damon some support, the knowledge of his own compassion.

"The worst of it is," Damon said at last, raising his ravaged face, "Elli thinks she has failed me, that she could not carry our daughter safely to life. If there is fault it is mine, who left her to care for this great house alone. Mine in any case! We are too near akin, doubly cousins, and in such close kinship there is often a heritage of death in the blood. I should never have married her! I should never have married her! I love her, I love her, but I knew she wanted children, and I should have known it was not safe, we were such close kin. . . . I do not know if I will dare to let her try again." Damon finally quieted a little, and stood up, saying wearily, "I should go back. When she wakes, she will want me beside her." For the first time since Andrew had known him, he looked his full age.

And he had envied Damon his happiness! Ellemir was young, they could have other children. But with this weight of guilt?

Later he found Callista in the small stone-floored stillroom, her hair tied up in the faded cloth she wore to keep away the herb-smells. She raised her face to him and he saw that it still bore the traces of tears. Had she shared that ordeal with her twin? But her voice had the remote calm he had grown to expect in Callista, and somehow it jarred on him now.

"I am making something which will lessen the bleeding; it must be freshly made or it is not so effective, and she must have it every few hours." She was pounding some thick grayish leaves in a small mortar. She scraped the mash into a cone-shaped glass and set it to filter through layers of closely woven cloth, carefully measuring and pouring a colorless liquid over it.

"There. That must filter before I can do anymore." She turned to him, raising her eyes. He asked, "But Elli—she will recover? And she can have other children, in time?"

"Oh, yes, I suppose so."

He wanted to reach out and take her in his arms, comfort the grief she shared with her twin. But he dared not even touch her hand. Aching with frustration, he turned away.

My wife. And I have never even kissed her. Damon and Ellemir have their shared sorrow; what have I shared with Callista?

Gently, pitying the grief in her eyes, he said, "Dear love, is it really such a tragedy? It's not as if she had lost a real baby. A child ready for birth, yes, but a fetus at this stage? How can it be so serious?"

He was not prepared for the horror and rage with which she turned on him. Her face was white, her eyes blazing like the flame beneath the retort. "How can you say such a thing?" she whispered. "How *dare* you? Don't you know that for twice a tenday, both Damon and Ellemir had been in contact with—with her mind, had come to know her as a real presence, their own *child*?" Andrew flinched at her anger. He had never thought of it, that in a family of telepaths, an unborn child would certainly be a presence. But so soon? So quickly? And what kind of thoughts could a fetus hardly more than a third of the way through pregnancy—But Callista picked up the scorn in that thought. She flung back at him, shaking, "Will you say, then, it is no tragedy if our son—or daughter—should die before he was strong enough to live outside my body?" Her voice trembled. "Is nothing real that you cannot see, *Terranan!*"

Andrew raised his head for an angry retort: *It seems we are never likely to know; you are not very likely to bear me a child as things are now*. But her white, anguished face stopped him. He could not return taunt for taunt. That thoughtless *Terranan* had hurt, but he had pledged her that he would never try to hurry her, never put her under the slightest pressure. He bit the angry words back, then saw, in the dismay that swept across her face, that she had heard them anyway.

Of course. She is a telepath. The taunt I did not speak was as real to her as if I had actually shouted it.

"Callista," he whispered, "darling, I'm sorry. Forgive me. I didn't mean—"

"I know." She stumbled against him, clung there, her bright head against him. She stood, shaking, within the circle of his arm. "Oh, Andrew, Andrew, I wish we had even *that*. . . ." she whispered, and sobbed aloud.

He held her, hardly daring to move. She felt taut, featherlike, like some wild bird which had flown to him and would take flight again at a word or an incautious move. After a moment her sobs quieted, and it was the old, still, resigned face she turned to him. She moved away, so gently that he hardly felt forsaken.

"Look, the liquid has all filtered through. I must finish the medicine I am making for my sister." She laid her fingertips lightly against his lips, in the old gesture; he kissed them, realizing that in an odd way this quarrel had drawn them closer.

How much longer? In the name of all the Gods at once, how much longer can we go on like this? And even as the thought tore through his mind, he realized he was not sure whether it was his own or Callista's.

Three days later, Andrew and Damon rode out, as planned, for Serrais. Ellemir was out of danger, and there was nothing more that Damon's presence could do for her. Nothing, Damon knew, could help Ellemir now but time.

Andrew felt strangely relieved, although he would

have been ashamed to say so, to get away. He had not realized how the tension between himself and Callista, the aura of silent grief, had weighed down on him at Armida.

The wide high plains, the mountains in the distance, all this could have been the Arizona horse ranch of Andrew's childhood. Yet he had only to open his eyes to see the great red sun, gleaming like a bloodshot eye through the morning fogs, to know that he was not on Terra, that he was nowhere on Earth. It was midmorning, but two small shadowy moons, pale violet and dim lime green, swung low beyond the crest of the hill, one nearing the full, another a waning crescent. The very smell of the air was strange, and yet it was his home now, his home for the rest of his life. And Callista. Callista, waiting for him. His mind's eye retained the memory of her face, pale, smiling from the top of the steps as he rode away. He cherished the smile in memory, that with all the grief their marriage had brought to her, she could still smile at him, give him her fingertips to kiss, bid him ride with the Gods in the soft speech he was beginning to understand: *"Adelandeyo."*

Damon, too, brightened perceptibly as the miles lengthened under their horses' hooves. The last few days had put lines in his face that had never been there before, but he no longer looked old, weighted down with anguish.

At midday they dismounted to eat their noon meal, tying their horses to graze on the new grass poking up sturdy leaves through the remnants of the last blizzard's snow. They found a dry log to sit on, surrounded by flower buds casting their snow pods and breaking out in riotous bud and leaf as if it were spring. But when Andrew asked about it, Damon said blankly, "Spring? Zandru's Hells, no, it's not even full winter yet, not till after Midwinter feast! Oh, the flowers?" He chuckled. "With the weather here, they bloom whenever there's a day or two of sun and warmth. Your Terran scientists have a phrase for it, evolutionary adaptation. In the Kilghard Hills, there are only a few days in high summer when it doesn't snow, so the flowers bloom whenever they get a little sun. If you think it looks odd here, you should go into the Hellers, and see the flowers and fruits that grow around Nevarsin. We can't grow ice-melons here, you know. It's too warm—they're a plant of the glaciers." And indeed, Damon had taken off his fur riding cape, and was riding in shirt sleeves, though Andrew was still muffled against what seemed a cold, biting day.

Damon unwrapped the bundle of food Callista had given them for their journey, and broke out laughing. "Callista says—and is very apologetic—that she knows very little of housekeeping. But we are in luck, since she has not yet learned what is suitable food to give to travelers!" There was a cold roast fowl, which Damon divided with the knife at his belt, and a loaf of bread still faintly warm from the oven, and Andrew could not imagine why Damon was laughing. He said, "I don't see what's funny about it. She asked me what I thought I would like to eat during a long ride, and I told her."

Damon laughed, handing Andrew a generous portion of the roast meat. It was fragrant with spices which the Terran had not yet learned to identify by name. "For some reason, just custom, I suppose, about all the food one can ever get for the road would be hard journey-bread, dried meat rolls, dried fruits and nuts, that sort of thing." He watched Andrew slicing up the bread, making a neat sandwich of the roast meat. "That looks good. I think I shall try it. And—will wonders never cease!—she gave us fresh apples too, from the cellar. Well, well!" He was laughing as he bit with gusto into the leg of the roast fowl. "It would never have occurred to me to question traveler's food and it would never have occurred to Elli to ask me if it was what I wanted! Maybe we can use some new ideas on our world!"

He sobered, lost in thought as he watched Andrew eating the sliced meat and bread. He himself had had heretical thoughts about matrix work outside the Towers. There ought to be a way. But he knew if he broached that to Leonie, she would be horrified, as horrified as if they were in the days of Regis the Fourth.

She would have known he was using a matrix, of course. Every legitimate matrix keyed to a Comyn telepath was monitored from the great screens in the Arilinn Tower. They could have identified Damon from his matrix, and Dezi, and, perhaps, though Damon was not sure, even Andrew.

If anyone had been watching. There was a shortage of telepathy for such inessential jobs as monitoring the matrix screens, so probably no one had noticed. But the monitor screens were there, and every matrix on Darkover was legally subject to monitoring and review. Even those like Domenic, who had been tested for *laran* and given a matrix, but never used it, could be followed.

That was another reason why Damon felt they should not waste such a telepath as Dezi. Even if his personality did not fit into the intimacy of a circle—and Damon was ready to admit Dezi would be hard to live with—he could be used to monitor a screen.

He thought wryly that today he was full of heresies. Who was he to question Leonie of Arilinn?

He finished off the leg of roast fowl, thoughtfully watching the Terran. Andrew was eating an apple, staring off thoughtfully at the far range of hills.

He is my friend. Yet he came here from a star so far away that I cannot see it in the sky at night. And yet, the very fact that there are other worlds like ours, everywhere in the universe, is going to change our world.

He looked at the distant hills, and thought, *I do not want our world to change*, then bleakly laughed at himself. He sat here planning a way to alter the use of matrices on Darkover, thinking of ways to reform the system of ancient Towers which guarded the old matrix sciences of his world, guarded them in safe ways established generations ago.

He said, "Andrew, why are you here? On Darkover?"

Andrew shrugged. "I came here almost by accident. It was a job. And then, one day, I saw Callista's face—and here I am."

"I don't mean that," Damon said. "Why are your people here? What does Terra want with our world? We are not a rich world to be exploited. I know enough about your Empire to know that most of the worlds they settle have something to give. Why Darkover? We are a world with few heavy metals, an isolated world with a climate your people find, I gather, inhospitable. What do the Terrans *want* with us?"

Andrew clasped his hands around his knees. He said, "There is an old story on my world. Someone asked an explorer why he chose to climb a mountain. And all he said was, 'Because it's there!' "

"That hardly seems enough reason to build a space-port," Damon said.

"I don't understand all of it. Hell, Damon, I'm no empire-builder. I'd rather have stayed on Dad's horse ranch. The way I understand it, it's *location*. You *do* know that the galaxy is in the form of a giant spiral?" He picked up a twig and drew a pattern in the melting snow. "This is the upper spiral of the galaxy, and this is the lower arm, and here is Darkover, making it an ideal place for traffic control, passenger transfers, understand?"

"But," Damon argued, "the travel of Empire citizens from one end of the Empire to the other doesn't mean anything to us."

Andrew shrugged. "I know. I'm sure Empire Central would have preferred an uninhabited world at the cross-roads, so they needn't have worried about who lived there. But here you are, and here we are." He shrank from Damon's frown. "*I* don't make their policy, Damon. I'm not even sure I understand it. That's just the way it was explained to me."

Damon's laugh was mirthless. "And I was startled by Callista giving us roast meat and fresh apples for journey-food! Change is relative, I suppose." He saw Andrew's troubled look and made himself smile. None of this was Andrew's fault. "Let's hope the changes are all for the better, like Callie's roast fowl!" He got off the log and carefully buried the apple core in a small runnel of snow behind it. Pain struck at him. If things had gone otherwise, he might have been planting this apple for his daughter. Andrew, with that uncanny sensi-tivity which he exhibited now and then, bent beside him, in silence, to bury his own apple core. Not till they were in the saddle again did he say, gently, "Some day, Damon, our children will eat apples from these trees."

They were away from Armida more than three ten-days. In Serrais, it took time to find ablebodied men who were willing to leave their villages, and perhaps their families, to work on the Armida estate for any-where up to a year. Yet they could not take too many single men, or it would disrupt the life of the villages. Damon tried to find families who had ties of blood or fosterage with people at Armida lands. There were many of them. Then Damon wished to pay a visit to his brother Kieran, and to his sister Marisela and her children.

Marisela, a gentle, plump young woman who looked like Damon, but with fair hair where his was red, ex-pressed grief at the news of Ellemir's miscarriage. She said kindly that if they had no better fortune in a year or two, Damon should have one of their children to foster, an offer which surprised Andrew, but which Damon took for granted.

"Thank you, Mari. It may be needful, at that, since the children of double cousins seldom thrive. I have no great need for an heir, but Ellemir's arms are empty and she grieves. And Callista is not likely to have a child very soon."

Marisela said, "I do not know Callista well. Even when we were all little maidens, everyone knew she was destined for the Tower, and she did not mingle much with the other girls. People are such gossips," she added vehemently. "Callie has a perfect right to leave Arilinn and marry if she chooses, but it is true we were all sur-prised. I know Keepers from the other Towers often leave to marry, but Arilinn? And Leonie has been there since I can remember, since our mother can remember. We all thought she would step directly into Leonie's shoes. There was a time when the Keepers of Arilinn could not leave their posts if they would. . . ."

"That day is hundreds of years gone," Damon said impatiently, but Marisela went on, unruffled. "I was tested for *laran* in Neskaya when I was thirteen, and one of the girls told me that if she was sent to Arilinn she would refuse, since the Keepers there were neutered. They were not women but *emmasca*, as the legend says that Robardin's daughter was *emmasca* and became woman for the love of Hastur. . . ."

"Fairy-tales!" said Damon, laughing. "That has not been done for hundreds of years, Marisela!"

"I am only telling you what they told me," Marisela said, injured. "And surely Leonie looks near enough to an *emmasca*, and Callista—Callista is thinner than Ellemir, and she looks younger, so you cannot blame me for thinking she might not be all woman. Even so, that would not mean she could not marry if she wished, although most do not want to."

"Marisa, child, I assure you that Andrew's wife is no *emmasca!*"

Marisela turned to Andrew and inquired, "Is Callista pregnant yet?"

Andrew laughed and shook his head. It was not the slightest use in being cross; standards of reticence differed enormously between cultures, and why should he blame Marisela, who was after all Callista's cousin, for asking what everyone wanted to know about a bride? He remembered what Damon had said about Ellemir and repeated it.

"I am content that she should have a year or two to be free of such cares. She is still very young."

But later he asked Damon in private, "What in the world is an *emmasca?*"

"The word *used* to mean one of the ancient race of the forests. They never mingle with mankind now, but there is said to be *chieri* blood in the Comyn, especially in the Hellers; some of the Ardais and Aldaran have six fingers on either hand. I am not sure I believe that tale— any horsebreeder will tell you that a half-breed is sterile— but the story goes that there is *chieri* blood in the Comyn, that the *chieri* in days past mingled with mankind and mixed their blood. It was believed that a *chieri* could appear as a man to a woman, or as a woman to a man, being both, or perhaps neither. So they say that in the old days some of the Comyn too were *emmasca*, neither man not woman, but neuter. Well, that was very long ago, but the tradition remains that these were the first Keepers, neither man nor woman. Later, when women took on the burden of being Keeper, they were made *emmasca*—surgically neutered—because it was thought safer for a woman to work in the screens if she had not the burden of womanhood. But in living memory—and I can say this positively, knowing the laws of Arilinn—

no woman has been neutered, even at Arilinn, to work in the Towers. A Keeper's virginity serves to guard her against the perils of womanhood."

"I still don't understand why that is," Andrew said, and Damon explained. "It's a matter of nerve alignment. The same nerves in the body carry both *laran* and sex. Remember that after we worked with the matrices we were all impotent for days? The same nerve channels can't carry both sets of impulses at once. A woman doesn't have that particular safety valve, so the Keepers, who have to handle such tremendous frequencies and coordinate all the other telepaths, have to keep their channels completely clear for *laran* alone. Otherwise they can overload their nerves and burn out. I'll show you the channels sometime, if you're interested. Or you can ask Callista about it."

Andrew didn't pursue the subject. The thought of the way in which Callista had been conditioned still roused an anger in him so deep that it was better not to think about it at all.

They rode to Armida after a long trip home, broken three times by bad weather which forced them to stay overnight in different places, sometimes housed in luxurious rooms, sometimes sharing a pallet on the floor with the family's younger children. Andrew, looking down at the lights of Armida across the valley, thought with a strange awareness, that he was truly coming home. Half a galaxy away from the world where he was born, yet this was home to him, and Callista was there. He wondered if all men, having found a woman to give meaning to life, defined home in that way: the place where their loved one was waiting for them. Damon, at least, seemed to share that feeling; he seemed as glad to return to Armida as he had been, almost thirty days before, to leave it. The great sprawling stone house seemed familiar now, as if he had lived there always.

Ellemir ran down the steps to meet Damon in the courtyard, letting him catch her up in his arms with an exuberant hug. She looked cheerful and healthy, her cheeks bright with color, her eyes sparkling. But Andrew had no time to spare for Ellemir now, for Callista was waiting for him at the top of the steps, still and grave. When she gave him her little half-smile, it somehow meant more to him than all Ellemir's overflowing gaiety. She gave him both her hands, letting him raise them to his lips and kiss one after the other, then, her finger-tips still lying lightly in his, she led him inside. Damon bent and greeted *Dom* Esteban with a filial kiss on the cheek, turned to Dezi with a quick embrace. Andrew, more reserved, bowed to the old man, and Callista came to sit close beside him while he gave *Dom* Esteban a report on their journey.

Damon asked after the frostbitten men. The less hurt ones had recovered and been sent to their families' care; the seriously wounded ones, the ones he had healed with the matrix, were still recovering. Raimon had lost two toes on his right foot; Piedro had never recovered feeling in the outer fingers of his left hand, but they were not wholly crippled, as had been feared.

"They are still with us," Ellemir said, "because Ferrika must dress their feet night and morning with healing oils. Did you know Raimon is a splendid musician? Almost every night, we have him up in the hall to play for us to dance, the servant girls and the stewards, and Callista and Dezi and I dance too, but now that you are back with us . . ." She snuggled against Damon's side, looking up at him with happy eyes.

Callista followed Andrew's gaze and said softly, "I have missed you, Andrew. Perhaps I cannot show it as Elli does. But I am more glad than I can tell you, that you are here with us again."

After dinner in the big hall, *Dom* Esteban said, "Shall we have some music, then?"

"I shall send for Raimon, shall I?" Ellemir said, and went to summon the men, and Andrew said softly, "Will you sing for me, Callista?"

Callista glanced at her father for permission. He motioned to her to sing, and she took her small harp and struck a chord or two.

> How came this blood on your right hand,
> Brother, tell me, tell me . . .

Dezi made a formless sound of protest. Looking at his troubled face as she returned, Ellemir said, "Callista, sing something else!" At Andrew's surprised, questioning look, she said, "It is ill luck for a sister to sing that in a brother's hearing. It tells the tale of a brother who slew all his kinfolk save one sister alone, and she was forced to pronounce the outlaw-word on him."

Dom Esteban scowled. He said, "I am not superstitious, and no son of mine sits in this hall. Sing, Callista."

Troubled, Callista bent her head over her harp, but she obeyed.

> We sat at feast, we fought in jest,
>   Sister, I vow to thee,
> A berserk's rage came in my hand
> And I slew them shamefully.

> What will become of you now, dear heart,
>   Brother, tell me, tell me . . .

Andrew, seeing Dezi's smoldering eyes, felt a wave of sadness for the boy, for the gratuitous insult *Dom* Esteban had put on him. Callista sought Dezi's eyes as if in apology, but the youngster rose and went out of the room, slamming the door into the kitchens. Andrew thought he should do something, say something, but what?

Later Raimon came hobbling into the hall on his canes and began to play a dance tune. The strain vanished as the men and women of the estate crowded into the center of the room, men in the outer ring, women in the inner, dancing a measure which wove into circles and spirals. One of the men brought out a drone-pipe, an unfamiliar instrument which, Andrew thought, made an unholy racket, for a couple of others to dance a sword-dance. Then they began to dance in couples, though Andrew noticed that most of the younger women danced only with one another. Callista was playing for the dancers; Andrew bowed to Ferrika and drew her into the dance.

Later he saw Ellemir and Damon dancing together, her arms around his neck, her smiling eyes lifted to her

husband's. It reminded him of his attempts to dance with
Callista, against custom, at their wedding. Well, nothing
forbade it now. He went in search of Callista, who had
yielded up her harp to another of the women and was
dancing with Dezi. As they drew apart, he came toward
them and held out his arms.

She smiled gaily and moved toward him, but Dezi
stepped between them. He spoke in a voice which could
not be heard three feet away, but there was no mistaking
the sneering malice in his tone: "Oh, we can't let you
two dance together *yet*, can we?"

Callista's hands dropped to her sides and the color
drained from her face. Andrew heard a clatter of broken
dishes and the shatter of a wineglass somewhere, under
the terrifying impact of her mental cry of pain. Evidently
everyone in the room with a scrap of telepathic awareness had picked up her outrage. Andrew didn't stop to
think. His fist smashed, hard, into Dezi's face, sending
the boy reeling.

Slowly Dezi picked himself up. He wiped the streaming blood from his lip, his eyes blazing fury. Then he
flung himself at Andrew, but Damon had grabbed him
around the waist, holding him back by force.

"Zandru's hells, Dezi," he breathed, "are you mad?
Blood-feud for three generations has been declared for
an insult less than you have put on our brother!"

Andrew looked around the ring of staring, shocked
faces until he saw Callista, her eyes staring and lost in
her drawn face. Abruptly she put her hands up to her
face, turned her back, and hurried out of the room. She
did not sob aloud, but Andrew could feel, like tangible
vibration, the tears she could not shed.

Dom Esteban's angry voice, cut through the lengthening, embarrassed silence.

"The most charitable explanation of this, Deziderio,
is that you have again had more to drink than you can
handle! If you cannot hold your drink like a man, you
had better limit yourself to *shallan* with your dinner, as
the children do! Apologize to our kinsman, and go sleep
it off!"

That was the best way to pass it off, Andrew thought.
Judging by their confusion, most of the people in the

room did not even know what Dezi had said. They had simply picked up Callista's distress.

Dezi muttered something—Andrew supposed it was an apology. He said quietly, "I don't care what insults you put on me, Dezi. But what kind of man should I be if I let you speak offensively to my wife?"

Dezi glanced over his shoulder at *Dom* Esteban—to make sure they were out of earshot?—and said in a low, vicious tone, "Your wife? Don't you even know that freemate marriage is legal only upon consummation? She's no more your wife than she is mine!" Then he went quickly past Andrew and out of the room.

All semblance of jollity had gone from the evening. Ellemir hastily thanked Raimon for his music and hurried out of the room. *Dom* Esteban beckoned Andrew and asked if Dezi had apologized. Andrew, averting his eyes—the old man was a telepath, how could he lie to him?—said uneasily that he had, and to his relief the old man let it pass. What could he do anyway? He could not declare blood-feud on his wife's half-brother, a drunken adolescent with a taste for insults that hit below the belt.

But was it true, what Dezi had said? In their own suite he put the question to Damon, who, though he shook his head looked troubled.

"My dear friend, don't worry about it. No one would have any reason to question the legality of your marriage. Your intentions are clear, and no one is worrying about the fine points of the law," he said, but Andrew felt that Damon had not even convinced himself. Inside their room he could hear Callista crying. Damon heard too.

"I would like to break our Dezi's neck for him!"

Andrew felt the same way. With a few vicious words, the boy had taken all the joy out of their reunion.

Callista had stopped crying when he came in. She stood before her dressing table, slowly unfastening the butterfly-clasp she wore at the nape of her neck, letting her hair fall down about her shoulders. She turned and said, wetting her lips, as if it were a speech she had rehearsed many times, "Andrew, I am sorry . . . I am sorry you were exposed to that. . . . It is *my* fault."

She sat down before the table and slowly took up her

carved ivory brush, running it slowly along the length of
her hair. Andrew knelt beside her, wishing desperately
that he could take her in his arms and comfort her.
"Your fault, love? How are you to blame for that
wretched boy's malice? I won't tell you to forget it—I
know you can't—but don't let it trouble you."

"But it is my fault." Even in the mirror, she would
not meet his eyes. "Because of what I am. It is my fault
that what he said was . . . true."

He thought, poignantly, of the way in which Ellemir
had snuggled into Damon's arms, the way her arms had
lain around Damon's neck while they danced. He said
at last, "Well, Callie, I won't lie to you, it's not easy. I
won't pretend that I'm enjoying the waiting. But I promised, and I'm not complaining. Leave it now, love."

Her small chin set in a stubborn line. "I can't leave it
like that. Can't you understand that you . . . your need
hurts me too, because I want you too, and I cannot, I
don't dare . . . Andrew, listen to me. No, let me finish,
do you remember what I asked you, the day we were
wedded? That if it were this hard for you, to . . . to
take another?"

He frowned at her in the mirror, displeased. "I
thought we'd settled that once and for all, Callista. In
God's name, do you think I care for any of the maids
or serving women?" Had it disturbed her, that he
danced with Ferrika tonight? Did she think . . .

She shook her head, saying faintly, "No. But if it
would make any difference . . . I have spoken to Ellemir
about this. She told me . . . she is willing."

Andrew stared at her, dismay and consternation mingling in his emotions. "Are you serious?"

But she was. Her grave face told him that, and anyway
she was not, he knew, capable of making that kind of
joke. "Ellemir? She is the last, the very last—your own
sister, Callista! How could I do such a thing to you?"

"Do you believe it makes me happy to see you so
miserable, to know that a brat like Dezi can shame you
that way? And how could I be jealous of my own sister?" He made a gesture of revulsion, and she put her
hand out to him. "No, Andrew, listen to me. This is our
custom. If you were one of us, it would be taken for

granted that my sister and I should . . . should share in this way. Even if things were . . . as they should be between us, if there was a time when I was ill, or pregnant, or simply not . . . not wanting you . . . it is very old, this custom. You have heard me sing the Ballad of Hastur and Cassilda? Even there, even in the ballad, it speaks of how Camilla took the place of her *breda* in the arms of the God, and so died when he was set upon. It was so that the Blessed Cassilda survived the treachery of Alar, to bear the child of the God. . . ." Her voice faded.

Andrew said flatly, "That kind of thing may be all very well in old ballads and fairy-tales. But not in real life."

"Even if I wish it, Andrew? I would feel less guilt because every additional day I delayed was adding to . . . to your suffering."

"Suppose you let me worry about that? There's no need for you to feel guilty." But she turned away, weary and defeated. She stood up, letting her released hair shower down to her waist, slowly took it in handfuls, separating it for braiding. She said, stifled, "I cannot endure this any longer."

He said gently, "Then it is for you to end it, Callista." He picked up a fine strand of her hair, pressing it to his lips, savoring the fine texture, the delicate fragrance. He felt dizzy at the touch. He had promised never to try to hurry her. But how long, how long . . . ?

"My darling, what can I say to you? Is the thought so frightening to you, even now?"

She sounded forlorn, wretched. "I know it shouldn't be. But I am afraid. I don't think I'm ready—"

He put his arms around her, very gently. He said, almost in a whisper, "How will you know, Callista, unless you try? Will you come and sleep beside me? No more than that—I swear to you I won't ask anything you're not ready to give me."

She hesitated, twisting a lock of her hair. She said, "Won't it . . . won't it make it worse for you, if I should decide I . . . I can't, I'm not ready yet?"

"Must I swear it to you, love? Don't you trust me?"

She said, with a heartbreaking smile, "It isn't you I

don't trust, my husband." The words made his breath catch in his throat.

"Then . . . ?" He held her loosely within the circle of his arms. After a long time, almost imperceptibly, she nodded.

He gently picked her up in his arms and carried her to his bed. He said, laying her down on the pillows, "Why, then, if you feel that way, isn't it proof that it's time, my darling? I promise you I will be gentle with you—"

She shook her head, whispering, "Oh, Andrew, if it were only as simple as that!" Her eyes filled and flooded with tears. Suddenly she put her arms up around his neck.

"Andrew, will you do something for me? Something you may not want to do? Andrew, promise?"

He said, aching with love, "I can't think of anything in this world or any other that I wouldn't do for you, Callie. My darling, my treasure, anything, anything that would make it easier for you."

She looked up at him, trembling. "This, then," she said. "Knock me unconscious. Take me by force, this time, while I cannot resist—"

Andrew drew back, looking down at her in blank horror. For a moment he literally could not speak his dismay and revulsion. At last he said stammering, "You must be mad, Callista! In God's name, how could I do such a thing to any woman alive? And least of all to you!"

She looked up in despair. "You promised."

Now he was angry. "What *are* you, Callista? What kind of mad, perverse—" Words failed him. Cold to his gentleness, did she crave his cruelty, then?

Her eyes were still flooding quiet tears. She said, picking up the thought, "No, no, I never thought you would *want* to. It was the only way I could think of—oh, Avarra pity me, I should have died, I should have died—"

She turned over, burying her head in the pillow, and began to cry so wildly that Andrew was terrified. He lay down beside her, tried to take her in his arms, but she wrenched violently away from him. Dismayed, in an agony almost as great as her own, Andrew picked her up, holding her against him, stroking and soothing her, trying to make contact with her mind, but she had slammed down the barrier against him. He held her, silent, letting her cry. At last she lay resistless in his arms as she had not done since he carried her out of the caves of Corresanti, and it seemed to him that some inner barrier had dissolved too. She whispered, "You're so good to me, and I'm so ashamed."

"I love you, Callista. But I think you've built this thing up in your mind, out of all proportion. I think we were wrong to wait then, and the longer we wait the worse it's going to be." He felt the familiar touch on his mind and he knew, now, that she welcomed it, as in that time of loneliness and fear. She said, "I wasn't afraid then."

He said, firmly and surely, "Nothing has changed since then except that I love you more."

He didn't know all that much about sexual inhibitions, but he did know there was such a state as pathological frigidity, and what little he had been told about a Keeper's training confirmed his suspicion that this must be what had been done to her: a total conditioning against any kind of sexual response. He was not naive enough to believe that a gentle seduction would ease all her fears and turn her into a passionate and responsive wife, but it seemed that was the only place to start. It might, at least, reassure her.

They were deeply in contact now. He sensed that she felt no trace of the physical arousal which was so strong in him, but he knew that she hungered for the closeness which could end this cold constraint between them. He drew her gently to him. He wanted her, yes, but not unwilling. He wanted her to share the tempest of passion that made him tremble. There was no need for words. She drew his face down to her, laying her lips against his in a shy hesitation, and he felt a sudden disquiet. He had never known an inexperienced woman before. Yet he could feel—they were deeply in contact now—the tremendous effort she was making not to shrink from his touch. It seemed that he would burst with tenderness. She was pliant in his arms, shyly touching him, not trying to conceal her lack of response. It was not the passivity of ignorance—she evidently understood what he expected of her—but there was not the faintest hint of physical arousal.

He reached out again for her mind. Then, through the familiar presence which was hers, he sensed a confusion, something else, alien yet familiar, strongly sexual. *Ellemir? Damon and Ellemir?* His first reaction was to withdraw, slam down mental barriers—*I'm no voyeur!*—but then, hesitant and still tentative, he could feel Callista drop into the fourway fusion, the old link among them reestablishing itself as it had done when they were all linked together within the matrix. And for the first time he felt a yielding in Callista, not a mental yielding alone, but a physical softening. She was less apprehensive, as if this was less frightening for her, shared with her twin. As he was drawn into the fourfold link, into intense participation in the lovemaking of the other couple, it seemed for an instant that it was Ellemir in his arms, that it was she who embraced him, opening herself wholly to him, warm, responsive—No, it was only that Callista had submerged herself in Ellemir's response, and through it he could feel Callista's shy surprise, the reassurance of Ellemir's excitement and pleasure. He pressed his mouth to hers, in a long, searching kiss, and for the first time felt a flicker of actual response. Callista was no longer passively permitting him to do what he would, she was actually sharing in the kiss for the first time.

Had she needed this kind of reassurance, then? At his urging whisper, she pressed herself warmly against him. He knew she was deeply merged now in Ellemir's consciousness, sharing Ellemir's response, letting it take over her own body. He could feel Damon too, and that was disquieting, or was it only that he could also feel and share Ellemir's response to Damon's strange, provokingly sensual mixture of gentleness and violence?

For a moment it seemed to him that this was enough for now, to drift on the surface of *their* passionate embrace, to seek no more, to let himself merge in this warm, welcoming multiple consciousness. But it was still too strange for him, and his own body, demanding now, urgent, insisted on completion. Like a swimmer coming up for air he gasped, trying to disentangle himself from the multiple mind-link, to narrow his consciousness down to Callista alone, Callista in his arms, fragile, vulnerable, wholly pliant, wholly yielding.

Suddenly, with unimaginable violence, the fragile mesh of consciousness shattered. All at once he felt a tearing, burning pain in his genitals. Shocked, crying out, he heard Callista scream in despair and wild protest and felt himself torn from her arms, hurtling through the air. His mind spun, dizzily. *This couldn't be real!* His head struck something sharp, and in a blaze of pain, crimson lights exploding like bombs inside his head, he lost consciousness.

CHAPTER EIGHT

He was lying on the floor.

Before consciousness came fully back, he was aware of that, and of the fuzzy protest, *How the hell did I get here?* There was a sharp pain in his head, and a worse one in his groin. Someone lifted his head. He made a noise of protest as his head exploded, and opened his eyes. Damon, stark naked, was kneeling beside him.

"Lie still," he said sharply, as Andrew struggled to rise. "Let me wipe the blood out of your eyes, you idiot!"

Andrew's main emotion, displacing even pain, was outrage. He pushed Damon's hand violently away. "What the bloody hell are you doing here? How dare you? Callista and I—"

"So," said Damon, with a wry half-smile, "were we. As you damn well know. Do you think we wanted to be interrupted like that? But better us than the servants, man, rushing up to find out who's being murdered. In hell's name, didn't you hear Callista screaming?"

All Andrew could hear was a sobbing whimper, but it seemed that somewhere in his mind was an awareness, not quite a memory, of shattering screams. He struggled to his feet, disregarding Damon's steadying hand.

"Callista! I must go to her—"

"Ellemir's with her, and I don't think she can face you just yet. Let me look at this." His probing hands were so impersonal that Andrew could take no offense. "Does this hurt?"

It did. Damon looked grave, but after some more probing, said, "No permanent damage to the testicles, I guess. No, don't try to look, you're not familiar with wounds and it will look worse to you than it is. Can you see all right?"

Andrew tried. "Fuzzy," he said. Damon mopped at

the cut on his forehead again. "Head wounds bleed like hell, but I think that needs a stitch or two."

"Never mind that." Callista's sobs tore at his consciousness. "Is Callista all right? Oh, God, did I hurt her?"

"Did *you* hurt *her?*" Ellemir said waspishly behind them. "She didn't quite manage to kill you, this time."

"Let her alone," said Andrew, fiercely protective. All he remembered was passion, and violent—terrifyingly violent—interruption. "What happened, an earthquake?"

Callista was lying on her side, her face swollen from crying. Naked, she seemed so defenseless that Andrew felt heartsick. He picked up her robe and spread it gently over her bare body.

"Darling—darling, what did I do to you?"

She broke out into the frantic weeping again. "I tried so hard . . . and I nearly killed him, Damon, I thought I was ready and I wasn't! I could have killed him . . ."

Damon smoothed her hair away from her wet face. "Don't cry any more, *breda*. All the smiths in Zandru's forges can't mend a broken egg. You didn't kill him, that's what matters now."

"Are you trying to tell me that *Callista*—"

"An error of judgment," Damon said matter-of-factly. "You shouldn't have tried without asking me to monitor her first and see if she was ready. I thought I could trust her."

Andrew heard the echo of Callista's words in his mind: "It isn't you I don't trust." And Damon, saying, "The man who rapes a Keeper takes his life and his sanity in his hands." Evidently Callista was still guarded by a set of completely involuntary psi reflexes, reflexes she could not control . . . and which made no differentiation between attempted rape and the tenderest love.

Damon said, "I've got to put a few stitches into Andrew's forehead, Elli. Stay with Callista, don't leave her for a moment." He caught Ellemir's eye, saying gravely, "Do you understand how important that is?"

She nodded. Andrew suddenly noticed that she was naked too, and seemed quite unconscious of it. After a moment, as if *his* awareness roused it in her, she turned away and slipped into a robe of Callista's that was hanging on a chair, then sat down beside her sister, holding her hand tightly.

"Come along, let me stitch that cut," Damon said. In the other half of the suite Damon got into a robe, unhurriedly went for a small kit in his bathroom, gestured to Andrew to sit under the lamp. He sponged the cut with something cold and wet which numbed it a little, then said, "Keep still. This may hurt a bit." As a matter of fact it hurt far more than that, but was over so quickly that almost before Andrew had time to flinch Damon was sterilizing the needle in a candle flame and putting it away. He poured Andrew a drink, got himself one, and sat down across from him, looking at him thoughtfully. "If the other injury bothers you much tomorrow, take a couple of hot baths. Damn it, Andrew, what *possessed* you? To try that now, without even asking—"

"What the hell is it to you when—or whether—I sleep with my wife?"

"The answer to that," Damon said, "would seem self-evident. You interrupted us at a critical moment, you know. I would have slammed down a barrier, but I thought it might help Callista. As it was, if I weren't Tower-trained, we'd both have been badly hurt. I *did* get the backlash, so it is my business, you see. Besides," he added, more gently, "I care a lot about Callista, and you too."

"I thought she was simply afraid. Because she had been sheltered, protected, conditioned to virginity—"

Damon swore. "Zandru's hells, how can things like this happen? All four of us telepaths, and not one of us with the sense to sit down and talk things over honestly! It's my fault. I knew, but it never occurred to me that you didn't. I thought Leonie had told you; she evidently thought I had. And I certainly thought Callista would warn you before trying—well, hell, it's done, it can't be undone now."

Andrew felt total failure, total despair. "It's no good, is it, Damon? I'm no good to Callie or anyone else. Shall I just . . . take myself quietly out of her life? Go away, stop trying, stop tormenting her?"

Damon reached out and gripped him hard. He said urgently, "Do you want her to *die?* Do you know how close she is to death? She can kill herself now with a thought, as easily as she almost killed you! She has no one else, nothing else, and she can put herself out of life with a single thought. Do you want to do that to her?"

"God, *no!*"

"I believe you," Damon said after a minute, "but you'll have to make *her* believe it." He hesitated. "I have to know. Did you penetrate her, even slightly?"

Andrew's outrage was so great that Damon flinched, even before he said, "Look, Damon, what the hell—"

Damon sighed. "I could ask Callie, but I thought I might spare her that."

Andrew looked at the floor. "I'm not sure. Everything's . . . blurred."

"I think if you had, you'd have been hurt worse," Damon said.

Andrew said, with a flare of uncontrollable bitterness, "I didn't know she was hating it so much!"

Damon laid a hand on the Terran's shoulder. "She wasn't. Don't let this spoil the memory of what *was* good. That part was real." He added, after a moment, "I know; I was there, remember? I'm sorry if that bothers you, but it happens, you know, with telepaths, and we've all been linked by matrix. It *was* real, and Callista loves you, and wants you. As for the rest, she simply miscalculated, must have thought she was free of it. You see, most Keepers, if they are going to leave, marry, fall in love, usually leave the Tower before their conditioning is complete. Or they find they can't work without too much trouble and pain, so their conditioning comes unstuck and they give up and leave. The training for a Keeper is awful. Two out of three girls who try it can't even manage it. And once it *is* complete, and properly done, it's very rare for it to disappear. When Leonie gave Callista leave to marry, she must have thought it was one of those rare cases, otherwise Callista would not have wished to leave the Tower."

Andrew turned white as he listened. "What can be done about it?"

"I don't know," Damon said honestly. "I'll do what I can." He passed a weary hand over his forehead. "I wish I had some *kirian* to give her. But for now, what she needs is reassurance, and only you can give her that. Come and try."

Ellemir had washed Callista's tear-stained face, combed and braided her hair, and put her into her nightgown. When she saw Andrew, her eyes filled with tears again.

"Andrew, I did try! Don't hate me! I nearly . . . nearly . . ."

"I know." He took her fingers in his. "You should have told me exactly what it was that you were afraid of, love."

"I couldn't." Her eyes were full of guilt and pain.

"I meant what I said before, Callista. I love you, and I can wait for you. As long as I have to."

She clung tightly to his hand. Damon bent over her. He said, "Elli will sleep with you tonight. I want her close to you all the time. Are you in any pain?"

She nodded, biting her lip. Damon said, "Ellemir, when you dressed her, were there any burns or blackening?"

"Nothing serious. A blackened patch on the inside of one thigh," Ellemir said, putting aside the nightgown, and Andrew, hovering, looked with horror at the scorched mark on the flesh. Did the psi force strike like lightning, then? Damon said, "No scarring, probably. But, damn it, Callie, I hate to have to ask, but . . ."

"No," she said quickly, "he did not penetrate me."

Damon nodded, obviously relieved, and Andrew, looking at the blackened burn mark, suddenly realized, in horror, why Damon had asked.

"Andrew's not hurt much, a bump on the head, no concussion. But if you're having pains, I'd better check you." At her half-voiced protest he said gently, "Callista, I was monitoring psi mechanics when you were only a child. That's right, lie on your back. Not so much light, Elli, I can't see much in this light." Andrew thought that sounded odd, but as Ellemir dimmed the lights, Damon nodded approval. He beckoned Andrew close. "I wish to hell I'd had the sense to show you this a long time ago."

He moved his fingertips over Callista's body, not touching her, about an inch above her nightgown. Andrew blinked, seeing a soft glowing light follow his fingertips, faint swirling currents, pulsing here and there with dim clouded spirals of color.

"Look. Here are the main nerve channels—wait, I want you to see a normal pattern first. Ellemir?"

Obediently she stretched out beside Callista. Damon said, "Look, the main currents, the channels on either side of the spine, positive and negative, and branching out from them, the main centers: forehead, throat, solar plexus, womb, base of the spine, genitals." He pointed out the spiraling centers of bright light. "Ellemir is an adult, sexually awakened woman," he said with quiet detachment. "If she were a virgin, the currents would be the same, only these lower centers would be less bright, carrying less energy. This is the normal pattern. In a Keeper, these currents have been altered, by conditioning, to cut off the impulses from the lower channels, the same channels which carry sexual energies and psi force. In a normal telepath—Ellemir has a considerable amount of *laran*—the two forces arise together at puberty and after certain upheavals, which we call threshold sickness, settle down to work selectively, carrying one or the other as the need arises, and all powered by the same force in the mind. Sometimes the channels overload. Remember how I warned you when we worked in the matrix about temporary impotence? But in a Keeper, the psi forces handled are so enormous that a two-way flow would be too strong for any single body to handle unless the channels are kept completely clear for psi force. So the upper channels are separated from the lower ones, which handle sexual vitality, and there are no backflows. What we have here"—he gestured to Callista, and Andrew was absurdly reminded of a lecture-demonstrator in anatomy—"is a major overload on the channels. Normally the psi forces flow *around* the sexual centers, without involving them. But look here." He gestured, showing Andrew that Callista's lower vital centers, so clear in Ellemir, were dully luminous, pulsing like inflamed wounds, a heavy, unhealthy, sluggish swirling. "There has been sexual awakening and stimulation, but the channels which would normally carry off those impulses have been blocked and short-circuited by the Keeper's training." Gently he laid his hands against her body, touching one of the swirling currents. There was a definite, audible *snap*, and Callista moaned.

"That hurt? I was afraid so," Damon apologized. "And I can't even clear the channels. There's no *kirian* in the house, is there? You'd never be able to stand the pain, otherwise."

This was all Greek to Andrew, but he could see the turgid, dull-red swirl which, in Callista, replaced the smooth luminous pulses he could see in Ellemir's body.

"Don't worry about it now," Damon said. "It may clear itself after you've slept."

Callista said faintly, "I think I could sleep better with Andrew holding me."

Damon replied compassionately, "I know how you feel, *breda*, but it wouldn't be wise. Once you have actually begun responding to him, there are two conflicting sets of reflexes trying to work at once." He turned to Andrew, with grave emphasis. "I don't want you to touch her, not at all, until the channels are clear again!" He added sternly to Callista, "That means both of you."

Ellemir got into bed beside Callista, covered them both. Andrew noticed that the swirling luminous channels had faded to invisibility again and wondered how Damon had made them visible. Damon, picking up the thought, said, "No trick, I'll show you how it's done sometime. You have enough *laran* for that. Why don't you get into Callista's bed and try to sleep? You look as if you need it. I'm going to stay here and monitor Callista until I know she's not going into crisis."

Andrew lay down in Callista's bed. It smelled, still, with the faint fragrance of her hair, the scent she always used, a delicate flowery perfume. For a time he lay awake in restless misery, thinking that he had done this to Callista. She had been right all along! He could see Damon, silent in the armchair, brooding, silent, watching over them, and it seemed for a moment that he saw Damon not as a physical being, but as a network of magnetic currents, electrical fields, a network, a crisscross of energies. At last he fell into a restless doze.

Andrew slept little that night. His head ached unendurably, and every separate nerve in his body seemed to be screaming with tension. Now and then he started awake, hearing Callista moan or cry out in her sleep, and he could not help nightmarishly reliving his failure. It was getting light outside when he saw Damon slip quietly from his chair and go toward his own room. Andrew slid out of bed and followed him. Damon, in the half-light looked exhausted and grave. "Couldn't you sleep either, kinsman?"

"I was asleep for a while." Andrew thought that Damon looked terrible. Damon picked up the thought and grinned wryly. "Riding all day yesterday, and all the hullabaloo last night . . . but I'm fairly sure she's not going into crisis or convulsions this time, so I can slip away and get a nap." He turned into his own half of the suite. "How do *you* feel?"

"I've got the great granddaddy of all splitting headaches!"

"And a few other aches and pains, I should imagine," Damon said. "Even so, you were lucky."

Lucky! Andrew heard that, incredulous, but Damon did not explain. He went to the window and flung it wide, standing in the icy blast and looking out into the white flurry of snow. "Damn. Looks like we're set for a blizzard. Worst thing that could possibly happen. Now, especially, with Callista—"

"Why?"

"Because, man, when it snows in the Kilghard Hills, it *snows*. We could be weathered in for thirty to forty days. I had hoped to send to Neskaya Tower for some *kirian*—I don't think Callista's made any yet—in case I have to clear her channels. But no man could travel in this; I couldn't ask it." He slumped, exhausted, on the windowsill. Andrew exclaimed, seeing the icy wind stirring his hair, "Don't go to sleep *there*, damn it, you'll get pneumonia," and closed the casement. "Go and rest, Damon. I can look after Callista. She's *my* wife, and *my* responsibility."

Damon sighed. "But with Esteban disabled I'm Callie's nearest kinsman. And I put you two in rapport under the matrix. That makes it *my* responsibility; by the oath I took." He stumbled, felt Andrew catch him by the shoulder and support him upright. He said blurrily, "But I'll have to try to sleep or I won't be able to help if she needs me."

Andrew steered him toward the tumbled bed, and he caught a thread of Andrew's thought, a troubled memory, conscience-stung, that Andrew had been for a time voyeur to Damon's lovemaking with Ellemir. Damon wondered fuzzily why that bothered Andrew, was too tired to care. He crawled into the disheveled bed. He forced himself to clarity for a moment. "Stay near the women. Let Callista sleep, but if she wakes and she's in pain, call me." He rolled over on his back, trying to see the Terran's face clear before his blurring eyes. "Don't touch Callista . . . damnably important . . . not even if she asks you to. It could be dangerous. . . ."

"I'll take my chances, Damon."

"Dangerous for *her*," Damon said urgently, thinking, *damn it, if I can't trust him I'll have to go back.* . . .

Andrew, picking up the thought, said, "All right, I promise. But I want you to explain that, when you can," and Damon said, with a weary sigh, "That's a promise," and let himself fall into the blankness of sleep. Andrew stood beside him, watching the drawn lines of weariness smooth into sleep, then covered his friend carefully and went away. He instructed Damon's body-servant to let him sleep, then, on an impulse, since Ellemir was always awake so early, and it would be awkward to have someone come looking for her, he told the man to send a message to the hall-steward that they had all been awake very late and no one was to disturb them until sent for.

He went back and lay down on Callista's bed. After a time he fell asleep again. He woke suddenly, aware that he had slept for hours. It was daylight but still dark, the snow blowing and flurrying past the windows. Callista and Ellemir were lying side by side in his bed, but as he watched, Ellemir sat up, crawled carefully over Callista and tiptoed to his side.

"Where is Damon?"

"Sleeping, I hope."

"Has no one sent for me?" Andrew explained what he had done, and she thanked him. "I must go dress. I will use Callista's bath if you don't mind, I don't want to disturb Damon. I'll borrow something of hers to wear too." Moving like a shadow, she collected clothes from Callista's wardrobe. Andrew watched with unfocused resentment—would she rather disturb Callista than Damon?—but evidently the familiar presence of her twin did not penetrate Callista's heavy sleep.

Without volition, Andrew recalled Ellemir standing over Callista last night, naked and unconcerned about it. He supposed that if someone was used to having his or her mind completely open, physical nakedness would not mean all that much. But he found himself recalling a moment last night when it seemed that it was Ellemir in his arms, warm, willing, responding to him as Callista could not. . . . Disquited, he turned away. Scalding heat flooded his face, and a twinge in his body reminded him painfully of last night's fiasco. Did Ellemir know, he wondered; that he was part of her lovemaking, was she aware of him too?

Ellemir watched him for a moment with a troubled smile, then, biting her lip, went into the bath, trailing an armful of blue and white linen.

Andrew, fighting for composure, looked down at his sleeping wife. She looked pale and tired, with great dark circles like bruises under her closed eyes. She was lying on her side, one arm partly covering her face, and Andrew recalled, with surging pain, how he had seen her lying like that, in the dim light of the overworld. Prisoner in the catmen's hands, her body in the dark caves of Corresanti, she had come to him in spirit, in sleep; bruised, bleeding, exhausted, terrified. And he could do nothing for her. His helplessness had maddened him then; now he felt again all the torment of helplessness, at her lonely ordeal.

Slowly she opened her eyes.

"Andrew?"

"I'm here with you, my love." He saw pain move visibly across her face, like a shadow. "How are you feeling, darling?"

"Terrible," she said with a wry grimace. "As if I had been caught in a stampede of wild *oudrakhi.*" Who but Callista, he wondered, could have made a joke at this moment? "Where is Damon?"

"Sleeping, love. And Ellemir went to bathe and dress."

She sighed, closing her eyes for a moment. "And I had thought today I would be truly a bride. Evanda be praised that it was Damon and Ellemir who heard us, and not that brat Dezi with his taunts." Andrew flinched at the thought. It had been Dezi's jeering, indeed, which had prompted the fiasco.

He said, with emphasis, "I wish I had broken his damn neck!"

She sighed, shaking her head. "No, no, it was not his doing. We are both grown people, we know enough to make our own decisions. What he said was a rudeness. Among telepaths, you learn very quickly not to pry into such matters, and if you should learn, unwillingly, of such a private matter, there are courtesies. It was unforgivable, but he is not to blame for what happened after, my love. It was our choice."

"My choice," he said, lowering his eyes. She reached for his hand. Her small fingers felt cold. Again he saw the pain, moving in her face, and said, "Damon said I was to call him if you woke in pain, Callista."

"Not yet. Let him sleep. He wearied himself for us. Andrew—"

He knelt beside her and she held out her arms. "Andrew; hold me; just for a moment. Let me lie in your arms . . . just let me feel you close to me. . . ."

He moved in swift response to the words, to the appeal in them, thinking that, even after last night, she still loved him, still wanted him. Then, remembering, he drew back. He said, heartwrung, "My darling, I promised Damon I would not touch you."

"Oh, Damon, Damon, always Damon," she said frantically. "I'm so sick and miserable, I just want you to hold me—" She broke off and let her eyes fall shut again with a forlorn sigh. He ached with the longing to fold her in his arms, not now with desire—that had receded very far—simply to hold her close, protect her, soothe her, comfort her pain. But his promise held him motionless, and she said at last, "Oh, I suppose he's right, damn him. He usually is." But he saw the pain again behind her eyes; aging her, drawing her face into hollows of exhaustion. Somehow, and the thought horrified him, he could think only of Leonie's face, worn, drawn, weary, old.

Again memory surged over him, the moment last night when for a moment they had been fully submerged in the lovemaking of Damon and Ellemir. She had wanted it, welcomed it, begun to respond to him, only after that full sharing with the other couple. Again the harsh throb of pain in his groins, the agonizing memory of failure, blurred the excitement. His love for Callista was not an atom less, but he felt an awful, indefinable sense that something had been spoiled. A breath of intrusion, as if Damon and Ellemir, dear and close as they were had somehow come between himself and Callista.

Callista's eyes were filled with tears. In another moment, heedless of his promise, he would have caught her into his arms, but Ellemir, fresh and rosy from her bath, dressed in something he had seen Callista wearing, came back into the room. She saw that Callista was awake and went directly to her.

"Feeling better, *breda*?"

Callista shook her head. "No. Worse, if anything."

"Can you get up, love?"

"I don't know." Callista moved tentatively. "I suppose I must. Will you call my maid, Elli?"

"No, I won't. No one else is to lay a finger on you, Damon said, and I won't have those silly girls gossiping. I'll look after you, Callie. Andrew, you had better tell Damon she's awake."

He found Damon already up, shaving in the luxurious bath which duplicated the one in their half of the suite. He gestured to Andrew to come in. "Does Callista seem any better?"

Then he noticed Andrew's hesitation. "Hell, I never thought . . . are there nudity taboos in the Empire?"

Andrew felt oddly that it was he and not Damon who ought to be embarrassed. "Some cultures, yes. Mine among them. But I'm in your world, so I guess it's up to me to get used to your customs, not you to mine."

It was stupid to feel embarrassed, Andrew knew, or angry, outraged at the memory of Damon last night, standing naked over Callista, looking down on her fragile bare battered body.

Damon shrugged, saying casually, "There aren't many taboos like that here. A few among the *cristoforos*, or for the presence of nonhumans or across generations. I wouldn't willingly appear naked in a group of my father's contemporaries, or *Dom* Esteban's, for instance. It's not forbidden, though, certainly not embarrassing the way you seem to be embarrassed. I wouldn't walk out naked among a group of the maid-servants for no reason either, but if the house was afire, or something, I wouldn't hesitate. A man my own age, married to my wife's sister . . ." He shrugged helplessly. "It never occurred to me."

Andrew realized he should have guessed last night, when Ellemir never seemed to notice.

Damon splashed water on his face, followed it with some green, pleasant-smelling herbal lotion. The smell reminded Andrew poignantly of Callista's little stillroom. Damon laughed, shrugging his shirt over his shoulders. He said, "As for Elli, you ought to be relieved. It means she has accepted you as part of the family. Would you want her to be embarrassed about you, and carefully keep herself covered in your presence, as if you were a stranger?"

"Not unless you would." But did that mean she did not see Andrew as a male at all, he wondered. A subtle way of unmanning him?

"Give yourself time," Damon said, "it will all sort itself out." He was getting unconcernedly into his clothes. "Is it still snowing?"

"Harder than ever."

Damon went to look, but when he cracked the casement to look out, the howling wind tore through the room like a hurricane. He hastily slammed it shut. "Callie's awake? Who's with her? Good, I'd hoped Ellemir would have sense enough to keep the maids away. In her condition, the presence of any nontelepath would be pretty nearly unendurable. That's why we never had human servants in the Towers, you know." He turned to the door. "Have any of you had anything to eat?"

"Not yet," Andrew said, realizing that it was past noon and he was very hungry.

"Go down, will you, and ask Rhodri to send something up. I think we all ought to stay near Callista," he said, then hesitated. "I'm going to put off a messy job on you. You'll have to go and give *Dom* Esteban some kind of explanation. One look at me and he'd know the whole story—he's known me since I was nine years old. I don't think he'll probe you for explanations. You're enough of a stranger that he still feels a little reserved with you. Do you really mind? I can't face explaining to him."

"I don't mind," Andrew said. He did, but he knew that some kind of explanation to the crippled Lord Alton was no more than courtesy. It was long past the hour when Ellemir should have been about the house, and *Dom* Esteban was accustomed to Callista's company.

He told the hall-steward that they had all been up very late and would breakfast in their rooms. Remembering what Damon had said about the presence of non-telepaths, he stipulated that no one should go into the suite, but the food should be set outside. The man said, "Certainly, *Dom* Ann'dra," without a flicker of curiosity, as if the request were commonplace.

In the Great Hall, *Dom* Esteban was in his wheeled-chair by the window, the guardsman Caradoc keeping him company. Andrew saw with relief that Dezi was nowhere to be seen. *Dom* Esteban and Caradoc were playing a board game something like chess that Damon had once tried to teach Andrew. It was called castles and had pawns of carved crystal which were not set in order on the board but shaken at random and moved from the spot where they fell, according to certain complex rules. *Dom* Esteban took a red crystal piece from the board, grinned triumphantly at Caradoc, then looked with raised eyes at Andrew.

"Good morning, or do I mean good evening? I trust you slept well?"

"Well enough, sir, but Callista is . . . is a little indisposed. And Ellemir is staying with her."

"And you're both staying with them, quite right and proper," said *Dom* Esteban, grinning.

"If there is anything which should be done, Father-in-law . . . ?"

"In this?" The old man gestured at the snowstorm. "Nothing, no need to apologize."

Andrew remembered that the old man was also a powerful telepath. If last night's disturbance had disrupted Damon and Ellemir even in their marriage bed, had it disturbed the old man too? But if so, not a flicker of the Alton lord's eyelids betrayed it. He said, "Give Callista my love, and tell her I hope she is well soon. And tell Ellemir to look after her sister. I have plenty of company, so I can manage without any of you for a day or so."

Caradoc made some remark in the thick mountain dialect about the blizzard season being the right time to stay indoors and enjoy the company of one's wife. *Dom* Esteban guffawed, but the joke was a little obscure for Andrew. He was grateful to the old man, but he felt raw-edged, indecently exposed. No one with a scrap of telepathic force could have slept through all that last night, he felt. It must have waked telepaths up all the way to Thendara!

Upstairs, food had been brought, and Damon had carried it to Callista's bedside. Callista was in bed again, looking white and worn. Ellemir was coaxing her to eat, in small bites as she would have coaxed a sick child. Damon made room for Andrew at his side, handed him a hot roll. "We didn't wait for you. I was hungry after last night. The servants probably think we're having an orgy up here!"

Callista said, with a small wry laugh, "I wish they were right. It would certainly be an improvement over present conditions." She shook her head as Ellemir proffered her a bite of hot bread, spread with the aromatic mountain honey. "No, really, I can't."

Damon watched her with disquiet. She had drunk a few sips of milk, but had refused to eat, as if the very effort of swallowing was too much for her. He said at last, "You've taken over the still-room, Callista, have you made any *kirian*?"

She shook her head. "I'd been putting it off, and there's no one here who needs it, with Valdir in Nevarsin. And it's troublesome to make, having to be distilled three times."

"I know. I've never made it, but I've watched it being done," Damon said, looking sharply at her as she shifted weight. "You're still in pain?"

She nodded, saying in a small voice, "I'm bleeding."

"That, too?" Wasn't she to be spared anything? "How much before the regular time is it? If it's only a few days, it might be simply the shock."

She shook her head. "You still don't understand. There is no . . . no regular time for me. This is the first time—"

He stared at her in shock, almost disbelieving. He said, "But you had turned thirteen when you first went to the Tower, were your woman's cycles not yet established?"

It seemed to Andrew that she looked embarrassed, almost ashamed. "No. Leonie said it was a good thing that they had not yet begun."

Damon said angrily, "She should have waited for that to begin your training!"

Callista looked away, turning red. "She told me . . . beginning so young, some of the normal physical processes would be disrupted. But she said it would make it easier for me if I was spared that altogether."

Damon said, "I thought *that* was a barbarism from the Ages of Chaos! For generations it has been taken for granted that a Keeper should be a woman grown!"

Callista rushed to the defense of her foster-mother. "She told me that six other girls had tried, and failed to make the adjustments, that it would be easier for me, with less pain and trouble. . . ."

Damon frowned, sipping at a glass of wine, staring into the depths as if he had seen something unpleasant there.

"Tell me, and think carefully. In the Tower, were you given any kind of drug to suppress your menses?"

"No, it was never necessary."

"I cannot think it of Leonie, but did she ever work with a matrix, on your body currents?"

"Only in the ordinary pattern-training, I think," Callista said doubtfully. Andrew broke in. "Look here, what is this all about?"

Damon's face was grim. "In the old days, a Keeper in training was sometimes neutered—Marisela said something like that, remember? I cannot believe—I cannot *believe*," he added with emphasis, "that Leonie would have blighted your womanhood that way!"

Callista said, stricken, "Oh, no, Damon! Oh, no! Leonie loves me, she would never . . ." But her voice faded out. She was afraid.

Leonie had been so sure that her choice was lifelong, had been so reluctant to release her. . . .

Andrew reached for Callista's cold hand. Damon said, frowning, "No, I know you were not neutered, of course not. If your cycles have come on, your clock is running again. But it was done sometimes in the old days, when they felt virginity was less of a burden to a girl still immature."

"But now it's begun, she'll be all right, won't she?" Ellemir asked anxiously, and Damon said, "We'll hope so." Perhaps the arousal of last night, abortive as it had been, had reawakened some of those blocked pathways in her body; if she had suddenly matured, it might be that her illness and physical discomfort might be the normal troubles of early development. He remembered from his years in the Tower that young women in Keeper's training, or for that matter any women working with psi mechanics above the level of monitor, were subject to recurrent and occasionally excruciating menstrual difficulties. Callista, following his thought, laughed a little and said, "Well, I have handed out golden-flower tea and such remedies to other women at Arilinn, and always thought myself lucky that I was immune to their miseries. It seems I have joined the ranks of normal women in *that* respect at least! I know we have golden-flower tea in the stillroom; Ferrika gives it to half the women on the estate. Perhaps a dose of that will be all I need."

Ellemir said, "I'll go and fetch you some," and after awhile she came back with a small cup of some steaming hot brew. It had a pungent herbal smell, strongly aromatic. Callista's voice held, for a moment, an echo of her old gaiety.

"Would you believe I have never tasted this? I hope it's not too dreadful a potion!"

Ellemir laughed. "It would serve you right if it were, you wretched girl, if you hand out such decoctions with no idea of what they taste like! No, actually, it's rather nice tasting. I never minded taking it. It will make you sleepy, though, so lie down and let it do its work."

Obediently Callista drank off the steaming stuff and settled down under her blanket. Ellemir brought some needlework and sat beside her, and Damon said, "Come along, Andrew, they'll be all right now," and let him out of the room.

Downstairs, in the stone-floored still-room, Damon began to look through Callista's supply of herbs, essences, distilling equipment. Andrew, looking at the oddly shaped flasks, the mortars and pestles and the bottles ranged on shelves, the bunches of dried herbs, leaves, stalks, pods, flowers, seeds, asked, "Are these all drugs and medicines?"

"Oh, no," Damon said absently, pulling a drawer open. "These"—he gestured to some crushed seeds—"are cooking spices, and she makes incense to sweeten the air, and some cosmetic lotions and perfumes. None of the stuff you can buy in the towns is half as good as what's made here by the old recipes."

"What was that stuff Ellemir gave her?"

Damon shrugged. "Golden-flower? It's a smooth muscle tonic, good for cramps and spasms of all kinds. It can't hurt her; they give it to pregnant women and to babies with the colic too." But, he wondered, frowning, if it could help Callista. Such serious interference with the physical processes . . . how could Leonie have done such a thing?

Andrew picked up the thought, as clearly as if Damon had spoken it aloud. "I knew Keepers underwent some physical changes. But this?"

"I am shocked too," said Damon, turning a bunch of white thornleaf in his hands. "It's certainly not customary these days. I had believed it was against the laws. Of course Leonie's intentions couldn't have been better. You saw the alterations in the nerve currents. Some of the girls do have a dreadful time with their woman's cycles, and Leonie probably could not bear to see her suffering. But what a price to pay!" He scowled and began opening drawers again. "If Callista had freely chosen . . . but Leonie didn't tell her! That is what I find hard to understand, or to forgive!"

Andrew felt an insidious dismay, a physical horror. Why should it, after all, shock him so much? Physical modification was not, after all, anything so unheard of. Most of the women who crewed Empire starships—they were made sterile by deep space radiations anyway—were spared the nuisance of menstruation. Hormone treatments made it unnecessary for women not actively engaged in childbearing. Why should it shock him so? It wasn't shocking, except that *Damon* found it so! Would he ever get used to this goldfish-bowl life? Couldn't he even think his own thoughts?

Damon was turning over bunches of herbs. He said, "You must understand. Callista is past twenty. She's a grown woman who has been doing difficult, highly technical work as a matrix mechanic for years. She's an experienced professional in the most demanding work on Darkover. Now none of her previous training, none of her skills, nothing is any good to her at all. She's struggling with deconditioning, and with sexual awakening, and she has all the emotional problems of any bride. And now, on top of all that, I discover that physically she's been held in the state of a girl of twelve or thirteen! Evanda! If I had only known. . . ."

Andrew looked at the floor. More than once, since the terrible fiasco of last night, he had felt as he imagined a rapist must feel. If Callista was, physically, an unawakened girl in her early teens—he felt a spasm of horror.

Damon said gently, "Don't! Callista didn't know it herself. Remember, for six years she's been functioning as an adult, experienced professional." Yet he knew this was not entirely true, either. Callista must have been aware of the enormous and ineradicable gulf between her and the other women. Leonie might have spared her protégée some physical suffering, but at what price?

Well, it was a good sign that the menstrual cycle had spontaneously reinstated itself. Perhaps other barriers would disappear with nothing more than time and patience. He picked up a bunch of dried blossoms and cautiously sniffed. "Good, here we are. *Kireseth*—no, don't smell it, Andrew, it does funny things to the human brain." He felt the faint guilt of memory. The taboo against the *kireseth*, among psi workers, was absolute, and he felt as if he had committed a crime in handling it. He said, speaking more to himself than Andrew, "I can make *kirian* from this. I don't know how to distill it as they do in Arilinn, but I can make a tincture. . . ." His mind was busy with possibilities: a strong solution of the resins dissolved out in alcohol. Perhaps with Ferrika's help he could make a single distillation. He put the stuff down, fancying that the smell of it was going to the roots of his brain, destroying controls, breaking barriers between mind and body. . . .

Andrew paced restlessly in the still-room. His own mind was filled with horrors. "Damon, Callista must have *known* what could happen."

"Of course she knew," said Damon, not really listening to him. "She learned that before she was fifteen years old, that no man can touch a Keeper."

"And if I could hurt or frighten her so terribly—Damon!" Suddenly he was overcome by the horror and revulsion which had gripped him last night. His voice dropped to a whisper. "Do you know what she wanted me to do? She asked me to . . . to knock her unconscious and rape her when she . . . when she could not resist." He tried to convey some of the horror that had awakened in him; but Damon only looked thoughtful.

"It just might have worked, at that," he said. "It was intelligent of Callista to think of it. It shows she has some grasp of the problems involved."

Andrew could not keep back a horrified "Good God! And you can say it like that, so calmly."

Damon, turning, suddenly realized that the younger man was at the edge of his endurance. He said gently, "Andrew, you do know what saved you from being killed, don't you?"

"I don't know anything any more. And what I do know doesn't help much!" He felt ragged despair. "Do you really think I could have—"

"No, no, of course not, *bredu*. I understand why you couldn't. I don't think any decent man could!" Gently, he laid a hand on Andrew's wrist. "Andrew, what saved you—saved you both—was the fact that she *wasn't* afraid. That she loved you, wanted you. So all she hit you with was the physical reflex she couldn't control. She didn't even knock you out; it was hitting your head on the furniture that did that. If she had been terrified and fighting you, if you had really been trying to take her unwilling, can you *imagine* what she would have thrown at you?" he demanded. "Callista is one of the most powerful telepaths on Darkover, and trained as a Keeper in Arilinn! If she had hated it, if she had thought of it as rape, if she had felt any . . . any fear or revulsion against your desire, you'd have been dead!" He repeated for emphasis, "You'd be dead, dead, *dead!*"

But she was afraid, Andrew thought, until Damon and Ellemir made contact. . . . It was the awareness of Ellemir's pleasure that made her want to share it! Even more disturbing was the thought of Damon, aware of Callista as *he* had been aware of Ellemir. Damon, sensing his distress, was for a moment shocked, experiencing it as a rebuff. They had all been so close, didn't Andrew want to be part of what they were? He laid his hand on Andrew's shoulder, a rare touch for a telepath, natural enough at this moment in the awareness of the intimacy they had shared. Andrew shrank from it, and Damon withdrew, troubled and a little saddened. Must he stay at such a distance? How long? How long? Was he brother or stranger?

But he said gently, "I know it's new to you, Andrew. I keep forgetting that I grew up as a telepath, taking this sort of thing for granted. It will be all right, you'll see."

All right? Andrew asked himself. To know that only the fact that he had become an involuntary voyeur kept his wife from killing him? To know that Damon—and Ellemir—both took this kind of thing for granted, expected it, welcomed it? Did Damon resent his wanting Callista all to himself? He remembered the suggestion that Callista had made, remembered the feel of Ellemir in his arms, warm, responsive—*as Callista could not be*. Shocked, in desperate confusion, he turned away from Damon, blundering with horror to get out of the room. He was overloaded with shame and horror. He wanted—needed—to get away, anywhere, anywhere out of here, away from Damon's too revealing touch, from the man who could read his most intimate thoughts. He did not know that he was virtually ill, with a very real illness known as culture shock. He only knew he felt sick, and the sickness took the form of furious rage against Damon. The heavy scent of the herbs made him afraid he would vomit. He said thickly, "I've got to get some air," and pushed the door open, stumbling through the deserted kitchens and into the yard. He stood with the heavy snow falling all around him, and damned the planet where he had come and the chances that had brought him here.

I should have died when the plane went down. Callie doesn't need me. . . . I'm never going to do anything but hurt her.

Damon said behind him, "Andrew, come and talk to me. Don't go off like this alone and try to shut it all out."

"Oh, God," Andrew said, drawing a breath like a sob, "I have to. I can't talk any more. I can't take it any more. Let me alone, damn it, can't you just let me alone for a little while?"

He felt Damon's presence like a sharp physical pain, a pressure, a compulsion. He knew he was hurting Damon; refused to know, to turn, to look. . . . Finally Damon said very gently, "All right, Ann'dra. I know you've had all you can take. A little while, then. But not too long." And Andrew knew without turning that Damon was gone. No, he thought with a shudder of horror, Damon had never been there at all, was still back in the little stone-floored still-room.

He stood in the courtyard, heavy snow blowing around him, its fury only a little abated by the enclosing walls. *Callista.* He reached for the reassurance of her touch, but she was not there, only a faint pulse, restless, and he dared not disturb her drugged sleep.

What can I do? What can I do? To his dismay and horror he began to weep, alone in the wilderness of snow. He had never felt so alone in his life, not even when the plane went down and he found himself alone on a strange planet, beneath a strange sun, in trackless unmapped mountains. . . .

Everything I ever knew is gone, useless, meaningless or worse. My friends are strangers, my wife the most alien

of all. My world is gone, renounced. I can never go back;
they think me dead.

He thought, *I hope I catch pneumonia and die,* then,
aware of the childishness of that, realized he was in very
real danger. Drearily, not from any sense of self-
preservation, but the remnant of vague duty, he turned
and went inside. The house looked alien, strange, not a
place where any Terran could manage to live. Had it
ever seemed welcoming, home? He looked with profound alienation around the empty hall, glad it was
empty. *Dom* Esteban must be taking his midday rest.
The maids were gossiping in soft voices. He sank down
wearily on a bench, let his head rest in his arms, and
stayed there, not asleep, but in retreat, hoping that if he
stayed very quiet it would all go away somehow and not
be real.

A long time later someone put a drink in his hands.
He swallowed it gratefully, found another, and another,
blurring his senses. He heard himself babbling, pouring
it all out to a suddenly sympathetic ear. There were
more drinks. He knew, and welcomed it, when he
passed out.

There was a voice in his mind, worming its way past his
barriers, deep into his unconscious, past his resistance.

No one wants you here. No one needs you here. Why
not go away now, while you can, before something dread-
ful happens. Go away now, back where you came from,
back to your own world. You'll be happier there. Go
now. Go away now. No one will know or care.

Andrew knew there was some flaw in his reasoning.
Damon had given him some good reason why he should
not go, then he remembered that he was angry with
Damon.

The voice persisted, gentle, cajoling:

You think Damon is your friend. Don't trust Damon.
He will use you, when he needs help, and then turn on
you. There was something familiar about the voice, but
it wasn't a voice at all. It was somehow inside his mind!
He tried in panic to shut it out, but it was so soothing.

Go away now. Go away now. No one needs you here.
You will be happy when you go back to your own people.
You will never be happy here.

With fumbling steps, Andrew went out into the side hall. He found his riding cloak, fastened it around his shoulders. Someone was helping him, buckling it around him. Damon, was it? Damon knew he couldn't stay. He couldn't trust Damon. He would be happy with his own people. He would get back to Thendara, back to the Trade City and the Terran Empire where his mind was his own. . . .

Go now. No one wants you here.

Even thickly drunk and blurred as he was, the violence of the storm struck him hard enough to take his breath away. He was about to turn back, but the voice pounded inside his head.

Go now. Go away. No one wants you here. You've failed. You're only hurting Callista. Go away, go to your own people.

His boots floundered in the snow, but he kept on, lifting and dropping them with dogged determination. *Callista doesn't need you.* He was drunker than he realized. He could hardly walk. He could hardly breathe, or did the flurrying snow take his breath away, snatch it, refuse to give it back?

Go away. Go back to your own people. No one needs you here.

He came a little to himself, with a final desperate attempt at self-preservation. He was alone in the storm, and the lights of Armida had vanished in the darkness. He turned desperately, stumbling, falling to his knees, realizing he was drunk, or mad. He stumbled to his feet, felt his mind blurring, fell full length in the snow. He must get up, go on, go back, get to shelter—but he was so tired.

I will just rest here for a minute . . . just a minute. . . .

Darkness covered his mind and he lost consciousness.

CHAPTER NINE

Damon worked for a long time in the narrow, stone-floored still-room, finally giving up in disgust. There was no way that he could make *kirian* as it was made in Arilinn. He had neither the skill nor, he suspected from a relatively thorough investigation of the equipment here, the proper materials. He regarded the crude tincture which he had managed to produce without enthusiasm. He didn't think he would care to experiment with it himself, and he was sure Callista would not. There was, however, a considerable amount of the raw material, and he might be able to do better another day. Perhaps he should have begun with an ether extraction. He would ask Callista. As he washed his hands and carefully disposed of the residues, he thought suddenly of Andrew. Where had he gone? But when he went upstairs again, to find Callista still sleeping, Ellemir answered his concerned question with surprise.

"Andrew? No, I thought him still with you. Shall I come—"

"No, stay with Callista." He thought Andrew must have gone down to talk to the men, or out to the stables through the underground tunnels. But *Dom* Esteban, alone at his frugal supper with Eduin and Caradoc, frowned when questioned.

"Andrew? I saw him drinking in the lower hall with Dezi. From the way they were pouring it down, I suppose he has passed out somewhere." The old man's gray eyebrows bristled with scorn. "Nice behavior, with his wife ill, to go off and get himself sodden drunk! How is Callista?"

Damon said, "I don't know." and thought suddenly that the old *Dom* knew. What else could it be, with Callista ill in bed and Andrew going off to get drunk? But one of the strongest sexual taboos on Darkover was that which separated the generations. Even if *Dom* Esteban had been Damon's own father instead of Ellemir's, custom would have forbidden him to discuss this.

Damon searched the house, in all the likely places, then, in growing panic, all the unlikely ones. Finally he summoned the servants, to hear that no one had seen Andrew since midafternoon, when he and Dezi had been drinking in the lower hall.

He sent for Dezi, suddenly afraid lest Andrew, drunk and not yet accustomed to Darkovan weather, should have gone out into the blizzard, underestimating its power. When the youngster came into the room, he asked, "Where is Andrew?"

Dezi shrugged. "Who knows? I'm not his guardian or his foster-brother!"

But at the unconcealable flash of triumph, a momentary glint before Dezi's eyes evaded his, suddenly Damon *knew*. "All right," he said grimly. "Where is he, Dezi? You were the last to see him."

The boy gave a sullen shrug. "Back to where he came from, I suppose, and good riddance!"

"In *this*?" Damon stared in consternation at the storm raging beyond the windows. Then he swung on Dezi with a violence that made the boy flinch and shrink away from him.

"*You* had something to do with this!" he said, low and furious. "I'll deal with you later. Now there is no time to lose!"

He ran, shouting for the servants.

Andrew woke, slowly, to burning pain in his feet and hands. He was rolled in blankets and bandages. Ferrika was bending over him with something hot. Holding his head, she got him to swallow it. Damon's eyes swam out of the fog, and groggily Andrew realized that Damon was really worried about him. He cared. It was not true, what Andrew had thought.

Damon said gently, "We found you just in time, I think. Another hour and we could never have saved your feet and hands; two hours and you would have been dead. What do you remember?"

Andrew struggled to remember. "Not much. I was drunk," he said. "I'm sorry, Damon, I must have gone mad for a little. I kept thinking, *Go away, Callista doesn't want you.* It was like a voice inside my head, so I tried to do just that, go away. . . . I'm sorry to have caused all this trouble, Damon."

"*You* don't need to be sorry," Damon said grimly, and his rage was like a palpable red glow around him. Andrew, sensitized, saw him as an electrical net of energies, not at all like the daily Damon he knew. He glowed, he trembled with fury. "*You* didn't cause the trouble. A very dirty trick was played on you, and it nearly killed you." Then he was Damon again, a slender stooping man, laying a gentle hand on Andrew's shoulder.

"Go to sleep and don't worry. You're here with us, and we'll look after you."

He left Andrew sleeping, and went in search of *Dom Esteban.* Rage was pulsing in his mind. Dezi had the Alton gift of forced rapport, of forcing mental links with anyone, even a nontelepath. Andrew, drunk, would be the perfect victim, and knowing Andrew, Damon suspected he had not gotten drunk of his own free will.

Dezi was jealous of Andrew. That had been obvious all along. But why? Did he feel that with Andrew out of the way, *Dom* Esteban might acknowledge him as the son he would then so desperately need? Or had he had it in his mind to seek Callista in marriage, hoping that would force the old man's hand, to admit Dezi was Callista's brother? It was a riddle beyond Damon's reading.

Damon might, perhaps, have forgiven an ordinary telepath under such temptation. But Dezi was Arilinn-trained, sworn by the oath of the Towers, never to meddle with the integrity of a mind, never to force the will of another, or his conscience. He had been entrusted with a matrix, with all the awsome power that entailed.

And he had betrayed it.

He had not done murder. Good luck, and Caradoc's sharp eyes, had found Andrew lying in a snowdrift, partly covered with the blowing snow. In another hour he would have been covered over, his body perhaps found in the spring thaw. And what of Callista, thinking Andrew had forsaken her? Damon shuddered, realizing that Callista might not have lived out the day. Thanks to all the gods at once, she had been deep in drugged sleep at the time. She would have to know—there was no way to keep such things secret in a telepathic family—but not yet.

Dom Esteban heard the story out with dismay. "I knew there was bad blood in the boy," he said. "I would have acknowledged him my son years ago, but I never quite felt I could trust him. I did what I could for him, I kept him where I could keep an eye on him, but there seemed something wrong with him somewhere."

Damon sighed, knowing the old man's bluster was mostly guilt. Secure, acknowledged, reared as a Comyn son, Dezi would not have had to bolster his enormous insecurities with envy and jealous spite, bringing him at last to attempt murder. More likely, though Damon tactfully barricaded the thought from the old man, his father-in-law had simply been unwilling to perpetuate, or take responsibility for, a sordid and drunken episode. Bastardy was no disgrace. For a woman to bear a Comyn son was honor, to her and the child, yet the most opprobrious epithet in the *casta* tongue was translated "sixfathered."

And even that could have been avoided, Damon knew, if while the girl was with child, she had been monitored to discover whose seed had kindled her to bear. Damon thought, in something very like despair, that there was something very wrong in the way they were using telepaths on Darkover.

But it was too late for any of this. For what Dezi had done there was only one penalty. Damon knew it, *Dom* Esteban knew it, and Dezi, Damon could see plainly, knew it. They brought him, tied hand and foot and half dead of fright, to Damon later that night. They had found him in the stables, making ready to saddle and be gone into the blizzard. It had taken three of Esteban's Guardsmen to overpower him.

Damon thought that would have been better. In the storm he would have found the same justice, the same death he had sought for Andrew, and death unmutilated. But Damon was bound by the same oath Dezi had violated.

Andrew felt that he too would have willingly faced

death in the blizzard, rather than the smoldering anger he could feel in Damon now. Just the same, paradoxically, Andrew felt sorry for Dezi when the boy was brought in, thin and frightened, looking younger than he was. He seemed like a boy hardly into his teens, so that the ropes binding him looked like monstrous injustice and torture.

Why didn't Damon just leave it to him? Andrew wondered. He would beat hell out of the kid and for somebody his age, that ought to be enough. He had said as much to Damon, but the older man had not even bothered to answer. It had been clear, anyway.

Andrew would never otherwise be safe again: from the knife in the back, the murderous thought. . . . Dezi was an Alton, and a murderous thought could kill. He had already come close to it. Dezi was not a child. By the law of the Domains, he could fight a duel, acknowledge a son, be held responsible for a crime.

He looked now at the shrinking Dezi, and at Damon, with dread. Like all men of swift but short-lived anger, Andrew had no experience with the held grudge; nor with the rage which turns inward, devouring the angry man as much as the victim of his wrath. It was this he sensed in Damon now, like a sullen red furnace-glow, dimly visible around him. The Comyn lord looked bleak, his eyes toneless.

"Well, Dezi, I hardly dare to hope you will make this easy for me or for yourself, but I'll give you the option, though it's more than you deserve. Will you match resonances with me willingly and let me take your matrix without a struggle?"

Dezi did not answer. His eyes blazed out bitter, hating defiance. Damon thought, what a waste it was. He was so strong. He flinched, shrinking from the intimacy that was being forced on him, the least welcome of all intimacies, that of torturer and tortured. *I don't want to kill him, and I probably will have to. Mercy of Avarra, I don't even want to hurt him.*

Yet, thinking of what he had to do, he could not keep himself from shuddering. His fingers closed, a spasmodic grip, over the matrix in its leather and silk insulation at his throat.

There, over the pulse, over the glowing center of the main nerve channel. Since it was given to Damon, at fifteen, and the lights in the stone wakened at the touch of his mind, it had never been beyond the reassuring touch of his fingertips. No other human being, except his Keeper, Leonie or, during a brief time in his Tower years, the young under-Keeper Hilary Castamir, had ever touched it. The very thought of having it taken from him, forever, filled him with a cold black terror worse than dying. He knew, with every fiber of the Ridenow gift, the *laran* of an empath, what Dezi was enduring now.

It was blinding. It was crippling. It was mutilation. . . .

It was the penalty invoked by the Arilinn oath for illegal use of a matrix. And it was what he must, by law, inflict now.

Dezi said, clinging to a last shred of defiance, "Without a Keeper present, it is murder that you do. Is murder penalty for attempted murder, then?"

Damon, though he felt Dezi's terror in his own bowels, kept his voice passionless. "Any halfway competent matrix technician—and I am rated a technician—can do this part of a Keeper's work, Dezi. I can match resonances and take it from you in safety. I won't kill you. If you try not to fight me, it will be easier for you."

"No, damn you!" Dezi spat out, and Damon steeled himself for the ordeal ahead. He could admire the boy's attempt to pretend courage, some dignity. He had to remind himself that the courage was a sham in a coward who had misused *laran* against a drunk and unprotected man, who had gotten him drunk for that purpose. To admire Dezi now, simply because he did not break down and plead for mercy—as Damon knew perfectly well he himself would do—made no sense at all.

He still felt Dezi's emotions—a trained empath, his *laran* honed to fine point at Arilinn, he could not block them out—but he steeled himself to ignore them, focusing on the ordeal ahead. The first step was to focus inward on his own matrix, to steady his breathing, let his consciousness expand into the magnetic field of his body. He let the emotions filter through and past him, as a

Keeper must do, feeling and accepting them, without entering into them in the slightest.

Leonie had told him once that if he had been a woman, he would have made a Keeper, but that, as a man, he was too sensitive, that this work would destroy him. Somehow, the remembrance made him angry again, and the anger strengthened him. Why should sensitivity destroy a man, if it was valuable for a woman, if it could have made a woman capable of the most difficult of all matrix work, that of a Keeper? At the time, the words had come close to destroying him; he had felt them an attack on his very manhood. Now they reaffirmed in him the knowledge that he could do this part of a Keeper's work.

Andrew, watching, lightly linked with Damon, saw him again as he had seen him for a moment the night before, watching over the sleeping Callista: a swirling field of interconnected currents with pulsing centers, dim colors glowing at the pulse spots. Slowly he began to see Dezi the same way, to sense what Damon was doing, bringing his own rate of vibration close to Dezi's own, to adjust the flows so that their bodies—and their matrix jewels—were vibrating in perfect resonance. This would, he knew, enable Damon to touch Dezi's matrix without pain, without inflicting physical or nervous shock strong enough to produce death.

For someone not keyed into the precise resonance, to touch someone else's matrix could produce shock, convulsions, even death; at the very least, incredible agony.

He saw the resonances match, pulse together as if, for a moment, the two magnetic fields blended and became one. Damon got out of his chair—to Andrew, it looked like a cloud of linked energy fields, moving—and went toward the boy. Abruptly Dezi wrenched control of the resonances away from Damon, shattering the blended rapport. It was like a clashing explosion of force. Damon gasped in anguish with the recoil, and Andrew felt the shattering pain that exploded in Damon's nerves and brain. Automatically, Damon stumbled out of reach of the clashing field, steadied himself to rematch resonances to the new field Dezi had created. He thought, almost in pity, that Dezi had panicked, that when it came to it, he couldn't quite endure it.

Again the matched resonances, the energy fields beginning to vibrate in consonance; again the attempt to reach out for Dezi, to remove the matrix physically from the magnetic field of his body. And again the shattering wrench as Dezi broke the resonances, thrust them apart with an explosion of pain cascading through them both.

Damon said compassionately, "Dezi, I know it's hard." Inwardly he thought that the boy could almost be a Keeper himself. Damon could not match resonances that way at his age! But then he had never been as desperate, either, nor as tormented. The breaking of resonances was obviously just as painful for Dezi as it was for Damon himself. "Try not to fight this time, my boy. I don't want to hurt you."

And then—they were open to one another—he felt Dezi's thrusting contempt for his attempt at pity, and knew this was not a panic reaction at all. Dezi was simply putting up one hell of a fight! Perhaps he thought he could outfight Damon, wear him down. Damon left the room and came back with a telepathic damper, a curious gadget which broadcast a vibration that could damp out telepathic emanations within a broad range of frequencies. Grimly he thought of Domenic's jest on the night he and Ellemir had been married. Such things were used, sometimes, to blur telepathic leakage, when there were others around, to protect privacy, to permit secret talk or prevent unwilling (or deliberate) telepathic eavesdropping. It was used sometimes in Comyn Council, or to protect others when there was an undeveloped, or uncontrolled, adolescent in psychic upheaval, before learning to control or focus powers. He saw Dezi's face change, take on real panic through the defiance.

Tonelessly, he warned Andrew, "Get out of range if you want to. This might hurt. I'm going to have to use it to damp out any frequencies he tries to raise."

Andrew shook his head. "I'll stick." Damon caught Andrew's thought: *I won't leave you alone with him.* Grateful for his friend's loyalty, Damon knelt down and began to set up the damper.

Before long, he had tuned it to damp out Dezi's assault on his consciousness. After that, it was simply a matter of matching his own resonances to Dezi's physical field of vibration. This time when he stepped into the interlocking fields, the damper blocked out Dezi's mental thrust to alter the frequencies, move him away. It was painful and hard to move under the damper, something he thought only a full-fledged Keeper could have done at all, with the damper full strength. It felt, physically, as if he were struggling through some thick, viscous fluid which dragged at his limbs and his brain. Dezi began to struggle like a mad thing as he came near. But it was hopeless, and he knew it. Dezi could exhaust himself with the effort to change frequencies, but he could not alter Damon's now, and the more he managed to alter his own, the more the ultimate shock would hurt.

Gently Damon laid his hand on the small silk insulating bag around Dezi's neck. His fingers fumbled to untie the thong. Dezi had begun to moan and struggle again, and his struggles, like a rabbit in a snare, wrenched at Damon with pity, even though the boy's terror was barricaded now by the damper. He managed to get the bag open. The blue stone, pulsing, glowing with Dezi's terror, fell into his fingers. As they closed over it, he felt the bone-cracking spasm within himself, saw Dezi slump as if felled by a crushing blow. He wondered wretchedly if he had killed the boy. He thrust the matrix within the field of the damper, saw it quiet down to a faint pulse, a resting rhythm. Dezi was unconscious, his head lolling to one side, froth on his bitten lips. Damon had to steel himself to remember Andrew, unconscious, in a deathly sleep in the snow, to think of Callista's agony if she had awakened to find herself abandoned, or widowed by treachery, before he could harden himself to say "That's done."

He thrust the matrix for a few minutes under the damper, saw it fade to dimness, the faintest of pulsing lights. It was still alive, but it had been lowered in strength to where it could not be used for *laran*.

He cast a pitying look at Dezi, knowing he had blinded the boy. Dezi was worse off now than Damon was when they sent him from Arilinn. In spite of Dezi's crime, Damon could not help feeling sorrow for the boy, so gifted, such a powerful telepath, potential higher than many now working in the screens and relays. Zandru's hells, he thought, what a waste. And he had crippled him.

He said wearily, "Let's finish this, Andrew. Hand me that lock-box, will you?"

He had gotten it from *Dom* Esteban, who had removed some small jewelry from it. As he thrust the matrix inside, closing the lid, he thought of the old fairytale: the giant kept his heart outside of his body, in the most secret place he could find, so that he could not be killed unless they sought out his hidden heart. He explained briefly to Andrew as he fiddled with the small matrix lock on the box, thrusting his own against it. He said, "We can't destroy the matrix; Dezi would die with it. But it is locked here with a matrix lock so nothing but my own matrix, attuned to this pattern, will ever open this box again." The box locked, he put it into a store-room, came back and bent over Dezi, checking the boy's breathing, his racing heart.

He would survive.

Mutilated . . . blinded . . . but he would survive. Damon knew he would rather have died, if it were he.

Damon straightened, listening to the quieting sound of the storm outside. He drew his dagger and cut the ropes binding the boy, thinking that it might be kinder to cut his throat. He wouldn't want to live. Was his terrible struggle only a way of attempting suicide?

He sighed, laying some money in a purse beside the boy. He said heavily to Andrew, "*Dom* Esteban gave me this for him. He'll probably go to Thendara, where Domenic promised him a cadet commission. He can't do much harm there, working in the City Guards and he can make himself some kind of career. Domenic will look after him—there's some sense of family loyalty, after all. Dezi won't even have to confess what's been done to him. He'll be all right."

Later, telling Ellemir what he had done, while Andrew watched over the still-sleeping Callista, he repeated it.

"I wouldn't have wanted to live. When I stood over him with the dagger, to cut the ropes they had tied him with, I wondered if it would have been kinder to kill

him. But I managed to live after they sent me from Arilinn. Dezi should have that chance too." He sighed, remembering the day he had left Arilinn, blind with pain,
dazed with the breaking of the bonds of the Tower circle, the closest bond known to those with *laran*, closer
than kin, closer than the bond of lovers, closer than husband and wife. . . .

"I got over wanting to die," he said, "but it was a
long time before I wanted to live again." Holding Ellemir close, he thought: *Not till I had you.*

Ellemir's eyes softened with tenderness, then, her
mouth hardening, she said, "You should have killed
him."

Damon, thinking of the sleeping Callista, who had
come, not knowing it, so close to death, thought this was
merely bitterness. Andrew was her sister's husband, she
had been linked to him by matrix during the long search
for Callista, and they had all come together in that brief,
spontaneous, fourfold moment of sharing, before the
frightening reflex Callista could not control had ripped
them apart. Like Ellemir, Damon too had been linked
to Andrew, feeling his strength and gentleness, his tenderness and passion . . . And this was the man Dezi had
tried, out of spite, to kill. Dezi, who had himself been
linked with Andrew when they healed the frostbite
cases, knew him too, knew his quality and his goodness.

Ellemir repeated implacably, "You should have
killed him."

Not for months did Damon know that this was not
merely bitterness, but precognition.

In the morning the storm had quieted, and Dezi, taking with him the money Damon had left at his side, his
clothing and his saddle horse, had gone from Armida.
Damon hoped, almost with guilt, that he would somehow manage to live, to find his way safely to Thendara
where he would be under Domenic's protection. Domenic, heir to Alton, was after all Dezi's half brother.
Damon was sure of it, now; no one not full Comyn could
have put up a fight like that.

Domenic would look after him, he thought. But it was
like a weight on his heart, and it did not lift.

CHAPTER TEN

Andrew was dreaming . . .

He was wandering in the blizzard he could hear outside, flinging heavy snow and sleet, driven by enormous winds, around the heights of Armida. But he had never seen Armida. He was alone, wandering in a trackless, houseless, shelterless wilderness, as he had done when the mapping plane went down and abandoned him on a strange world. He was stumbling in the snow and the wind tore at his lungs and a voice whispered like an echo in his mind: *There is nothing for you here.*

And then he saw the girl.

And the voice in his mind whispered. *This has all happened before.* She was wearing a flimsy and torn nightdress, and he could see her pale flesh dimly through the rents in the gown, but it did not flutter or move in the raging winds that tore him, and her hair was unstirring in the raging storm. She was not there at all, she was a ghost, a dream, a girl who never was, and yet he knew, on another level of reality, she was Callista, she was his wife. Or had that been only a dream within a dream, dreamed while he was lying in the storm, and he would lie there and follow the dream until he died . . . ? He began to struggle, heard himself cry out . . .

And the blizzard was gone. He was lying in his own bedroom at Armida. The storm was raging and dying away outside, but the bedroom fire had burned to dim coals. By its light he could dimly see Callista—or was it Ellemir, who had slept at her side ever since the night when the psi reflex she could not control had blasted them both down, in the midst of their love?

For the first few days after Dezi's attempted murder

he had done little except sleep, suffering from the after-effects of mild concussion, shock, and explosure. He touched the unhealed cut on his forehead. Damon had taken out the stitches a day or two ago, and the edges were beginning to scab cleanly. There would be a small scar. He needed no scar to remind him of how he had been torn from Callista's arms, a force like lightning striking through her body. He recalled that it used to be a favorite form of torture, in the old days on Terra, an electrode to the genitals. It hadn't been Callista's fault though, the shock of knowing what she had done had nearly killed her too.

She was still abcd, and it seemed to Andrew that she grew no better. Damon, he knew, was worried about her. He dosed her with odd-smelling herbal potions, discussing her condition at length in words of which Andrew understood perhaps one in ten. He felt like the fifth leg on a horse. And even when he began to mend, to want to be out and about, he could not even lose himself in the normally heavy work of the horse ranch. With the blizzard season, all had come to a dead halt. A handful of servants, using underground tunnels, tended the saddle horses and the dairy animals which provided milk for the household. A handful of gardeners cared for the greenhouses. Andrew was nominally in charge of all these, but there was nothing for him to do.

Without Callista, he knew, there was really nothing to hold him here, and he had not been alone with Callista for a moment since the fiasco. Damon had insisted that Ellemir sleep at her side, that she must never, even in sleep, be allowed to feel herself alone, and that her twin was better for this purpose than any other.

Ellemir had nursed her tirelessly, night and day. On one level Andrew was grateful for Ellemir's tender care, there being so little he could do for Callista now. But at the same time he resented it, resented his isolation from his wife, the way in which it emphasized the fragility of the thread that bound him to Callista.

He would have cared for her, nursed her, lifted her . . . but they would never leave him alone with her for a moment, and this too, he resented. Did they really think that if they left Callista alone, Andrew would fall on her again like a wild animal, that he would rape her? Damn it to hell, he thought, it was more likely that he was always going to be scared to touch her even with a fingertip. I just wanted to be with her. They told him she needed to know that he still loved her, and then they acted as if they didn't dare leave them together for a minute. . . .

Realizing that he was merely going over and over, obsessionally, frustrations about which he could do nothing, he turned over restlessly and tried to sleep again. He heard Ellemir's quiet breathing, and Callista's restless sigh as she turned over. He reached for her with his thoughts, felt the touch dimly on his mind. She was deep asleep, drugged with another of Damon's or Ferrika's herb medicines. He wished he knew just what they were giving her, and why. He trusted Damon, but he wished Damon would trust *him* a little more.

And Ellemir's presence too was a low-keyed irritation, so like her twin, but healthy and rosy where Callista was pale and ill . . . Callista as she should have been. Pregnancy, even though frustrated so soon, had softened her body, emphasizing the contrast to Callista's sharp thinness. Damn it, he shouldn't think about Ellemir. She was his wife's sister, his best friend's wife, the one woman of all women forbidden to him. Besides, she was a telepath, she'd be picking up the thought, and it would embarrass hell out of her. Damon had told him once that among a telepathic family a lustful thought was the psychological equivalent of rape. He didn't care a damn about Ellemir—she was just his sister-in-law—it was just that she made him think of Callista as she might be if she were healthy and well and free of the grip of the forever-bedamned Tower.

She was so gentle with him. . . .

After a long time he drifted off to sleep and began to dream again.

He was in the little herdsman's shelter where Callista, moving through the overworld, the world of thought and illusion, had led him through the blizzard, after the crash of the plane. No, it was not the herdsman's shelter; it was the strange illusory walled structure that Damon had built up in their minds, not real except in their visualization, but having its own solidity in the realm of thought, so he could see the very bricks and stones of it. He woke, as he had done then, in dim light, to see the girl lying beside him, a shadowy form, stilled, sleeping. As he had done then, he reached for her, only to find that she was not there at all, that she was not on this plane at all, but that her form, through the over-world, which she had explained as the energy-net double of the real world, had come to him through space and perhaps time as well, taking shape to mock him. But she had not mocked him.

She looked at him with a grave smile, as she had done then, and said with a glimmer of mischief, "Ah, this is sad. The first time, the very first time, I lie down with any man, and I am not able to enjoy it."

"But you are here with me now, beloved," he whispered, and reached for her, and this time she was there in his arms, warm and loving, raising her mouth for his kiss, pressing herself to him with shy eagerness, as once she had done, but only for a moment.

"Doesn't this prove to you that it is time, love?" He drew her against him, and their lips met, their bodies molded one to the other. He felt again all the ache and urgency of need, but he was afraid. There was some reason why he must not touch her . . . and suddenly, at the moment of tension and fear, she smiled up at him and it was Ellemir in his arms, so like and so unlike her twin.

He said "No!" and drew away from her, but her hands, small and strong, drew him down close to her. She smiled at him and said, "I told Callista to tell you that I am willing, as it was told in the ballad of Hastur and Cassilda." He looked around, and he could see Callista, looking at them and smiling. . . .

And he woke with a start of shock and shame, sitting up in bed and staring wildly around to reassure himself that nothing had happened, nothing. It was daylight, and

Ellemir, with a sleepy yawn, slid from the bed, standing there in her thin nightgown. Andrew quickly looked away from her.

She did not even notice—he was not a man to her at all—but would continue to walk around in front of him half dressed or undressed, keeping him continually on edge with a low-keyed frustration that was not really sexual at all. . . . He reminded himself that he was on *their* world, and it was for him to get used to *their* customs, not force his own on them. It was only his own state of frustration, and the shaming realism of the dream, which made him almost painfully aware of her. But as the thought clarified in his mind, she turned slowly and looked full at him. Her eyes were grave, but she smiled, and suddenly he remembered the dream, and *knew* that she had shared it somehow, that his thoughts, his desire, had woven into *her* dreams.

What the hell kind of man am I, anyhow? My wife's lying there sick enough to die, and I'm going around with a lech for her twin sister. . . . He tried to turn away, hoping Ellemir would not pick up the thought. *My best friend's wife.*

Yet the memory of the words in the dream hung in his mind: *I told Callista to tell you that I am willing.* . . .

She smiled at him, but she looked troubled. He felt that he ought to blurt out an apology for his thoughts. Instead she said, very gently, "It's all right, Andrew." For a moment he could not believe that she had actually spoken the words aloud. He blinked, but before he thought what to say, she had gathered up her clothes and gone away into the bath.

He went quietly to the window and looked at the dying storm. As far as he could see, everything lay white, faintly reddened with the light of the great red sun, peering faintly through the stained edges of the clouds. The winds had whipped the snow into ice-cream ridges, lying like waves of some hard white ocean, sweeping back all the way to the distant blurring hills. It seemed to Andrew that the weather refuted his mood: gray, bleak, insufferable.

How fragile a tie, after all, bound him to Callista! And yet he knew he could never go back. He had discovered too many depths within himself, too many alien strangenesses. The old Carr, the Andrew Carr of the Terran Empire, had wholly ceased to exist on that faraway day when Damon placed them all in rapport through the matrix. He closed his fingers on it, hard and chill in the little insulated bag around his neck, and knew it was a Darkovan gesture, one he had seen Damon make a hundred times. In that automatic gesture, he knew again the strangeness of his new world.

He could never go back. He must make a new life for himself here, or go through what years remained to him as a ghost, a nothingness, a nonentity.

Until a few nights ago he had believed himself well on the way to building his new life. He had worthwhile work to do, a family, friends, a brother and sister, a second father, a loving and beloved wife. And then, in a blast of unseen lightning, his whole new world had crumbled around him and all the alienness had closed over him again. He was drowning in it, sinking in it. . . . Even Damon, usually so close and friendly, his brother, had turned cold and strange.

Or was it Andrew himself who now saw strangeness in everything and everyone?

He saw Callista stir, and, suddenly apprehensive lest his thoughts should disturb her, gathered up his clothes and went away to bathe and dress.

When he came back, Callista had been wakened, and Ellemir had readied her for the day, dressing her in a clean nightgown, washing her, braiding her hair. Breakfast had been brought, and Damon and Ellemir were there, waiting for him around the table where the four of them had taken their meals during Callista's illness.

But Ellemir was still standing over Callista, troubled. As Andrew came in, she said, and her voice held deep disquiet, "Callista, I wish you would let Ferrika look at you. I know she is young, but she was trained in the Amazon's Guildhouse, and she is the best midwife we have ever had at Armida. She—"

"The services of a midwife," said Callista, with a trace of wry amusement, "are of all things the last I need, or am likely to need!"

"All the same, Callista, she is skilled in all manner of

women's troubles. She could certainly do more for you than I. Damon," she appealed, "what do you think?"

He was standing at the window, looking out into the snow. He turned and looked at them, frowning a little. "No one has more respect than I for Ferrika's talents and training, Elli. But I do not know if she would have the experience to deal with this. It is not commonplace, even in the Towers."

Andrew said, "I don't understand this at all! Is it still only the onset of menstruation? If it is as serious as this, perhaps," and he appealed directly to Callista, "could it do any harm for Ferrika to look you over?"

Callista shook her head. "No, that has ended, a few days ago. I think"—she looked up at Damon, laughing— "I am simply lazy, taking advantage of a woman's weakness."

"I wish it were that, Callista," Damon said, and he came and sat down at the table. "I wish I thought you would be able to get up today." He watched her slowly, with lagging fingers, buttering a piece of the hot nut-bread. She put it to her mouth and chewed it, but Andrew did not see her swallow.

Ellemir broke a piece of bread. She said, "We have a dozen kitchen maids, and if I am out of the kitchen for a day or two, the bread is not fit to eat!"

Andrew thought the bread was much as usual: hot, fragrant, coarse-textured, the flour extended with the ground nut-meal which was the common staple food on Darkover. It was fragrant with herbs, and tasted good, but Andrew found himself resenting the strange coarse texture, the unfamiliar spices. Callista was not eating either, and Ellemir seemed troubled. She said, "Can I send for something else for you, Callista?"

Callista shook her head. "No, truly, I can't, Elli. I am not hungry—"

She had eaten almost nothing in days. In God's name, Andrew thought, what ails her?

Damon said, with sudden roughness, "You see, Callista? It is what I told you! You have been a matrix worker how long—nine years? You know what it means when you cannot eat!"

Her eyes looked frightened. She said, "I'll try, Damon.

Really I will," and took a spoonful of the stewed fruit on her plate, choking it down reluctantly. Damon watched her, troubled, thinking that this was not what he had intended, to force her to pretend hunger when she had none. He said, staring out over the whipped-cream ridges of snow, purpling with the light, "If the weather would clear, I would send to Neskaya. Perhaps the *leronis* could come to look after you."

"It looks like clearing now," Andrew said, but Damon shook his head.

"It will be snowing harder than ever by tonight. I know the weather in these hills. Anyone setting forth this morning would be weathered in by midday."

And indeed, soon after midday the snow began to drift down from the sky again in huge white flakes, slowly at first, then more and more heavily, in a resistless flood that blotted out the landscape and the ridge of hills. Andrew watched it, as he went from barn-tunnels to greenhouses, going through the motions of supervising stewards and handymen, with outrage and disbelief. How could any sky hold so much snow?

He came up again in late afternoon, as soon as he had completed the minimal work which was all that could be done these days. As always when he had been away from Callista for a little while, he was dismayed. It seemed that even since this morning she had grown whiter and thinner, that she looked ten years older than her twin. But her eyes blazed at him with welcome, and when he took her fingertips in his, she closed them over his hand, hungrily.

He said, "Are you alone, Callista? Where is Ellemir?"

"She has gone to spend a little time with Damon. Poor things, they have had so little time together lately, one or the other of them is always with me." She shifted her body with that twinge of pain which seemed never to leave her. "Avarra's mercy, but I am weary of lying in bed."

He stooped over her, lifted her in his arms. "Then I will hold you for a little while in my arms," he said, carrying her to a chair, near the window. She felt like a child in his arms, loose and limp and light. Her head leaned wearily against his shoulder. He felt an aching tenderness, without desire—how could any man trouble this sick girl with desire? He rocked her back and forth, gently.

"Tell me what is going on, Andrew. I have been so isolated; the world could have come to an end and I would hardly have known."

He gestured at the white featureless world of snow beyond the window. "Nothing much has been happening, as you can see. There is nothing to tell, unless you are interested in knowing how many fruits are ripening in the greenhouse."

"Well, it is good to know that they have not yet been destroyed by the storm. Sometimes the windows break, and the plants are killed, but it would be early in the year for that," she said, and leaned wearily back against him, as if the effort of talking had been too much for her.

Andrew sat holding her, content that she did not draw away from him, that she seemed now to crave contact with him as much as she had feared it before. Perhaps she was right: now that her normal mature cycles had begun again, with time and patience, the conditioning of the Tower could be overcome. Her eyes were closed, and she seemed asleep.

They sat there for some time, until Damon, abruptly coming into the room, stopped, in dismay and shock. He opened his mouth to speak, and Andrew caught directly from his mind the frightened urgency:

Andrew! Put her down, quickly, get away from her!

Andrew raised his head angrily, but at the very real distress in Damon's thought he acted quickly, rising and carrying Callista to her bed. She lay still, unconscious, unmoving.

"How long," Damon said evenly, "has she been like this?"

"Only a few minutes. We were talking," Andrew said defensively.

Damon sighed. He said, "I thought I could trust you, I thought you understood!"

"She is not afraid of me, Damon, she *wanted* me to hold her!"

Callista's eyes flickered open. In the room's pale snow-light they looked colorless. "Don't scold him, Damon, I was weary of lying in bed. Truly, I am better. I thought tonight I would send for my harp and play a little. I am so tired of having nothing to do."

Damon looked at her skeptically. But he said, "I will send for it, if you ask."

"Let me go for it," Andrew said. Surely if she felt well enough to play her harp, she must be better indeed! He went down into the Great Hall, found a steward and asked for the Lady Callista's harp. The man brought the small instrument, not much larger than a Terran guitar, in its carved wood case.

"Shall I carry it up for you, *Dom* Ann'dra?"

"No, I will take it."

One of the woman servants, behind the steward, said, "Bear our congratulations to the lady, and say that we hope she will soon be well enough to accept them in person."

Andrew swore, unable to stop himself. Quickly he apologized—the woman had meant no harm. And what else could they have thought? She had been abed for ten days, and no one had been asked to come and nurse her, only her twin sister being allowed near. Could anyone blame them if they thought that Callista was pregnant, and that her sister and her husband were taking great care that her child did not meet the fate of Ellemir's? At last he said, and knew his voice was unsteady, "I thank you for your . . . your kind wishes, but my wife has no such good fortune . . ." and he couldn't go on. He accepted their murmured sympathy, and escaped quickly upstairs.

In the outer room of the suite, he stopped, hearing Damon's voice raised in anger.

"It's no good, Callista, and you know it. You can't eat, you don't sleep unless I drug you. I hoped it would all sort itself out, after your cycles came on of their own accord. But look at you!"

Callista murmured something. Andrew could not hear the words, only the protest in them.

"Be honest, Callista. You were *leronis* at Arilinn. If someone had been brought to you in this state, what would you do?" A brief pause. "Then you know what I must do, and quickly."

"Damon, no!" It was a cry of despair.

"*Breda*, I promise you, I will try—"

"Oh, Damon, give me a little more time!" Andrew heard her sobbing. "I'll try to eat, I promise you. I *am* feeling better, I sat up today for more than an hour, ask Ellemir. Damon, can't you give me a little more time?"

A long silence, then Damon swore and came out of the room. He started to stride past Andrew without speaking, but the Terran grasped his arm.

"What's wrong? What were you saying to get her so upset?"

Damon stared past him and Andrew had the unsettling thought that to Damon he was not really there at all. "She doesn't want me to do what I have to do." He caught sight of the harp in the case and said scornfully, "Do you really think she is well enough for that?"

"I don't know," Andew said angrily. "I only know that she asked me for it." Abruptly, remembering what the servants had said, he felt he could endure no more.

"Damon, what is wrong with her? Every time I have asked, you have evaded me."

Damon sighed and sat down, leaning his head on his hands. "I doubt if I can explain. You're not matrix-trained, you haven't the language, you don't even have the *concepts*."

Andrew said grimly, "Just put it in words of one syllable."

"There aren't any." Damon sighed and was silent, thinking. Finally he said, "I showed you the channels, in Callista and in Ellemir."

Andrew nodded, remembering those glowing lines of light and their pulsing centers, so clear in Ellemir, so inflamed and sluggish in Callista.

"Basically, what ails her is overload of the nerve channels." He saw that Andrew did not understand. "I told you how the same channels carry sexual energies and psi forces, not at the same time, of course. When she was trained as Keeper, Callista was taught techniques which prevented her from being capable of—or even aware of—the slightest sexual response. Is that clear so far?"

"I think so." He pictured her whole sexual system

made nonfunctional so that she could use her whole body as an energy-transformer. God, what a thing to do to a woman!

"Well, then. In the normal adult the channels function selectively. Turning off the psi forces when the channels are needed for sexual energies, turning off sexual impulses when psi is being used. After matrix work you were impotent for a few days, remember? Normally, when a Keeper gives up her work, it is because the channels have reverted to normal levels, and normal selectivity. Then she is no longer able, as a Keeper *must* be able, to remain totally and completely free of the slightest trace of sexual energy remaining in the channels. Evidently Callista must have thought this had already happened in her channels, because she could feel herself reacting to you. She did for a moment, you know," he said, looking at Andrew hesitantly, and Andrew, unwilling to remember that fourfold moment of contact, to acknowledge that Damon could have been part of it, could not raise his eyes. He only nodded, without looking up.

"Well, then, if an ordinary Keeper—a fully functioning Keeper, with conditioning intact and channels clear—is attacked, she can protect herself. If, for instance, you had not been Callista's husband, someone to whom she had given the right, if you had been a stranger attempting rape, she would have blasted straight *through* you. And you would have been very, very dead, and Callista would have been . . . well, I suppose she would have been shocked and sick, but after a good meal and some sleep she would not have been much the worse. But that didn't happen."

Andrew said numbly "God!"

It isn't you I don't trust, my husband. . . .

"She must have believed she was ready, or she would never have risked it. And when she realized she was *not* ready—in that split second before she blasted you with the reflex she couldn't control—she took a backflow through her *own* body. And that saved your life. If that whole flow of energy had gone through you, can you imagine what would have happened?"

Andrew could, but discovered he would much rather not.

"It must have been that shock which brought on her menstruation. I watched her carefully until I knew she wasn't going into crisis, but after that I thought the bleeding, and the normal energy drain of that time in women, would carry off the overloading and clear the channels. But it hasn't." He frowned. "I wish I knew precisely what Leonie had done to her. Meanwhile, I asked you not to touch her. And you must not."

"Are you afraid she will blast me again?"

Damon shook his head. "I don't think she has the strength for that now. In a way it's worse. She is reacting to you physically, but the channels are not clear so there is no way to carry off the sexual energies through the channels in the normal way. There are two sets of reflexes operating at once, each jamming the other, inhibiting either of the normal functions."

"I feel more muddled than ever," Andrew said, dropping his head in his hands, and Damon set to work to simplify further.

"A woman trained as Keeper sometimes has to coordinate eight or ten telepaths. Working in the energon rings, she has to channel all that force *through* her own body. They handle such *enormous* psi stresses, like"— he picked up the analogy neatly from Andrew's mind— "an energy-transformer. So they can't, they *dare* not, rely on the normal selectivity of the ordinary adult. They have to keep those channels totally, completely, and permanently cleared for the psi forces. Do you remember what my sister Marisela said?"

They heard it together, an echo in Damon's mind: *In the old days the Keepers of Arilinn could not leave their posts if they would. . . . The Keepers of Arilinn are not women but* emmasca. . . .

"Keepers aren't neutered anymore, of course. They rely on vows of virginity, and intensive antisexual conditioning, to keep the channels totally free. But a Keeper is, after all, a woman, and if she falls in love, she is likely to begin to react sexually, because the channels have returned to normal selectivity, for psi or for sex. She has to stop functioning as a Keeper, because her channels are no longer completely clear. She could handle ordinary psi, but not the enormous stresses of a Keeper, the energon rings and relays—well, you don't know much about that, never mind it. In practice, a Keeper whose conditioning has failed usually gives up *laran* work altogether. I think that's foolish, but it's our custom. But this is what Callista was expecting: that once she had begun to react to you, she would begin to use the channels selectively, like any normal mature telepath."

"So why didn't she?" Andrew demanded.

"I don't know," Damon said, in despair. "I have never seen anything like it before. I would not like to believe that Leonie had altered the channels so they could never function selectively, but I cannot think of anything else it could be. Since Leonie evidently altered her channels in some way, to keep her physically immature, I can only think it was that. But do you understand now why you must not touch her, Andrew? It's not because she would blast you again—and probably kill you this time—for she would let herself die before she would do that. It would be so easy for her that it terrifies me to think about it. But it's because the reflexes are still *there*, and she's fighting them, and it's killing her."

Andrew covered his face with his hands. "And I begged her . . ." he said almost inaudibly.

"You couldn't know," said Damon gently. "She didn't know either. She believed she was deconditioning normally, or she would never have risked it. She was willing to give up the psi function of the channels entirely, for you. Do you know what that meant to her?"

Andrew muttered, "I'm not worth it. All that suffering."

"And so damned unnecessary!" Damon broke off. He was talking blasphemy. No law was stricter than that which prevented a Keeper, her oath once given back, her virginity lost or even suspect, from ever again doing any serious matrix work. "It was what she wanted, Andrew. To give up her work as Keeper, for you."

"So what's to be done?" Andrew demanded. "She can't go on like this, it will kill her!"

Damon said reluctantly, "I will have to clear her channels. And this is what she does not want me to do."

"Why not?"

Damon did not answer at once. Finally he said, "It's

usually done under *kirian*, and I have none to give her. Without it, it's hellishly painful." This made Callista sound like a simple coward, and he was reluctant to give that impression, but he did not feel capable of explaining to Andrew what Callista's real objection was. His eyes fell with relief on the *rryl* in its case.

"But if she is well enough to ask for that, perhaps she is really better," he said with a glimmer of hope. "Take it to her, Andrew. But," and he paused, said at last, reluctantly, "don't touch her. She's still reacting to you."

"But isn't that what we want?"

"Not with the two systems overloading and jamming," Damon said, and Andrew bent his head, saying in a low voice, "I promise."

He went past Damon, into the room where Callista lay—and stopped in shock. Callista lay silent, unmoving, and for a dreadful moment he could not see her breathing. Her eyes were open, but she did not see him, and her eyes did not move to follow him as his shadow fell between her and the light. A terrible fear gripped him; he felt a soundless scream tightening his throat. He whirled to shout for Damon, but Damon had already picked up the telepathic impact of his panic and was running into the room. Then a great sigh of relief, almost a sob, burst from Damon.

"It's all right," he said, catching at Andrew as if dizzy, "she's not dead, she's . . . she's left her body. She's in the overworld, that's all."

Andrew whispered, staring at the wide-open sightless eyes, "What can we do for her?"

"In her present physical state she won't be able to stay long," Damon said, trouble, concern, and hope mingling in his voice. "I did not even know she was strong enough for this. But if she is . . ." He did not say it aloud, but they could both hear what he did not say: *If she is, perhaps it is not as bad as we fear.*

Moving in the gray spaces of the overworld, Callista sensed their cries and their fear, but dimly, like a dream. For the first time in an eternity, she was free from pain. She had left her racked body behind, stepping out of it like a too-large garment, slipping on to the familiar realms. She felt herself formulate in the gray spaces of the overworld, her body cool and quiet and at peace as it had been before. . . . She saw herself wrapped in the airy translucent folds of her Keeper's robe, a *leronis*, a sorceress. *Do I still see myself like this?* she wondered, deeply troubled. *I am not a Keeper, but a wedded woman, in thought and heart if not in fact. . . .*

The emptiness of the gray world frightened her. She reached out, almost automatically, for a landmark, and saw in the gray distance the faint glimmer that was the energy-net equivalent, in this world, of the Arilinn Tower.

I cannot go there, she thought, *I have renounced it*, yet with the thought she felt a passionate longing for the world she had left forever behind her. As if the longing had created its own answer, she saw it brighten, then, almost with the swiftness of thought, and she was *there*, within the Veil, in her own secret retreat, the Garden of Fragrance, the Keeper's Garden.

Then she saw the veiled form before her, slowly taking shape. She did not need to see Leonie's face to recognize her here.

"My darling child," Leonie said. Callista knew it was only a tenuous contact in thought, but so real was their presence to one another in this familiar realm that Leonie's voice sounded rich, warm, tenderer than ever in life. Only on this nonphysical plane, she knew, could Leonie risk this kind of emotion. "Why have you come to us? I had thought you gone forever beyond our reach, *chiya*. Or have you strayed here in a dream?"

"It is no dream, *Kiya*." Anger washed through her, like a cold shock bathing every nerve. She controlled it, as she had been taught from childhood, for the anger of the Altons could kill. Her voice cold and demanding, rejecting Leonie's tenderness, she stated, "I came to seek you, to ask you why you spoke a blessing without truth! Why did you lie to me?" Her own voice was like a scream in her ears. "Why did you bind me in bonds I could not break, so that when you gave me in marriage it was mockery? Do you grudge me happiness, who knew none of your own?"

Leonie flinched. Her voice was filled with pain. "I had hoped you happy and already a bride, *chiya*."

"You know what you had done to make that impossible! Can you swear that you have not neutered me, as was done in old days to the lady of Arilinn?"

Leonie's face was filled with horror. She said, "The Gods witness it, child, and the holy things at Hali, you have not been neutered. But Callista, you were very young when you came to the Tower. . . ."

Time seemed to flow backward as Leonie spoke and Callista felt herself dragged back to a time half forgotten, her hair still curling about her cheeks instead of braided like a woman's, felt again the frightened reverence she had felt for Leonie before she had become mother, guide, teacher, priestess. . . .

"You succeeded as Keeper when six others had failed, my child. I thought you proud of that."

"I was," Callista murmured, bending her head.

"But you misled me, Callista, or I would never have let you go. You made me believe—though I hardly felt it possible—that already you were responding to your lover, that if you had not lain with him it would only be a little while. And so I thought perhaps I had not really succeeded, that perhaps your success as Keeper came because you *believed* yourself free of such things as tormented the other women. Then, when love came into your life and you found where your heart lay, then, as has happened with many Keepers, it was no longer possible to remain unawakened. And so I blessed you, and gave you back your oath. But if this is not true, Callista, if it is not true. . . ."

Callista remembered Damon flinging the angry taunt at her: *Will you spend your life counting holes in linen towels and making herbs for spice-bread, you who were Callista of Arilinn?* And Leonie heard it too, in her mind, an echo.

"I said it before, my darling, now I offer it again. You can return to us. A little time, a little retraining, and you would be one of us again."

She gestured, the air rippled, and Callista was clothed in the crimson of a Keeper, ritual ornaments at her brow and her throat.

"Come back to us, Callista. Come back."

She said, faltering, "My husband—"

Leonie gestured that away as nothing. "Freemate marriage is nothing, Callista, a legal fiction, meaningless until consummated. What binds you to this man?"

Callista started to say "Love," and under Leonie's scornful eyes could not get the word out. She said, "A promise, Leonie."

"Your promise to us came first. You were born to this work, Callista, it is your destiny. Do you remember, you consented to what was done to you? You were one of seven who came to us that year. Six young women failed, one after another. They were already grown, their nerve channels matured. They found the clearing of the channels and the conditioning against response too painful. And then there was Hilary Castamir, do you remember? She became Keeper, but every month, when her woman's cycles came upon her, she went into convulsions, and the cost seemed too great. I was desperate, Callista, do you remember? I was doing the work of three Keepers, and my own health began to suffer. And for this reason I explained it to you, and you consented—"

"How could I consent?" Callista cried in despair. "I was a child! I did not even know what it was you asked!"

"Yet you consented, to be trained when you were not yet full-grown and the channels still immature. And so you adjusted easily to the training."

"I remember," Callista said, very low. She had been so proud, that she should succeed where so many failed, that she should be Callista of Arilinn, take her place with the great Keepers of legend. She remembered the exhilaration of seizing the direction of the great circles, of feeling the enormous stresses flow unhindered through her body, of seizing and directing the enormous energon rings. . . .

"And you were so young, I thought it unlikely you would ever change. It was pure chance. But, my darling, this can all be yours again. You have only to say the word."

"No!" Callista cried. "No! I have given back my oath—I do not want it!" And yet in a curious sense she was not sure.

"Callista, I could have forced you to return. You were virgin still, and the law permitted me to require you to come back to Arilinn. The need is still great, and I am old. Yet it is as I said, it is too heavy a burden to be borne unconsenting. I released you, child, even though I am old and this means I must struggle to bear my burden till Janine is old enough and strong enough for this work. Does this sound as if I wished you ill, or lied when I blessed you and bade you live happily with your lover? I thought you already free. I thought that in giving back your oath I bowed to the inevitable; that you were already freed in fact and there was no reason to hold to the word and torture you by the attempt to make you return, to clear your channels and force you to try again."

Callista whispered, "I hoped . . . I believed I was free. . . ."

She could feel the horror in Leonie, like a tangible thing. "My poor child, what a risk to take? How could you care so much for some man, when you have all this before you? Callista, my darling, come back to us! We will heal all your hurts. Come back where you belong—"

"No!" It was a great cry of renunciation. As if it had reverberated into the other world, she could hear Andrew's voice, crying out her name in agony.

. "Callista, Callista, come back to us . . ."

There was a brief, sharp shock, the shock of falling. Leonie was gone and pain arrowed through her body. She found herself lying in her bed, Andrew's face white as death above hers.

"I thought I'd lost you for good this time," he whispered.

"It might be better . . . if you had," she murmured in torment.

Leonie was right. Nothing binds me to him but words . . . and my destiny is to be Keeper. For a moment, time swam out of focus and she saw herself sheltered behind a strange unfamiliar wall, not Arilinn. She seized the strands of force within her hands, cast the energon rings. . . .

She reached out for Andrew, instinctively shrank away. Then, feeling his dismay, reached for him, disregarding the knifing, warning pain.

She said, "I will never leave you again," and clung to his hands in desperation.

I can never go back. If there is no answer I will die, but I will never go back.

Nothing binds me to Andrew but words. And yet . . . words . . . words have power. She opened her eyes, looking directly into her husband's, and repeated the words he had said at their wedding.

"Andrew. In good times and in bad . . . in wealth and in poverty . . . in sickness and health . . . while life shall last," she said, and closed her hands over his. "Andrew, my love, you must not weep."

CHAPTER ELEVEN

Damon felt he had never before been quite so frustrated as now. Leonie had acted for reasons which seemed good to her at the time, and he could, a little, understand her motives.

There must be a Keeper at Arilinn. All during Leonie's life, that had been the first consideration, nothing could be allowed to supersede it. But there was no way he could explain this to Andrew.

"I'm sure if I were in your place, I should feel much the same," he said. It was late at night, Callista had dropped into an exhausted, restless sleep, but at least she was sleeping, undrugged, and Damon tried to find a shred of hope in that. "You cannot blame Leonie—"

"I can and I do!" Andrew interrupted, and Damon sighed.

"Try to understand. She did what she thought best, not only for the Towers but for Callista too, to save her the pain and suffering. She could hardly have been expected to foresee that Callista would want to marry—" He had started to say, "to marry an out-worlder." He caught himself and stopped, but of course Andrew picked up the thought anyway. A dull red flush, half anger, half embarrassment, spread over the Terran's face. He turned away from Damon, his face looking closed and stubborn, and Damon sighed, thinking that this had to be settled quickly or they would lose Andrew too.

The thought was bitter, almost intolerable. Since that first moment of fourfold meshing within the matrix, while Callista was still prisoner, Damon had found something he had thought irrevocably lost to him when he was sent from the Tower, the telepathic bond of the circle.

He had lost it when Leonie sent him from Arilinn, to resign himself to live without it, and then, beyond hope, he had found it again in his two girl cousins and this out-worlder. . . . Now he would rather die than let the bond be broken again.

He said firmly, "Leonie did this, for whatever reasons, good or bad, and she must bear the responsibility for it. Callista was not strong enough to get the answer from her. But Leonie, and Leonie alone, may hold the key to her trouble."

Andrew looked out into the black, snow-shot darkness beyond the window. "That's no help. How far is Arilinn from here?"

"I don't know how you would reckon the distance. We calculate it at ten days ride," Damon said, "but I had no thought of going to her there. I shall do as Callista has done and seek her out in the overworld." His narrowed lips sketched a bleak smile. "With *Dom* Esteban disabled and Domenic not yet grown, I am her nearest kinsman. I have right and responsibility to call Leonie to account."

But who could call a Hastur to account, Hastur, and the Lady of Arilinn?

"I feel like going along with you and raising a little hell myself," said Andrew.

"You wouldn't know what to say to her. I promise you, Andrew, if there is an answer to be found, I'll find it."

"And if there isn't?"

Damon turned away, not even wanting to think about that. Callista slept restlessly, tossing and moaning in her sleep. Ellemir was doing some needlework in an armchair, frowning over the stitches, her face bright in the oval of the lamp. Damon reached for her, feeling the quick response in her mind, a touch of reassurance and love. *I need her with me, and I must go alone.*

"In the other room, Andrew, we would disturb them here. Keep watch for me," he added, leading the way into the other room, arranging himself half lying in a great chair, Andrew at his side. "Watch . . ."

He focused on the matrix, felt the brief, sharp shock of leaving his body, felt Andrew's strength as he hovered briefly in the room . . . Then he was standing on the gray and formless plain, seeing with surprise that behind

him, in the overworld, there was a landmark, a dim
structure, still shadowy. Of course, he and Dezi and Andrew had built it for shelter when they worked with the
frostbitten men, a refuge, a protection. *My own place. I
have no other now.* Firmly he put that aside, searching
in his bodiless formation for the glimmering beacon-light
of Arilinn. Then, literally with the speed of thought, he
was there, and Leonie before him, veiled.

She had been so beautiful. . . . Again he was struck
with the old love, the old longing, but he armored himself with thoughts of Ellemir. But why did Leonie veil
herself from him?

"I knew when Callista came that you would not be
far behind her, Damon. I know, of course, in a general
way, what you want. But how can I help you, Damon?"

"You know that as well as I. It is not for myself that
I need help, but for Callista." ·

Leonie said, "She has failed. I was willing to release
her—she has had her chance—but now she knows her
only place is here. She must come back to us at Arilinn, Damon."

"It is too late for that," Damon said. "I think she will
die first. And she is near it." He heard his own voice
tremble. "Are you saying you will see her dead before
releasing her, Leonie? Is the grasp of Arilinn a death-
grip, then?"

He could see the horror in Leonie, like a visible cloud,
here where emotions were a solid reality. "Damon, no!"
Her voice trembled. "When a Keeper is released it is
because she can no longer hold the channels to a Keeper's pattern, that they are no longer clear for psi work.
I thought this could not happen with Callista, but she
told me otherwise and I was willing to free her."

"You knew you had made that impossible!" Damon
accused.

"I . . . was not sure," said Leonie, and the veils stirred
in negation. "She said to me . . . she had touched him.
She had . . . Damon, what was I to think? But now she
knows otherwise. In the days when a girl was trained to
Keeper before she was fullgrown, it was taken for
granted that the choice was for life and there could be
no return."

"You knew this, and still made that choice for Callista?"

"What else could I do, Damon? Keepers we must have, or our world goes dark with the darkness of barbarism. I did what I must, and if Callista is even reasonably fair to me, she will admit it was with her consent." And yet Damon heard, like an echo in Leonie's mind, the bitter, despairing cry:

How could I consent? I was twelve years old!

Damon said angrily, "Are you saying it is hopeless, then? That Callista must return to Arilinn or die of grief?"

Leonie's voice was uncertain; her very image in the gray world wavered. "I know that once there was a way, and the way was known. Nothing from the past can be wholly concealed. When I myself was young I knew a woman who had been treated so, and she said that a way was known to reverse this fixing of channels, but she did not tell me how and she has been dead more years than you have lived. It was known everywhere in the days when the Towers were as temples, and the Keepers as their priests. I spoke truer than I knew," she said, abruptly putting the veil back from her ravaged face. "Had you lived in those days, Damon, you would have found your own true vocation as Keeper. You were born three hundred years too late."

"This does me little good now, kinswoman," Damon said. He turned aside from Leonie's face, seeing it waver and change before him, half Leonie as she had been when he was in the Tower, when he loved her, half the aging Leonie of today, as he had seen her at his wedding. He did not want to see her face, wished she would veil herself again.

"In the days of Rafael II, when the Towers of Neskaya and Tramontana were burned to the ground, all the circles died, with the Keepers. Many, many of the old techniques were lost then, and not all of them have been remembered or rediscovered."

"And I am supposed to rediscover them in the next few days? You have extraordinary confidence in me, Leonie!"

"What thought has ever moved in the mind of humankind anywhere in this universe can never be wholly lost."

Damon said impatiently, "I am not here to argue philosophy!"

Leonie shook her head. "This is not philosophy but fact. If any thought has ever stirred the stuff of which the universe is made, that thought remains, indelible, and can be recaptured. There was a time when these things were known, and the fabric of time itself remains. . . ."

Her image rippled, shook like a pool into which a stone had been dropped, and was gone. Damon, alone again in the endless, formless gray world, asked, *How in the name of all the Gods at once can I challenge the very fabric of time?* And for an instant he saw, as from a great height, the image of a man wearing green and gold, the face half concealed, and nothing clear to Damon's eyes except a great sparkling ring on his finger. Ring or matrix? It began to move, to undulate, to give out great waves of light, and Damon felt his consciousness dimming, vanishing. He clutched at the matrix around his neck, trying desperately to orient himself in the gray overworld. Then it was gone, and he was alone in the blankness, the formless, featureless nothingness. Finally, dim on the horizon, he perceived the faint and stony shape of his own landmark, what they had built there. With utter relief, he felt his thoughts drawing him toward it, and abruptly he was back in his room at Armida, Andrew bending anxiously over him.

He blinked, trying to coordinate random impressions. *Did you find an answer?* He sensed the question in Andrew's mind, but he did not know yet. Leonie had not pledged to help, to free Callista from the bondage, body and mind, to the Tower. She could not. In the overworld she could not lie, or conceal her intention. She wanted Callista to return to the Tower. She genuinely felt that Callista had had her chance at freedom and failed. Yet she could not conceal it, either, that there was an answer, and that the answer must lie in the depths of time itself. Damon shivered, with the deathly cold which seemed to lie inside his bones, clutching his warm overtunic around his shoulders. Was that the only way?

In the overworld Leonie could not tell a direct lie.
Yet she did not tell him all the truth either, he sensed,
because he did not know where to look for all the truth,
and there was still much she was concealing. But why?
Why should she need to conceal anything from him?
Didn't she know that Damon had always loved her,
that—the Gods help him—he loved her still, and would
never do anything to harm her? Damon dropped his face
in his hands, desperately trying to pull himself together.
He could not face Ellemir like this. He knew that his
grief and confusion were hurting Andrew too, and Andrew didn't even understand how.

One of the basic courtesies of a telepath, he reminded
himself, was to manage your own misery so that it did
not make everyone else miserable. . . . After a moment
he managed to calm himself and get his barriers back in
shape. He raised his face to Andrew and said, "I think
I have a hint at the answer. Not all of it, but if we have
enough time, I may manage it. How long was I out?"
He stood up and went to the table where the remnants
of their supper still stood, pouring himself a glass of
wine and sipping it slowly, letting it warm him and calm
him a little.

"Hours," Andrew said. "It must be past midnight."

Damon nodded. He knew the time-telescoping effect
of such travel. Time in the overworld seemed to run on
a different scale and was not even consistent, but something else entirely, so that sometimes a brief conversation would last for hours, and at other times a lengthy
journey which, subjectively, seemed to endure for days,
would flash by in the blink of an eye.

Ellemir appeared in the doorway, saying anxiously,
"Good, you are still awake. Damon, come and look at
Callista, I don't like the way she keeps moaning in her
sleep."

Damon set the wineglass down, steadying himself
against the table with both hands. He came into the
inner room. Callista seemed asleep, but her eyes were
half open, and when Damon touched her she winced,
evidently aware of the touch, but there was no consciousness in her eyes. Andrew's face was drawn. "What
ails her now, Damon?"

"Crisis. I was afraid of this," Damon said, "but I thought it would happen that first night." Quickly he moved his fingertips over her body, not touching her. "Elli, help me turn her over. No, Andrew, don't touch her, she's aware of you even in her sleep." Ellemir helped him turn her, sharing with him a moment of shock as they stripped the blankets from her body. How wasted she looked! Hovering jealously near as the lines of light built up in Callista's body, Andrew saw the dull, faded currents. But Damon knew he did not completely understand.

"I knew I should have cleared her channels at once," he said with hopeless anger. How could he make Andrew understand? He tried, without much hope, to put it into words:

"She needs some kind of . . . of discharge of the energy overload. Yet the channels are blocked, and the energy is backing up—leaking, if you like—into all the rest of her system, and is beginning to affect all her life functions: her heart, her circulation, her breathing. And before I could—"

Ellemir drew a harsh gasp of apprehension. Damon saw Callista's body stiffen, go rigid, arch backward with a weird cry. For several seconds a twitching, shuddering tremor shook all her limbs, then she collapsed and lay as if lifeless.

"God!" Andrew breathed. "What was *that*?"

"Convulsion," Damon said briefly. "I was afraid of that. It means we've *really* run out of time." He bent to check her pulse, listen to her breathing.

"I knew I should have cleared her channels."

"Why didn't you?" Andrew demanded.

"I told you: I have no *kirian* for her, and without that I don't know if she would be able to stand the pain."

"Do it now, while she's unconscious," Andrew said, and Damon shook his head.

"She has to be awake and consciously cooperating with me, or I could damage her seriously. And . . . and she doesn't want me to," he said at last.

"Why not?"

Damon said it at last, reluctantly: "Because if I clear the channels, that means she goes back to the normal state for *her*, a normal state for a Keeper, with the channels completely separated from the normal woman's state—cleared for psi and fixed that way. Back to the way she was before she ever left the Tower. Completely unaware of you, sexually unable to react. In effect, back to square one."

Andrew drew a harsh breath. "What is the alternative?"

"No alternative now, I'm afraid," Damon said soberly. "She can't live long like this." He touched the cold hand briefly, then went into his room where he kept the supply of herb medicines and remedies he had been using. He hesitated, but finally chose a small vial, came back, loosened the cap and poured it between Callista's slack lips, holding her head so that it ran down her throat.

"What is that? What are you giving her, damn it?"

"It will keep her from going into another convulsion," Damon said, "at least for the rest of the night. And tomorrow . . ." But he shrank from finishing the sentence. Even when he was doing this work regularly in the Tower, he had no liking for it. He shrank from the pain he must inflict, shrank, too, from the need to face Callista with the stark knowledge that she must sacrifice what little gain had been made with her maturing, and return to the state Leonie had imposed on her, unresponsive, immature, neuter. He walked away from Callista, rinsing and replacing the vial, trying to calm himself. He sat down on the other bed, looking at Callista in dismay, and Ellemir came to his side. Andrew still knelt by Callista, and Damon thought that he should send him away, because even in sleep Callista was conscious of him, her channels reacting to his physical presence even if her mind did not. For a moment it seemed as if he could see Andrew and Callista as a series of whirling, interlocking magnetic fields, reaching out toward one another, grasping, intertwining polarities. But where the energies should reinforce and strengthen one another, the forces were swirling and backing up in Callista, draining her strength, unable to flow freely. And what was this doing to Andrew? It was draining him too. By main force Damon turned off the perception, forcing himself to come back to the surface, to see Callista just as a desperately sick woman who had collapsed after a convulsion and Andrew as a concerned man, bending over her in dread and despair.

It was for this kind of thing that Leonie sent him from the Tower, he knew. She said he was too sensitive, that it would destroy him, he recalled, and then, for the first time in his life, rebellion came. It could have been a strength, not a weakness. It could have made him even more valuable to them.

Ellemir came and sat down beside him. He stretched out a hand to her, though, with an almost anguished need, how long it had been since they had come together in love. Yet the long discipline of the matrix mechanic held firm in his mind. It did not occur to him to think of breaking it. He drew her down, kissed her gently, and said, "I have to save my strength, darling, tomorrow is going to be demanding. Otherwise . . ." He laid a kiss into the palm of her hand, a private memory and a promise.

Ellemir sensed that he was pretending a cheerfulness and confidence he did not feel, and for a moment she was outraged, that Damon did not believe she knew, or that he thought he could pretend or lie to her. Then she realized the hard discipline behind that optimism, the rigid courtesies of a telepath worker. To give any mental recognition to such dread would reinforce it, create a kind of positive feedback, spiraling them down into a self-perpetuating chaos of despair. She was, she reflected with a touch of cynicism, getting some hard lessons in what it was like to be bound so closely to a working telepath. But her love and concern for Damon overflowed. She knew he did not want pity, but his greatest need, just now, was to be freed of concern about whether he would have to compensate for *her* dread.

She must carry her own burden of fears, she cautioned herself. She could not lay them on Damon. She took his hands in hers, leaning over to return his kiss very lightly.

Gratefully, he drew her down beside him, holding her in the curve of his arm, a comforting, wholly undemanding touch.

Andrew glanced around at them, from where he knelt beside Callista, and Damon caught his emotions: fear for Callista, dread, uncertainty—*can Damon really help her?*—distress at what it would mean if she were to be wholly Keeper again, all her old conditioning intact with the cleared channels. And, seeing Ellemir lying close against Damon, curled up in his arm, a confused emotion that was not, really, even jealousy. Callie and he had never had even this much. . . . Damon's pity for Andrew went so deep he had to cut it off, stifle it lest it tear at him and lessen his strength for what he had to do tomorrow.

"You stay close to Callista. Call me if there's any change, no matter how slight," he said, and saw Andrew draw a chair close to Callista, lean forward, lightly holding her limp wrist in his own.

Poor devil, Damon thought, *he can't even disturb her now. She's too far gone for that, but he has to feel he's doing something for her, or he'll crack. And the comfort he felt in Ellemir's closeness was gone.* With rigid discipline, he made himself relax, lie quietly at her side, loosen his muscles and float into the calm state needed for what he had to do. At last, floating, he slept.

It was well after daylight when Callista stirred, opening her eyes in confusion.

"Andrew?"

"I'm here, love." He tightened his fingers on hers. "How are you feeling?"

"Better, I think." She could not feel any pain. Somewhere a long time ago—someone had told her that was a bad sign. After the suffering of the last days she welcomed it. "I seem to have slept a long time, and Damon was worrying because I didn't."

Did she even know she had been drugged? Aloud he said, "Let me call Damon," and stepped away. On the other bed Damon lay stretched out, lightly holding Ellemir with one arm. Andrew felt that cruel stab of agonized envy. *They seemed so secure, so happy in the knowledge of one another. Would Callista and he ever have this? He had to believe it or die.*

Ellemir's blue eyes opened. She smiled up at him, and Damon, as she stirred, was instantly awake.

"How is Callista?"

"She seems better."

Damon looked at him skeptically, got up and went to Callista's side. Following him, Andrew suddenly saw Callista through Damon's eyes: white and emaciated, her eyes deeply sunken into her cheeks.

Damon said gently, "Callista, you know as well as I what has to be done. You're a Keeper, girl."

"Don't call me that!" she flared at him. "Never again!"

"I know you have been released from your oath, but an oath is only a word, Callista. I tell you, there is no other way. I cannot take the responsibility—"

"I have not asked you to! I am free—"

"Free to die," Damon said brutally.

"Don't you think I'd rather die?" she said, and began to cry for the first time since that night, sobbing stormily. Damon watched her, his face like stone, but Andrew took her up in his arms, holding her against him, protectively.

"Damon, what in the hell are you doing to her!"

Damon's face was red with anger. He said, "Damn it, Callista, I'm tired of being treated like a monster coming between you, when I've exhausted myself trying to protect you both."

"I know that," she wept, "but I can't bear it. You know what this is doing to Andrew, to me, it's killing us both!"

Andrew could feel her hands shaking as she clung to him, cradled in his arms, her body light as a child's. From somewhere he seemed to see her as a strange web of light, a kind of electrical energy net. Where was this strange perception coming from? His body no longer seemed real, but was trembling in a nowhere, and he too was no more than a fragile web of electrical energies, sparking and sputtering, with a deathly, growing weakness. . . .

Now he could no longer see Damon—Damon, too, was lost behind the swirling electrical nets. No, Damon was flowing, changing, glowing with anger, a dull crimson like a furnace. Andrew had seen this before, when he confronted Dezi. Like all men of easygoing temperament and flaring, easily dispelled anger, Andrew was shocked and horrified at the deep-down furnace-red glow of Damon's. Dimly behind the shifting colors and electrical energies, the swirling pulses and lights, he knew that the man Damon walked to the window and stood, his back to them, staring out into the snowstorm, struggling to master his wrath. Andrew could feel the rage from inside, as he felt Callista's agony, as he felt Ellemir's confusion. He fought to get them all solid again, all hard and human, not swirling confusions of electrical images. What was real? he wondered. Were they really nothing more than swirling energy masses, fields of energy and moving atoms in space? He fought to hold on to human preception, through Callista's frenzied, feverish grip. He wanted to go to the window. . . . He *did* go to the window and touch Damon. . . . He did not move, anchored by the weight of Callista across his lap. Fighting for human speech, he said, entreating, "Damon, no one thinks you are a monster. Callista will do whatever you think is best. We both trust you, don't we, Callista?"

With an effort Damon managed to control his wrath. It was rare for him to let it have even a moment's mastery over him. He felt ashamed. At last he came to their side and said gently, "Andrew has a right to be consulted in your decision, Callista. You cannot keep doing this to all of us. If it were only your own decision—" He broke off with a gasp. "Andrew! Put her down, quickly!"

Callista had gone limp in Andrew's arms. Shaken by the fright in Damon's voice, Andrew made no protest when Damon lifted Callista from his arms, laid her back in bed. He motioned Andrew to move away. Puzzled, resentful, Andrew obeyed. Damon bent over the woman.

"You see? No, don't cry again, you haven't the strength. Don't you know you went into crisis last night? You had a convulsion. I gave you some raivannin—you know what that means as well as I do, Callie."

She hardly had the strength to whisper, "I think . . . we would all be better off . . ."

Damon held her wrists lightly in his hand, such slender wrists that even Damon's hands, which were not large, could wholly encircle them. Feeling Andrew's resentful stare, he said wearily, "She hasn't the strength for another convulsion."

Andrew said, at the end of endurance, "Was this my doing, too? Is it always going to be unsafe for me to touch her?"

"Don't blame Andrew, Damon . . ." Callista's voice was only a thread. "It was I who wanted . . ."

"You see?" Damon said. "If I keep you away from her she wants to die. If I let you touch her, the physical stress gets worse and worse. Quite apart from the emotional strain, which is tearing you both to pieces, physically she can't endure much more. Something must be done quickly, before—" He broke off, but they all knew what he did not say: Before she goes into convulsions again and we can't stop it this time.

"You know what has to be done, Callista, and you know how much time you have to make up your mind. Damn it, Callie, do you think I want to torment you when you're in this state? I know you are physically in the state of a girl of twelve, but you are *not* a child, can't you stop behaving like one? Can't you somehow manage to behave like the adult professional you have learned to be? Stop being so damned emotional about it! What we have here is a physical fact! You are a Keeper—"

"I am not! I'm not!" she gasped.

"At least show some of the good sense and courage you learned as one! I'm ashamed of you. Your circle would be ashamed of you. Leonie would be ashamed—"

"Damn it, Damon," Andrew began, but Ellemir, her eyes blazing, grabbed his arm. "Keep out of this, you fool," she whispered. "Damon knows what he's doing! It's her *life* at stake now!"

"You are afraid," Damon said, taunting, "you are afraid! Hilary Castamir was not fifteen, but she endured having her channels cleared every forty days for more than a year! And you are afraid to let me touch you!"

Callista lay flat on her pillows under Damon's hard grip, her face dead white, her eyes beginning to blaze with a lambent flame none of them had ever seen in her before. Her voice, weak as it was, trembled with such rage that it was like a shout.

"You! How dare you talk to me that way, you that Leonie sent from Arilinn like a whimpering puppy because you had not the courage. Who do you think you are, to talk to me like that?"

Damon stood up, releasing her, as if, Andrew thought, he was afraid he might strangle her if he didn't. The dull-red furnace glow of rage was around him again. Andrew clenched his hands until he could see blood beneath the nails, trying to keep them all from disintegrating into whirling fields of energy again.

"Who am I?" Damon shouted. "I am your nearest kinsman, and I am your technician, and you know very well what else I am. And if I cannot make you see reason, if you will not use your knowledge and good judgment, then I swear to you, Callista of Arilinn, that I shall have *Dom* Esteban carried up here and let you try your tantrums on him! If your husband cannot make you behave, and if a technician cannot, then, my girl, you may try conclusions with your father! He is old, but he is still Lord Alton, and if I explain to him—"

She said, white with fury, "You wouldn't dare!"

"Try me," Damon retorted, turning his back and standing firm, ignoring all of them. Andrew stood by, uneasy, looking from Damon's turned back to Callista, white and raging against her pillows, holding to consciousness by that very thread of rage. Could either give way, or would they remain locked in that terrible battle of wills till one of them died? He caught a random thought—from Ellemir?—that Damon's mother was an Alton, he too had the Alton gift. But Callista was the weaker, Andrew knew she could not long sustain this fury which was destroying them all. He must break this impasse and do it quickly. Ellemir was wrong. Damon could not break her will that way, even to save her life.

He went to Callista and knelt at her side again. He begged, "Darling, do what Damon wants!"

She whispered, the cold anger breaking so that he could see the terrible grief behind it, "Did he tell you it would mean I could not . . . that we would lose even what little we have had?"

"He told me," Andrew said, trying desperately to

show somehow the aching tenderness that had swallowed up everything else in him. "But my darling, I came to love you before I had ever set eyes on you. Do you think that is all I want of you?"

Damon turned around slowly. The anger in him had melted. He looked down at them both with a deep and anguished pity, but he made his voice hard. "Have you found enough courage for this, Callista?"

She said, sighing, "Oh, courage? Damon, it is not that I lack. But what is the reason for it? You say it will save my life. But what life have I now that is worth keeping? And I have involved you all in it. I would rather die now before I bring you all to where I am."

Andrew was aghast at the bottomless despair in her voice. He made a move to take her in his arms again, remembered that he endangered her by the slightest touch. He stood paralyzed, immobilized by her anguish. Damon came and knelt beside him. He did not touch Callista, either but nevertheless he reached for her, reached for both of them, and drew them all around him. The slow gentle pulse, the ebb and flow of matched rhythms, naked in the moving dark, closely entangled them in an intimacy closer than lovemaking.

Damon said in a whisper, "Callista, if it were only your own descision, I would let you die. But you are so much a part of all of us that we cannot let you go." And from one of them, Andrew never knew whether himself or another, the thought wove through the multiplex joining that was their linked circle: *Callista, while we have this, surely it is worth living in the hope that somehow we will find a way to have the rest.*

Like surfacing from a very deep dive, Andrew came back to separate awareness again. Damon's eyes met his, and he did not shrink from the intimacy in them. Callista's eyes were so bruised, so dilated with pain that they looked black in her pallid face, but she smiled, stirring faintly against his arm.

"All right, Damon. Do what you have to. I've hurt you all . . . too much already." Her breath faded and she seemed to struggle for awareness. Ellemir brushed a light kiss over her sister's brow.

"Don't try to talk. We understand."

Damon rose and drew Andrew out of the room with him.

"Damn it, this is work for a Keeper. There were male Keepers once, but I haven't the training."

"You don't want to do this at all, do you, Damon?"

"Who would?" His voice was shaking uncontrollably. "But there's nothing else to do. If she goes into convulsions again she might not live through the day. And if she did, there might be enough brain damage that she'd never know us again. The overload on all life functions—pulse, breathing—and if she deteriorates much further . . . well, she's an Alton." He shook his head despairingly. "What she did to you would be nothing to what she might do to all of us, if her mind stopped functioning, and all she knew was that we were hurting her . . ." He flinched with dread. "I've got to hurt her so damnably. But I have to do it while she's aware, and able to control and cooperate intelligently."

"What is it you're afraid of? You can't really hurt her, can you, using—what is it, psi?—on those channels? They aren't even physical, are they?"

Damon shut his eyes for a moment, an involuntary, spasmodic movement. He said, "I won't kill her. I know enough not to do that. That's why she has to be conscious, though. If I make any miscalculations, I could damage some of the nerves, and they are centered around the reproductive organs. I could damage them just enough to impair her chances of ever bearing a child, and she can tell me better than I can myself just where the main nerves are."

"In God's name," Andrew said in a whisper, "can't you do it while she's unconscious? Does it *matter* if she can have children?"

Damon looked at him in shock and horror. "You can't possibly be serious!" he said, desperately making allowances for his friend's distress. "Callista is Comyn, she has *laran*. Any woman would die before risking *that*. This is your wife, man, not some woman of the streets!"

Before Damon's real horror, Andrew fell silent, trying to conceal his absolute bafflement. He'd stomped all over some Darkovan taboo again. Would he ever learn? He said stiffly, "I'm sorry if I've offended you, Damon."

"Offended? Not exactly, but . . . but shocked." Damon was bewildered. Didn't Andrew even think of this as the most precious thing she could give him, the heritage, the clan? Was his love only a thing of rut and selfishness? Then he was bewildered again. No, he thought, Andrew had endured too much for her; it was not only that. Finally he thought, in despair: *I love him, but will I ever understand him?*

Andrew, caught up in his emotion, turned and put an embarrassed hand on Damon's shoulder. He said hesitantly, aloud, "I wonder if . . . if anyone ever understands anyone? I'm trying, Damon. Give me time."

Damon's normal reaction would have been to embrace Andrew, but he had grown accustomed to having these natural gestures rebuffed, to knowing that they embarrassed his friend. Something would have to be done about that, too. "Just now we're agreed on one thing, brother, we both want what's best for Callista. Let's get back to her."

Andrew returned to Callista's side. In spite of everything he had felt that Damon *must* be exaggerating. These were psychological things, how could they have a genuine, physical effect? Now he knew that Damon was right, Callista was dying. With a shudder of dread he realized that she no longer attempted even to move her head on the pillow, although her eyes moved to follow him.

"Damon, swear that afterward there will be a way to bring me back to . . . to normal. . . ."

"I swear it, *breda*." Damon's voice was as steady as his hands, but Andrew could see he was struggling for control. Callista, though, looked peaceful.

"I have no *kirian* for you, Callista."

Andrew could sense the tensing of fear in her, but she said, "I can manage without it. Do what you have to."

"Callista, if you want to risk it, you have *kireseth* flowers . . . ?"

She made a faint gesture of negation. Damon had known she would not agree to that; the taboo was absolute among the Tower-trained. Yet he wished she had been less scrupulous, less conscientious. "You said you were going to try . . ."

Damon nodded, taking out the small flask. "A tincture. I filtered off the impurities, and dissolved the resins in wine," he said. "It might be better than nothing."

Her laughter was soundless, no more than a breath. Andrew, watching, marveled that even now she could laugh! "I know that is not your major skill, Damon. I'll try, but let me taste it first. If you've gotten the wrong resin . . ." She sniffed cautiously at the flask, tasted a few drops, and finally said, "It's safe. I'll try it, but—" She calculated, finally saying, showing a narrow space between thumb and forefinger, "Only about that much."

"You'll need more than that, Callista. You'll never be able to stand the pain," Damon protested. She said, "I have to be maximally aware of the lower centers and the trunk nerves. The major discharge nodes are overloaded, so you may have to do some rerouting." Andrew felt a chill of horror at her detached, clinical tone, as if her own body were some kind of malfunctioning machine, her own nerves merely defective parts. What a hell of a thing to do to a woman!

Damon lifted her head, supported her while she swallowed the indicated dose. She stopped at precisely what she had judged, obstinately closing her mouth. "No, no more, Damon, I know my limits."

He warned colorlessly, "It's going to be worse than anything you've ever had."

"I know. If you hit a node too close to the"—Andrew could not understand the term she used—"I may have another seizure."

"I'll be careful of that. How many days ago did the bleeding completely stop? Do you know how deep I'm going to have to take you?"

She sketched a grimace. "I know. I cleared Hilary twice, and I have more overload than she ever did. There is still a residue—"

Damon caught Andrew's look of horror. He said, "Do you really want him here, darling?"

She tightened her fingers on his hand. "He has a right."

Damon's voice was so strained that it sounded harsh, but Andrew, still linked strongly to the other man, knew it was only the inner stress. "He's not used to this, Callista. He'll only know that I'm hurting you terribly."

God! Andrew thought. Did he have to watch any more of her suffering? But he said quietly, "I'll stay if you need me, Callista."

"If I were bearing his child he would stay in rapport and share more pain than this."

"Yes," Damon said gently, "but if it were that—Lord of Light, how I wish it were!—you could reach out to him and draw on his strength with no hesitation. But now, you know this, Callista, I would have to forbid him to touch you, whatever happened. Or *you*, to reach out to *him*. Let me send him away, Callista."

She nearly rebelled again then, through her own misery sensing Damon's dread, his desperate unwillingness to hurt her, she reached up her hand, with a sort of pained surprise that it felt so heavy, to touch his face. "Poor Damon," she said in a whisper. "You hate this, don't you? Will it make it easier for you this way?"

Damon nodded, not trusting himself to speak. It was hard enough to inflict pain of that kind without having to stand up to the reactions of others who hadn't the faintest idea what he was doing.

Resolutely, Callista looked up at Andrew. "Go away, love. Ellemir, take him away. This is a matter for trained psi technicians and with the best will in the world, you can't help and might do damage."

Andrew felt mingled relief and guilt—if she could endure this he should be strong enough to share it with her—but he also felt that Damon was grateful for Callista's choice. He could sense the effort Damon was making to create in himself the same clinical, unemotional attitude Callista was trying to display. In mingled horror and guilt, together with a shamed relief, he rose quickly and hurried out of the room.

Behind him, Ellemir hesitated, glancing at Callista, wondering if this would be easier if they could all share it in rapport. But a single glance at Damon's face decided her. This was bad enough for him. If he must inflict it on her too, it would be even worse. She deliberately broke the remaining link with Damon and Callista, and without turning to see what effect this had on the other two—but she could sense it, relief almost as great as Andrew's—she followed him quickly across the hall of the suite. She caught up with him in the central hall.

"I think you need a drink. What about it?" She led him into the living room of their half of the suite and rummaged n a cabinet for a square stoneware bottle and a couple of glasses. She poured, sensing Andrew's remorseful thoughts: *Here I sit enjoying myself over a drink and God only knows what Callista's going through.*

Andrew took the drink she handed him and sipped. He had expected wine; instead it was a strong, fiery, highly concentrated liquor. He took a sip, saying hesitantly, "I don't want to get drunk."

Ellemir shrugged. "Why not? It might just be the best thing you can do."

Get drunk? With Callista . . .

Ellemir's leveled eyes met his. "That's why," she said. "It's some assurance for Damon that you will stay out of this, letting him do what he has to. He hates it," she added, and the tension in her voice made Andrew realize that she was as worried about Damon as he was about Callista.

"Not quite." But her voice shook. "Not in quite . . . quite the same way. We can't help, all we can do is . . . stay out of it. And I'm not . . . used to being shut out this way." She blinked ferociously.

So like Callista and so unlike, Andrew thought. He'd grown so used to thinking of her as stronger than Callista, yet Callista had lived through that ordeal in the caves. She was no fragile maiden in distress, not half as frail as he thought she was. No Keeper could be weak. It was a different kind of strength. Even now, refusing the drug Damon offered to give her.

Ellemir said, sipping the fiery stuff, "Damon has always hated this work. But he'll do it for Callie's sake. And," she added after a moment, "for yours."

He replied in a low voice, "Damon's been a good friend to me. I know it."

"You seem to find it hard to show it," Ellemir said, "but I suppose that is the way you were taught to react to people in your own world. It must be very hard for you," she added. "I don't suppose I can even imagine how hard it is for you here, to find everyone thinking in strange ways, with every little thing different. And I suppose the little things are harder to get used to than the big ones. The big ones you get used to, you make up your mind to them. The little things come along unexpectedly, when you aren't thinking about them, aren't braced against them."

How perceptive of her to see that, Andrew thought. It was, indeed, the little things. Damon's—and Ellemir's own—careless nudity which made him awkward and self-conscious as if all the unthinking habits of a lifetime were constrained and somehow rude; the odd texture of the bread; Damon kissing *Dom* Esteban, without self-consciousness, in greeting; Callista, in the early days when they had shared a room, not embarrassed when he saw her half dressed about the room or once, by accident, wholly naked in her bath, but coloring and stammering with embarrassment when once he came up behind her and lifted up the long strands of loosened hair from her bare neck. He said in a low voice, "I'm trying to get used to your customs. . . ."

She said, refilling his glass, "Andrew, I want to talk to you."

It was Callista's own phrase, and it made him somehow braced and wary. "I'm listening."

"Callista told you that night"—instantly he knew the night she meant—"what I had offered. Why did it make you angry? Do you really dislike me as much as that?"

"Dislike you? Of course not," Andrew said, "but—" and he stopped, literally speechless. "It hardly seems fair for you to tempt me like this."

"Have you been fair to any of us?" she exclaimed. "Is it fair for you to insist on remaining in such a state when we all have to share it, like it or not? You are— you have been for a long time—in an appalling state of sexual need. Do you think I don't know it? Do you think Callista doesn't know it?"

He felt stung, invaded. "What business is that of yours?"

She flung her head back and said, "You know perfectly well why it is my affair. Yet Callista said you refused . . ."

Damn it, it had been an outrageous suggestion, but Callista at least, had had the decency to be a little different about it! And Ellemir was so like Callista that he could hardly help reacting to her very presence. He set his mouth and said tersely, "I can control it. I'm not an animal."

"What are you? A cabbage plant? Control it? Maybe I wasn't suggesting that otherwise you might go out and rape the first woman you see. But that doesn't mean the need isn't there. So in essence you are lying to us with everything you do, everything you *are*."

"God almighty!" he exploded. "Is there no privacy here?"

"Of course. Have you noticed? My father hasn't been asking any questions that would make any of us feel awkward. It really isn't *his* business, you see. He won't pry. *None* of us will ever know whether he knows anything about this at all. But the four of us—it's different, Andrew. Can't you be honest with us, at least?"

"What am I supposed to do then? Torment her for what she can't give me?" He remembered the night when he had done just that. "I can't do that again!"

"Of course not. But can't you see that's part of what's hurting Callista? She was terribly aware of your need, so that at last she risked . . . what finally *did* happen, because she knew your need, and that you couldn't accept anything else. Are you going to go on like that, adding to her guilt . . . and ours?"

Sleeplessness, worry and fatigue, and the strong cordial on an empty stomach, had hit Andrew hard, blurring his perceptions till the outrageous things Ellemir was saying almost made sense. If he had done what Callista asked, it would never have come to this. . . .

It wasn't fair. So like Callista and so terribly unlike . . . you could strike sparks off this one! "I am Damon's friend. How could I do that to him?"

"Damon is *your* friend," she retorted, real anger in her voice. "Do you think he enjoys your suffering? Or are you arrogant enough to think"—her voice shook— "that you could make me care less for Damon because I do for you what any decent woman would want to do, seeing a friend in such a state?"

Andrew met her eyes, matching her anger. "Since we're being so overwhelmingly honest, did it occur to you that it isn't you I want?" Even now it was only because she was *there*, so like Callista as she should have been.

Her anger was suddenly gone. "Dear brother"—*bredu* was the word she used—"I know it is Callista you love. But it was I in your dream."

"A physical reflex," he said brutally.

"Well, that's real too. And it would mean, at least, that you need no longer torment Callista for what she cannot give you." She reached to refill his glass. He stopped her.

"No more. I'm already half drunk. Damn it, does it matter whether I torment her that way, or by going off and falling into bed with someone else?"

"I don't understand." He felt that Ellemir's confusion was genuine. "Do you mean that a woman of your people, if she could not for some reason share her husband's bed, would be angry if he found . . . comfort elsewhere? How strange and how cruel!"

"I guess most women think that if they . . . if they have to abstain for some reason, it's only fair for the man to share the . . . the abstention." He fumbled. "Look, if Callista's unhappy too, and I go off to get myself laid—oh, hell, I don't know the polite words— isn't it pretty rotten of me to act as if *her* unhappiness doesn't matter, as long as my own needs are met?"

Ellemir laid a gentle hand on his arm. "That does you credit, Andrew. But I find it hard to imagine that a woman who loved a man wouldn't be glad to know he was satisfied somehow."

"But wouldn't she feel as if I didn't love her enough to wait for her?"

"Do you think you would love Callista less if you were to lie with me?"

He returned her gaze steadily. "Nothing in this world could make me love Callista less. *Nothing*."

She shrugged slightly. "So how could she be hurt? And think about this, Andrew. Suppose that someone other than yourself could help Callista break the bonds she did not seek and cannot break. Would you be angry with her, or love her less?"

Touched on the raw, Andrew remembered the moment when it seemed that Damon had come between them, his almost frantic jealousy. "Do you expect me to believe a man wouldn't mind that, here?"

"You told me only now that nothing could make you love her less. Would you forbid her, then?"

"Forbid her? No," Andrew said, "but I might wonder how deep *her* love went."

Ellemir's voice was suddenly shaking. "Are you Terrans like the Dry-Towners, then, who keep their women behind walls and in chains so that no other man will touch them? Is she a toy you want to lock in a box so that no one else can play with it? What *is* marriage to you, then?"

"I don't know," Andrew said drearily, his anger collapsing. "I've never been married before. I'm not trying to quarrel with you, Elli." He fumbled with the pet name. "I . . . just . . . well, we were talking, before, about things being strange to me, and this is one of them. To believe Callista wouldn't be hurt . . ."

"If you had abandoned her, or if you had forced her to consent, unwilling—as with *Dom* Ruyven of Castamir, who forced Lady Crystal to harbor his *barragana* wife and to foster all the bastards the woman bore—then, yes, she might have cause to grieve. But can you believe it is cruelty, that you do her will?" She met his eyes, reached out, gently, and took his hand between her own. She said, "If you are suffering, Andrew, it hurts all of us. Callista too. And . . . and me, Andrew."

His barriers were down. The touch, the meeting of their eyes, made him feel wholly exposed to her. No wonder she had no hesitation in simply walking around without her shift, he realized. This was the real nakedness.

He had reached that particular stage of drunkenness where preconceptions blur and people do outrageous things and believe them commonplace. He could see Ellemir, now as herself, now as Callista, now as a visible sign of a contact he was only beginning to understand, the four-way link between them. She bent and laid her mouth against his. It went through his body like a jolt of electricity. All his aching frustration was behind the strength with which he pulled her into his arms.

Is this happening, or am I drunk, and dreaming about it again? Thought blurred. He was aware of Ellemir's body in his arms, slender, naked, confident, with that curious matter-of-fact acceptance. In a moment's completely sober insight, he knew that this was her way of cutting off awareness of Damon too. It was not only his need, but hers. He was glad of that.

He was naked, with no memory of shedding his clothes. She was warm, pliant in his arms. *Yes, she has been here before, for a moment, the four of us, blended, just before catastrophe struck. . . .* At the back of her mind he sensed a warm, welcoming amusement: *No, you are not strange to me.*

Through growing excitement came a sad strange thought: *It should have been Callista.* Ellemir felt so different in his arms, so *solid* somehow, without any of the shy fragility which so excited him in Callista. Then he felt her touch, rousing him, blotting out thought. He felt memory blurring and wondered for a moment if this were her doing, so that for now the kindly haze obscured everything. He was only a feeling, reacting body, driven by long need and deprivation, aware only of an accepting, responding body in his arms, of excitement and tenderness matching his own, seeking the deliverance so long denied. When it came it was so intense that he thought he would lose consciousness.

After a time he stirred, carefully shifting his weight. She smiled and brushed her hair from his face. He felt calm, released, grateful. No, it was more than gratitude, it was a closeness, like . . . yes, like the moment they had met in the matrix. He said, quietly, "Ellemir." Just a reaffirmation, a reassurance. For the moment she was clearly herself, not Callista, not anyone else. She kissed him lightly on the temple, and suddenly exhaustion and release of long denial all fell together at once, and he slept in Ellemir's arms. An indefinable time later he woke to see Damon looking down at them.

He looked weary, haggard, and Andrew thought, in shock, that here was the best friend he had ever had, and here he was, in bed with his wife.

Ellemir sat up quickly. "Callista—?"

Damon's sigh seemed dragged up from the roots of

his body. "She's going to be all right. She's asleep." He stumbled and almost fell on top of them. Ellemir held out her arms, gathering him to her breast.

Andrew thought he was in the way there, then, sensing Damon's exhaustion, how near the older man was to collapse, realized that his preoccupation with himself was selfish, irrelevant. Clumsily, wishing there was some way to express what he felt, he put his arm around Damon's shoulders.

Damon sighed again, and said, "She's better than I dared hope for. She's very weak, of course, and exhausted. After all I put her through . . ." he shuddered, and Ellemir drew his head to her breasts.

"Was it so terrible, beloved?"

"Terrible, yes, terrible for *her*," Damon muttered, and even then—Ellemir sensed it with heartbreak—he was trying to shield her, shield them both from the nakedness of his own memory. "She was so brave, and I couldn't bear having to hurt her like that." His voice broke. He hid his face on Ellemir's breasts and began to sob, harshly, helplessly.

Andrew thought he should leave, but Damon reached out for Andrew's hand, clinging to it with an agonized grip. Andrew, putting aside his own discomfort at being present at such a moment, thought that right now Damon needed all the comfort he could get. He only said very softly, when Damon had quieted, "Should I be with Callista?"

Damon caught the overtone in the words: *You and Ellemir would rather be alone.* In his worn, raw-edged state it was painful, a rebuff. His words were sharp with exhaustion.

"She won't know whether you're there or not. But do as you damn please!" and the unspoken part of his words were as plain as what he said aloud: *If you just can't wait to get away from us.*

He still doesn't understand . . .

Damon, how could he? Ellemir hardly understood herself. She only knew that when Damon was like this it was painful, exhausting. His need was so much greater than she could meet or comfort in any way. Her own inadequacy tormented her. It was not sexual—*that* she could have understood and eased—but what she sensed in Damon left her exhausted and helpless because it was not any recognizable need which she could understand. Some of her desperation came through to Andrew, though all she said was, "Please stay. I think he wants us both with him now."

Damon, clinging to them both with a desperate, sinking need for physical contact which was not, though it simulated it, the real need he felt, thought, *No, they don't understand.* And, more rationally, *I don't understand it either.* For the moment it was enough that they were there. It wasn't complete, it wasn't what he needed, but for the moment he could make it do, and Ellemir, holding him close in despair, thought that they could calm him a little, like this. But what was it he really needed? Would she ever know? She wondered. How could she know when he didn't know himself?

CHAPTER TWELVE

Callista woke and lay with her eyes closed, feeling the sun on her eyelids. In the night, through her sleep, she had felt the storm cease, the snow stop, and the clouds disappear. This morning the sun was out. She stretched her body, savoring the luxury of being wholly without pain. She still felt weak, drained, though it now seemed to her that she had slept for two or three whole days without intermission, after that dreadful ordeal. Afterward she had remained abed for a few days, recovering her strength, although she felt quite well. She knew that the first thing necessary was to recover her health, which, always before, had been excellent, and it would take time.

And when she was well, what then? But she caught herself. If she began to fret about that, she would have no peace.

She was alone in the room. That was luxury too. She had spent so many years alone that she had come to crave solitude as much as she had once dreaded it during the difficult years of her training. And while she was sick she had never been alone for an instant. She knew the reason—she would unhesitatingly have ordered the same treatment for anyone in her condition—and she had welcomed their care and unceasing love. Now, however, it was good to wake again and know herself once more left alone.

She opened her eyes and sat up in bed. Andrew's bed was empty. Dimly she remembered, through her sleep, hearing him moving around, dressing, going out. With the storm over, there would be all manner of things to be attended to around the estate. Around the house too. Ellemir had spent so much time at her side during the days of her illness that she had neglected the running of the household.

Callista decided that she would go downstairs this morning.

Last night Andrew had been with Ellemir again. She had sensed it dimly, by the old discipline turning her mind away from it. He had come in softly, near midnight, moving quietly so as not to disturb her, and she had pretended sleep.

I am a fool and unkind, she told herself. *I wanted this to happen, and I am honestly glad, yet I could not speak to him and say so.* But that line of thought led nowhere, either. There was only one thing she could do, and she must summon up the strength to do it: to live every day as best she could, recovering her health, trusting Damon's promise. Andrew still loved and wanted her, though, she thought with a detachment so clinical she did not even know it was bitter, she could not imagine why he should. Again, why dwell on the one thing they could not yet share? Resolutely she got out of bed and went to bathe.

She dressed herself in a blue woolen skirt and a white knitted tunic with a long collar which could be wound about her like a shawl. For the first time since she could remember she actually felt hungry. Downstairs, the maids had cleared away the morning meal. Her father's chair had been rolled to the window and he was looking out into the heavily drifted courtyard, where a group of serving men, heavily bundled, were clearing away some of the snow. She went and brushed his forehead with a dutiful kiss.

"Are you well again, daughter?"

"Much better, I think," she said, and he motioned her to sit beside him, scanning her face carefully, narrowing his eyes.

"You're thinner. Zandru's hells, girl, you look as if you'd been gnawed by Alar's wolf! What ailed you, or shouldn't I ask?"

She had no idea what, if anything, Andrew or Damon might have told him. "Nothing very much. A woman's trouble."

"Don't give me that," her father said bluntly, "you're no sickling. Marriage doesn't seem to agree with you, my girl."

She recoiled, saw in his face that he had picked up

the recoil. He backed off quickly. "Well, well, child, I have known it a long time, the Towers do not easily let go their hold on those they have taken. I remember well how Damon went for more than a year like a lost soul blundering in the outer hells." Clumsily he patted her arm. "I won't ask questions, *chiya*. But if that husband of yours is no good to you . . ."

Quickly she put out her hand to him. "No, no. It has nothing to do with Andrew, Father."

He said, his frown skeptical, "When a bride of a few moons looks as you do, her husband is seldom blameless."

Under his concentrated study she flushed, but her voice was firm. "On my word, Father, there has been no quarrel, and Andrew is no way to blame." It was the truth, but not the whole truth. There was no way to tell the whole truth to anyone outside their closed circle, and she was not sure she knew it herself. He sensed that she was evading him, but he accepted the barrier between them. "Well, well, the world will go as it will, daughter, not as you or I would have it. Have you breakfasted?"

"No, I waited to keep you company."

She let him call servants and order them to bring her food, more than she wanted, but she knew he had been shocked by her thinness and pallor. Like an obedient child, she forced herself to eat a little more than she really wanted. His eyes dwelt on her face as she ate, and he said at last, more gently than was his custom, "There are times, child, when I feel that you daughters of Comyn who go into the Towers take risks no less than those of our sons who go into the Guard, and fight along our borders . . . and it's just as inevitable, I suppose, that some of you should be wounded."

How much did he know? How much did he understand? She knew he had said just about as much as he could say without breaking one of the strongest taboos in a telepathic family. She felt obscurely comforted, even through her embarrassment. It could not have been easy for him to go this far.

He passed her a jar of honey for her bread. She refused it, laughing. "Would you have me fat as a fowl for roasting?"

"As fat, maybe, as an embroidery needle," he scoffed. Her eyes on his face, she saw that he too was thinner, drawn and worn, and his eyes seemed set deeper behind cheekbones and brow.

"Is there none here to keep you company, Father?"

"Oh, Ellemir is in and out, about the kitchens. Damon has gone to the village, to see to the families of the men who were frostbitten during the great storm, and Andrew is in the greenhouse, seeing what the frost has done there. Why not join him there, child? I am sure there is work enough for two."

"And it is certain I am no help to Ellemir about the kitchens," she said, laughing. "Later, perhaps. If the sun is out they will be doing a great wash, and I must see to the linen rooms."

He laughed. "To be sure. Ellemir has always said that she would rather muck out barns than use a needle! But later maybe we can have some music again. I have been remembering how, when I was younger, I used to play a lute. Perhaps my fingers could get back their skill. I have so little to do, sitting here all the day. . . ."

The women of the household, and some of the men, had dragged out the great tubs and were washing clothes in the back kitchens. Callista found her presence superfluous and slipped away to the small still-room where she had made her own work. Nothing was as she had left it. She remembered that Damon had been working here during her illness, and, surveying the disorder he had left, she set to work to put everything to rights. She realized too that she must replenish stocks of some common medicines and remedies, but while her hands were busy with some of the simplest herbal mixtures, separating them into doses to be brewed for tea, she realized that there was a more demanding task before her: she must make some *kirian*.

She had thought when she left the Tower that she would never do this again; Valdir was too young to need it and Domenic too old. Yet she realized soberly that whatever happened, no household of telepaths should be without this particular drug. It was by far the most difficult of all the drugs she knew how to make, having to be distilled in three separate operations, each to dispose of a different chemical fraction of the resin. She had set everything to rights in the still-room and was taking out her distilling equipment when Ferrika came in and started, seeing her there.

"Forgive me for disturbing you, *vai domna*."

"No, come in, Ferrika. What can I do for you?"

"One of the maids has scalded her hand at the wash. I came to find some burn salve for her."

"Here it is," Callista said, reaching a jar from a shelf. "Can I do anything?"

"No, my lady, it is nothing serious," the woman said, and went away. After a little while she returned, bringing back the jar.

"Is it a bad burn?"

Ferrika shook her head. "No, no, she carelessly put her hand into the wrong tub, that is all, but I think we should keep something for burns in the kitchen and washing rooms. If someone had been severely hurt it would have been bad to have to come up here for it."

Callister nodded. "I think you are right. Put some into smaller jars, then, and keep it there," she said. While Ferrika at the smaller table, began to do this, she frowned, opening drawer after drawer until Ferrika finally turned and asked, "My lady, can I help you to find something? If the Lord Damon, or I myself, have misplaced something for you . . ."

Callista frowned. She said, "Yes, there were *kireseth* flowers here . . ."

"Lord Damon used some of those, my lady, while you were ill."

Callista nodded, remembering the crude tincture he had made. "I have allowed for that, but unless he wasted or spoiled a great deal, there was far more than he could have used, stored in a bag at the back of this cabinet." She went on searching cabinets and drawers. "Have you used any of it, Ferrika?"

The woman shook her head. "I have not touched it." She was smoothing salve into a jar with a small bone paddle. Watching her, Callista asked, "Do you know how to make *kirian*?"

"I know how it is done, my lady. When I trained in the Guild-house in Arilinn, each of us spent some time apprenticed to an apothecary to learn to make medicines and drugs. But I myself have never made it," the woman said. "We had no use for it in the Guild-house, though we had to learn how to recognize it. You know that the . . . that some people sell the by-products of *kirian* distillation, illegally?"

"I had heard this, even in the Tower," Callista said dryly. *Kireseth* was a plant whose leaves, flowers and stems contained various resins. In the Kilghard Hills, at some seasons, the pollen created a problem, having dangerous psychoactive qualities. *Kirian*, the telepathic drug which lowered the barriers of the mind, used the only safe fraction, and even that was used with great caution. The use of raw *kireseth*, or of the other resins, was forbidden by law in Thendara and Arilinn, and was regarded as criminal everywhere in the Domains. Even *kirian* was treated with great caution, and looked on with a kind of superstitious dread by outsiders.

As she counted and sorted filtering cloths, Callista thought, with a peculiar homesickness, of the faraway plains of Arilinn. It had been her home for so long. She supposed she would never see it again.

It could be her home again, Leonie had said. . . . To dispel that thought, she asked, "How long did you live in Arilinn, Ferrika?"

"Three years, *domna*."

"But you are one of our people from the estate, are you not? I remember that you and I and Dorian and Ellemir all played together when we were little girls, and had dancing lessons together."

"Yes, my lady, but when Dorian went to be married, and you to the Tower, I decided I did not want to stay at home all my life, like a plant grown fast to the wall. My mother had been midwife here, you remember, and I had, I thought, talent for the work. There was a midwife on the estate at Syrtis who had been trained in the Arilinn Guild-house, where they train healers and midwives. And I saw that under her care, many lived whom my mother would have consigned to the mercy of Avarra—lived, and their babies thrived. Mother said these newfangled ways were folly, and probably impious as well, but I went to the Guild-house at Neskaya and

took oath there. They sent me to Arilinn to be trained.
And I asked leave of my oath-mother to come here and
take employment, and she agreed."

"I did not know there was anyone at Arilinn from my
home villages."

"Oh, I saw you now and again, my lady, riding with
the other *vai leroni*," Ferrika said. "And once the *domna*
Lirielle came to the Guild-house to aid us. There was a
woman there whose inward parts were being destroyed
by some dreadful disease, and our Guild-mother said
that nothing could save her except neutering."

"I had thought that illegal," Callista said with a shudder, and Ferrika answered, "Why, so it is, *domna*, except
to save a life. More than illegal, it is very dangerous as
it is done under a surgeon's knife. Many never recover.
But it can be done by matrix—" She broke off with a
rueful smile, saying, "But who am I to say that to you,
who were Lady of Arilinn and know all such arts?"

Callista said, shrinking, "I have never seen it."

"I was privileged to watch the *leronis*," said Ferrika,
"and I felt it would be greatly helpful to the women of
our world if this art was more widely known."

With a shudder of revulsion, Callista said, "Neutering?"

"Not only that, *domna*, although, to save a life, that
too. The woman lived. Though her womanhood was destroyed, the disease had also been burnt out and she was
free of it. But there are so many other things which
could be done. You did not see what Lord Damon did
with the crippled men after the storm, but I saw how
they recovered after—and I know how men recover
when I have had to cut off their toes and fingers to save
them from the black rot. And there are women for
whom it is not safe to bear more children, and there is
no safe way to make it impossible. I have long thought
that partial neutering might be the answer, if it could be
done without the risks of surgery. It is a pity, my lady,
that the art of doing such things with a matrix is not
known outside the Towers."

Callista looked dismayed at the thought, and Ferrika
knew she had gone too far. She replaced the cap on the
jar of burn salve with strong fingers. "Have you found

the *kireseth* that was missing, Lady Callista? You should ask Lord Damon if he put it somewhere else." She put away the salve, glanced through the herbal teas Callista had divided into doses, and looked along the shelves. "We have no more blackfruit root when this is gone, my lady."

Callista looked at the curled scraps of root in the bottom of the jar. "We must send to the markets at Neskaya when the roads are clear. It comes from the Dry Towns. But surely we do not use it often?"

"I have been giving it to your father, *domna*, to strengthen his heart. For a time I can give him red-rush, but for daily use this is better."

"Send for it, then, you have the authority. But he has always been a strong, powerful man. Why do you think he needs stimulants for his heart, Ferrika?"

"It is often so with men who have been very active, *domna*, swordsmen, riders, athletes, mountain guides. If some injury keeps them long abed, their hearts weaken. It is as if their bodies developed a need for activity, and when it is too suddenly withdrawn, they fall ill, and sometimes they die. I do not know why it should be so, my lady, I only know that very often it is so."

This was her fault too, Callista thought in sudden despair. It was in fighting with the catmen that he lost the use of his limbs. And, remembering how tender her father had been with her that morning, she was seized by grief. Suppose he should die, when she had just begun to know him! In the Tower she had been insulated from grief and joy alike. Now it seemed that the world outside was filled with so many sorrows she could not bear it. How could she ever have had the courage to leave?

Ferrika watched her with sympathy, but Callista was too inexperienced to realize it. She had been taught to rely so wholly upon herself that now she was unable to turn to anyone else for advice or for comfort. After a time, Ferrika, seeing that Callista was lost in her own thoughts, went quietly away, and Callista tried to resume her work, but what she had heard left her so shaken that her hands would not obey her. Finally she replaced her materials, cleaned her equipment and went out, closing the door.

The men and maids had finished the washing, and in the rare bright sun, were out in the courtyards, pegging up sheets and towels, linens and garments, from lines strung everywhere. They were laughing gaily and calling jokes back and forth, tramping about in the mud and melting snow. The courtyard was full of wet flapping linens, blowing in the gusty wind. They looked merry and busy, but Callista knew from experience that if she joined them it would put a damper on their high spirits. They were used to Ellemir, but to the women of the estate—and even more to the men—she was still a stranger, exotic, to be feared and revered, a Comyn lady who had been a *leronis* at Arilinn. Only Ferrika, who had known her as a child, was capable of treating her as another young woman like herself. She was lonely, she realized as she watched the young girls and women running back and forth with armfuls of wet wash for the lines and dry sheets for the cupboards, making jokes and teasing one another.

She was lonely, belonging nowhere, she felt, not in the Tower, not among them.

After a time she went off to the greenhouses. Heaters were always kept inside the greenhouses, but she could see that some of the plants near the window had been frostbitten, and in one of the buildings the weight of snow had broken several panes. Although it had been hastily boarded up, some fruit bushes had died. She saw Andrew at the far end, showing the gardeners how to cut away damaged vines, looking for live wood.

She rarely *looked* at Andrew, being so accustomed to being aware of him in other ways. Now she wondered if Ellemir thought him handsome or ill-looking. The thought annoyed her disproportionately. She knew Andrew thought her beautiful. Not being a vain woman, and, because of the taboo which had surrounded her all her adult life, unaccustomed to masculine attention, this always surprised her a little. But now, she felt that since Ellemir was so lovely, and she was so thin and pale, he must certainly think Ellemir more beautiful.

Andrew looked up, smiled and beckoned to her. She came to his side, politely nodding to the gardener. "Are these bushes all dead?"

He shook his head. "I think not. Killed to the root, maybe, but they'll grow again this spring." He added to the man, "Mind you mark where you've cut them back, so you don't plant anything else there and disturb the roots."

Callista looked at the cut bushes. "These leaves should be picked and sorted, and those which aren't frost-damaged must be dried, or we'll have no seasoning for our roasts till spring!"

Andrew relayed the order. "A good thing you were here! I may be a good gardener, but I'm no cook, even on my world."

She laughed. "I am no cook at all, on any world. I know something of herbs, that is all."

The gardener bent to take away the cut branches, and behind his back Andrew bent to kiss her quickly on the forehead. She had to steel herself not to move out of reach, as long habit and deep reflexes prompted. He was aware of the abortive movement and looked at her in pained surprise, then, remembering, sighed and smiled.

"I am glad to see you looking so well, my love."

She said, sighing, feeling nothing in his kiss, "I feel like that bush there, killed down to the roots. Let's hope I'll grow again in spring too."

"Should you be out? Damon said you should rest again today."

"Well, Damon has a bad habit of being right, but I feel like a mushroom in a dark cellar," Callista said, "it's so long since I've seen the sunlight!" She halted in a patch of sun, savoring the warmth on her face, while Andrew moved along, checking the rows of vegetables and pot-herbs. "I think everything here is still in good order, but I'm not familiar with these. What do you think, Callista?"

She came and knelt beside the low bushes, checking their roots. "I told Father years ago that he should not plant the melons so close to the wall. It's true that there's more sunlight here, but there isn't really enough insulation in a bad storm. This one will die before the fruit is ripe, and if this one survives"—she pointed— "the cold has killed the fruit. The rind may do for pickle, but it will not ripen and must be taken away before it rots." She called the gardener back to give orders.

"We will have to ask for some more seed from one of the lower lying farms. Perhaps Syrtis has been protected from the storm. They have good fruit trees and we can ask them for some melons, and some slips from their vines. And these should be taken to the kitchens. Some can be cooked before they spoil, others salted and put by."

As the men went to carry out the orders, Andrew slipped his hand between her arm and her body. She tensed, went rigid, then quick color flooded her face. "I am sorry. It is only a . . . a reflex, a habit . . ."

Back to square one. All the physical reflexes, so slowly and carefully obliterated in the months since their marriage, were returned in full strength. Andrew felt helpless and defeated. He knew that this had been necessary to save her life, but seeing it actually in action again was another shock, and a severe one.

"Don't look like that," Callista begged. "It's only for a little while!"

He sighed. "I know. Leonie warned me of this." His face tightened, and Callista said edgily, "You really hate her, don't you?"

"Not her. But I hate what she did to you. I can't forgive that, and I never will."

Callista felt a curious inward trembling, a shaking she could never quite control. She kept her voice even with an effort. "Be fair, Andrew. Leonie put no compulsion on me to be Keeper. I chose of my free will. She simply made it possible for me to follow that most difficult of paths. And it was also of my free will that I chose to endure the . . . the pain of leaving. For *you*," she added, looking straight at Andrew.

Andrew sensed that they were perilously close to a quarrel. With one part of himself he craved it, a thunderclap which would clear the air. The thought came unbidden that with Ellemir that would be the way: a short, sharp quarrel, and a reconciliation which would leave them closer than ever.

But he could never do that with Callista. She had learned, with what suffering he could never guess, to keep her emotions deeply guarded, hidden behind an impermeable barrier. He breached that wall at his peril.

He might now and then persuade her briefly to lower it or draw it aside, but it would always be there and he could never risk destroying it without destroying Callista too. If she seemed hard and invulnerable on the surface, he sensed that behind this she was more vulnerable than he could ever know.

"I won't blame her, sweetheart, but I wish she could have been more explicit with us, with both of us."

That was fair enough, Callista thought, remembering—like a bad dream, like a nightmare!—how she had railed at Leonie in the overworld. Still she felt compelled to say, "Leonie didn't know."

Andrew wanted to shout, well, why in hell didn't she? That's her business, isn't it? But he dared not criticize Leonie to her either. His voice was shaking. "What are we to do? Just go on like this, with you unwilling even to touch my hand?"

"Not unwilling," she said, forcing the words past a lump in her throat. "I *cannot.* I thought Damon had explained it to you."

"And the best Damon could do only made it worse!"

"Not worse," she said, her eyes blazing again. "He saved my life! Be fair, Andrew!"

Andrew muttered, his eyes lowered, "I'm tired of being fair."

"I feel that you hate me when you talk like that!"

"Never, Callie," he said, sobered. "I just feel so damnably helpless. What are we to do?"

She said, lowering her eyes and looking away from him, "I cannot think it is so hard for you. Ellemir—" But she stopped there, and Andrew, overcome with all the old tenderness, reached out for the deeper contact, wanting to reassure her, and himself, that it was still there, that it could endure through the separation. It occurred to him that because of their deep-rooted cultural differences, even telepathy was no guarantee against misunderstanding. But the closeness was there.

They must start from that. Understanding could come later.

He said gently, "You look tired, Callie. You mustn't overdo on your first day out of bed. Let me take you upstairs." And when they were alone in their room, he asked gently, "Are you reproaching me for Ellemir, Callista? I thought it was what you wanted."

"It was," she said, stammering. "It was only . . . only . . . it should make it easier for you to wait. Do we have to talk about it, Andrew?"

He said soberly, "I think we do. That night—" And again she knew just what he meant. For all four of them, for a long time, "that night" would have only one meaning. "Damon said something to me that stuck. All four of us telepaths, he said, and not one of us with enough sense to sit down and make sure we understood each other. Ellemir and I managed to talk about it," he said, adding with a faint smile, "even though she had to get me half drunk before I could manage to break down and talk honestly to her."

She said, not looking at him, "It has made it easier for you. Hasn't it?"

He said quietly, "In a way. But it's not worth it if it's made you ashamed to look at me, Callista."

"Not ashamed." She managed to raise her eyes. "Not ashamed, no, it is only . . . I was taught to turn my thoughts elsewhere, so that I would not be . . . vulnerable. If you want to talk about it"—Evanda and Avarra forbid she should be less honest with him than Ellemir—"I will try. But I am not . . . not used to such talk or such thoughts and I may not . . . may not find words easily. If you will . . . will bear with that . . . then I will try."

He saw that she was biting her lip, struggling to force her words through the barrier of her inarticulateness, and felt a deep pity. He considered sparing her this, but he knew that a barrier of silence was the only barrier they might never be able to cross. At all costs—looking at her flushed cheeks and trembling mouth, he knew the cost would be heavy—they must manage to keep a line of communication open.

"Damon said you must never be allowed to feel yourself alone, or think yourself abandoned. I can only wonder, does this hurt you? Or make you feel . . . abandoned?"

She said, twisting her slender fingers in her lap. "Only if you had truly . . . truly abandoned me. Stopped caring. Stopped loving me."

He thought that it was such an intimate thing, it could not help but bring him closer to Ellemir, make even more distance between Callista and himself.

His barriers were down, and Callista, following the thought, flared up in outrage: "Do you want me only because you thought I would give you more pleasure in our bed than my sister?"

He turned a dull red. Well, he had wanted directness; he had it. "God forbid! I never thought of it that way at all. It's only . . . if you think I am going to be wanting you any less, I would rather forget the whole thing. Do you really think that because I sleep with Ellemir I have stopped wanting *you*?"

"No more than I have stopped wanting *you*, Andrew. But . . . but now we are equal."

"I don't understand."

"Now your need of me is like mine for you." Her eyes were level and tearless, but he sensed that inside she was weeping. "A . . . a thing of the mind and heart, a grief like mine, but not a . . . a torment of the body. I wanted you to be content, because"—she wet her lips, struggling against inhibitions which had lasted for years—"*that* was so terrible to me, to feel your need, your hunger, your loneliness. And so I tried to . . . to share it and I . . . I nearly killed you." The tears spilled over, but she did not cry, flicked the tears away angrily. "Do you understand? It is easier for me when I need not feel *that* in you, so I would do anything, risk anything to quiet it. . . ."

The desolation in her face made him want to weep too. He ached to take her in his arms and comfort her, though he knew he could not risk anything but the lightest touch. Gently, almost respectfully, he lifted her slender hand to his lips and laid the lightest breath of a kiss on the fingertips. "You are so generous you put me to shame, Callista. But there is no woman in the world who can give me what I want from you. I am willing to . . . to share your suffering, my darling."

This was such a strange thought that she stopped and looked at him in amazement. He meant that, she thought with a queer excitement. His world's ways were different, she knew, but in their terms he was really trying to be unselfish. It was the first awareness she had ever had of his total *alienness*, and it came as a deep, wrenching shock. She had always seen only their similarities; now she was faced, shockingly, with their differences.

He was trying to say, she realized, that because he loved her, he was willing to suffer all that pain of deprivation. . . . Perhaps he did not even know, that night, how much his need had tormented her, could still torment her.

She tightened her fingers on his hand, remembering in despair that for a little while she had known what it was to desire him, but now she could not even remember what it had been like. She spoke, trying to match his gentleness: "Andrew, my husband, my love, if you saw me bearing a heavy burden, would you weigh me down with your own burden as well? It will not lighten my suffering if I must endure yours too."

Again the shock, strangeness, amazement, and Andrew realized, with sudden insight that in a telepathic culture, it meant something different, to share suffering.

She said, with a quick smile, "And don't you realize that Damon and Ellemir are part of this too, and that they will also be miserable, if they have to share your misery?"

He was slowly making his way through that, like a labyrinth. It wasn't easy. He had thought he had shed a great deal of his cultural prejudice. Now, like an onion, stripping off one layer seemed only to reveal a deeper layer, thick and impregnable.

He remembered waking in Ellemir's bed to find Damon standing over him, had expected, almost craved Damon's reproaches. Perhaps he wanted Damon to be angry because a man of his own world would have been angry, and he wanted to feel something familiar. Even guilt would have been welcome. . . .

"But Ellemir. You simply *expected* this of her. No one consulted her, or asked if she was willing."

"Has Ellemir complained?" Callista asked, smiling.

Hell, no, he thought. She seemed to enjoy it. And that bothered him too. If she and Damon were all that happily married, how could she seem to get so much pleasure— damn it, so much fun—out of going to bed with him? He felt angry and guilty, and it was all the worse because he knew Callista didn't understand that either.

Callista said, "But of course, when Elli and I married and agreed to live under one roof, we took that for granted. Certainly you know that if either of us had married a man the other could not . . . could not accept, we would have made certain—"

Somehow that rang a warning bell in Andrew. He did not want to think about the obvious implications of that.

She went on. "Until a few hundred years ago, marriage as we know it now simply did not exist. And it was not considered right for a woman to have more than one or two children by the same man. Do the words *genetic pool* mean anything to you? There was a period in our history when some very valuable gifts, hereditary traits, were almost lost. It was thought best for children to have as many different genetic combinations as possible, to guard against the accidental loss of important genes. Bearing children to only one man can be a form of selfishness. And so we didn't have marriage then, in the sense that we do now. We do not, as the Dry-Towners do, force our wives to harbor our concubines, but there are always other women to share. What do you Terrans do when your wives are pregnant, if a woman is too far advanced in pregnancy, too heavy, or weary, or ill? Would you demand that a woman violate her instincts for your comfort?"

If it had been Ellemir asking this, Andrew would have felt he had scored a point, but as Callista said it there was no challenge. "Cultural prejudices aren't rational. Ours is against sleeping with other women. Yours, against sex in pregnancy, makes no sense to me, unless a woman is really ill."

She shrugged. "Biologically, no pregnant animal desires sex; most will not endure it. If your women have been culturally conditioned to accept it as the price of retaining a husband's sexual interest, I can only say I am sorry for them! Would you demand it of me after I had ceased to take pleasure in it?"

Andrew suddenly found that he was laughing. "My love, of all our worries, it seems that one is the easiest to put off until it is at hand! Do you have a saying . . . can we cross that bridge when we come to it?"

She laughed too. "We say we will ride that colt when

he has grown to bear a saddle. But truly, Andrew, do you Terran men—"

He said, "God help me, love, I don't *know* what most men do. I doubt if I could ask you to do anything you didn't want to. I'd probably . . . probably take the rough with the smooth. I guess some men would go elsewhere, but make damn sure their wives didn't find it out. There's another old saying: what the eye doesn't see, the heart doesn't grieve over."

"But among a family of telepaths, such deceit is simply not possible," Callista said, "and I would rather know my husband was content in the arms of someone who gave us this out of love, a sister or a friend, than adventuring with a stranger." But she was calmer, and Andrew sensed that removing their talk from an immediate problem to a distant one had made it less troubling to her. He said, "I'd rather die than hurt you."

As he had done earlier, she lifted his fingertips to her lips and kissed them, very lightly. She said with a smile, "Ah, my husband, dying would hurt me worse than anything else you could possibly do."

CHAPTER THIRTEEN

Andrew rode through melting snow, a light flurry still falling. Across the valley he could see the lights of Armida, a soft twinkle against the mountain mass. Damon said these were only foothills, but to Andrew they were mountains, and high ones, too. He heard the men talking behind him in low voices and knew that they were also looking forward to food, and fire, and home, after eight days in the far pastures, noting the damage of the great blizzard, the condition of the roads, the damage to livestock.

He had welcomed this chance to be alone with those who could not read his thoughts. He had not yet grown wholly accustomed to life within a telepathic family, and he had not, as yet, quite learned to guard himself against accidental intrusion. From the men he picked up only a small, slight background trickle of thought, surface, undisturbing, inconsequential. But he was glad to be coming home. He rode through the courtyard gates and servants came to take his horse's bridle. He accepted this now without thought, though there were times when, stopping to think, it still disturbed him somewhat. Callista ran down the steps toward him. He bent to kiss her lightly on the cheek, then discovered though it was too dark in the courtyard, that it was Ellemir he held. Laughing, sharing her amusement at his mistake, he hugged her hard and felt her mouth under his, warm and familiar. They went up the steps holding hands.

"How are all at home, Elli?"

"Well enough, though Father has grown short of breath and eats little. Callista is with him, but I would not let you go ungreeted," she said, giving his fingers a slight squeeze. "I've missed you."

Andrew had missed her too, and guilt surged in him. Damn it, why did his wife have to be twins? He asked, "How is Damon?"

"Busy," she said, laughing. "He has been buried in the old records of the Domains, of those of our family who were Keepers or technicians at Arilinn or Neskaya Tower. I do not know what he is looking for, and he has not told me. In this last tenday I have seen little more of him than of you!"

Inside the hallway Andrew shrugged off his great riding cloak and gave it to the hall-steward. Rhodri drew off his snow-clogged boots and gave him fur-lined ankle-high indoor boots to put on. Ellemir on his arm, he went into the Great Hall.

Callista was seated beside her father, but as she came through the door she broke off, laid her harp unhurriedly on a bench and came to meet him. She moved quietly, the folds of her blue dress trailing behind her, and against his will he found himself contrasting this with Ellemir's eager greeting. Yet he watched her, spellbound. Every movement she made still filled him with fascination, desire, longing. She held out her hands and at the clasp of those delicate cool fingertips he was baffled again.

What the hell was love anyway? he asked himself. He had always felt that falling in love with one woman meant falling out of love with others. Which of them was he in love with anyway? His wife . . . or her sister?

He said, holding her hands gently, "I've missed you," and she smiled up into his face. *Dom* Esteban said, "Welcome back, son, hard trip?"

"Not so much." Because it was expected, he bent and kissed the old man's thin cheek, thinking that he looked paler, not well at all. He supposed it was to be expected. "How is it with you, Father?"

"Oh, nothing ever changes with me," the old man said as Callista brought Andrew a cup. He took it, raised it to his lips. It was hot spiced cider, and tasted wonderful after the long ride. It was good to be home. At the lower end of the hall the women were laying the table for the evening meal.

"How is it out there?" *Dom* Esteban asked, and Andrew began his report.

"Most of the roads are open again, though there are heavy drift-falls, and pack-ice at the bend in the river.

All things considered, there's not much stock lost. We found four mares and three foals frozen in the shed beyond the ford. Ice had drifted over the fodder there and they had probably starved before they froze."

The Alton lord looked grim. "A good brood mare is worth her weight in silver, but with such a storm, we might have expected more losses. What else?"

"On the hillside a day's ride north of Corresanti, a few yearlings were cut off from the rest. One with a broken snow-leg could not get to the shelter, was covered by a snow-slide. The rest were hungry and shivering, but they'll do well enough, all fed and tended now, and a man left to look after them. Half a dozen calves were dead in the farthest pasture, in the village of Bellazi. The flesh was frozen, and the villagers asked for the carcasses, saying the meat was still good, and that you always gave it to them. I told them to do what was customary. Was that right?"

The man nodded. "It's custom for the last hundred years. Stock dead in a blizzard is given to the nearest village, to make what use they can of meat and hides. In return they shelter and feed any livestock that makes its way down in a storm, and bring them back when they can. If in a hungry season they slaughter and eat an extra one, I don't worry that much about it. I'm no tyrant."

The serving women were bringing in the meal. The men and women of the household gathered around the long table in the lower hall, and Andrew pushed *Dom* Esteban's rolling-chair to his place at the upper table, where the family sat with a few of the upper servants and the skilled professionals who managed the ranch and the estate. Andrew was beginning to wonder if Damon would not appear at all when he suddenly thrust open the doors at the back of the hall and, apologizing briefly to Ellemir for his lateness, came to Andrew with a welcoming smile.

"I heard in the court that you were home. How did you manage alone? I kept thinking I should have come with you, this first time."

"I managed well enough, though I would have been glad of your company," Andrew said. He noted that

Damon looked weary and haggard, and wondered what the other man had been doing with himself. Damon volunteered nothing, beginning to ask questions about stock and fodder sheds, storm damage, bridges and fords, as if he had never done anything in his life except help to manage a horse ranch. While they talked ranch business with *Dom* Esteban, Callista and Ellemir talked softly together. Andrew found himself thinking how good it would be when they were all alone together again, but he did not grudge the time spent with his father-in-law on the ranch affairs. He had feared, when he first came here, that he would be received only as Callista's husband, penniless and alien, useless for the strange affairs of a strange world. Now he knew that he was accepted and valued as a born son and heir to the Domain would have been.

The business of repairs to buildings and bridges, of replacements for lost stock, occupied most of the meal. The women were clearing away the dishes when Callista leaned over and spoke in an undertone to her father. He nodded permission, and she stood up, rapping briefly on the edge of a metal tankard for attention. The servants moving in the hall looked at her respectfully. A Keeper was the object of almost superstitious reverence, and though Callista had given up her formal status, she was still looked on with more than ordinary respect. When the hall was perfectly quiet, she spoke in her soft, clear voice, which nevertheless carried to the furthest corners of the hall:

"Someone here, without authority, has been trespassing in my still-room and has taken some of an herb from there. If it is returned at once, and no unauthorized use made of it, I will assume that it was taken by mistake, and not pursue the matter any further. But if it is not returned to me by tomorrow morning, I will take any action I think suitable."

There was a confused silence in the hall. A few of the people murmured to one another, but no one spoke aloud, and at last Callista said, "Very well. You may think about it overnight. Tomorrow I will use any methods at my command"—with an automatic, arrogant gesture her hand went to the matrix in its concealed place at her throat—"to discover who is guilty. That is all. You may go."

It was the first time Andrew had seen her deliberately call upon her old authority as Keeper, and it troubled him. As she came back to her seat he asked, "What is missing, Callista?"

"*Kireseth*," she said briefly. "It is a dangerous herb, and its use is forbidden except to the Tower-trained or under their express authority." Her smooth brow was wrinkled with a frown. "I do not like the idea of some ignorant person going around crazed with the stuff. It is a deliriant and hallucinogen."

Dom Esteban protested, "Oh, come, Callista, surely not so dangerous. I know you people in the Towers have a superstitious taboo about the stuff, but it grows wild here in the hills, and it has never been—"

"Just the same, I am personally responsible for making certain that none of it is mishandled by my neglect."

Damon raised his head. He said wearily, "Don't trouble the servants, Callista, *I* took it."

She stared at him in astonishment. "You, Damon? Whatever did you want with it?"

"Will it be enough for you to know that I had my reasons, Callista?"

"But why, Damon?" she insisted. "If you had asked, I would have given it to you, but—"

"But you would have asked why," Damon said, his face drawn into lines of exhaustion and pain. "No, Callie, don't try to read me." His eyes were suddenly hard. "I took it for reasons that seemed good to me, and I am not going to tell you what they are. I may not need it, and if I do not I will return it to you, but for the moment I believe I may have a use for it. Leave it there, *breda*."

She said, "Of course, if you insist, Damon." She raised her cup and sipped, watching Damon with a troubled look. Her thoughts were easy to read: *Damon is trained in the use of* kirian, *but he cannot make it, so what could he want with the raw herb? What can he possibly be going to do with it? I cannot believe he would misuse it, but what does he intend?*

The servants dispersed. *Dom* Esteban asked if someone would care to play cards with him, or castles, the chess-like game Andrew was learning to play. Andrew agreed and sat studying the small cut-crystal pawns with surface absorption, but his mind was busy elsewhere. What could Damon have wanted with the *kireseth*? Damon had warned him not to handle or smell it, he remembered. Moving a pawn, and losing it to his father-in-law, it seemed that he could feel Damon's thoughts leaking around the perimeter of his own emotions. He knew how much Damon hated and feared the matrix work he had been trained to do, had been forced to renounce, and had returned to against his will. *Until Callista is free. And even then . . . There is so much that a telepath can do, so much undone. . . .* Cutting off Damon's thoughts by main force, Andrew forced himself to concentrate on the board before him, lost three pawns in rapid succession, then made a major mistake in moving which cost him the major piece called the dragon. He conceded, saying apologetically, "Sorry, the shapes of those two still confuse me a little."

"Never mind," said the old man, graciously returning the mistakenly moved piece. "You are a better player, at that, than Ellemir, though she is the only one who has patience to play with me. Damon plays well, but seldom has the time. Damon? When Andrew and I have played this out, will you play the winner?"

"Not tonight, Uncle," said Damon, rousing himself from deep abstraction, and the old man, glancing around the hall, noted that most of the housefolk had dispersed to their beds. Only his own body-servant, yawning, lingered before the fire. The Alton lord sighed, glanced at the angle of moonlight beyond the windows.

"I am selfish. I keep you young people here talking half the night, and Andrew has had a long ride, and has been parted a long time from his wife. I sleep so badly now, and the nights seem endless with no one to keep me company, so I tend to cling to you. Go along, all of you, to your own beds."

Ellemir kissed her father good night and withdrew. Callista lingered to say a word to the old man's body-servant. Damon turned to follow Ellemir, then hesitated in the doorway and came back.

"Father, there is an important piece of work to be done. Can you spare us for a few days?"

"Do you need to be away?"

"No away, no," Damon said, "but I might need to put up dampers and a barrier and isolate the four of us. I can choose what time is best, but I would rather not delay too long." He glanced at Callista, and Andrew caught the thought he tried to guard: *She will die of grief* . . .

"We will need at least three or four days, uninterrupted. Can that be arranged?"

The old man nodded, slowly. "Take what time you need, Damon. But for any long periods of work, it would be better to wait till Midwinter is past, and until the repairs from the storm have been completed. Is that possible?"

Andrew saw *Dom* Esteban's disquieted gaze at Callista, and heard what he did not say: *A Keeper who has given back her oath?* He knew Damon heard it too, but Damon only said, "Possible, and we will do that. Thank you, Father." He bent and embraced the older man. He watched him, frowning a little, as his servants wheeled him out of the room.

"He misses Dezi, I think. Whatever the lad's faults, he was a good son to the old man. For his sake, perhaps, I wish we could have forgiven Dezi." He sighed as they went up the stairs. "He is lonely. There is no one here now who is really company for him. I think, when the spring thaw comes, we must send for some kinsman or friend to bear him company."

Callista was coming up the stairs behind them. Damon paused before turning away to go to his own suite.

"Callie, you were made Keeper very young, too young, I think. Did you take training for the other grades too? Are you monitor, mechanic or technician? Or did you only work in the central relays as *tenerésteis*?" He used the archaic word usually rendered in *casta* as "Keeper" although "warden" or "guardian" would have been equally accurate.

"Why, you taught me to monitor yourself, Damon. It was my first year in the Tower and your last. By certificate I am only a mechanic; I never tried to do a technician's work. There was no lack of technicians, and I had enough to do in the relays. Why?"

"I wanted to know what skills we had between us," Damon said. "I reached the level of technician. I can build what lattices and screens we need, if I have the crystals and blank nodes. But I may need a mechanic, and I will certainly need a monitor, if I am to look for the answer I promised you, so be sure you don't let yourself get out of condition to monitor if it is needed. Have you kept up your breathing?"

"I could not sleep without it. I suspect all of us trained there will do it all our lives," she said, and Damon smiled, leaning forward and kissing her cheek very lightly.

"How well you know, sister. Sleep well. Good night, my brother," he added to Andrew, and went away.

It was obvious that something was bothering Damon. Callista was sitting at her dressing table, braiding her long hair for the night. It reminded Andrew poignantly of another night, but he turned his thoughts away. Callista, still preoccupied with Damon, said, "He is more troubled than he wants us to know. I have known Damon for a long time. It is no use asking him anything he does not want to tell . . ."

But what could he possibly want with kireseth?

Andrew remembered with a flicker of jealousy that she had not shrunk from Damon's light kiss on her cheek, but he knew what would happen if he tried it. Then, against his will, Andrew found himself thinking of Damon and Ellemir, together, reunited.

She was his wife, after all, and he, Andrew, had no rights . . . none at all.

Callista put out the light and got into her own bed. Sighing, Andrew lay down, watching the four moons move across the sky. When he finally fell asleep he was not aware of it. It was as if he moved into some state of consciousness between reality and dreams. Damon had told him once that at times, in sleep, the mind moved into the overworld, without any conscious thought.

It seemed to him that he left his body behind and moved through the formless grayness of the over-

world. Somewhere, everywhere, he could see and
be aware of Damon and Ellemir making love, and
while he knew they would welcome it if he joined
them, linked with their joyous rapport and closeness, he kept turning away his eyes and his mind
from the sight. He wasn't a voyeur; he wasn't that
depraved, not yet, not even here.

After a long time he found the structure they had
built for working with the frostbitten men. He was
afraid he would find them there too, as they seemed
to be everywhere at once, but Ellemir was sleeping
and Damon was sitting on a log, dejectedly, a bunch
of dried *kireseth* flowers lying at his side.

He asked, "What did you want with them,
Damon?" and the other man said, "I am not sure.
Why do you think I could not explain it to Callista?
It is forbidden. Everything is forbidden. We should
not be here at all."

Andrew said, "But we are only dreaming about
it, and how can anyone forbid dreaming?" But he
knew, guiltily, that a telepath must be responsible
even for his dreams, and that even in dreams he
could not go to Ellemir as he longed to do. Damon
said, "But I told you, it is only a part of being what
we are," and Andrew turned his back on Damon
and tried to get out of the structure, but the walls
shut him in and enclosed him. Then Callista—or
was it Ellemir? He could no longer be sure anymore, which of them was his wife—came to him,
with a bunch of the *kireseth* flowers in her hand,
and said, "Take them. Our children will eat of these
fruits some day."

Forbidden fruit. But he took them in his hand,
biting the blossoms which were soft as a woman's
breasts, and the smell of the flowers was like a sting
inside his mind. Then lightning struck the walls, and
the structure began to tremble and shake asunder,
and through the collapsing walls Leonie was cursing
them, and obscurely Andrew knew that it was all his
fault because he had taken Callista away from her.

And then he was alone on the gray plain, and the
landmark was very far away on the horizon. Al-

though he walked for eternities, days, hours, aeons, he could not reach it. He knew that Damon and Callista and Ellemir were all inside, and they had found the answer and they were happy, but he was alone again, a stranger, never to be part of them again. As soon as he drew near the grayness expanded, elastic, and he was far away and the structure was on the far horizon again. And yet somehow at the same time he was inside his walls, and Callista was lying in his arms—or was it Ellemir, or somehow was he making love to them both at once?— and it was Damon who was wandering outside on the horizon, struggling to come near to the landmark, and never reaching it, never, never. . . . He said to Ellemir, "You must take him some of the *kireseth* flowers," but she turned into Callista, and said, "It is forbidden for the Tower-trained," and he could not decide whether he was there, lying between the two women, or whether he was outside, wandering on the distant horizon. . . . Somehow he knew he was trapped inside Damon's dream, and he could not get out.

He woke with a start. Callista slept restlessly in the gray darkness of the room. He heard himself say, half aloud, "You will know what to do with them when it is time . . ." and then, wondering what he had meant, knew the words were part of Damon's dream. Then he slept again, wandering in the gray and formless realms until dawn. Partly aware that it was not his own consciousness at all, he wondered if he were himself, or if he had somehow become entangled with Damon as well.

He found himself thinking that precognition was almost worse than having no gift at all. If it were a warning, you could be guided by it. But it was just time out of focus, and even Leonie did not understand time. And Andrew in his own awareness wished Damon would keep his damned troubling dreams to himself.

It was a cold, bitter morning, with sleet falling. Damon felt that the sky reflected his own mood.

He had avoided this work for many years, now he was

being forced into it again. And he knew, now, that it was not only for Callista's sake. He had been wrong to renounce it so completely.

He had been misled by the taboo barring telepaths from matrix work outside the Towers. That taboo might, after the Ages of Chaos, have made some sense. But now he felt, with every nerve in him, that it was wrong.

There was so much work for telepaths to do. And it was being left undone.

He had built himself a new career, of sorts, in the Guardsmen, but it had never satisfied him completely. Nor could he find, as Andrew did, satisfaction and fulfillment in helping to manage the estate of his father-in-law. He knew that for many a younger son, without an estate of his own, this would have been a perfect solution: landless himself, to have an estate where his sons would share in the heritage. But it was not for Damon. He knew that any halfway skilled steward could do his work as well. He was there simply to assure that no unscrupulous paid employee took advantage of his wife's father.

He did not begrudge the time spent on the work of the estate. His life was here with Ellemir, and it would tear him into fragments to be parted, now, from Andrew or from Callista.

It was different for Andrew. He had grown to manhood in a world not unlike this, and for him it was recovering a world he had thought lost forever when he left Terra. But Damon now had begun to guess that *his* real work was this, the work he had been trained in the Towers to do.

"Your part and Ellemir's," he told Andrew, "is simply to guard us against intrusion. If there are any interruptions—though I have tried to arrange that there will be none—you can deal with it. Otherwise you must simply remain in rapport and lend me your strength."

Callista's work was far more difficult. At first she had been reluctant to take part in this way, but he had managed to persuade her, and he was glad, for he could trust her completely. Like himself, she was Arilinn-trained, a skilled psi monitor, and knew precisely what was wanted. She would watch over his life functions and make sure that his body continued to function as it should while his essential self was elsewhere.

She looked pale and strange, and he knew she was reluctant to return to this work she had abandoned forever, not, like himself, out of fear or distaste, but because it had been such a wrench to abandon it. Having made the renunciation, she was reluctant to compromise.

Yet this was her own true work, Damon knew. It was what she was born and trained to do. It was wrong and cruel that a woman could not do this work without renouncing womanhood. For anything less than working among the great relays and screens, Callista would be completely qualified, were she married a dozen times and as many times a mother! Yet she was lost to the Towers, and it was no less a loss to her. It was a foolish notion, he considered, that with the loss of virginity she would be deprived of all the skills so painstakingly trained into her, and all the knowledge learned at such cost during all those years in Arilinn!

He thought, *I do not believe it*, and caught his breath. This was blasphemy, sacrilege unthinkable! Yet he looked at Callista and thought defiantly, *Nevertheless, I do not believe it!*

Yet he was violating the Tower taboo even in using her as a monitor. How stupid, how appallingly stupid!

Of course, legally he was doing nothing wrong. Callista, though she had declared intent to marry by a freemate ceremony, was not, in fact, Andrew's wife. She was still a virgin, and therefore qualified. . . . How stupid the whole thing was! How tragically stupid!

Something was wrong, he thought once again, terribly and tragically wrong with the whole concept of training telepaths on Darkover. Because of the abuses of the Ages of Chaos, because of the crimes of men and women dead so long that even their bones were dust, other men and women were condemned to a living death.

Callista asked gently, "What's wrong, Damon? You look so angry!"

He could not explain it to her. She was still bound by the taboos, deep in her bones. He said, "I'm cold," and left it at that. He had wrapped himself in a loose robe, which would at least protect his body from the awful chilling of the overworld. He noted that Callista had also substituted a long, warm wrapper for her ordinary housedress. He lay back in a padded armchair, while Callista made herself comfortable on a cushion at his feet. Andrew and Ellemir were a little further away, and Ellemir said, "When I kept watch for you, you had me stay physically in contact with the pulse spots."

"You're untrained, darling. Callista has been doing this work since she was a little girl. She could even monitor me from another room, if she had to. You and Andrew are basically superfluous, though it's a help to have you both here. If something should interrupt us—I've given orders, but if, the Gods forbid, the house should take fire or *Dom* Esteban fall ill and need help—you can deal with it, and protect Callista and me from disturbance."

Callista had her matrix in her lap. He noted that she had fastened it to the pulse spot with a bit of ribbon. There were different ways of handling a matrix, and at Arilinn everyone was encouraged to experiment and find the way most congenial. He noted that she contacted the psi jewel without physically looking into the stone, while he himself gazed into the depths of his own, seeing the swirling lights slowly focus. . . . He began to breathe more and more slowly, sensing it when Callista made contact with his mind, matching the resonances of her body's field to his own. More dimly and at a distance he felt her bring Andrew and Ellemir into the rapport. For a moment he relaxed into the content of having them all around him, close, reassuring, in the closest bond known. At this moment he knew that he was closer to Callista than to anyone in the world. Closer than to Ellemir, whose body he knew so well, whose thoughts he had shared, who had so briefly and heartbreakingly sheltered their child. Yet Callista was close to him as twin to unborn twin, and Ellemir somewhere in the outside distance. Beyond her he sensed Andrew, a giant, a rock of strength, protecting them, safeguarding them. . . .

He felt the walls of their sheltering place enclosing them, the astral structure he had built while he worked with the frostbitten men. Then, with that curious upward thrust, he was in the overworld, and he could *see* the walls taking shape around them. When he had built it with Andrew and Dezi it had resembled a travel-shelter of rough brown stone, perhaps because he had regarded it as temporary. Structures in the overworld were what you thought they were. He noticed that the rough brick and stone had now become smooth and lucent, that there was a slate-colored stone floor beneath his feet, not unlike that of Callista's little still-room. From where he stood, in the green and gold colors of his Domain, he could see an array of furnishings. Noticed like this, they looked curiously transparent and insubstantial, but he knew that if he tried to sit on them they would take on strength and solidity. They would be comfortable and would, furthermore, provide whatever surface he wanted—velvet or silk or fur at his own will. On one of these Callista lay, and she too looked oddly transparent, though he knew she would solidify too, as they were here longer. Andrew and Ellemir looked more dim, and he saw that they were asleep on the other furniture, because they were here only in his mind, not conscious on the overworld level at all. Only their thoughts, drifting through his in the rapport where Callista held them, were strong and present. They were passive here, lending all their strength to Damon. He floated for a moment, enjoying the comfort of a support circle, knowing it would keep him from some of the awful draining he had known before. He noted how Callista held in her hands a series of threads like a spiderweb, and he knew this was how she visualized the control she was keeping over his body where it lay in the more solid world. If his breathing faltered, if his circulation was impaired by the cramped position, if, even, he developed an itch which could disturb his concentration here in the overworld, she could repair the damage long before he was conscious of it. Guarded by Callista, his body was safe, here behind the shelter of their landmark.

But he could not linger here, and even as he was aware of it he felt himself move through the impalpable walls of the shelter. His thoughts provided exit, though no outsider could ever enter, and he was out on the gray and featureless plain of the overworld. In the distance he could see the peaks of the Arilinn Tower, or, rather, the duplicate of that Tower in the overworld.

For a thousand years, perhaps, the thoughts of every psi-technician who moved into the overworld had created Arilinn as a safe landmark. Why was it so far away? Damon wondered, then knew: this was Callista's visualization, working in link with his own, and to her Arilinn seemed very far indeed. But here in the overworld space had no reality and with the swiftness—literally—of thought, he stood before the gates of Arilinn.

He had been driven forth. Could he get in now if he tried? With the thought he was inside, standing on the steps of the outer court, Leonie before him in her crimson robes, veiled.

"I know why you have come, Damon. I have searched everywhere for the records you want, and I have learned, in these days, more of the history of Arilinn than I had ever guessed. I had known, indeed, that in the first days of the Towers, many Keepers were *emmasca*, of *chieri* blood, neither man nor woman. I had not known that when such births grew rare, as the *chieri* mingled less and less with humankind, some of the earliest Keepers were neutered to resemble them. Did you know, Damon, that not only neutered women, but castrated males were used at some times for Keepers? What a barbarism!"

"And not needed," Damon said. "Any halfway competent psi-technician can do most of a Keeper's work, and pay no higher price than a few days of impotence."

Leonie smiled faintly and said, "There are many men who think even that price too high, Damon."

Damon nodded, thinking of his brother Lorenz, and the contempt in his voice when he said of Damon: "Half monk, half eunuch."

"And for women," Leonie said, "it was discovered that a Keeper need not be neutered, though they had not yet discovered the training techniques we use. It was sufficient to fix the channels steadily clear, so they would not carry any impulses save the psi impulses. So it was done, without the barbarism of neutering. But in our age, even that seemed too much an impairment of a woman." Leonie's face was scornful. "I think it was only the pride of the men of Comyn, who felt that a woman's most precious attribute was her fertility, her ability to pass on their male heritage. They became squeamish about any impairment of a woman's ability to bear children."

Damon said, in a low voice, "It also meant that a woman who thought as a young girl that she wished to be Keeper need not make a lifetime choice before she fully knew the burden it demanded."

Leonie dismissed that. "You are a man, Damon, and I do not expect you to understand. It was to spare the women this heavy burden of choice." Suddenly her voice broke. "Do you think I would not rather have had all that cut cleanly from me in childhood, rather than going all my life imprisoned, knowing I held the key to my prison, and that only my own oath, my own honor, the word of a Hastur, kept me so . . so prisoned." He could not tell whether it was grief or anger that made her voice tremble. "If I had my way, if you men of Comyn were not so concerned with a woman's precious fertility, any girl-child coming to the Tower would be neutered at once, and live her life as Keeper happy, and free of the burden of womanhood. She would be free of pain and the never-ending reminders of choice—that she can never choose once and for all, but must make that choice anew every day of her life."

"You would make them slaves lifelong to the Tower?"

Leonie's voice was almost inaudible, but to Damon it was like a cry. "Do you think we are not slaves?"

"Leonie, Leonie, if you felt it so, why did you bear it all these years? There were others who could have taken it from your shoulders when it grew too heavy to be borne."

"I am a Hastur," she said, "and I have given oath never to lay down my burden until I had trained another to take it from me. Do you think I did not try?" She looked straight at him, and Damon tensed with remembered anguish, for as his thoughts formed her, so she was in the overworld, and it was the Leonie of his first years in the Tower who stood before him. He would never know if any other man thought her beautiful, but to him she was infinitely beautiful, desirable, holding the very strings of his soul between her slender hands. . . . He turned away, fighting to see her only as he had seen her last in the flesh, seen her at his wedding: a woman calm, aging, controlled, past rage or rebellion.

"I thought you content with power and reverence, Leonie, with the highest place of all, equal to any Comyn lord—Leonie of Arilinn, Lady of Darkover."

She said, the words coming from immense distances, "Had you known I rebelled, then would I have been a failure, Damon. My very life, my sanity, my place as Keeper, depended on that, that I should hardly know it myself. Yet I tried again and again to train another to take my place, so I could lay down a burden too heavy for me. Always when I had trained a Keeper, some other Tower would discover that their Keeper had chosen to leave them, or that her training had failed and she was fit for nothing but to leave and marry. A fine lot of weak and aimless women they were, none with the strength to endure. I was the only Keeper in all the Domains who held my office past twenty years. And even when I began to grow old, three times I gave up my own successor, twice to go to Dalereuth and once to Neskaya, and I who had trained a Keeper for every Tower in the Domains wished to train one for Arilinn, so that I might have some rest. You were there, Damon, you saw what happened. Six young girls, each with the talent to work as Keeper. But three were already women and, young as they were, had known some sexual wakening. Their channels were already differentiated and could not carry such strong frequencies, though two of them later became monitors and technicians, in Arilinn or in Neskaya. Then I began to choose younger and younger girls, almost children. I came near to success with Hilary. Two years she worked with me as underKeeper, *rikhi*, but you know what she endured, and at last I felt I must take pity on her and let her go. Then Callista—"

"And you made sure *she* would not fail," Damon said, enraged, "by altering her channels so she *could* not mature!"

"I am a Keeper," Leonie said angrily, "and responsible only to my own conscience! And she consented to what was done. Could I foresee that her fancy would

light on this *Terranan*, and her oath would be as nothing
to her?"

Before Damon's accusing silence she added, defensively, "And even so, Damon, I love her, I could not
bear her unhappiness! Had I believed it only a childish
fancy, I would have brought her back here to Arilinn
with me. I would have showered her with so much love
and tenderness that she would never regret her Terran
lover. And yet . . . and yet she made me believe . . ."
In the fluid levels of the overworld, Damon could see
and share with Leonie the image Leonie had seen in
Callista's mind: Callista lying in Andrew's arms, spent
and vulnerable, as he carried her from the caves of
Corresanti.

Now that he had seen her, if only reflected in Leonie's
mind, as, she might have been, undamaged, unchanged—
having once seen Callista like that—he knew he would
never be content until he had seen her so again. He said
quietly, "I cannot believe you would have done this if
you did not believe it could be undone."

"I am a Keeper," she repeated indomitably, "and responsible only to my own conscience."

This was true. By the law of the Towers, a Keeper
was infallible, her lightest word law where every member
of her circle was concerned. Yet Damon persisted.

"If it was so, why did you not neuter her, and have
done with it?" She was silent. At last she said, "You
speak so because you are a man, Damon, and to you
a woman is nothing but a wife, an instrument to give
you sons, to pass on your precious Comyn heritage. I
have other purposes. Damon, I was so weary, and I
felt I could not bear to spend my energy and strength,
to put all my heart into her for years and years, and
then watch her waken, and go from me into some
man's arms. Or, like Hilary, to sicken and suffer the
tortures of a damned soul with every waxing moon. It
was not selfishness, Damon! It was not only a longing
to lay down my own work and have rest! I loved her
as I had never loved Hilary. I knew she would not fail,
but I feared she was too strong to give way, even under
such suffering as Hilary's, that she would endure it—
as I did, Damon—year after long year. So I spared her

this, as I had the right to do." She added defiantly, "I was her Keeper!"

"And you removed her right to choose!"

"No woman of the Comyn has choice," Leonie said almost in a whisper, "not truly. I did not choose to be Keeper, or to be sent to a Tower. I was a Hastur, and it was my destiny, just as the destiny of my playmates was to marry and bear sons to their clans. And it was not irrevocable. In my own childhood I knew a woman who had been treated so, and she told me it was reversible. She told me it was lawful, where neutering was not, so that women might be reclaimed, if their parents chose, for those dynastic marriages so dear to Comyn hearts, and there was no chance of impairing the precious fertility of a Comyn daughter!" The sarcasm in her voice was so bitter that Damon quailed.

"It is reversible—how?" Damon demanded. "Callista cannot live like this, neither Keeper nor free."

"I do not know," Leonie said. "When it was done, I never believed it would have to be reversed, and so I made no plans for this day. But I was glad—as near as anything could make me glad—when she told me I had wrought less well than I thought." Again he shared with Leonie the brief vision of Callista in Andrew's arms as he carried her from Corresanti. "But it seems she was mistaken."

Leonie looked wrung and exhausted. "Damon, Damon, let her come back to us! Is it so evil a thing, that she should be Lady of Arilinn? Why should she give that up, to be wife to some *Terranan* and bear his half-caste brats?"

Damon answered, and knew his voice was shaking, "If she wished to be Lady of Arilinn, I would lay down my life defending her right to remain so. But she has chosen otherwise. She is wife to an honorable man I am proud to call brother, and I do not want to see their happiness destroyed. But even if Andrew were not my friend, I would defend Callista's right to order her life as she will. To lay down the title of Lady of Arilinn, if she so desires, to be wife to a charcoal-burner in the forest, or to take up sword like the Lady Bruna her foremother and command the Guards in her brother's place! It is *her* life, Leonie, not mine or yours!"

Leonie buried her face in her hands. Her voice was sick and choked. "Be it so, then. She shall have choice, though I had none, though you had none. She shall choose what you men of Darkover have called the only fit life for a woman! And it is I who must suffer for her choice, bearing the weight of Arilinn till Janine is old enough and strong enough to bear the burden." Her face was so old and bitter that Damon shrank from her.

But he thought that it was no true burden to her. Once, perhaps, she might have laid it down. But now she had nothing else, and it was everything to her, to have this power of life and death over them all, all the poor wretches who gave their lives for the Towers. It meant much to her, he knew, that Callista had to come to her and beg for what should be hers by right!

He said, making his voice hard, "It has always been the law. I have heard you say that the life of a Keeper is too hard to be borne unconsenting. And it has always been so, that a Keeper is freed when she can no longer do her work in safety. You said it, yes, you are a Keeper and responsible only for your own conscience. But what is it to be a Keeper, Leonie, if the conscience of a Keeper does not demand an honesty worthy of a Keeper, or of a Hastur!"

There was another long silence. At last she said, "On the word of a Hastur, Damon, I do not know how it is to be undone. All my search of the records has told me only that in the old days, when this was commonly done—it was done after the Towers had ceased to neuter their Keepers, so that the sacred fertility of a *Comynara* need not suffer even in theory—such Keepers were sent to Neskaya. So I sought there for the records. Theolinda, at Neskaya, told me that all the manuscripts were destroyed when Neskaya was burned to the ground during the Ages of Chaos. And so, although I still feel Callista should return to us, there is only one way to rediscover what must be done for Callista. Damon, do you know what is meant by Timesearch?"

He felt a curious rippling coldness, as if the very fabric of the overworld were wavering beneath his feet. "I had heard that technique, too, was lost."

"No, for I have done it," said Leonie. "The course

of a river had shifted, and farms and villages all along
the watershed were threatened with drought or flood
and famine. I did a Timesearch to discover precisely
where it had run a hundred years before, so that we
could divert it back into a course where it could run,
and not waste energy trying to force it to flow without
a natural channel. It was not easy." Her voice was
thinned and afraid. "And you would have to go further
than I went. You would have to go back before the
burning of Neskaya, during the Hastur rebellions. That
was an evil time. Could you reach that level, do you
think?"

Damon said slowly, "I can work on many levels of the
overworld. There are others, of course, to which I have
no access. I do not know how to reach the one where
Timesearch can be done."

"I can guide you there," Leonie said. "You know,
of course, that the overworlds are only a series of
agreements. Here in the gray world it is easier to visualize your physical body moving on a plain of gray
space, with thoughtforms for landmarks"—she gestured to the dimly glowing form of Arilinn behind
them—"than to approach the truth, which is that your
mind is a tenuous web of intangibles moving in a realm
of abstractions. You learned as much, of course, during
your first year in the Tower. It is possible, of course,
that the overworld is nearer the objective reality of the
universe than the world of form, what you call the real
world. Yet even there any good technician can see, at
will, bodies as webs of atoms and whirling energy and
magnetic fields."

Damon nodded, knowing this was true.

"It is not easy to get your mind far enough from the
agreements of what you call the real world to be free of
time as you know it. Time itself is probably no more
than a way of structuring reality so that our brains can
make some sense out of it," Leonie said. "Probably in
the ultimate reality of the universe, to which our experiences are approximations, there is no experience of time
as a sequence, but past and present and future all exist
together as one chaotic whole. On a physical level—of
course that includes the level where we are now, the

world of images, where our visualization constantly re-creates the world we prefer to see around us—we find it easier to travel along a personal sequence from what we call past to present to future. But in reality even a physical organism probably exists in its entirety at once, and its biological development from embryo to senility and death is merely another of its dimensions, like length. Am I confusing you, Damon?"

"Not much. Go on."

"On the level of Timesearch that whole concept of linear sequence disappears. You must create it for yourself so that you do not become lost in the chaotic reality, and you must anchor yourself somehow so that you will not regress your physical body through the resonances. It is like wandering blindfold in a mirror-maze. I would rather do anything in this universe than try it again. Yet I fear that only in such a quest into time can you find an answer for Callista. Damon, *must* you risk it?"

"I must, Leonie. I made Callista a promise." He would not tell Leonie of the extremity in which the promise had been made, or of the agony she had endured, when it would have been easier to die, because she trusted that promise. "I am not a Hastur, but I will not forswear my word."

Leonie sighed deeply. She said, "I am a Hastur, and a Keeper, responsible for everyone who has given me an oath, man or woman. I feel now that if it were for me to choose, no woman would be trained as Keeper unless she first consented to be neutered, as was done in the ancient days. But the world will go as it will, and not as I would have it. I will take responsibility, Damon, yet I cannot take all the responsibility. I am the only surviving Keeper at Arilinn. Neskaya is often out of the relays because Theolinda is not strong enough even now, and Dalereuth is using a mechanic's circle with no Keeper, so that I feel guilty keeping Janine at my side in Arilinn. We cannot train enough Keepers as it is now, Damon, and those we train often lose their powers while still young. Do you see why we need Callista so terri-bly, Damon?"

It was a problem with no answer, but Damon would not have Callista made a pawn, and Leonie knew it. She

said at last, in wonder, "How you must love her,
Damon! Perhaps it is to you I should have given her."

Damon replied, "Love? Not in that sense, Leonie.
Though she is dear to me, and I who have so little courage admire it above all else in anyone."

"You have little courage, Damon?" Leonie was silent
for a long time and he saw her image ripple and waver
like heat waves in the desert beyond the Dry Towns.
"Damon, oh, Damon, have I destroyed everyone I love?
Only now do I see that I broke you, as I broke
Callista. . . ."

The sound of that rang, timeless, like an echo, in
Damon. *Have I destroyed everyone I love? Everyone I
love, everyone I—everyone I love?*

"You said it was for my own good that you sent me
from Arilinn, Leonie, that I was too sensitive, that the
work would destroy me." He had lived with those words
for years, had choked on them, swallowed them in bitterness, hating himself for living to hear them or repeat
them. He never thought to doubt them, not for an
instant . . . the word of a Keeper, a Hastur.

Trapped, she cried out, "What could I possibly have
said to you?" Then, in a great cry of agony: "Something
is wrong, terribly wrong, with our whole system of training psi workers! How can it possibly be right to sacrifice
lives wholesale this way? Callista's, Hilary's, yours!" She
added, with indescribable bitterness, "My own."

If she had the courage or the honesty, Damon thought
bitterly, to tell him the truth, to say to him, "One of us
must go, and I am Keeper, and cannot be spared," then
he would have lost to Arilinn, yes, but he would not
have been lost to himself.

But now he had recovered something lost when he
was sent from the Towers. He was whole again, not broken as he was when Leonie cast him out, thinking of
himself as weak, useless, not strong enough for the work
he had chosen.

Something was desperately wrong with the system of
training psi workers. Now even Leonie knew it.

He was shocked by the tragedy in Leonie's eyes. She
whispered, "What do you want of me, Damon? Because
I came near to destroying your life in my weakness, does

the honor of a Hastur demand I must stand unflinching and let you destroy mine in turn?"

Damon bowed his head. His long love, the suffering he had mastered, the love he had thought burned out years ago, lent him compassion. Here in the overworld, where no hint of physical passion could lend danger to the gesture or the thought, he reached for Leonie, and as he had longed to do through many hopeless years, he took her in his arms and kissed her. It did not matter that only images met, that they were, in the real world, a tenday ride apart, that no more than Callista could she ever have responded to his passion. None of this mattered. It was a kiss of such despairing love as he had never given, would never again give to any living woman. For a moment Leonie's image wavered, flowed, until she was again the younger Leonie, radiant, chaste, untouchable, the Leonie for whose very presence he had hungered for so many anguished, lonely years, and tormented himself with guilt for the longing.

Then she was the Leonie of today, faded, worn, ravaged by time, weeping with a helpless sound he thought would break his heart. She whispered, "Go now, Damon. Return after Midwinter, and I will guide you to where you may seek in time for Callista's destiny and your own. But for now, if there is any pity left in you, go!"

The overworld trembled as if in a storm, vanished in grayness, and Damon found himself back in the room at Armida. Callista was looking at him in dismay and consternation. Ellemir whispered, "Damon, my love, why are you crying?" But Damon knew he could never answer.

Needless, Cassilda and all the Gods, needless, all that suffering, his, Callista's. Poor little Hilary's. Leonie's. And the pitying Avarra alone knew how many lives, how many telepaths in the Towers of the Domains, condemned to suffer. . . .

It would have been better for the Comyn, better for all of them, he despaired, if in the Ages of Chaos every son of Hastur and Cassilda had blown themselves to bits and their starstones with them! But there must be an end to it, an end to this suffering!

He clung desperately to Ellemir, reached beyond her to clutch at Andrew's hands, at Callista's. It wasn't enough. Nothing would ever be enough to wipe out his awareness of all that misery. But while they were all around him, close, he could live with it. For now. Maybe.

CHAPTER FOURTEEN

Dom Esteban had asked them to delay the psi work until Midwinter was past and the repairs of the storm completed. Damon welcomed the respite, even while he felt sick with apprehension, with the need to have it over. He knew that a lot would depend on the weather. If there were another storm, Midwinter festival would be celebrated with only the housefolk, but if the weather were fine, all the people within a day's ride would come, and many of them would spend the night. Midwinter eve dawned red and pleasant, and Damon could see *Dom* Esteban visibly brightened by the prospect. He was ashamed of his own reluctance. A break in winter isolation meant a great deal, in the Kilghard Hills, and more to an old man, crippled and chair-bound. At breakfast Ellemir chattered gaily about plans for the festival, taking up the holiday spirit.

"I will set the kitchen girls to baking festival cakes, and one of the men must ride down to the South Valley and ask old Yashri and his sons to come play for the dancing. And if many are going to be sleeping overnight, we must have all the guest rooms opened and aired. And I suppose the chapel is shamefully filled with dust and dirt. I have not been down there since . . ." She faltered and looked away, and Callista said quickly, "I will tend the chapel, Elli, but are we to make the fire?" She glanced at her father and he said, "I dare say it's foolishness, in this day and age, to kindle sun-fire." He looked at Andrew, his eyebrows raised, as if, Damon thought, he expected the younger man to jeer. But Andrew said, "It seems to be one of the most universal customs of mankind, on most worlds, sir, some form of Midwinter festival marking the return of the sun after the longest night, and some form of Summer festival for the longest day."

Damon had never thought of himself as a sentimental man, had trained himself harshly to leave the past buried, yet now he remembered all the winters he had spent at Armida, as Coryn's friend. He used to stand beside Coryn at Midwinter festival, with all the little girls around them, and think that if he ever had a family of his own, he would keep to this custom. His father-in-law picked up the memory and raised his eyes, smiling at Damon. His voice was gruff: "I thought all you young people thought it a pagan nonsense and better forgotten, but if someone can carry my chair into the court we will have it done, then, if there is enough sun for the purpose. Damon, I cannot go choose wine for the feast, so here is the key to the cellars. Rhodri says the wine was good this year, even if I had no hand in the making."

Andrew was returning from the daily task of inspecting the saddle horses when Callista intercepted him. "Come down and help me tend the chapel. No servant may do this, but only one connected by blood or marriage to the Domain. You have never been down here before."

Andrew had not. Religion did not seem to play a very great part in the daily life of the Domains, at least not here at Armida. Callista had tied herself up in a big apron, explaining as they went down the stairs, "This was my only task as a child; Dorian and I used to tend the chapel at festivals. Elli was never allowed down here, because she was boisterous and broke things."

It was easy to see Callista as a small, grave little girl, trusted to handle valuable and fragile things without breaking them. She said as they went into the chapel, "I have not been home for the festival since I went to the Tower. And now Dorian is wedded and has two little daughters—I have never seen them either—and Domenic away in Thendara commanding the Guard, and my youngest brother in Nevarsin. I have not seen Valdir since he was a babe in arms. I do not suppose I will see him now until he is grown." She stopped and suddenly shivered, as if she had seen something frightening.

"Is Dorian much like you and Elli?"

"No, not much. She is fair, as many of the Ridenows are. Everyone said she was the beauty of the family."

"I am reluctant to think all your family had defective eyesight," Andrew said, laughing, and she colored, leading him into the chapel.

At the center was a four-sided altar, a stone slab of translucent white stone. It looked very old. On the walls of the chapel were old paintings. Callista pointed, explaining quietly, "These are the Four, the old Gods: Aldones, the Lord of Light; Zandru, who works evil in the darkness; Evanda, lady of spring and growing things; and Avarra, the dark mother of birth and death." She took up a broom and began to sweep the room, which was, indeed, very dusty. Andrew wondered if she herself believed in these gods, or whether her religious observance was merely formal. Her very contempt of religion must be something different from what he believed about it.

She said, hesitating, "I am not sure what I believe. I am a Keeper, a *tenerésteis*, a mechanic. We are taught that the order of the universe does not depend upon any deities and yet . . . and yet who knows if it was not the Gods who ordained these laws which built things as they are, the laws we cannot refuse to obey." She stood quietly for a moment, then went to sweep in the corner, calling Andrew to help her brush up the dust, gather the small dishes and vessels from the altar. In a niche on the wall was a very old statue of a veiled woman, surrounded by roughly sculptured children's heads in blue stone. She said in a low voice, "Perhaps I am superstitious after all. This is Cassilda, called the Blessed, who bore a son to the Lord Hastur, son of Light. They say that from *his* seven sons were descended the seven Domains. I have no idea whether the tale is true, or only legend or fairy-tale, or garbled memory of some old truth somewhere, but the women of our family make offerings. . . ." She was silent, and in the dust of the neglected altar Andrew saw a bunch of flowers, left to wither there.

Ellemir's offering, when she thought she was to bear Damon's child. . . .

Silently he put his arm around Callista's waist, feeling

closer to her than at any time since the dreadful night
of catastrophe. Many strange threads went to the making
of a marriage. . . . Her lips were moving, and he wondered if she was praying, then she raised her head,
sighed and took the withered posy between her fingers,
dropping it tenderly into the pile of rubbish.

"Come, we must clean all these vessels and make the
altar clean for the new fire to burn there. We must
scrape all these candlesticks—how came they to leave
all the dead wax in them last year, I wonder?" The gaiety was back in her voice again. "Go out to the well,
Andrew, and bring in some fresh water."

By noontime the great red disk of the sun hung clear
and cloudless overhead, and two or three of the strongest Guardsmen carried *Dom* Esteban into the courtyard,
while Damon set up the arrangement of mirror, burning-
glass and tinder which would kindle the fire in the ancient stoneware fire-pan. They could smell the balsam
incense Callista had kindled on the altar inside, and
Damon, looking at Callista and Ellemir, could almost
see them as little girls in tartan dresses, their hair curling
around their cheeks, solemn and well behaved. Dorian
had sometimes brought her doll to the ceremony—he
could not remember ever seeing either Callista or Ellemir with a doll. He and Coryn had stood beside *Dom*
Esteban for this ceremony. Now the old man could not
kneel beside the fire-pan, and it was Damon who held
the burning-glass, stood waiting while the brilliant focus
of light crawled across the tinder and resin-needles, raising a thin trail of fragrant smoke. For a long time the
spot smoldered, the smoke rising. Then a crimson spark
echoed the glare of the sun in the mirror, and a tiny
flame leaped to life at the center of the smoke. Damon
crouched over the fire-pan, coaxing the flame, carefully
feeding it with resin-needles and shavings, until it blazed
up, to an accompaniment of cheers and cries of encour-
agement from the watchers. He handed the fire-pan to
Ellemir, who carried it inside to the altar. Then, laughing
and exchanging good wishes and season's greetings, they
began to leave the court, passing one by one past the
old man's chair to receive small gifts. Ellemir, standing
beside him, handed them out, trinkets of silver and

sometimes copper. In a few cases—the more valued servants—she gave certificates entitling them to livestock or other property. Callista and Ellemir bent one after another to kiss their father and wish him the joy of the season. His gifts to his daughters were valuable furs which they could have made into riding cloaks for the worst weather.

His gift to Andrew was a set of razors in a velvet case. The razors were made of some light metal alloy, and Andrew knew that on metal-starved Darkover this was a handsome gift. He bent, feeling awkward, and embraced the old man, feeling the whiskered cheeks against his with a curious sense of warmth, of belonging.

"A good festival to you, son, and a joyous New Year."

"And to you, Father," said Andrew, wishing he could think of more eloquent words. Just the same, he felt as if he had taken another small step toward finding his place here. Callista held his hand tightly, as they went into the house to make preparation for the feast later that day.

All afternoon guests were arriving from outlying farms, from small estates nearby, many of them guests at the wedding. Going up to dress for the festival dinner, Damon found himself exiled from his own half of the suite. Ellemir, drawing him into the rooms shared by Andrew and Callista, told him, "I have given our rooms to the folk from Syrtis, Loran and Caitlia and their daughters. You and I will spend the night in here with Andrew and Callista. I have your holiday clothes here."

Andrew, sharing the cramped quarters in holiday spirit with Damon, lowered his shaving mirror so that the smaller man could look into it. He crouched, fingering the hair that had grown long on his neck. "I should get someone to cut my hair," he said, and Damon laughed.

"You're neither a monk nor a Guardsman, so you surely don't want it any shorter than it is *now*, do you?" His own hair was trimmed smoothly, about the length of his collar; Andrew shrugged. Custom and dress were completely relative. His own hair now seemed enormously long, shaggy, unkempt, yet it was shorter than

Damon's. Shaving with the new razors, he found himself wondering why, on a freezing planet like Darkover, only old men went bearded against the cold. But then, customs made no sense.

Downstairs, looking at the hall hung with green boughs, and spiced festival cakes smelling not unlike the gingerbread of his Terran Christmases, it seemed poignantly like a childhood celebration on Terra. Most of the guests were people he had seen at his wedding. There was a lot of dancing, and enough heavy drinking to surprise Andrew, who had thought of the Darkovan hillmen as sober people. He said so to Damon, and his brother-in-law nodded. "We are. That's why we save our drinking for special occasions, and those occasions don't come very often. So make the best of them. Drink up, brother!" Damon was taking his own advice; he was already half drunk.

There were some of the boisterous kissing games he remembered from his wedding. Andrew remembered something he had read years ago, how urban societies with a great deal of leisure developed highly sophisticated amusements, not needed for the rare leisure of people who spent a lot of time in hard manual work. Remembering what he had heard of frontier days on his own world, quilting parties, corn-husking bees, where hardworking farmers whiled the time with what would later be considered games for young children— bobbing for apples, blindman's buff—he realized he should have expected this. Even here in the Great House there was plenty of hard work to be done and festivals like this were few, so if the games seemed childlike to him, it was his fault, not the fault of these hardworking farmers and ranchers. Most of the men had calloused hands betraying plenty of hard physical labor, even the noblemen. His own hands were hardened as they had not been since he left the horse ranch in Arizona, at nineteen. The women worked too, he thought, remembering the days Ellemir spent supervising in the kitchens, and Callista's long hours in stillroom and greenhouse. Both of them joined gaily in the dancing, and in the simple games. One of them was not unlike blindman's buff, with a man and a woman blindfolded and made to seek through the crowds for one another.

When the dancing began he was much in demand as a partner. He found out why when a youngster still in his teens swept Callista into the dance, saying over his shoulder to his previous partner, a girl who looked no more than fourteen, "If I dance with a bride at Midwinter, I shall be married before the year is out!" The girl—a child really, in a child's flowered frock, her hair in long curls about her cheeks—came up to Andrew, saying with a pert smile to hide her shyness, "Why, then, I'll dance with the groom!" Andrew let the child pull him on to the dance floor, warning her that he was not a good dancer. Later he saw the girl again, in a corner with the youngster who had wanted to be married that season, kissing with what seemed to be unchildlike passion.

As the night wore on there was a lot of pairing off in corners and wandering away in couples into the dark outer part of the halls. *Dom* Esteban got very drunk and was eventually carried off to bed, senseless. One by one the guests took their leave, or said good night and were escorted to their beds. Most of the servants had joined in the party and were as drunk as the other guests, not having a long ride in the cold ahead of them. Damon had fallen asleep on a bench in the Great Hall, and was snoring. It was the dimness before dawn when they looked around the Great Hall, with its drooping greenery, scattered bottles and cups, discarded sweets and refreshments, realizing that their duties as hosts were ended and they could seek their own beds. After a few halfhearted efforts to rouse Damon, who muttered drunkenly at them, they left him there and went upstairs without him. Andrew was amazed. Even at his wedding, Damon had drunk sparingly. Well, even a sober man had a right to get drunk at the New Year, he supposed.

In the rooms which the two couples were to share that night because of the house party, he felt a knifelike frustration, intensified by his half-drunken state, amorous and disappointed. It was a hell of a life, married like this and sleeping alone. A hell of a marriage, so far, and what felt like a travesty of a Christmas party. He felt let-down, dismal. Maybe with Damon drunk, Ellemir—but no, the women had climbed together into his big bed, as they had done during Callista's long illness. He supposed he would sleep again in the small one that was usually Callista's, and Damon, if he came upstairs at all, in the sitting room of the suite.

The women were giggling together like little girls. Had they been drinking too? Callista called his name softly and he came over to them. They were lying close together, laughing in the dim light. Callista reached up and pulled him down to them.

"There's room for you here."

He hesitated. Did this make any sense, tantalizing himself this way? Then he laughed, climbing in beside them. The bed was an enormous one that would have held half a dozen without crowding. Callista said softly, "I wanted to prove something to you, my love," and gently pushed Ellemir into his arms.

He felt furious embarrassment that seemed to burn through his whole body, dousing his passion like ice water. He had never felt so naked, so exposed, in his life.

Oh hell, he felt. He was behaving like a fool. Wasn't this the next logical step anyway? But logic had no part in his feelings.

Ellemir felt warm, familiar, comforting in his arms.

"What's the matter, Andrew?"

The matter, and damn it, she had to know it, was Callista's presence. He supposed that to some people this would be especially exciting. Ellemir followed his thoughts, which associated this kind of thing with erotic exhibitions, attempts to rouse jaded tastes, decadence. She said in a whisper, "But it isn't at all like that, Andrew. We are all telepaths. Whatever we do, the others will know it, be part of it, so why pretend that any of us can ever completely shut out any of the others?"

He felt Callista's fingertips touching his face. Strange that in the dark, though their small hands were almost identical, he could be so sure it was Callista's hand and not Ellemir's on his cheek.

Among telepaths the concept of that kind of privacy could not exist, he knew, so shutting doors and going away in isolation was only a pretense. There came a time when you stopped pretending. . . .

He tried to bring back his previous amorous state, but drunkenness and embarrassment conspired to defeat him. Ellemir laughed, but it was perfectly clear that the laugh did not intend ridicule. "I think we've all had too much to drink. Let's sleep, then."

They were all almost asleep when the door of the room opened and Damon came in, moving unsteadily. He looked down at them, smiling. "Knew I'd find you all here." He flung his clothes this way and that. He was still blundering drunk. "Come on, make room, where do I "

"Damon, you want to sleep it off," Callista said. "Won't you be more comfortable—"

"Comfortable be damned," Damon said drowsily. "Nobody ought to have to sleep alone at festival time!"

Laughing, Callista made room at her side and Damon crawled in, was instantly asleep. Andrew felt a mad laughter blowing away his embarrassment. As he fell asleep he became aware of a dim thread of rapport, weaving among them, as if Damon, even in sleep, reached out for the comfort of their presence, drawing them all close together, intertwined, close folded, their hearts beating in rhythm, a slow pulse, an infinite comfort. He thought, not knowing whether it was his own thought or another's, that Damon was there, it was all right now. That was the way it ought to be. He felt Damon's awareness: *All my loved ones. . . . I will never be alone again. . . .*

It was late when they woke, but the drawn curtains made it dark in the room. Ellemir was still folded in his arms. She stirred, turned sleepily toward him, enfolded him with her woman's warmth. The sense of closeness, of unique sharing, was still there, and he let himself be swept into it, accepting the welcoming of her body. It was not only himself and Ellemir, somehow, but the very awareness, somewhere below conscious level, that they were all part of it, they fitted together, uniquely and without analysis. He felt like shouting to the world, to everyone, "I love you, I love all of you." In his exulta-

tion he did not distinguish his sexual awareness of Ellemir, the tenderness for Callista, the strong, protective
warmth he felt for Damon. They were all one emotion,
and it was love. He floated in it he drowned in it, he lay
spent, luxuriating in it. He knew they had wakened the
others. It didn't seem to matter.

Ellemir moved first, stretching, sighing, laughing,
yawning. She raised herself a little, kissed him quickly.
"I would like to stay here all day," she said ruefully,
"but I am thinking of the chaos downstairs in the hall.
If any of our guests are to have breakfast, I must go
down and make sure something is done!" She leaned
over and kissed Damon and, after a moment, kissed Callista too, then slid from the bed and went to dress.

Damon, less physically involved, sensed the effort Callista was making to keep herself barriered. So it was not
complete, after all. She was still outside. He touched a
light fingertip to her closed eyes. Andrew had gone into
the bath. They were alone, and he felt the gallant pretense dissolve.

"Crying, Callie?"

"No, of course not. Why should I?" But she was.

He held her, knowing at this moment they shared
something from which the others were excluded, that
shared experience, that painful discipline, the sense of
apartness.

Andrew had gone to dress. Damon caught a fragment
of his thought, contentment mingled with chagrin, and
thought how for a little while Andrew was one of them.
Now he was apart from them too. He sensed Callista's
emotions too, not begrudging Ellemir anything, but desperately needing to know before she could share it. He
sensed her desperate grief, the sudden mad impulse to
tear at herself with her nails, beat herself with her fists,
turn against this useless mutilated body which was so far
from what it should have been. He held her against him,
trying to calm and soothe her with his touch.

Ellemir came back from her bath, the ends of her hair
dripping, and sat at Callista's dressing table. "I will wear
one of your housedresses, Callie, there is so much clearing away to be done," she said. "That is the only bad
thing about a party!" She saw Callista, hiding her face

against Damon, and for a moment she was wrung by Callista's grief. Ellemir had been brought up thinking of herself as having little of the *laran* of her clan, but now, taking the full impact of her twin's sorrow, she knew it was more of a curse than a blessing. And when Andrew came back she sensed his sudden apartness.

Andrew was thinking that you just had to be brought up to that kind of thing. He interpreted Ellemir's tense silence as shame or regret for what had happened and wondered if he ought somehow to apologize. For what? To whom? Ellemir? Damon? He saw Callista lying in Damon's arms. Where would he get any right to complain? Turn about was fair play, but he still felt an almost physical queasiness and disgust, or was it only that he had drunk too much the night before?

Damon saw his eyes on them and smiled.

"I suppose *Dom* Esteban has a head worse than mine this morning. I'll go douse some cold water on mine, and go down and see if I can do something for our father. I haven't the heart to leave him to his body-servant today." He added, disentangling himself slowly and without haste from Callista, "Have your Terrans any suitable expression for the morning after the night before?"

"Dozens," Andrew said glumly, "and every one as revolting as the thing itself." Hangovers, he thought.

Damon went into the bath and Andrew stood jerking a comb through his hair, glowering at Callista. He did not even see that her eyes were red. Slowly she got out of bed and into her flowered chamber robe. "I must go help Ellemir. The maids will hardly know where to start. Why are you staring at me, my husband?"

The phrase made him angry, quarrelsome. "You will not even let me touch your fingertips, and if I kiss you, you draw away as if I meant rape, yet you were lying in Damon's arms—"

She lowered her eyes. "You know why I dare . . . with him."

Andrew remembered the intense awareness, sexuality, he had sensed, *shared* with Damon. It was disquieting, flooding him with vague unease. "You cannot say that Damon is not a man!"

"Of course he is," said Callista, "but he has learned—and in the same hard school as I—when and how *not* to seem so."

That was somehow, to Andrew's hypersensitive guilt, like a taunt, as if he were some kind of brute, animal, who could not control his sexual urges but must be accommodated. She had literally pushed him into Ellemir's arms, but Damon needed no such concessions. Suddenly, angrily, he took Callista in his arms, forced his mouth on hers. For a moment she fought him, twisting her mouth away from his, and he could feel the wild upheaval in her. Suddenly she went wholly passive in his arms, her lips cold, unmoving, so far away she might not have been in the same room with him at all. Her low voice tore at him like fangs.

"Whatever you feel you must do, I can bear. As I am now, it would make no difference. It will not damage me now, nor stir me to the point where I will react or strike at you. Even if you felt you must . . . must take me to bed . . . it would mean nothing to me, but if it gave you any pleasure . . ."

Cold, shocked to the very bones, he let her go. Somehow this was more horrible than if she had resisted him madly, torn at him with teeth and fingernails, struck him again with the lightning bolt. Before, she feared her own arousal. Now she knew that nothing would get through her defenses . . . nothing.

"Oh, Callista, forgive me! Oh, God, Callista, forgive me!" He fell to his knees before her, gathering up her small fingertips in his, pressing them to his lips in an agony of remorse. Damon came from the bath, standing appalled at the tableau, but neither of them heard or saw him. Slowly Callista laid her hands on either side of Andrew's face. She said in a whisper, "Ah, love, it is I should ask you to forgive me. I do not want . . . I do not want to be indifferent to you." Her voice was filled with such grief that Damon knew he could not wait any longer.

He knew why he had gotten so drunk last night. It was because, with Midwinter past, he could no longer delay the ordeal. Now he must go into the overworld, into time itself, and search for help there, for a way to bring Callista back to them. Now, before her frantic grief, he felt he would risk more than this for her, for Andrew.

Very quietly, he withdrew and went out of the suite the other way.

CHAPTER FIFTEEN

After Midwinter, surprisingly, the weather moderated and repairs from the great storm went forward rapidly. Within a tenday they were complete, and Andrew felt that he could leave everything in the hands of the *coridom* for some time.

He thought he had never seen Damon as overwrought and irritable as during that morning, after Damon had isolated the suite with telepathic dampers and warned the servants not to approach them. Since Midwinter Damon had been edgy, silent, but now, as he adjusted the dampers, prowling around the suite nervously, they could all sense it. Callista finally broke into his nervous fretting with, "That's *enough*, Damon! Lie down flat and breathe slowly. You can't start like this, and you know it as well as I do. Get yourself calmed first. Do you want some *kirian*?"

"I don't *want* it," said Damon irritably, "But I suppose I'd better have it. And I want a blanket or something. I always come back half frozen."

She gestured to Ellemir to cover him with a blanket and went for the *kirian*. "Taste it first. My distilling apparatus here isn't as efficient as what I had at Arilinn, and there may be residues, though I filtered it twice."

"You can't be worse at that sort of thing than I am," Damon said and sniffed carefully, then laughed, remembering Callista doing almost the same thing with the crude tincture he had made. "Never mind, my dear, I don't suppose we'll poison one another." He let her measure a careful dose, adding, "I don't know what the time-distortion factor is, and you'll have to stay in phase to monitor me. Hadn't you better take some yourself?"

She shook her head. "I have an awfully low tolerance for the stuff, Damon. If I took enough for phasing, I'd have serious trouble. I can key it with you without it."

"You'll get awfully cramped and cold," Damon

warned, but he realized that after so many years as Keeper she probably knew her tolerances for the telepathic drug to the narrowest margin. She smiled, measuring her dose by a few drops. "I'm wearing an extra warm shawl. If I'm monitoring life functions, when do you want me to pull you out?"

He didn't know. He had no experience with the stresses of Timesearch. He had no idea what he might be called on to endure in the way of side effects. "Better not pull me back unless I go into convulsions."

"That far?" Callista felt a sharp stab of guilt. It was for her he was incurring this terrible risk, returning to this work he so feared and hated. They were already close in linkage. He laid a light hand on her wrist. "Not only for you, darling. For all of us. For the children."

And for the Keeper, the one who will come. Callista did not say the words aloud, but time had slipped out of focus, as it did sometimes for an Alton, and she saw herself from a great distance, here, elsewhere, standing knee-deep in a great field of flowers; looking down at a delicate girl lying unconscious before her, standing in the chapel at Armida before the statue of Cassilda, a wreath of crimson flowers in her hand. She laid the flowers on the altar, then she was back with them again, dizzied, flushed, exalted. She whispered, "Damon, you saw . . ."

Andrew had seen too, all of them had seen, and he remembered Callista's look of pity and grief as she removed Ellemir's forgotten offering from the chapel. "Our women still lay flowers at her shrine. . . ." Damon said gently, "I saw, Callie. But it's a long way from here to there, you know."

She wondered if Andrew would mind very much, then brought herself back, with firm discipline, to her work. "Let me check your breathing." Lightly she passed her fingertips above his body. "Take the *kirian* now."

He swallowed, making a wry face. "Ugh! What did you flavor it with, horse piss?"

"Nothing, you've forgotten the taste, that's all. How many years since you took it? Lie back and stop clenching your hands; you'll only knot your muscles and give yourself cramps."

Damon obeyed, looking around the three faces surrounding him: Callista, sober and commanding; Ellemir looking a little scared; Andrew, strong and calm, but he sensed with an undercurrent of dismay. But again his eyes came back to Callista's confident face. He could absolutely rely on her, Arilinn-trained. His breathing, his life functions, his very life was in her hands, and he was content to have it there.

Why must she renounce this, because she wanted to live in happiness, and bear children?

Callista was bringing Ellemir and Andrew into the circle. He felt them slip into the rapport, meshing. Already he was adrift, floating, very distant. He looked at Ellemir as if she were transparent, thinking how much he loved her, how happy she was.

Callista said quietly, "I'll let you go as far as crisis, first stage, not as far as convulsions. That wouldn't do you any good, nor any of us."

He didn't bother to protest. She had been trained at Arilinn; it was her decision to make. Then he was in the overworld, sensing it as their landmark formed around him, a tower like Arilinn, less solid, less brilliant, not a beacon but a shelter, very remote, yet solid around him, a protection, a home here. For a moment, as he looked around the gray world and sheltered, delaying, within its walls, he found himself wondering with an absurd flippancy what the other telepaths who wandered in the gray world would think, to find a new tower there. Or would the others ever notice, ever come to this remote place where Damon and his group were working? Resolutely, he formed his thoughts to bear him swiftly to Arilinn, and found himself standing in the court before Leonie. He saw with relief that her face was veiled and her voice cool and remote, as if the moment of passion had never been.

"We must first reach the level where motion through time is possible. Have you taken sufficient precaution to keep yourself monitored?" He felt that she was looking *through* him, to the overworld, to the world behind him where his body lay, Callista silently watching by his side. She looked oddly triumphant, but she said only, "You may be away for a very long time, and it will seem longer than it is. I will guide you as far as the Timesearch level, though I am not sure I will be able to stay there. But we must move through the levels, a little at a time. I usually try to think of it as a flight of steps," she added, and he saw that the grayness around them had lifted enough to reveal a shadowy flight of steps, curving away upward and vanishing into thicker grayness above them, like fog shrouding a riverbed. He noted that the stairs had a gilt bannister, and wondered what staircase in Leonie's childhood, perhaps in Castle Hastur, was revived here in her mental image.

He knew perfectly well, as he set his foot on the first step behind Leonie, that in actuality only their minds moved through the formless atoms of the universe, but the firm visualization of the staircase felt reassuringly solid under his feet, and gave them a focal point for moving from level to level. Leonie knew this path and he was content to follow.

The stairs were not steep, but as he climbed it seemed that he began to breathe more heavily, as if climbing in a mountain pass. The stairs still felt firm, even carpeted under foot, though his feet themselves, he knew, were only mental formulations. It became harder and harder to feel them, to lift them from step to step. The stairs felt fuzzier and dimmer, leading into thick gray fog just a little ahead of him. Leonie's form was only a crimson-veiled wisp.

The thick fog closed in. He could see a few inches of the staircase under his feet, but he was walking in grayness which made his body disappear. The grayness darkened into a blackness crisscrossed by racing blue lights.

The level of energy-nets. Damon had worked on this level as a psi technician, and with a sharp effort he managed to solidify it, making it into a dark cavern with narrow lighted trails and footpaths leading upward through a maze of falling water. Leonie was dim and shadowy here, her robes colorless. He did not hear her now in words:

Go carefully here. We are in the level of monitored matrices. They will watch us so that no harm comes to me. But follow closely, I know where matrix work is being done and we must not intrude.

Silently Damon threaded his way along the blue-lighted paths. Once there was a burst of blue light, but Leonie's thought reached him urgently:

Turn away from it!

And he knew that somewhere a matrix operation was under way, of such a delicate nature that even a random thought—"looking" at it—could throw it out of balance and endanger the mechanics. He visualized physically turning his back on the light, closing his eyes so that he could not see it even through his eyelids. It seemed a long time before Leonie's thought-touch recalled him:

It is safe to go on now.

Again the staircase formulated beneath his feet, though he could not see it, and he began climbing. Only dogged concentration could now force the illusion of a physical body which could climb, and the stairs were like mist under his feet. His pulse began to labor as he struggled upward, and his breath came heavily. It was like climbing a mountain pass, like the steep rock-stairs leading upward to Nevarsin Monastery. He felt about in the thick darkness for the ice-rimed rail, felt it burn his fingers, but was grateful for the sensation. It helped him solidify the terrible, chaotic formlessness of this level. He had no idea how Leonie, who was untrained in climbing, was managing here, but he sensed her near him in the darkness, and knew she must have her own mental techniques for coping with the rising levels. His breath was thinning now, and he felt that his heart was pounding in acute, dizzy distress. He felt the vertigo of terrible height beneath him. He could not force himself to go on. He clung to the railing, feeling it numbing his hands with cold.

I cannot go on, I cannot. I will die here.

Slowly his breathing began to come more smoothly, his laboring heart calmed. He knew with the remotest consciousness that Callista had gone into phase with him, regulating his heart and breathing, Now he could struggle upward again, although the stairs were gone. As his sense of struggling upward and upward grew more intense he began, desperately, to formulate the memory of the cliff-climbing, ice-and-rock techniques he had learned as a boy at Nevarsin, as if he were dragging himself up rough-cut hand- and footholds, fixing imaginary ropes and pitons to help him haul his reluctant body upward. Then he lost his body again, and all track of levels and effort, moving only by fierce concentration from darkness to darkness. In one of them there were strange, formless cloud masses and he seemed to wallow through bogs of cold slime. In another there were presences everywhere, crowding him, thrusting their intangible shapelessness against him, crowding. . . . The very concept of *form* was lost. He could not remember what a body was, or what it felt like to have one. He was as shapeless, as everywhere-and-nowhere as *they*, whatever they were, everywhere interpenetrating. He felt sick and violated, but he struggled on, and after eternities this too was gone.

Finally they reached a curious, thin darkness, and Leonie, close beside him in the nowhere spaces, said, but not in words:

This is the level where we can slip loose of linear time. Try to think of moving along a river upstream. It will be easier if we find a single fixed place and move back from there. Help me find Arilinn.

Damon thought *Is Arilinn here too?* and knew he was being absurd. Every place which physically existed must stretch upward through all the levels of the universe. Intangibly, a hand gripped his and Damon felt his own hand materializing where it might have been if, here, he had one. He focused his mind on Arilinn, saw a dim shadow and found himself in Leonie's room there.

Once, in his last year there, Leonie had collapsed inside the relays. He had carried her to her room and laid her on her bed. He had not at the time consciously noted a single detail of that chamber, yet he saw it now, dimly outlined on his mind and memory. . . .

No, Damon! Avarra have pity, no!

He had had no notion of calling up that forgotten day, no desire to remember—Zandru's hells, no! The memory had been Leonie's, and he knew it, but he accepted blame for it and sought a more neutral memory. In the matrix chamber at Arilinn he watched Callista, at thirteen, her hair still down her back. He guided her fingers gently, touching the nodes where the nerves surfaced against the skin. He could see the embroidered butterflies on the wrists of her smock; he had not noticed them then. Dimly, but with a realness which unnerved him— were these revived thoughts of years ago or was the present-day Callista remembering?—he saw that she was docile, but frightened of this stern man who had been her dead brother's sworn friend but now seemed impassive, old, alienated, distant. A stranger, not the familiar kinsman.

Was I so harsh with her, so distant? Were you frightened of me, Callie? Zandru's hells, why are we so harsh with these children?

Leonie's hands touched him across Callista's. How austere she had been, even then, how stern and lined her face had grown in a few years. But time swept backward and Callista was gone, had never been there. He stood before Leonie for the first time, a young psi monitor seeing for the first time the face of the Keeper of Arilinn. *Evanda! How beautiful she had been! All Hastur women were beautiful, but she had the legendary beauty of Cassilda.* He felt again the agony of first love, the despair of knowing it was hopeless, but time was still flowing backward with merciful swiftness. Damon lost awareness of his body, it had never existed, he was a dim dream in a dimmer darkness, seeing the faces of Keepers he had never known. (Surely that fair-haired woman was a Ridenow of his own clan.) He saw a monument built in the courtyard to honor Marelie Hastur, and knew with a spasm of terror that he was watching an event which had taken place three centuries before his own birth. He kept on, moving upstream, felt Leonie swept away from him, tried to fight his way to her. . . .

I can go no further, Damon. The Gods guard you, kinsman.

He reached for her in panic, but she was gone, would not be born for hundreds of years. He was alone, dazed, wearied, in a vast twinkling foggy darkness, only the shadow of Arilinn behind. *Where can I go? I could wander forever through the Ages of Chaos and learn nothing.*

Neskaya. He knew that Neskaya was the center of the secret. He let Arilinn dissolve, felt himself move with thought to the Tower of Neskaya, outlined against the Kilghard Hills. It was like fording a cold mountain stream against a current which was trying to sweep him downstream to his own time. In the dim struggle he had almost lost track of his objective. Now, desperately, he reformed it: to find a Keeper in Neskaya before it was destroyed in the Ages of Chaos and then rebuilt. He struggled backward, backward, and saw Neskaya Tower lying in ruins, destroyed in the last of the great wars of that age, burned to ashes, the Keeper and all her circle slaughtered.

It was there again, not the sturdy cobblestone structure he had seen rising behind the walls of Neskaya City, but a tall, luminous, dim-glowing tower of pallid blue stone. Neskaya! Neskaya in the ages of its glory, before the Comyn had fallen to the poor remnant of today He felt himself shuddering somewhere at the knowledge that he saw what no living man or woman of his time had ever seen, the Tower of Neskaya in the heyday of the Comyn.

A twinkling light began to dawn in the courtyard, and by its sparkle Damon saw a young man and remembered, in startlement and welcome, that he had seen this once before. He chose to interpret it as a sign. The young man was wearing green and gold, with a great sparkling ring on his finger—ring or matrix? Surely that delicate face, the green and gold clothing of an ancient cut, marked the young man as a Ridenow? Yes, Damon had seen him before, though briefly. He felt himself formulate with a curious emotional sense of relief. He knew that the body he wore on this complicated astral level was only an image, the shadow of a shadow. He was briefly aware of his own body, cold, comatose, cramped, a gasping tormented piece of flesh unimaginably *elsewhere*. The body he wore here in the higher level was unfettered, calm, easy. After such exhausting eternities of formlessness, even the shadow of form was a release of tension, almost an explosion of pleasure. A solid weight, blood he could feel pulsing in his veins, eyes that could see. . . . The young man wavered, became firm. Yes, he was a Ridenow, a lot like Damon's brother Kieran, the only brother Damon loved rather than tolerated with civility for their common blood.

Damon felt a rush of love for the stranger, who must

have been one of his own remote forebears. He wore a
long loose golden robe, cinctured with green, and sur-
veyed Damon with a calm, kindly stare. He said, "By
your face and your garments you are surely one of my
own clan. Do you wander in a dream, kinsman, or do
you seek me from another Tower?"

Damon said, "I am Damon Ridenow." He began to
say that he was not now a Tower worker, but it occurred
to him that on this level time had no meaning. If all
time co-existed—as it must—then the time when he had
been psi technician was as real, as present, as the time
when he lay in Armida, searching. "Damon Ridenow,
Third in Arilinn Tower, technician by grade, under
Wardship of Leonie of Arilinn, Lady Hastur."

The young man said gently, "Surely you dream, or
you are mad, or astray in time, kinsman. All the Keepers
from Nevarsin to Hali are known to me, and there is no
Leonie among them, nor no Hastur woman." He smiled,
not unkindly. "Shall I dismiss you to your own place,
cousin, and your own time? These levels are dangerous,
and no mere technician can tread them in safety. You
may return when you have won the strength of Keeper,
cousin, and that you have come here now shows me you
have already that strength. But I can send you to a level
that is safe for you, and wish for you as much caution
as you have courage."

"I am neither mad nor dreaming," Damon said, "nor
am I astray in time, though truly I am far from my own
day. My Keeper sent me here, and it may be that you
are whom I seek. Who are you?"

"I am Varzil," said the young man, "Varzil of
Neskaya, Keeper of the Tower."

Keeper. Damon had been told of times when men
were made Keepers. The young man used the word in
a form he had never heard, however, *tenerézu.* When
Leonie had told him of male Keepers, she had used the
common form of the word, which was invariably femi-
nine. Coming from Varzil, the word was a shock. *Varzil!*
The legendary Varzil, called the Good, who had re-
deemed Hali after the Cataclysm destroyed the lake
there. "In my day you are a legend, Varzil of Neskaya,
remembered best as Lord of Hali."

Varzil smiled. He had a calm, intelligent face, but it was alive with curiosity, without the withdrawn, remote, isolated quality of every Keeper Damon had ever known. "A legend, cousin? Well, I suppose legends lie in your day as in mine, and it might be well for me to know nothing of what lies ahead, lest I grow afraid, or arrogant. Tell me nothing, Damon. Yet one thing you have told already. For if a woman is Keeper in your day, then has my work succeeded and those who refused to believe a woman strong enough for Keeper have been silenced. So I know my work is not futile and will succeed. And since you have given me a gift, Damon, a gift of confidence, what can I give you in return? For you would not undertake a journey so far without some terrible need."

"The need is not mine but my kinswoman's," Damon said. "She was trained to be Keeper at Arilinn, but has been released from her vows, to marry "

"Need she be released for that?" Varzil asked. "But what is your need? Even in my day, kinsman, a Keeper is no longer surgically mutilated, or do you think me a eunuch?" He laughed with a gaiety which for some reason reminded Damon of Ellemir.

"No, but she is held halfway between Keeper and normal woman," Damon said. "Her channels were fixed to the Keeper's pattern when she was too young, before maturing, and she cannot readjust the channels to select for normal use."

Varzil looked thoughtful. He said, "Yes, this can happen. Tell me, how old was she when she was trained?"

"Between thirteen and fourteen, I think."

Varzil nodded. "I thought so. The mind writes deeply in the body, and the channels cannot readjust with the imprint of many, many years as a Keeper in her mind. You must lead her mind back to the days when her body was free, before the channels were altered and locked, and many years as Keeper froze the imprint into her nerve channels. Her mind once free, her body will free itself. When you take her through the sacrament next— But wait, are you sure the channels have not been surgically altered, nor the nerves cut?"

"No, it seems to have been done in pattern training with a matrix—"

Varzil shrugged. "Unnecessary, but not serious," he said. "There are always some of the women who let their channels lock that way, but at the Year's End festival the release comes. Some of our early Keepers were *chieri*, neither man nor woman, *emmasca*, and they too found themselves locked or frozen into that pattern. This, of course, is why we instituted the old sacramental rite of Year's End. How you must love her, cousin, to come so far! May she bear you children who will be as much credit to your clan as their brave father."

"She is not my wife," Damon said, "but wedded to my sworn brother. . . ." As soon as he had said that, he felt confused, for the words seemed to have no meaning to Varzil, who shook his head dismissingly.

"You are her Keeper; it is for you to be responsible."

"No, it is she who is Keeper," Damon protested, feeling a sudden frightening irritability, and Varzil looked at him sharply. The overworld shook, trembled, and for a moment Damon lost sight of Varzil, even the great sparkle of his ring dimming out into a faint, distant point of blue. *Was it a matrix?* He felt as if he was smothering, drowning in the darkness. He heard Varzil in the distance, calling his name, then with relief felt Varzil's hand close faintly upon the image of his hand. His body came into focus again, but he felt faint and sick. He could only see Varzil dimly, and beyond him a circle of faces, a glittering ring of stones, faces of Comyn who must have been his forgotten ancestors. Varzil sounded deeply concerned.

"You must not remain here longer, cousin, this level is death for the untrained. Come back, if you must, when you have won your full strength as *Tenerézu*. Do not fear for your cherished one, Damon. It is for you, as her Keeper, to take her into the ancient sacrament of Year's End, as if she were half-*chieri* and *emmasca*. I fear you must wait for the festival, if she must work as Keeper in the time between, but after that, all will be well. And not in three hundred years or a thousand will any child of the Towers forget the festival." Damon swayed, dizzy, and Varzil steadied him again, saying with kindly concern, "Look into my ring. I will return you to a level that is safe for you. Do not fear, this ring has none of the dangers of the ordinary matrix. Farewell, kinsman, bear my love and greetings to the one you cherish."

Damon said, feeling his consciousness thinning and groping, "I do not . . . do not understand." Nothing remained clear now but Varzil's ring, glowing, coruscating, wiping out the darkness. *I saw this before, like a beacon.*

Speech had gone. He could no longer formulate words. But Varzil was close beside him in the darkness. *Yes, I shall go now and set a beacon to guide you here . . . this ring.*

Damon thought, confusedly, *I saw it before.*

Do not struggle with definitions for time, cousin. When you are Keeper you will understand.

Men are not Keepers in my day.

Yet you are Keeper, or could never have come here without death. Now I may delay no longer for your safe return, cousin, brother. . . .

The glow of the ring filled Damon's consciousness. Sight vanished, light left him, his body went formless. He was floating, struggling to maintain balance over a gulf of nothingness. He fought to cling to some foothold, felt himself swept away, falling. *All those levels I climbed so painfully, must I fall down them all. . . . ?*

He fell, and knew he would go on falling, falling, for hundreds of years.

Darkness. Pain. Formless weariness. Then Callista's voice, saying, "I think he's coming around now. Andrew, lift his head, will you? Elli, if you don't stop crying, I'll send you out of here, I mean that!" He felt the sting of *firi* on his tongue, and then Callista's face moved into his range of vision. He whispered, and knew his teeth were chattering, "Cold . . . I'm so cold. . . ."

"No you aren't, love," Callista said gently. "You're wrapped in all the blankets we have, and there are hot bricks at your feet, see? The cold is *inside* you, don't you think I know? No, no more *firi*. We'll have hot soup for you in a minute."

He could see now, and every detail of his journey, of the conversation with Varzil, came flooding back into his mind. Did he truly meet an ancestor so long dead that even his bones were dust by now? Or did he dream, dramatize knowledge deep in his unconscious? Or did his mind reach deep into time to see what was written on the fabric of the past? What *was* reality?

But what festival did Varzil mean? He had said that not in three hundred years or a thousand would the Comyn forget the festival and the sacrament, but Varzil had not counted on the Ages of Chaos, on the destruction of Neskaya Tower.

Still, the answer was there. As yet it was obscure, but he could already see where it was leading. *The mind writes deeply in the body.* Somehow, then, he must lead Callista's mind back to a time when her body was free of the cruel constraints of the years as Keeper. *It is for you as her Keeper to lead her into the ancient sacrament of Year's End, as if she were half-*chieri *and* emmasca.

Whatever the lost festival, it could be recaptured or reconstructed somehow—a ritual to free the mind of its constraints? If all else failed—what had Varzil said? *Come back when you have won your full strength as Keeper.*

Damon shuddered. Must he, then, continue this frightening work, outside the safety of a Tower, to make himself Keeper in truth, as well as in the potential Leonie had seen in him? Well, he was pledged, and for Callista there was, perhaps, no other way.

It might not be that bad, he thought hopefully. There must be records of the festival of Year's End in the other Towers, or perhaps at Hali, in the *rhu fead*, the holy place of the Comyn.

Ellemir looked over Callista's shoulder. Her eyes were red with crying. He sat up, clutching the blankets about him. "Did I frighten you, my dearest love?"

She gasped. "You were so cold, so stiff, you didn't even seem to be breathing. And then you would start gasping, moaning—I thought you were dying, dead—oh, Damon!" Her hands clutched at him. "Never do this again! Promise me!"

Forty days ago he would have promised her, with pleasure. "My darling, this is the work I was trained for, and I must be free to do it at need." Varzil had hailed him as Keeper. Was that his destiny?

But not at a Tower again. They had made an art of deforming the lives of their workers. In seeking to free Callista, would he free all his sons and daughters to come?

Callista raised her head at a slight sound. "That will be the food I sent for. Go and fetch it, Andrew, we don't want outsiders in here." When he returned, she poured hot soup into a mug. "Drink it down as quickly as you can, Damon. You are as weak as a bird newly hatched."

He grimaced, saying, "Next time I think I'll stay inside the egg." He began to drink in hesitant sips, not sure, at first, that he could swallow. His hands would not hold the mug, and Andrew steadied it for him.

"How long was I out?"

"All day, and most of the night," Callista said. "And of course I could not move during that time either, so I'm stiff as planks nailed into a coffin!" Wearily she stretched her cramped limbs, and Andrew, leaving Ellemir to hold Damon's mug, came and knelt before her, pulling off her velvet slippers and rubbing her feet with his strong hands. "How cold they are!" he said in dismay.

"About the only advantage the higher levels have over winter in Nevarsin is that you don't get frostbite," Callista said, and Damon grinned wryly. "You don't get frostbite in the hells, either, but I never heard that advanced as a good reason not to stay out of them." Andrew looked puzzled, and Damon asked, "Or do your people have a hot hell, as I heard the Dry-Towners do?"

Andrew nodded, and Damon finished his soup and held out his mug for more. He explained, "Zandru supposedly rules over nine hells, each colder than the last. When I was in Nevarsin they used to say that the student dormitory was kept about the temperature of the fourth hell, as a way of showing us what might be in store for us if we broke too many rules." He glanced at the harsh darkness outside the window. "Is it snowing?"

Andrew asked, "Does it ever do anything *else* here at night?"

Damon cradled his cold fingers around the stoneware mug. "Oh, yes, sometimes in summer we have eight, ten nights without snow."

"And I suppose," Andrew said, straight-faced, "that people start to collapse with sunstroke and die of heat exhaustion."

"Why, no, I never heard that—" Callista began, then, seeing the twinkle in Andrew's eyes, broke off and laughed. Damon watched them, exhausted, weary, at peace. He wriggled his toes. "I wouldn't be surprised to find I had frostbite, after all. On one level I was climbing on ice—or thought I was," he added, with a reminiscent shiver.

"Take off his slippers and look, Ellemir."

"Oh, come, Callie, I was joking—"

"I wasn't. Hilary was caught once on a level where there seemed to be fire, and came back with burns and blisters on the soles of her feet. She could not walk for days," Callista said. "Leonie used to say, 'The mind writes deeply in the body.' Damon, what is it?" She bent to look at the bare feet, smiled. "No, there seems no physical injury, but I am sure you *feel* half frozen. When you have finished your soup, perhaps you should get into a hot bath. It will make certain your circulation is not really impaired."

She sensed Andrew's questioning look, and went on. "Truly, I do not know if it is the cold of the levels reflected in his body, or something in the mind, or whether the *kirian* makes it easier for the mind to reflect into the body, or whether *kirian* slows down the circulation and makes it easier to visualize cold. But whatever it is, the subjective experience in the overworld is *cold*, icy cold, chill to the bone, and without arguing where the cold comes from, I have experienced it often enough to know that hot soup, hot bricks, hot baths, and plenty of blankets should be all ready for anyone who returns from such a journey."

Damon felt unwilling to be alone, even in his bath. While lying flat he felt fine, but when he tried to sit up, to walk, it seemed that his body thinned to insubstantiality, his feet did not feel the floor, he walked bodiless and fading in empty space. He heard, ashamed, his own soft wail of protest.

He felt Andrew's strong arm under his, holding him up, making him solid, *real* again to himself. He said, half in apology, "I'm sorry. I keep feeling as if I'm disappearing."

"I won't let you fall." In the end Andrew almost had to carry him to his bath. The hot water brought Damon back to consciousness of his physical self again. Andrew, warned of this reaction by Callista, looked relieved as Damon began to look like himself. He sat on a stool beside the tub, saying, "I'm here if you need me."

Damon was filled with overflowing warmth, gratitude. How good they all were to him, how kind, how loving, how careful of his well-being! How he loved them all! He lay in his bath, floating, euphoric, an elation as great as his former misery, until the water began to cool. Andrew, disregarding the request to send for his bodyservant, lifted him bodily out of the tub, dried him, wrapped him in a robe. When they came back to the women he was still floating in euphoria. Callista had sent for more food, and Damon ate slowly, cherishing every bite, feeling that food had never tasted so fresh, so sweet, so good.

At the back of his mind he knew that his present elation was simply part of the reaction and would sooner or later give way to enormous depression, but he clung to it, enjoying it, trying to savor every moment of it. When he had eaten as much as he could possibly hold (Callista, too, had eaten like a horse-drover, after the exhaustion of the long monitoring session) he begged, "I don't want to be alone. Can't we all stay together as we did at Midwinter?"

Callista hesitated, then said, with a glance at Andrew, "Certainly. None of us will leave you while you need us close to you."

Knowing that the presence of nontelepathic servants would be intensely painful to Damon and Callista in their present state, Andrew went to carry the dishes and the remnants of the supper from the room. When he came back they were all in bed, Callista already asleep next to the wall, Damon holding Ellemir in his arms, his eyes closed. Ellemir looked up, drowsily making room for him at her side, and Andrew unhesitatingly joined them. It seemed right, natural, a necessary response to Damon's need.

Damon, Ellemir held close to him, felt Andrew and then Ellemir drop off to sleep, but he lay awake, unwilling to leave them even in sleep. He felt no hint of desire—knew that under present conditions he would feel none for some days—but he was content simply to feel Ellemir in his arms, her hair against his cheek, to reassure himself that he, himself, was *real*. He could hear and sense Andrew, just beyond, a strong bulwark against fear. *I am here with my loved ones, I am not alone. I am safe.*

Gently, without desire, he fondled her, his fingers caressing her soft hair, her warm bare neck, her soft breasts. His awareness was tuned so high that he could feel through her sleep her awareness of the touch, the new tingle there. As he had been taught long ago when he was a monitor, he let his awareness sink down through her body, feeling the changes in the breasts, deep in the womb, without surprise. He had been so careful since she lost their child, it must have been of Andrew's making. It was just as well, he felt. She and he were such close kin. He kissed the nape of her neck, so warmed and filled with love that he felt he would burst with its weight. He had by instinct guarded Ellemir from the danger of a child of long generations of inbreeding, and now she could have the child she hungered for, without fear. He *knew*, with a deep inner knowledge, that this child would not be lost too soon to live, and rejoiced for Ellemir, for all of them. He reached past Ellemir to touch Andrew's hand in the darkness. Andrew did not wake, but clasped his fingers on Damon's in his sleep. *My friend. My brother. Do you know, yet, of our good fortune?* Clasping Ellemir tightly, he realized with a shudder that he could have died out there on the higher levels of the overworld, that he might never again have seen any of these whom he so loved, but even that thought did not long disturb him.

Andrew would have cared for them, all their lives. But it was good to be with them still, to share this warmth, to think of the children who would be born to them here, of the life before them, the endless warmth. He would never be alone again. Falling asleep, he thought, *I have never been so happy in my life.*

When Damon woke hours later, the last dregs of warmth and euphoria had been squeezed from his mood. He felt cold and alone, his body dim and vanishing. He could not feel his own body, and clutched at Ellemir in a spasm of panic. His touch woke her at once, and she reacted to his hungry need for contact, folding herself against him, warm, sensual, alive against his cold deathliness. He knew, rationally, that he had nothing sexual for her now, but he still clung, desperately trying to stir in himself some flicker, some shadow, some hint of the love he felt for her. It was an agony of need, and Ellemir knew in despair that it was not really sexual at all. She held him and soothed him, and did what she could, but in his drained state of exhaustion he could not sustain even the momentary flickers of arousal that came and went. She was terribly afraid that he would exhaust himself still more in this despairing attempt, but she could think of nothing to say which would not hurt him still more. Under that frenzied tenderness, she felt her heart would break. At last, as she had known he must, he sighed, releasing her. She wanted to say that it did not matter, that she understood, but it mattered to Damon, and she knew it, and there would never be any way to change that. She simply kissed him, accepting the failure and his desperation, and sighed.

But now he sensed that the others were awake. He reached out gently, gathering the fourfold rapport around him, reassuring him more than the desperate attempt at sex. Intense, aware, closer than the touch of bodies, beyond words, beyond sex, they felt themselves blending into one. Andrew, feeling Damon's need in himself, reached for Ellemir, who came eagerly into his arms. The blended excitement grew, spreading out shivering ripples through all of them, engulfing even Callista, melting them into a single entity, touching, enfolding, surging, responding. Whose lips touched and crushed, whose thighs clasped, whose arms held which body in a fierce embrace? It overflowed, spread like a wave, a flood of fire, a scalding, shivering explosion of pleasure and fulfillment. As the excitement subsided—stabilized, rather, at a less intense level—Ellemir slipped out of Andrew's arms, caught Callista close, holding her, generously opening her mind to her sister. Callista clung to the mental contact hungrily, trying to hold something of that closeness, that togetherness she could share only this way, at second hand. For a moment she was actually unaware of her own unresponding body, so closely circled in the unbroken chain of emotion.

Andrew, sensing when Callista's mind opened wholly, so that in a sense it *had* been Callista in his arms, felt a dizzy exaltation. He felt as if he overflowed, spread out so that he seemed to occupy all the space in the room, to encircle all four of them in his arms, and both Damon and Callista picked up his impulsive thought: *I wish I could be everywhere at once! I want to make love to all of you at once!* Damon moved close to Andrew, holding him in a confused desire to share, somehow, in this intense delight and closeness, sharing, actually participating in the slow repeated rise of excitement, the gentle, intense caresses. . . .

Then shock, dismay—*What the hell is going on?*—as Andrew realized whose were the caressing hands. The fragile web of contact shattered like breaking glass, smashed with harsh physical shock. Callista gave a short, shaking cry, like a sob, and Ellemir almost cried it aloud: *Oh, Andrew, how could you . . . !*

Andrew lay very still, rigidly forcing himself not to move physically apart from Damon. *He is my friend. It isn't that important.* But the moment was gone. Damon turned away, burying his face in the pillow, and his voice came hoarsely:

"Zandru's hells, Andrew, how long do you and I have to be afraid of each other?"

Andrew, blinking, surfaced slowly from the confusion. He realized only dimly what had happened. He turned and laid a hand on Damon's shaking shoulder, saying awkwardly, "I'm sorry, brother. You startled me, that's all."

Damon had control of himself again, but he had been caught at the deepest moment of vulnerability, wholly open to all of them, and the rebuff had hurt unimaginably. Even so, he was a Ridenow, and an empath, and he grieved at Andrew's regret and guilt. "Another of your cultural taboos?"

Andrew nodded, shaken. It had never occurred to him that anything he could do, *anything*, could hurt Damon so enormously. "I'm—Damon, I'm sorry. It was just sort of . . . sort of a reflex, that's all." Awkward, still scared at the immensity of what he had done to Damon, he bent and hugged him a little. Damon laughed, returned the hug, and sat up. He felt drained, aching, but the disorientation was gone.

Shock treatment, he realized. Soothing was effective in hysteria. So was a good hard slap. When he got up to wash and dress he felt gratifyingly solid, real to himself again. He thought, soberly, that it was not so bad, after all. This time, when Andrew received a shock to one of his ingrained taboos, he didn't run away or try to shake loose. He knew he'd hurt Damon, and accepted it.

They both lingered a moment in the outer room of the suite when the women had dressed and gone. Andrew glanced at Damon with constraint, wondering if Damon was still angry with him.

"Not angry," Damon said aloud. "I should have expected it. You have always been afraid of male sexuality, haven't you? That first night, when you and Callista went into rapport with Ellemir and me. I sensed that. There was so much else to worry about that night, I'd forgotten, but when we touched by accident, in the link, you panicked." He felt again Andrew's tentative response, his troubled withdrawal. "Is it culturally necessary to regard all male sexuality except your own as a threat?"

"Not afraid," said Andrew, with a glint of anger, "repelled when it's directed at me."

Damon shrugged. "Humans are not herd animals who regard every other male as a rival or a threat. Is it impossible for you to take pleasure in male sexuality?"

Andrew said, with distaste, "Hell, yes. Do *you*?"

"Of course," Damon said, bewildered. "I cherish the . . . the awareness of your maleness as I cherish the femininity of the women. Is that so hard to understand? It makes me more aware of my own . . . own manhood—" He broke off with an uneasy laugh. "How can we get into a tangle like this? Even telepathy is no good, there are no mental images to go with the words." He added, more gently, "I'm not a lover of men, Andrew. But I find it hard to understand that kind of . . . fear."

Andrew muttered, not looking at him, "I guess it doesn't matter all that much. Not here."

Damon felt dismay that something so simple to him should cause such enormous self-doubt, real fear, in his friend. He said, troubled, "No, but Andrew, we're married to twin sisters. We will probably spend a lot of our lives together. Am I always going to have to fear that a moment of . . . of affection will alienate you, upset you to the point where all of us, even the women, are hurt by it? Are you always going to fear that I will . . . will overstep some invisible boundary, try to force something on you which . . . which repels you like this? How long"—his voice broke—"how long are you going to be on guard against me?"

Andrew felt intense discomfort. He wished he were a thousand miles away, that he need not stand like this, exposed to Damon's intensity, his closeness. He had never realized what it was to be a telepath and part of a group like this, where there was no way to hide. Every time they tried to hide from each other they got into trouble. They had to face things. Abruptly he raised his head and looked straight at Damon. He said in a low voice, "Look, you're my friend. Anything you want is . . . is always going to be okay with me. I'll try not to . . . get so upset about things. I"—not even their hands touched, but it felt somehow as if he and Damon were close together, embracing like brothers—"I'm sorry I hurt your feelings. I wouldn't hurt you for the world, Damon, and if you don't know it, you ought to."

Damon looked up at him, tremendously touched and moved, sensing the enormous courage it had taken for Andrew to say this. An outsider; and he had come so far. Knowing that Andrew had gone more than halfway to heal the rift he had made, he touched him lightly on the wrist, the feather-touch telepaths used among themselves to intensify closeness. He said, very gently, "And I'll try and remember that this is still strange to you. You are so much one of us now that I forget to make allowances. And now enough of that. There is work to be done. I must look everywhere in the archives of Armida to find if there is any record of the old Year's End festival before the Ages of Chaos and the burning of Neskaya. Failing that, I must look in the records of all the other Towers, and some of that must be done through the telepath relays. I cannot travel to Arilinn and to Neskaya and to Dalereuth, but truly, I think now that we will some day have the answer."

He began to tell Andrew about it. He still felt weary and depressed, the residual fatigue from the long over-world journey overwhelming him with the inevitable re-action. He told himself that he must not blame Andrew for his own state of mind. It would be easier when they were all back to normal.

But at least, he thought, there was now something like a hope for that.

CHAPTER SIXTEEN

The search in the archives of Armida was unproductive. There were records of all kinds of festivals which had at one time or another been customary in the Kilghard Hills, but the only Year's End festival he could discover was an old fertility ritual which had died out considerably before the time of the burning of Neskaya and which seemed to have rather less than no bearing at all on Callista's problem. Now that the search was underway, however, she was patient, and her health continued to improve.

Her menstruation had returned twice, but although Damon insisted that she should spend a precautionary day in bed each time, and he had been prepared to clear her channels again if needed, they remained clear. It was a good sign for her physical health, but a poor one for the eventual development of normal selectivity of the channels!

The normal winter work at Armida moved on, a mild winter, toward the spring thaw. As usual in winter, Armida was isolated, with few tidings of what happened in the outside world. Small bits of news took on major importance. A brood mare in one of the lower pastures gave birth to twin foals, both fillies. *Dom* Esteban gave them to Callista and Ellemir, saying that they should have matched saddle horses in a few years if they chose. The old minstrel Yashri, who had played for the dancing at Midwinter, broke two fingers of his hand in a fall during a drunken birthday party in the village, and his nine-year-old grandson came proudly to Armida, carrying his grandsire's harp—which was nearly as tall as he was—to play dances for them in the long evenings. A woman on the further edge of the estate gave birth to four children at a single birth, and Callista rode with Ferrika out to the village where it had happened, to deliver gifts and good-will wishes. An overnight storm forced her to spend two nights away from home, to Andrew's dread and worry. When she returned and he asked why this had been necessary, she told him gently, "It is needful for the safety of the babes, my husband. In the far hills the people are ignorant. They regard such a birth as a portent of luck, evil or good, and who is to know how it will take them? Ferrika can *tell* them this is nonsense, but she is one of themselves and they will not listen to her, though she is a midwife trained in Arilinn, a Free Amazon, and probably much more intelligent than I am. But I am *Comyn*, and a *leronis*. When I take gifts to the children, and comforts to the mother, the people know I have them under my protection, and at least they will not treat them as some frightful omen of catastrophe to come."

"What were the babies like?" Ellemir asked eagerly, and Callista grimaced. "All newborn babes look to me like hairless rabbithorns for the spit, Elli, surpassingly ugly."

"Oh, Callie, how can you *say* that!" Ellemir reproached. "Well, I shall simply have to go and see them for myself! Four at a birth, what a marvel!"

"Still, it is hard for the poor woman. I managed to encourage two women of the village to share the suckling, but even before they are weaned, we shall have to send them a dairy animal."

News of the quadruple birth spread far and wide around the hills, and Ferrika said she was glad it was still winter and the roads not too good—though indeed it was a mild winter—or the poor woman would be bothered to death by people coming to see this marvel. Andrew found himself wondering what a severe winter would be like, if this was a mild one. He supposed that some year he would find out.

He had lost track of the passing time, except insofar as he carefully registered expected dates of foaling in the horse ranch's studbooks and got into long, involved discussions with *Dom* Esteban and old Rhodri about the breeding of the best mares. The days were lengthening perceptibly when he had the passing of time brought forcibly to his attention.

He had come in from a long day in the saddle, and

was going upstairs to ready himself for the evening meal. Callista, in the Great Hall, was with her father, teaching the old man to play her harp. Ellemir met him at the door of the suite they shared and drew him into her half of the rooms.

This was not uncommon. Damon had been absorbed in research, and now and again made lengthy journeys into the overworld. His efforts were fruitless so far, but it had the normal consequence of matrix work, and Ellemir had, matter-of-factly, welcomed Andrew into her bed at these times and others. At first he had accepted this for what it had always been, a substitute for Callista's inability. Then, one night, when he merely slept at her side—she had turned away intimacy, saying she was too tired—he had realized that it was not only this he desired of Ellemir.

He loved her. Not as a substitute for Callista, but for herself. He found this intensely disturbing, having always thought that falling in love with one woman meant falling out of love with others. He carefully concealed the thought, knowing it would trouble her, and only when he was far out in the hills, away from them all, did he let his mind carefully explore the thought: *God help me, have I married the wrong woman?* And yet when he saw Callista again, he knew he loved her no less than ever, that he would love her forever even if he could never again touch even her fingertips. He loved both of them. What could he do about it? Now, as he looked at Ellemir, small and smiling and flushed, he could not forbear taking her in his arms and kissing her heartily.

She wrinkled her nose at him. "You smell of the saddle."

"I'm sorry, I was going to bathe—"

"Don't apologize, I like the smell of horses, and in winter I can never get out and ride. What were you doing?" When he told her, she said, "I'd think the *coridom* could handle that."

"Oh, he could, but if they get used to seeing me handle their problems, they'll be willing to come to me instead of bothering *Dom* Esteban. And he looks so tired and worn lately. I think the winter is weighing on him."

"On me too," Ellemir said, "but I have something

now to make the waiting worthwhile. Andrew, I wanted to tell you first of all: I am pregnant! It must have happened shortly before Midwinter—"

"God almighty!" he said, shocked and sobered. "Ellemir, I'm sorry, love—I should have been—"

It was like a slap in the face. She moved away from him, her eyes flashing with anger. "I wanted to thank you for this, and now I find you begrudge me this greatest of gifts. How can you be so cruel?"

"Wait, wait—" He felt confused. "Elli, little love—"

"How dare you call me love-names after . . . after slapping me in the face like that?"

He put out a hand to her. "Wait, Ellemir, please. I don't understand again, I thought . . . Are you trying to tell me you are *pleased* about being pregnant?"

She felt equally confused. "How could I possibly *not* be pleased? What sort of women have you known? I was so happy, so very happy when Ferrika told me this morning that now it was sure, not just my own wishes confusing me." She looked ready to cry. "I wanted to share my happiness and you treat me like a prostitute, as if I were unfit to bear your child!" She sobbed suddenly. Andrew drew her against him. She pushed him away, then lay weeping against his shoulder.

He said helplessly, "Oh, Ellemir, Ellemir, will I ever understand any of you? If you are happy about this, then of course I am happy too." He realized that he meant it as he had never meant anything in his life.

She sniffed, raising her head, like a day in springtime, all showers and sunshine. "Really, Andrew? Really glad?"

"Of course, darling, if you are." Whatever complications this might cause, he added to himself. It must be his child or she would have told Damon first.

She picked up his confusion. "But how *could* Damon feel? He shares my happiness, of course, and is glad!" She leaned back, looked up into his face and said, "Would this also be something wrong for your people? I am glad I do not know any of them!"

Repeated shocks of this kind had made Andrew almost numb to them. "Damon is my friend, my best friend. Among my people this would be considered treachery, a betrayal. My best friend's wife would be the one woman forbidden to me."

She shook her head. "I do not think I like your people *at all*. Do you think I would share my bed with any man my husband did not know and love? Would I bear a child for my husband to father, by a stranger or an enemy?" After a moment, she added, "It is true, I wished to bear Damon a child first, but you know what happened, and might happen again. We are too closely kin, so now we may decide to have no children between us, since he does not need an heir of Ridenow blood, and a child you give us is likely to be healthier and stronger than one he might give me."

"I see." He could admit it made some sense, but he paused to examine his own feelings. A child of his own, by a woman he loved. But not by his beloved wife. A child who would call some other man father, on whom he would have no claim. And how would Callista feel? Would it seem another mark of her distance, her exclusion? Would she feel betrayed?

Ellemir said gently, "I am sure she will be glad for me too. Surely you do not think I would add a feather's weight to her sorrow when she has had so much to bear."

He still felt uncertain. "Does she know?"

"No, though she may suspect, of course." She hesitated. "I always forget you are not one of us. I will tell her if you wish, though one of our own would want to tell her himself."

The complex courtesies of such things were beyond him, but suddenly he wished to do what was right in his adopted world. He said firmly, "I will tell her."

But he would choose his own time, when she could not doubt his love.

He went into his own room, in confusion, and while he made himself ready for the evening meal, his thoughts ran a strange counterpoint to the mundane business of bathing, trimming the beard which, in defiance of custom, he had begun to grow, putting on his neat indoor clothing.

His own child. Here, on a strange world, and not even the child of his own wife. But Ellemir did not think it strange, and Damon had, evidently, known for some time and approved. A strange world, and he was part of it.

Before he was ready, he heard riders in the courtyard, and when he came downstairs he found Damon's brother Kieran, returning from a wintertime visit to Thendara with his eldest son, a redheaded, bright-eyed boy of fourteen or so, and half a dozen Guardsmen, paxmen and hangers-on. Andrew had not liked Damon's eldest brother Lorenz, but he found Kieran likable, and welcomed news from the outside world, as did *Dom* Esteban.

"Tell me how Domenic fares," demanded the old man, and Kieran smiled, saying, "As it happens, I saw a good deal of him. Kester"—he indicated his son—"is due to go into the cadet corps this summer, so I felt it best to refuse his offer to take Danvan's place as cadet-master; no man can be master to his own son." He smiled to take the sting from the words, and said, "I do not wish to be as hard on my son as you had to be on yours, Lord Alton."

"Is he well? Does he manage the Guards competently?"

"As near as I can tell, you could hardly do better yourself," Kieran said. "He sits long and listens to wiser heads. He has asked much advice from Kyril Ardais and from Danvan, and even of Lorenz, though I do not think"—he smiled sidelong at Damon, a shared joke—"that he really thinks much more of Lorenz than we do. Still, he is wary, and diplomatic, has made the right friends, and has no favorites. His *bredin* are well-behaved lads both, young Cathal Lindir, and one of his *nedestro* brothers—I think the name is Dezirado?"

"Desiderio," said *Dom* Esteban, with a smile of relief. "I am glad to hear that Dezi is safe and well too."

"Oh, aye, the three of them are always together, but no brawling, no whoring, no roistering. They are as sober as monks all three. You would think Domenic realized, like a man three times his age, that such a young lad in the command will be watched night and day. Not that they are sad-faced prigs either—young Nic always has a laugh or a jest—but he is holding down the responsibility with both hands," Kieran told them, and Andrew remembering the merry boy who had stood beside him at his wedding, was glad Domenic was doing so well. As for Dezi, well, perhaps a responsible and challenging job, and knowing that Domenic acknowledged his family status as the old man would never do, might at last help the boy find himself. He hoped so. He knew what it was to feel you did not belong anywhere.

"Is there other news, brother-in-law?" Ellemir asked eagerly, and Kieran smiled. "No doubt I should have taken heed of the ladies' gossip in Thendara, sister. Let me think . . . There was a riot in the street where the Free Amazon's Guild-house stands, and the story goes that some man claimed his wife had been taken there unwilling—"

"That is not true," Ferrika said angrily. "Forgive me, *Dom* Kieran, but a woman must come herself and beg admission there!"

Kieran laughed good-naturedly. "I do not doubt it, *mestra*, but so the tale runs in Thendara, that he sent hired swords to take her back, and they say his wife fought alongside the Amazons defending her house, and wounded him. The tale grows ever greater with each mouth that repeats it. Someday, no doubt, they will say she killed him and nailed his head to the wall. Someone was exhibiting the body of a two-headed foal in the market, but my paxman told me it was a fake, and a clumsy one at that. In his boyhood he was apprentice for a time to a harness-maker and knows their tricks. And, let me think a moment, oh, yes. As I rode through the hills, I heard of a field of *kireseth* in bloom with the warm days, not a true Ghost Wind as in the summertime, but a winter blooming."

Dom Esteban nodded, smiling. He said, "It is rare, but it happens, and it used to be thought fortunate."

Callista explained in a low voice to Andrew: "*Kireseth* is a flower which blooms but rarely in the hills. The pollen and flowers are the source from which we make *kirian*. When it blooms in high summer, with the heat and wind in the hills, it sweeps down from the hills in a wind of madness, a Ghost Wind they call it. Men do strange things under its influence, and when there is a

true Ghost Wind we ring the alarms and barricade ourselves in our homes, for the beasts run mad in the forests, and sometimes nonhumans come down out of the
hills and attack mankind. I saw them once as a child,"
she said, shuddering.

Dom Esteban went on: "But with a winter blooming,
it cannot last long enough to be serious. A village's folk
will forget their sowing and ploughing, leave their gardens untended for a day or two while they play the fool,
but after a few hours the rain comes to settle the pollen
to the ground. The worst thing I ever heard during a
winter blooming was that the scavenger wolves in the
forest grew bold—the pollen affects the brain of man
and beasts alike—and came into the fields to attack cattle or horses. Mostly a winter blooming is only an unexpected holiday."

Andrew remembered that he had been warned by
Damon not to handle or smell the *kireseth* flowers in the
still-room.

"It has one other side effect," said Ferrika, with a
broad smile. "There will be more work in that village
for the midwife, when autumn comes. Women who have
chosen not to have children, or even old matrons whose
children are grown sometimes find themselves with
child."

Dom Esteban guffawed. "Ah, yes, when I was a lad
they used to make jokes at weddings, if the marriage
had been arranged by the families and the bride was
reluctant. Then one summer there was a wedding—oh,
off to the north, near Edelweiss—and a Ghost Wind
blew during the feasting. The festivities were rowdy,
feasting and drinking and . . . well it was indecorous,
and went on for days. I was too young, alas, to take
much good from it, but I remember seeing some things
usually shielded from children's eyes." He wiped tears
of laughter from his face. "And then, more than half a
year later, many children were born about whose parent-
age there was, to say the very least, a question. Now
they do not make such jokes at weddings any more."

"How disgusting!" Ferrika said with a grimace, but
Damon could not help laughing, thinking of the wedding
whose vulgar jokes and rowdy games, made in jest, had

turned to an orgy under the influence of the Ghost Wind.

"I don't suppose *they* thought it was funny," Ellemir said soberly, and *Dom* Esteban said, "No indeed, chiya. As I told you, they do not ever make such jokes at weddings there now! But indeed, there used to be tales in the hills that in summer, when the Ghost Winds blew, some people in the Domains would hold festival, an old festival of fertility. Those were barbarian days, before the Compact, perhaps even before the Ages of Chaos." He added, "But, of course, a winter blooming is nothing serious."

"Nor any laughing matter," Ferrika said, "for the women who find themselves bearing an undesired child!"

Andrew saw Ellemir frown a little in puzzlement. He followed her thoughts easily enough: Could any woman *not* want a child? Callista said, "I could wish for a winter blooming here. I must make more *kirian*, because what we have is nearly gone and we should keep it in the house."

One of the stewards, eating his meal at a side table where he could be quickly summoned at need, raised his head and said, in a diffident, rusty voice, "*Domna*, if that is truly your wish, there are *kireseth* flowers on the hillside above the pasture where the twin foals were born, the one where the old stone bridge stands. I do not know if they are in bloom still, but my brother saw them when he rode that way three days ago."

"Truly?" Callista said. "I thank you, Rimal. If the weather holds fine—though it is not likely to—I shall ride that way tomorrow and replenish my store."

That night there was neither rain nor snow, and after breakfast, when Kieran Ridenow had taken his leave— *Dom* Esteban urged him to stay for a few days, but he said he must take advantage of the good weather—Callista ordered her horse saddled. *Dom* Esteban frowned when he saw her in her riding skirt.

"I do not like this, Callista. *Chiya*, when I was a lad it was always said that no woman should ride alone in the hills when the *kireseth* is in bloom."

Callista laughed. "Father, do you truly think—"

"You are *comynara*, child, and none of our own would harm you, mad or sane, but there might be strangers or outlaws in the hills."

"I will take Ferrika with me," she said gaily. "She has had the training of an Amazon Guild-house, and can defend herself against any man born, whether he intend robbery or rape."

But Ferrika, summoned in half seriousness, refused to go. "The dairyman's wife is near her term and may give birth today, *domna*," she said. "It would hardly be seemly to leave my proper task and go pleasure-riding into the hills. You have a husband, my lady, ask *him* to ride with you."

There was not much for Andrew to do about the estate—the repairs from the storm had been completed, and the ranch was still in its winter dormancy, despite the fine weather. He had his horse saddled.

Away from the household, he thought, when they were together, he might find the right moment to tell her about Ellemir. And the baby.

It was still early when they set out. To the east, the sky was layered with purple and black flaps of thick clouds, latticed with crimson from the sun behind. As they rode along the steep trails, looking down into the valleys below, with patches of snow clinging below the trees, and the horses on every hillside cropping the sprigs of new-sprung grass, his heart lightened. Callista had never seemed merrier, more beautiful. She sang snatches of old ballads as they rode, and once paused, childlike, at the mouth of a long valley to send a long, sweet "Hallooo—ooo—ooo" down the slope, laughing gaily when the echo came back a hundredfold from the high rocky slopes. As they rode the sun climbed the sky and the day grew warmer. She unfastened her dark blue riding cape and slung it across her saddle horn.

"I did not know you could ride so well," Andrew said.

"Oh, yes, even at Arilinn I rode a great deal. We spend so much time indoors, in the screens and the relays, that if we did not get out of doors for exercise, we would be as stiff and lifeless as the paintings of Hastur and Cassilda in the chapel! We used to take our hawks, on holidays, and ride out into the country around Arilinn—it is not hill country like this, but flat plain—and fly them at birds and small game. I was proud that I could handle a *verrin* hawk, a big bird, like this"—she spread her hands apart—"not a lady-bird as most of the women did." She laughed again, a ringing sound. "Poor Andrew, I have been captive, and ill, and house-bound, so much that you must think me some delicate fairy-tale maiden, but I am a country girl, and very strong. When I was a child I could ride as well as my brother Coryn. Now I think my mare can beat your gelding to that fence yonder!" She clucked to the horse and was off like the wind. Andrew dug in his heels and raced after her, his heart in his mouth—she was not accustomed to riding now; she would be off in a moment—but woman and horse seemed to blend into a single creature. When she reached the fence, instead of pulling up her horse, she went flying over, with a laughing cry of excitement, the gray mare rising like a bird in the air and coming down lightly on the far side. As Andrew followed, she drew her horse to a walk and they moved along more slowly, side by side.

Perhaps this was what it was to be in love, Andrew thought. Every time he saw Callista it was like the first time, always all new and surprising. But that thought stirred the guilt which was never very far away. After a few minutes she noticed his silence, turned to him reaching her small gloved hand to his. "What is it, my husband?"

"I had something to tell you, Callista," he said abruptly. "Did you know Ellemir is pregnant again?"

Her face was suffused with her smile. "I am so glad for her! She has been so brave, but now she will have an end to mourning and sorrow."

"You don't understand," Andrew said doggedly. "She says it is my child—"

"Oh, of course," Callista said. "She told me Damon had not wanted her to try again so soon, for fear she would . . . would lose it. I'm very glad, Andrew."

Would he ever get used to their customs? He supposed it was lucky for him, but still . . . "Don't you mind, Callista?"

She started to say—he almost *heard* the words—"Why should I mind?" but then he saw her suppress them. He was still a stranger in some ways, in spite of everything. She said at last, slowly, "No, Andrew. I truly don't mind. I don't suppose you do understand. But look at it this way." She smiled again, her mirthful smile. "There will be a baby in the house, your child, and although I am fond enough of babies, I do not really want to have one yet. In fact, and this is ridiculous, Andrew," she added, laughing, "although Ellemir and I are twins, I am not old enough to have a baby yet! Don't you know that the midwives say no woman should bear a child until her body has been mature a full three years? And for me it is not half a year yet! Isn't that funny? Elli and I are twins, and she is pregnant the second time, and I am not really old enough to have a baby!"

He flinched at the joke. How could she make jokes about the way in which her body had been held, immature, and yet, he realized soberly, it was her very ability to find something funny, even in this, which had saved them all from despair.

They reached the valley with the old stone bridge, where the twin foals had been born. Together they rode up the long slope, tethered their horses to a tree, and dismounted.

"*Kireseth* is a flower of the heights," Callista said. "It does not grow in the tilled valleys, and probably it is a good thing. Men sometimes even weed it out when it grows on the lower slopes, because the pollen causes trouble: when it blooms, even horses and cattle are likely to behave like mad things, stampede, attack one another, mate out of season. But it is very valuable, for we make the *kirian* from it. And look, it is beautiful," she said, pointing to the lone grassy slope, covered with a cascade of blue flowers, shimmering with their golden stamens. Some were still blue, others like bells of gold, covered with the golden pollen.

She tied a piece of thin cloth, like a mask, over the lower part of her face. "I am trained to handle it without reacting much," she said, "but even so, I do not want to breathe too much of it."

He watched while she made preparations to gather

the flowers, but she warned him away. "Don't come too close, Andrew. You have never been exposed to it before. Everyone who lives in the Kilghard Hills has been through a Ghost Wind or two and knows how they will react, but it does very strange things. Stay here under the trees with the horses."

Andrew demurred, but she repeated her injunction firmly. "Do you think I need help picking a few flowers, Andrew? I brought you with me to have your company on the long ride, and to soothe my father's fears about bandits or robbers lurking in the hills with intent to rob me of the jewels I am not wearing, or to attempt rape, which might," she added, with a touch of grim laughter, "be worse for them to attempt than for me to suffer."

Andrew turned his face away. He was glad Callista could find some amusement, but that particular joke struck him as being in questionable taste.

"It will not take long for me to gather what I need of the flowers; they are already blooming and are heavy with the resin. Wait here for me, my love."

He did as she said, watching her move away from him and into the flowers. She stooped and began cutting the flower heads, putting them into a thick bag she had brought. Andrew lay down on the grass beside the horses and watched her moving lightly through the field of gold and blue flowers, her red-gold hair falling in a single braid down her back. The sun was warm, warmer than he could remember for any day on Darkover. Bees and insects buzzed and whirred softly in the field of flowers, and a few birds swooped down overhead. Around him, with sharpened senses, he could smell the horses and their saddle leather, the heavy scent of the resin-trees, and a sweet, sharp, fruity smell which, he supposed, must be the scent of the *kireseth* flowers. He could feel it filling his head. Remembering that Damon had warned him against handling or smelling even the dried flowers, he conscientiously moved the horses a little further away. It was a still, windless day, with not the slightest breeze blowing. He drew off his riding jacket and wadded it under his head. The sun made him drowsy. How graceful Callista was, as she bent over the flowers, cutting a blossom here and one there,

stowing them in her bag. He closed his eyes, but behind
his eyelids it seemed he could still see sunlight, splinter-
ing into brilliant colors and prisms. He knew he must
have had a whiff of the resin; Damon had said it was an
hallucinogen. But he felt relaxed and content, with no
impulse to do any of the dangerous things he had been
warned that men and animals did under its influence.
He was completely content to lie here on the warm
grass, dimly conscious of the shifting rainbow colors behind his eyelids. When he opened his eyes, the sunlight
seemed brighter, warmer.

Then Callista was coming toward him, the mask fallen
from her face, her hair flowing. She seemed to wade,
waist deep, through shimmering golden waves of the
star-shaped flowers, a delicate girlish woman in a cloud
of bright copper hair. For a moment her form shim-
mered and wavered as if she were not there at all, not
his wife in a riding skirt, but the ghostly image he had
seen while her body lay prisoner in the caves of Corresanti and she could come to him only in insubstantial
form in the overworld. But she was real. She sat beside
him on the grass, bending her glowing face over him
with a smile so tender that he could not forbear to draw
her down to him and kiss her lips. She returned his kiss
with an intensity which dimly surprised him . . . although,
half asleep and his senses half sharpened, half dulled by
the pollen, he could not remember quite why this should
surprise him so much.

He reached for her, drew her down beside him in the
grass. He held her in his arms, kissing her passionately,
and she gave him back his kisses without hesitation or
withdrawal.

A random thought crossed his mind, like a flicker of
wind stirring the glowing flowers: *Did I ever dream that
I had married the wrong woman?* This new, responsive
Callista in his arms, glowing with tenderness, made the
very thought absurd. He knew that she shared the
thought—he no longer cared to try to conceal it from
her, no longer cared to conceal *anything* from her—and
that it amused her. He could feel the little glimmering
ripples of laughter through the waves of desire which
swept them both.

He knew, positively, that now he could do what he would and she would not protest, but compunction stayed him from anything further than this, the kisses she shared and gave back so intensely. Whatever she felt, it might be dangerous for her. That night . . . she had wanted him then too. And that had ended in catastrophe and near-tragedy. He would not risk it again until he was certain, more for her sake than his own.

He knew she was beyond fear, but she accepted this, as she had accepted the kisses, the caresses. Strangely, there seemed no compulsion to go further, no ache of frustration. He was also swept with ripples of laughter which seemed somehow to heighten the ecstatic quality of this moment, of sun and warmth and flowers and singing insects in the grass all around him, a laughter, a mirth which shook Callista too, along with desire.

His wife and he were perfectly content to lie here in the grass beside her, with his clothes on, and she hers, and do nothing more than kiss her, as if they were children in their teens. . . . It was absurdly hilarious and delightful.

The politest of the Darkovan words for sex was *accandir* which meant simply to lie down together and was so noncommittal that it could be used in the presence of young children. Well, he thought, again swept by the little ripples of mirth, that was what they were doing. He never knew how long they lay there side by side in the grass, kissing or gently caressing one another, while he played with the strands of her hair or watched the soft prisms of color behind his eyes crawl across her glowing face.

It must have been hours later—the sun had begun to angle down from noon—when a cloud darkened the sun and a wind sprang up, blowing Callista's hair across her face. Andrew blinked and sat up, looking down at her. She lay resting on one elbow, her under-tunic opened at the throat, bits of grass and flowers caught in her hair. It was suddenly cold, and Callista looked at the sky regretfully. "I am afraid we must go, or we will be caught in the rain. Look at the clouds." With reluctant fingers she fastened her tunic-laces, picked leaves from her hair, and braided it loosely. "Just enough for decency," she said, laughing. "I do not want to look as if I had been lying down in the fields, even with my own husband!"

He laughed, gathering up the bag of flowers at her side, laying it on the pommel of her saddle. What happened to them? he wondered. The sun, the pollen, what was it? He was ready to lift her on her horse when she delayed, suddenly catching at him, putting her arms around his neck.

She said, "Andrew, oh, please—" and glanced at the edge of the field, the shelter of the trees. He knew her thoughts; there was no need to put them into words.

"I want to . . . I want to be all yours."

His hands tightened about her waist, but he did not move.

He said, very gently, "Darling, no. No risks."

It seemed that it would be all right, but he was not sure. If the channels overloaded again . . . He could not bear to see her suffer that way. Not again.

She drew a long, deep breath of disappointment, but he knew she accepted his decision. When she raised her eyes to him again they were filled with tears, but she was smiling. *I will cast no shadow on this wonderful day by asking for more, like a greedy child.*

He put her riding cloak around her shoulders, for a sharp wind was blowing from the heights and it was cold. As he lifted her into the saddle he could see the field of flowers, now chill blue, without the golden shimmer that had been on them. The sky was darkening into a drizzle of rain. He lifted Callista into her saddle, and beyond her, as he mounted, could see that on the other slope across the valley the horses were beginning to bunch up, moving restlessly, looking for shelter also.

The ride back was silent, Andrew feeling let down, distressed. He felt that he had been a fool. He should have taken advantage of Callista's yielding, the sudden disappearance of fear or hesitation. What stupid compunction had made him hesitate?

After all, if it was Callista's response to him which overloaded the channels, there had already been as much of that as if he had actually taken her. As she had wished! What a fool he had been, he thought, what a damnable fool!

Callista was silent, also, glancing now and then at him with an inexpressible look of guilt and dread. He picked up her fear, fear that came to wipe out the gladness.

I am glad I have known, again, what it was to desire him, to return his love . . . but I am afraid. And he could feel the paralyzing texture of her fear, the memory of pain when she had allowed herself, before, to respond to him. *I couldn't endure that again. Not even with* kirian. *And it would be dreadful for Damon too. Merciful Avarra, what have I done?*

It was raining hard by the time they reached Armida, and Andrew lifted Callista from the saddle, sensing with dismay the way her body stiffened against his touch. Again? He kissed her wet face under the soaked hood. She did not draw away from the kiss, but she did not return it, either. Puzzled, but trying to be sympathetic— she was afraid, poor girl, and who could blame her after that awful ordeal?—Andrew carried her up the steps and set her on her feet.

"Go and dry yourself, my precious, don't wait for me. I must make sure the horses are properly seen to."

Callista went slowly and regretfully up the stairs. Her gaiety had vanished, leaving her feeling tired and sick with apprehension. One of the strongest taboos in Arilinn was that which made the raw *kireseth* plant, untreated, a thing wholly forbidden. Although she was no longer bound by those laws, she felt guilty and ashamed. Even when she knew she was being affected by the flowers, she had remained to enjoy the effect, not moving out of range or withdrawing. And through the guilt was fear. She did not feel as she had felt with channel overload before—she had seldom felt better—but knowing what she did about herself, she was deathly frightened.

She went in search of Damon, and he guessed at once what had happened. "Were you exposed to *kireseth*, Callista? Tell me."

Stumbling, ashamed, frightened, she managed to convey to Damon a little of what had happened. Damon, listening to the faltering words, thought in an anguished empathy that she sounded as shamed as a repentant harlot, not a married woman who had spent the day innocently with her own husband. But he was troubled. After the events of the early winter, Andrew would never have approached her like this, without an explicit invitation. *Kireseth*, as a matter of fact, had quite a reputation for breaking down inhibitions. But whatever the cause, she might again have overloaded her channels with two conflicting sets of responses. "Well, let us see what harm has been done."

But after monitoring her briefly, he felt confused. "Are you *sure*, Callista? Your channels are a Keeper's, undisturbed. What sort of joke is this?"

"Joke? Damon, what do you mean? It happened just as I said."

"But that is impossible," Damon said. "You could *not* react like that. If you had, your channels would be overloaded and you would be very ill. What do you feel now?"

"Nothing," she said wearily, defeated, "I feel nothing, nothing, *nothing*!" For a moment he thought she would burst into tears. She spoke again, her voice tight with unshed tears. "It is gone, like a dream, and I have broken the laws of the Tower. I am outcaste for nothing."

Damon did not know what to think. A dream, compensating for the deprivations of her life? The *kireseth* was, after all, an hallucinogenic drug. He stretched his hands to her. Her automatic withdrawal from the touch verified his guess: she and Andrew had merely shared an illusion.

Later he questioned Andrew, which he could do more thoroughly and specifically, discussing the physical responses involved. Andrew was distressed and defensive, though he willingly admitted he would have been responsible if Callista had been harmed. Zandru's hells, Damon thought, what a tangle! Andrew already had so much guilt about wanting Callista when she could not respond to him, and now he must be deprived even of the illusion. Laying his hand on his friend's shoulder, he said, "It's all right, Andrew. You didn't hurt her. She's all right, I tell you, her channels are still wholly clear."

Andrew said stubbornly, "I don't believe it was a dream, or an illusion, or anything like that. Damn it, I didn't invent the leaves in my hall!"

Damon said, wrung with pity, "I've no doubt you were lying somewhere on the ground. *Kireseth* contains one fraction which stimulates *laran*. Evidently you and Callista were in telepathic contact, much more strongly than usual, and your . . . your frustrations built a dream. Which could happen without . . . without endangering her. Or you."

Andrew hid his face with his hands. It was bad enough to feel like a fool for spending the whole day kissing and caressing his wife without anything more intimate, but to be told that he had simply gone off on a drugged dream about doing it that was worse. Stubbornly he looked up at Damon. "I don't believe it was a dream," he said. "If it was a dream, why didn't I dream of what I *really* wanted to do? Why didn't *she*? Dreams are supposed to *relieve* frustrations, not make new ones, aren't they?"

That, of course, was a good question, Damon admitted, but what did he know of the fears and frustrations which might inhibit even dreams? One night, during his early manhood, he had dreamed of touching Leonie as no Keeper might be touched even in thought, and he had spent three sleepless nights for fear of repeating the offense.

In his own room, readying himself for the evening meal, Andrew looked at his garments, crumpled and stained. Was he fool enough to have erotic dreams about his own wife? He didn't believe it. Damon wasn't there; he was. And he knew what happened, even if he could not explain it. He was supremely glad Callista was not harmed, though he could not understand that either.

It was that night at dinner when *Dom* Esteban said, in a worried tone, "I wonder . . . do you suppose all is well with Domenic? I feel something menaces him, something evil . . ."

"Nonsense, Father," Ellemir said gently. "Only this morning *Dom* Kieran told us he was well and happy, and surrounded by his loving friends, behaving himself and carrying out his responsibilities as best he could! Don't be silly!"

"I suppose you are right," the old man said, but still he looked troubled

"I wish he were at home."

Damon and Ellemir exchanged frowning glances. Like all Altons, *Dom* Esteban had occasional flashes of precognition. God grant he was only worrying, Damon thought, not seeing the future. The old man was crippled and ill. It was probably only worry.

But Damon found that he too had begun to worry, and he did not stop.

CHAPTER SEVENTEEN

All night Damon's dreams had been haunted by the sound of horse's hooves, galloping—galloping toward Armida with evil tidings. Ellemir was dressing, preparing to go downstairs for her early work in supervising the kitchens—this pregnancy attended with none of the sickness and malaise of her first—when she suddenly turned pale and cried out. Damon hurried to her side, but she brushed past him and ran down the stairs, into the hall and the courtyard, standing at the great gates, bareheaded, her face white as death.

Damon, feeling the premonition grip him and take hold, followed her, pleading, "Ellemir, what is it? Love, you must not stand here like this . . ."

"Father," she whispered. "It will kill our father. Oh, blessed Cassilda, Domenic, Domenic!"

He urged her gently back toward the house, through the fine mist of the morning rain. Just inside the doors they found Callista, pale and drawn, Andrew troubled and apprehensive at her side. Callista went toward her father's room, saying quietly, "All we can do now is be with him, Andrew." Andrew and Damon stayed close beside the old man while his body servant dressed him. Gently Damon helped lift him into the wheeled chair. "Dear Uncle, we can only wait for tidings. But whatever may come, remember that you still have sons and daughters who love you and are near you."

In the Great Hall, Ellemir came and knelt beside her father, weeping. *Dom* Esteban patted her bright hair and said hoarsely, "Look after *her*, Damon, don't worry about me. If . . . if evil has come to Domenic, that child you bear, Ellemir is next heir to Alton."

God help them all, Damon thought, for Valdir was not yet twelve years old! Who would command the Guards? Even Domenic was thought too young!

Andrew was thinking that his son, Ellemir's child,

would be heir to the Domain. The thought seemed so wildly improbable that he was gripped with hysterical laughter.

Callista put a small cup into the old *dom's* hand. "Drink this, Father."

"I want none of your drugs! I will not be put to sleep and soothed until I know—"

"Drink it!" she commanded, standing pale and angry at his side. "It is not to dim your awareness, but to strengthen you. You will need all your strength today!"

Reluctantly the old man swallowed the draught. Ellemir rose and said, "The housefolk and workmen must not go hungry for our griefs. Let me go see to their breakfast."

They brought the old man to the table and urged him to eat, but none of them could eat much, and Andrew felt himself straining to hear beyond the range of his ears, to listen for the messenger, bringing the tidings they now took for granted.

"There it is," said Callista, laying down a piece of buttered bread, starting to her feet. Her father held out his hand, very pale but in command of himself again, Lord Alton, head of the Domain, Comyn.

"Sit still, daughter. Ill news will come when it will, but it is not seemly to run to meet it."

He lifted a spoonful of nut porridge to his mouth, put it down again, untasted. None of the others were even pretending to eat now, hearing the sound of hoofbeats in the stone courtyard, the booted feet of the messenger on the steps. He was a Guardsman, very young, with the red hair which, Andrew already knew, meant that somewhere, nearby or far back, he had Comyn blood. He looked tired, sad, apprehensive.

Dom Esteban said quietly, "Welcome to my hall, Darren. What brings you at this hour, my lad?"

"Lord Alton." The messenger's voice seemed to stick in his throat. "I regret that I bear you evil tidings." His eyes flickered around the hall. He looked trapped, miserable, unwilling to break the bad news to this old man, frail and drawn in his chair.

Dom Esteban said quietly, "I had warning of this, my boy. Come and tell me about it." He held out his hand,

and the young man came, hesitantly, toward the high table. "It is my son Domenic. Is he . . . is he dead?"

The young man Darren lowered his eyes. *Dom* Esteban drew a hoarse, shaking breath like an audible sob, but when he spoke he was under control.

"You are wearied with the long ride." He beckoned to the servants to take the young Guardsman's cloak, remove his heavy riding boots and bring soft indoor slippers, set a mug of warmed wine before him. They set a chair for him near the high table. "Tell me all about it, lad. How did he die?"

"By misadventure, Lord Alton. He was in the armory, practicing at swordplay with his paxman, young Cathal Lindir. Somehow, even through the mask, he was struck a blow on the head. None thought it serious, but before they could fetch the hospital officer, he was dead."

Poor Cathal, Damon thought. He had been one of the cadets during Damon's year as cadet master, as had young Domenic himself. The two lads had been inseparable, had been paired off everywhere: at sword-practice, on duty, in their leisure hours. They were, Damon knew, *bredin*, sworn brothers. Had Domenic died by any mischance or accident, it would have been bad enough, but for a blow struck by his sworn friend to be the instrument of his death—Blessed Cassilda, how the poor lad would suffer!

Dom Esteban had managed to pull himself together, was questioning the messenger about other arrangements. "Valdir must be brought from Nevarsin at once, designated heir."

Darren told him, "Lord Lorill Hastur has already sent for him, and he urges you to come to Thendara if you are able, my lord."

"Able or not, we shall ride this day," *Dom* Esteban said firmly. "Even if I must travel by horse-litter, and you must come with me, Damon, Andrew."

"I too." Callista's face was pale but her voice firm, and Ellemir said, "And I." She was crying noiselessly.

"Rhodri," Damon said, beckoning the old steward, "find a place for the messenger to rest, and send one of our men at once to ride for Thendara on the fastest horse available, to tell Lord Hastur that we will be there within three days. And ask Ferrika to come at once to Lady Ellemir."

The old man nodded acquiescence. Tears were streaming down old Rhodri's wrinkled face, and Damon remembered that he had been here at Armida all his life, had held both Domenic and the long-dead Coryn on his knees when they were children. But there was no leisure to think of any of these things. Ferrika, brought to Ellemir, admitted that the ride would probably do no harm. "But you must travel at least part of the time in a horse-litter, my lady, for too much riding would be wearying." When Ferrika was told that she must accompany them, she protested.

"There are many on the estate who need my services, Lord Damon."

"Lady Ellemir bears the next heir to Alton. It is she who most needs your care, and you are her childhood friend. You have taught other women on the estate, now they must justify their training."

This was so obvious, even to the Amazon midwife, that she spoke the polite phrase of respect and acquiescence, and went to speak to her subordinates. Callista had set the maids to packing what they would need for a possibly lengthy stay in Thendara. When Ellemir asked why, she said briefly, "Valdir is a child. Comyn Council may not be content to allow our father, crippled and with an ailing heart, to serve as head of the Domain; there may be a protracted struggle over a guardian for Valdir."

"I should think Damon would be the logical guardian," Ellemir said, and Callista's lips stretched in a bleak smile. "Why, so he should, sister, but I have sat as Leonie's surrogate in Council, and I know that to these great lords, nothing is ever simple or obvious if there is political advantage to some other way of settling it. Remember how Domenic said they were fighting over his right to command the Guards, young as he was? Valdir is younger still."

Ellemir quailed, with an automatic gesture laying a protective hand over her belly. She had heard old tales of bitter feuds in Comyn Council, of struggles more cruel than blood-feud because the ones who struggled were not enemies but kinsmen. As the old saying went, when *bredin* were at odds, enemies stepped in to widen the gap.

"Callie! Do you think . . . do you think Domenic was *murdered*?"

Callista said, faltering, "Cassilda, Mother of Seveners, I pray it is not so. If he had died by poison, or of some mysterious illness, I would fear so indeed—there was so much strife over the heirship of Alton—but struck down by Cathal in play? We *know* Cathal, Elli, he loved Domenic as his own life! They had sworn the oath of *bredin*. I would sooner believe Damon an oath-breaker than our cousin Cathal!" She added, her face white and troubled, "If it had been Dezi . . ."

The twin sisters looked at one another, not willing to speak their accusation, yet remembering how Dezi's malice had come close to costing Andrew's life. At last Ellemir said in a shaking voice, "Where, I wonder, was Dezi when Domenic died?"

"Oh, no, no, Ellemir." Callista caught her sister close, cutting off the words. "No, no, do not even *think* it! Our father loves Dezi, even if he would not acknowledge him, so do not make it worse than it is! Elli, I beg you, I beg you, do not put that thought into Father's head!"

Ellemir knew what Callista meant: somehow she must manage to guard her thoughts, so that the careless accusation would not reach her father. But the thought troubled her, as she went about the business of preparing the women servants to care for the household in their absence. She found a moment to slip down to the chapel, laying a small garland of winter flowers before the altar of Cassilda. She had wanted her child to be born at Armida, where he would live surrounded by the heritage which must be his some day.

All she had ever wanted in life was to be wedded to Damon, to bear sons and daughters to her clan and his. Was that so much to ask? she thought helplessly. She was not like Callista, ambitious to do *laran* work, to sit in Council and settle affairs of state. Why couldn't she have that much peace? And yet she knew that in the days to come, she could not fall back on this refuge of womanhood.

Would they demand that Damon must command the Guards in his father-in-law's place? Like all Alton daughters, she was proud of the hereditary post of commander which her father had borne, which she had thought would be Domenic's for years to come. But now Domenic was dead and Valdir too young, and who would it be? She looked around the chapel at the painted gods on the walls, on the representation, stiff and stylized, of Hastur, Son of Aldones, at Hali with Cassilda and Camilla. They were the forebears of the Comyn; life was easier in their day. Wearily she left the chapel and went upstairs to talk about which of the maids should come with them, which be left to care for the estate in their absence.

Andrew too had much to occupy his mind as he talked to the old *coridom*—like all the other servants, stricken with grief at the news of their young master's death—about managing the stock and the estate business during his absence. He thought that he ought to stay back, for he had no business in Thendara, and the ranch should not be left in the hands of servants. But he knew that part of his reluctance was because the Terran Empire HQ was at Thendara. He had been content that the Terrans should think him dead; he had no kin to mourn, and there was nothing there that he wanted. But now there was, unexpectedly, conflict again. He knew rationally that the Terrans had no claim on him, that they would not even know he was in the old city of Thendara, and certainly would not come after him. Just the same he felt apprehensive. And he too wondered where Dezi had been when Domenic died, and dismissed the thought as unworthy.

Damon had told him that Thendara was not much more than a day's ride for a single man on a fast horse, in good weather, traveling alone. But for a large party, with servants, baggage, a pregnant woman and an elderly cripple who must travel in horse-litters, it might take four or five times that. Much of the work of readying the party's horses and baggage came to Andrew, and he felt wearied but satisfied when at last the party rode forth between the great gates. *Dom* Esteban was in a litter drawn between two horses; another awaited Ellemir when she was weary of riding, but now she rode beside Damon, shrouded in a green riding cloak, her eyes swollen with crying. Andrew remembered Domenic teasing Ellemir at the wedding, and felt deeply saddened; he had had so little time to know this merry brother who had so quickly accepted him.

Then there was a long straggle of pack animals, servants riding the antlered beasts which had a surer gait on the mountain roads than most horses, and half a dozen Guardsmen at the rear to protect them against the dangers of travel in the hills. Callista looked tall, pale, otherworldly in her black riding cape. Looking at her haunted face under the dark hood, it was hard to remember the laughing girl in the golden flowers. Had it been only yesterday?

And yet, beneath the mourning solemnity of her dark garments and her pale face, she was still that laughing woman who had given and received his kisses with such unsuspected passion. Some day—soon, soon, he pledged himself fiercely!—he would free her and have her always with him. He looked at her bent head and she raised her face with a wan smile.

The journey took four cold and exhausting days. On the second day Ellemir took to her litter and did not ride horseback again till just before they entered the city gates. In the notched pass which overlooked the city she insisted on leaving the horse-litter and mounting again.

"The litter jolts me, and the baby, worse than Shirina's gait," she insisted pettishly, "and I will not be carried into Thendara as if I were a spoiled queen or a cripple. I want them to know my child is no weakling!" Ferrika, appealed to, said that Ellemir's comfort was more important than anything else, and if she felt comfortable and able to ride, ride she should.

Andrew had never seen the Comyn Castle except distantly from the Terran Zone. It stood high above the city, immense and ancient, and Callista told him how it had stood there since before the Ages of Chaos, how it had not been built by human hands at all. The stones had been lifted into place by matrix circles from the Towers, working together to transform the forces.

Inside it was a labyrinth, with enormous long corridors, and the rooms to which they were shown—rooms, Callista told him, reserved since time immemorial for the Altons at Council season—were almost as spacious as the adjoining suites they occupied at Armida.

Outside the Alton suite the castle seemed deserted. "But Lord Hastur is here," Callista told him. "He remains in Thendara most of the year, and his son Danvan is helping to command the Guards. I suppose they will summon council to act on the heirship of Alton. There are always questions, and Valdir is so young."

As *Dom* Esteban was carried into the main hall of the Alton rooms, a slender, sallow boy with a sharp, intelligent face and hair so dark it hardly seemed red, about twelve years old, came forward to meet him.

"Valdir." *Dom* Esteban held out his arms, and the boy knelt at his feet.

"You are so young, my boy, but you will have to be a grown man already!" As the boy rose, he clasped him close. "Do you know what has become of your brother's . . ." He choked on the word. Young Valdir said quietly, "He rests in the chapel, Father, and his paxman is with him. I did not know what I ought to do, but"—he gestured, and Dezi came hesitantly into the main room—"my brother Dezi has been such a help to me, since I came from Nevarsin."

Damon thought, uncharitably, that Dezi had lost no time, now that his protector was dead, in worming himself into the good graces of the next heir. Next to the thin, sallow Valdir, Dezi, with his bright red hair and freckled face, looked far more like a member of the family than did the legitimate son. *Dom* Esteban embraced Dezi, weeping.

"My dear, dear boy—"

Damon wondered how he could deprive the old man of the comfort of his only other remaining son, deprive Valdir of his only living brother? It was a true saying, bare is back without brother. In any case, Dezi, deprived of his matrix, was harmless.

Valdir came and hugged Ellemir. "I see you finally did marry Damon. I thought you would." But before Callista he hung shyly back. Callista held out her hands, explaining to Andrew, "I went to the Tower when

Valdir was an infant in arms; I have seen him only a few times since, and not since he was a tiny child. I am sure you have forgotten me, brother."

"Not quite," said the boy, looking up at his tall sister. "I seem to remember a little. We were in a room with colors, like a rainbow. I must have been very small. I fell and hurt my knee, and you took me on your lap and sang to me. You were wearing a white dress with something blue on it."

She smiled. "I remember now, it was when you were presented in the Crystal Chamber, as every Comyn son must be so that they may be sure he has no hidden defect or deformity, when later he is pledged for marriage. I was only a psi monitor then. But you were not even five years old; I am surprised you should even remember the blue veil. This is my husband, Andrew."

The child bowed courteously but did not offer Andrew his hand, retreating to Dezi's side. Andrew bowed coldly to Dezi; Damon gave him a kinsman's embrace, hoping the touch would dispel the suspicions he could not be rid of. But Dezi was well barricaded against him. Damon could not read his mind even a little. Then Damon admonished himself to be fair. At their last meeting he had tortured Dezi, nearly killed him; how could he greet Damon with much friendship?

Dom Esteban was taken to his rooms. He looked pleadingly at Dezi, and the young man followed his father. When they had gone Andrew said with a grimace, "Well, I thought we were rid of him. But if it comforts our father to have him near, what can we do?"

Damon thought it would not be the first time that a bastard son, rascally in his youth, had become the prop and mainstay of a father who had lost his other children. He hoped for *Dom* Esteban's sake, and for Dezi's own, that it might prove to be so.

He joined Andrew and Callista, saying, "Will you come with me to the chapel, to see what has been done with Domenic? If all is seemly, we can spare our father this, and Ellemir. Ferrika has put her to bed. She knew Domenic best . . . there is no need to harrow her feelings more."

The chapel was in the deepest part of the Comyn Castle, carved from the living rock of the mountain on which it stood. It had the cold, earthy chill of an underground cavern. Domenic lay in the echoing silence on a long trestled bier, before the carved image Andrew could already recognize as the Blessed Cassilda, mother of the Domains. In the carved stone figure Andrew fancied he could actually see a faint likeness to Callista's own features, and to the cold and lifeless face of the young man who lay dead.

Damon bowed his head, burying his face in his hands. Callista gently bent and kissed the cold brow, murmuring something Andrew could not hear. A dark form, crouched kneeling beside the bier, suddenly stirred and rose. It was a short, sturdily built young man, disheveled and heavy-eyed, his eyelids reddened with long weeping. Andrew knew who he must be, even before Callista held out her hands.

"Cathal, dear cousin."

He stared at them pitifully for a moment before he found his voice. "Lady Ellemir, my lords . . ."

"I am not Ellemir, but Callista, cousin," she said quietly. "We are grateful that you should have remained with Domenic till we could come. It is right there should be someone near who loved him."

"So I felt, and yet I felt guilty, I who was his murderer—" His voice broke. Damon embraced the shaking lad.

"We all know it was mischance, kinsman. Tell me how it happened."

The red-eyed stare was pitiable. "We were in the armory, working with wooden practice swords as we did every day. He was a better swordsman than I," Cathal said, and his face came apart. He too, Andrew noticed, had Comyn features; "cousin" was not just politeness.

"I didn't know I had hit him so hard, truly I didn't. I thought he was shamming, teasing me, that he would spring up and laugh—he did that so often." His face twisted. Damon, remembering a thousand pranks during Domenic's cadet year, wrung Cathal's hand. "I know, my boy." Had the lad gone like this, uncomforted, burdened since the death?

"Tell me about it."

"I shook him." Cathal was white with horror. " I said, 'Get up, you silly donkey, stop playing the fool.' And then I took off his mask and I saw he was unconscious. But even then I didn't think much about it—someone is always getting hurt."

"I know, Cathal, I was knocked senseless half a dozen times in my cadet years, and look, my middle finger is still crooked where Coryn broke it with a practice sword. But what did you do then, lad?"

"I ran off to fetch the hospital officer, Master Nicol."

"You left him alone?"

"No, his brother was with him," Cathal said. "Dezi was putting cold water on his face, trying to bring him around. But when I came back with Master Nicol he was dead."

"Are you sure he was alive when you left him, Cathal?"

"Yes," Cathal said positively. "I could hear him breathing, and I felt his heart."

Damon shook his head, sighing. "Did you notice his eyes. Were the pupils dilated? Contracted? Did he react to light in any way?"

"I . . . I didn't notice, Lord Damon, I never thought to look."

Damon sighed. "No, I suppose not. Well, dear lad, head injuries do not always follow the rules. A Guardsman in my year as hospital officer was knocked against a wall in a street fight, and when they picked him up he seemed quite well, but at supper he went to sleep with his head on the table, and never woke, but died in his sleep." He stood up, his hand resting on Cathal's shoulder.

"Set your mind at rest, Cathal. There was nothing you could have done."

"Lord Hastur and some of the others, they questioned and questioned me, as if anyone could ever believe I could hurt Domenic. We were *bredin*—I loved him." The boy went and stood before the statue of Cassilda, saying vehemently, "The Lords of Light strike me here if I could ever harm him!" Then he turned and knelt for a moment at Callista's feet. "*Domna*, you are a *leronis*, you can prove at will that I held no malice toward my dear lord, that I would have died myself to shield him, would that my hand had withered first!"

Tears had begun to flow again. Damon bent and raised him, saying firmly, "We know that, my lad, believe me." Grief and guilt flooded him. The boy was wide open to Damon's mind, but the guilt was only for the careless blow, there was no guile in Cathal. "Now a time has come when more weeping is only self-indulgence. You must go and rest. You are his paxman; you must ride at his side when he is laid in the earth."

Cathal drew a long breath, looking up into Damon's face. "You *do* believe me, Lord Damon. Now, now I really think I can sleep."

He watched the boy turn away, sighing. Whatever reassurances he might give, Cathal would live the rest of his life with the knowledge that he had slain his kinsman and his sworn friend by evil chance. Poor Cathal. Domenic died quickly and without pain. Cathal would suffer for years.

Callista was standing before the bier, looking down at Domenic, dressed in the colors of his Domain, his curly hair combed unnaturally smooth, his eyes peacefully closed. She felt at his throat.

"Where is his matrix? Damon, it should be buried with him."

Damon frowned. "Cathal?"

The boy, at the very threshold of the chapel, stopped. "Sir?"

"Who laid him out for burial? Why did they take his matrix from his body?"

"Matrix?" The blue eyes were uncomprehending. "I heard him say often enough that he had no interest in such things. I didn't know he had one."

Callista's fingers strayed to her throat. "He was given one when he was tested. He had *laran*, though he used it but seldom. When I last saw him it was around his neck, in a little bag like this."

"Now I remember," Cathal said. "He did have something around his neck, I thought it a lucky charm or some such thing. I never knew what it was. Perhaps whoever laid him out for burial thought it too shabby a trinket to bury with him."

Damon let Cathal go. He would ask who had prepared Domenic's body for burial. Surely it should be buried with him.

"How could anyone take it?" Andrew asked. "You have told me, and shown me, that it is not safe to touch another's matrix. When you took Dezi's, it was nearly as painful for you as for him."

"In general, when the owner of a keyed matrix dies, the stone dies with him. After that it is only a dead piece of blue crystal, without light. But it is not suitable that it should remain to be handled." The chances were overwhelming that some servant had simply thought it, as Cathal said, a shabby trinket not fit to bury with a Comyn heir.

If Master Nicol, not understanding, had touched it, perhaps loosened it, trying to give Domenic air, *that* could have killed him, but no, Dezi was there. Dezi would have known, being Arilinn-trained. If Master Nicol had tried to remove the matrix, Dezi, who, as Damon had cause to know, could do a Keeper's work, would surely have chosen to handle it himself, as he could do so safely.

But if Dezi had taken it . . .

No. He would *not* believe that. Whatever his faults, Dezi had loved Domenic. Domenic alone in the family, had befriended him, had treated Dezi like a true brother, had insisted on his rights.

Brother had slain brother before this, but no. Dezi had loved Domenic, he loved his father. It would have been hard, indeed, not to love Domenic.

For a moment Damon stood beside the bier of the dead boy. Come what might, this was the end of the old days at Armida. Valdir was so young, and if he must be heir so soon, there would be no time for the usual training of a Comyn son, the years in cadet corps and Guardsmen, the time spent in a Tower if he was fit for it. He and Andrew would do their best to be sons to the aging Lord Alton, but despite their best intentions, they were not Altons steeped in the traditions of the Lanarts of Armida. Whatever happened, it was the end of an era.

Callista followed Andrew as he went to examine the paintings on the walls. They were very old, done with

pigments that glowed like jewels, depicting the legend
of Hastur and Cassilda, the great myth of the Comyn.
Hastur in his golden robes wandering by the shores of
the lake; Cassilda and Camilla at their looms; Camilla
surrounded by her doves, bringing him the traditional
fruits; Cassilda, a flower in her hand, proffering it to the
child of the God. The drawings were ancient and stylized, but she could recognize some of the fruits and
flowers. The blue and gold blossom in Cassilda's hand
was the *kireseth*, the blue starflower of the Kilghard
Hills, colloquially called the golden bell. Was this sacred
association, she wondered, why the *kireseth* flower was
taboo to every Tower circle from Dalereuth to the Hellers? She thought, with a pang of regret, how she had
lain in Andrew's arms, unafraid, during the winter
blooming. They used to make jokes about it at weddings,
if the bride were reluctant. Her eyes stung with tears,
but she swallowed them back. While the heir of the Domain, her dearly loved younger brother, lay dead, was
this any time to be fretting about her private troubles?

CHAPTER EIGHTEEN

It was a gray morning, the sun hidden behind banks of fog and little spits and drizzles of sleet blowing around the heights, as the funeral procession rode northward from Thendara, bearing the body of Domenic Lanart-Alton to lie beside his forefathers of the Comyn. The *rhu fead* at Hali, the holy place of the Comyn, lay an hour's ride northward from the Comyn Castle, and every lord and lady of Comyn blood who could come to the Council in the last three days rode with them to do honor to the heir to Alton, killed by tragic mischance so young.

All except Esteban Lanart-Alton. Andrew, riding with Cathal Lindir and young Valdir, remembered the scene which had broken out that morning when Ferrika, summoned by the old man to give him something to strengthen him for the journey, had flatly refused.

"You are not fit to ride, *vai dom*, not even in a horse-litter. If you follow him to his grave, you will lie there beside him before a tenday is out." More gently, she had added, "The poor lad is beyond all helping or hurt, Lord Alton. We must think now of your own strength."

The old man had flown into such a rage that Callista, hastily summoned, had feared that his very anger would bring on whatever catastrophe Ferrika feared for him. She had tried to mediate, saying tentatively, "Can it harm him as much as this kind of disturbance?"

"I will hear no woman's ruling," *Dom* Esteban had shouted. "Send for my body-servant and get out of here, both of you! Dezi—" He had turned to the lad for confirmation, and Dezi said, his smooth face flushing with color, "If you will ride, Uncle, I will go with you."

But Ferrika had slipped away, and returned in a moment with Master Nicol, the hospital officer of the Guards. He felt the old man's pulse, turned down his eyelid to look at the small veins there, then said curtly,

"My lord, if you ride out today, you are not likely to return. There are others here who can bury the dead. Your heir has not even been formally accepted by Council, and in any case he is but a lad of twelve years. Your task, *vai dom*, is to save your own strength till that boy is grown to manhood. By a last sentimental service for your dead son, will you risk leaving your living one fatherless?"

Before these unwelcome truths there was nothing to say. Dismayed, *Dom* Esteban had allowed Master Nicol to put him back to bed. He clung to Dezi's hand and the boy remained docilely at his side.

Now, riding northward to Hali, Andrew recalled the calls of condolence, the long talks with other members of the Council which had taxed Lord Alton's strength to the utmost. Even if he survived the coming Council season and the homeward journey, could he live until Valdir was declared a man at fifteen? And how could a boy of fifteen possibly cope with the complex policies and politics of the Domain? Certainly not this sheltered, scholarly lad from a monastery!

Valdir rode at the head of the procession, in drab formal mourning, his face very pale against the dark garments. Beside him rode his sworn friend Valentine Aillard, who had come with him from Nevarsin, a big, sturdy boy with hair so blonde it looked white. Both boys looked solemn, but not deeply grieved. Neither of them had known Domenic well enough for that.

On the shores of the Lake of Hali, where legend said that Hastur, son of Light, had first come to Darkover, Domenic's body was laid in an unmarked grave, as the custom demanded. Callista leaned heavily on Andrew as they stood beside the opened grave, and he picked up her thought: *It does not matter where he lies, he has gone elsewhere. But it would have comforted my father, if he could rest in Armida soil.*

Andrew looked around the burying ground and shivered. Here beneath his feet lay all that was mortal of countless generations of Comyn, with no sign to tell where they lay except for the irregular mounding of the ground, thrust into heaps by spring thaw and winter snow. Would his own sons and daughters lie here one day? Would he, himself, some day rest here under the strange sun?

Valdir, as nearest of kin, stepped first to the graveside. His voice was high and childish, and he spoke hesitantly.

"When I was five years old, my brother Domenic lifted me from my pony and said I should have a horse fit for a man. He took me to the stables, and helped the *coridom* choose a gentle horse for me. Let that memory lighten grief."

He stepped back and Valentine Aillard took his place. "In my first year in Nevarsin I was lonely and miserable, as all the boys are, only more so, because I have neither mother nor father living, and my sister was fostered far away. Domenic had come to visit Valdir. He took me into the town and bought me sweets and gifts so that I would have what the other boys had after a visit from kinfolk. When he sent Valdir gifts at Midwinter festival he sent me a gift too. Let that memory lighten grief."

One by one, the members of the funeral party stepped forward, each with some memory or tribute of the one who lay in his grave. Cathal Lindir could only stand silent, swallowing his sobs, and finally he only blurted out, "We were *bredin*. I loved him," and stepped back, hiding himself in the crowd, unable even to speak the ritual words. Callista, taking his place at the graveside, said, "He was the only one in my family to whom I was not . . . not something apart and strange. Even when I dwelt at Arilinn, and all my other kinsfolk treated me as a stranger, Domenic was always the same to me. Let that memory lighten grief." She wished that Ellemir were here, to hear the tributes to her favorite brother. But Ellemir had chosen to remain with her father. Domenic, she said, was past all help or hurt, but her father needed her.

Andrew stepped in his turn to the graveside. "I came a stranger to Armida. He stood beside me at my wedding, for I had no kinsman at my side." As he ended with "Let that memory lighten grief," he felt saddened that he had had so little time to know his young brother-in-law.

It seemed that every lord and lady of Comyn who had ridden to Domenic's grave had searched their memory for some small kindness, some pleasant encounter for the mourners to remember the dead. Lorenz Ridenow, who, Andrew remembered, had schemed to oust Domenic from his command of the Guards on the grounds of his youth, spoke of how modest and competent the boy had been under the authority thrust on him so young. Danvan Hastur, a short, sturdy young man, with silver-gilt hair and gray eyes, cadet-master in the Guards, told how the young commander had interceded for the victim of a cruel prank among the cadets. Damon, who had been Domenic's cadet-master when he was fourteen and new to the cadets, remembered, and told them, that in spite of Domenic's perpetual pranks and mischief, he had never heard Domenic make a joke with any malice, or play a prank with anything of cruelty in it. Andrew realized, with a sorrowful pang, how much the boy would be missed. It would be hard on Valdir, to fill the place of a young man so universally liked and respected.

As they rode home the fog began to lift. Riding through the gap in the hills leading down into Thendara, Andrew looked again across the valley to the buildings which had begun to thrust upward within the enclosed walls of the Terran Zone, the hum of machinery, perceptible even from this distance, for the building there. Once he had been Andrew Carr and dwelt in a compound like that, yellow lights blotting out the color of whatever sun he lived under, and he had not cared what lay beyond. Now he looked indifferently at the small distant shapes of spaceships, the skeleton ribs of the unfinished skyscrapers. All that had nothing to do with him.

As he turned away he saw the eyes of Lorill Hastur resting on him. Lorill was Regent of Comyn Council, and Callista had explained that he was more powerful than the King, a man of middle age, tall, commanding, with dark-red hair fading to white at the temples. His eyes caught and held Andrew's for a moment. The Terran remembered that Lorill was supposed to be a powerful telepath and looked quickly away. He knew that was foolish—if the Hastur lord wished to read his mind, he could do it without looking him in the eye! And he knew enough of the courtesies of telepaths now to know Lorill would not do so uninvited without good reason. Yet he felt ill at ease, knowing he was there under false pretenses. No one knew he was Terran. But he tried to appear indifferent, listening as Callista pointed out the banners of the Domains to him.

"The silver fir tree on the blue banner is Hastur, of course, you saw it when Leonie came to Armida. And that is the Ridenow banner with the green and gold, where Lorenz is riding. Damon has the right to a banner-bearer, but he seldom bothers with it. The red and gray feathers are the banner of Aillard, and the silver tree and crown belong to the Elhalyn. They were once a sept of the Hasturs." Prince Duvic, Andrew thought, who had come to honor the heir to Alton, looked less regal than Lorill Hastur, or even young Danvan. Duvic was a spoiled, dissolute-looking youth, foppishly dressed in fur.

"And that is old *Dom* Gabriel of Ardais, and his consort Lady Rohana; see the hawk on their banner?"

"That's only six counting Armida," Andrew said, counting. "What is the seventh Domain?"

"The Domain of Aldaran was exiled long ago. I have heard all kinds of reasons given, but I suspect it was simply that they lived too far away to come to Council every year. Castle Aldaran is far away in the Hellers, and it is difficult to govern folk who live so far in the mountains that no man can tell whether or not they keep the laws. Some say the Aldarans were not exiled but seceded of their free will. Everyone you ask will tell a different tale of why the Aldarans are no longer the seventh Domain. I suppose some day one of the larger Domains will divide again, so that there are seven. The Hasturs did so when the old line of the Elhalyn died out. We are all akin anyway, and many of the minor nobility have Comyn blood. Father spoke once of marrying Ellemir to Cathal . . ." She was silent and Andrew sighed, thinking of the implications. He had married into an hereditary caste of rulers. Ellemir's coming child, any child Callista might bear, would inherit an awesome responsibility.

And I started on a horse ranch in Arizona!

He felt equally overawed when, later that day the

Comyn Council gathered in what Callista called the Crystal Chamber, a room high in one of the turrets, fashioned of translucent stone, cut in prisms which flashed with the light of the sun, so that it was like moving in the heart of a rainbow. The room was octagonal, with tiers of seats, each of the Comyn Domains under their own emblem and banner. Callista whispered that every member of a family holding Council-right, and known to have *laran*, had an indisputable right to appear and speak in Council. As Keeper of Arilinn she had held such a right, though she had seldom bothered to come.

Leonie was there with the Hasturs; Andrew looked away from her. But for her, Callista might now be his wife in more than name and perhaps it would be Callista, not Ellemir, bearing his child.

But then, he thought, he would never have known Ellemir. How could he wish for that?

Dom Esteban, pale and drawn but straight and dignified in his wheeled chair, sat in the lowest ranks of seats, at floor level. On either side his sons were seated, Valdir pale and excited, Dezi's face smooth and unreadable. Andrew saw the lifted eyebrows, the curious glances at Dezi. The family resemblance was unmistakable, and for *Dom* Esteban to seat Dezi at his side in the Crystal Chamber was like a belated public acknowledgment.

Lorill Hastur's voice was deep and solemn. "This morning we paid our respects to the heir to Alton, tragically killed by misadventure. But life goes on, and we must now designate the next heir. Esteban Lanart-Alton, will you—" He amended, looking at the old man in the wheeled chair, "Can you take your place among us? If not, you may speak from where you are."

Dezi rose and wheeled the chair forward, returning unobtrusively to his seat.

"Esteban, I call upon you to designate the next heirs to your Domain, that we may know them and accept them all."

Esteban said quietly, "My nearest heir is my youngest legitimate son, Valdir-Lewis Lanart Ridenow, by my lawful wife *di catenas*, Marcella Ridenow." He beckoned Valdir to come forward; the boy knelt at his father's feet.

"Valdir-Lewis Lanart-Alton," *Dom* Esteban said, for

the first time giving him the Domain title used only by
the head of the Domain and his nearest heir, "as a
younger son you were not sworn to Comyn even by
proxy, and because of your youth, no formal oath may
be required or accepted. I ask you only, then, if you will
abide faithfully by vows sworn in your name, and repeat
them for yourself when you are lawfully of an age to
do so."

The boy's voice was shaking. "I will."

"Then," and he gestured to Valdir to rise and formally
embraced him, kissing him on both cheeks, "I name you
heir to Alton. Is there any to challenge this?"

Gabriel Ardais, a man in his sixties, tall and soldierly
but graying and gaunt, with the pallor of ill-health, said
in a harsh and rusty voice, "I do not challenge, Esteban,
that the boy is lawfully born and looks healthy, and my
fosterling Valentine, who was his playmate at Nevarsin,
tells me he is quick and intelligent. But I like it not, that
the heir to so powerful a Domain should be a minor
child. Your health is uncertain, Esteban; you must consider the possibility that you may not live for Valdir to
reach manhood. A regent to the Domain should be
appointed."

"I am ready to appoint a regent," Esteban said. "My
next heir after Valdir is the unborn son of my daughter
Ellemir. By your leave, my lords, I will designate her
husband, Damon Ridenow, as regent of Alton, and
guardian of Valdir and the unborn child."

"He is not an Alton," Aran Elhalyn protested, and
Esteban answered, "He is nearer kin than many others;
his mother was my youngest sister Camilla. He is my
nephew, and bears *laran*, and he holds marriage-right in
the Domain."

Aran said, "I know Lord Damon. He is no youth, but
a responsible man nearing his fortieth year. He has
borne honorably many responsibilities given to Comyn
sons. But we were not informed in Council of this marriage. May we ask why a marriage between Comyn son
and *comynara* was made in such unseemly haste, and
under only a freemate bond?"

"It was not Council season," Esteban said, "and the
young people did not want to wait half a year."

"Damon," said Lorill Hastur, "if you are to be named regent to a Domain, it would seem more suitable for your marriage to be made lawfully under Council law, *di catenas*. Are you willing to marry Ellemir Lanart with full ceremony?"

Damon replied good-naturedly, his hand on Ellemir's, "I will marry her a dozen times if you will, under any ritual you like, if she will have me."

Ellemir laughed aloud, a merry little ripple. "Can you doubt that, my husband?"

"Then come forward, Damon Ridenow of Serrais." Damon made his way into the central space of the room, and Lorill asked solemnly, "Damon, are you free to accept this obligation? Are you heir to your own Domain?"

"Not within a dozen places," said Damon. "I have four older brothers, and among them, I believe, they have eleven sons, or had when I last counted; it may be more by now. And Lorenz is already twice a grandfather. I will swear allegiance to Alton willingly, if my brother and Lord of Serrais will give me leave."

"Lorenz?" Lorill asked with a glance at the side of the room where the Ridenow lords sat. Lorenz shrugged. "Damon may do as he will. He is of responsible years, and not likely to succeed to the heirship of Serrais. He is married into the Alton Domain. I consent."

Damon glanced at Andrew with a comical lift of one eyebrow, and Andrew picked up his thought: *Surely that is the first time Lorenz has ever approved entirely of anything I did.* But outwardly he was solemn, as befitted this most serious of occasions.

"Kneel, then, Damon Ridenow," Lorill said. "You have been named regent and guardian to the Alton Domain, as nearest of male kin to Valdir-Lewis Lanart-Alton, heir to Alton, and to the unborn son of Ellemir, your lawful wife. Are you prepared to swear allegiance to the lord of the Domain, Warden of Alton, and to renounce all other loyalties save that to the King and the Gods?"

Damon said steadily, "I do so swear."

"Are you prepared to assume wardship of the Domain, should the lawful head of the Domain be unable through age, illness or infirmity to act in such capacity;

and to swear that you will guard and protect the next heirs to Alton with your own life, if the Gods shall ordain it so?"

"I do so swear."

Ellemir, watching from her place, could see the fine sweat at Damon's hairline, and knew that Damon did not want this. He would do it for the sake of the children, Valdir and her son, but he did not want it. And fiercely, to herself, she hoped her father knew what he was doing to Damon!

Lorill Hastur said, "Do you solemnly declare that to the best of your knowledge you are fit to assume this responsibility? Is there any man who will challenge your right to this solemn wardship of the people of your Domain, the people of all the Domains, the people of all Darkover?"

Kneeling, Damon thought, *Who would be truly fit for such a responsibility? Not I, Aldones, Lord of Light, not I! Yet I will do the best I can, I swear it before all the Gods. For Valdir, for Ellemir and her child.*

He said aloud, "I will abide the challenge."

Danvan Hastur, commander of the Honor Guard for the Council, strode to the center of the room, where Damon still knelt, the rainbow light playing over his face. Sword in hand, he called in a loud voice, "Is there any to challenge the wardship of Damon Ridenow-Alton, Regent of Alton?"

Into the silence a young voice said, "I challenge." Damon, startled, feeling Andrew's consternation even from where he sat at the very back of the Alton seats, raised his head to see Dezi step forward, take the sword from Lorill's hand.

"On what grounds?" Lorill inquired. "And by what right? You are not known to me, young man."

Dom Esteban looked at Dezi in dismay. His voice trembled. "Do you not trust me, Dezi, my son?"

Dezi ignored the words and the tenderness in them. "I am Desiderio Leynier, *nedestro* son of Gwennis Leynier by Esteban Lanart-Alton, as the only surviving grown son of the lord of the Domain, I claim the right to act as guardian to my brother and the unborn son of my sister."

Lorill said sternly, "We have no records of any acknowledged *nedestro* sons of Esteban Lanart-Alton save for the two sons of Larissa d'Asturien, who are without *laran* and thus by law excluded from this Council. May I ask why you were never acknowledged?"

"As for that," said Dezi, with a smile that barely escaped insolence, "you must ask my father. But I call the Lady of Arilinn to witness that I am Alton, and bear the gift of the Domain in full measure"

At Lorill's question, Leonie rose, her frown showing her distaste for this proceeding. "It is none of my affair to designate heirships in Comyn, yet since I have been called to witness, I must state that Desiderio speaks truth: he is son to Esteban Lanart and bears the Alton gift."

Esteban said heavily, "I am ready and willing to acknowledge Dezi as my son if this Council will have it so; I brought him here for that purpose. But I do not feel him the most appropriate Guardian for my young son or my unborn grandson. Damon is a man of mature years, Dezi but a youth. I ask Dezi to withdraw the challenge."

"With all respect, Father," Dezi said deferentially, "I cannot."

Damon, kneeling, wondered, what would happen now. Traditionally the challenge could be settled by combat, a formal duel, or one challenger could withdraw, or either one could present evidence to be examined by Council, purporting to prove that the other was unfit. Lorill was explaining this.

"Have you reason to think Damon unfit, Desiderio Leynier, *nedestro* of Alton?"

"I have." Dezi's voice was shrill. "I submit that Damon attempted to murder me, to make his own claim more secure. He knew me Esteban's son, while he was but son-in-law to Alton, and therefore he stripped me of my matrix. It was only my own skill at *laran* which kept him from blood-guilt on a brother-by-marriage."

Oh, my God, thought Andrew, feeling the breath catch in his throat. *That bastard, that Goddamned stinking young bastard. Who but Dezi could cook up something like this?*

Lorill Hastur said, "That is an extremely serious accusation, Damon. You have honorably served the Comyn for many years. We need not even listen to it, if you can give us some explanation."

Damon swallowed and looked up, conscious of the eyes of all of them on his face. He said steadily, "I was sworn to Arilinn; I took oath there to prevent misuse of any matrix. I took it from Dezi under that oath, for he had misused *laran* by forcing his will upon my sister's husband, Ann'dra."

"True," Dezi said defiantly without waiting for the challenge. "My sister Callista is besotted by this come-by-chance from nowhere, a *Terranan*. I sought only to get rid of this fellow from nowhere who has cast such an evil spell on her, so that she may make a marriage worthy of a Comyn lady, not disgrace herself in the bed of a *Terranan* spy."

General uproar. Damon sprang to his feet, enraged, but Dezi stood facing him, defiant, slightly mocking. It seemed that everyone in the Crystal Chamber was talking, shouting, questioning at once. Lorill Hastur again and again vainly commanded silence.

When some semblance of order was restored he said, looking grave, "We must inquire into this matter privately. Very serious charges and counter-charges have been laid. For now, I bid you to disperse, and not to discuss this matter among yourselves. Gossip will not better it. Beware of careless fire in the forest; beware of careless talk even among the wise. But be assured, we will look into the rights and wrongs of this matter, and present it for your judgment within three days from now."

Slowly the room emptied. Esteban deathly pale, looked sadly at Damon and Dezi. He said, "When brothers are at odds, strangers step in to widen the gap. Dezi, how can you do this?"

Dezi set his jaw. He said, "Father, I live only to serve you. Do you doubt me?" He looked at Ellemir, clinging to Damon's arm, then said to Callista, "Some day you will thank me, my sister."

"Sister!" Callista looked Dezi full in the eyes, then, deliberately, she spat in his face and turned away. Laying her fingertips on Andrew's arm, she said clearly, "Take me out of here, my husband. The place stinks of treachery."

"Daughter—" *Dom* Esteban pleaded, but Callista turned her back and Andrew had no choice but to follow. But his heart was pounding, and his thoughts seemed to echo the troubled rhythm: *What now?*

CHAPTER NINETEEN

In their own rooms, Callista turned to Andrew, saying vehemently, "He killed Domenic! I do not know how he managed it, but I am sure of it!"

"There is only one way it could have been done," Damon said, "and I am afraid to believe he was that strong!"

Ellemir asked, "Could he have forced Cathal's mind, made him strike Domenic at a vulnerable spot? He has the Alton gift and can force rapport . . ." But she sounded hesitant, and Callista shook her head.

"Not without killing Cathal, or inflicting so much brain damage that Cathal's very condition would tell the tale."

Damon's face was bleak and unreadable. "Dezi has the talent to do a Keeper's work," he said, "we all saw that when I took his matrix from him. He can handle or modify another's stone, adapt it to his own resonances. I think, left alone with Domenic, injured, but alive, he could not resist the temptation to have one in his hands again. And when he took Domenic's from his throat"— he flinched, and Andrew saw that his hands were shaking—"Domenic's heart stopped with the shock. A perfect, undetectable murder, since there was no known Keeper there, and most people did not know Domenic even possessed a matrix. And it would explain why Dezi is barricaded from me."

Callista's voice shook. "Among telepaths he must go barricaded till the day of his death, a dreadful fate indeed!"

Ellemir said savagely, "Not half so dreadful as the death he gave Domenic!"

"It is worse than you realize," Damon said in a low voice. "Do you think, now that he knows his power, that Valdir is safe? How long will he spare Valdir, now that only Valdir lies between him and the heritage of Alton?

And when he has *Dom* Esteban's ear and perfect trust, who else lies between him and the lordship of the Domain?"

Ellemir turned white, her hands going to her body as if to shield the child who cradled there. "I told you you should have killed him," she said, beginning to cry. Callista looked at Ellemir in consternation.

"It would be all too simple, a few fragile blood vessels to sever, and the unborn child bleeds to death, his link to life gone."

"Don't!" Ellemir cried.

"Why do you think we are so careful, in teaching psi monitors?" Callista asked. "Women in the Towers are careful not to get pregnant during their term of work, but it does happen, of course. And Dezi learned there to monitor—Avarra's mercy, it was I who taught him! And learning the vulnerable spots, learning how *not* to damage mother or child, makes it easy to learn to violate them."

"I wouldn't put it past him," Andrew said, speaking for the first time, "but I wouldn't hang a dog without more proof than we have here. Will there ever be any way to prove it?" Even if Dezi had killed Domenic by taking the matrix from the stunned and unconscious boy, he had only to fling away a bit of dead crystal.

Damon's face was set. "I believe Dezi's own weakness will expose him. True, he could have disposed of the proof, but I do not believe he could give up that kind of power. Would he be able to resist the temptation to have one again in his own hands? Not if I know our Dezi. And he could modify the stone to his use, which means there is still a witness against him. Silent. But a witness."

"Fine," said Andrew sarcastically. "We have only to go to him and say hand over the matrix you killed Domenic to get, like a good boy."

Damon's hand clutched his own matrix as if for reassurance. "If he is carrying a modified matrix the relay screens in Arilinn and the other Towers will show it."

"Fine," Andrew said again. "How far is Arilinn from here? A tenday's ride, or more?"

"It is simpler than that," Callista told him. "There are

relay screens here in the Old Tower of Comyn Castle. In time past, so they say, technicians could teleport themselves between Towers by use of the great screens. It isn't done much anymore. But there are also monitor screens, attuned to those in the other Towers. Any mechanic can link into those and trace any licensed matrix on Darkover." She hesitated. "I cannot . . . I have given back my oath."

Damon was impatient with this technicality. Such a loss to the Towers, such a loss to Callista, but whatever Keeper or mechanic was now in charge of the Old Tower, *she* would observe the prohibition, and there was nothing to be done.

"Who keeps the Old Tower, Callista? I cannot believe that the Mother Ashara would receive us on such an errand."

"No one within living memory has seen Ashara outside the Tower," Callista said. "I think she could no longer leave it if she would, she is so old. I myself have never seen her, except in the screens, nor, I think, has even Leonie. But when last I heard, Margwenn Elhalyn was her under-Keeper; she will tell you what you want to know."

"Margwenn was psi monitor at Arilinn when I was Third there," Damon said. "She went from us to Hali; I did not know she had come here." Technicians, mechanics, monitors were moved from Tower to Tower, as the need was greatest. If Margwenn Elhalyn was not precisely an old friend, at least she knew who he was and it saved lengthy explanations about what he wanted.

He had never been inside the Old Tower of Comyn Castle. Margwenn admitted him to the matrix chamber, a place of ancient screens and lattices, machinery whose very existence had been forgotten since the Ages of Chaos. Damon, his errand forgotten for a moment, stared at it in avid curiosity. Why had all this technology, the ancient science of Darkover, been allowed to sink into obscurity? Even at Arilinn he had not learned to use all these things. True, there were too few technicians and mechanics even to staff the relays which provided communications and generated essential energy for certain technologies, but even if matrix workers were no longer willing, in these self-indulgent days, to give up their lives and live guarded behind walls, surely *some* of these things could be done outside!

Strange heretical thoughts to be thinking in the very center of the ancient science. When their forefathers forbade that very thing, they must have had their reasons!

Margwenn Elhalyn was a slim fair-haired woman of unguessable age, though Damon thought she was a little older than he was himself. She had the cold withdrawnness, the almost hieratic decorum, of all Keepers. "The Mother Ashara cannot see you, her mind sojourns elsewhere much of the time in these days. How may I serve you, Damon?"

Damon hesitated, unwilling to explain his errand and charge Dezi, without proof, of what he suspected. Margwenn had not attended the Council, though she had every right to do so. Many technicians were not interested in politics. Damon had once felt that way himself, that his work was above such base considerations. Now he was not so sure.

Finally he said, "Some confusion has arisen about the whereabouts of certain matrices in the hands of the Alton clan, legitimately issued, but their fate uncertain. Are you familiar with Dezi Leynier, who was admitted to Arilinn for something under a year, some time ago?"

"Dezi?" she said without interest. "Some bastard of Lord Alton's, wasn't he? Yes, I remember. He was dismissed because he could not keep discipline, I heard." She went to the monitor screen, standing motionless before the glassy surface. After a little time lights began to wink, deep inside it, and Damon, watching her face without attempting to follow her in thought, knew she was linked into the relay to Arilinn. Finally she said, "Evidently he has given up his matrix. It is in the hands of a Keeper, not inactivated, but at a very low level."

In the hands of a Keeper. Damon, who had himself lowered its level and put it into a locked and sealed box, metal-bound and tamperproof, understood that perfectly well.

Hands of a Keeper. But any competent technician

could do a Keeper's work. Why should it be surrounded with taboo, ritual, superstitious reverence? Concealing his thoughts from Margwenn, he said, "Now can you check what has become of the matrix of Domenic Lanart?"

"I will try," she said, "but I thought he was dead. His matrix would have died with him, probably."

"I had thought so too," Damon said, "but it was not found on his body. Is it possible that it is also in the hands of a Keeper?"

Margwenn shrugged. "That seems unlikely, although I suppose, knowing Domenic unlikely to use *laran*, she might have reclaimed it and modified it to another's use, or to her own. Although most Keepers prefer to begin with a blank crystal. Where was he tested? Not at Arilinn, surely."

"Neskaya, I think."

Margwenn raised her eyebrows as she went to the screen. It took no telepathic subtlety to follow her thought: *At Neskaya they are likely to do anything.* At last Margwenn turned and said, "Your guess is right, it is in the hands of a Keeper, though it is not in Neskaya. It must have been modified and given to another. It did not die with Domenic, but is fully operative."

And there it was, Damon thought, his heart sinking. A small thing for positive proof of a cold-blooded, fiendish murder.

Not premeditated. There was that small comfort. No one alive could have foreseen that Cathal would strike Domenic unconscious as they practiced. But a sudden temptation . . . and Domenic's matrix survived him, to point unerringly to the one person who could have taken it from his body without himself being killed by it.

Gods above, what a waste! Had *Dom* Esteban been able to overcome his pride, admit to the somewhat shameful circumstances of Dezi's begetting, had he been willing to acknowledge this gifted youngster, Dezi would never have come to this.

Damon thought, with wrenching empathy that the temptation must have been sudden, and irresistible. For a trained telepath being without a matrix was like being deaf, blind, mutilated, and the sight of the unconscious

Domenic had spurred him on to murder. Murder of the one brother who had championed his right to be called brother, who had been his patron and friend.

"Damon, what ails you?" Margwenn was staring at him in amazement. "Are you ill, kinsman?"

He made some civil excuse, thanked her for her help, and went away. She would know soon enough. Zandru's hells, there would be no way to hide this! All the Comyn would soon know, and everyone in Thendara! What scandal for the Altons!

Back in their rooms, his drawn face told Ellemir the truth at once. "It's true, then. Merciful Avarra, what will this do to our father? He loved Dezi. Domenic loved him too."

"I wish I could spare him the knowledge," Damon said wretchedly. "You know why I cannot, Elli."

Callista said, "When Father knows the truth, there will be another murder, that is sure!"

"He loves the boy, he spared him before," Andrew protested. Callista pressed her lips tightly together.

"True. But when I was a little girl Father had a favorite hound. He had reared it by hand from a puppy and it slept on his bed at night, and lay at his feet in the Great Hall. When it grew to be an old dog, however, it became vicious. It took to killing animals in the yards, and once it bit Dorian and drew blood. The *coridom* said it must be destroyed, but he knew how Father loved the old dog, and offered to have it quietly made away with. But Father said, 'No, this is my affair.' He went out into the stables, called the brute to him, and when it came he broke its neck with his own hands." She was silent, thinking of how her Father had cried afterward, the only time she ever saw him weep, except when Coryn died.

But he did not ever shrink from doing what he must.

Damon knew she was right. He might have preferred to spare his father-in-law, but Esteban Lanart was Lord Alton, with wardship, even to life and death, over every man, woman, and child in the Alton Domains. He had never dealt out justice unfairly, but he had never failed to deal it out.

"Come," he said to Andrew, "we must lay it before

him." But when Callista rose to follow them, he shook his head.

"*Breda*, this is an affair for men."

She turned pale with anger. "You dare speak so to me, Damon? Domenic was my brother, so is Dezi. I am an Alton!"

"And I," said Ellemir, "and my child is next heir after Valdir!"

As they turned to the door, Damon found a snatch of song running in his head, incongruous, with a sweet, mournful memory. After a moment he identified it as the song Callista had begun to sing, and had been rebuked:

> How came this blood on your right hand,
>   Brother, tell me, tell me . . .
> It is the blood of my own brothers twain
>   Who sat at the drink with me.

Ellemir had spoken more truly than she knew: It was ill-luck for a sister to sing that song in a brother's hearing. But, looking at the women, Damon thought that like the sister in the old ballad, who had condemned the brotherslayer to outlawry, they would not shrink from the sentence.

It was only a few steps into another part of the suite, but to Damon it seemed a long journey, across a gulf of misery, before they stood before *Dom* Esteban, who looked at them in bewilderment.

"What means this? Why are you all so solemn? Callista, what is wrong with you, *chiya*? Elli, have you been crying?"

"Father," said Callista, white as death, "where is Valdir? And is Dezi near?"

"They are together, I hope. I know you have a grudge against him, Damon," he said, "but after all, the lad has right on his side. I should have done years ago what I propose to do now. He is not old enough to be regent of the Domain, of course, or Valdir's guardian, the idea is preposterous, but once acknowledged he will see reason. And then he will be such a brother to Valdir as he was to my poor Domenic."

"Father," Ellemir said in a low voice, "that is what we fear."

He turned to her in anger. "I thought you, at least, would show a sister's forebearance, Ellemir!" Then he met the eyes of Damon and Andrew, fixed steadily on him. He looked from one to the other and back again, in growing distress and annoyance.

"How dare you!" Then, impatiently, he reached out for contact, read directly from them what they knew. Damon felt the knowledge sink into the old man's mind in one great surge of pain. It was like death, a blinding moment of physical agony. He felt the old man's last thought: *My heart, my heart is surely breaking. I thought that was only an idle word, but I feel it there*, before he slipped into merciful unconsciousness. Andrew, moving swiftly, caught the limp body in his arms as he pitched out of his wheeled chair.

Too shocked to think clearly, he laid him on his bed. Damon was still paralyzed with the, backlash of the Alton lord's pain.

"I think he's dead," Andrew said, shocked, but Callista came and felt his pulse, laid her ear briefly against his chest. "No, the heart still beats. Quickly, Ellemir! Run and fetch Ferrika, she is nearest, but one of you men must go down to the Guard Hall and search for Master Nicol."

She waited beside her father, remembering that Ferrika had warned her about his weakening heart. When the woman came, she confirmed Callista's fear.

"Something has gone wrong in the heart, Callista." In her sympathy she forgot the formal "my lady," remembering that they had played together as children. "He has had too many shocks to endure." She brought stimulant drugs and when Master Nicol came, between them they managed to get a dose into him.

"It's touch and go," the hospital officer warned. "He might die at any moment, or linger like this till Midsummer. Has he had a shock? With respect, Lord Damon, he should have been guarded from the slightest stress or bad news."

Damon felt like demanding how do you guard a telepath against evil news. But Master Nicol was doing his

best, and he would have had no more answer than
Damon himself.

"We will do what we can, Lord Damon, but for now . . .
it is fortunate he had already chosen you regent."

It was like a flood of ice water. He was regent of
Alton, with wardship and sovereignty over the Domain,
till Valdir was declared a man.

Regent. With power of life and death.

No, he thought, flinching with revulsion. It was too
much. He did not want it.

But looking down at the stricken old man, he knew
that duty lay on him. Confronted with proof of Dezi's
treachery, the Alton lord would have acted unflinchingly
to protect the children, young boy and unborn babe, who
were the next heirs to. Alton. As Damon must act. . . .

When Dezi came back with Valdir, he found them all
waiting for him.

"Valdir," said Ellemir gently, "our father lies very ill.
Go and find Ferrika and ask news of him." To their
great relief, the child ran off at once, and Dezi stood
waiting, defiant.

"So now you have your will, Damon. You are regent
of Alton. Or are you? I wonder."

Damon found his voice. "I am warned. Dezi. You cannot serve me as you served Domenic. As regent of Alton
I demand that you give up to me the matrix you stole
from Domenic's body."

He saw comprehension sweep over Dezi's face. Then,
to Damon's horror, he laughed. Damon thought he had
never heard a sound so shocking as that laughter.

"Come and take it, you Ridenow half-man," he
taunted. "You will not find it so easy this time! You
could not take me that way now, even with your Nest
about you!" Damon flinched at the ancient obscenity,
for the women's sake. "Come, I called your challenge in
Council, let us have it here and now! Which of us is to
be regent of Alton? Have you that much strength? Half
monk, half eunuch, they call you!"

Damon knew he had picked up the taunt from Lorenz,
or was it from Damon himself? He found his voice. "If
you kill me, you prove yourself even less fit to be regent.
It is not strength alone, but right and responsibility."

"Oh, have done with that cant!" Dezi scoffed. "Such *responsibility*, I suppose, as my loving father took for me?"

Damon wanted to say that the *dom* had truly loved Dezi enough for his treachery almost to kill him too. But he wasted no words, grasping his own matrix, focusing, striking to alter the resonances of the one Dezi wore. Had stolen.

Dezi felt the touch, struck out a blinding mental blow. Damon went physically to his knees before the impact. Dezi had the Alton gift, the anger which could kill. Fighting panic, he realized that Dezi had grown, was stronger. Like a wolf with a taste for man's flesh, he had to be destroyed at once, lest this ravening beast get among the Comyn. . . .

The room began to cloud, thicken with swirling lines of force between them. He felt himself falter, felt Andrew's strength behind him, even as Andrew was physically holding him upright. Dezi glowed within the fog. He hurled lightnings at the men. Damon felt the ground thinning beneath his feet, felt himself beaten down toward the floor.

Callista stepped between them. She seemed to tower above them all, tall and commanding, her matrix blazing at her throat. Damon saw the matrix in Dezi's hand glow like a live coal, felt it burn through his tunic and into his flesh. Dezi yelled in pain and rage, and for an instant Damon saw Callista as she had been in Arilinn, flickering with the crimson of a Keeper's robes. With the small dagger she wore at her waist she struck at the thong about Dezi's throat. The matrix fell to the floor, blazed like fire when Dezi grabbed for it. Damon felt with Dezi the flare of agony as Dezi's hand began to burn in the flame. The matrix rolled to one side, a useless black dead thing.

And Dezi *disappeared!* Andrew, for a fraction of a second, watched the place where Dezi had vanished, the air still trembling behind him. Then it rang in all their minds, a terrible dying scream of despair and rage. And they *saw* it, as if they had been physically present in that room at Armida.

When Callista had destroyed Domenic's stolen matrix, Dezi could not face being without one again. With his last strength he had teleported himself through the over-world, to materialize at that place where Damon had placed his own for safekeeping—a panic reaction, without rational thought. A moment of considering would have told him it was safely locked away inside a solid, metal-bound strongbox. Two solid objects could not occupy the same space at the same time, not in the solid universe. And Dezi—they all saw it and shuddered with horror—had materialized half in, half out of the box holding the matrix. And even before that despairing dying scream died away, they had all heard the echo in Damon's mind. Dezi lay on the floor of the strong-room at Armida, very completely and very messily dead. Even through his horror Damon found a moment to pity whoever would have to deal with that dreadfully materialized corpse, half in and half out of a solidly locked strongbox which had split his skull like a piece of rotten fruit.

Ellemir had sunk to the floor, moaning with shock and dread. Andrew's first thought was for her. He hurried to her, holding her, trying to pour his strength into her as he had poured it into Damon. Damon slowly picked himself up, staring into nowhere. Callista was staring at her matrix, in horror.

"Now I am truly forsworn . . ." she whispered. "I had given back my oath . . . and I used it to kill. . . ." She began to scream wildly, beating at herself with her fists, tearing at her face with her nails. Andrew thrust Ellemir gently into a low chair, ran to Callista. He tried to grasp her flailing arms. There was a shower of blue sparks and he landed, stunned, against the opposite wall. Callista, looking at him, her eyes wide and half mad with horror, shrieked again, and her nails ripped down her cheeks, blood following them in a thin, scarlet line.

Damon sprang forward. He grasped her wrists in one hand, held the struggling, screaming woman immobile, and with his open hand slapped her, hard, across the face. The screams died in a gasp. She slumped and he held her upright, cradling her head on his shoulder.

Callista began to sob. "I had given back my oath," she whispered. "I could not refrain. . . . I moved against him *as Keeper*. Damon, I am still Keeper despite my oath . . . my oath!"

"Damn your oath!" said Damon, and shook her. "Callista! Stop that! Don't you even know you saved all our lives?"

She stopped crying, but her face, ghastly with streaked blood and tears, was drawn into a mask of horror. "I am forsworn. I am forsworn."

"We're all forsworn," Damon said. "It's too late for that! Damn it, Callie, pull yourself together! I have to see if that bastard has managed to kill your father too. And Ellemir—" His breath caught in his throat. Shocked into compliance, Callista went quickly to where Ellemir lay motionless in the chair.

After a moment she raised her head. "I do not think the child has suffered. Go, Damon, and see if all is well with our father."

Damon moved toward the other rooms of the suite. But he knew without moving that *Dom* Esteban was so near death that nature had provided its own shield. He had been spared all knowledge of that battle to the death. Damon, however, needed a moment alone, to come to terms with this new knowledge.

Without thought, he had moved against a Keeper, an Alton, had moved, automatically, to shake her out of her hysteria, to take the full responsibility.

It is I who am Keeper of these four. Whatever we may do, it is on my responsibility.

Before long, he knew, he would be called to account for what he had done. Every telepath from Dalereuth to the Hellers must have witnessed that death.

And already he had alerted them to what was happening among the four of them, when with Andrew and Dezi he had built that landmark in the overworld, to heal the frostbitten men. Sorrow gnawed at him again, for the boy so terribly and tragically dead. Aldones, Lord of Light . . . Dezi, Dezi, what a waste, what a tragic waste of all his gifts. . . .

But even sorrow gave way to the knowledge of what he had done, and what he had become.

Exiled from Arilinn, he had built his own Tower. And Varzil had hailed him as *tenerézu*. Keeper. He was Keeper, Keeper of a forbidden Tower.

CHAPTER TWENTY

Damon had known it would not be long in coming, and it was not.

Ellemir had quieted. She sat in the chair where Andrew had laid her, only gasping a little with shock. Ferrika, summoned, looked at her with dismay.

"I don't know what you have been doing, my lady, but whatever it is, unless you want to lose this baby too, you had better go to bed and stay there." She began gently to move her hands over Ellemir's body. To Damon's surprise, she did not touch her, keeping an inch or two between Ellemir's body and her fingertips, finally saying with a faint frown, "The baby is all right. In fact, *you* are in worse case than *he* is. I will send for a hot meal for you, and you eat it and go to—" She broke off, staring at her hands in astonishment and awe.

"In the name of the Goddess, what am I doing!"

Callista, recalled to responsibility, said, "Don't worry, Ferrika, your instinct is good. You have been around us so much, it is not surprising. If you had a trace of *laran* it would surely have wakened. Later I will show you how to do it very precisely. On a pregnant woman it is a little tricky."

Ferrika blinked, staring at Callista. Her round, snub-nosed face looked a little bewildered, and she took in the dreadfully bloody scratches down Callista's face, blinking. "I am no *leronis*."

"Nor am I now," Callista said gently, "but I have been taught, as you shall be. It is the most useful of skills for a midwife. I am sure you have more *laran* than you know." She added, "Come, let us take Ellemir to her room. She must rest, and," she added, raising her hands to her bleeding face, "I must see to these, too. And when you send for food for Ellemir, Damon, send for some for me too; I am hungry."

Damon watched them go. He had long suspected Ferrika had some *laran*, but he was grateful it was Callista who had decided to take the responsibility for teaching her.

There was no reason that any person with the talent should not have the training, Comyn or no. Because things had been done this way since the Ages of Chaos was no reason they must continue to be done this way till Darkover sank into the Last Night! Andrew had become one of them, and he was a Terran. Ferrika had been born on the Alton estates, a commoner and, worse, a Free Amazon. But she had everything that was needful to make her one of them too: she had *laran*.

Comyn blood? Look what it had done for Dezi!

Aware that after the terrific matrix battle he too was famished, he sent for some food and when it came he ate it without caring what it was, watching Andrew do the same. Neither spoke of Dezi. Damon thought that at some future time *Dom* Esteban would have to know that the bastard son he had cherished and defended had died for his crimes. But he need never know the dreadful details.

Andrew ate without tasting, aware of the terrible hunger and draining of matrix linking, but he felt sick even while his starved body put away the food with mechanical intensity. His thoughts ran bitter counterpoint; he saw again Damon shaking Callista, holding her against self-mutilation. The memory of Callista's bleeding face made him sick.

He had left it to Damon to care for her, thinking of no one but Ellemir. Elli, bearing his child. He had touched Callista and she had thrown him across the room. Damon had grabbed her like a caveman, and she had quieted right down. He wondered, despairing, if they had *both* married the wrong women.

After all, he thought, his mind plodding miserably along an all too familiar track, they were both Tower-trained, both top-rank telepaths, understanding each other. Elli and he were on a different level, just ordinary people, not understanding these things. He glanced at Damon with a sense of resentful inferiority.

He killed a boy this morning. Horribly. And he sat there calmly eating his dinner!

Damon was aware of Andrew's resentment, but did not try to follow his thoughts. He knew and accepted that there were times, perhaps there would always be times, when Andrew, for no reason he could understand, suddenly went apart from them, no longer a beloved brother but a desperately alienated stranger. He knew it was part of the price they both paid for the attempt to extend their brotherhood across two conflicting worlds, two very different societies. It might always be this way. He had tried to bridge the gap, and it always made things worse. Now all he could do, and he knew it sadly, was to leave it to run its course.

When the door opened again, Damon raised his head in irritation which he quickly controlled—the servant, after all, had his work to do. "Do you want to take the dishes? A moment . . . Andrew, have you finished?"

"Su serva, dom," the man said, "the Lady of Arilinn and her *leroni* from the Tower have begged the favor of a word with you, Lord Damon."

Begged? Damon thought skeptically, not likely. "Tell them I will see them in the outer chamber in a few minutes." Privately he thanked whatever God might be listening that Callista was with Ellemir and they had not asked for her. If Leonie saw those scratches on her face . . . "Come along, Andrew," he said. "They probably want all four of us, but they don't know it yet."

Leonie led the group. Margwenn Elhalyn was with her, and a couple of telepaths from Arilinn who had come since Damon's time, and one, a man named Rafael Aillard, who had been there with him, though he was now stationed at Neskaya. It was incredible, Damon thought, that at one time this man was part of his circle, closer to Damon than blood kin, a beloved friend. Leonie was veiled and this struck Damon with irritation. Surely it was seemly for a *comynara* and Keeper to go veiled among strangers. He could have understood it if Margwenn had veiled herself. But Leonie?

But he spoke as if it were an ordinary thing to have his chamber invaded by four strange telepaths and the Keeper of Arilinn. "Kinswoman, you lend me grace. How may I serve you?"

Leonie said bluntly, "Damon, you were sent from Arilinn years ago. You have *laran*, and you have been trained in the use of a matrix, so you may not be forbidden to use it for such personal purposes as are lawful. But the law forbids that any serious matrix operations shall be undertaken outside the safeguards of a Tower. And now you have used your matrix to kill."

As a matter of fact, he thought, it had been Callista who killed Dezi. But that didn't matter. It was his responsibility. He said so.

"I am regent of Alton. I put to death, lawfully, a murderer who had killed one and attempted to kill another within the Domain. I claim privilege."

"Privilege denied," Margwenn said. "You should have slain him in a lawful duel, with legitimate weapons. You are not empowered, outside a Tower, to use a matrix for an execution."

"The attempted murder, and the murder, were both done by matrix. Being Tower-trained, I am sworn to prevent such misuse."

"Misuse to prevent misuse, Damon?"

"I deny that it was misuse."

"That decision was not yours to make," Rafael Aillard said. "If Dezi had broken the laws of Arilinn—and from what I knew of him I find it easy to believe, but that is neither here nor there—you should have laid it before us, and left it to us to take action."

Damon's answer was monosyllabic and obscene. Andrew had never believed Damon would speak so in the presence of women. "The first offense was committed in my presence. He sought to force his will on my sworn brother, driving him into a storm without shelter; only good luck saved him from death. And now he has slain my wife's brother, the heir to Alton, and everyone came near to letting it pass as an unlucky accident! Who but I should deal the punishment? All my life I have been taught that it is my responsibility to deal with an offense against kin. Or what else is Comyn?"

"But," said Leonie, "your training was given you for use within a Tower. When you were sent forth—"

"When I was sent forth, was I to spend the rest of my life without the knowledge and skill of my training? If I could not be trusted with the knowledge, why was it given? Should I live the rest of my life like a toddler in a walking-harness, not moving unless my nurse holds the reins?" He looked directly at Leonie. He did not say it aloud, but everyone there could follow it: *I should never have been sent from Arilinn. I was dismissed upon a pretext which I now know to have been false.* Aloud he said, "When I was sent away, I was set free to act upon my own responsibility, like any Comyn son."

And even now, Leonie, you will not face me.

How dare you! The woman put back her veil. She had, Damon thought with detachment, quite lost the last remnants of her remarkable beauty. She drew herself to her full height—an inch or two taller than Damon—and said, "I will not hear this quibbling!"

Damon said with cold, deliberate insolence, "I did not invite any of you here. Is the guardian of Alton to listen and keep his tongue behind his teeth, like a naughty child being scolded, in his own chamber?"

Leonie frowned. "Would you rather we formally lay these matters before all the Comyn in the Crystal Chamber?"

Damon shrugged and said, "Speak, then." He nodded to chairs about the room. "Will you sit? I have no taste for discussing weighty matters while I stand shifting from one foot to another like a cadet on punishment detail. And may I offer you refreshment?"

"Thank you, no." But they took chairs, and Damon sank into another. Andrew remained standing. Without knowing it, he had fallen into the traditional stance of a paxman behind his lord, a step behind where Damon sat. The others saw it and frowned, as Leonie began.

"When you left Arilinn, we trusted you to observe the laws, and in general we made no complaint. From time to time we followed your matrix in the monitor screens, but most of the things you had done were minor and lawful."

"Excellent," said Damon with sarcastic emphasis. "I am relieved to know you thought it lawful for me to use my matrix to lock my strongbox, to find my way through a wood if I mistook my path, or to stanch the bleeding of a friend's wound!"

Rafael Aillard scowled at Damon. "If you will hear

us without trying to make bad jokes, we will have done with this painful task more quickly!"

Damon said, "I am not short of time to bear what you have to say. Still, my wife is ill and pregnant, and my father-in-law at death's very threshold, so it is true I could spend what remains of this day more profitably than listening to this pile of stable-sweepings you are mouthing at me!"

"I am sorry Ellemir is not well," Leonie said, "but is Esteban so seriously ill as all that? In the Council chamber but this day, he was hearty and strong."

His mouth set in hard lines, Damon said, "The news of the treachery done by the bastard son he had loved laid him low. It is possible he will live through the day, but he is not likely to see another winter's snow."

"So you took it on yourself to avenge him and act as Dezi's executioner," Leonie said. "I have no grief for him. He had not been in Arilinn a tenday before I saw such flaws in his character that I knew he would not stay."

"And, knowing this, you took the responsibility of training him? Who picks a tool unsuited to a task should not complain if it does nothing more than cut the hand that holds it." Remotely he realized that as recently as Midwinter, it would have been unthinkable to question the motives and decisions of any Keeper, certainly not the Lady of Arilinn.

Margwenn said impatiently, "What would you have had us do? You know it is not easy to find Comyn sons and daughters with full *laran*, and whatever Dezi's faults, his gifts were great."

"You would have done better to train a commoner with less of noble blood, and more of decency and character!"

Rafael said, "You know that no one not of Comyn blood can come within the Veil at Arilinn."

"Then, damn it," said Damon, thinking of Ferrika's gentle touch as she monitored Ellemir, "maybe it's time to tear down the Veil and make some changes at Arilinn!"

Leonie's lip curled in distaste. "Where do you get these ideas, Damon? Is this what comes of taking a *Ter-*

ranan into your household?" But she gave him no time
to answer.

"We did not complain when you used your matrix
lawfully. Even when you took Dezi's matrix from him,
we made no complaint. But you were not content with
that. You have done many things unlawful. You have
taught this *Terranan* some rudiments of matrix technology. You will recall that Stefan Hastur decreed, when
first they came here, that no Terran was even to be
allowed to witness any matrix operation."

"May he rest in peace," Damon said, "but I am not
willing to give to a dead man the right to be the warden
of my conscience."

Rafael said angrily, "Should we reject the wisdom of
our fathers?"

"No, but they lived as they chose when they were
alive, and did not consult me about my wishes and
needs, and I shall do the same with them. Certainly I
will not enshrine them as gods, and treat their lightest
word as the *cristoforos* treat the nonsense from their
Book of Burdens!"

"What is your excuse for training this *Terranan*?"
Margwenn asked.

"What excuse do I need? He has *laran*, and an untrained telepath is a menace to himself and to everyone
around him."

"Was it he who encouraged Callista to break her
sworn word? She had pledged to lay down her work
forever."

"I am not the warden of Callista's conscience either,"
Damon said. "The knowledge is in her mind, I cannot
take it from her." Again, with great bitterness, he flung
the question at Leonie: "Should she spend her life
counting holes in linen towels, and making spices for
herb-bread?"

Margwenn grimaced with contempt. "It seems that
was Callista's choice. She was not forced to give back
her oath. She was not even raped. She made a free
choice, and she must live with it."

You are all fools, Damon thought wearily, and made
no effort to conceal the thought. He saw it reflected in
Leonie's eyes.

"One charge is so serious that it makes all the others trivial, Damon. You have built a Tower in the overworld. You are working an unlawful mechanic's circle, Damon, outside a Tower built by Comyn decree, and outside the oaths and safeguards ordained since the Ages of Chaos. The penalty for that is a dreadful one. I am reluctant to impose it on you. Will you, then, dissolve the links of your circle, destroy the forbidden Tower you have made, and swear to us that you will do so no more? If you will pledge this to me, I will ask no further penalty."

Damon rose to his feet. He was standing braced, as he had done when he faced Dezi's murderous onslaught *This*, he thought, *I face standing up*.

"Leonie, when you sent me from the Tower, you ceased to be my Keeper, even the keeper of my conscience. What I have done, I have done on my own responsibility. I am a matrix technician, trained at Arilinn, and I have lived all my life under the precepts taught to me there. My conscience is clear, I will make no such pledge as you ask."

"Since the Ages of Chaos," Leonie said, "it has been forbidden for any circle of matrix workers to operate except in a Tower sanctioned by Comyn decree. Nor can we allow you to take into your circle a woman who once was Keeper and who has given back her oath. By the laws handed down since the days of Varzil the Good, this is not allowed. It is unthinkable, it is obscene! You must destroy the Tower, Damon, and pledge me never to work with it again. As regent of Alton, and Callista's guardian, I call upon you to make certain that she never again violates the conditions upon which her oath was given back."

Damon said, keeping his voice steady with an effort, "I do not accept your judgment."

"Then I must invoke a worse," Leonie said. "Do you wish me to lay this before the Council, and the workers in all the Towers? You know the penalty if you are adjudged guilty there. Once all this is set in motion, even I cannot save you," she added, looking directly at him for the first time since the conversation had begun. "But I know that if you give your word, you will not break

it. Give me your word, Damon, to break this unlawful
circle, to withdraw all force from your Tower in the
overworld, and pledge me personally to use your matrix
from this day forth only for such things as are lawful
and come within the limits allotted; and I give you my
word in turn that I will proceed no further, whatever
you have done."

Your word, Leonie? What is your word worth?

It was like a blow in the face. The Keeper turned pale.
Her voice was trembling. "You defy me, Damon?"

"I do," he said. "You have never inquired into my
motives, you have chosen to ignore them. You talk of
Varzil the Good. I do not think you know half as much
about him as I do. Yes, I defy you, Leonie. I will answer
these charges at the proper time. Lay them before the
Council, if it pleases you, or before the Towers, and I
will be ready to answer them."

Her face was deathly white. *Like a skull*, Damon
thought.

"Be it so then, Damon. You know the penalty. You
will be stripped of your matrix, and so that you cannot
do as Dezi has done, the *laran* centers of your brain
will be burned away. On your own head be it, Damon,
and all of these may bear witness that I tried to save
you."

She turned, moving out of the chamber. The others
followed in her wake. Damon stood unmoving, his face
rigid and unyielding, till they were gone. He managed
to maintain the cold dignity until the sound of their steps
in the outer rooms had died away. Then, moving like a
drunken man, he reeled into the inner room of the suite.

He heard Andrew cursing, a steady stream of exple-
tives in what he supposed was Terran—he did not know
a word of the language—but no one with *laran* could
possibly misunderstand their meaning. He moved past
Andrew, flung himself facedown on a divan, and lay
there, his face in his hands, not moving. Horror surged
in him; his stomach heaved with nausea.

All his defiance now seemed a child's bravado. He
knew, beyond doubt or question, that he would find no
way to answer the charges, that they would find him
guilty, that he would incur the penalty.

Blinded. Deafened. Mutilated. To go through life without *laran*, prisoner forever in his own skull, intolerably alone forever . . . to live as a mindless animal. He clutched himself in agony. Andrew came and stood beside him, troubled, only partially aware what was distressing him.

"Damon, don't. Surely the Council will let you explain; they'll know you did the only thing you could do."

Damon only moaned in dread. It seemed that all the fears of his life, which he had been taught it was not manful to acknowledge, surged over him in one great breaking wave which was drowning him. The fears of a lonely, unwanted child, of a lonely boy in the cadets, clumsy and unloved, tolerated only as Coryn's chosen friend; all his life holding fear at bay lest he be thought, or think himself, less than a man. The fear and self-doubt lest Leonie should somehow look beneath his control, detect his forbidden passion and desire, the guilt and loss when she had sent him from Arilinn, telling him he was not strong enough for this work, feeding the knowledge of his own weakness, the fear he had smothered always. The repressed fear of all the years in the Guards, knowing himself no soldier, no swordsman. The dreadful guilt of fleeing, leaving his Guardsmen to face death in his place. . . .

All his life. All his life he had been afraid. Had there ever been so much as a day when he was not aware that he was a coward vainly pretending not to be afraid, pretending bravado so no one could see what a cringing worm he was, what a helpless sham, what a poor thing wearing the shape of a man? His life mattered so little to him, he would rather have faced death than expose himself as the craven, shameful weakling he was.

But now they had threatened the one thing he truly could not bear, would not bear, would not endure. It would be easier to die now, to put his knife through his throat, rather than live blinded, mutilated, a corpse walking in the pretense of life.

Slowly he became aware, through the fog of panic and dread, that Andrew was kneeling at his side, troubled and pale. He was pleading, but the words could not reach Damon through the deadly fog of fear.

How Andrew must despise him, he thought. He was so strong. . . .

Dismayed, Andrew watched Damon's silent struggle. He tried to reason with him, but he knew he simply wasn't getting through. Did Damon even *hear* him? Trying to break through to him, he sat beside Damon, bent to put an arm around him.

"Don't, don't," he said, clumsily. "It's all right, Damon, I'm here." And then, feeling awkward and shy as he always did at any hint of the closeness between them, he said, almost in a whisper, "I won't let them hurt you, *bredu*."

Damon's agony of frozen terror broke, overwhelming them both. He sobbed convulsively, the last remnants of self-control gone. Shaken, Andrew tried to withdraw, thinking that Damon wouldn't want Andrew to see him like this, then he realized that was the last vestige of his Terran thinking. He *could not* withdraw from Damon's pain, because it was his own pain, a threat to Damon a threat to himself. He must accept Damon's weakness and fear as he accepted everything else about him, as he accepted his love and concern.

Yes, love. He knew now, holding Damon sobbing against him, Damon's terror washing through him like an invading tidal wave, he loved Damon as he loved himself, as he loved Callista and Ellemir—he was a very part of them. From the very beginning, *Damon* had known and accepted this, but he, Andrew, had always held back, had told himself Damon was his friend, but that there were limits to friendship, places never to be touched.

He had resented it when Damon and Ellemir had merged with his attempt to make love to Callista, had tried to isolate himself with her, feeling that his love for her was something he couldn't, didn't want to share. He had resented Damon's closeness to Callista, and had never, he knew now, understood precisely what had prompted Ellemir to make the offer she had made. He had been embarrassed, shamed when Damon found him with Ellemir, even though he had taken his consent for granted. He had regarded his relationship with Ellemir as something apart from Damon, as it was apart from

Callista. And when Damon had tried to share his euphoria, his overflowing love for them all, had tried to express Andrew's own unspoken wish—*I wish I could make love to you all*—he had rebuffed him with unimaginable cruelty, disrupting the fragile link.

He was even wondering if they had both married the wrong women. But Andrew was the one who was wrong, he knew now.

They were not two couples, changing partners. It was the four of them, all of them. They belonged together, and the link was as strong between Damon and him as between either of them and the women.

Maybe even, and he felt the thought surface in absolute terror, daring a kind of self-knowledge he had never allowed himself before, stronger. Because they could see themselves reflected in each other. Find a kind of affirmation of the reality of their own manhood. He knew now what Damon meant when he said he cherished Andrew's maleness as he cherished the femininity of the women. And it wasn't what Andrew was afraid it was.

For it was just this, suddenly, that he knew he loved in Damon, gentleness and violence combined, the very affirmation of manhood. It now seemed incredible that he could ever have found Damon's touch a threat to his manhood. It confirmed, rather, something they shared, another way of stating to one another what they both *were*. He should have welcomed it as a way of closing the circle, of sharing the awareness of what they all meant to one another. But he had rebuffed him, and now Damon, in the terror which he could not share with the women, could not even turn to him to find strength. And where would he turn, if not to a sworn brother?

"*Bredu*," he whispered again, holding Damon with the fierce protectiveness he had felt from the first toward him, but had never known how to express. His own eyes were blinded with tears. The enormity of this commitment frightened him, but he would not turn back.

Bredin. There was nothing like this relationship on earth. Once, trying for analogy, he had mentioned to Damon the rite of blood brotherhood. Damon had shud-

dered with revulsion, and said, his voice trembling with
loathing, "That would be the ultimate forbidden thing
between us, to shed a brother's blood. Sometimes *bredin*
exchange knives, as a pledge that neither can ever strike
at the other, since the knife you bear is your brother's
own." Yet, trying to understand, through the revulsion,
what blood brotherhood meant to Andrew, he had conceded that, yes, the emotional weight was the same. Andrew, thinking in his own symbols because he could not
yet share Damon's, thought now as he held him that he
would give the last of his blood for Damon, and that
would horrify him, as what Damon had tried to give him
had frightened Andrew.

Slowly, slowly, all that was in Andrew's mind filtered
through to Damon. He understood now, he was one of
them at last. And as Andrew held him, letting the barriers slowly dissolve, Damon's terror receded.

He was not alone. He was Keeper of his own Tower
circle, and he drew confidence from Andrew, finding his
own strength and manhood again. No longer bearing the
burden of all the others, but *sharing* the weight of what
they were.

He could do anything now, he thought and, feeling
Andrew's closeness, amended out loud, "*We* can do anything." He drew a long breath, raised himself, and drew
Andrew to him in a kinsman's embrace, kissing him on
the cheek. He said softly, "Brother."

Andrew grinned, patted him on the back. "You're all
right," he said. The words were meaningless, but Damon
felt what was behind them.

"What I said about blood brotherhood once," said
Andrew, struggling for words, "it's . . . the same blood,
as of brothers . . . blood either would shed *for* the
other."

Damon nodded, accepting. "Kin-brother," he said
gently, "Blood brother, if you wish. *Bredu.* Only it is life
we share, not blood. Do you understand?" But the
words didn't matter, nor the particular symbols. They
knew what they were to one another, and it didn't
need words.

"We have got to prepare the women for this," Damon
said. "If they bring those charges in Council—and make

those threats—and Ellemir is not warned, she could miscarry or worse. We must decide how we will face this. But the important thing"—his hand went out to Andrew again—"is that we face it together. All of us."

CHAPTER TWENTY-ONE

For three days Esteban Lanart hung between life and death. Callista, watching at his side—Ferrika had forbidden Ellemir to sit up with him—monitoring the apparently dying man, ascertained that the great artery from the heart was partially blocked. There would be a way to reverse the damage, but she was afraid to try.

Late in the evening of the third day he opened his eyes and saw her at his side. He tried to move, and she put out a hand to prevent him.

"Lie still, dear Father. We are with you."

"I missed . . . Domenic's funeral . . ." he whispered, then she saw memory flood back, with a spasm of sorrow crossing his face. "Dezi," he whispered, "wherever I was, I . . . I think I felt him die, poor lad. I am not guiltless. . . ."

Callista enfolded his rough hand in her own slender fingers. "Father, whatever his crimes or wrongs, he is at peace. Now you must think only of yourself, Valdir needs you." She could see that even this little talking had exhausted him, but under the faded lips and bluish pallor the old giant was still there, rallying. He said, "Damon . . ." and she knew what he wanted and reassured him quickly. "The Domain is safe in his hands and all is well."

Satisfied, he slipped back into sleep, and Callista thought that Council must accept Damon as regent. There was no one else with the slightest claim. Andrew was a Terran; even if he had had any skills at government, they would not have accepted him. Dorian's young husband was a *nedestro* of Ardais, and knew nothing of Armida, whereas it had been Damon's second home. But Damon's regency still hung under the shadow Leonie had threatened, and even as she wondered how soon the showdown would come, Damon opened the door in the outer suite and beckoned.

"Leave Ferrika with him and come."

In the outer room he said, "They have sent for us in the Crystal Chamber, an hour from now, for me and Andrew. I think we should all go, Callista."

In the bleak light her eyes hardened, no longer blue but a cold flashing gray. "Do I stand accused of oath-breaking?"

He nodded. "But as regent of Alton I am your guardian, and your husband is my sworn man. You need not face the charges unless you choose." He grasped her shoulders between his own. "Understand this, Callista, I am going to defy them! Have you the courage to defy them too? Are you strong enough to stand by me, or are you going to collapse like a wet rag and lend strength to our accusers?"

His voice was implacable, and his hands on her shoulders hurt her. "We can have the courage of what we have done, and defy them, but if you do not, you will lose Andrew, you know, and me. Do you want to go back to Arilinn, Callista?" He put his hand up to her face and traced, with a light finger, the red nail-marks on her cheek. He said, "You have still the option, for you are still a virgin. That door remains open until you close it."

Her hand went to the matrix at her throat. "I gave back my oath of my own free will; I never thought to break it."

"It would have been easy to make a clear choice, once and forever," Damon said. "It is not so easy to do when you must do so now. But you are a woman and under wardship. Is it your will that I answer for you to the Council, Callista?"

She flung off his hand. "I am *comynara*," she said, "and I was Callista of Arilinn. I need no man to answer for me!" She turned and walked toward the room she shared with Andrew. "I will be ready!"

Damon went toward his own room. He had roused her defiance deliberately, but he faced the knowledge that it might as easily turn against them.

His own instinct of defiance was high too. He would not face his accusers like some sneak thief dragged to judgment! He dressed in his best, tunic and breeches of leather dyed in the colors of his Domain, a jeweled dagger belted at his waist. He rummaged in his belongings for a neck-ornament set with firestones, and in a drawer came upon something wrapped in a cloth.

It was the bundle of dried *kireseth* blossoms he had taken from Callista's still-room, without knowing why.

He had acted on an impulse he still did not understand, not sure whether it had been a flash of precognition or something worse. He had not been able to explain to her, or to anyone else, why he had done it.

But now, as he stood holding them in his hands, he knew. He never knew whether it was the faintest whiff of the resins from the cloth—it was widely known to stimulate clairvoyance—or whether it was just that his mind, now holding all the information, had suddenly moved to synthesize it all without his conscious effort. But suddenly he *knew* what Varzil had been trying to tell him, and what the Year's End ritual must have been.

Unlike Callista, he knew precisely *why* the use of *kireseth* was forbidden, except when distilled and fractioned into the volatile essence known as *kirian*. As *Dom* Esteban's stories had reminded them, *kireseth*, the blue starflower traditionally given by Cassilda to Hastur in the legend—called the golden bell when the flowers hung covered with their golden pollen—*kireseth*, among other things, was a powerful aphrodisiac, breaking down inhibitions and controls, and now all the links in the chain were clear.

The paintings in the chapel. *Dom* Esteban's stories, and the indignation they had roused in Ferrika, sworn to the Free Amazons, who did not marry and regarded marriage as a form of slavery. The singular illusion shared by Andrew and Callista at the time of the winter blooming, only now Damon knew it had *not* been an illusion, despite the clearing of Callista's channels immediately afterward. And Varzil's advice. . . .

The key was the taboo. Not forbidden because of uncleanness and lewd associations, as he had always thought, but forbidden because of sanctity.

Ellemir said behind him, nervously, "It is time. What have you there, beloved?"

Guilty with the memory of the taboo which had lain

heavy on him since childhood, he thrust the flowers quickly into the drawer, still wrapped in their cloth. The same instinct which had prompted him to dress in his best for his accusers had prompted her too, he was glad to see. She wore a gown fit for a festival, cut low across the breasts. Her hair, low on her neck, was a heavy, gleaming coil. Her pregnancy was obvious even to the most casual observer by now, but she was not ungainly. She was beautiful, a proud Comyn lady.

When he met with Andrew and Callista in the outer room of the suite, he saw that the same instinct had prompted them all. Andrew wore his holiday suit of dull grayed satin, but Callista outshone them all.

Damon had never thought the formal crimson of a Keeper became her. She was too pale, and the brilliant color made her look washed out, a dimmer reflection of her beautiful twin. He had never thought Callista beautiful; it confused him that Andrew thought her so. She was too thin, too much like the stiff child he had known in the Tower, with a virginal rigidity which made her, to Damon, unattractive. At Armida, she chose her clothes carelessly, thick old tartan skirts and heavy shawls. He sometimes wondered if she wore Ellemir's castoffs because she had so little interest in her appearance.

But for the Council she had put on a dress of grayed blue, with a veil of the same color, only thinner, woven with metallic threads that gleamed and twinkled as she moved, and her hair blazed like flame. She had done something to her face to conceal the long red scratches there, and there was an abnormally high color in her cheeks. Was it vanity or defiance which had prompted her to paint her face this way, so that her paleness would not seem the pallor of fear? Star-sapphires gleamed at her throat and she wore her matrix bared, blazing out from among them. As they paced into the Council chamber, Damon felt proud of them all, and willing to defy all of Darkover, if need be.

It was Lorill Hastur who called them all to order, saying, "Serious charges have been laid against you all. Damon, are you willing to answer these charges?"

Looking up at the Hastur seats, and Leonie's implacable face, Damon knew that to explain and justify, as he had intended, would be a waste of time. His only chance was to seize and hold the initiative.

"Would any hear me, if I did?"

Leonie said, "For what you have done there can be no explanation and no excuse. But we are inclined to be lenient, if you will submit yourself to our judgment, you and these others whom you have led into rebellion against the most sacred laws of Comyn." She was looking at Callista as if she had never seen her before.

Through the silence Andrew thought, *Prisoners at the bar, have you anything to say before judgment is passed on you?*

It was on him that Lorill first turned his eyes.

"Andrew Carr, your offense is serious, but you acted in ignorance of our laws. You shall be turned over to your own people, and if you have broken none of *their* laws, you shall go free, but we will ask that you be sent off our world at once.

"Callista Lanart, you have merited a sentence equivalent to Damon's. But Leonie has interceded for you. Your intended marriage, being unconsummated"—how, Damon wondered, had Lorill known that?—"has no force in law. We declare it null and void. You shall return to Arilinn, with Leonie making herself personally responsible for your good behavior.

"Damon Ridenow, for your own offenses, and the offenses of these whom you have led into disobedience, you merit death or mutilation under the old laws. You are here offered a choice. You may surrender your matrix at once, with a Keeper to safeguard your life and reason, so that you may live out your life as regent of Alton, and guardian of the Alton heir your wife bears. If you refuse this, it will be taken from you by force. Should you survive, the *laran* centers of your brain will be burned away, to prevent any further abuse."

Ellemir gave a low cry of dismay. Lorill looked at her with something like compassion, and said, "Ellemir Lanart, as for you, being misled by your husband, we impose no sentence save this: that you shall cease to meddle in matters outside the sphere of women, and turn your thoughts to your only duty at this time, to safeguard your coming child, who is heir to Alton. Since your father lies ill and your only surviving brother is a minor child, and your husband under our sentence, we place you under wardship of Lord Serrais, and you shall return to Serrais to bear your child. Meanwhile, I have chosen three respectable matrons of Comyn to care for you until sentence has been carried out on your husband: Lady Rohana Ardais, Jerana, Princess of Elhalyn, and my own son's wife, Lady Cassilda Hastur. Allow them now to take you from this chamber, Lady Ellemir. What is to come may prove disturbing, even dangerous for a woman in your condition."

Lady Cassilda, a pretty, dark-haired woman, about Ellemir's age, and herself heavily pregnant, held out her hand to Ellemir. "Come with me, my dear."

Ellemir looked at Cassilda Hastur and back at Damon. "May I speak, Lord Hastur?"

Lorill nodded.

Ellemir's voice sounded as light and childish as ever, but determined. "I thank the matrons for their kind concern, but I decline their good offices. I will stay with my husband."

"My dear," Cassilda Hastur said, "your loyalty does you credit. But you must think of your child."

"I *am* thinking of my child," Ellemir said, "of all our children, Cassilda, yours and mine, and the life we want for them. Have any of you bothered to think, really *think* about what Damon is doing?"

Damon, listening incredulously—he had poured his heart out to her, the night he healed the frostbitten men, but he had not believed she really understood—heard her say:

"You know and I know how hard it is to find telepaths in these days, for the Towers. Even those who have *laran* are reluctant to give up their lives and live behind walls, and who can blame them? I would not want to do it myself. I want to live at Armida and have children to live there after me. And I do not want to see *their* lives torn by that terrible choice, either, to know that they must shirk one or the other duty to their Domain. But there is so much for telepaths to do, and no one is doing it. They need not all be done behind the walls of a Tower, indeed some of them *cannot* be done there. But because so many people believe that is the only way to use *laran*, the work is simply not being done at all, and the people of the Domains are suffering because it is not done. Damon has found a way to make it available to everyone. *Laran* need not be a kind of . . . of mysterious sorcery, hidden inside the Towers. If I, who am a woman, and uneducated, and the lesser of twins, can be taught to use it, as I have been, a little, then there must be many, many, who could do, it. And—"

Margwenn Elhalyn rose in her place. She was very pale. "Must we sit and listen to this . . . this blasphemy? Must we who have given our lives to the Towers sit here and hear our choice blasphemed by this . . . this ignorant woman who should be home by her fireside making baby clothes, not standing before us prattling like a silly child of things she cannot understand!"

"Wait," said Rohana Ardais, "wait, Margwenn. I too was Tower-trained, and the choice was forced on me, to give up this work I loved, to marry and give sons to my husband's clan. There is some wisdom in what Lady Ellemir says. Let us hear what she is saying to us, without interrupting."

But Rohana was silenced by outcry. Lorill Hastur called them to order, and Damon remembered with a sinking heart that Lorill too had been trained in Dalereuth Tower, and had been forced to renounce it when he inherited the position as Council Regent. "You have no Council voice, Lady Ellemir. You may choose to go with the matrons we have chosen to care for you, or you may remain here. You have no other options."

She clung to Damon's arm. "I stay with my husband."

"Sir," Cassilda Hastur said, troubled, "Has she the right to choose, when this choice may endanger the child she bears? She has miscarried once, and this child is heir to Alton. Is not the child's safety more important than her sentimental wish to stay with Damon?"

"In the name of all the Gods, Cassilda!" Rohana protested. "She is not a child! She understands what is at stake here! Do you think she is a dairy animal, that by leading her out of sight of her child's father you can make her indifferent to his fate? Sit down and let her alone!"

Rebuked, the young Lady Hastur took her seat.

"Damon Ridenow, choose. Will you surrender your matrix without protest, or must it be taken from you?"

Damon glanced at Ellemir, holding his arm; at Callista, blazing jeweled defiance; at Andrew, one step behind him. He said to them, not to Lorill, "May I speak, then, for you all? Callista, is it your will to return to Arilinn in Leonie's care?"

Leonie was looking at Callista with a hungry eagerness, and Damon suddenly understood.

Leonie had never allowed herself to love. But Callista, like herself a pledged virgin lifelong, Callista she might love safely, with all the repressed hunger of her starved emotions. It was no wonder that she could not let Callista go, that she had made it impossible for Callista to leave the Tower. Her love for the girl had not the faintest hint of sexuality, but it was love, nevertheless, as real as his own hopeless love for Leonie.

Callista was silent, and Damon wondered which would be her choice. Did Arilinn seem more attractive to her than what they offered, less troubling, less painful? And then he knew that Callista's silence was only compassion, reluctance to fling Leonie's offered love and protection back into her face. Unwillingness to hurt the woman who had cherished and protected the lonely child in the Tower. When she spoke there were tears in her eyes.

"I have given back my oath. I will not receive it again. I too will remain with my husband."

Now, indeed, they stood as one! Damon's voice rang defiant:

"Hear me then!" He drew Ellemir close, fiercely protective. "For my wife, I thank the noble ladies of Comyn, but none but I shall care for her while I live. As for Andrew, he is my sworn man, and you yourself, Lorill Hastur, during the building of the spaceport, judged that Terrans might enter into private agreements with Darkovans, and the reverse, and these shall be treated like any other contract under Domain law. I have taken the oath of *bredin* with Andrew, and I shall be personally responsible for his honor as for my own. This means that as regent of Alton I shall hold his marriage to Callista to be as valid as my own. And as for myself," and now he faced Leonie and flung the words, deliberately, straight at her, "I am Keeper, and responsible only to my own conscience."

"You? Keeper?" Her voice was scornful. "You, Damon?"

"You yourself guided me in Timesearch, and it was Varzil the Good who named me *tenerézu*." With deliberation, he used the archaic male form of the word.

Lorill said, "You cannot call to witness a man who has been dead for hundreds of years."

"You have called me to judgment on laws which have stood since those days," Damon said, "and the structure I have built in the overworld stands for all to witness who have entry there. And this was the law and the test in those days. I am Keeper. I have established my Tower. I will abide the challenge."

Leonie's face paled. "That law has been dead since the Ages of Chaos."

You live by laws which should have been dead long ago too. He did not speak the words aloud, but Leonie heard them, and so did everyone with *laran* in the Crystal Chamber. She said, as white as a skull, "So be it. You have invoked the old test of a Keeper's right and responsibility. You and Callista are renegades of Arilinn, so this shall be Arilinn's affair, to answer the challenge. It will be a duel, Damon, and you know the penalty if you fail. Not only you and Callista, but your consorts— if any of you survive the ordeal, which is unlikely—shall be stripped of your matrices and the *laran* centers burned away, so that you may live as an example and a warning to anyone who would stretch out his hand, unfit, for a Keeper's place and power."

"I see you know the consequences, Leonie," said Callista. "Would that you had known them equally well when I was made Keeper."

Leonie ignored her, staring fixedly into Damon's eyes.

"I will abide the ordeal and its penalties, Leonie," Damon said, "but you do realize, Leonie, that you invoke them on yourself and all of Arilinn, should you fail to conquer."

She said, furiously, "I think we would all risk more than that, to punish the insolence of those who would build a forbidden Tower on our threshold!"

"*Enough!*" Lorill held out his hands to silence them. "I declare challenge and ordeal between Arilinn Tower and its Keeper, Leonie Hastur, and"—he hesitated a moment—"and the forbidden tower with him who stands self-proclaimed as its Keeper, Damon Ridenow. It shall begin at sunrise tomorrow."

Leonie's face was like stone. "I shall await the ordeal."

"And I," said Damon. "Until sunrise, Leonie."

He gave a hand to Ellemir, the other to Callista. Andrew paced one step behind them. Without looking back, they left the Crystal Chamber.

Until sunrise. He had spoken bravely. But could they face Leonie, and all the forces of Arilinn?

They must, or die.

CHAPTER TWENTY-TWO

Damon's first act, when they returned to the Alton suite, was to fetch a telepathic damper and isolate *Dom* Esteban's room behind it. He gently told Ferrika what he was doing.

"At sunrise there may be a . . . a telepathic disturbance," he warned her, thinking how ridiculously inadequate the words were. "This will make certain he will not be drawn into it, for he is too weak for any such thing. I leave him in your care, Ferrika, I trust you."

He found himself wishing he could isolate Ellemir too behind such a safe barrier, with her unborn baby. He told her this when he returned to the rooms they shared with Callista and Andrew, and she smiled wanly.

"Why, you are no better than the ladies of Comyn Council, my husband, feeling I must be shielded and excused because I am a woman, and bearing. Don't you think I realize that we are all fighting together, for the right to live together and bring up our children to a better life than most Comyn sons and daughters can have? Do you think I want *him*"—she laid her hand, with that expressive gesture, on her pregnant body—"to face the crippling choice you faced, or Callista, or Leonie? Do you think I am unwilling to fight, as well as you?"

He held her close, realizing her intuition was sounder than his own. "My darling, all the Gods forbid I should be the one to deny you that right."

But as they rejoined Callista and Andrew, he realized that the coming battle was more than life and death. If they lost—and survived—they would be worse than dead.

"It will be fought in the overworld," he warned, "like the last battle with the Great Cat. We must all be very sure of ourselves, because only our own thoughts can defeat us."

Ellemir sent for food and wine and they dined together, trying to make it a festive occasion, forgetting they were strengthening themselves for the ordeal of their lives. Callista looked pale, but Damon was relieved to see that she ate heartily.

There were two of them Keeper-trained, he thought, Keeper-strong. But that also roused an uncomfortable thought. If they lost, it would be all the same, but if they won there was a matter still unsettled.

"If we win," he said, "I shall have won the right to work as I will with my chosen circle, then Ellemir as my wife, and Andrew as my sworn man, are beyond the reach of Council meddling. But you, Callista, you are close to the heirship of Comyn; nearer than you are only two children, and one is still unborn. Council will argue that my duty as regent of Alton is to have you married off to some suitable man, someone of Comyn blood. A woman of your years, Callista, unless actually working in a Tower, is usually married."

"I am married," she flared at him.

"*Breda*, the marriage will not stand if anyone contests it. Do you really trust Council not to contest it? Old *Dom* Gabriel of Ardais has already spoken to me about marrying you to his son Kyril—"

"Kyril Ardais?" Her nostrils flared in disdain. "I had as soon marry some bandit of the Hellers and be done with it! I have not spoken with him since he was a bully intimidating us all at children's parties, but I do not suppose he has improved by aging!"

"Still, it is a marriage Council would approve. Or they might follow through on Father's wish and give you, as he meant to give Ellemir, to Cathal. But marry you off they certainly will. You know the law about freemate marriage as well as I do, Callista."

She did. Freemate marriage was legal upon consummation and could be annulled by act of Council, as long as it was childless.

"Avarra's mercy," she said, looking around the table at them all, "this is worse than being put to bed in the sight of half the Domain of Alton, and I thought *that* was embarrassing!"

She laughed, but it was not a mirthful sound. Ellemir

said gently, "Why do you think a woman is put to bed so publicly? So that all may see and know that the marriage is a legal fact. But in your case a question has been raised. I do not doubt Dezi has talked freely on the matter, damn him!"

"I doubt not he is already damned," Damon said, "but the mischief is done."

"Are you telling us," Andrew said, laying his hand over Callista's, and noting with dread that she drew it away, with the old automatic reflex, "that Dezi's taunt was true after all and our marriage is not lawful?"

Reluctantly Damon nodded. "While Domenic lived and *Dom* Esteban was healthy, no one would question what his daughters did, far away in the Kilghard Hills. But the situation has changed. The Domain is in the hands of a child and a dying man. Even if Callista were still Keeper, legally they could not force her to marry, but any persuasion short of force would be used. And since she has already given back her oath, and publicly refused to return to Arilinn, her marriage is a legitimate concern of Council."

"Have I no more rights in the matter than a horse led to the marketplace?" Callista demanded.

"Callie, I did not make the laws," he said tenderly. "I will unmake some of them, if I can, but I cannot do it overnight. The law is what it is."

"Callista's father agreed to give her to me," Andrew said. "Does that decision have no legal merit?"

"But he is a dying man, Andrew. He may die tonight, and I am only warden of Alton under the Council, no more." He looked deeply troubled. "Only if we could go to Council with an established marriage under the Law of Valeron—"

"What is *that*?" Andrew demanded, and Callista said tonelessly, "A woman of the Aillard Domain, from the plains of Valeron, won a Council decision which has served as a precedent ever since. Whether the marriage is freemate or otherwise, no woman can be separated unwilling from the father of her child. Damon means that if you could take me to bed—and preferably make me pregnant at once—we would have a way to contest the Council." She made a face. "I do not want a child yet—still less do I want it at the bidding of Council like this, like a mare being taken to stud—but better that, than that I should marry someone chosen by Council for political reasons, and to bear *his* children." She looked miserably from Damon to Andrew and said, "But you know that it is impossible."

Damon said quietly, "No, Callista. This marriage, and you know it, stands or falls on whether you can go before Council tomorrow and swear that the marriage has been consummated."

She cried out, trapped, terrified, "Do you want me to kill him this time?" and buried her face in her hands.

Damon came around the table, gently turned Callista to face him. "There is another way, Callista. No, look at me. Andrew and I are *bredin*. And I am stronger than you. You could hit me with everything you threw at Andrew, and more, and you could not hurt me!"

She turned away, sobbing, "If I must. If I must. But, oh, merciful Avarra, I wanted that to come in love, when I was ready, not in a battle to the death!"

There was a long silence, with only Callista's stifled weeping. The sound tore at Andrew's heart, but he knew he must trust Damon to find a way for them. At last Damon said quietly, "Then there is only one way, Callista. Varzil told me that the answer for you was to free your mind from the imprint of years as Keeper on your body. I can free your mind, and your body will be freed, as it was in the winter blooming."

"You told me that was only an illusion . . ." She faltered.

"I was wrong," Damon said quietly. "I did not put everything together until a little while ago. I wish, for your sake, that you and Andrew had been able to trust your instincts. But now . . . I have some *kireseth* flowers, Callista."

Her hands flew to her mouth in apprehension, terror, understanding. "It is taboo, forbidden to anyone Tower-trained!"

"But," Damon said, and his voice was very gentle, "*our* Tower does not live by the laws of Arilinn, *breda*, and I am not a Keeper by *those* laws. Why do you think it became taboo, Callista? Because, under the impact of the *kireseth*—as you have seen—even a Keeper could not retain her immunity to passion, desire, human need. It is a telepathic catalyst drug, but it is much, much more than that. After the training given to Keepers in the Towers, it is frightening, unthinkable, to admit that there is no *reason* for a Keeper to be chaste, except temporarily, for strenuous work. Certainly there is no need for such lifetime loneliness and withdrawal. The Towers have imposed cruel and needless laws on their Keepers, Callista, from the Ages of Chaos, when the Year's End ritual was lost. I think it must have been at the time of Midsummer festival then. At our festival, all through the Domains, women are given flowers and fruit in commemoration of Cassilda's gift to Hastur, but how is the Lady of the Domains always pictured? With the golden bell of *Kireseth* in her hands. This was the ancient ritual, so that a woman might work as Keeper in the matrix circles, with her channels clear, and then return to normal womanhood when she chose."

He took her two hands in his. She tried, in the old, automatic way, to draw them away, but he held them firmly in his own, controlling her. "Callista, have you the courage to turn your back on Arilinn and explore, with us, a tradition which will allow you to be Keeper and woman at once?"

He had struck the right note when he appealed to her courage. Together they had tested it to the outermost limits. She bowed her head, consenting. But when he brought the *kireseth* flowers, folded into a cloth, she hesitated, holding the bundle in her hands.

"I have broken every law of Arilinn save this. Now I am truly outcaste," she said, near to tears again.

Damon said, "They have called us both renegades. I will not ask you to do anything I am not willing to do first, Callista."

He took the cloth from her hand, unfolded it and raised it to his face, deeply inhaling the dizzying scent. Fear rushed through him—the forbidden thing, the taboo—but he recalled Varzil's words:

"This is why we instituted the old sacramental rite of Year's End. . . . You are her Keeper; it is for you to be responsible."

Callista was white and shaking, but she took the *kireseth* from Damon's hands, breathing in deeply. Damon meanwhile thought of the Arilinn circle, which would strike them at sunrise. Was he making a tragic mistake?

During his years there, when serious work was contemplated any kind of stress was prohibited, anything like sexual contact above all. *They* would spend this night in solitary concentration, preparing for the battle ahead of them.

But Damon was not working along those lines. He knew he could not defeat Arilinn by doing what they did. His Tower was building something wholly new, built upon their fourfold rapport. It was only right that they should spend this night in completing the bond, helping Callista to be part of it, to share it fully.

Andrew took the flowers from Callista's hands. As he breathed their scent—dried, powdery, but still reminiscent of the field of golden flowers under the crimson sunlight—he seemed to see Callista coming through the field of flowers again, and the memory made him faint with longing. As Ellemir took them in her turn, he felt moved to protest—was this safe for her, in her condition? But she had the right to choose. She should share whatever this night brought them.

Damon felt a rush of expanding outward consciousness, a heightened awareness. It seemed that the matrix at his throat was flickering, throbbing like a live thing. He cradled it in his hand and it seemed to speak to him, and for the moment he wondered if the matrices were, after all, a form of alien life, experiencing time at a fantastically different rate, symbiotic with mankind?

Then he seemed to rush backward as he had done during Timesearch, and experience, with curious clairvoyance, what he had heard of the history of the Towers, at Arilinn and at Nevarsin. After the Ages of Chaos, centuries of decadence, corruption, and conflicts which had decimated the Domains and raged over half a world, the Towers had been rebuilt and the Compact formed, forbidding all weapons save those within hand's reach of the wielder, and forcing anyone who would kill to take an equal chance at death. Matrix work had been relegated to the Towers and to those of Comyn blood, sworn to the Towers and the Keepers. The Keepers, vowed to chastity and without allegiance even to family ties, were required to be disinterested, without political or dynastic interest in the rule of the Domains. The training of Tower workers was based on strong ethical principles and the breaking of all other bonds, creating strength and integrity in a world corrupt and laid waste.

And the Keepers were sworn to protect the Domains, to guard against further misuse of the matrix stones. Without political power, they had nevertheless taken on tremendous personal and charismatic force, priestesses, sorceresses, with a vital spiritual and religious ascendancy, controlling all the matrix workers on Darkover.

But had this in itself become an abuse?

It seemed to Damon that he was in telepathic contact across the centuries with his distant kinsman Varzil—or was it a faint racial memory? When had the Towers abandoned the Year's End ritual which kept them in touch with their common humanity? The ritual had allowed a Keeper, celibate by harsh necessity for her incredibly difficult and demanding work—and in those days, at the height of the Towers, it had been far more demanding still—to become periodically aware of her common humanity, sharing the instincts and desires of her fellow men and women.

When had they abandoned it? Even more, *why* had they abandoned it? At some time during the Ages of Chaos had it become a kind of debauchery? For whatever reasons, good or bad, it was gone, and with it the knowledge of how to unlock the channels frozen for psi work at such a high level. So the Keepers, no longer neutered, had been forced to rely on a kind of training basically inhuman, and the power of the Keepers lay in the hands of such women who were capable of withdrawing themselves thus completely from their instincts and desires.

It seemed to Damon, as he traversed the years, that he could feel within himself all the suffering of these men and women, alienated, despairing, many failing because they could not so fully separate themselves from the human lot. And those who succeeded had had to adopt impossible standards for themselves, training of an inhuman rigor, total alienation even from their own circles. But what choice had they had?

But now they would rediscover what the old rite could have done. . . .

He was not looking at Callista but he *felt* her frozen decorum dissolving, felt the lessening physical rigidity, tension running out of her like running water. She had dropped into a chair. He turned and saw her smiling, stretching like a cat, holding out her arms to Andrew. Andrew went and knelt beside her, and Damon watched, thinking with longing of a lovely child in the Tower, all her exquisite spontaneity leaving her day by day, slowly changing to a prim tense silence. Now, his heart aching, he could see a little of that child in the sweet smile Callista gave Andrew. Andrew kissed her hesitantly, then with growing passion. As the fourfold rapport began to weave among them again, they all shared, for a moment, in the kiss. But Andrew, his own inhibitions broken by the *kireseth*, moved a little too quickly. His arms tightened around Callista, crushing her against him, and the growing demand of his kisses frightened her. In sudden panic she broke away from him, thrusting him away with the full strength of her arms, her eyes wide with dread.

Damon felt the double texture of her fear: partly she feared that what had happened before would happen again, that the reflex she could not control would strike Andrew, hurt him, kill him; partly she feared her own arousal, strange, unfamiliar. She looked at Andrew with something like terror, stared at Damon with a numb, trapped look which bewildered him.

Ellemir's thoughts moved quickly through the growing rapport. *Have you forgotten how young she is?*

Andrew stared at her without comprehension. After all, Callista was Ellemir's twin!

Yes, and after so many years as a Keeper, in some ways she is older, but all of that is gone from her mind now. She is, essentially, the little girl of thirteen who went to the Tower. For her, sex is still a memory of terror and pain, and how she nearly killed you. She has nothing good to remember except a few kisses among the flowers. Leave her to me for a little, Andrew.

Reluctantly Andrew drew away from Callista, and Ellemir put an arm around her twin's shrinking shoulders. None of them needed to speak aloud now, and didn't bother.

Come with me, darling, it won't hurt them to wait until you are ready. She led her into the inner room, telling her, *This is your real wedding night, Callista, and there will be no crude horseplay and jokes.*

Pliant as a child, and to Ellemir she seemed almost like a child, Callista allowed her twin to undress her, to remove the paint with which she had concealed the red marks on her face, to brush out her long hair over her shoulders, put her into a nightgown. The touch laid them open to one another, Ellemir's guard also going down under the growing influence of the *kireseth.* She felt the flood of memories her twin had not been able to share when they had tried, on the night before their wedding, to exchange hesitant confidences.

Ellemir felt and *experienced*, with Callista, the conditioning to withdrawal, the harsh discipline against even a random touch of any other human hand. With overwhelming horror, she looked at the small healed scars on Callista's wrists and hands, awash with the physical and emotional anguish of those first terrible years in the Tower. *And Damon had a part in this!* For a moment she shared Callista's agonized resentment, the rage never given voice or outlet, poured into a tension and force whose only outlet was through the focused energy of the matrix screens and relays.

She reexperienced with Callista the slow, inexorable deadening of normal physical responses, the numbing of bodily reflexes, the hardening of tensions in mind and body into a rigid armoring. Callista, by the third year in Arilinn, had no longer been lonely, had no longer craved human contact or emotional nourishment.

She was a Keeper.

It was a miracle, Ellemir realized, that she had any human compassion, any real feeling left at all. In a few more years it would have been too late; even *kireseth* could not have dissolved away the hard armor of the years, the imprint in the mind of so much tension.

But the *kireseth* had dissolved the patterning in Callista, leaving her a trembling child. Her mind was freed, and her body was no longer bound by the inexorable reflexes of the training, but with it had gone all the intellectual acceptance and maturity with which Callista had overlaid her inexperience, and she was a frightened little girl. Essentially, Ellemir thought with deep compassion, Callista was younger than she herself had been when she took her own first lover.

After being freed like this, Callista should have had a year or two to grow up normally, to come first to emotional and then to physical awareness of love. But she did not have that much time. She had only tonight, to cross a gulf of years.

With anguished empathy, cradling the shaking girl in her arms, Ellemir wished she could give Callista some of her own acceptance. Callista did not lack courage—no one who had been able to endure that kind of training could be thought lacking in courage. She would harden herself, go through with the consummation, so that she could face the Council tomorrow and swear that it had been done, but, Ellemir feared, it would be an ordeal, a test of courage, not the joyous thing it should have been.

It was cruel, Ellemir decided. They were asking a child to consent to her own rape—for in essence that was what it would be!

She would not be the first. So many women of Comyn were married, almost as children, to men they hardly knew and did not love. Callista had courage, so she would not rebel. And she really loved Andrew. But still, Ellemir thought, it would be a wretched wedding night for her, poor child.

Time was the one thing she needed, and the one thing Ellemir could not give her.

She felt Callista's tentative touch on her mind, a reaching for reassurance, and suddenly realized that there *was* a way to share her own experience with her twin. They were *both* telepaths. Ellemir had always been doubtful, hesitant about her own *laran*, but under the *kireseth* she too was discovering a new potential, a new growth.

Confidently, holding Callista's hands in hers, she let

her mind drift back to her fifteenth year, the time of
Dorian's pregnancy, her growing closeness to Dorian's
young husband, the agreement of the sisters that Ellemir
should take Dorian's place in his bed. Ellemir had been
a little afraid, not of the experience itself, but that Mikhail might think her ignorant or childish, too young, too
inexperienced, not a fit substitute for Dorian. When he
first came to her, and Ellemir had not remembered this
in years, she had been paralyzed with fright, almost as
frightened as Callista was now. Would he find her awkward, ugly?

And yet how easy it had been, how simple and pleasant, after all, how foolish her apprehension had seemed.
When Dorian's child was born and the time was at an
end, she had regretted it.

Slowly she moved forward in time, blending her
awareness with Callista's, sharing the growth of her love
for Damon. The first time they had danced together in
Thendara, at Midsummer festival, he had seemed
middle-aged to her, only one of her father's officers, silent, withdrawn, showing attention to his cousin out of
politeness, no more. Not until Callista was imprisoned
among the catmen and she had sent for him in panic,
had it occurred to her that Damon was anything but a
friendly older kinsman, the friend of her long-dead elder
brother. And then she had known what he meant to her.
She shared with Callista, as she could never have done
in words, the growing frustration of waiting, the dissatisfaction with kisses and chaste embraces, the ecstasy of
their first coming together. *If I could have known then,
Callie, how to share this with you!*

She reexperienced, with mingled joy and the memory
of dread, her first suspicion of pregnancy: happiness, the
fear and sickness, the turmoil of her body which had
turned into a hostile strange thing, but through it all, the
joyfulness. She felt herself sobbing again uncontrollably
as she relived the day the fragile link had given way and
Damon's daughter had died unborn. And then, more
hesitantly—*are you able to accept this? Do you resent
it?*—she felt again her growing awareness of Andrew's
need, welcoming him into her bed, for a little almost
fearing it would lessen her closeness to Damon; again

the delight of learning that it heightened it, because now
it was a matter of choice and not merely custom, that
her relationship with Damon had developed even more
deeply with what she had learned about herself and her
own desires from Andrew.

*I knew you wanted me to do this, Callista, but I
couldn't help wondering if it was because you really did
not know what it meant to me.*

Callista sat up in bed, put her arms around Ellemir
and kissed her, reassuringly. Her eyes were wide with
wonder and awe. Ellemir was struck by her beauty. She
knew Damon loved Callista too, sharing something with
her that Ellemir never could. Yet she could accept it, as
she knew Callista accepted that Ellemir and not she herself would give Andrew his first child. Independently she
came to the conclusion Andrew had reached: they were
not two couples changing partners now and then, like
some figure in a complicated dance. They were something else, and each of them had something unique to
give the others.

She knew Callista's fear had gone, that she was eager
to become part of this thing they were, and she did not
need to raise her eyes to know that Andrew and Damon
had come to join them. For a moment she wondered if
she and Damon should withdraw, leaving Andrew alone
with Callista, then almost laughed at herself for the idea.
They were all a part of this.

For a little the contact was only of their minds, as
Damon began to reach out and weave the fourfold rapport among them, close, intertwining, complete as it had
never been before. Ellemir thought in musical images,
and to her it was like blending voices, Callista's clear
and golden like the singing to the harp, Andrew's a
strong bass undercurrent, Damon's a curiously many-
voiced harmony, her own weaving them together, blending with each. Even as she visualized this rapport as
music, as harmony, she shared the images of the others:
a sunburst of blending colors in Callista's mind; the close
tactile sense of Andrew's private imagery, so that for a
little it seemed that they all curled naked together in a
strange darkness, touching everywhere; sparkling spiderweb threads from Damon's consciousness, weaving them

all into one. For a long time they seemed to need no more than this. Callista, floating in the glowing colors, was faintly amused to feel Damon's touch and knew he had kept enough separate awareness to monitor her channels. Then, as he touched her, the emotional rapport deepened, became a stronger awareness in her body, something new and strange, but not frightening.

Vaguely, at the edge of her mind, she remembered her father's stories. *Kireseth* was given to reluctant brides. Well, she was reluctant no more. Was the effect of the resin on body or mind? Was it the opening of the mind which had freed her to be so aware of her body, of the closeness to Ellemir, who was roused and aware of all of them? Or was it the body's hunger for closeness which opened the mind to the deeper communion of minds? Did it matter? She knew Andrew was still afraid to touch her. Poor Andrew, she had hurt him so much. She reached out to him, drawing him into her arms, felt him cover her with kisses. This time she gave herself up to them, feeling as if she were drowning in the ecstatic shimmer of lights, and at the same time woven into a trembling darkness.

In a sudden bewilderment of sensuality it was simply not enough to be in Andrew's arms. She did not move away from him, but she reached for Damon, felt his touch, kissed him and suddenly, in a flash, remembered how she had found herself wanting to do this during her first year in the Tower, had stifled the memory in a frenzy of terror and shame. Touching both hard male bodies, she felt her fingertips tracing down the curve of her sister's breast, down the pregnant body, letting her consciousness sink deeper, just touching the faint, faint stir of the unborn child's dreamless sleep. Somehow she felt enfolded like that, safe, surrounded by love, and she knew she was ready for the rest too.

Andrew, sharing this with her, knew that for Callista, Ellemir's accepting sexuality would always be the key, that it had bridged the gap for Callista as it had almost done on their first catastrophic attempt. He knew that if he had welcomed the rapport, even then Ellemir might have managed to bring them all safely through. But he had wanted to be alone with Callista, separate.

If I could only have trusted Ellemir and Damon then . . . and through his regret felt Damon's thoughts, *That was then, this is now, we have all changed and grown.*

And that was the last moment of separate awareness for any of them. Now, as it had almost been at Midwinter, the rapport was complete. None of them ever knew or wanted to know, none of them ever tried to separate out or untangle isolated sensations. Details did not matter at that point—whose thighs opened or clasped, whose arms held close, who moved away for a moment, only to come closer, who kissed, probing, whose lips opened to the kiss, who penetrated or was penetrated. It seemed that for a little while they all touched everywhere, sharing every closeness so deeply that there was no separate consciousness at all. Callista was never sure, afterward, whether she had shared Ellemir's awareness of the act of love or had experienced it for herself, and for a little while, briefly dropping into rapport with one of the men, saw and embraced *herself*—or was it her twin? She felt one of the men explode into orgasm, but was not sure whether or not she had participated in it. Her own consciousness was too diffuse. She felt her own awareness expanding, with Damon and Andrew and Ellemir like more solid spots in her own body, which had somehow expanded to take up all the space in the room, pulsing in multiple rhythms of excitement and awareness. Whether she herself had known pleasure or whether she had simply shared the intense pleasure of the others, she was never wholly sure; she did not want to know. Nor did any of them ever know which of them had first possessed Callista's body. It did not matter; none of them wanted to know. They floated, they submerged in ecstasy, so blended from sensuality and the sharing of intense love that such things were irrelevant. Time had gone completely out of focus. It seemed to have gone on for years.

A long time later Callista knew she was drowsing, in tremendous content, still surrounded by them all. Ellemir was asleep with her head on Andrew's shoulder. Callista felt weary, strange, and blissful, dropping now into Damon's consciousness, now into Andrew's, now submerging for minutes at a time into Ellemir's sleep. Drifting between past and future, aware of her own body as she had never been since childhood, she knew she would be able to go into Council and swear her marriage had been consummated, and then, with a reluctance which actually made her laugh a little, that she had come from this night pregnant. She did not really want a child, not yet. She had wanted a little time to learn about herself, to know the kind of growth Ellemir had known, to explore all the new and unexplained dimensions in her life.

But I'll live through it, women do, she thought with secret laughter, and the laughter spilled over to Damon. He reached out, enlacing her fingers with his.

Thank the Gods you can laugh about it, Callie!

It isn't as if it had to be a choice, as I feared. As if I could never use my own particular skills again. It's a broadening of what I am, not a narrowing of choices.

She still resented the need to have a child by the Council's choice and not her own—she would never forgive the Council for their attitude—but she accepted the necessity and knew she would easily manage to love the unwanted child, enough to hope that the coming daughter would not know, until she was old enough to understand, just how very much she had been unwanted.

But I want never to know who fathered it. . . . Please, Elli, even in monitoring, never, never let me be sure. And they promised one another, silently, that they would never try to know whether the child conceived this night was Damon's daughter or Andrew's. They might suspect, but they would never know for certain.

For hours they lay dozing, resting, sharing the fourfold rapport, feeling it come and go. Although all the others had drifted into sleep toward morning, Damon found himself wakeful and a little fearful. Had he weakened them, or himself, for the coming battle? Could Callista clear her channels quickly enough?

And then, dropping into Callista's consciousness, he knew that they would always be wholly clear, for whichever force she chose to use them. She would not need the *kireseth*; now she knew within herself how it *felt* to switch them over from sexual messages to the full strength of *laran*. And Damon knew, with surging confidence, that he could meet whatever came.

And then he knew, reluctantly, why the use of *kireseth* had been abandoned. As a rare and sacramental rite, it was safe and necessary, helping the Keepers reaffirm their common humanity, reaffirming the close bond of the old Tower circles, the closest bond known, closer than kin, closer than sexual desire.

But it could all too easily become an escape, an addiction. Would men, with this freedom accessible, ever accept the occasional periods of impotence after demanding work? Would women accept the discipline of learning to keep the channels clear? *Kireseth*, with overuse, was dangerous. A thousand stories of the Ghost Winds in the Hellers made that clear. And the temptation to overuse it would be almost irresistible.

So it had first fallen into a taboo, for rare and sacramental use, later the taboo being enlarged to total disuse and disrepute. With regret for what he would always remember as one of the peak experiences of his life, Damon knew that even as a Year's End ritual it might be too tempting. It had brought them, undamaged, through the last barrier to their completion, but in future they must rely on discipline and self-denial.

Self-denial? Never, when they had one another.

And yet, if all of time coexisted at once, this magical hour would always be present and real to them as it was now.

Sadly, lovingly, feeling their presence all around him and regretting the necessity to separate, he sighed. One by one, he woke them.

"Sunrise is near," he said soberly. "They will observe the terms precisely, but they will not give us a moment's advantage, so we must be ready for them. It is time to prepare for the challenge."

CHAPTER TWENTY-THREE

It was the thin darkness which preceded the dawn. Damon, standing at the still-dark window, not even grayed with the coming light, felt ill at ease. The exultation was still with him, but there was a small gnawing insecurity.

Had this, after all, been the wrong thing to do? By all the laws of Arilinn, this should have weakened them, made them unfit for the coming conflict. Had he made the most tragic and irrevocable of all mistakes? Had he, loving all of them, condemned them to death and worse?

No. He had staked all their lives on the rightness of what they were doing. If the old laws of Arilinn were right after all, then they all deserved to die and he would accept that death, if not gladly, at least with a sense of justice. They were working in a new tradition, less cruel and crippling than the one he had rejected, and his belief that they were right must triumph.

He had wrapped himself in a warm robe against the cold of the overworld. Callista had done the same, and had wrapped a fluffy shawl around Ellemir's shoulders. Andrew, shrugging into his fur riding cloak, asked, "What exactly is going to happen, Damon?"

"*Exactly?* There's no way I can tell you that," Damon said. "It is the old test for a Keeper: we will build our Tower in the overworld, and they will try to destroy it, and us with it. If they cannot destroy it, they must acknowledge that it is lawful and has a right to be there. If they destroy it . . . well, you know what will happen then. So we must not allow them to destroy it."

Callista was looking pale and frightened. He took her face gently between his hands.

"Nothing can hurt us in the overworld unless you believe that it can." Then he knew what was troubling her: all her life she had been conditioned to believe that her power rested in her ritual virginity.

"Take your matrix," he commanded gently.

She obeyed hesitantly.

"Focus on it. See?" he told her, as the lights slowly gathered in the stone. "And you know your channels are clear."

They were. And it was not only the *kireseth*. Freed of the enormous tensions and armoring of the Keeper's training, the channels were no longer frozen. She could command their natural selectivity. But why had no instinct told her this?

"Damon, how and why could they allow a secret like this to be forgotten?"

It meant that no one ever had to make the cruel choice Leonie had forced on her as a child, which other Keepers for ages past had accepted in selfless loyalty to Comyn and Towers.

"How could they abandon *this*"—her words took in all the wonder and discovery of the night just past— "for *that*?"

"I do not know," Damon said sadly, "nor do I know if they will accept it now. It threatens what they have been taught, makes their sacrifices and their suffering useless, an act of folly."

And he felt a clutch of pain at his heart, knowing that in what he did, as with all great discoveries, there were the seeds of bitter conflict. Men and women would die to champion one or the other side in this great struggle, and he knew, with a great surge of anguish, that a daughter of his own, with the face and the name of a flower, a daughter born to him by neither of these women here in this room, would be brutally murdered for daring to try to bring this knowledge into Arilinn itself. Mercifully the knowledge blurred again; the time was *now*, and he dared not concern himself with past or future.

"Arilinn, as all the other Towers, is locked into a decision our forefathers made. They may have been guided by reasons which were valid then, but are not valid now. I am not forcing the Tower circles to abandon their choice, if it is truly their choice and if, after knowing the cost, knowing there *is* now an alternative, they choose to keep to their own ways. But I want them to know that there is an alternative, that if I, working alone and outcast, have found one alternative, then there may be others, dozens of others, and some of these others might even be more acceptable to them than the one I have found. But I am claiming the right, for myself and my circle, to work in my own way, under such laws as seem right and proper to us."

It seemed so simple and so rational. How could others threaten them with death or mutilation for that? Yet Callista knew that they had threatened and they would carry out the threat.

Andrew said to Ellemir, "I am not concerned for you, but I wish I could be sure this would not threaten your child."

He knew he had hit on Ellemir's own fear. But she said steadfastly, "Do you trust Damon or not? If he felt there was danger, he would have explained it to me, and let me make the choice in full knowledge."

"I trust him." But, Andrew wondered, did Damon simply feel that if they lost the coming battle it would be useless for any of them to survive anyway, including Ellemir and the baby? Firmly he cut off that line of thought. Damon was their Keeper. Andrew's only responsibility was to decide whether or not Damon was worthy of trust and then to trust him and follow his directives, without mental reservations. So he asked, "What do we do first?"

"We build the Tower, and we establish it firmly with all our strength. It has been there for a long time, but it is what we imagine it to be." He added to Ellemir, "You have never been in the overworld; you have only kept watch for me here. Link with me, and I will bring you there."

With a strong mental thrust he was in the overworld, Ellemir beside him in the featureless grayness. Dimly at first, but with more clarity moment by moment in the overlight, he could make out the sheltering walls of their landmark.

At first it had been a rude shelter, like a herdsman's hut, visualized almost accidentally. But with each successive use it had grown and strengthened, and now a true, declared Tower rose around them, with great lucent blue-shining walls, as real to his touch and step as the room in Comyn Castle where they had consummated their fourfold bond. Indeed they had brought much of that world with them, because, Damon thought, the fourfold bond and its completion was in a way the most important thing that had ever happened to any of them.

As always in the overworld he felt taller, stronger, more confident, which was the essence of it all. Ellemir, at his side, did not resemble Callista nearly as much as she did in the solid world. Physically, she and Callista were very much alike, but here where the mind determined the physical appearance, they were very unlike. Damon knew enough of genetics to wonder briefly if they were not identical twins after all. If they were not, it might mean that Callista could bear him a child without as much risk as Ellemir. But that was a thought for another time, another level of consciousness.

After an instant Callista and Andrew joined them in the overworld. He noticed that Callista had not clothed herself in the crimson robe of a Keeper. As the thought reached her she smiled and said, "I leave that office to you, Damon."

For a duel between Keepers, perhaps he should be clothed in the ritual crimson sacrosanct to a Keeper, but he shrank from the blasphemy and suddenly knew why.

He would not fight this battle by Arilinn's laws! He was not Keeper by their cruel life-denying laws, but he was *tenerézu* of an older tradition, defending his right to be so! He would wear the colors of his Domain and no more.

Andrew took up the stance of a paxman or bodyguard, just two steps behind him. Damon reached for Ellemir's hand on his right, for Callista's on his left, felt their fingertips lightly as a touch in the overworld always felt. He said in a low voice, "The sun rises over our Tower. Feel its strength around us. We built it here for shelter. Now it must stand here, not only for us, but as a symbol for all matrix mechanics who refuse the cruel constraints of the Towers, a shelter and a beacon for all those who will come after us."

It seemed to Andrew, although the lucent blue walls of the Tower rose around him, that he could see the sun of the overworld *through* its walls. Callista had once explained it to him:

In the world of the overlight, where they were now, there was no such thing as darkness, because the light did not come from a solid sun. It came from the energy-net body of the sun, which could shine right through the energy-net body of the planet. To Andrew the red sun was enormous, a pale rim rising beyond and somehow *through* the Tower, shedding scattered crimson light, dripping bloody clouds.

Lightning flared around them, blinding them, and for a moment it seemed that the Tower rocked, trembled, that the very fabric of the overworld shook into grayness. *It has come* Damon thought, the attack they awaited. Strongly linked to one another, they felt the Tower's walls strong and sheltering around them, while Damon flicked an explanation to Andrew and Ellemir, less experienced than himself.

They will try to destroy the Tower, but since it is our visualization *of the Tower which holds it firm here, they cannot budge it unless our own perception of it falters.*

One of the games of technicians in training was to fight duels in jest in the overworld, where the thought stuff was endlessly pliable and all of their constructs could be wiped out with a thought as quickly as they had been brought into being. Although he knew it was only an illusion, Damon still felt a purely irrational twinge of physical fright as lightning bolt after lightning bolt struck the Tower, seeming to shake it with deafening thunderclaps. This could be a dangerous game, for whatever happened to the astral-world body could also happen, by repercussion, to the physical self. But behind the walls of their Tower they were safe.

They cannot harm us. And I do not want to harm them, only to be safe with my friends . . . but he knew they would not accept that. Sooner or later the endless attack from outside must weaken them. His only defense was to attack.

As quickly as thought they were standing together on the highest battlement of their Tower. To Andrew it felt like rock beneath his feet. He was clothed, as always in the overworld, in the grayish silvery fabric of a Terran Empire uniform, and as he became aware of it, he felt it alter. *No, I am really not Terran now.*

He realized, with just a flicker of consciousness, that he was wearing the saddle-rubbed leather breeches and the furred riding jacket he wore for work around the estate. Well, that was now his truest self; he *belonged* to Armida now.

As they stood at the top of the Tower they could see the loom of Arilinn, like a flaming beacon. How, Damon wondered, had it come so near? Then he realized it was the visualization of Leonie and her circle, who had spoken of the forbidden Tower as built on their very threshold. To Damon it had seemed very distant, worlds away. But now they were close together, so close that he could *see* Leonie, a crimson veiled statue, grasp handfuls of plastic thought-stuff and hurl lightning. Damon struck it in midair with his own lightning, saw it explode, crash over the circle standing on the pinnacle of Arilinn, saw a crack in the fortress Tower of Arilinn.

They perceive us as a threat to them! Why?

Only a moment, and the thunder was crashing around them again, a fierce duel of lightning bolts, hurled and intercepted, and he felt a random thought—it must be Andrew's—*I feel like Jove hurling his thunders.* He wondered with an infinitesimal fragment of his consciousness who or what Jove was.

I can batter down the Tower of Arilinn, because for some reason they are afraid of us. But Leonie abruptly changed her tactics. The lightnings died and they were suddenly smothering, drowning as a rain of sickening slime cascaded over them, suffocating them, making them retch with disgust. Like dung, semen, horse manure, the trails left by the slugs who invaded the greenhouse in a wet season . . . they were drowning in foulness. *Is this how they see what we have done?* Damon struggled to clear his mind of sickness, wiping his face free of the—No, that was to give it reality. Quickly, linking hands and minds with his circle, he thickened the slime, made it the richness of fertilized soil, let it fall from their bodies until from its rich depths flowers and growing things sprang up, covering the roof of the Tower where they stood in the rioting life of an early spring blooming. They stood triumphant in the field of flowers, reaffirming life out of ugliness.

I fought the Great Cat from outside the Tower, and I triumphed. As if to affirm the act which had brought him the awareness of his own psi power, undiminished by the years he had spent outside the Tower, he called up the Great Cat, pouring their linked minds into the image, sending it out to hover over the heights of Arilinn. *While the Great Cat ravaged the Kilghard Hills and brought darkness and terror and hunger to all our people, you sat safe in Arilinn and you did nothing to help them!*

The two Towers stood now so close that he could see Leonie's face *through* her veil, shining with wrath and despair. In the overworld, Damon thought detachedly, she was still as beautiful as she had ever been. But he could see her for only a moment, for her face vanished in a swirling darkness which wiped out sight of her circle. Where Leonie had stood, a dragon reared upward, roaring and breathing flame. Golden-scaled, golden-clawed, towering to the sky above Arilinn, its fire showered down on the forbidden Tower. Damon felt the blistering heat, felt as if his body were crisping and withering in the fire, heard Callista cry out in agony, felt Ellemir's terror, and for a moment wondered if Leonie must succeed after all in driving them from the overworld, forcing them back into their physical bodies. . . .

But with the flame he also felt the awareness of a legend in Andrew's mind: *Burn us and we will rise again like a phoenix from the ashes.* . . . Reaching with all his last strength through the fire and the burning which threatened to drive them all from the overworld, Damon linked them closer still. Together they poured all their psychic force into the shifting stuff of the overworld, linking into a giant bird, feathers blazing, burning up in the ecstatic union which consumed them, their four linked minds joined. In Andrew's mind Damon felt them curled naked together, inside a darkness; inside an unhatched egg, while the flames wholly consumed them, burned them down into ash. Then, in an ever-expanding ecstasy, the shell around them broke and they burst upward from the ashes, spreading mighty wings in a single, linked burst of flaming energy, soaring over Arilinn, triumphant. . . . From the phoenix beak came thunder, lightning, shaking and rumbling the Tower of Arilinn.

Damon saw, as if far below, the small forms of Leonie and her circle, watching in despair and dread.

Leonie! You cannot destroy us! I ask truce.

Damon knew that he did not wish to destroy Arilinn. It had been his home. He had suffered there unendurably, as Callista had suffered, yet he had been trained there too, disciplined, taught to use the utmost strength and control. His training in Arilinn was at the basis of what he was now, of what he might eventually become. Arilinn should stand forever, in overworld and real world, a home for telepaths, a symbol of what Tower training had been and might some day be again. The strength and power of the Domains.

But Leonie's voice was shaken, almost inaudible.

"No, Damon, strike us down. Destroy us utterly, as you have destroyed all we stand for."

"No, Leonie." And now, suddenly, they stood facing one another on the gray plain of the overworld. And he knew—and knew that Leonie shared the thought—that he could never harm her. He loved her, had always loved her, would always love her.

"And I love you too," Callista said tenderly at his side. She stretched her hands to Leonie, then, as she had never done in the real world, she took Leonie in her arms, holding the woman against her in a tender, loving embrace. "But Leonie, my beloved foster-mother, can you not see what it is that Damon has done?"

Leonie said, shaking, "He has destroyed the Towers. And you, Callista, you have betrayed us all!" She shrank from the girl, staring at her in horror. Damon, linked with her now, knew that she could *see* what had happened to Callista, that she was a woman, loving, loved, fulfilled—not Keeper in the old sense at all, yet wielding the full power of her training and her strength. "Callista, Callista, what have you done?"

Damon answered, gently but unyielding, "We have discovered the old way of working, where a Keeper need not sacrifice life and all the joy of living."

Then my life was useless, my sacrifice needless. And, with a despair Damon could neither measure nor endure: *Let me die now.*

He could see *through* her, with the new sight of a

Keeper, and he saw in horror what she had done to herself. Why had he never guessed? She had sent him from the Tower to remove forever the temptation that he might lose control and reveal his desire for her. But to remove her *own* temptation? The laws forbade the neutering of a Comyn woman, and she had stopped short of that with Callista.

But for herself?

He said with an anguished compassion, "Not needless, Leonie. You and all those like you have kept the tradition alive, kept the matrix sciences of Darkover alive, so that some day this rediscovery might be made. Your heroism has made it possible for our children and grandchildren to use the old sciences without so much suffering and tragedy. I do not want to destroy the Towers, only to take some of the burden from you, to make it possible to train others outside the Towers, so that you need not give up your lives, so that the price need not be so cruelly high. You, and all of us who have come from Arilinn and the other Towers, have kept the flame alive, even though you fed it with your own flesh and blood." He stood disarmed before them all, knowing they could strike him down now, but also *knowing*, with that deep inner knowledge, that now they heard what he said.

"Now the living flame can be rekindled, and it need not feed on your very lives. Leonie"—he turned to her again, his hands held out in pleading—"if you could break under the strain, you, a Hastur, and Lady of Arilinn, then it is surely a burden too heavy for any mortal man or woman. No one alive could have borne it without breaking. Let us work, Leonie, let us go on as we have begun, so that a day will come when once again the men and women who come to the Towers can find joy in their work, not endless sacrifice and a living death!"

Slowly Leonie bowed her head. She said, "I acknowledge you Keeper, Damon. You are beyond harm or vengeance at our hands. We merit any penalty you choose to invoke."

He said, his heart aching, "I can inflict on you no penalty greater than you have laid on yourself, Leonie, the self-chosen sentence you must continue to bear until another generation is strong enough to carry it. Avarra grant in her mercy that you will be the last Keeper of Arilinn to face such a living death, but Keeper of Arilinn you must remain, until Janine can bear the burden alone."

And your only punishment will be to know that for you it is too late. Torn with Leonie's agony, he knew it had always been too late for her. It was too late when, at fifteen, she went into the Dalereuth Tower under the vows of a Keeper. He saw her receding, further and further, like a star dimming out in the morning light. He saw the Tower of Arilinn itself receding on the fluid horizon of the overworld, till it dwindled in the distance, shone with a faint blue light, was gone. Damon and Andrew, Ellemir, and Callista were alone in the forbidden Tower, and then, with a sharp shock, the overworld too was gone, and they were in the suite in Comyn Castle. The peaks beyond the window were flooded with sunlight, but the great red sun had barely cleared the horizon.

Sunrise. And the fate of the four of them, and the fate, perhaps, of all the telepaths on Darkover, had been settled in an astral battle lasting less than a quarter of an hour.

EPILOGUE

"You are a fool, Damon," said Lorenz, Lord of Serrais, with deep disgust. "You have always been a fool and you will always be a fool! You could have been regent of Alton and commanded the Guards long enough to break the hold of the Altons on that office and give it to the Domain of Serrais!"

Damon laughed good-naturedly. "But I do not want to be commander," he said, "and now there is no need. *Dom* Esteban is likely to live as long as needful to bring Valdir to manhood, and perhaps more."

Lorenz looked at him with suspicion and distrust. "How did you do that? We had heard he was at death's door!"

"Exaggerated," Damon said with a shrug, knowing that this would be his lifework, to study the ways of healing with matrix and monitor.

The principle once vindicated, it had not been difficult to go into the damaged heart, remove the blockages and restore the heart to full function. Esteban Lanart, Lord Alton, would be paralyzed for the rest of his life, but a man could command the Guards from a wheeled chair. When it was needful to take the field, young Danvan Hastur or Kieran Ridenow could command in his place. Damon was regent of the Domain only in name now, as a contingency against accident or ill luck. Precognition was not the main gift of either Alton or Ridenow, but he had a flash of it now, knowing that Valdir would assume the wardship of Alton as a grown man, and that he would be one of the most innovative Altons ever to rule the Domain.

Lorenz said in disgust, "Have you no ambition at all, Damon?"

"More ambition than you can imagine," Damon said, "but it takes a different form than yours, Lorenz.

And now, I fear, we must part, since we have a long way to ride. We are returning to Armida. Ellemir's child is next heir to the Domain, and he must be born there."

Lorenz bowed with an ill grace. Andrew, riding just behind Damon, he ignored, but he saluted Ellemir courteously, and Callista with something like real respect. Damon turned to embrace his brother Kieran.

"You will visit us at Armida in the autumn, when you return to Serrais?"

"I will indeed," Kieran said, "and I hope then to see Ellemir's son. Who knows, he may command the Guards someday!" He dropped back, leaving the Guardsmen who were to accompany Damon and his party on their journey to ride ahead of them. Damon was about to give the signal for the rest to ride when he saw a slender woman, cloaked and hooded as was seemly for a *comynara* before this great company, coming down the stairs from the courtyard of Comyn Castle. Instinct told him who she was, or was it only that nothing now could have hidden Leonie of Arilinn from his sight?

So he did not mount, but signaled to his groom to hold the horse ready and went toward her, meeting her at the foot of the steps.

"Leonie," he said, bowing over her hand.

"I came to say farewell, and to give Callista my blessing," she said quietly.

Andrew bowed deeply as Damon led her past, toward Callista, who stood ready to mount her gray mare. Leonie raised her head, and it seemed to Andrew that the old woman's eyes burned out from the depths of a skull, blazing resentment at him, but she inclined her head formally, saying, "Good fortune attend you." She reached out her hands then, and Callista just touched her fingertips, the faint feather-touch of telepath to telepath.

Leonie said quietly, "Take my blessing, child. You know now how deeply I mean it, and how much good fortune I wish for you."

"I know," Callista whispered. The resentment had gone. What Leonie had done had been difficult to endure, but it had made this deeper breakthrough possible, had brought her to what she now knew was the deepest possible fulfilment. She and Andrew might have come together without harm, and lived together happily, but she would have given up her *laran* forever, as it was always assumed a Keeper must do. She knew now that she would have lived the rest of her life only half alive. She raised Leonie's fingertips to her lips and kissed them, reverently and with deep love.

It was too late for Leonie, Callista knew, but now she no longer grudged their happiness.

Leonie turned to Ellemir, making a gesture of blessing. Ellemir bowed her head, accepting without returning the greeting, and Leonie turned to Damon. Again, in silence, he bowed over her hand, not raising his eyes to hers. It had all been said; there was nothing further to be said or done between them. He knew they would not meet again. Enormous, uncrossable distances lay between Arilinn and the forbidden Tower, and it had to be so. From Damon's work a whole new science of matrix mechanics would spring, to remove the terrible burden from the Towers. She made the gesture of blessing again, and turned away.

Damon mounted his horse in silence and they rode through the gates, Andrew riding with Callista at the head of the party, then servants, retainers, and banner-bearers. At the end rode Damon, with Ellemir at his side. He felt that his heart would break. He had his happiness, such happiness as he had never deemed possible. But his happiness was built on the lives of Leonie and others like her, who had kept the knowledge alive. Cassilda, mother of the Domains, he prayed, grant that we never forget, or hold their sacrifice lightly. . . .

He rode with his head bent, grieving, until he saw Ellemir's sorrowful eyes on his and knew that he must not continue to sorrow like this.

For the rest of his life he would remember and regret, but it must be a private grief, almost a secret luxury. Now his face must be turned firmly toward the future.

There was work to do. Work perhaps too trivial for the Towers, but important: work like the repair to

Dom Esteban's heart, like the work he had done to save the feet and hands of the frostbitten men. And more important still, testing the outer limits of who could actually be matrix-trained. Callista, as promised, had already taught Ferrika to monitor. She was an apt pupil and would learn more. And in the years to come there would be others.

Ellemir shifted her weight in the saddle and Damon said anxiously, "You must not tire yourself, my love. Should you truly ride now?"

Ellemir laughed gaily. "Ferrika is waiting to order me into the horse-litter, but for now I will ride in the sunshine."

Together they rode forward, past the servants, the piled pack animals, to where Callista and Andrew rode side by side.

As they went through the pass, Andrew took a last, fleeting look at the Terran spaceport. He might never see it again, but surely the Terrans would be there for the rest of his life. Perhaps Valdir's attitude toward the Terrans would be different, because he had known Andrew well, not as a strange alien, but a man like themselves, the husband of his sister.

But all that was the future. He turned his eyes from the spaceport without a backward look. His world lay elsewhere now.

They rode down from the pass and the spaceport was gone. But Callista could hear the thunder of one of the great ships, and trembled a little. It made her think, too, much, of the changes which had come to Darkover, of all the changes which would come, whether she knew of them or not. But she thought that if she could have endured all the changes of the last year, surely she could face what would come after this. She also had work to do, sharing Damon's work, and thinking, as well, of her coming child.

She too is being called unwanted into a world she does not want, even as I was. . . .

But the coming world would be for her children to face. All she could do was prepare them, and try to make a better world for them to live in. She had already begun. She reached for Andrew's hand, enjoying the simple awareness that it could lie in hers and she felt no need or desire to pull it away. As Damon and Ellemir joined them, she smiled. Whatever changes would come, they would face them together.

MERCEDES LACKEY

The Novels of Valdemar

To Order Call: 1-800-788-6262

CJ Cherryh

EXPLORER

0-7564-0086-4

The *Foreigner* novels introduced readers to the epic story of a lost human colony struggling to survive on the hostile world of the alien atevi. In the final installment to this sequence of this series, can diplomat Bren Cameron, trapped in a distant start system, facing a potentially bellicose alien ship, help prevent interspecies war, when the secretive Pilot's Guild won't even cooperate with their own ship?

Be sure to read the first five books in this action-packed series:

To Order Call: 1-800-788-6262

Julie E. Czerneda

Web Shifters

"A great adventure following an engaging character across a divertingly varied series of worlds."—*Locus*

Esen is a shapeshifter, one of the last of an ancient race. Only one Human knows her true nature—but those who suspect are determined to destroy her!

BEHOLDER'S EYE
0-88677-818-2
CHANGING VISION
0-88677-815-8

Also by Julie E. Czerneda:

IN THE COMPANY OF OTHERS
0-88677-999-7
"An exhilarating science fiction thriller"—
Romantic Times

To Order Call: 1-800-788-6262

DAW 11

OTHERLAND

TAD WILLIAMS

"The Otherland books are a major accomplishment."
–Publishers Weekly

"It will captivate you."
–Cinescape

In many ways it is humankind's most stunning achievement. This most exclusive of places is also one of the world's best-kept secrets, but somehow, bit by bit, it is claiming Earth's most valuable resource: its children.

CITY OF GOLDEN SHADOW (Vol. One)
0-88677-763-1

RIVER OF BLUE FIRE (Vol. Two)
0-88677-844-1

MOUNTAIN OF BLACK GLASS (Vol. Three)
0-88677-906-5

SEA OF SILVER LIGHT (Vol. Four)
0-75640-030-9

To Order Call: 1-800-788-6262